# After Alice

# Also by Gregory Maguire

*Confessions of an Ugly Stepsister*
*Mirror Mirror*
*Lost*
*Making Mischief: A Maurice Sendak Appreciation*
*Matchless*
*The Next Queen of Heaven*

### Books in the Wicked Years
*Wicked*
*Son of a Witch*
*A Lion Among Men*
*Out of Oz*

# After Alice

## Gregory Maguire

*wm*

**WILLIAM MORROW**
*An Imprint of* HarperCollins*Publishers*

HarperCollins books may be purchased for educational, business, or sales promotional use. For information please e-mail the Special Markets Department at SPsales@harpercollins.com.

FIRST EDITION

Designed by Jamie Lynn Kerner

Library of Congress Cataloging-in-Publication Data has been applied for.

ISBN 978-0-06-054895-7 (hardcover)
ISBN 978-0-06-243767-9 (international edition)
ISBN 978-0-06-244264-2 (B&N signed edition)
ISBN 978-0-06-244265-9 (BAM signed edition)

15 16 17 18 19   OV/RRD   10 9 8 7 6 5 4 3 2 1

*For Natacha Liuzzi*

Alice took up the fan and gloves, and, as the hall was very hot, she kept fanning herself all the time she went on talking: "Dear, dear! How queer everything is to-day! And yesterday things went on just as usual. I wonder if I've been changed in the night? Let me think: *was* I the same when I got up this morning? I almost think I can remember feeling a little different. But if I'm not the same, the next question is 'Who in the world am I?' Ah, *that's* the great puzzle!" And she began thinking over all the children she knew that were of the same age as herself, to see if she could have been changed for any of them.

"I'm sure I'm not Ada," she said, "for her hair goes in such long ringlets, and mine doesn't go in ringlets at all; and I'm sure I can't be Mabel, for I know all sorts of things, and she, oh! she knows such a very little! Besides, *she's* she, and *I'm* I, and oh dear, how puzzling it all is!"

—Lewis Carroll, *Alice's Adventures in Wonderland*

I appreciate the kind advice of early readers: Ann Fitch, Betty Levin, Andy Newman, Jill Paton Walsh, and of course my editor, Cassie Jones. Any errors of fact, tone, or interpretation are my own. The portion of *The History of the Fairchild Family,* quoted nearly verbatim here in chapter 5, is by Martha Mary Butt Sherwood; the text comes from the chapter called "The Story on the Sixth Commandment," a section often deleted in later editions of that popular children's novel. The scrap of Victorian poetry recited in chapter 28 is from a chapter header in *Middlemarch;* I'm unable to identify poem or author.

# PART THE FIRST

———— ✦ ————

The meteorological records for these parts assure us that July 4, 1862, was "cool and rather wet": but on that day Lewis Carroll first told the tale of *Alice in Wonderland* to four people in a Thames gig, rowing upstream for a picnic tea, and to the ends of their lives all four remembered the afternoon as a dream of cloudless English sunshine.

—JAMES/JAN MORRIS, *OXFORD*, PAGE 18

# CHAPTER 1

———— ✎ ————

$W$ere there a god in charge of story—I mean one cut to Old Testament specifics, some hybrid of Zeus and Father Christmas—such a creature, such a deity, might be looking down upon a day opening in Oxford, England, a bit past the half-way mark of the nineteenth century.

This part of Oxfordshire being threaded with waterways, such a god might have to make a sweep of His mighty hand to clear off the mists of dawn.

Now, to the human renewing the pact with dailiness, Oxford at matins can seem to congeal through the fogs. A process of accretion through light, the lateral sedimentation of reality. A world emerging, daily, out of nothing, a world that we trust to resemble what we've seen previously. We should know better.

To a deity lolling overhead on bolsters of zephyr, however, the city rises as if out of some underground sea, like Debussy's *La cathédrale engloutie,* that fantasia about the sub-

merged Breton cathedral rising once ever hundred years off
the island of Ys. (Yes, Debussy is early twentieth century,
but time means nothing to Himself.) Spires and domes like
so much barnacled spindrift poke through first. Gradually,
as the sun coaxes the damp away, the coving spaces emerge.
From above, not only the lanes and high street, but also the
hidden places wink into being. Nooks and wells of secret
green in college quadrangles scarcely imagined by the farrier
on his way to the stable, the fishmonger to his stall.

An underworld, all exposed by light.

Even Jehovah, presuming Jehovah, must find the finicky
architecture of his Oxford too attractive to notice the hum-
bler margins of the district. At least at first. Gods have to
wake up, too. But this story starts on the northeast side of
town. People are rousing in an old rectory, here, and an even
older farmhouse, over there. Night-time is being brushed
aside like so much cobweb. The day is wound up and begins
even before the last haunted dreams, the last of the fog, those
spectral and evanescent residues, have faded away.

# CHAPTER 2

─────── ❧ ───────

$\mathrm{A}$lice is missing."

A sigh, a clink of porcelain on porcelain. "Again?"

# CHAPTER 3

———— ✖ ————

Depending upon the hour, a governess in a troubled household is either a ministering angel or an ambulatory munitions device. Behold Miss Armstrong, foraying in the upstairs corridor toward her employer.

"Reverend Boyce? It's about Ada. The child is underfoot and making of herself a nuisance. Underfoot and underhanded; I believe she pesters the poor creature when our backs are turned. Ada must be got outdoors for some healthful exercise. I won't say *mischief,* I just won't. But her absence would allow the household some calm. I assume you've tried Dalby's Carminative? Or Mrs. Winslow's Soothing Syrup? Opium has such a tender effect."

Miss Armstrong hovered in the doorway to the nursery where Ada's brother was not, just now, sleeping. Not anymore. The governess stood to let the night nurse pass. The infant castoff reeked with a vegetable accent as the nurse hurried by. She swung the tin pail at the end of her extended arm.

The Vicar mumbled something. It was hard to be sure just what he meant. He specialized in tones of such subtlety that one could hear in it whatever one chose. "Ada . . ." He backed against the distempered wall, allowing his voice to drift into a nearly musical ellipsis. Miss Armstrong paused, an ear uplifted, waiting for an epiphany. He might have meant anything by it. He faded without clarifying.

Miss Armstrong took his vatic murmur as agreement that an outing for Ada would do the household good. So the governess cornered Ada on the stair landing, crowding her into the aspidistra. A pot of Mama's best rough-cut would be dislodged from the larder so the child might deliver it somewhere. Perhaps to the benighted family at the Croft? As a mercy. "We shall go together along the river if you take care not to stumble into the brink and drown," suggested Miss Armstrong. The river was slow here, our old Cherwell, but kitted out with treacherous tree roots and crumbling banks, and just enough depth to scare one toward salvation. "Go say farewell to your mother whilst I collect the marmalade."

Since members of the household staff argued over competing therapies with which to treat the pink smudge of infant, Mama had repaired to the sewing room. Keeping out of the fray. On this bright morning, the room was still dusky, the curtains not yet drawn back. "Stay quite a long time if you like. If they'll have you," said Mama. "Your brother sorely needs some quiet."

"It's not my fault if Father likes me to practice my hymns," said Ada.

"You may practice them all you like in the cow pasture."

Ada, not a deeply imaginative child, believed the cows were resistant to conversion. She didn't reply.

"If they press you to take tea, accept."

Ada thought it unlikely that the cows would propose afternoon tea. She blinked, noncommittal. Mama sighed and continued. "*Ada*. Attend. Make yourself a comfort to the Clowds. Endeavor to help in all matters. Play with Alice, perhaps."

"Alice is a flaming eejit." Ada gave the word a spin such as Cook, from County Mayo, was wont to do. Mama might have boxed Ada's ears for impertinence: cruelty as well as a mocking Irishry of tone. But her mother knew Ada's outburst was misplaced emotion. An infant in peril affected everyone in the house. And during ordinary hours, Ada was known to be fond of Alice, who was Ada's best friend and her only one. So Mama waggled her fingers in the air, *Go, go,* and settled her crown of hair, the color of browning roses, upon the bolster of the davenport. A miasma of lavender toilet water couldn't mask the hint of madeira wafting from the open decanter though it was not yet eleven in the morning. Mrs. Boyce lay squalid in self-forgiveness.

Ada considered refusing to be dismissed. But she was a good girl. On the way out, she slammed the sewing room door only a little.

In the front passage, Miss Armstrong handed the marmalade to Ada. "Off and away with the fairies once again," said the governess, "for our sins," and then she turned to plunge down a few steps toward the kitchen, to hector Cook into warming some milk. His Lordship the Infant Tyrant must be cozened. No alcoholic pap for *him*.

But *off and away with the fairies?* Ada was prosaic. She didn't know to whom the governess referred. The Tiny Interruption, who preferred screaming rather than observing the newborn's usual practice of sleeping round the clock? Or perhaps Ada herself, hulked upon the Indian-red Kidderminster by the front door, staring at her face in the looking-glass? The face appearing between ringlets, Ada thought, *might* be considered innocent and blameless as a fairy. Though ugly. A bad fairy, perhaps. A rotten packet of fairy. She opened the front door without permission, the quicker to get away from the sight of herself standing all clumpedy-clump and iron-spined in the front hall.

"Off and away with the fairies . . ." Without much remorse, Ada decided to behave as if she'd been sent packing, and left.

Cook, hearing the front door bang, gave Miss Armstrong a piece of her mind. "Sure and ye've dispatched that lummoxing gallootress to foul mischief by tramps and peddlers or to a watery grave, Jaysus mercy are ye out of yer mind like the rest of us?" She threw a marrow at the governess. Miss Armstrong didn't care to take bosh from someone beneath her. Yet Cook had a point. Miss Armstrong, whose skills as a governess were heightened by a permanent agitation of the nerves, rushed to hunt for her gloves so she could pursue Ada with adequate decorum.

The river seen between full-headed trees caught snips of sunlight and flashed brazen glints. Willows twitched in the wind. Ada noticed and didn't notice. She had never before ventured outside without a chaperone. All too soon Miss

Armstrong would ambush her, so through the gate of the Vicarage of Saint Dunstan's Ada torqued and bumbled. A rare treat, to snatch a few moments alone. From an upstairs window, her brother's sedition: serrated syllables, all caw and no coo.

Even here, on the city's northeast edge, where the river and sky could aspire to eternal bucholia, clouds of stone dust dulled the view. The grit of hammered Oxford under construction. Matthew Arnold, today, or soon, might be writing his "Thyrsis" somewhere or other, about Oxford, "sweet city with her dreaming spires." But in Ada Boyce's 186_, Oxford was anything but static picturesquerie. Oxford earth was sliced open into canyons, as foundation pits were sunk in the familiar fields. Oxford air was thickened with scaffolds for masons working to rival those spires. Everywhere, Headington limestone folded double upon itself, yeasting away.

Of course, like many children, Ada was oblivious of the world in her immediate view. Cowslips and colleges, willows on the Isis and Cherwell, morning bells rung on the summer wind: What meant these to Ada? She paid no heed to those inflexible cows on the other side of the water, standing in Marston fields; or to that boat on the current, some curate rowing giddy girls about all on a midsummer's morning. Ada was encased in the husk of Ada, which consisted, largely, of these: parents distracted and obscure; Miss Armstrong, not obscure enough, in fact screechy, bothersome, and all too adjacent; and the new Boy Boyce, with his tiny boyness perched between his legs. Ada wished it might fly away. Or sting itself. Quite hard.

She climbed a stile, huffing and grunting. *Grace* is not a word that comes to mind when Ada lurches into view. But this morning, Ada sacrificed any hopes for proper comportment in order to put a distance between herself and the Bickerage, as she called the Vicarage of Saint Dunstan's.

She paused at a spinney of juvenile ashes. She held her breath a moment to be able to hear over her own exertions. Was that a cry from Miss Armstrong, requiring Ada to halt? Ada wouldn't halt, of course, but it might seem more like fun if she were being chased.

Only the sound of church bells, Christ Church perhaps. Descants of sonorous bronze coin. Falling, falling; where did they pile up? But this is not a question Ada asked herself.

# CHAPTER 4

How hateful Miss Armstrong was. "Pitiable," Ada's father would have suggested, as a more suitable, a more *benign* adjective. But Ada thought of *hateful* as a scientific term: "The Hateful Nanny," and so on, *See page XXIX*. A steel engraving in the marginalia might depict Miss Armstrong's distended nostrils and gaspy mouth, marked as *Fig. A*.

Oh, but Miss Armstrong. A highly strung martinet, smelling of lavender and camphor. She once struck the Vicar's wife as not unlike a comic illustration from the pages of the latest number of *Punch*, and so Mrs. Boyce had made the mistake of muttering "Miss Armstrong Headstrong" in Ada's hearing. But the child could have no notion of the battery of affronts that this governess catalogued nightly, after her prayers. On many a grim morning, Miss Armstrong reviewed her trials as she repaired the threadbare lacing of a severe bonnet. *Stitch*, for the times the Reverend Everard Boyce neglected to say good morning on the stairs. *Stitch double stitch*, for the times

Mrs. Boyce dropped her walking stick and it had to be picked up rather than left lame on the floor where it had fallen. Picked up and repositioned, only to fall again. *Three stitches* and a *prick* of the pin for the tedium of overseeing Ada Boyce, a child parceled out by a lapse in heaven's supervision, as far as Miss Armstrong was concerned. The guarded eye in that child. That torso. When other girls of Ada's age were gleeful English roses on swaying stems, Ada was a glum, spastic heifer. Sooner or later she'd require a wheeled chair. Miss Armstrong hoped to be well on her way to a new position by the time this happened to Ada. Otherwise the governess might guide such a chair along the banks of the Cherwell and accidentally give it a mighty shove.

No, Miss Armstrong would never stoop to murder. Certainly not. To conceive a crime was not to commit one. Miss Armstrong was aware that imagination, often a cause of temptation and unrest, could also serve the soul: It provided images of morbid behavior to which one might practice resistance.

A reservoir of resistance: She had built up a huge fund. She needed it.

Miss Armstrong suffered a complaint common among staff engaged in homes rich in rectitude though meager in physical comforts. She felt overlooked as a woman. Of sisterly company there was, effectively, none. (Ada didn't count.) Reverend Boyce's wife, frankly, would have been considered disreputable had Miss Armstrong been one to gossip. (Had the governess anyone to gossip with. Wolverhampton was a long way from Oxford.) But consider: a Vicar's wife, lounging about with her morning robe opened onto terraces of unabashed bosom! Miss Armstrong observed, she didn't comment, she wiped her own nose dry, tightened her own corset. In the matter of Mrs. Boyce and dipsomania, Miss Armstrong had perfected a look of restraint and kept her distance as she could.

The governess was grateful not to be homely. Her own color was as good as her references. But it made no difference. The pious rector treated Miss Armstrong as if she were made of bamboo or clay. As she stood aside in the vestibule when he came in from haunting the parish poorhouse, he all but hung his scarf upon her forearm. Miss Armstrong sometimes tried to communicate her yearning for recognition as a feminine entity by the tilting of an eyebrow. This was too obscure a hieroglyphic for the Vicar to decipher, no matter how Miss Armstrong concentrated the pure fire of her being in the muscles of her forehead. One day she would self-immolate, like Krook in *Bleak House*. Spontaneous combustion caused by an eyebrow left to smolder a moment too long.

Ada could know none of this, of course, but in cooler moments Ada saw Miss Armstrong clearly enough. Severe, knobby, left-handed, Chapel rather than Church, chiding and churlish by turns, pliant only where Ada's father was concerned. Untapped fervors.

The girl tried to be patient. Vexing though the new baby was proving to be, he might thrive long enough to require a governess. He might pivot Miss Armstrong's attentions away from Ada. Currently the infant had a wet nurse, a nanny, and a steady visitation of doctors, who all thought something might be achieved for the boy, eventually. Or that's what they said. If it lived.

But enough of Miss Armstrong and the dreadful baby. Ada is outside, alone: She is scraping against life the way her brother is. She is newly in the world.

# CHAPTER 5

———— ❦ ————

Had Ada known anything of painting, she might have approved of the view before her as a suitable subject for Constable. A vitality in the clouds suggested muscular air, though just now the riverside poplars stood still, as if holding their breath. The world pauses for royalty and deformity alike, and sometimes one can't tell the difference.

Oxfordshire was not *very* like Essex or Suffolk, of course. But Ada was not thinking of Constable and rural English landscapes, but of Hell, and how the city of Oxford, its edges braided with rivers and its atmosphere close and clammy at times, was comfortably unlike Hell.

Since the arrival of her brother, Ada had become better educated in the atmospherics of the underworld. On the night of the bloody nappy, her parents had grown distracted enough for Ada to get her hands on her father's volume of Dante's *Inferno,* the first French edition of 1861. Ada could read no French but she could understand French pictures.

The sensational illustrations were by Doré. They weren't yet popularized in England; this edition had been procured in Paris by some clerical colleague of the Reverend Boyce. She had pored over the pages of the purloined book. She could glean little of the story of Dante's journey underground. But what a tale the pictures told. Everywhere gloom, and mystery, and oddment. Barren landscapes of slag-slope; creatures rare and frightening; and firm-fleshed nakedness throughout. Miss Armstrong, coming athwart Ada, had pounced. She'd impounded the book under her own pillow. She'd declared that worry had deranged the Master and sherry the Mistress, and for the nonce they were unfit to supervise their own children.

But too late. Ada had been vouchsafed a glimpse of the underworld. What glustery, ghastly improbabilities might open up beneath the roots of the Iffley yew, should the Boyces have to dig a grave in the family plot at the Church of Saint Mary for the burial of Infant Male! Ada hoped she might be excused from attending the interment. If any of those scaly-tailed figures were to emerge from the soil, let them grasp Miss Armstrong and drag *her* down, Persephone in Pluto's dirty palace. Miss Armstrong might find a new position, one more to her liking.

Children tread the line between worlds. "Suffer the little children to come unto me" isn't just the granting of permission, but the announcement of privilege, preferment.

So here we are. On her way to her friend's house, Ada rounded a copse of copper beeches along the riverbank. She came upon Alice's older sister sitting in the shade. Lydia had a big book in her lap. She looked up at Ada, startled. Perhaps lulled by the wind on the water, the morning light in the leaves, Lydia had been about to drowse. "Oh, you," Lydia said, with little affection. "You must be looking for Alice."

"Must I?" asked Ada. "I've been sent to deliver a gift of marmalade to the household."

"I shouldn't go there, were I you. Mr. Darwin of great renown is visiting today, and he and Papa are arguing about stuff and nonsense. They sent Alice and me away as they thought us too impressionable. Alice is about somewhere. She was here a moment ago. What is that dreadful odor?"

"It's the opodeldoc. For my rheumatism. What are you reading?" The book was splayed in full view. It featured nothing like the thrilling pictures of Doré. Only paired columns of type. There seemed to be no dialogue.

"You're too young for rheumatism. I should revolt if they tried to rub me with an unguent that nasty. Oh, the book? Papa thrust it at me and told me to read to Alice, but you know Alice. I was trying to do as I was told. The piece is about a Shakespeare play, *A Midsummer Night's Dream*. I doubt you've heard of it."

"Father deplores the stage. 'Vice in Three Acts,' he says."

"Curious. I didn't know there *were* that many acts of vice." Lydia had fifteen years to Ada's ten, and everything the older girl said sounded as if it meant more than Ada could understand. "Ah, well. It would be easier to watch this folderol than it is to read about it." Lydia yawned. "Alice was here a moment ago. Perhaps she has wandered over to look at the stork nest. You might find her there." Lydia pointed to some imprecise horizon. "You know our Alice. She plays hide-and-seek but sometimes forgets to ask someone to look for her."

"I'll continue on to your house and perform my duty."

"What a little prig you are. Stay out of Darwin's way or he'll turn you into a monkey. Or maybe an ass." Lydia flapped one hand at Ada. She turned a page of her book with the other. Then she paused. "Is someone calling after you?"

"Surely not," said Ada.

"Is that your governess? What is her name? Miss Armstrong? The tightly sprung woman from *Wolverhampton*?" She made Wolverhampton sound like Purgatory.

"Holy Hell," said Ada. "I'll be going now."

"The language of you young people." Lydia sighed. So few years on Ada, yet such opportunity for condescension. "Hide-and-seek, you too? I may pretend to be dozing so as not to have to speak to your governess. Though I suppose in any case she will sniff you out. Your medicinal cologne."

Ada didn't reply. She hurried to the other side of the tree, where a companion tree joined it at the ankle. The pair leaned out over the water, and Ada tried to lean along with them so they would conceal her. The double trunk split into tuberous roots, forming a proto-Gothic archway in the sandy bank just inches above the river. From that join, Ada saw a nose and then a face emerge, twitching. A denizen of the riverbank worried himself out. Adjusting his waistcoat and standing erect, he turned this way and that. He seemed not to notice Ada. She was in the shadows. She didn't dare call out to Lydia for fear she would startle the creature, but really: a white rabbit in a gentleman's waistcoat! Who could possibly have run up that snug apparel and struggled him into it?

"Miss Lydia," called Miss Armstrong, brisking along the path that meandered toward the riverbank from the outcrop of distant homes. "I was to accompany Miss Ada on her perambulations, but she left the Vicarage before I was ready. I am quite cross with her."

Ada didn't dare move. She watched Lydia expertly drop her head back upon the grassy bolster as if in slumberland. Good. She would not give Ada away. Ada leaned farther along the slant of the trees, trying to become more shadow-covered. The rabbit had hopped a few feet toward the sunlight, but at the sound of Miss Armstrong's voice he froze. "The time has got away from me," cried Miss Armstrong, "I couldn't locate my gloves. Miss Lydia, is Ada about? Have you seen her?" Then her voice dropped; she had noticed Lydia's closed eyes. "Beg pardon," whispered Miss Armstrong, and turned this way and that, as if sniffing for Ada.

All at once Ada found that she'd stepped into the rabbit-hole. If she didn't get loose, she'd be stuck here, clenched by soil and tree-root, pounced upon by her persecutrix. She put the marmalade jar in the pocket of her pinafore and reached down to dig her foot out. Though mere inches from the river, the sandy soil was dry and easily shoveled away. Still, bending at the waist was hard labor for Ada. Before she could retract her ankle, a sub-flooring of rotted root-mass gave way. She was in as far as her knee. She knelt, she had no choice, and she scrabbled at the yielding earth. She was swallowed up by the ground, just as she had hoped would happen to Miss Armstrong in Iffley churchyard. She found herself falling into darkness.

# CHAPTER 6

——— ⸙ ———

Another curious thing happened then.

A month ago Ada had noticed that she was outgrowing her iron corset, that penitential vest intended to tame the crookedness in her spine. Due to the fuss around her mother's troublesome pregnancy and the wretched offspring it produced, a new device had yet to be fabricated. Now, as Ada fell, the contraption underneath her outer clothes sprang open of its own accord. Ada was accustomed to such relief only in the bath or in dreams. How could the cord slip free from the grommets while she tumbled? The articulated halves of her portable prison were ripping through the cotton husking of her clothes. The appendages flapped behind her. Tatters of fabric—her camisole, her chemise—rippled. She was so shocked at the sense of liberty that it took her a moment to notice that this was a tumble without a stop.

In time—and when does a fall take time, except for the drift of a leaf or a snowflake, or perhaps a lapse into perdition?—Ada's attention turned to her plight. She was dropping down the middle of a cylindrical shaft shaped like a very long, very clean smoke-stack. What furnace but the fires of Hell might require such a column? In any event, all ought to have been Stygian darkness if she'd sunk more than a yard from the tree roots. But a pellucid gleam struck the walls at regular intervals. She couldn't tell where the subtle light came from. It seemed inherent rather than solar.

The sides of the vertical tunnel were paved neatly in Cotswold stone. This shaft must have taken laborers seven years to build, she guessed. Goodness, but it was lengthy. Perhaps she had slipped into some sort of sleeve inside a wheel-rim that went all the way around the globe, under the surface of the world, and joined up with itself in an endless circuit. The wheel that made the world turn. Eventually she would meet up with the hole she had first slipped into. Maybe she'd pop out again, head-first like that rabbit. Or maybe, while she was making her orbit, workers were sealing the breakage. When she reached the spot she'd entered, it would just be more stone, more brick. No doorway out. She'd fall forever and never land. She'd be the world's first internal asteroid.

Or what if she actually was dropping straight down, and would come out in the Antipodes? She might have to learn to walk on her hands. It could scarcely be harder than balancing on her feet, she supposed. Balance, as Miss Armstrong often reminded Ada, was a gift from the Lord to those who deserved it.

She heard a distant scream. Not terrified, but startled. Was it some screech she had made herself, an echo still ricocheting along the walls? Ada couldn't tell from which direction the sound had come. Might it be, perhaps, Alice? Was she here, too? If so, had she already fallen, or was she above Ada, just starting her descent?

Nothing to be done about it now, but wait till they met up. If they did.

She began to notice alcoves in the stonework. Some of them had been used as shelves. She must be falling more slowly than she thought, for by training herself to concentrate, Ada could make out some of the items. A candle snuffer like the one she'd once smuggled outside, in an attempt to catch a minnow while Miss Armstrong was lost in rue. Ada had dropped it in the water. How had it ended up here? Well, *down* here? And then a row of books. They looked suspiciously like those astringent volumes that Miss Armstrong had tried to read aloud until, one by one, Ada had misplaced them under sofa cushions or in the fireplace. Why, there was *The History of the Fairchild Family*! Ada recognized the scuffed bands on the spine of brown roan. How Miss Armstrong had shivered over the moral depravity exhibited by little lisping Henry, Emily, and Lucy Fairchild. Surely Ada had lost *that* book, thoroughly, in the grate? She'd stood there for some time, poking the pyre of coals so that no evidence of her own corruption survived to thrill her governess.

Ada was now falling so languorously that the book was within her reach. She could grab it to see if her name was written in the flyleaf. But she left it where it was. Should she be falling into Hell, she wouldn't be surprised to see *The History of the Fairchild Family* as a set text for the instruction of the juvenile damned. She felt she could almost quote her father's favorite passage. The one where pious Mr. Fairchild takes his sin-weakened children to see a corpse hanging on a gibbet. "The body of a man hung in chains; it had not yet fallen to pieces, although it had hung there some years. It had on a blue coat, a silk handkerchief round the neck, with shoes and stockings and every other part of the dress still entire; but the face of the corpse was shocking, that the children could not look upon it. 'When people are found guilty of stealing, or murder, they are hanged upon a gallows . . . till the body falls to pieces, that all who pass by may take warning by the example.'" Ada felt she could wait a while longer to meet this passage anew, and so she left the book where it was.

If she truly *were* falling in some sort of circuit, vast or immediate, she would pass this location again. Why shouldn't she place something else here and see if she came across it later? That would prove circularity of a sort. Should she leave behind her corset? No—while it had sprung free like an open trap, tearing her clothes, its iron webbing was still affixed to her arms. Perhaps the jar of marmalade in the pocket of her pinafore? Very well. If she deposited it here without delivering it to Alice's family at the Croft, it would become something she'd stolen. It would belong in this treasury of ill-gotten goods. So, soon enough, *voilà,* an empty ledge. As she reached to put the jar on the shelf, though, she dropped it. It fell more swiftly than she did, disappearing beneath her in the ill-lit gloom. She didn't hear anything like a smash, or anyone crying out, "Oy! Watch it up there!" Oh well. Marmalade has to make its own way in life, like the rest of us, she thought.

What with her tormented spine, she'd never been allowed to swim. She wondered if this was the time to try. She raked her limbs. She only succeeded in inching her corset farther off her arms. It wouldn't come off unless she undressed herself almost entirely. If I am headed to Hell, where's the harm, she thought. According to Doré, everyone is naked there. She wriggled out of her pinafore and then her smock and her torn chemise. The back brace, which often rubbed her raw despite the shift that she wore underneath it, began to clink and clatter. Twisting in the air, like Jacob wrestling with the angel, Ada managed to remove one arm from the iron sleeve-hole. The second arm slipped out much more easily. "Goodbye!" she said to the device as it arched its grommety iron spine and extended its ribs. It took to solo flight. It didn't fall as she fell, but began to rise. Soon it was out of sight. What that sourpuss Lydia would think of the iron brace emerging from the rabbit-hole without its cargo of twisted child, Ada couldn't begin to imagine. Up until ten minutes ago, Ada had not had much experience in the practice of imagination.

She was dropping faster. Since she was now falling face forward, she saw that she was catching up with the marmalade jar. Shortly she reached it and snatched it out of the air. Now she *would* store it, and see if it showed up again. Upon the next ledge she came across, two mice were larking about. They were dressed in blue denim caps and chewing on stems of grass. As if they'd been expecting her for most of eternity, they accepted the jar of marmalade she thrust their

way with brisk, businesslike nods. One of them winked. The
other tipped his cap. "It's meant for the Croft," she told them,
in case they were going toward Alice's house. However, Alice's house was home to that wicked cat, Dinah, so perhaps
mice would be unwilling to make deliveries to that particular
larder.

Would she see the marmalade again, and the *Fairchild
Family*? Would her flying corset come sweeping toward her
from below? If so, that would be proof she was falling in an
endless circle. She'd have to take up a hobby of some sort if
she were to fall for eternity.

Would she become lonely? Now there was an interesting question. She'd never been alone long enough to imagine what being lonely might be like. Perhaps she'd have the
chance to try. She might even like it.

Before she could decide whether or not she was pleased at
this possibility, her fall ended suddenly. Not in a bloody splat-
ter, as she might have feared had she got around to thinking
about it, but in a shattering splash. Salt water closed over
her head before she knew what was happening. A liquid ceiling divided her from the crepuscular tunnel above. Her eyes
closed of their own accord. Gone were the mice, and marmalade, and much else she had not yet had a chance to examine
closely.

Death, Ada's father had begun recently to insist, comes
to us all.

# CHAPTER 7

———— ✌ ————

Lydia. The sister who sits and reads in a book "with no pictures and no conversation."

Lydia's charade of napping has worked. Her eyelids are aware of a blond blur, a diffusion of sunlight. Miss Armstrong, the pinch-nosed spinster from the Vicarage, has passed by, hastening through the grass.

Having let the volume fall closed, Lydia leaves it like that. It pinches her finger. She doesn't mind if she loses her place. She has only the dimmest sense of what Shakespeare is on about in *A Midsummer Night's Dream*. Yet, almost against her will, Lydia has begun to absorb a notion proposed by the essayists. Shakespeare's farrago of a comedy, they suggest, is a series of nested stories. The maestro Shakespeare wants the theatregoer to see them as if cupped one within the next, or at least contiguous: a royal couple at their leisure; the court of magical Titania and Oberon and fierce Puck; the rustics practicing for their crude theatrical; the performance of that

sketch itself, which is another world. Does it go further in?
Lydia has lost track.

As she lolls in a state of sleep-like abandon (it is not sleep,
it is not a dream), Shakespeare's embedded narratives begin
to merge and overlap. Does the lion played by Peter Quince
have any significance to Puck? Do Puck's tricks matter in the
lives of Theseus and Hippolyta, crowned heads of Athens?
Does Shakespeare matter to a pubescent girl? Lydia, Lydia,
one hip nudging the bole of a tree, half sprawled on sweet
summer grass.

She almost dozes. The degrees of difference between
sleep and wakeful alertness are multiple. The closed book
makes a papery mouth upon her hand.

Now her thoughts jostle, like blossoms in a vase, blossoms
that someone has cupped with her palms, to refresh; but has
gone away again. The same flowers, the same thoughts, in
nearly but not exactly the same arrangement as before.

Instead of that Elizabethan rigmarole, Lydia's mind stut-
ters toward her own mid-Victorian world. She is dimly aware
of invisible systems and enterprises that hold her and all
whom she knows. Categories. She doesn't name them for she
isn't an encyclopaedist: Indeed, if she turned her full attention to this sidelong thought, it would evaporate. But we can
guess, we can glean.

The dramatis personae, first. Her father is a failed
scholar. Mr. Clowd is cerebral and uncertain, groping in
a world of shattered statues. Armless blind maidens, un-
manned kouroi. Lydia suspects he suffers the temptation
toward Rome, as this year he has dragged his family through

the broken arches of dissolved monasteries. Yet he is at the same time a distant friend of Darwin, through the Thomas Huxley connection—Huxley an outlier cousin of some sort. Lydia's father worries over the scandalous notion of natural selection with appalled fascination. In politics he claims no allegiance; he has become inured to Whig and Tory alike. Lately he's been known to stay up all night in the kitchen and bake himself a pie. Mrs. Brummidge was no end of startled when she found him one morning over the Kitchener range, floured to the elbows.

Lydia is old enough to picture her father dispassionately, or so she thinks. The pockety skin afore his ears, where he makes a hopeless attempt to trim his own sideburns. The spectacles always askew because, it seems, one ear is higher than the other. He is tall and scant of hair except on his chin and cheeks. From a distance he has the appearance of a walking cucumber that has gone deliquescent in the middle. He has always been cheerful to his daughters if distracted of late.

Darling Mama within her own moments. In Lydia's dozing mind we must allow only present tenses; there is no backstory in dream. Time slips all its handcuffs.

So: airs and portents for Mama. Scandals implied and denied in a single gesture involving the shoulder and the wrist. Mesmerism. An obscure form of what in a few decades will come to be known as aestheticism, though Mama's skirmishes toward beauty involve ecstatic poetry and plumes of drying marsh grass. She adores Lydia, is baffled by Alice, and never lets on that she is aware the neighbors call the girls the Iceblock Sisters, for the hydrocephalic proportions of their skulls. What are we learning? That this family is a family of courtesies, and secrets. But so is every family. The girls have overheard the titters, the muttered phrases meant to redden their ears. They've pretended to believe their mother hasn't heard them, too. They walk on, Mama in front with her hands folded, her daughters tottering along behind with their heads, like under-set puddings, wobbling as if they might tumble.

And Alice, ah, Alice. But Alice is largely missing from Lydia's thoughts.

Lydia has begun to dream of other networks of thought. They interpenetrate and interrupt, like great angled dials of diaphanous webbing. Faith and its horrors. The furtive lore of sex. The quirkish worlds of Andersen and Hoffmann and the unexpurgated Chaucer. It might as well be Puck, and Nick Bottom, and Oberon and Titania, and Hermia and Lysander: coordinates superimposed one upon the other, in this netherworld of not-quite-dream-not-yet-waking . . . until Lydia is hooked homeward by the sound of a hawking voice.

"Miss Lydia, I beg your pardon. I am disturbing your studies."

She had let down her guard; she opened her eyes. She regretted it at once. Again, that dreadful governess from the Vicar's house, cantering along the path. In accord to the laws of propriety as they pertain to servants, Lydia allowed a cool, cerebral, "Miss Armstrong."

Miss Armstrong had to catch her breath before replying. Lydia was already forgetting her daydreams. She was aware of the bright stamp of sunlight on the sky behind the trees. And Miss Armstrong a grotesquerie, a foreshortened ogress looming overhead.

Lydia sat up, thinking: It is like a tree, is it not, this business of *position*. I am like a squirrel in a tall tree. I have no squirrel words for how high the tree is or how to name my particular perch, but I know my relative position precisely. It is a good deal lower than Pater's, because he is the paterfamilias. Pater is lower than Darwin. Darwin in all his genius idiosyncrasy is nonetheless lower than the Queen. I am, however, on a higher branch than Miss Armstrong, despite her superior years. We both recognize that.

"How lucky for me, you're awake. Where might Alice be?" asked Miss Armstrong.

Ah, Alice, thought Lydia. Now, of children and *their* whereabouts, it is harder to speak. "Good morning, Miss Armstrong."

Lydia's courtesy was cutting. Miss Armstrong flushed. "You must forgive me. I have forgotten my manners. Good morning, Miss Lydia. You are keeping well, I trust?"

"You're looking for Alice?" asked Lydia. Rudeness to a servant from another household was unbecoming; Lydia had lost a little of her ranking. She made up for it. "You're out of breath, Miss Armstrong. Would you care to pause for a moment?" How careful, that *for a moment*.

"I mustn't interfere with your meditations." She opened her palm upon her waist in a casual way. "In actual fact, I wasn't really looking for Alice."

"Very wise," said Lydia. "Alice isn't easy to pin down.

She was here a few moments ago. We've been sent out of the house. Perhaps to escape contagion by blasphemy. Pater has several visitors, one of them a certain Mr. Darwin." She looked up to see if Miss Armstrong registered the name of Mr. Darwin. Miss Armstrong didn't seem to appreciate the outrageous prestige of such a visitor.

"Actually, it is our Ada I require," said Miss Armstrong. "The new lord of the family is fussing this morning, so Ada and I were to pay a call on your household and contribute a token of esteem. A jar of Mrs. Boyce's Seville marmalade. Ada left the Vicarage before I had found my gloves."

Lydia yawned.

"But Ada isn't generally allowed to wander the riverbanks alone, what with her—" Miss Armstrong looked into the hems of both gloves, as if the acceptable description of Ada's monstrousness were stitched thereupon. "Her condition," she concluded.

"Ada is able to move about quite well on her own," observed Lydia.

"Or so she *thinks*," said Miss Armstrong darkly. As if Ada were an amputee who hadn't yet cottoned on to the fact that walking was out of the question. "At any rate, I tiptoed past you here on my way to the Croft. Your cook said that Ada hadn't been seen there today, so perhaps she'd met up with Alice on the riverbank. And Alice would be with you, she said. So I've returned to find Alice, and I hope Ada with her."

Lydia looked about theatrically. "Alice is missing. Generally."

"That is unkind. Ada has her struggles, and Alice has hers. And so do you and I."

Lydia didn't want to be part of a compound subject conjoined with Miss Armstrong. "I don't know where Alice is. She was kicking last year's chestnuts into the water a while ago but has run off. It's true that Ada came by as I was reading, but I didn't see in which direction she headed. I'm sure the girls met up, and are larking about."

"Ada doesn't *lark*. It's not in her nature. And she hasn't the strength."

"Well, then," said Lydia, shrugging.

# CHAPTER 8

———— ✺ ————

Who first, upon sensing the backward rush of memory said to signal the moment of death, was able to telegraph this apprehension to the family gathered around? Maybe the original gentleman descended from ape said the equivalent of "falling out of tree" to his common-law ape wife, and she interpreted his words as "just as he left for the dusty world beyond, his whole life passed before his eyes. Then he hit the ground." After all, falling out of the tree is the first and the last thing we do.

And what might death seem like for those prior to language? Infants, say. Or for those incapable of memory, the simple folk known as God's beloveds? What can the final moments be like for humans who are now beyond both language and memory, like certain great-aunts in bonnets that went out of fashion a half-century ago?

For Ada, who was only a decade old, the memories came as illustrations in books. She saw first a dense and beautifully crisp illustration from that collection of Doré's engravings for *The Inferno*: specifically, **Plate 10** from Canto III, Charon supervising the embarkation of sinners in a boat on a dark lake. Unlike Ada, the sinners were magnificent human specimens, swollen into adult sensuousness with citrus-round breasts, if female, and mathematically beautiful abdomens and buttocks, if male. Without complaint the damned must have worn their iron spines in childhood, to die with such correct posture. Still, it wasn't the divine bodies of sinners that Ada now recalled, but the netherworld itself. Beyond the slopes of scree, Doré had limned a black sky pasted across with blacker, underground clouds. The landscape looked like certain sections of Cumberland she'd seen once on a family mission of mercy to an ailing great-aunt near Coniston. ("No rest for the Vicar'd," her father had muttered.) But Ada couldn't figure out Doré's sky under the earth, a sky that wasn't a heaven. It must be a holy mystery, to borrow a phrase from Cook. Or a damned mystery.

Twisting deep within the Lake Amniosis into which she had fallen, her mind flipped some page backward, to other illustrations she had seen. Because less pertinent, perhaps, to her effort of dying, they were less clearly apprehended. Some blotty woodcuts of *The Rational Brutes; or Talking Animals,* by Dorothy Kilner. The frontispiece from *Goody Two-Shoes,* published once upon a time at John Newbery's shop. Though it more often served the cause of mirth, that greasy volume had been passed down through her mother's family for the instruction of several generations already. One might live out an uplifting, book-length life if one was lucky. Or out-live one, if one was luckier. (*The Short Life and Inspiring Death of Ada Boyce: Presto to Finis, with Hand-tinted Woodcuts for Instruction and Delight, etc.*)

The oldest picture Ada could recall was a representation of Noah's Ark, on a page stained with oatmeal. Earlier than that she could not remember.

Drifting underwater, Ada felt as if she must have missed the Ark, along with the unicorns and behemoths and centaurs and other failed species. She was doomed to extinction any minute now. In the picture as she recalled it, bearded Noah looked like her reverend father, making no effort to notice his daughter flailing beneath the waves. Her mother was below-decks with her chin in an Old Testament chalice of madeira. There was no Cook on board the Ark as far as Ada knew; Ireland hadn't been invented yet. She had a suspicion that Noah's newborn infant son had trotted along on all fours and tripped up his big ungainly sister, making her sprawl and tumble overboard into the flood. Sororicide.

Then, to her surprise, she broke through.

But broke through what? It seemed, at least, to be the surface of the water. Perhaps more. As in the landscape by Doré, an impossible, outlandish sky lolled overhead with an unsettling suggestion of eternity.

She was naked. But she suspected she hadn't been made corporeally perfect in her plunge.

"I say," called a voice, "I do hope you're not drowning."

She looked about for a boat, for Noah and his Ark, for Charon and his bark, anyone on duty. She saw no boat, but as she pivoted—how much easier it was to move in water than on land!—she discovered that she was close to a strand. A couple of peculiar-looking creatures were making their way along the beach, from left to right. A Walrus walking hand in hand with a laborer of some sort. A difficult thing to accomplish, given that walruses sport nothing approximating a hand. Still, there was no other way to put it. The human had some obscure tools of his trade poking from a pocket in his laborer's leather apron.

Neither of them looked like Charon. Nor like Noah. Perhaps the human, who seemed to be a joiner, had learned shipbuilding from Noah, while the Walrus had survived the flood because, of course, walruses swim adequately enough.

"I may be drowning," she called.

"Please don't," came a reply. They had stopped and were peering at her. The Walrus was speaking. "We just saw a sign that said DROWNING IS FORBIDDEN AND PUNISHABLE BY DEATH."

"The Queen is ruthless about misbehavior of that sort," added his companion.

"If one drowns, one can't then be put to death," said Ada. She polliwogged nearer the shore, keeping her bare shoulders submerged.

"I don't know why you say that. One can drown one's sorrows in a flask of herring cordial, but the sorrows always return," said the Walrus. "They don't stay drowned. They can be put to death again happily enough."

He was a Walrus who looked as if he knew something considerable about sorrow. Then again, thought Ada, perhaps most walruses look like that.

"Why is an oyster like a writing desk?" asked the tradesman.

"Ah. My friend," said the Walrus to Ada, "is a Carpenter, and he knows many useful things about writing desks. As we are just returning from a breakfast with oysters, perhaps he intends to write about it." To the Carpenter, the Walrus said, "An excellent riddle, my dear man. The very wet child beyond may have an opinion on the matter."

"Why is an oyster like a writing desk?" called the Carpenter in a voice keyed to falsetto.

Ada had found purchase with her feet now, so she could stop rotating her arms and knees. She said musingly, "*Why* is an oyster like a writing desk?"

"That's *our* riddle," remarked the Walrus. "Don't ask it back to us. You can ask us one of your own. If you have one."

"I'm pondering. Why is an oyster like a writing desk?" She reviewed the conversation they'd had. "I think I know. An oyster is like a writing desk because neither can be drowned."

"That's the correct answer," said the Walrus. He drooped his moustaches farther than usual. "You're good."

"Do I get a prize?" asked Ada. "Where I come from, riddles are sometimes tests to prove the merit of the hero. If the hero guesses the answer correctly, very often a door is opened unto him."

"Well, if a hero comes along, we'll open the door for him," said the Walrus. "That's your prize."

"And if there isn't a door, I'll build one," said the Carpenter. "Do you have a riddle for us?"

Ada only knew one riddle. "When is a door not a door?"

The pair of beachcombers looked at each other from

beneath whiskery eyebrows. The Walrus shrugged. "It is a dreadful mystery," whispered the Carpenter. "No one can *ever* know the answer to that question. It is existentially, hyperbolically, quintessentially unknowable."

"I know it, and I'll tell you," said Ada proudly. "A door is not a door when it is ajar."

"A jar of what?" asked the Walrus. "Jellyfish jam, I hope? Mackerel marmalade?"

"No, *ajar*—it's a word that means *open*. Standing open."

The Carpenter slapped his palm against the Walrus's upturned flipper, and they danced a bit of a quadrille, as well as they could without six partners.

"Well, that settles that, then!" said the Carpenter. "Am I right or am I right?"

"Is that another riddle?" asked Ada. "What do I get if I answer it correctly?"

"A further chance to fail," said the Carpenter. He stopped cavorting and the two of them began to trudge away. Oyster shells, the ones that had fallen from their pockets as they danced, cracked when trod upon. They made a sound like the splintering of fine porcelain.

When the pair of ambassadors had passed from view, and Ada couldn't see another creature about, she clambered out of the salt sea. The air was cool on her skin. Her clothes waited on the strand, dry and neatly folded. They showed no sign of damage. A sprig of seaweed was attractively arranged upon the top like a spray of rosemary. Ada dressed with little pain and an ease that approached the gymnastic. The sensation was so novel as to be nearly troubling. Once appropriately clothed, she walked along the sand in the direction from which her interlocutors had come. She didn't care to encounter them again, at least not just yet. She wasn't sure why. Her gait was still lopsided, but so was the world, so she kept on.

# CHAPTER 9

It seemed there was nothing to be done but that Miss Armstrong must sit down. Lydia would be spared the essay analyzing Shakespeare's comedy. Trying not to feel grateful to Miss Armstrong about that, Lydia made the briefest of nods. The gesture was an unconscious imitation of her mother's, once upon a time.

Lacking awkward crinolines, Miss Armstrong collapsed to the grass with a flump. Yes, Lydia thought: As the poet contends, God's in His heaven—All's right with the world. The hillside's dew-pearled and slightly greasy. The governess's skirts will be creased, quite probably stained, she noted with satisfaction. She allowed herself to say, "I'm certain Ada Boyce is lurching about somewhere."

"Oh, yes, well. *Somewhere*," said Miss Armstrong dolorously, waving her arms. She looked alarmed. "I can hardly return to that—that *place*—with the news that I've lost track of her. I shall be let go if I am seen to have let *her* go."

"I expect you are referring to the Vicarage. How is Boykin Boyce getting on?"

"Assessments differ, but in any case, the little prince is croupy. That means Cook is unpleasant, and Ada is unpleasant, and Mrs. Boyce is—" She jumped over the treacherous gulf of that unspoken remark and landed on the other side. Which proved a still more perilous terrain. "And the Master of the house is my bête noire, Miss Lydia." But Miss Armstrong hadn't meant to utter those words. They'd been spoken from depths she believed to be beyond language. Knowing that she couldn't easily retract them or make them mean other than what they seemed to suggest in mile-high letters, she burst into tears.

Lydia didn't claw for the slip of handkerchief she kept in her pocket. Miss Armstrong would have her own. Sure enough, here it came, useful for blotting the nasal symphonics and the patting of eyelashes gone gluey in a monsoon of feeling sufficient to dampen all Rangoon. "Miss *Armstrong*. If you please."

That was all that was needed. Miss Armstrong regained her bearings as if she'd been arrested by a constable and brought before a magistrate under charges of public incoherence.

"My, my. I don't know what came over me, Miss Lydia. Perhaps the crying of Baby Boyce has become infectious. He's a right little runtling, he is."

Lydia, having caught the thread, was inclined to pull it. "Tell me about your Reverend Everard Boyce," she said. "I've hardly been introduced." The *your* was salt salt salt.

"I'm sure I don't gossip." Despite the testimony, Miss Armstrong looked entirely unsure.

"From a distance, the good Reverend Boyce cuts a fine figure."

"Oh, well, if it is figures you want, take up skating on ice." Miss Armstrong, proud of the riposte, straightened her spine.

"Is it true that Mrs. Boyce repaired to her chamber after the happy event and that she refuses to emerge?"

"From whom would you have heard such calumny? Yes, it's true."

"Which must put a certain pressure upon the rest of the household."

"I am happy to say clockwork could not run more smoothly than at the Boyce establishment."

"But the poor Vicar. I hope he isn't deprived of his wife's affections."

"You scandalize me, Miss Lydia."

"It was not I who burst into tears at his name."

Miss Armstrong cast her head away. The angle suggested she had avian forebears. When she relaxed and returned to glance at Miss Lydia, she said, "You are a wicked child, to tempt me toward an allowance of intimacy you've no intention of returning. My respect for my employer is unbounded, and exactly appropriate to my station and to his. I shall thank you not to return to the subject."

Lydia plucked at some grass and petted it as if it were the forelock of a Tennyson-besotted youth lying in her lap.

The tone she employed was languorous. "I have known un-requited love."

Miss Armstrong was stronger than that. "I suspect there are few girls of your affectionate nature who couldn't say the same. Miss Lydia, I am loath to return to the Bickerage—the Vicarage for the reasons given. I must find Miss Ada. But *your* home is in a state, your servants busy with the guests who have come to call on your father. Your Mrs. Brummidge said there was a child in the house but it wasn't Ada."

"I don't know who that might be. Perhaps the kitchen maid's sister has come to observe how to do no housework."

"Do you think there's any possibility Ada could be lurking about the Croft in the hopes of engaging that visiting child in play? Ada is lonely, you understand. And your sister can be fickle about including Ada in the romps of childhood."

Lydia felt a rare moment of guilt. "Ada shouldn't consider herself singled out for snubbing. Our little Alice often lives in her own world."

"She's not alone in that practice." Miss Armstrong rose and smoothed her skirts as best she could. Yes, grass stains a-plenty, but they didn't fill Lydia with the glee she'd antic-ipated. "If you have no recommendation on where I might find either of them, Alice or Ada, I shall continue to look on my own. But if Ada *should* come by, would you ask her to wait with you until I return? I shall be sure to pass by on my way home."

"I may not still be here."

"I wouldn't hold you here on my account." She gazed along the riverbank in the direction of the University Parks,

Christ Church Meadows, and beyond that Iffley, Bourne-
mouth, Majorca, Patagonia. "I suppose it's possible that,
giddy in her liberation, Ada decided to go see the Iffley oak.
It's a popular destination for those on a mission of picnic.
I only hope she hasn't slipped in the water and fetched up
against the milldam." She set out with a purpose, but turned
when Miss Lydia called her name.

"Miss Armstrong," said Lydia, smiling with a contemptu-
ous vagueness, "you mustn't fret. Your secret is safe with me."

"My secret?" said Miss Armstrong in a rush, as if she
had revealed something sinister about milldams and damp
ruined children. Then, remembering her admission about
Everard Boyce, she blushed a rogue scarlet.

Lydia settled back into the arms of the tree, and Shakespeare, and the lost romantics in the forests around Athens.

# CHAPTER 10

———— ❧ ————

$P$erhaps she dozed a little. It was that kind of an early summer day. In dreams, time may eddy and distort, but even when it traffics in the past, it does so in the guise of the present moment.

No breeze stirs. Water in slow motion. The glop of a tench breasting for a dead beetle. The river, so slow and murmurous as nearly to be mute, sealing the wound. The shriek of children at play across the fields, pestering a cow, whose bell makes jaundiced comment as she hustles away. Now a breeze arises. In the subtlest of commotions, poplar leaves shift and touch one another, and subside. A frog out of sorts with its social life croaks, but only once, as if thinking the better of it.

Dreams ride in us, frictionless, dark reflections in bright water.

Against the mutability of dream, the natural laws advocated by our bewigged Enlightenment forebears are powerless. Newton, for instance, insists on gravity and other prohibitions of the physical world, from which (while we are awake) we are never free. But we can fly in dreams.

Other bearded potentates—Jehovah, Cronos, all their ilk—they sort time through their fingers. They never confuse the strands: But dreams play havoc with sequence.

Of course, these days, the accepted sequence is under revision. Six decades and some into the century, though Browning does indeed reassure us God is still in His heaven, Darwin is taking tea in the Croft. Heaven shudders as Cambrian creatures shake mud from their gills, rewriting history. Sequence, and consequence.

Consider this moment. Queen Victoria, newly mourning the death of Albert the Prince Consort, has cast a spell of propriety, sentiment, and moral rigor throughout England and Scotland. *Consequentiality.* Lydia will spend her entire life in a nexus of Victorian social understandings too near to be identified by the naked eye, like viruses, or radiation.

At the same time, with ink staining his forefingers, and crumbs from his hard roll upon his lower lip, Karl Marx is hunched over in the Reading Room of the British Library. He frets, and lays dynamite. History has its own evolutionary strategy, toward consequentialities we cannot anticipate.

In 186_, faith is largely put in *structure*. Slice apart cadavers. Dig up Attic Greece. Examine gluey plant cells under magnification. Color another corner of Africa the geographer's salmon-pink of Empire, and install the new district commissioner in some obscure equatorial colony to the strains of a dark-skinned military band. Everything that exists is *intact*. Look at it. The established church, with the

Queen as its head. Righteous in faith! The British civil service in its first decade of rule of the Asian sub-continent, following the demise of the East India Company. Firmly in control. And social life: As rigid as the ironwork supporting the glass canopies of the great London railway termini— Waterloo, Charing Cross, Paddington—the class system keeps the London poor separate from the gentry. Mostly. Though some systems can be secretly porous, especially in certain neighborhoods after midnight.

Meanwhile, strictest of all, and affected by everything already mentioned, the rising middle class hold notions of childrearing that are hemmed round with creeds of nation, faith, and family. Children are cornered and dragooned even by those who adore them. For their own good. For the good of their characters and their immortal souls.

But what is character? How solid? We cut our hair, we shave our beards, we lose a limb. We remain ourselves. In dreams, however, we swap identities licentiously. We sabotage the structures of our character without a thought.

None of this occurs to Lydia in so many words. A little lost ladybird stumbled into great concentric spider-webs. Yet, as she drowses, sunlight pinking her bared forearms, she nearly wonders, where in all these enterprises of thought and institution is Lydia herself? What is the character of Lydia, and where the soul of Lydia, were there still such a thing as a soul?

And where, for that matter, *is* Alice?

# CHAPTER 11

Ada hadn't gone much farther along the strand when she came upon a door standing upon a wooden sill. The door was closed cleanly in its framing, but its jamb was unattached to any wall. Possibly a door that had been built in a shop and abandoned upright upon a beach. When is a door not a door?

Ada found it just as handsome and finished on the far side as on the near. Indeed, it was hard to tell if there was an inside or an outside to the thing. She tried the handle, but the door was locked. Then she looked more closely at the knob. Inscribed in tiny letters across the brass bulb, words so small she could just read them:

KEEP OUT.

Nothing would do, then, but to check the knob on the far side of the door. It said:

OUT KEEP.

Well, she thought, Miss Armstrong's favorite words for me are *outlandish* and *outrageous*. If through that door is where the *out* is kept, perhaps I have no business going there. She stumped on, disgruntled at having been denied entry to a portion of beach she could reach just as well by ignoring the door altogether.

Still, what sort of Hades might this be, if she were barred from certain sacrosanct sections? Maybe it wasn't actually Hell, just hellish?

Around a soft promontory, she came upon a stand of roses prospering in the lee of a stony slope. They tossed their heads in a salt wind. Ada didn't know much about horticulture. That would involve asking questions of Miss Armstrong and enduring her endless answers. On their daily marches, Ada could never spare the breath to gabble. She needed all her strength for walking.

The flowers were quietly talking amongst themselves as she neared them.

Ada had heard of the language of the flowers. Her parents had sent roses to the Croft that time. They had said that roses spoke of sympathy. But Ada hadn't understood that floriology had an actual tongue. In fact, Ada found symbolic language vexing. When Miss Armstrong Headstrong lunged toward a window, claiming that the sun was a golden chariot drowning in a flaming Tyrrhenian Sea, Ada humped across the room after her and saw only an evening sun partly covered by dark blue and orange clouds. On the basis of her inclination to be literal, Ada had had to relinquish her copy of the *Household Tales* of the Grimm brothers. She would find it worryingly fantastical and unscientific, no doubt, and probably pagan, too. Best not to risk it.

"I do so love a day served up like this. It suits my palate," said the tallest of the rose-trees, flexing her petals, which were a varnished, carmeline pink.

"Days like this, Rosa Rugosa, are a penny a pound," replied a second, a thorn-pronged cousin nearby whose blossoms were colored an apoplectic plum. "Cheap and cheerful, if you like that sort of thing; and, if you'll allow me to say it, common."

"It's a strain, pretty days," said a low-limbed third rose-tree, gloomily. "Frankly, I don't know why we bother."

"Ninny. We air our blossoms to signify the passion of the world," snapped the thorny purple. "Though what is passion but blood and *sorrow?*"

Ada knew that eavesdropping was very poor form indeed. As she inched closer, she turned her face to the sea so she wouldn't be caught staring. The horizon seemed to be nearer than it had been before.

At the crest of a strong spine about four feet high, the pink-blossomed creature called Rosa Rugosa bobbed. "You two would complain at being dipped in liquid gold. What's wrong with buttery sunlight and a vivid wind? I've rarely enjoyed a more gratifying light." She turned her upper leaves, as if opening her hands. "A day like this nourishes one."

"Well, Miss Happy Happiness! Such self-satisfaction," remarked the plum-violet blossom. "Preening all day, and for what? *I* never would. Wait till a lovesick courtier or a grieving widow comes by and tries to pluck *me*. I'll give them what-for with my thorns. Mark my words, Rosa Rugosa, you're becoming blowsy."

Rosa Rugosa took no offense, but rotated her sepal neckline the better to spread her pink petals about in the light.

"You're right, Rosinathorn," said the low-growing third to the second. "Rosa Rugosa looks like a hoyden behind a shop counter."

"Of course I'm right," snapped Rosinathorn. "She's parked right in front of me, Rosadolorosa, I can hardly see the shoreline for all her primping. I've a good mind to lean forward and stab her."

"Oh, why bother?" Rosadolorosa, the third tree, was a no-nonsense confusion of collapsing hoops and canes. Her few petty blossoms were arrayed without conviction on a single drooping spear. The blossoms meant to be white, Ada thought, but against Rosa Rugosa's pinks, they looked dingy and lacking in starch. "It's my belief that our lives are stolen from us. Ornamented with pinnate leaves and colored frills, we exist only as a consolation for others. I don't feel fulfilled. Indeed, some days I scarcely feel at all."

"If you begin to weep again from some nameless ontological grief, Rosadolorosa, I'll call for a pruning," declared dusky Rosinathorn. "Bad enough I have Little Honeysweet Sunshine to one side. To have the Flower of Death to the other side is more than stem can bear. I'm not sure which of you is worse."

Ada found arguing roses to be unsettling. It was so like

the Bickerage. "I think you're all lovely, each in her own way," she said peaceably.

"Horrors! A spy, listening in at our backstairs nattering!" said Rosa Rugosa. "Attitudes, girls!" She rearranged herself in as relaxed an odalisque's posture as she could, given she was outfitted with woody stems. Ada knew what *that* felt like.

"This is *such* a charade," muttered Rosinathorn. Her stems brushed against one another, clicking thorns.

Rosadolorosa made no attempt to compose herself, but sagged in the wind like a white shroud dropped upon the sands.

"I never met flowers who could speak," said Ada.

"You have not yet met us," said the first. "I am Rosa Rugosa."

"I don't mean to be impertinent," said Ada, "but can you tell me what you signify? I mean, in the language of flowers?"

The roses exchanged glances. "Why do you ask?" barked Rosinathorn.

"Some months ago my parents sent roses to the Croft. They told me the flowers conveyed a message. But I don't know flowers. Do different colors signal different messages?"

"Pink is for happiness," said Rosa Rugosa promptly. "*Tra la la* and all that."

"Purple red is for passion, but in my experience that usually means pain," snarled Rosinathorn. "Come close to my thorns and I'll show you."

"White is—but why should I signify anything to anyone?" murmured Rosadolorosa vaguely. "White is the absence of significance."

The Boyce family had sent the Clowds a bouquet of yellow roses. Literature, even of roses, remained a mystery. Ada dropped the matter. "It's a pleasure to meet you. My name is Ada."

"Was that Ada, did you say?" Rosa Rugosa leaned upon the available breeze; it looked something like a curtsey.

"Or Ardour?" snickered Rosinathorn, with a certain menace.

"Or Adder?" ventured Rosadolorosa. "The worm, the worm, he comes for us all."

"Ada. Miss Ada Boyce, of the Vicarage of Saint Dunstan's, Oxfordshire."

"A very low address," said Rosa Rugosa, "if *I've* never heard of it."

"Rosa Rugosa has pretensions," pointed out Rosadolorosa, sniggering. "Uppity."

"Isn't it rewarding to have friends of the heart?" asked Rosa Rugosa in a bright, hysterical tone. "Mine are always having fun with me." She beckoned Ada with a spray of leaves.

Ada came nearer, but not too near.

"Now, tell us how you like our little patch of heaven," said Rosa Rugosa. "Don't you admire it? I'm sure you've never before seen the likes of us."

"I don't mean to be contrary, but I've been to the Isle of Wight," said Ada. "I've seen roses along the beach before."

"Oh," said Rosa Rugosa. She sounded insulted, as if perhaps she had thought herself one of a kind. However, she rallied and continued in a sweet diatribe. "But have roses seen you? You can't be said to have properly established yourself in a place until you have been *seen* there."

Ada didn't know how to answer this. When she was out in public, passersby sometimes averted their faces, if not out of disgust then, as she preferred to think, out of charity. Perhaps Rosa Rugosa had a point. She turned her face from the roses so as not to give away her sense of disorientation, both at home and here. "Is it my imagination or is the sea shrinking?"

"There is no sea," said Rosa Rugosa. "This is only a very wide salt-water well. May I present my ladies-in-waiting, Rosinathorn and Rosadolorosa?"

"Who died and made you princess? I'm not waiting upon *you*," said Rosinathorn. "I just happen to be rooted in the same neighborhood."

Rosadolorosa added, "*I'm* waiting for your pink petals to go beige, Rosa Rugosa. If you must know. Death comes to us all. You first, I hope."

Rosa Rugosa seemed accustomed to the insurrection of her court, if that's what it was. They could get no nearer to her than fate had planted them; anyway, she was the largest and benefited from the best situation. Ada said to her, "Are you the queen who forbids drowning?"

"If she's a queen, I'm a sack of anthracite biscuits," snorted Rosinathorn.

"If she's a queen, I'm a hornet with a head cold," said Rosadolorosa.

Ignoring the rabble, Rosa Rugosa said loftily to Ada, "I suppose you could call me a princess. The royalty of beauty.

While you . . . well, you aren't beautiful at all. Indeed, you're not like any child I've ever seen before."

"Have you seen many little girls?"

"Never a one."

"Then I couldn't be like her. There's no one to be like."

"And indeed you aren't. Couldn't be more different if you tried."

Ada tried again. "Have you noticed someone named Alice come along?"

"Let me think," said Rosa Rugosa. "No. Rosinathorn, Rosadolorosa, have you seen an Alice?"

Perhaps they didn't know what an Alice was. Rosinathorn and Rosadolorosa refused to reply.

Ada hurried on. "It's just that—well, if she's here, I seem to have lost her."

"Perhaps *she* has lost *you*," said Rosa Rugosa. "You aren't much in the way of sparkling companionship so far. You're new here, aren't you?"

"I'm sorry that I've intruded," said Ada. "I'll just ask that gardener coming along the strand."

"Gardener?" shrieked Rosa Rugosa. She began to furl her petals. A creature was making his way toward them at a great speed. He was shaped something like a sail, but bothered by a wind that turned him sideways and showed him to be paper-thin. As he drew closer, Ada could see that he was a playing card about her own height. Which meant either he was a large card or she'd become a very little girl. The Ace of Spades, he seemed, on spindly legs. In one hand he carried a flower basket made of wicker, and in the other a spade.

"They *will* choose to live on the outskirts of respectable society, this lot," he huffed as he drew nearer. "Stand aside, child, or you'll be flecked with sand as I dig. I assume you want to keep your frock tidy for the afternoon affair."

"What are you doing?" asked Ada.

"She calls for roses, and roses she must have," said the Ace of Spades. Strong for a paper creature, he set to work in the sandy soil near the roots of Rosa Rugosa.

"I am being abducted!" shrieked the princess (if indeed she was one, and not just putting on airs). "Rosinathorn, to arms!"

Rosinathorn smirked as she retracted her jagged backbone.

Ada asked the gardener, "Who calls for roses?"

"The Queen."

"Queen Victoria?"

"Whosoever *that* is, she has no standing here. I'm talking about the Queen of Hearts, don't you know," said the Ace of Spades. "We ran low in our count of roses, and I am dispatched to swell the population."

"This is rape, this is plunder," shrilled Rosa Rugosa. "Rosinathorn, ready your thorns! Rosadolorosa, strangle this miscreant with your creepers!"

Rosinathorn and Rosadolorosa attempted nothing of the sort, but remained as still and mute as an arrangement upon a tombstone.

The Ace of Spades began to cantilever Rosa Rugosa's root system upon the spade. A fringe of airy brown threads came to light with a scatter of soil.

"Down below, she's dirty as the rest of us," sniggered Rosinathorn under her breath.

"Come to stay, have you?" the Ace of Spaces asked of Ada. Ada hadn't yet considered the duration of her visit to this peculiar place. The question made her uneasy. "I couldn't say," she replied. "I started out by looking for a friend."

"You'll find no friend *here*," said the Ace of Spades. "These are a heartless lot, roses. Very selfish. I'd suggest you try the royal family, the Hearts. But they're worse."

"Replant me at once or I'll tell the Queen you said that!" said Rosa Rugosa.

"You shut your gob or I'll paint you white," said the Ace of Spades. Rosa Rugosa obeyed, or perhaps she had fainted. The gardener threw the uprooted princess into his wicker carryall. "Any other volunteers?" The mean-spirited companions were shocked into silence. Rosinathorn shed all her thorns; they dropped to the ground around her. Rosadolorosa went from white to grey. She appeared to have died of grief, instantly. Before Ada could ask if she might join the Ace of Spades, he was hurrying around the promontory in the direction from which she'd come.

# CHAPTER 12

She left Rosinathorn and Rosadolorosa. There was nothing she could do for them. If they revive, let them learn to comfort one another with the language of flowers, she thought. Passion and Annihilation in the absence of Happiness. I have Alice to find.

She followed the Ace of Spades. She was just in time to see him arrive at the door in the sand. He located a key tied to a cord that looped through the handle of his wicker basket. He unlocked the door on the OUT KEEP side and went through, slamming it shut behind him. Ada had been calling to him, calling as in a dream, but her voice was small and lost in the wind. By the time she got to the door, it was locked again. When she walked around the door, the Ace of Spades and Rosa Rugosa were nowhere in sight.

She looked out to the horizon, puzzling. The sea was shrinking. The world on the other side of the ocean became visible. She'd always wondered where Noah's flood went when it was done. Now she knew. Underground.

This sea was gurgling with a murky slurp, as if draining into a section of the new London sewers. Everyone said
they were such a miracle, those sewers, relegating the Great
London Stink to history. Ada didn't know about that, but
she was familiar with an ebb tide at the Isle of Wight. She
expected a pungency of fish rot. She smelled only opodeldoc.
The blur of the incoming world was a wave of forest, green
heads of elm and oak a sort of leafy spume. I shall be crushed
by a marauding wood, she thought. This did not terrify her.
Something outlandish would be on the other side of that experience, another OUT KEEP, no doubt.

Still, she made herself rigid in case the force of the green
tide broke all her bones. She didn't want her limbs to be
scattered so far apart as to make reassembly difficult. She
understood that personal integrity was a matter of finding
the proper cage; she'd been broken before, yet her iron corset
had kept her contained.

The crowns of the trees reared back on all sides like the
heads of stallions at dressage. The limbs of onrushing trees
linked arms. The sea had become the size of a puddle and it
was still shrinking. Ada peered, hoping that if it disappeared
completely she'd be able to spy the drain. What could be
under the underworld? But when there was hardly more than
a cupful of salt water left in the sand, it resolved itself into
the bowl of a teacup set upon a saucer. Tied to the porcelain
handle was a tag. Words were written upon it.

Ada groaned at the effort of bending, but the groan was
only habit; bending hardly hurt at all. Before she could lift

the cup and saucer from the sand, however, a breeze blew the sand away, revealing a shiny disk. This turned into the glass top of a rosewood table that thrust itself out of a wooden floor much as a fountain rises when the spigots are first opened. The table grew to the height of a pergola, elevating the teacup far out of Ada's reach. In the shade of the closing forest, only a cup of ocean, and it was over her head.

I ought to be able to see what the tag says, even if it just says NO BATHING FOR THREE HOURS AFTER LUNCHEON, thought Ada. Try as she might, she couldn't climb the pedestal of the table high enough to read the tag through the glass. She looked about to find some fallen tree limb that she might prop against the tabletop and thereby scale the slope to the glass plateau. Only now did she realize that, though the approaching forests had halted in time to keep from crushing her, they'd come dreadfully close. They'd boxed her into a sort of capacious coffin. And the forest was turning itself inside out. It assumed the look of an attractive beveled paneling that lined four sides of a windowless salon. She could find only one door in this long, high chamber, the previously isolated door that said KEEP OUT. It was now properly fitted into a wall. Snug, and no doubt still locked.

Overhead, what Ada had thought were intertwining boughs turned out to be a pale green ceiling, done over in a plaster molding that emulated the fan-vaulting in Brasenose College Chapel. The effect was faintly pietistic. In the center of the ceiling, the branches twisted themselves into another instruction: DON'T LOOK UP.

# CHAPTER 13

There is no earthly reason why I ought to stay here for the benefit of that Miss Armstrong, thought Lydia. If Ada falls into mischief through lack of supervision, her governess will be shown the door. Then that poor woman's struggles over her feelings for the Vicar will be a matter of the past. In any event, it isn't my duty to play watchguard for Ada Boyce. I'm nobody's servant.

So with a determination to be brusque and to enjoy it, she rose to her feet and turned back toward her own home.

The day was continuing warm, indeed warm enough that showers might follow by tea-time. A certain broodiness of cumulus out toward the Cotswolds as Lydia picked her way along the path. She avoided the eyes of strolling summer scholars and Saturday marketgoers, hustling by with their baskets and barrows, as assiduously as they attempted to catch hers.

Pater had said to keep out from underfoot until the guests left. She expected he had *meant* to say, "Keep Alice away, as she will only ask vexing questions." Lydia wasn't certain, but in any case, she was hardly dragging Alice back before teatime. Lydia would slip in through the kitchen garden and disturb no one. If Alice had already come home and was interrupting affairs, Lydia could claim to have become lost with Theseus and Hippolyta in the forests around Athens. Pater would allow that much.

She made her way past the rangy yews and into the kitchen garden. Upon the margins of the grounds surrounding the house, newer neighborhoods were encroaching—the elegant terrace houses in the crescents of Park Town were almost visible through the distant phalanx of trees. But, dating from some previous century, the Croft lingered on, lacking style and symmetry. An undistinguished stone farmhouse with halfhearted stucco chipped away in patchwork pieces to reveal glimpses of a frame timber construction, oak beams filled in with a crazy quilt of brick, rubble, stone. The house seemed to list in the sunlight. An effect of irregular eaves, perhaps. The back door was open. Hens were wandering about like ladies at a lyceum tea trying to find their friends before selecting their seats. The dovecote was silent. The heat made doves dozy.

Mrs. Brummidge was slapping dough on the pastry table. Great whuffs of flour paled the air. The room reeked of stewed celery and onion broth. "Thought you was Carter with that brace of hares, I did," said the cook, wiping straying hairs away from her brow with the front of her wrist. "But it's the likes of Miss Lydia inspecting the kitchens, no less." Her tone was less mocking than it may sound. She was, perhaps, a bit intimidated by the young mistress of the house. "Where's Alice at, then?"

"Isn't Alice at home?"

"If she's not with you, she's missing again. I worried as much to your father this morning, but then I decided she'd gone with you."

"I expect she's wandered back. Must be loitering somewhere."

"Miss Lydia, I made a jam pasty and left it steaming on the sill; that always draws Alice for a nibble if she's haunting a place. But she's not come around, I notice. Mayhaps the child has taken Dinah and her kittens up the back stairs to the nursery? My back has been turned what with a luncheon for guests to manage, so nothing is impossible. Nip up them steps and have a look-see. If she's not crooning to the kittens, I'd say she's still out and about."

Lydia gripped an unpainted chair and sat down. "If she's home, we'll hear her in good time. How are things in the parlor?"

Mrs. Brummidge gave Lydia a look the girl could not read, waited a moment before continuing. "You'd have to ask Rhoda. She's been doing the coming and going."

Rhoda sat in the corner unthreading the runner beans. "Lot of talky-talk in there, they had to open the windows to let the words out," she said.

"How is the mighty Darwin? Is this part of a delayed victory lap?" The Great Oxford Debate several years ago, in which Darwin's theories had been attacked by Bishop Wilberforce (and defended by the family's distant cousin Thomas Huxley,

among others), was by now old news but still fun. Even boot-
blacks, disagreeing about the proper practice of their trades,
threatened to rent out the Oxford University Museum of Natural History to argue their positions. Still, those who regarded
the book of Genesis as factual took the notion of transmutation
from beast to mankind very seriously indeed. Sedition, calumny, apostasy. There were some who said Darwin would be
ill-advised to wander in dark Oxford lanes without a cosh and
a pistol or, barring that, an agreeable gorilla to defend him
against attacks from the spiritual thinkers of the day.

"I try not to overhear when I am retrieving the tray," replied Rhoda, full of self-admiration, as if listening to Darwin
hypothesize on pre-history might irritate her morals. "He has
added inches and fullness to his beard since his last visit. I'll
say no more."

"Perhaps he means to serve as a walking exhibit of Early
Man before Tonsorial Parlors." Lydia had her hands full
with her own talents, appetites, delusions, and curiosities
about life as it was lived in high June of 186_. Pre-history
to a fifteen-year-old girl child means nothing further back
in time than the courtship of her parents. "I don't suppose
Alice is in there with them? Rhoda?"

"No; just the master, and Darwin, and an associate visiting from Philadelphia or Boston, I believe, and his little
black beetle."

"Another specimen to examine? Is it pricked into a page
with pins?"

"We don't gossip in my kitchen," snorted Mrs. Brummidge.
Rhoda bent ostentatiously to her work. Lydia, included in the

condemnation, felt chafed under instruction. She was imagining a campaign of insurrection, though had not settled on a strategy, when a knock sounded on the door from the passage.

"Goodness, could they not *ring* when they need attention?" hissed Mrs. Brummidge. "And me not done up proper to conduct a tour through the operations." She adjusted her apron. She wiped some apple peels from where they'd clung to the cloth. She added, "The master is bringing Darwin through to examine lower life-forms, Rhoda. Straighten your spine or you'll be mistook for a mollusk."

"Maybe it's Alice's nurse, back early," said Lydia.

"Miss Groader has gone to Banbury to deal with her ailing mother. She won't return until the morrow. That's why *you* were to be looking after Alice." Arriving at the door to the passage, Mrs. Brummidge opened it with a brusque gesture, part genuflection and part defensive crouch.

It was neither beardy Darwin nor the master, after all, but a younger gentleman in fine enough clothes to make both Rhoda and Lydia sit up. "Ah, I've come to the right place," he said. "Always an exercise in temptations, which closed door to approach." He spoke in one of the American accents; Lydia couldn't distinguish among them. To her they all sounded dry and tinny. Almost quack-like.

"What can I do for you sir." Mrs. Brummidge was immune to the charms of a well-fitting waistcoat upon a trim male form if the form was a foreigner. The visitor had removed his coat, as the parlor took the morning sun punishingly. In his shirt-sleeves and buttoned vest he seemed the very grocer.

"I wondered if you might have some milk."

Lydia stood and folded her hands together so the full impact of her juliette sleeves might register. "I'm Lydia. The mistress of the house, more or less."

"I beg your pardon." He bowed and blushed. "I'd been told you would not be at home today, and I assumed—how foolish of—" He all but swallowed his collar. "Mr. Winter, at your service."

So now, an impasse. No further conversation was possible. Lydia despite her status in the household was no more than a hostage standing in the center of this flour-strewn flagstone floor. This was Mrs. Brummidge's domain.

The cook sniffed. "We don't hold with milk drinking in this house unless there is a sick child. Too many vile particules. I could supply you with a glass of nut ale. Or a barley water. Take your choice. Unless the child is sick?"

"Child?" said Lydia. Affecting too maternal a tone would be a strain, and unconvincing; she tried merely for the investigative.

"Barley water would do nicely. Miss Lydia," said Mr. Winter, and bowed. "Cook." He glanced over at Rhoda and gave up, and disappeared.

"*Child?*" said Lydia, turning to Mrs. Brummidge with lifted nostrils, suggesting outrage at not having been informed. But of course: Hadn't Miss Armstrong mentioned another young scalawag on the premises today?

"You do *such* a job keeping track of Alice," retorted Mrs. Brummidge. "How mortifying, was you to lose a visiting child in the bargain. And one traveling with His Noxiousness Mr. Darwin, no less." (Mrs. Brummidge did not care to imagine chimpanzees swinging from the branches of *her* family tree.)

"I'll take the lemon barley through when it is ready," said Lydia.

"I wouldn't hear of it. A scandal. Rhoda, off your rump and look smart." Though the *Mrs.* was an honorific, Mrs. Brummidge maintained a matron's sense of decorum. She enjoyed wielding it as a weapon. It was more effective than irony.

# CHAPTER 14

———— ❧ ————

$A$da sat and leaned against the pedestal of the table. To judge by the solitary piece of furniture, she seemed to be in a hall for giants. Yet she could spy no entrance for them. The KEEP OUT door in the baseboard looked like one from a writing-desk cubby. Ada felt very small indeed. But agile, like a mouse, not like a broken toy lost under the settee. Surely she could worry her way through that door somehow? It seemed to be the only exit.

She scurried forward and tried the knob again, in case it had changed its mind and wanted to open. It did not. But this time she thought to look through the keyhole.

What began as undifferentiated sheen organized itself into patches of green and blue. A lawn of some sort, a sky. A wall of topiary hedge clipped into the shapes of domesticated hens, as far as Ada could tell. Along came the Ace of Spades with the basket containing Rosa Rugosa, who was trailing her roots through the grass in a most unladylike display. Ada cupped her hands around the keyhole and called, "Hallo, over here! Open the door!" But the Ace of Spades, if he even heard Ada, kept traipsing. His head was down, possibly to find a burying plot for Rosa.

Until now, Ada had been drifting through this unusual day with disregard for what she'd left behind and for what might lie ahead. Had it occurred to her to ask the question— *what is this adventure like?*—she might have concluded that her visit seemed like a story or a dream. In any case, it didn't correspond to life as she had known it so far.

A story in a book has its own intentions, even if unknowable to the virgin reader, who just lollops along at her own pace regardless of the author's strategies, and gets where she will. After all, a book can be set aside for weeks, or for good. (Burned in the grate.) Alternatively, a story can be adored for centuries. But it cannot be derailed. A plot, whether abandoned by a reader or pursued rapturously, remains itself, and gets where it is headed even if nobody is looking. It is progressive and inevitable as the seasons. Winter still comes after autumn though you may have died over the summer.

As for dreams, they are powered by urgent desire, even if that desire is only to escape the quotidian. Ada, who lived with a sense of disappointment and failure, thanks to her misshapen form, suffered from a flat dream-life, one that seemed poorly differentiated from her waking hours. As a stolid child, her dreams were of static things, almost still-lifes: a lump of cheddar on a board, a goat roped to a tinker's cart, a curving road.

Now, however, Ada no longer felt like the passive observer of an unfolding fiction or of a dream daguerreotype. Something new rose in her, a thrill of ambition. She had to get into that garden. She *would* get into that garden. She didn't know why she felt so strongly about it. Usually she didn't much care for gardens. The garden at the Vicarage was a mess, what with the monkey-puzzle tree needing pruning and the orange hawkbit colonizing the verge. But this garden looked entrancing, something like a college garden glimpsed through forbidding gates. Such Oxford gardens would remain off-limits to the likes of Ada, both for her gender and for her crab-gaited form. And probably for her latent sinfulness. All the more important that she gain access to this paradise in the keyhole.

She peered again. Beyond the door, the lawn was shorn and rolled to Pythagorean precision. The clouds were perfect, neither too many nor histrionic. As she watched hungrily, the cumuli began sliding down the side of the world and changing places with the lawn. This proved disconcerting, like a picture in a book turned upside down. Why, there was the Ace of Spades digging a hole in the lawn-sky, and stuffing Rosa Rugosa root-first into the green-fringed heaven hovering over a blue eternal sky-sea. It was amusing to see the Ace of Spades sprinkle water upward. "This *is* a day I'm having," said Ada to herself.

"No, it's not," said a voice behind her. "It's a day *I'm* having. You're only decoration. A sort of mousy, apprentice Erinys detached from her clot of spectres, I imagine. Lose your way?"

She turned and discovered a lopsided crescent moon hanging above and to one side of the glass tabletop. "Did you speak?" she asked it. "You, moon?"

The moon distorted itself to answer. "You were expecting a Pantagruel come through for his cup of ocean? The instructions tell you: Don't look up."

"I was always taught to look a person in the eye when addressing them. Though it's difficult to do now. Your eyes are invisible."

The moon-mouth said, "I'm feeling hungry, but harpy or mouse, you are extremely odd-looking. I hope you don't taste untoward."

"I am no mouse. I am a little girl."

"You are either a *very* little girl or an indecisive Fate or an argumentative and dissembling mouse." The sliver-moon began to seem more like a cat's mouth. Ada was glad the rest of the cat wasn't present, as a cat that size would scarcely leave room for her.

"Do you know how to get into the garden?" she asked, to change the subject.

"Through the door, of course. When it's ajar."

A guttural hiss or a purr, Ada couldn't decide which, rumbled from behind the smiling moon-mouth. Then a tongue emerged from between pin-teeth. It angled to lick some invisible part of the implied cat. When Ada realized that the cat was probably bathing its particulars, she was glad the body was absent. Gigantic feline organs of any variety weren't included in the list of classic panoramas she might hope to glimpse before she died.

She thought it would be polite to divert attention from the practice of hygiene. "The garden beyond that door is circling itself somehow."

"No it isn't," said the cat-mouth. "It's the keyhole that's rotating."

Ada looked again. Sure enough, the keyhole was moving in a clockwise direction, one complete rotation to the minute. "I met a gardener who had a key. But he's already inside. Is there another key?" she asked.

"There may be, or may not be, but either way it means nothing to me. This is my day, after all, not yours. I have no interest in attending a garden party."

"I should think we share the day equally," ventured Ada.

"Impossible," came the reply. "I'm much larger than you are. So we can't share anything equally. Grow up a little and you'll see what I mean."

"I would like to know what the tag on the teacup says. Since you are much more lofty than I, you could read it and tell me."

One orange cat-eye appeared, and squinted at the table-top. "It says: DRINK ME."

"I find that hard to believe."

A bit more of the cat appeared, nearly its whole face, including a pair of twitching ears. A mask floating against walnut wainscoting. "I could carry you in my mouth and deposit you on the tabletop if you like, and you could see for yourself if I'm lying." The smile now looked like a leer.

Ada was afraid if she walked into the cat's mouth she might fall out the other side. What would Miss Armstrong say? "I'd better not," she said. "I know a little bit about the damned crowding into Charon's boat, but I don't know much about ghosts, including ghost cats. There might be some contagion, and I don't think I'm ready to be a ghost."

"No time like the present. Can't I interest you in a little bite?" The mouth loomed. "I think you are wearing a tag that says EAT ME, but you have hidden it in your clothes. That's why mice shouldn't wear clothes."

Ada said, "I have only one life. I need to take care of it."

"Very well said. Off and away with the fairies, indeed. *That* was a smart move." Ada couldn't tell if the spectral cat was mocking her. It continued. "They buried *me* under the Iffley yew. A new grave was open and they packed me on top of a coffin before they filled in the hole. It's true cats have nine lives, you know. But cats can't count. So I don't know where I am."

"I don't know where I am either. But I know where I want to be. Won't you please tell me where I can find another key?"

The cat-head didn't reply, but set to licking the ocean out of the teacup. As it beaded up on the cat's whiskers, it no longer looked like drops of salty sea, but like cream. "Since this is *my* day, by and large, I have no reason to satisfy the urges of the most peculiar mouse I have ever met. Still, I'm feeling fat and satisfied. *Do* climb into my mouth, my dear. More than one way to get into that garden, you know."

At great speed, the mouth dipped very close to her. The smile looked less hungry than kind, but Ada stepped back. "I am too timid," she said, "and we've hardly been introduced. Another time, perhaps."

The haunted mouth began to fade. "Very well. I can wait. May I give you a bit of advice?"

"Please do."

"Don't take the advice of anyone you meet here. We're all mad."

Ada thought about it. I've just met *you*, and your advice is not to trust you. If I *don't* take your advice, then I *should* trust you. I guess I have to trust you and not trust you. Your advice wheels about like the keyhole. There's no way in.

Watching the cat-head dissolve much as daylight does, by unnamable degrees, Ada's eyes fell again on the words in the ceiling tracery. DON'T LOOK UP. Why trust *that* advice? Noticing that the plaster tracery had sent tendrils down the paneling, and that they were beginning to take root in the floor, she found a foothold and then a second. She began to climb toward the green heaven.

# CHAPTER 15

Mrs. Brummidge poured; Mrs. Brummidge squeezed the lemons; Mrs. Brummidge scooped the sugar; Mrs. Brummidge took a great wooden spoon and stirred the concoction. "Whilst you was out reading and losing track of Alice," she said to Lydia, "that governess from the Vicarage came sniffing about for Ada Boyce, who'd been sent here with a jar of marmalade. But we never seen her, nor the marmalade, which will be welcome should it ever arrive."

"Young ladies these days," said Lydia, deciding how to proceed. "One would think there were gypsies about, the way small girls disappear."

"Well, our Alice has her own compass, no doubt about that and don't we know it well. But Ada Boyce is docile as a lambkin."

"A mammoth, compromised lambkin."

"Don't be snarky. Ada's lighting out on her lonesome

vexes her governess no end. You've not seen the poor afflicted child, did you?"

"Well, I did. And then I did not," said Lydia. "I said as much to Miss Armstrong as she flurried by me after having accosted you for news. She's a high-spirited ostrich, not made for patience, I think."

"Well, that *household*," said Mrs. Brummidge darkly.

"What do you mean?"

"I once went by to borrow some malt vinegar? That time the grocer was gone away? Due to his old gaffer's getting his head split open by a falling chamber pot? The kitchen door of the Vicarage was open to the sun and their cook didn't hear my knock, so I stepped inside." Mrs. Brummidge looked this way and that, as if there were agents who might hear her spilling testimony against the House of Boyce. "She was drinking *tea* from the *spout*. Oh, it's an ill-run house, from garret to cistern. I don't wonder Miss Armstrong flusters so." At this she caught herself. Too much had been said. She finished up with the lemon barley. She whisked a tray from the shelves beneath the window. "Rhoda, look smart. They'll be waiting for this."

Lydia stood. "Rhoda, keep at your beans." The kitchen maid was flummoxed, as if caught between a constable and a clergyman and unsure whom to obey. At Lydia's insurrection Mrs. Brummidge took a sluice of air between her teeth and backward-whistled it in. But she said no more about it. She placed the tray with the lemon barley and some drinking glasses and a plate of morning cake upon the pastry table.

She retreated, as if the refreshments were about to detonate. She trained her eyes on the floor. Rhoda settled her rump back on her three-legged stool.

Lydia didn't speak again, but picked up the tray. She led with her shoulder through the swinging door into the passage. When she was halfway along, she heard Mrs. Brummidge hiss at Rhoda, "Unseemly!" with the same tone of scandal she might have used had she been saying "Strumpet!" or "Baptist!" She does have her opinions, does our Mrs. Brummidge, thought Lydia. She was stymied for a moment at the parlor door, which was closed. How does one knock and open a door while carrying a tray? How did Rhoda ever manage? Balancing one edge of the tray against her bosom, Lydia freed her right hand to knock. Then she went through, into the male preserve of Pater, Mr. Darwin, and that handsome Mr. Winter.

The light was bright. The breeze off the Cherwell delivered an odor of June mud, backwashed with essence of meadow-grass and a whiff of cow. Mr. Winter was quiet and attentive, lifting on his toes before the open window. His hands were clasped in downward prayer. His eyes did not tilt toward the door. Nor did those of Pater or of Darwin. But Lydia could hardly blame them. They were expecting no one more exotic than Rhoda.

She set the tray down on top of the closed harmonium. Her back turned to them, Lydia listened intently to the men. Darwin seemed to be reading from his own manuscript, line by line. Pater was commenting in words of solemn circumspection. It reminded Lydia of the way the local boys would beat the bounds of the parish every year, with peeled willow wands and high hilarity. Of hilarity there was none from Darwin, nor from dear father, but the intensity of thrashing seemed to her the same. Every yard of statement needed to be tested for soundness. What Mr. Winter was adding, other than devotion to the holy cause of thought, was unclear.

Lydia rotated at the hip, waiting for a pause in the proceedings so she could offer to serve. Mr. Winter against the bright window was a silhouette. His hair was silvery blond and sleek. His form was neater even than it had seemed in the kitchen. How nice that he wasn't lost in one of those sexless black gowns in which the scholars tramped about, hooting in sunshine and huddling in rain.

A patch of shadow in a darker corner of the room shifted from beside the aureole afforded Mr. Winter. Lydia started, making a small, contained movement. Was Alice hiding in here all along? Impossible. But the shape was childlike. "Mercy upon us," she said with displeasure. Darwin paid no mind. Pater looked up. She could not turn toward Mr. Winter.

"Lydia, whatever are you doing?" said her father.

"I am here to deliver a beverage, Pater, as requested by your other guest. I had been told there was a child. I see I had not been told everything."

The creature came forward. His countenance was of a very un-English hue. He was of Africa, or from some plantation in Hispaniola or Barbados or the like. His skin was shiny as oiled mahogany. Hair cropped as if for nits. With undisguised thirst, he cast his glance upon the drink. "Yes, this is meant for you," she said. His hands came out to clasp the glass before she had filled it. For an instant she saw his hands were gammon-pink upon the palms. This surprised her, as the boy was otherwise as coal-dusty as a sweep at the end of his fourth flue of the day.

Darwin went back to his text, her father to his exegetic murmuring. Mr. Winter moved across the carpet so he could speak in a lowered tone. "Miss Lydia, you honor us," he said.

"No one mentioned the child was a boy," she replied, in tones even lower, "and an aboriginal at that."

"May I present him to you? Miss Lydia, this is Siam." The boy didn't meet her eyes. He downed the lemon drink like a Berber lately crawled from hot Sahara sands.

"What is he doing here? With—with them? With you?" She realized it might sound uncouth, her inquiry, but she could be considered the mistress of the house, by some accountings anyway. She threw back her shoulders to suggest authority.

"Well, miss, the lad's traveling with me, you see. I'd arrived at Down House to meet the great man. I'd a letter of introduction. To my surprise, despite his recent aversion to travel, Darwin announced he'd made a previous appointment to visit your father"—at this Mr. Winter's voice became a whisper—"in his bereavement. My unexpected arrival was timely. I was invited to come along and assist, as Darwin is too frail to travel alone."

"Yes," said Lydia, also in private tones, "but—but. This boy. He seems young to be your servant."

"No, no; not a servant, you're right about that," said Mr. Winter hastily, as if that explained everything.

"Mother has been dead for several months. Why has Darwin come now? And why have you bothered to come with him?" Lydia felt she was asking questions too grand for the custom of the parlor; she might well continue with *And why did Mother die, and where did she go?* But she stood looking at Mr. Winter with a ferocity that, though she had no idea of it, was nearly glamorous.

"I understand that your father was kind to Huxley when he was here defending Darwin's theories against the charges of heresy. Darwin has his head in natural science, but everyone has lost someone," explained the guest, hushedly. "Darwin his daughter Annie, this house its beloved matriarch. The heart is a construct of any waking creature, and Darwin has a heart, too."

"A heart *and* a mind. I suppose Pater wants to discuss the immortal soul with Mr. Darwin." She sighed, as if it was a recurrent argument about interior plumbing.

"The great man is not well," said Mr. Winter. "He lives in his sickroom. Had I not shown up opportunely upon his doorsill, he'd never have managed this trip. I can see it is taking a toll. I should go back to his side."

The little boy had finished a second glass. "There will be none for the others," said Lydia rudely. "Though I suppose I can negotiate a fresh supply. How does this scamp come to be with you?"

"He can speak for himself. He speaks English quite well.

Perhaps you would like to show him around, now he is comfortable here? He's slightly bored."

The world of men, always reconvening, asserting itself. The pull of her father's susurrus, Darwin's cautious replies. Mr. Winter preferred that over conversation with her. "Very well," she said. "Master Siam, is it? You may accompany me. You may tell me something about yourself."

The lad followed her willingly enough, only pausing at the door to glance bright eyes at his guardian. Mr. Winter had returned to the window. He'd struck up again the posture of acolyte. An Athenian harkening to Socrates. "Come along lest you get lost, too," said Lydia to the child.

# CHAPTER 16

————— ✑ —————

$A$da hadn't climbed more than a few yards up the strut-work of the great hall before she saw that the flanking curlicues of plaster were no longer symmetrical. Now they seemed to be teased into variety. The cold molded surface fragmented in her hands as she climbed. It crumbled like old moss, revealing the suppleness of living wood. She turned to look about her. She realized that the hall had turned back into a forest. She was climbing one of dozens of trees growing so closely together that she could see no horizon.

What about the teacup, the tag, she thought. She looked down. Perhaps she could read it from above? But she'd achieved too great a height already. The table below her had lengthened, and covered itself with a cloth, upon which several dozen teacups and quite a few pots of tea were set about in a higglety-pigglety fashion. She couldn't identify the original teacup among them from this vantage. Well, when

I finish seeing where I am, she thought, I shall climb back down and have a spot of tea.

It felt wonderful to climb. Her feet possessed a new and certain stepping-knowledge that they had never had on paving stones or staircases. At home, the very pattern in the carpet could trip her up, it seemed.

Ada wasn't the type to analyze her moods, generally. Even now she didn't dwell on the idea of elation. But she felt it as she climbed. A promised view often lifts the heart.

She was reaching a point where the canopy was becoming thinner. She had to be careful to settle her foot squarely in each forking branch for fear of cracking it and tumbling earthward. The light intensified. The sky, a peerless blue, seemed very much a shire and not a London sky, she observed. She hoped she might somehow see into the garden where the Ace of Spades had been busy planting Rosa Rugosa.

"I imagine you have the right papers for this neck of the woods?" asked a voice curtly.

Ada craned. "I never thought of the neck of the woods as being near the top of the trees, but I suppose it makes sense."

"You're approaching the crown of the tree, so of course you're at the neck of the woods," snapped the voice. Its owner fluttered near. "We've had a serpent scare recently. We can't be too careful. We've hired an agent to ensure security. I imagine he grilled you right proper before allowing you access."

"That cat with the floating smile?"

"Cat! Mind your tongue! Cat indeed! As if!" The bird shook her wings like a creature emerging from a birdbath.

"While serpents are a menace to eggs in the nest, cats are notorious for slaying birds. No, I'm talking about the Head Egg below, the one who cleared your travel papers."

"I have no papers, and no one cleared them."

"Perhaps he saw them and cleared them away, and that's why you haven't got them anymore," said the bird. "If you haven't got any papers, though, do you actually recall who you are and what you are doing here?"

"If you please, my name is Ada."

"Adder! I knew it! And a very fat adder at that. You shall find no mercy from *me*!" At this the little bird began to fly in Ada's face, beating and shrieking.

"I'm not an adder, please! I'm a girl."

The bird returned to a branch and cocked her head to look with one eye, then twisted about to look with a second. "*Another* girl? I'm not sure I believe you. The serpent said she was a girl, too, but I never saw a girl with such a long neck. I imagine she thought *she* was being the neck of the woods. She was only drawing attention to herself in an unseemly fashion, if you ask me."

Ada had almost forgotten about Alice. "*Have* you seen another girl? Was she called Alice, by any chance?"

"If I knew I wouldn't say. You are all in cahoots, a league of serpents. Go away or I'll call the Head Egg."

Ada was about to suggest that the bird do just that, as Ada rather liked the notion of a large egg in charge of domestic tranquility. She wanted to see how such a campaign might be carried out. However, just then she heard the noise, not too far off, of breaking branches. A disorganized mechanical

ruckus, more or less at the same height as Ada and her inter-
locutor, though out of sight behind screens of foliage.

"There it is again, that infernal groaning and thwacking.
Something has been worrying itself into conniptions over
that way. I would go to look but I dassn't leave my nest, not
with serpents about."

"You *can* trust me. I'm no serpent, I'm a girl."

"A serpent can change its skin, you know, and appear
to us in all manner of guises." This sounded like something
the Reverend Boyce would declare. Before Ada could ask
herself whether perhaps she *was* a kind of serpent without
knowing it, the bird continued. "Whatever it is over there, I
hope it comes and catches you. It ratchets, it creaks, it breaks
branches. The Bandersnatch, for all I know. Frumiouser
and frumiouser, by the sound of it. I wish it would go away.
Would you care to be engaged as a Bandersnatch-snatcher?"

"No, thank you." Ada shuddered. A storm of tattered
leaves rose in the air a short distance away, suggesting proximity of danger. "I may have to do without the view that I'd
climbed all the way up here to see. Perhaps I should have
minded the instructions. The ceiling did advise me not to
look up."

"That was my doing," said the bird. "I thought I would
advertise against craning and preening, so as to prevent serpents from noticing the eggs in my nest. A new mother would
kill to protect her young, you know." Her feathers drooped.
"Of course my strategy didn't keep you out."

"I've been advised not to take advice," said Ada, to
soothe her.

The bird replied promptly, "Then may *I* advise that you stay and join me in the rearing of my latest clutch of eggs."

"No, thank you," said Ada. "I'm afraid of the Bandersnatch, or whatever it is. And I may be late for tea." She could no longer see the table laid out beneath the limbs of the trees, but she hoped it was still there, and that the tea was still hot.

"It's acceptable to be late for tea in this neck of the woods," said the bird. "Indeed, it's inevitable, as we never serve tea here. Did you mention you were leaving? If you see the Head Egg, tell him he has fallen down on the job."

"Oh, I hope he hasn't," said Ada, beginning to reverse her footsteps. "When an egg falls, well, it can't easily be repaired, even with Mrs. Winslow's Soothing Syrup. 'All the king's horses and all the king's men couldn't put Humpty together again.'"

"You *are* a serpent, always on about fallen eggs," said the bird. "We birds live above reproach."

"I hope I am not descending to meet reproach," said Ada, being clever.

"All who descend meet reproach," said the bird, with fine moral feeling.

# CHAPTER 17

───────  ❧  ───────

The boy followed Lydia down the steps to the kitchens. She had no interest in exposing him to the gawps of Rhoda or Mrs. Brummidge, but what else was she to do with him?

"More to drink, more cake," Lydia announced as she came through, like a regular domestic. "I left the pitcher and the other glasses behind, but this little prince is ravenous."

"Poor tyke," said Mrs. Brummidge, bustling. Rhoda jumped with a start. She looked as if she'd been reading up on cholera in London and the filthy well at Broad Street, and she'd become a convert to Snow's theory of germ contagion. She inched away from the boy as if she might catch something wretched from him.

The kitchen door stood open to cucumber frames and a few ill-trimmed old fruit trees whose heavy arthritic limbs were supported with crutches. The light that slanted in, the taint of meadowsweet upon the aqueous breeze, the sound of doves now at their elevenses, these all conferred upon Siam an air of normalcy. He looked like a boy who might need Dinah the cat, or her kittens, to play with. For a moment Lydia hated him for his ordinariness. There ought to be a credit of the exotic about him, but his eyes looked just like a boy's eyes, no different.

She was tired of playing Mother after just a few moments. She was after all hardly fifteen. Finding this novelty of humanity upon her threshold, what *would* Mama have done?

But questions of that sort could have no answer. The subjunctive mood was not Logic Lane. It was no detour, only a cul-de-sac. Answers to the question *what Mama would have done*: They did not exist, for one could never know. Had Mrs. Clowd not died at the end of Michaelmas term, her husband wouldn't have received a belated visit of condolence from the great Darwin. Some gibbering American named Winter wouldn't have come up from London to hold Darwin's elbow at every step. This ebony boy would be scratching the backs of his knees in some other room than this.

"I don't suppose you have a name," said Mrs. Brummidge offhandedly to the boy.

"Do too."

"So do I, it's Mrs. Brummidge." As if she talked to specimen children every day of the week, as natural as that. She lumbered about, cutting an extra large slice of cake for him. "Now you tell me your moniker, and we'll be done with this little bit of business."

"Siam," he said. "Siam Winter. Winter," he repeated.

Lydia couldn't bring herself to ask how he came by Mr.

Winter's name. "Shall I get Dinah from upstairs? She's probably dozing on Alice's window-bench, or on Nurse Groader's coverlet."

"I'll go," said Rhoda, and fled.

"Are you visiting in England or have you come to live?" asked Mrs. Brummidge.

Siam shrugged. His neck was bony but his chin lovely and stunted. When he glanced around, Lydia slid an extended peek. She hadn't imagined such ruddiness possible in a boy of his origins. He caught her looking. He pursed his lips, as if trying to keep his tongue from sticking itself out at her.

"Not Egyptian, I'd guess, nor Italian," said Mrs. Brummidge. "Would you be from the sugar islands then?"

"Siam is in the Far East, Mrs. Brummidge," said Lydia.

"No, I ain't," said the boy.

"Where—do—you—come—from?" asked Lydia, as if addressing the deaf.

"The parlor," he said, crooking a thumb over his shoulder.

Stifling a smile, Mrs. Brummidge commenced to dicing the rhubarb for her syllabub. "Either very quick or very slow, that one," she commented, "but luncheon wants to be ready when they ring for it. Why don't you take the boy for a stroll, Lydia? Whilst you're about it, you *will keep an eye out for Alice.* Do you hear me? Her father will notice her absence sooner or later, and you'll answer to him if anything happens to her." A clucking of tongues, a soft shaking of the head at the sorrows of incompetent parenting.

It wasn't that Lydia objected to being seen with a child of equatorial origins. It was that she wouldn't know what to say should anyone meet her in the lane down to the meadows. While Lydia didn't think she was insensitive to the plight of others—the color of his skin, his curious rubicund health!— she was careful of her own profile in the community. Anyone might note her discomfiture and take it to be for the wrong reason. "Alice would be some help right now," complained Lydia. Alice wouldn't bother with Siam's race; she wouldn't notice it. Just as she had never commented on Ada's bracing armature.

Mrs. Brummidge *would* go on and on about a thing. "Miss Alice was in your charge. It's fine for her to be larking about all lonesome, but she's too young to be gone for too long."

"I dozed and she dawdled off," said Lydia. "She'll dawdle back, as usual. She doesn't go near the water, and everyone knows her, so there's no need to fret."

"I worry for Miss Alice, I worry for her father. We're taking care of him now, mind." But before Mrs. Brummidge could work up to a fine hectoring, Rhoda came back with Dinah's two kittens, the black and the white.

They brought Siam up from his somnolent caution, those kittens. They capered and tottered and mewed with great fantastic faces on their frail necks. He fell on his knees to adore them. They pounced upon his thighs and bounced away again, as if everything they touched were shot through with static, the sort promised by dry air and thready cotton blankets. "They's a pair of little demons," he cried. Scrapping like Lucifer and Michael, the black and the white, over and over so fast they might almost have been two grey kittens.

They paused, suddenly mature, studying. The black one

deigned to lick its uneven fur. Siam took something out of
his coat pocket to dangle and attract its twin. His back was
turned to the room, and Lydia couldn't make out what he
had—a toy of some sort, a worsted ball perhaps, or a scrap of
rasher filched from some breakfast platter? Then a knock on
the door sounded. In came Mr. Winter, less tentatively this
time.

"They've begun to talk on personal matters," he said,
"and it seemed proper for me to leave them in peace. I shall
take a constitutional. Siam, come. It'll do you good to stretch
your legs after your long morning."

"I'll come, too," said Lydia. Mrs. Brummidge shot her
quite the look. "You *suggested* I take the boy out, and that
I collect Alice," she continued, "so I'll escort Mr. Winter
around the path toward Parks Road and the great case of
reptilian bones. Have you yet seen the University Museum,
Mr. Winter?"

Mrs. Brummidge couldn't contain herself. "But Miss
Lydia! Walking about with a gentleman you've just met? Not
without your father's say, and I'll march in there and—"

"Oh, he can't be disturbed. He is indisposed," said Mr.
Winter. He made a gesture, a finger at the lips, a *shhhh*. It was
unseemly for being intimate.

"You'll need a chaperone then at the very least. Rhoda,
off your posterior, and no jaw."

"We have a chaperone," said Lydia sweetly. "Little Siam,
don't you know."

She stood and pressed down the front of her skirt. It
was too warm to require a shawl, though a bonnet would be

proper. She would get one presently. For the moment, she stood bareheaded, willing a stiff sudden breeze to come in off the water and meadow and stir her hair just so. And you might have guessed her a minor goddess, for all that, because the breeze did as she imagined it might. Her hair blew fetchingly about her pale cheeks and severe expression.

# CHAPTER 18

———— ✺ ————

$A$da had climbed down to where there were no more branches. She could see the green grass below. It looked generous and soft, like feather blankets. Previously, in the world above worlds (DON'T LOOK UP), had she been able to scale a tree in the first place, she'd have been paralyzed on the descent. She'd have had to summon a gardener with a ladder to rescue her. Had she jumped, her legs would have been too rigid to provide coil and spring upon landing. They'd have absorbed the impact like ivory jackstraws, and shattered.

Ada was, however, not above-world, and so she jumped down.

She landed without disaster. Indeed, it was almost fun. No, it *was* quite fun, pleasurable. She had half a mind to climb back up and do it again, but the other half of her mind was ready for a refreshment. The tea was laid out for a party of several dozen, as far as she could tell. She brushed herself off to make herself presentable. She pushed through ferny underbrush to approach the table set out *en plein air*.

More than one table pushed together, it seemed. At various places they jutted out, at one point making a T. Unmatching chairs were arrayed, some helter-skelter, pushed back as if guests had fled in haste. Elsewhere, chairs were neatly aligned in sequence, awaiting company. At the far end, at a particularly dingy patch of tablecloth, a couple of characters were nattering away. They froze when they heard her approach.

"Don't look now," said a small, intense man in a top hat, "but I believe we have a burglar."

"When may I look?" replied his companion, who had promptly clasped paws over its eyes. It was a Hare of some variety, naked of ornament but for a key on a chain around its neck.

"I'm not a burglar," said Ada.

"Clever alibi," said the man, chomping on a bit of bread. "Many would believe you. I, for one, am not fooled."

"Ooh," said the Hare, peeking. "She *is* beautiful. She has stolen my heart."

"I rest my case," said the Hatter, for that's what he seemed to be, now that Ada could see a card reading *10 / 6* jauntily stuck in the silken hatband that announced the price as ten shillings sixpence. "Have some tea, but don't steal the spoons."

"I would welcome some tea, but I would never steal a spoon," said Ada.

"So you're a liar now, too. What's that you've got in your pocket?"

"How do you know I have anything in my pocket?" asked Ada.

"I can see the handle sticking out."

Ada felt in her pinafore. She withdrew a spoon. "Oh, this. Yes, well they were dosing the baby with some corrective. I cadged a portion. I put this in my pocket to bring downstairs, but I forgot. I promise that it doesn't belong to you."

"It doesn't *now*," said the Hare. "I'd recognize that pattern anywhere, though."

Ada laid it on the table next to the nearest spoon. "They're as near twins as spoons can be," said the Hatter.

"They're nothing at all alike," said Ada.

"Not all twins are identical," said the Hatter. "I have a twin called Hatta, and *he* has a twin called Hatter. You can imagine the confusion when we all try to reserve a table at one of the finer establishments." He looked about dolefully.

"*Are* there any establishments around here?" asked Ada.

"They wouldn't dare," said the Hatter. "How do you find the tea?"

"It's quite—well, it seems quite salty, I'm afraid."

"It's an awful curse to be frightened of salt. You must jump at your own tears."

"It's all a matter of taste, I expect," replied Ada. "How do *you* find it?"

"Why, I look down in my cup, and there it is. If it were a bear it would bite me."

At this the lid of a teapot fell off. A Dormouse poked its nose up. Its whiskers twitched. It said drowsily, "Is she gone?"

"She's right here," said the Hare, waving a spoon of its own toward Ada.

The Dormouse craned its thick furry neck. "That's not Alice. That's a different one."

"Must be her twin," said the Hare. "Don't touch the brioches, darling, we're saving them for the Duchess, if she ever arrives."

"You've seen Alice," said Ada. "She's been here!"

"She marched through a little while ago," said the Hare. "How long ago was that, Hatter?"

"Not as long as all that," said the little man, munching on toast.

"Were you already in the middle of your tea?" asked Ada.

"We don't know, do we," said the Hatter. "Until we're done, we don't know when the middle might be. We may be just beginning. Eternity is grueling—not that we're serving gruel, mind. But this tea party may go on for hundreds of years. Right now, I couldn't possibly say."

"I could," said the Dormouse. "But I won't." It clamped the lid on top of its head like a little beanie and sunk into the teapot. However its friends cajoled, it would not come out again. It whistled a popular melody through the tea-spout, though, which unsettled Ada. It sounded ghostly.

"I had forgotten that I was looking for Alice," she said. "Which way did she go, do you know?"

"She went forward," said the Hare decisively, "for no one has yet found a way to go back." He began to sing to the tune of the Dormouse.

*"Though many would reclaim their youth,*
*They soon must learn the dreaded truth*
*That even should they homeward stray*
*They'd find their youth had been stolen away."*

"If their youth had been stolen and they found it, they'd have it again," said Ada.

"Cleverness becomes a thief. I suspect she's up to mischief." The Hatter pointed his spoon at Ada and turned to the Hare. "I'd keep my thumb upon the *Kuchen, mein* Hare. Remember what happened to the tarts. A messy business, that. We haven't seen the end of it yet. Child, why are you looking for Alice?"

"Because she is lost," said Ada.

"She did not look lost to me," said the Hare. "All the while she was here, she was as solid a little janissary as you'd care to see. Every time I looked over at her, there she was. With that alarming forehead. You could hardly miss her. It was like having Gibraltar to tea."

"Did she say where she was going?" asked Ada. "She has a tendency to wander about, you see. Someone will be worrying about her."

"No doubt," said the Hare. "I can't say I noticed where she went, Hatter, did you? We were deep in conversation when she left."

"We were talking about where she might go if she ever got up from the chair," said the Hatter. "Then, we looked up, she was gone. So we never found out."

Ada felt a twinge of impatience. "This is important. If I

could just steal a moment of your time and ask you, please, to
try to remember—"

"Stealing again. And time is all we have, really," said the
Hare sadly.

"Time for tea," declared the Hatter. "The madeira cake
beckons. Shall we?"

They moved a few places to the right, where new cups
were set cleanly upon unmatching saucers. Farther along the
table, the ornamental cake stand got up. It humped itself a
few places away and squatted again.

"All this talk about stealing," said Ada. "Have *you* stolen
her?"

"I stole a glance at her," admitted the Hare. "So shoot me."

"She was an honest soul," said the Hatter, "if a bit dim."

"That's not a very nice thing to say."

"No, it isn't," he agreed. "Nor is it very tufted, or char-
treuse, or miasmic, or palindromic. It's actually quite a dim
thing to say, but that's what she was. Dim."

"You are making me quite cross," said Ada. "I'm leaving."

"She's trying to steal away," whistled the Dormouse
through the spout.

"She'd take anything that isn't nailed down. The damson
*gâteau* is at grave risk of abduction. After her," said the Hatter,
pouring a new cup of tea.

"After *you*," said the Hare politely.

"After all is said and done," said the Dormouse, "there is
nothing to be done. Or said." It fell silent, a little wistfully.

The Hatter lifted his cup and examined the dregs intently. The Hare took advantage of its companion's abstrac-

tion to spring from its chair. In a few bounds it had caught up with Ada. It pulled the chain from around its neck and put it around Ada's. "Here," said the Hare. "I shall give you this in exchange for the spoon you left behind. I wouldn't like anyone to think I had stolen it. The Queen maintains the stiffest penalty for stealing. The death sentence. You will find this key uncommonly poor for measuring out treacle, but perhaps you can learn to do without treacle. Many do."

Before Ada could thank the Hare, she heard a loud crashing in the woods behind her, as if a piece of the Hythe Bridge had fallen out of the trees. An iron sound, dangerous. She didn't ask the Hare where Alice might have been heading, but ran in the opposite direction of the crash. When she looked back, the Hare had returned to the table and was tying the edge of the tablecloth around its neck like a sort of bib. The Hatter was weeping bitterly. Ada thought she heard him say, "She has stolen the *Stollen*." She didn't pause to object, but pressed on through the forest, which was growing darker.

# CHAPTER 19

O ut of doors they assembled, a most uncommon grouping in Lydia's experience. This child in his
easy loping amble, his splendid coffee-bean skin not exactly a
novelty in these lanes, but not so common as to go unnoticed.

This boy, this Siam; and Lydia, in her own weeds of
mourning. How well her fair hair showed as it spilled upon
the dark shoulders of her summer shawl.

And then this American reed, quicksilver and grave
at once, this Mr. Winter. He must have a Christian name,
though Lydia had no idea if it might be proper to ask about
it outright. With the death of Lydia's mother had come, alas,
the loss of maternal guidance. Mrs. Brummidge groused
and grumbled, of course; a cook doesn't count. Old Nurse
Groader had opinions, and shared them. Still, a nurse can
be relied upon to be old-fashioned, raised up, as such terma-
gants always are, to promote the mores of a hundred years
past.

Other nearby female influences? Disconcertingly few. The wives of some neighbors, who found Alice less winsome than weird, and treated Lydia like a Cerberus, skirting her as they approached the Croft with platters of cold sliced roast something or buckets of summer pudding, meant to console and attract the poor widower. Also an elderly spinster cousin in Cumnor, whose dislike for Lydia was returned in spades. Of other relatives there remained none except Lydia's maternal grandmother. Upon the death of her only child, though, the dame had been struck with an affliction binding her tongue to silence. For her own good care she'd been removed to a lying-in home up the Banbury Road. If she had opinions about Lydia's deportment, ailment required the scold to keep her thoughts to herself.

And so I'm on my own, Lydia thought, as they passed through the gate and into the lane toward the river meadows and, eventually, the University Parks and the Oxford University Museum of Natural History. If conversation lagged she could take Mr. Winter and young Siam through and show them the claw of the dodo, so sensibly extinct.

In silence she began to assemble what she knew of the Museum. It wasn't much. The construction had been funded by the sale of Bibles, a strategy intended to console those who found the close study of nature unseemly if not heretical. Nature is the second book of God, she reminded herself, preparing a defense in case Mr. Winter was religious to a fault, like so many Americans as she'd heard it told. Or was God the second book of Nature? She couldn't remember.

Perhaps she'd better avoid the Museum altogether. They'd keep to the riverbank.

She needn't have worried. Once free of the scholastic silence of the old Croft, Mr. Winter became expansive. His heels scuffed at the gravelly track with such force that stones skipped about. He talked of the excitement of being in London for the first time, so far from home, so warmly welcomed thanks to the letters of introduction he had carried.

"But where is your home, when you are at home," Lydia asked, and even more bravely, "where is his?" Siam was skipping ahead down the path, eager as a beagle to see what lay around the next turn.

"Here, and thereabouts, and wherever," said Mr. Winter. "We move as we might. Those in allegiance to abolition show boundless courtesy."

"I'd thought that slavery matter settled, what with your proclamations and amendments and such. I mean, I know about your war, but isn't your Lincoln the local Lord Mansfield?" Lydia hoped they wouldn't become bogged down in a discussion of the times. The only current affair that mattered was the death of her mother. "Our nation gave up the slave trade forty years ago, when Bishop Wilberforce's father made a forceful case against it."

"The law says one thing, and custom another," replied Mr. Winter. "What the assemblies legislate and what happens on the back roads of small towns are not always in agreement. Put another way, history takes a long time to happen."

"I have always lived *here*," said Lydia, trying to draw him back to the subject. "When you go home, where will you go?"

But he appeared not to hear her. "Will you stay on in Oxford, now that your mother has passed on?"

She felt impatient. "Of course. We are not tinkers in caravans. And my father has his work."

"What work is that, besides support to the defenders of Darwinism?"

"Pater crawls back and forth in underground corridors, retrieving books requested by scholars in the Bodleian." She didn't want to talk about her father. "Have you a Christian name, Mr. Winter, or are you so deeply Darwinist that you have become a pagan?"

"You shock me, as you intend." His tone was mocking.

She considered behaving as if chastised. She dropped her eyes to her hands, which were clasped at her waist. He took mercy, though. He said, "Yes, I am Josiah Winter. I do not know if local practice permits you to call me Josiah, but I would permit it, if I may address you as Lydia."

"Americans take liberties," she acknowledged. "Josiah."

How far down the primrose path will I stray today? she wondered.

"He is in my care, is Siam," said Josiah Winter. "He has been so, Lydia, ever since a member of our New England congregation received a packet containing the severed ear of a recovered slave."

"I don't understand." She hoped he would recognize in her voice a request for restraint. He carried on, as Americans will, deaf to certain subtleties.

"Have you heard of the Underground Railroad?" he asked her.

"I presume you are not talking about those tunnels being dug about Paddington and such." She was trying to be light-hearted.

"Siam and some of his kin were headed for Canada West, where slavery has been outlawed several decades now," he said. "But bounty hunters caught up with them. Siam alone escaped. He has been under my protection since. He is likely to remain with me until his liberty can be promised by civil law. And so I've brought him abroad, for his own safety."

"He has taken your name," she said.

"I have given it to him." A mild correction, saying much she could not interpret.

It was nearly as far as she felt prepared to go on the matter. Siam Winter was leaping about, laughing at bovinity. "I cannot imagine his ordeals, but he has survived them well," she said. "I assume Mrs. Winter has skills in the kitchen, or she has engaged a cook who knows what boys require to thrive."

"Oh, there is no Mrs. Winter," replied Mr. Winter.

# CHAPTER 20

———— ✦ ————

$A$da stopped a short way into the forest.
She could no longer hear the Hatter and the Hare. The light
was low, but it was a green gloaming rather than a dusky one.
The woods grew dense. Huge clusters of flowers of a pale
soapsuds color, almost lavender grey, drooped from aged
vines. "They are something like wisteria," she found herself
saying aloud, "and something not."

"A gentleman out strolling in the meadow!" cried an
eager voice. "Just what I hoped to see."

It took Ada a few moments to locate the source of that
remark. An elderly man in a rusty coat of chain mail was
rooted to the earth by thick ropes of vine. They had grown
up around him, coiling woody tendrils around his legs and
waist and arms. Even as Ada watched, new fingerlets of green
stretched to explore his ears and the wispy white hair upon
his pate.

"I'm hardly a gentleman," she replied, "and this is hardly a meadow."

"And I am hardly surprised," he replied. "I tend to muddle. Dear sir, would you be so kind as to untwist this vine from me? I fear I shall be late for the occasion."

Ada went to work with a will. She tugged at the newest shoots because they were most supple. When they snapped, she began struggling with the more rigid coils. "How did you come to be entrapped?"

"I've always been susceptible to the beauties of nature," he replied. "Nature knows it, and takes advantage. I heard your utterance—that the hanging blossoms were something like wisteria and something not—and I was trying to decide what they were most *not* like. It was either a raven or a writing desk. As I paused to decide, nature got the better of me. There, you are a brave young gentleman. I'm sorry for any damage to your skirts. Your wife must send the bill to my accountant. My solicitors will counter-sue. The whole merry game will begin again. I am the White Knight, by the way."

"I am Ada. I am looking for my friend, named Alice. I have no wife. I am no gentleman."

"Oh, you protest, but quality will out, sir. Look what a comfort you're being."

Ada had freed his arms. He helped her pick at the thickest parts of the vine around his legs. Eventually he was able to pull his feet out of his metal shoes, leaving them trapped. His stockings were in need of a good rinsing. But he wrenched two bunches of drooping flowers from the nearby vines. He thrust a foot into the midst of each of them. They looked like festive, silvery lilac footwear, more suitable for a visit to the baths than to a court of arbitrage.

"Given your armor, I assume you're a knight with a *K*."

"Sometimes," he said, "though I have lost my helmet and visor. For all I know I have misplaced the *K* in my name, too. But I would answer to a White Night, sans the *K*, without blushing."

"Night as in night-time? I never heard of a White Night."

"The more common name of that animal, I believe, is Noon."

"But there is no night-time in Noon."

"Ah yes," he said, sadly and kindly, "the elderly militia know that there is, there always is. One can die at any moment, you see. Noon is a disguise of whiteness put on by the eternal Night behind it."

He was old. She didn't want him to talk about death. "Here is your helmet." As she picked it up from the ferns, a feathery white plume at its crest detached. It flew itself away, looking for all the world like an escaping moustache.

"My love to your devoted mother," cried the Knight to his plume. To Ada, he said, "That's a fine valet I have, none better. But you've been a good lad, too. I shall put in for a promotion to the Queen. Very likely you shall be made Sergeant-at-the-Lower-Extremities, as you helped release my legs and feet."

"I doubt it," said Ada.

"Well, they already have a Sergeant-at-Arms, as far as I've heard. In any case, the Queen will decide. She always does."

"Are you on your way to see the Queen?" asked Ada.

"In a manner of speaking," said the old man, looking about dubiously. "That is, I go out of my way *not* to see the Queen, as she has quite a temper, but I am rarely successful."

"I had heard the Queen was temperate," said Ada.

"Ill-tempered, temperate, a distinction without a difference," said the Knight. "As *illiterate* can refer to a cat who refuses to deliver a litter of kittens and instead delivers newspapers it has no capacity to read."

"Ill-tempered and temperate *are* most certainly different states. They are opposites."

"The Queen has become quite raveled over the theft of her tarts," insisted the Knight. "And you know what *that* means."

"No."

"It means unraveled. I rest my case."

Ada did not care to be rude. Still, she insisted, "Opposites cannot mean the same thing."

"Do you cleave to your belief about that?"

"Of course, or I shouldn't have made the remark."

"Then cleave yourself from your beliefs. It's much of a muchness, or such of a suchness."

"Well," said Ada, "in *any* case, I've never known an illiterate cat!"

"Don't become raveled or unraveled over it. Sir, shall we go?"

Ada took his arm, as he seemed a bit wobbly on his pins. They made their way through the underbrush. "I have always heard that Queen Victoria was moderate in her tastes," ventured Ada.

"I never heard that at all," replied the Knight. "Then, I have never heard of Queen Victoria."

"But you mentioned the ill-temper of the Queen."

"I was referring to the Queen of Hearts," he replied. "Ever since her tarts were stolen clean away, she's been in a foul disposition. No one wants to attend her *fête* today, but if everyone sent in regrets she'd be left alone on the playing ground. She'd have to call for her own head to be cut off."

"That sounds rather extreme."

"She never earned high marks for civility, I'm afraid. She's ruthless, though great fun at a beheading. Now, for whom did you say you were looking?"

Ada kept nearly forgetting. "Alice, a little girl. Like me. I believe she came this way, or nearby. Have you seen her?"

"I have never seen a little girl. I wouldn't recognize one if she stepped on me."

"I'm a little girl," she replied.

"If you're a little girl, I'll be a monkey's aunt." He took off a thick leathern glove and fished about in his breastplate. He withdrew a magnifying glass on a chain, which he put to his eye. A glaucous eye, and runny. "Well, timber my shivers, what an odd element you are," he said. "A most unconvincing-looking gentleman to stride the meadows. But then, the code of manliness requires us not to make comments on the intolerable ugliness of others. So I shall say no more about your condition, sir. But I do hope you manage to find some professional help. The bow in your hair is lopsided. Shall I?"

"I'll manage," said Ada. "I could never fix it myself before this, for my arms would not go all the way up and around. I too wore an iron armature, you see. Not unlike yours, though more private. I seem to have lost it."

"I would lose my own suit of armor, though the Brigade to Preserve Morals in the Wilderness would probably have something to say about my choice of drawers. I favor an India-printed pattern of capering codfish. Are you going as far as the Queen's garden?"

Ada said, "I never know where anything begins and ends here. So I don't know quite where I am going. But I am looking for Alice."

"So you said. Well, if I should come across another gentleman kitted out as nonconformistly as you are, I shall ask if he is Alice. If he answers 'Yes,' he may be lying, so I shall pay no attention. If he answers 'No,' he may also be lying, so I shall send him directly to you with my compliments. What address shall I use?"

"I have no address," she said. "So I may as well continue along with you. Perhaps we shall find her together."

"You have no chattel, no impedimenta," observed the White Knight. "I presume you have come to stay?"

She didn't know the answer. She'd embarked upon her unexpected journey without luggage of any variety, if one discounted the pot of marmalade. She felt only distant associations with the world of her dropsical mother and her father the Vicar, of Boykin Boyce the Screaming Wonder of the Nursery, and of Miss Armstrong Headstrong. Yet mentioning Alice to the old Knight made her friend come alive in Ada's thoughts, much as the unexpected whiff of balsam sap can revive all manner of Yuletide memories and hopes.

It occurred to Ada that Alice might be having a more difficult time of it in this peculiar wilderness than she was herself. She began to draw a distinction between them.

Ada had only one friend, and that was Alice. The Croft, where Alice's family lived, was near enough the Bickerage that Ada, chaperoned, could walk there by the river path, avoiding the crowds of Carfax or the High in Oxford proper. It was an untroubled route. In the center of town, Ada was too likely to be jostled by hurrying dons or by housemaids with paper packets of suet tied with string. Or she might be stared at, which was another sort of annoyance.

Calm Alice never stared balefully at Ada, but talked and played in her own lively way. She included Ada when Ada turned up at the gate, but she ran off to follow a calf or a honeybee if it sang out to her, forgetting to bid Ada "Good-bye!" or to say "I'll return presently!" If Ada lived in portable iron stocks, Alice lived in the portable moment. They were well suited to be friends with each other. But if less constrained by the world than Ada was, Alice was also less tethered. Up until now.

Ada had been relieved of her exoskeleton. She was walking about with the freedom—well, the freedom of a young gentleman, actually. Perhaps that is what the old Knight was seeing in her, a jolly liberty, a certain being at-large. Whereas Alice, who knew? Through this unreliable landscape Alice might herself still be moving. Blundering, with no sense of direction, no recollection of her origins. It is what made Alice amazing, and also why she tended to get lost. She needed Ada, even if she didn't know it. It was Ada who would bring her home, if it could be managed.

"This wood is becoming insistent," said the Knight. He took out his sword and tried to prise a space between the tree trunks. They were growing closer together. On all sides the gloom thickened. The voluted bark pressed in. The forest seemed more like a paneled chamber than a dense glade. As the Knight drew his sword back, breathing heavily, he knocked over a glass-topped table. A teacup fell and shattered on the marble floor, which was tiled like a chessboard in alternating squares of black and white. "I say, sir," he said to Ada, "is that a keyhole I spy in yon chestnut bole? If so, would that key on the chain around your manly neck insert itself usefully therein?"

# CHAPTER 21

The sun dispensed the sort of heat that presses against the skin and makes it itch. Lydia allowed her shawl to fall to her elbows. She was sorry she had brought it, but she had to have something to fiddle with. Her hands rarely knew how to keep still.

They had reached the banks of the Cherwell. A skirting of plummy black shadow was dropped below each exhausted riverbank tree. A few cows were standing hock-deep in the shallows, perhaps mesmerized by their reflections. Siam was flying at the water's edge and beginning to splash, as if he were in Brighton. Noon bells sang out with their usual ignorance of mood, marking out moments of grief and worry, elation and confusion. The bells said that at its core, human life was fundamentally a sort of organic clockwork, while the winds and skylarks that swept against the sound of metronomic iron timekeeping argued for variety, subtlety, epiphany. What the sun thought, or meant, or said, was too high overhead to be heard. Like the vasty deity to which Lydia's father tried to pray, the sun shouted its light and simultaneously kept its magnificent silence.

What *might* her mother have made of Mr. Winter? It was a question that Lydia could neither answer nor let go. Against her reservations she forced herself to think in the funereal subjunctive. How *would* Mama have proceeded to chat with this unexpected American visitor?

Mrs. Clowd might not have waited for Pater to introduce the guest. Mrs. Clowd would have exchanged pleasantries at the outset. She'd have spoken with a lively good humor, at once teasing and tender, asking droll questions that could summon no sensible reply. Mrs. Clowd would have embarrassed her husband, who would have been happy to be embarrassed. Mrs. Clowd dashed a room with fancy. Mrs. Clowd was dead. What lesson here for Lydia?

Josiah Winter seemed satisfied to stroll in silence. He clasped his hands behind his back. Lydia didn't have her mother's bravado. As she understood the protocol, Lydia must wait until Mr. Winter felt ready to speak again. She couldn't imagine how she might bring herself to address him first. She pictured, mostly in fun, how she might stumble so he would have to reach out a steadying hand. Though he was an American, surely he would be at least *that* gallant?

"As we weren't presented to each other formally," said Mr. Winter at last, "I haven't had the occasion to express my condolences on the loss of your mother."

She was so relieved he'd spoken at last that she had to clutch her stomach muscles with her hands. *Oh, we never lost her; we know precisely the plot of ground in which her casket was laid.* To keep from saying that, she began to giggle. But humor is anarchic. She snorted. Her nose blew out and her eyes ran. *Losing your mother.* Wasn't that exactly what Pater wanted and needed, to revoke that loss, to correct that error of misplacing someone for eternity? And Pater required the reassurance of Darwin himself, of all people. Pater required some declaration of persisting faith, so that as Jane Isabel Clowd, late of this parish and removed to Iffley Churchyard, drew further away in time and in memory from her husband and daughters, the chances of her salvation and of the resurrection of her soul should not be equally adrift.

For time had changed its terms, no matter what the bells of Oxford said. The one-sided eternity of the afterlife, only a few years after the Oxford Debate, was now guessed to have a secret twin, a mirrored flank, beginning, if eternities could begin, as long a time before a life as the Scriptures proposed it would continue after.

"Oh, Miss Lydia," said Mr. Winter. He pulled from a waistcoat pocket a clean kerchief. "I have upset you, when I meant only to console you."

"It is the silly pollen," she cried. She accepted his attentions and wiped her eyes. "The great Darwin himself cannot cozen my father back into his faith. The lock has sprung and it will not hitch again."

"Your father is a brave man. He seems to be an honest one. I mean honest in his mind," he continued. "I mean in his *thinking*. I am not saying this at all well."

"Pater says it ought not make a difference if man's place in nature, as Mr. Darwin recently insists, has a different origin than we understood before. Do you know what I mean?"

"I have heard Mr. Darwin use the phrase 'the descent of man,'" remarked Josiah Winter.

She frowned. "Some days I do not know how much farther down we could go."

"Those are dark words for a young lady as pretty as you. Darwin doesn't mean those words in a spiritual or moral sense, but only in terms of our history as primates. You are descended from your parents. It is *that* use of the word he means to imply."

"If we concede a different past, must we conclude a different future?" protested Lydia.

"That's your father's question. I see that. And made intense by the loss of his wife, whom I wish I had had the fortune to meet. But you must not take upon yourself your father's struggle. Remember your own English hymn, so popular in my country and, I believe, sung at the funeral of your Prince Albert. 'Rock of Ages.' It has the most encouraging conclusion."

The stranger then began to sing, right out in the open air.

> *"While I draw this fleeting breath,*
> *When mine eyes shall close in death,*
> *When I soar to worlds unknown,*
> *See Thee on Thy judgment throne,*
> *Rock of Ages, cleft for me,*
> *Let me hide myself in Thee."*

Lydia hardly knew what to say. She supposed she had asked for this. Soaring to worlds unknown sounded like an ascent, but becoming a plug in the Rock of Ages was surely not a celestial event, but a granitic one, the sepulchral descent of man.

She didn't know if she should return his handkerchief, damp as it was. But he might think she was clinging to it as a souvenir. Perhaps she would do just that. "He's getting a good deal ahead," she managed, pointing at Siam.

"I will not lose him. I am all he has."

"He is lucky, I suppose."

"I do not think often about luck, except the quirk of accident that brought his soul into the world as a Negro in Georgia, and mine as a white man in the Commonwealth of Massachusetts."

"I should have imagined that was no accident." Lydia attempted a sweetness that was, perhaps, not entirely successful. "Don't you think, rather, the Almighty decides, at His sacred whim, which of us shall ascend and which descend? Shan't we pay homage to His mastery by enduring the circumstances of our lives?"

He didn't speak for a while. He smiled at her sideways, quizzically. Then he said, "I see you are your father's daughter, possessed of a quick mind. What a pity that, with all these great chapels of learning tottering about on every side of you, you will not have a chance to argue with some dean of divinity."

"We must conclude that my gender is another decision of the Almighty," she said. Her tone was more muted. "I don't discuss such matters with my father, though I listen when he speaks. Upon occasion, Pater tutors local grammar school boys hoping to sit the exams. He is especially interested in biblical history."

"I'm surprised he doesn't teach at one of the colleges."

"We're not all equally gifted," was all she would say. "He enjoys his work in the archives of the Bodleian. He absorbs whatever he can by glancing at the volumes he locates for the scholars, who require them for their study."

"An education in scraps and moments."

"All that is afforded most of us. Did you attend a college, Mr. Winter?"

Before he could answer, a fluting voice hailed Lydia from across the rich meadow. Miss Armstrong was bowling along, carrying a parasol to protect her noble nose from the sunlight. "Oh, Miss Lydia, how glad I am to see you again," she cried. "I must confer with you, if you can spare me the time."

The governess descended upon them, huffing. "The descent of woman," muttered Lydia. She was certain that Mr. Winter had not heard her.

# CHAPTER 22

―――― ❧ ――――

The key that the rattled Hare had given Ada: Would it fit in the door? It would. Would it swivel in the lock? Indeed it would, with a self-satisfied and industrious little click.

But then, would the door open?

This was a different matter. Though the key had turned, the brass doorknob would not. Ada looked at the words engraved on its shiny surface. They were even smaller than before. She had to kneel and put her face close to the doorknob to try to make them out.

"I left my spectacles on the mantelpiece, little man. What does it say?" asked the White Knight.

"I think it says ALL YE WHO ENTER HERE, ABANDON HOPE," replied Ada, "though I can't be sure. The letters are *very* small and imprecise."

"I suspect its advice is to abandon *home*," said the Knight.

"As it turns out, I left home this morning. I refused to bring
it along however much it whined. I believe I am qualified for
admittance. Step away, let me try the door."

"It was my key," said Ada, perhaps sullenly.

"Ah, but you have not abandoned quite enough home,"
said the White Knight. "You are a very young gentleman.
Some habits are hard to shake off until you are old and frail
like me. I have shaken off romance, ambition, and curly locks
along with the accoutrements of the domestic life. I will not
be denied. Aside, I say."

She moved aside. The White Knight took off his glove.
He tried the doorknob. It would not turn. He tried to push
the door in with his shoulder, but he could not budge it. He
tried to pull it. Since he had braced his feet against the door
for leverage, this proved a doomed strategy.

"Perhaps if we both pushed at once," he said. Ada returned to her position. Unaccustomed to being asked to perform physical assistance of any sort, she was pleased. "On the
count of three, we shall rush at the door with all our might,"
he said. "Five, four, three."

They both hurtled themselves forward. A curious thing
happened then. The door opened, but not by swinging wide,
as a book swings open on its hinged spine. Instead, fixed upon
a central horizontal axis, the door behaved like a flywheel.
The top half fell inward. The White Knight tumbled head-
first through the doorway like a sack of chain-mail laundry
tossed in a chute. At the same time, the bottom half of the
door kicked up and outward. Ada was struck in the elbows

and knees. She tumbled backward as the White Knight fell forward. She righted herself in time to see his heels disappear behind the closing door, which slammed shut with a snap that had a vindictive character to it.

The door had revolved. There was still a keyhole, but no key dangled from it. The key was stuck in the keyhole on the other side. The door was locked again. Ada went on her knees once more to try to peer through the keyhole, to call to the Knight, to tell him to open the door from that side. But the keyhole was blocked by the key. She could see nothing more of the serene garden, the Knight, the roses, or the playing cards setting up for the grand *fête*.

She stood up. The letters on the doorknob were scrambling about to form a new message. She didn't care to read depressing messages. She turned away from it.

The paneled hall was a forest again, but a dull, cloistered sort of forest. Gone were the hot spots of green and gold that sunlight loves to scatter as a corrective against boskiness. Yet it didn't feel like evening. It took Ada a moment to realize that she was a little clammy. A mist had begun to seep through the woods. Had she wanted to backtrack toward the Hatter and the Hare at their tea party, she wouldn't have known which way to go. Moisture was collecting on her skin and her upper lip the way it did when fog crept in at the seaside. She had no shawl. For warmth, she began to walk through the gloom, swinging her arms martially as any perfect little soldier might do.

The mist curled and tried to rub against her, but she wouldn't let it touch. She kept up her spirits by reciting cer-

tain nursery plaints that Miss Armstrong had been accustomed to delivering in regretful tones.

*"Little Jack Horner and Little Boy Blue*
*Fell into trouble and sank in the stew.*
*Old Mother Hubbard soon had the pot covered*
*And served them for supper. Her dog had some, too."*

That did not sound entirely as it ought. She tried again.

*"Little Miss Muffet and Mary Contrary*
*Found in the garden a spider most scary.*
*It stung them and hung them to save them for dinner,*
*A fate that awaits the conventional sinner."*

She hadn't recalled that the nursery characters knew
one another so well. Nor that they were all so bent on
dining.

She hurried along the path, thinking that the fog itself
was like a toothless mouth trying to close upon her. A mouth
without a body attached. But how odd—she never thought in
sloppy images like this.

*"Robin a'Bobbin, a big-bellied wren*
*Ate more meat than forty men can.*
*He ate a church, he ate a steeple,*
*He opened the doors and gobbled the people.*
*He ate the future and the past,*
*And all the days as they galloped past.*

*He ate the prophets, stars, and sky,*
*And fell down dead and refused to die."*

"I am beginning to feel I grew up in the wrong nursery, as these rhymes won't behave," she said aloud, to give herself courage. "I wonder if nursery rhymes do lasting damage?" Before she could answer her own question, the path dropped in a steep decline. She found herself rushing downslope into a clearing in the mist. Her new agility failed her. She tumbled.

A group of travelers turned to her. "Oh, my, a guardian angel," cried one. "How welcome, for we are quite lost. I fear we will arrive late for our performance."

Ada drew herself up short. The figure addressing her was flat and sharp, possibly cut out of a sheet of metal and painted in carnival colors. A Tin Ballerina, with one leg lifted and a beribboned tambourine pinched in her tin fingers. She was accompanied by a Tin Bear with a valise upon his upturned nose. Sauntering along behind was a large, sour-looking, fully ovoid Egg, wearing a necktie and little else.

"What a remarkable family you have," said Ada to the Tin Ballerina.

"We have no family, we simply have careers. We are in the theatre," replied the Tin Ballerina, a little sadly.

"I thought there seemed a bit of Punch and Judy to you. Where are you going?"

"We are going to perform, of course, but we have lost our way in this purgatorial soup. You are good to show up and lead us forward, you heavenly creature."

"I am not that good," said Ada. "And I am not a guardian angel."

"You came from above, didn't you? That's the origin of angels," replied the Tin Ballerina.

Ada didn't know if the Tin Ballerina was referring to the slope or to the world of upper Oxford. "Well. I came from above. Yes. But only in a manner of speaking."

"She has no strings," said the Tin Bear. "She's a guardian angel, all right."

"No one asks me my opinion," snapped the Egg, "but if they should, I might have something sharp to say!"

"Dear Humpty Dumpty, what is your opinion?" asked the Tin Ballerina.

"I have no idea," he replied. "Perhaps she is a guardian ornament, intended to revolve in the wind like other tin weathervanes." Oh, thought Ada, *that's* what the Tin Bear and the Tin Ballerina most resemble: weather-vanes. While the Egg resembled nothing so much as a refugee from a luncheon platter.

"You're players meant to entertain at the garden party of the Queen of Hearts!" guessed Ada.

"If you say so," said the Tin Bear. "*I* would have said we were cheap ornaments intended for the decoration of joyless holiday endeavor, destined for the rubbish bin, but you know best, dear guardian angel."

"Please don't think me a guardian angel. For one thing—"

"You are hardly a guardian mongoose," said Humpty Dumpty. "And a good thing, too, for mongooses eat raw eggs."

"Alas," said the Tin Bear, "guardian angel or not, you cannot join our band. You have no strings. So you are not a marionette."

"*You* have no strings," said Ada. "If I am not a guardian angel, neither are you marionettes. I think you're weather-vanes. I mean, except Mr. Egg."

"We are poor soothsayers, I'm afraid. We cannot tell whether the weather will hold for the party," said the Tin Ballerina. "In any case, we do have strings. I don't mean in *any* case, really, I mean in *that* case." She revolved upon her toe so her extended leg pointed toward the valise balanced atop the Tin Bear. "We keep them coiled in the satchel until they are needed. Now, tell us whether or not you are going to guide us to the party."

Ada said, "If you are weather-vanes, you ought to be able to sort out your location from which way the fog is blowing in. No?"

"I thought I told you. We're whether-vanes, with an *h*," said the Tin Ballerina. "We don't know whether we're coming or going. It's supposed to be charming, but it makes our professional appearances alarmingly impromptu."

Ada put a finger to her lips. "Aren't *you* a guardian Egg?" she asked the one called Humpty Dumpty. "I had been told a Head Egg like you was serving as a lookout to protect birds' nests from hungry serpents."

"I've been told *you* went out walking in the lane without a chaperone!" he retorted. "Mind your own business. I left the position of guardian Egg to take up a higher calling. Art is all. You will rarely have seen a performance in which an Egg has such an exalted role."

"I've never seen any performance in which an Egg was featured at all," admitted Ada.

"Exactly," said Humpty Dumpty. "I rest my case."

"I wish I could rest *my* case," said the Tin Bear. His valise was soldered to his nose.

"Prepare to be astounded," continued Humpty Dumpty to Ada. "If we ever get there, I mean."

"Perhaps I could join your troupe. I should like to go to the garden party, too," said Ada. "I am hunting for a friend, you see. I'm afraid that she may be lost."

"She's no more lost than Paradise," said the Tin Bear. Everyone looked at him. "Do you think even Paradise Lost could find itself in this fog? *Really.*"

"Well, we can't get any more lost than we are," decided Ada. "So I'll come along with you. We'll see where we get."

"That will never do," said the Tin Ballerina. "*We'll* come along with *you*, and we'll see where we get."

The Egg muttered something bitter that Ada couldn't quite catch. Then that noise, like the ongoing collapse of an industrial artifact, sounded again, and too near for comfort. Without choosing a path, they all ran in single file: Ada first, the Tin Ballerina hopping *en pointe*, the Tin Bear stumping behind. Humpty Dumpty was last, glancing over the great flanks of his even jowls (he had no shoulders to speak of). The forest grew indistinct with fog. The leafy branches of trees seemed like great mittened claws eager to scrape at the party. It couldn't be denied that the clangorous monster was following them. "The Jabberwock!" hissed the Tin Bear. "A Guardian Demon!" They all closed their eyes as they ran. The fog was so close they couldn't see more than a foot ahead of themselves anyway.

# CHAPTER 23

———— ❧ ————

.

The governess again! A riverbank nixie gone mad for interruption into human affairs. Puck's countervalence. Lydia could spit. But the manifestation of Miss Armstrong snapped Lydia to attention. So far, Mr. Josiah Winter had proven little more than an unexpected aspect of Lydia's morning. If, in time to come, this June day would be picked out in her memory for special notice, it would be because she had strolled upon the riverbank with a young American gentleman. True, their duet of comments and potent pauses had been only an experiment at grown-up conversation. But they *were* together as a pair, strolling. A first, for Lydia.

With Miss Armstrong hieing into view, however, the dalliance of this walk, the private silly adventure of it, was now beaten into something public and coarse. This encounter on the Cherwell bank would lie between Lydia and Miss Armstrong, unmentioned, every time their paths crossed for the rest of their lives.

She glared at Miss Armstrong swooping across the meadow, cutting the diagonal the more quickly to meet them. Miss Armstrong was watching where she placed her feet. She didn't notice Lydia's ferocity. And Lydia thought: The court and the rabble of Athens move so quickly into the woods, stung and shifted by magic, abused by Puck. Shakespeare was showing how any social event is composed of separate simultaneous experiences, whose meanings differ, and must be negotiated into commonality if history is to occur.

She had no intention of negotiating with Miss Armstrong, but Lydia was stuck like a wasp in honey. The stroll was no longer hers alone. Hers, and Mr. Winter's.

"I was hoping to waylay you, Miss Lydia," huffed Miss Armstrong. She put out her hand to grasp Lydia by the wrist, in friendship or worry. Lydia offered no wrist. After a moment Mr. Winter held out his hand. Miss Armstrong recoiled with flare, as if she hadn't noticed the gentleman till his hand appeared. "Begging your pardon, sir; I am interrupting your meander. I am —"

"Mr. Winter, may I present Miss Armstrong," said Lydia. It was not a question. "A governess from the Vicarage along the way." The tone in which she said *governess* had a likeness to iron.

"How do you do." Mr. Winter bowed from the waist.

Rallying, Miss Armstrong became downright Bohemian. "Miss Lydia, the Vicarage has gone turnips to toast! Ada has

not returned, but that's the least of it. The infant is squalling as if being pricked with invisible needles. The doctor has
been sent for. Mrs. Boyce has taken the boy to her bosom.
She has turned the Vicar out of the sewing room. He is *beside*
himself, and you know what he is *like!*"

Lydia had no idea what the Vicar was like. She was not
interested in learning. She couldn't decipher this story, with
its needles and bosoms and squallings. Oh, so the infant had
the hiccups. To judge by the look on Miss Armstrong's face,
the Pennines would now collapse and the Hebrides float away
toward Norway. But all this drama couldn't deter Lydia from
her obligations, much as she tried to resist them. "Miss Armstrong, this is Mr. Winter, lately of London though originating in those pestered States across the ocean."

"I understand," said Miss Armstrong in a tone of regret.
She put a hand to her bonnet brim as if to brush away a
horsefly. "Miss Lydia, I am beside myself."

"So I see," said Lydia. "I have no words of advice for you,
though. We are engaged in our own campaigns. We're out
looking for Alice, as she hasn't returned either. No one has
reached a state of alarm, mind you. Alice never goes far. She
merely goes . . ." She thought. "Deep."

Miss Armstrong murmured, "Where is the boy who looks
after the sheep, but under the haystack, fast asleep." They
began to walk together, a hateful trio.

"I know that nursery ditty," said Mr. Winter. "It is sung
at the cots of Concord babes. Interesting how the word *fast*
suggests, in that instance, a way of holding. From the word
*fastened*, I suppose. Locked in sleep, kept."

"Is it possible that Ada is locked in sleep somewhere with her head on Alice's shoulder?" said Miss Armstrong. "Has *anyone* seen Ada today?"

"One might imagine she'd been pushed into the river and drowned, to simplify her life and everyone else's," said Lydia.

"No one could imagine such a thing," protested Miss Armstrong.

"You did," said Lydia. "You told me earlier. You pictured Ada fetched up against the milldam, as I re—"

"The marmalade—"

"Ada and her marmalade!" Lydia made an airy, dismissive sound like a French laundress. How Miss Armstrong could jabber as she walked! "Miss Lydia, Ada can't have gone far. But some forbidden destination would have appealed to her more strongly than the company of Alice." In an aside to Mr. Winter, Lydia said, "My sister isn't always attentive. Oh, she's never unkind, but she's easily distractible. If she and Ada were playing a game of hide-and-search, and Ada had closed herself in a wardrobe, Alice might decide to go dig worms in the garden and drop them in the well. Ada could spend the day waiting to be found."

"Don't say that!" Miss Armstrong took a fright. "Mr. Winter, Ada Boyce has never gone out alone before today. It's always been my pleasure to walk with her endlessly, endlessly, hither and yon, *endlessly*; but what with turmoil at home, Ada escaped me. The Vicar—oh, possessed of such piety!" She shook her head; her shoulders wobbled, too. "And Mrs. Boyce, distracted by the nuisance of a newborn, and all her natural feeling for her husband channeled elsewhere. It is a harlequinade, a harlequinade enacted in a torched and smoking rectory, by people devastated with terror and madeira." She had said too much, of course, she had flung her*self* into the river and drowned. She blinked two or three times like a Guernsey surprised to have just delivered an aria. She lowered her parasol, closed it. She stabbed the ground with it as if to kill the very earth upon which she walked. She lifted both hands in a gesture of defeat that didn't fool Lydia for a moment. "I am not myself today," said Miss Armstrong by way of apology, in a softer tone.

"Few are," said Mr. Winter. Lydia couldn't tell if he was being amusing or rude. "Of course, we'll look for your Ada while we keep an eye out for Miss Lydia's sister. Would you care to walk along with us?"

Lydia couldn't bear it. "I suspect, Miss Armstrong, that having escaped you, Ada took the chance to engage a boatman to take her across the river. I seem to think she said something of the sort. To explore the other side, she said. And look, there's a boatman lolling down on that spit. Just there. Perhaps you should hire him yourself, and go have a look around that side of the river. We'll check out this side. One *never knows*." The tone was ominous. "Of course if we find Ada we'll send her home at once. I have already told you that, Miss Armstrong."

But now Miss Armstrong was weeping. Lydia could have given her a good hard kick. "I can't begin to tell you what it would mean—to us—if I were sent away!" she sobbed. Mr. Winter stopped, pale. Had he never encountered a volatile woman before? He put out his hand and settled it upon Miss

Armstrong's shoulder. She couldn't look up, but she raised one hand and rested it upon his as if they had known one another for twenty years. The bells began to sound the quarter hour. The sun blinked behind a cloud. For a moment the colors took on a hasty intensity. The first cloud after a session of blinding sunlight is a shade of the underworld, a hint of the grave and even how it might smell. Lydia felt a shiver of dread, but overcame it.

"I understand what you feel," said Mr. Winter. "Should anything happen to my lad, I would be beside myself."

"Your lad," chimed Miss Armstrong questioningly.

"Siam." Lydia spoke with a ferocious oratorical clarity. "Ahead of us on the path. Halloo, Siam!" she called to the boy, who turned and waved.

Miss Armstrong lost some ground. It was too much. "You may be right," she said to someone, to herself. Who knew what she meant? She pivoted away from the riverbank path and began beating down the shallow slope to the water's edge. Lydia turned her shoulder; the subject was closed. As the moment passed, the dome of the Radcliffe Camera in the distance came out of shadow into the sun. The stodgy beauties of the colleges, and all these comic barbarians at their finialed gates.

"What a passionate creature," said Mr. Winter.

"She's an utter lunatic."

"But look, she's left behind her parasol. She'll need it, with the sun on the water. Miss Armstrong," he called, with what Lydia thought was perhaps not a full-throated effort. Distance, and the noise of the governess's rushing skirts, must have kept her from hearing. "I shall go after her and deliver it," he decided. "I shall ambush her by the launch, hand her the thing, and return, like so. Keep on along the riverbank." He indicated with a nod of his head a path ahead by which he'd come back to Lydia. "I shall rejoin you along the way, having made a triangle of it. With your permission."

Lydia didn't give permission, but he was off on his own, gamboling like an idiotic April lamb. She didn't want to witness the reunion from this distance, any distance. She suspected he would loiter. She hated him, she hated them both. She turned her face into the wind. She looked for black Siam, a sentimental silhouette against the diamond-dashed glitter and glare of a backwash of the Cherwell. She cupped her hands at her mouth. "I say," she called to him, at a volume she knew the adults couldn't hear. "We're told to head back. Come with me."

# CHAPTER 24

————— ✣ —————

We must now, if only for a moment, consider Siam on the riverbank, and what he sees. He examines life as intently as anyone else in this history. That the puzzlingly kind Mr. Josiah is loping along the bank, away from him—this causes in Siam a mix of relief and anxiety at the same instant. And what of Miss Lydia, the half-adult missie, with her flaxen hair pulled forward in a way that fails to disguise the vastness of her forehead? She puts Siam in mind of the white cliffs of Albion, as Mr. Josiah had named them, on the vessel that brought them from Oostende.

Persons like Miss Lydia are an unknown element in Siam's life. His experience with white females of that age has been so chaperoned as to kill conversation. He doesn't think in terms of vixen, virago, or virgin. He thinks she is attractive, though perhaps an aberration, like one of those new barnacles or orchids about which Mr. Josiah has yammered with Mr. Darwin. They broke the mold before they cast her, he thinks. That is perhaps not quite right. Still, it seems fitting.

Of Miss Armstrong he has no opinion. She is a wild improbability whom he can see but has not met. He watched Mr. Josiah loping down a sloping bank toward her. Miss Lydia is hollering something to Siam. He ventures a few feet nearer to see if he can understand her words beneath her accent.

# CHAPTER 25

————— ❦ —————

The woods began to thin. The sound of hastening footsteps in the fog took on sloshy echo. They were running through marsh grass now, wetlands. Their feet were soaked. Perhaps we are at the side of the ocean, thought Ada. "The salt air will do you no good," she panted to the Tin Ballerina and the Tin Bear. "You will come down with a pox."

"I adore salt," huffed Humpty Dumpty. "Salt completes me."

"We mustn't plunge into the sea or we would have to consider drowning," said the Tin Bear. "And I'm not sure I'm capable of that. I'd be an utter failure."

The noise of their pursuer only intensified. They heard a hunger in that racket, or some other ambition. The Jabberwock, if such it was, must be lost in the fog, too. They cringed at the creak and clang of its limbs, which seemed in the thickening air to be all around them.

"We are but poor players a-wandering in the muck and the mire," said the Tin Ballerina. "It's time we relied upon a higher power. We must put ourselves in the hands of loftier management."

"All right," said the Tin Bear. He unfolded from his valise a baker's dozen of brightly colored kites, in patterns of red and black and white. Each had a string attached to one corner. The Tin Bear tied the other ends of the strings to various limbs of the traveling troupe.

"I'm afraid we don't have any extras," said the Tin Ballerina to Ada. "But you may hold my hand for comfort and guidance, if you like. Perhaps you will be lifted up by our society."

"There does not seem to be much uplift in my day today," said Ada, "but I'm willing to try."

"Good. You run ahead. When the wind catches the kite, launch it," said the Tin Ballerina.

"How do you do this when you're all alone?" she asked.

"Privately," said the Tin Ballerina. "Run!"

Ada ran. When the string stretched taut and a wind came up, she tossed the kite up into the fog. Before it rose and disappeared into the mist, it turned once or twice. The kite was made of a playing card.

"That was a Three of Diamonds," she shouted to the troupe of players.

"The sky is improved by additional diamonds," said Humpty Dumpty. "Next kite, hurry! That creature is getting closer."

It took only a few moments before all thirteen kites were launched. They disappeared into the low cloud cover. Ada now saw that the creatures had been transformed into marionettes. The tin cutouts and Humpty Dumpty were each suspended a few feet in the air by four kite-card strings. Humpty clenched the string to the Ace between his teeth, perhaps because he was top-heavy.

"We are now in fine hands," said the Tin Ballerina, glancing skyward.

"My hand is finer than yours," mumbled Humpty Dumpty. "I have a royal flush."

"Oh," said the Tin Bear to Ada, "I forgot; we do have one final kite. We rarely use it, but you are welcome to it if you like. It is a Joker."

"Ah." Ada wasn't sure if this was a good idea. It seemed impolite to turn the offer down, though, so she launched herself a kite. She gripped the string as the wind began to lead them in a direction that had no whether-or-not to it. They weren't lifted far off the ground but skipped and hopped as marionettes do, untroubled by gravity, drawn by strings directing them from the sky.

"How do you know this is the right way?" she asked.

"We do not question our higher power," said Humpty Dumpty. "It knows best."

"We are but tugged at the whim of the Creator," agreed the Tin Bear.

"Though we struggle in fog, our fate is in the cards," called the Tin Ballerina. And who knew but that she was right, for the sound of the menacing creature that pursued them began to recede a little. The kites dragged Ada, the Tin Ballerina, the Tin Bear, and Humpty Dumpty so quickly that there was no more breath for talking. It reminded Ada of going for a walk with Miss Armstrong.

At length the mist began to dissipate. It seemed they must have covered many miles. The wind slackened. The kites drooped and failed. They found themselves pausing in a mature beech woods, right at the door of a small, stately home made of stone and, it seemed, crumpets and old boots.

They untied their strings and rolled them up, and they crammed the kites back in the valise of the Tin Bear. "You are most admirable marionettes," admitted Ada.

"We have no say in the matter," said the Tin Ballerina, without remorse. "Life blows us where it will. Hither, thither, and whether. We play our little witty roles. I should have liked to run a boardinghouse, but life has not given me that."

"Hush," said the Tin Bear. "Is that the wind, or has the Terror of the Fog followed us even here?"

Sure enough, a strangled iron cry reverberated a good ways off. If it had followed them this far, alas, it would come nearer. Ada rapped on the door, hoping for the best.

In short order the door was opened by a sleepy-looking housemaid in a mob-cap. "They've all gone off," she said grumpily. "Go away."

"They've gone, and we've come," said the Tin Bear. "Let us in."

"I'm not scared of a dancing bear with a portmanteau stuck on his noodle," said the housemaid, but she opened the door just the same. "Very well, if there's no stopping you."

"Who's gone off?" asked Ada as they crowded into the filthy kitchen. A pot of soup had bubbled down to grime and was gently scorching upon the hob.

"Why, the Duchess, of course, and the Cook. The Duchess went to the garden party in high dudgeon, but the Cook wasn't invited, so she went to her sister's in low spirits."

"High Dudgeon and Low Spirits," said Humpty Dumpty. "Very fine addresses, both. I don't suppose you have a bite to offer us?"

"There's naught to eat, what with that pig about," said the housemaid, "so keep a proper tongue in your head or we'll see how large a *soufflé* you might make." She sat on a stool and picked up her knitting. She seemed to be devising a morning coat out of seaweed.

A terrible roar, all too close, descended upon the house. Through the window they could see crumpets falling off the roof. A glory of soot emitted from the chimney. Ada and the marionettes clung to one another, but the housemaid only yawned. "I wonder if that's the Baby wanting its brekky," said the housemaid. "Baby *likes* eggs."

"I adore babies myself," said Humpty Dumpty, flashing some pointy teeth.

"Is that the noise of the Jabberwock?" asked Ada.

"I couldn't say. I wouldn't know a Jabberwock from a Wockerjab. Could be Baby in a state. Perhaps Baby knows." The housewife opened a little iron door to a bread oven. A pig poked his head out the aperture.

"Is that you making such a horrid row?" asked the housemaid. The pig shook his snout. The stertorous commotion seemed to have landed on the eaves, as the room was showered with crumbs and dust. The housemaid said to the guests, "Baby has a wicked chest cold, but that cough belongs to something else. Maybe that Jockerwab you was collecting, for a specimen, was it?"

"And what *is* a Jabberwock?" asked Ada.

At this the Baby turned his little snout up and rolled his little piggy eyes at her. He began to speak.

> *"And what's a Jabberwock, you ask?*
> *To answer is a gruesome task.*
> *It is not ape though ape it may.*
> *To be a bee it cannot be.*
> *'Not carp?' you carp; 'Not carp,' I say.*
> *Nor dog, though dogged, I decree.*
> *It is not ewe—how you amuse!—*
> *Nor fish, although you fish for clues—"*

"Intolerable nonsense," interrupted Humpty Dumpty.

"You've ruined my line of thought," snapped the Baby.

"Just finish up, and then we'll know what a Jabberwock truly is," said Ada peaceably enough. "Knowledge comes at the end."

"The end part goes like this," said the Baby sharply.

> *"The only sound it makes is sproink,*
> *And on the matter, by my bladder, that's my final oink."*

Then the Baby wiggled out of the bread oven, fell on the floor, and turned and bit his own curly tail in annoyance.

"We didn't hear all the *other* animals it isn't," said Ada. "So how will we recognize it when we find it?"

"It'll find you," said the Baby grimly, snuffling for crumbs under the pastry table.

"Does either of you know the way to the garden party?" said Ada. "That's where we are headed. The marionettes are performing, and I am looking for a friend."

"*You'll* never find a friend, not with that attitude!" said Humpty Dumpty.

The housemaid said to Ada, "I'll show you how to get to the garden gate, though I'd not go inside myself. I'm not invited."

"And a good thing, too," said the Baby, eating a tea towel off the airing rack. "*You'd* bring the tone down, you would."

"No sugar-water for you," said the housemaid, "if you're going to make personal remarks."

"It's the only kind I know how to make." The Baby began to run around the table, oinking up a storm. "I think the Jabberwock is eating the roof! Everybody hide."

"Quick," said the housemaid. She stood and put on the seaweed jacket. It now seemed as broad as a cape, and somehow it was capacious enough for all of them to huddle under. Crumbs of plaster dust like caster sugar showered upon them as she drew the edges of the coat together. "I always find if you're caught at home without a vorpal blade, a seaweed frock serves as a fine caution against germs and Jabberwocks." She fastened a snap somehow. They plunged into darkness.

# CHAPTER 26

———— ✑ ————

$L$ydia had had no difficulty persuading
Siam to return with her to the Croft. "Your Mr. Winter will
find us there," she said. "He's on an errand of foolishness or
mercy, or perhaps both."

Siam made no reply. Perhaps, Lydia thought, that description characterizes Mr. Winter's attention to Siam, too.

Lydia thought it wouldn't be proper for them to walk
abreast, though she wasn't sure why. She pressed ahead, re-
marking over her shoulder, "Mind the burrs," and "We'll turn
here, it's quicker." They passed into a grove of saplings. For
a moment they were out of sight of any rooftops or chimney
pots, cows or river. The June greenery gave off its smell of sour
and sweet fervor. She almost felt drunk. How wild the world
was, when you paused to look over the stile, out any window,
across the herbaceous borders of propriety, 1860s version.

She stopped and turned, without forethought. She faced
Siam. He had just leaped over a spot of puddle and so he was

right at her chin. He couldn't back up because of the mud. She didn't retreat either.

"How do you find it, traveling about with him?" she said.

How fast the shutters flew up, how fast the drapes were drawn! A look of uncomprehending stiffness such as one might catch from a Welshman. Siam said, "Mr. Josiah he make all the bookings and such."

"Tell me about where you were born. Tell me about your family."

"Nothing to say 'bout that. It's all—" He made a gesture with his hand. "All gone."

"We have little in common, but we have that," she said. "My mother is gone, too. She died some months ago."

He shrugged. She guessed that he knew there was nothing to say. They had nothing to give to each other. Grief cocoons the newly bereaved, and sometimes they never escape.

"I am going mad," said Lydia. "Always responsible for Alice, always tending to my desperate father. Neither the matron of the house nor the daughter." Oh, but she was sounding like Miss Armstrong now. "How do you manage, going from here to there? Are you escaping owners who would enslave you and bring you back to whichever southern state you fled from? Or do you have a destination? Is there a home for you ahead?"

"Mr. Josiah my home," he said. His eyes were glazed. He looked over Lydia's shoulder. A wind pushed the leaves about. It was like being swamped in a green tide rolling in.

"Are you being followed even in England?" she asked. He would not answer.

"You was looking for your sister," he said at last.

"She can look after herself. She'll show up when she's hungry. I want to know more about Mr. Winter."

"I can't say. He away with that blue jay woman."

She took that to be a caution. Calling Miss Armstrong a blue jay! "Is he often scarpering off with single women?"

"Let's go."

"I see," she said. It wasn't so much pity as irritation that turned her heel once more. She heard in his avoidance of the subject something untoward about the character of Mr. Winter. Her annoyance was shot through with a surge of bile and regret. The resulting admixture might have been called rage. She kept her voice still as a tyrant adult might. "Very well. Back to the morgue."

A tension had arisen between them. When he stopped to pick up a stone or a feather or whatever attracted him, she didn't wait. By the time she reached the Croft, he was quite a few steps behind. She didn't hold the gate.

"Well?" asked Mrs. Brummidge.

"Alice is out larking somewhere with Ada Boyce, it seems. Miss Armstrong is rounding them up."

"Quite right, too. And Mr. Winter's young charge? What did you do with him?" Mrs. Brummidge looked foul and censorious.

"What do you think I did? I slaughtered him and pushed him in the river."

"You need a nostrum for your wild panics, my girl. But one distress at a time. Mr. Darwin rang for your Mr. Yankee to walk him to the privy. His bowels are unsettled, he said."

"Father will have to do it. For all I know, Mr. Winter has gone into town with Miss Armstrong. Perhaps they have eloped."

Along, now, came Siam. Shuffling at the door.

"I think not. My laddio, *you* can attend Mr. Darwin. Go to the parlor and see if he will come with you."

"T'aint my place," he said.

"Well, it certainly isn't mine!" snapped Mrs. Brummidge. "This house is in an uproar today. Go and offer some help. I've luncheon to get on the table." She turned back to the oven and peered inside, batting against the steam and sniffing judiciously. "Not one of my better efforts, but it'll have to do." She turned. "What are you waiting for, child? Do as I say."

Still he did not move. He juggled his hands in his pockets.

"What do you have there?" said Mrs. Brummidge, all glower. "Pocketed something from the Master's vitrine, have you? Turn out your pocket, let me see, or I'll be sacked for theft. I won't find another position at my age, not like this one."

Siam brought out a handful of treasures. Rather than hold them out in his open palm, he dropped them on the tabletop. Two stones from the riverbank. A bit of old conker shell, its auburn shine from last September all weathered to grey. A black ebony pawn from a chessboard.

"That *isn't* from the set in the parlor. Upon my word, I believe it is." Mrs. Brummidge turned pale. "Mr. Clowd's chess game is useless without all its pieces. As I've been told often enough and no mistake. You've no right to go sneaking about and lifting things from us. I don't care what your heathen background. You ought to know better by now. You're in *England*." She pronounced that with especial force, as if every knee should bow. "Miss Lydia, make him put it back, and bring him to apologize to the Master."

"I only holded it," said Siam. "I warn't taking it."

"You took it out of the house."

"Didn't know I was going out. Anyhows, now it's back."

Mrs. Brummidge wouldn't discuss it further. "Miss Lydia." In that tone, the cook's word was law. She turned to withdraw the joint from the oven. "Drawing room, young lady. Have him replace the object at once. Then to the parlor, where you will see that this fellow apologizes for his behavior, and offers to help Mr. Darwin, poor soul, with his cramps and ailments."

Lydia had been docile, almost amused at seeing Siam upbraided. "Come along," she said. She led him up the steps and through the passage to the front of the house. Her father was in the parlor with Mr. Darwin. The door across the corridor, the door to the drawing room, was closed. "We don't even *come* in here anymore," she said. "I can't think when you found the moment to steal around our house on your own. You might have opened any door and . . . found me unprepared for company."

"When Mr. Josiah took Mr. Darwin out to visit the necessary. I just standing in the hallway. And your father, he crying or something. I coon't go back in there. So I look around in this room 'stead." His hand on the doorknob.

"Very well. Go in again."

He opened the door. The drawing room was still shaded

with curtains. Outlines, dust, a faint odor evocative of Mama. It had been Mama's room primarily. They did not use this room now.

"Why they cloths up on the picture?"

"It's not a picture. It's a mirror," said Lydia at the door-way, gasping in small silent intakes, keeping her voice level. "A practice in this country to drape the mirrors when some-one dies. It's outrageous that you've made me come into this place. Put back the piece now, I don't like to be here."

"Who do," he muttered.

"That's a rude thing to say as a guest, in this house, in this nation."

"I'd leave iffen I could."

"You may get your chance." She felt light-headed and fiery. "I'll tell your dallying Mr. Winter, when and if he ever returns, that you've stolen from us. Perhaps he'll reconsider whether to keep on endorsing your *bid* for *freedom*." She went further then, swayed into recklessness by the miasma of loss in this chamber. "I do believe it may be the law of the land that thieves are exported. Certainly a fair number of felons have been marched to World's End and sent down under, never to return."

"Down under." He said it with the sound of an oracle, slow and horrified at what was emerging from his mouth. He set the pawn upon the chessboard so softly there was no little click of ebony upon marble tile square. None of the other ebony pieces, nor their ivory twins, shuddered or flinched. The world was dead.

"Down under," she said again. "Oh, what's the bother?"

There was noise from the kitchen, a warm deep note, Mr.
Winter. He'd expected to meet up with Lydia again but she
rejected him summarily, for his courtly attention to that
stupid governess. He deserved whatever he got. "There he is.
I shall go tell him at once of your perfidy. Wait here."

She closed the door. He was alone in the dark, waiting.

Down under. Back home. What was the difference, what
difference did it make? In a half hour, had he undone everything merciful that had happened to him in his otherwise
merciless existence?

Who had he become, just by menacing this jittery white
girl? He felt altered, other than himself. Nothing was like
it had been before. *Am I even Siam?* he wondered. He had
not always been Siam, he'd had another name. At Dover,
the minister of customs had examined his papers and then
asked a question in an accent too quaint for an American
boy to understand. Mr. Winter had given the tiniest nod of
his head, so he'd murmured, "Yes I am." But the officer had
heard "Siam." He'd written that down on the paper. Siam
had had a ready-made alias he hadn't intended to choose.

The room was so dark. He felt gone, invisible, as if he
had no more presence. All for a little black toy that had no
face. He went past the checkered board on its table. He ventured to the mantelpiece and found a footstool by the hearth.
He climbed up, and pushed aside the purple cloth that hung
over the looking-glass.

The light was poor. Siam couldn't see himself at first.

"He's in the drawing room," came Lydia's sharp voice in
the passage. "Go say your piece, Mr. Winter."

A knock at the door. "Are you in here?" Mr. Winter's voice angry.

The boy might have answered "Yes I am," or "Siam," or even "Samuel," had he been in there. But the drape was settling across the looking-glass. The room was empty.

# PART THE SECOND

There are bits and pieces of the Thames all over Oxford, runnels and reaches and backwaters—"more in number than your eyelashes," Keats said—and beneath the very centre of the city runs the Trill Mill stream, a gloomy underground waterway in which it was discovered, one day in the 1920s, a rotted Victorian punt with two Victorian skeletons in it.

—JAMES/JAN MORRIS, *OXFORD*, PAGE 31

# CHAPTER 27

A noisy place and dark, the world has always seemed to Siam. A millstone working upon its quern not grain but shale, or glass, something splintery. The last light with any real warmth had been at home, long ago, in a place and a time that no longer existed, with people whose names he didn't say even inside his own mind. As if by thinking of them he might betray them anew. Might put them to some further punishment beyond that which had been accorded them by the slave-hunters.

Now, the boy is momentarily impressed by the silence. The drape on the other side hasn't fallen all the way back, it seems. An uncovered triangle of glass, hardly the size of his hand, remains. He climbs down onto a footstool placed in *this* room just where he had positioned it in the *other*. Curious. He is stealthy, a cat making no noise. The room is very like the one he has just left; equally dark, shrouded. It's too gloomy to know what sort of room it is. Possibly a second parlor. He hopes this isn't the room where Mrs. Clowd is laid. He wouldn't want to be in a dark place with a spooky corpse.

He puts his hand to his face, palm side in because he knows the back of his hand is darker and will reflect less. Creeping up to the mantel and keeping as low as he can, he peers through his fingers across into the room from which he has escaped. Beyond the dark room with the chessboard, out in that passageway, a vector of summery light suddenly sluices, describing a wedge of golden swimming motes. Into the glare, struck as if by fire, Miss Lydia advances, and steps a foot into the dark other room. Her ghoulish pale hair falls upon her neck. Her hand lingers on the doorknob uncertainly. She opens her mouth and says something. Her expression betrays vexation, perhaps the start of worry. She may be calling his name, but he can't hear it.

In the absence of sound, he hears traces of things that he heard in a handful of hidey-holes from Georgia to Tennessee to Pennsylvania and other places. He and his party had learned to disappear in a split moment, sometimes stowed all together, sometimes separately. But he'd always been with one or the other of them, never alone. A smokehouse in the Blue Ridge steeps, a sugaring shed in Brooklyn. Smoke and sugar. And once in the gritty mouth of a coal mine, where they'd huddled in darkness, afraid to strike a match for fear of firedamp, that methane monster.

Disembodied words from the memory of those moments attach themselves to the soundless speaking of Lydia, who is addressing someone in the corridor behind her.

*Don't know the names they'd be using, farmer; but
when you got black rats in the woodpile no need to know
their names before you trap them.*

*If we find you're harboring stolen property, we'd
not be averse to burning this ham house down.*

*Sending cargo up north, ma'am? Ma'am? Why, you
look like you near swallowed a sack of saltpeter, ma'am.
Not going to harm a whisker on your old chin, ma'am.
Put down your gun, it's liable to make a row and waken
the cooey-doves.*

Behind Lydia, into the room, comes Mr. Josiah. Siam can't
see his face clearly; Lydia is in the way, and so are the tears in
Siam's eyes. He doesn't dare wipe them; the movement of his
hand would attract attention. He squeezes his lids shut. Even
through closed eyes he can sense when the light has gone out
of that other room. When he cautiously looks about, he sees
the light has largely disappeared from this room, too.

There is no telling when that missie will come back,
hunting him. Siam doesn't want to plot an escape route in
the bright sunshine of an Oxford noon. He'll hide here till
tempers cool and his brains warm up. He has to think about
what next. He hunches down to his haunches and makes his
way forward, feeling the edges of tables. He brushes against
the chess set. But that was in the room he just evacuated.
Another set here, an identical one? Even in the anonymous
dark, he can feel the forward pawn, just like the one he has

just replaced. A little thing to bring him such trouble. It meant no harm—as if things could have meanings.

Oh, but now he's knocked it on the carpet, and can't make it out in the gloom. He leaves it be.

As much out of habit as not, he backs up into the open hearth, which is clean, clear of andirons and ashes. If someone opens the door, he'll be simply shadows, no more, the ghost of smoke.

In Cheapside last week, in London, he'd come across a chimney sweep at dusk, fresh from his day of labor. Boy or stunted man, bowed by a hawking cough, that person stared at Siam. Bright eyes alert in his sooty face. He'd said something to Siam. Blessing or curse, neither Siam nor Mr. Josiah had known, for the fellow's mouth seemed thick with growths that made an already difficult accent into an impossible language. But though his words had been hooded, and the spit on the paving stones viscous and bloody, the sweep's eyes had looked full of pity and mercy. When he gathered up his brooms and his brushes and turned away, it seemed to Siam like losing another brother.

At this memory, Siam thinks he might climb the flue. He has done this before, once, stealing through the big house with Clem the time he was loaned to pick the cotton fields of Bellefleur or Bellerive or Bellefuck or wherever it was. Clem had later been found out and beaten, but he'd never let on Siam was trespassing in there, too. Siam wonders if the chimneys here are made the same way, with protrusions for the hands to grasp. He'll find out.

He makes a start of it by feeling to make sure the space

is wide enough for his head and his shoulders. He stands up, gingerly, into the darker dark. He raises his hands and gropes, and locates a hold. With one hand on the brick and the other pressed against the wall of the flue, he pulls himself up so his feet are not standing in the hearth anymore. He wedges himself a few feet upward, angled in the flue like a twig in the neck of a brown glass bottle. But he can't find a second brick with which to pull himself higher. Then the first one breaks in his hand. With a mighty crash, he slips to the hearth. Somehow, against his plans and hopes, he smashes through the hearth, or maybe it opens on a hinge for the dumping of ashes into a cellar. He continues falling through the dark. Eventually I'll reach the kitchens and fetch up in a pot of stew, and ruin their lunch, he thinks, and almost begins to laugh, as if his despair has a bright aspect to it. Still he falls. The kitchen must be a long way down, he thinks, halfway to Hell.

# CHAPTER 28

Lydia remarked, "How curious of the child. Where has it gone?" She could hear her own voice taking a public, amused sound, as if Siam were a toddler scurrying under tabletops, and she were pretending ignorance of it, for his delight.

"Why would he come in here?" asked Mr. Winter.

"I sent him to replace something he had"—Lydia hadn't clarified for herself just how far she was going to go with this—"collected." She glanced first at the chessboard. Her eyes hadn't adjusted to the gloom. She couldn't tell if all the pieces were there. "He is playing a game on us."

"He's not the type to play games. Siam, come forward, if you're here."

Nothing stirred in the room. Lydia was confused. After these months, this terrible space still seemed the laying-out room, and would remain so until her father stirred the grief out of it. It wasn't her place to throw open the drapes. Yet she

crossed to the windows and did just that, for the weasel child
had got the better of her. "I can't believe he's slipped out a
window. Look, they are latched, each one." She turned. The
two dozen chess pieces stood in their proper ranks. "Is he
that stealthy that he might have slipped out behind my back?
But it was scarcely turned."

"You under-guess his capacity for intrigues." Mr. Winter
took the room by eminent domain. He strode to check the
shadowed side of the dish cupboard, where the brown and
white pieces had wakened and were winking dustily in the
surprise light. The Staffordshire leech jar, its perforated lid
set aside, held a clump of dead flowers set there in memoriam
months ago. Brown stalks and curled petals. So little color
left that Lydia couldn't remember what sort of flowers they'd
been. Rhoda must be frightened of this room, and avoided it
since the occasion. What a failure of a maid she was. Lydia
crossed the room. She twitched the violet drape into place
around the over-mantel looking-glass. She smoothed the
cloth.

"I asked him about his escapades," she said. "My, how he
husbands his story. If you're the one who has trained him to
hold his tongue, you've done your job well."

"As a guardian, I can only reinforce lessons that his life
has allowed him," said Mr. Winter. "The boy has a history he
would sooner forget. I know some of it, and I would let go of
it if I could. Some realities are too onerous to be borne by
nations, let alone by children. But we are all chained in this."
He sounded cross yet his words rolled out smoothly, as if
he'd prepared his statement for a sympathetic congregation.

How fond of his own sonorities, for a young man.

"Lydia, Mr. Winter." That was her father's voice beyond the door to the drawing room. "I insist. Mr. Darwin requires assistance at once."

She was all daughter, that was all she was. "Yes, Father, of course."

She swept the American abolitionist out of the room. "But this is not right at all," said Mr. Winter in a backstairs voice to Lydia. "Siam is too petrified to go off on his own."

"I shall find Siam playing with our Alice, no doubt. She's about somewhere. I shall make it my chief aim to locate them, right now. Oh, but isn't the day filled with missing children!" She spoke lightly and with a hushed voice. This focus, this emphasis required her to lean into Mr. Winter's shoulder. She overbalanced, though. She had to catch herself on her fingertips against his broadcloth, an accident of poise. Her blood leapt in her arteries to counterweigh the advance.

The great man was in the passage, his broad famous hands flat upon his waistcoat, thumbs touching, little fingers pointing to the floorboards. She allowed herself to sense the presence of illness, intellectual temerity, and theological scandal. He moved by in a froth of white whiskers. Fame and mystery, they are two sides of any earthbound prophet. There was a hint of sharp mustard in his wake. She pulled the door to the drawing room closed. She leaned against it, hands clasped behind her back. She watched Mr. Winter grasp Darwin's elbow and lead him toward the side door and the privy.

"Lydia."

She turned to look at her father, who raised an eyebrow. It was not her foray into the unused parlor that he was commenting on, but that she had been there with Mr. Winter. Unchaperoned. "Remember who you are," he told her, before turning his face away.

Ah, but that was easier said than done, she thought. In order to remember who you are, you have to have known it in the first place.

Her father stood in the passage by the parlor door. He was distracted by both his colloquy with Darwin and his concern for Lydia. What he said next—she could hear it quite clearly—may have served two lines of thought at once.

He said gently,

> "*Genus holds species,*
> *Both are great or small.*
> *One genus highest, one not high at all.*
> *Each species has its differentia, too,*
> *This is not that, and He was never You.*"

He may have been talking about the Savior. Or about Mr. Winter. Or possibly about dinosaur relics in the Oxford Museum and great apes in the Congo basin.

"Shall I tell Mrs. Brummidge to bring out the luncheon?"

He rubbed his face. This may have been a nod, or a grimace. He said, "Alice is keeping herself quiet today, anyway." He passed back into his parlor. He closed the door upon Lydia's caution and her anger.

In the kitchen, Mrs. Brummidge said, "So you've mis-

placed the visiting heathen creature, too?" She heaved the
joint out of the oven and onto the butcher's board. It was
blackened on one side like a log removed from the hearth.
Mrs. Brummidge chose some words unsuitable for Rhoda's
ears and the maid went rash red. But Lydia refused to flinch at
the assault, which barreled on. "For Lord's sakes! The young
scamp must've scarpered up the front stairs whilst you was
tossing your ribbons at his master. He's playing with Alice
in some quiet way, and that's not right. Not in this house,
with no Missus to remind you or Alice what's done or not to
be done. Go up at once, and if they're around, bring them
both down. I'll dish up some scraps and milk gravy when I've
done sorting out the platters. Perhaps a dark boy will prefer
the charred bits."

Lydia flew up the stairs. The day seemed to be coming un-
stitched. It reminded her of her first and only trip to London
in a railroad car. They'd crowded into a carriage with other
passengers. Everyone, without considerations of privacy,
talked their business across strangers. All their plans of what
was doing in the City, and who was up from the country
stopping in Lincoln's Inn Fields, and when someone would
return, today or another, and alone or not. Lydia tried not to
listen but her ears insisted. The railroad carriage rocked, at
the stupendous speed of quite a few miles in an hour, and the
railroad company didn't seem to care if someone dropped a
ham on the floor, and which child had forgotten to use the
loo, and whether Auntie Pretzel would remember to collect
them in Paddington. On lolloped the carriage, as if time
would work out all concerns eventually, with remorseless ac-

curacy, no matter how the passengers barracked about their lives. Alice had sat and looked out the window at the rushing world, and she hadn't seemed to notice that she wasn't alone. Lydia noticed.

Lydia glanced in the nursery. She knew Alice wasn't there. Lydia could feel Alice in the house as one could feel a spirit or an intruder. But Lydia might be wrong about Siam. Who knew if he was readying to make off with something more valuable? That the Clowd family had little of value but what was broken among them didn't occur to Lydia. She sensed trickery and slippyness in Siam, as if he had evaporated in order to implicate her somehow. In something. She loathed him for it. She wanted to find him out at a greater crime, and cry foul.

Dinah the cat and her two kittens slept in a lazy, shedding heap upon a trunk in a sunny window. Lydia nearly pitched a shoe at them. It would have felt satisfactory to let a shoe go, but she didn't. She gritted her teeth and passed by, opening chamber doors and even wardrobes in case he was hiding therein.

He couldn't have climbed out upon the roof, surely? The window over the front portico was flung open, wide enough for a limber lad to scramble out, and woody vines around the lattice might have allowed him to climb down. But in the heat of June that window was always open.

She went up another half-flight to the box room under the eaves. This dusty space featured only one window. Union cloth was tacked across it. She ripped it down. The view from atop the house gave out over the heads of trees to the river and meadows. She might see Siam on the run. She could hurry downstairs with news for Mr. Winter about his miscreant.

No boy to be seen; nor Alice; nor Ada; nor that pesky Miss Armstrong. They had all been swallowed up in their own escapades. Ought Lydia start to be anxious for Alice? It wasn't unusual for the child to wander off, but this day was beginning to feature a comedy of absences. What Puck might be bewitching the neighborhood with metamorphoses, parliaments, evaporations and misalliances?

She saw Mr. Winter waiting a few feet off from the privy house. He was studying the bees that hovered and swam over the snapdragons. She might have hallooed, did girls her age do that. She lifted her face in case he felt her gaze and saw her staring, so she might be caught looking statuesquely into the distance. The glassy summer noontime paused, trembled upon its long silent note of heat and anticipation. A few clouds over the Cotswolds cast upon that horizon a rich, regal grey, with a nap like Parisian velvet.

# CHAPTER 29

———— ✦ ————

The housemaid had pulled closed the drapes of the cloak of seaweed. The fronds interlaced and locked like iron mesh around Ada, the maid, and the performing troupe.

The seaweed, though dead and dry, was still growing. It seethed and twitched densely. Soon it had filled in all the spaces among the strands. With no horizon to settle her eyes upon, without little sense of up-and-down or here-and-there, Ada was unmoored. Blood pounded in her eyelids but devoid of the orangey pulse that happens when one closes one's eyes at the bright seaside. She seemed motionless, in an attitude like a figure in a tableau vivant intended to reprove. *The Virtues of Modesty, Restraint, and Perspicacity at Play in Elysium.* Though struck with paralysis in the dark, she had the uncomfortable sense of velocity. As if she and her companions were moving at a remarkable speed, and unaware of it. As if they were ignorant, decorous creatures painted around the rim of a dinner plate that had been sent hurtling through the air toward someone's head. Ada was not accustomed to thinking in such terms. Such aggressive equations. But crash they did not, or not so they noticed. The housemaid opened a button to let in some air. Though some peculiar sounds caught Ada's attention, none of them seemed to be Jabberwockian, as she had come to think of it.

"I always find a change of clothes so brightens the mood, don't YOU?" asked the housemaid as she released Ada into the daylight. The child fell out of confinement onto her knees, which hurt like the dickens. It took her a moment to straighten up and turn around. In her new agility she still favored one leg.

She found herself on a gravel walk. But for the housemaid, Ada was alone. "Where is this?"

"The path you find yourself upon," answered the housemaid.

"What happened to the marionettes and to Humpty Dumpty?"

"Oh, they were wanted at the garden party. They were afraid of being late. Humpty Dumpty didn't want to be turned into a devil egg, which in the annals of kitchen science is the same thing as an angel egg. The Queen of Hearts has a robust temper, you see. And anger gives one an appetite. So her edible guests do try to keep her from losing her temper."

"But I wanted to go there, too," said Ada. "I'm sure that's where my friend Alice will be. She is ever one for a party, especially if there are charades, or games and prizes."

The housemaid had finished removing her seaweed robe. She was folding it into a small square, about the size of a pincushion. She popped it into her mouth. "How unfortunate if it starts to rain at the party, as I've just eaten my weather apparel," she said. "Then again, seaweed gets so very wet in the rain."

Her voice was different than it had been. Ada realized that her young fresh face was now lined. She had turned pale. Her eyes blinked, rheumy and kind. She had shrunk, and her shoulders were hunched. She looked like the sort of aged matron who might be in charge of collecting tickets at a parish luncheon. "You're not yourself," said Ada.

"Travel tires one, don't you agree?" replied the old woman. "So I've changed my clothes. It seems to go on forever, life. Still, when I get home, no doubt I'll feel sprightly again. Take my arm, dear, as I have trouble navigating over this treacherous gravel."

"Where are we?" asked Ada, looking about.

"I have no idea. It seems perhaps to be a Zoological Plantation of some sort. I think we are the exhibit. Do you see the bars behind which we are caged?"

The old woman indicated a set of low hoops, like croquet wickets, set in the ground along the edges of the path. They formed an airy, imbricated fringe between well-kept lawns on either side.

Ada said, "Those aren't the bars of a cage. They are fences meant to keep us from walking upon the grass."

The old woman demurred. "They are for our own protection. Otherwise, visitors who come to stare at our peculiarities would pluck us to shreds and turn us into decorative items for their homes. What type of specimen are you?"

"Begging your pardon, but I am no specimen."

"Oh, you most certainly are. I believe you may be a fine example of a Rogue Child. No one seems to be hunting after *you* to fetch you from this durance vile," said the old woman. "As for me, I am a White Queen. Very rare in these parts. I frighten the natives. Quite often I frighten myself, but that is only for practice so I can do my job in the public *mêlée*."

Ada knew she ought to be polite to a member of the royalty. "I believe travel has made you confused. This is simply a garden path. We could step over that low ridge of iron hoops and trespass upon the grass whenever we wanted."

"Such ignorance in the young. If you think you are so free, try straying from your path. You should know the truth about captivity. Go ahead, my dear. Try."

Ada went to the edge of the walk and began to step over. The lifelong stiffness that had been absent since her fall through the shaft now seemed to afflict her in the hip, however, and she couldn't raise her ankle more than a few inches. She turned to explain about her ailment to the White Queen, who smiled wincingly. Then the old woman directed her alabaster scepter toward her own feet. Ada saw that the Queen's shoes were affixed to a dial of some sort, like a plaster stand.

"Why, you're a chess piece, more or less," said Ada in amazement. "No wonder you are having a hard time walking."

"I glide but I do not jump. Shhhh, I believe we have company." The White Queen cocked her head and rolled her eyes to one side meaningfully.

Along the grass on the other side of the hooped edging strolled a Lion, a Unicorn, and an elderly Sheep. The Sheep was trailing some undone knitting out of a carpetbag.

"Don't look now," said the Unicorn, "but the most revolting creatures are on display over there. Don't look. Don't."

All three of them turned and rushed to the edge of the path and leaned over, making faces at Ada and the Queen.

"Just ambling along as if it owned the road. I call that sass!" said the Lion.

The Sheep adjusted a pince-nez. "I recognize a Queen when I see one in captivity. Would that all Queens met the same fate!" Her companions laughed halfheartedly but sent glances over their shoulders to make sure such sedition had not been overheard. "But what in nature or out of it could that other revolting thing be?"

"It's a mere trifle, no less," said the Lion. "Either that or a plum pudding."

"I never saw a plum pudding with such a foul expression on its face. I do believe it's not a comestible at all," said the Unicorn. "It's a mythical creature, I suspect. It doesn't exist. It's a child."

"We saw a child just a little while ago," the Lion reminded him. "*She* existed."

"Ah, but where is she now?" The Unicorn shrugged. "Imaginary, I tell you. A matter of legend and superstition with no basis in fact. So is this one. Swords and swordfish, but it's an ugly brute."

"I am not," said Ada.

"It thinks it's talking!" said the Sheep. "Isn't that droll, isn't it queer! Hello, whiddle whillikums, how is your hawwible life today? Blah blah, it replies, as if it can understand us!"

"Was the mythical creature you saw called Alice?" asked Ada.

"It thinks it knows all about our lives. Did its owners give it a pamphlet to study before prodding it out of its Creature House to parade its ugliness before the paying public?" asked the Unicorn.

"I think it's rather dear," said the Sheep. "I should like to take it home and hang its head on the wall above my occasional table."

"What is your occasional table when it occasionally is something else?" asked the White Queen politely, as if trying to change the subject from Ada to something less offensive.

"I choose not to recognize it when we pass in the street," replied the Sheep. "Sometimes it is an ornamental iron fawn in a dubious coiffure, sometimes a wheelbarrow putting on airs. I cut it severely."

"I *like* that one," said the Lion, pointing. "Here, Queeny Queeny, if I point a stick at you will you snap at it with your little royal dentures?" He could see no stick at hand so he grabbed the Unicorn around the neck. With swiping motions he thrust the horn of his friend over the side of the path at Ada and the White Queen.

"I'll make a pudding of *you*," said the White Queen. "When I hang my crown up, I spend my leisure time as a housemaid, so I have learned many tricks of the kitchen, believe me! I'll thank you to mind your manners."

"It's so real, yet so banal," said the Sheep.

"Let go of my horn," said the Unicorn. "It's ticklish."

"Did you fail to board the Ark? And did you drown?" Ada asked of the Unicorn. "Did Noah even *try* to save you?"

"Rescue is a myth. Don't believe a word of it," said the Unicorn.

"We mustn't linger," said the Lion, releasing the Unicorn. "Zoos are a form of happy diversion, but the light is lengthening. We ought to push on. I hope you still have the invitation to the party?" he asked the Sheep.

"Oh, dear, yes," she said. "I understand there is to be an execution."

"What is to be executed?" asked the Lion.

"Manners and fine taste, among other things. Let's hurry along."

"Tell Alice!" cried Ada. "Tell Alice I am coming for her!"

"Aren't children so like real life?" said the Lion as they all opened up parasols and began to ascend in the breeze. "And yet so *not*, too."

"I still think it's a trifle," said the Unicorn.

# CHAPTER 30

————— ❧ —————

It is an ordinary day in Oxford, just one midsummer day in the early 1860s. The clock has struck one. Mrs. Brummidge has finished laying out the luncheon. She has let her employer know the table is set. She has dumped the water used for boiling the pudding into the stones of the soakaway, and she has sat down in the shade outside the kitchen doorway. She is sucking on a horehound drop.

This story is spattering along on unregistered reaches of the edges of the famous town. The town hardly acknowledges the likes of Mrs. Brummidge. For her part, Mrs. Brummidge knows nothing, and will never know anything, about Charles Ryder and Sebastian Flyte and Zuleika Dobson, Harriet Vane and Lyra Belacqua and Jay Gatsby, George Smiley and James Bond, or even Captain Jas. Hook. They are yet to be imagined. In any case, Mrs. Brummidge doesn't read fiction. She hasn't the patience for it.

It might be worth considering for a moment if the built

landscape inspires in authors the invention of romantic individuals. Of course, architecture is impervious to rants, petitions, to shrieks of rape and the murder of martyrs and all the other human noise. But is one of the satisfactions of carved space—that is, massive stone laid just so—that it calls out for the creation of heightened characters to live up to it? Even if those outsize characters are ourselves, our own cleansed, resolved natures? The ancient Greeks may have thought so. (Drama was perhaps invented by the natural amphitheatre, and not the other way round.) The medieval masons of Chartres and Reims built windowed bluffs that laddered light into heaven; and peasants, in perceiving their own rights to salvation, began to imagine other rights, too. So Oxford, at its inception a huddle of theologicians and divines, grew into a city of dreams, and much good may come of that. Little surprise that Middle-earth and Narnia were both discovered here.

Yet this story takes place outside of the most famous sites. No murder in the Sheldonian, no undergraduate lust in the reading room of the Radcliffe Camera, no academic intrigue in the Senior Common Room of Balliol, no capering over the leads of Christ Church, no spicy infidelities in the back passage at the Ashmolean, no spiritual remorse before William Holman Hunt's *The Light of the World*. Most of this story takes place on Oxford's margins, the area where the maps of famous buildings and renowned sites tend to pale and give out. The undifferentiated reaches marked *HC SVNT DRACONES*. Beyond the old town walls. You won't identify the exact mile of riverbank that ties together the lives of those in the Vicarage and the Croft. The river changes its course by grains of mud every day, imperceptibly. A rural district yields indifferently to development, plot by plot. And once the colleges open to women, fifteen, twenty-five years hence, the late-Victorian houses of Norham Gardens and the like, those anxiously fanciful, tall brick ships moored behind their garden gates up and down each lane, will obliterate this scrap of unsanctified north Oxford. It will remain only here, on these pages.

Perhaps we love our Oxford because it seems eternal, and we can return arm in arm; while our private childhoods are solitary, unique to each of us alone, and lost. We cannot point them out to one another. Only, sometimes, in the text of a book here and there, we tap the page with a finger and say, "This is what my lost days were like. Something like this." But even as we turn to the fellow in the bed beside us to say, "Yes, this passage here," whatever it is we recognized has already disguised itself, changed in that split instant. There is no hope that our companion can see what we, just for a moment, saw anew and hailed with a startled, glad heart. Literary pleasure, and a sense of recognition and identification, real though they are, burn off like alcohol in the flame of the next heated moment.

# CHAPTER 31

———— ✎ ————

So, yes, the luncheon is set, and the great man is brought to table. He is not sat at the foot, for that was Mrs. Clowd's place and will never be used again. He is placed at Mr. Clowd's right hand. Mr. Josiah Winter sits at Mr. Clowd's left. Rhoda brings forward the first course, a mock turtle soup. She retires to hover in the pantry. She listens to spoons clink upon porcelain. The men speak intermittently, affably, but without the race of competitive chatter Rhoda knows from meals at the boardinghouse in Jericho where on her off-days she sometimes shares a meal with her sister, who is in service to an addlepated old cleric hunkered down among the other rubbishy types there.

Rhoda has nothing to do with the disappearance of Alice. She has paid little attention to the child. The little girl, a bit of a pill. Rhoda pulls up Alice's bedding every morning and wonders at the doll left on the chest. Alice never sleeps with a doll as other girls might. Was she always this rigid,

Rhoda wonders, or am I only seeing her as she is today, these months after the passing of her mother? Alice? Eager to put every foot right, to live every moment correctly, to balance or redress that slashing crime perpetrated by an unfeeling universe? Or to forestall it happening again? Strange little Alice, playing in the penumbra of her father's moral consternation. She can't help but absorb some of the stress of that man's grief. Put plainly: If we aren't made of eternal stuff by a Creator who bent low upon the earth to fashion us, how can we hope for an eternal soul that might return to Him? And how can we hope for the promised reunion of souls when this created universe has run its course?

Of course Rhoda doesn't put Alice's situation like this. She thinks, scatteredly, Peculiar mite, that Alice. Whatever haze of apprehension attends the thought of the missing child is quickly dissipated. In the moments before the soup bowls must be removed—they dine à la Russe, in stages, unlike the hobbledehoyfreeforall service at the boardinghouses—Rhoda goes to soak the tea towels in an enamel basin. She studies her own cuticles. She has moved on from any further reflection about Alice's character.

Mrs. Brummidge and Rhoda: These two people are here, too, in the story, along with the newborn Boy Boyce, that squalling infant, the presence of whom first sent his sister Ada hustling out of the Vicarage with a jar of marmalade. The dropsical Mrs. Boyce, the distractible Vicar; they inhabit their own Oxfords. They don't realize that they might remember this day for the rest of their lives. The fatal day rarely announces itself, but comes disguised as mid-summer.

Our private lives are like a colony of worlds expanding, contracting, breathing universal air into separate knowledges. Or like several packs of cards shuffled together by an expert anonymous hand, and dealt out in a random, amused or even hostile way.

# CHAPTER 32

———— ❧ ————

Lydia wasn't hungry. It was too hot, she thought. Still, Mrs. Brummidge would report to Mr. Clowd if Lydia neglected to eat anything. So she sat at the kitchen worktable with a hunk of bread and some cheese. She didn't care for soup, but Mrs. Brummidge delivered a portion to her regardless. Lydia was put out at not having been invited to dine with the gentlemen, but in truth, Mr. Darwin scared her a little. And Mr. Winter probably would have ignored her over the joint and the peas, or been condescending. So perhaps it was best she stayed in the kitchen. With the residual heat of the oven, however, she felt dizzy and not entirely herself.

"We can't get rid of you, it seems," said Mrs. Brummidge in a here's-trouble voice. Lydia looked up. She wasn't surprised to see Miss Armstrong once more. That woman seemed yoked to this household today by a gum-rubber cord. She lowered her parasol and entered without invitation.

"I am on the edge of being alarmed." In the absence of a gesture of welcome, she sat down.

"Only on the edge?" replied Lydia. "Is there any way I can help . . . ?"

But the woman was calmer than she'd been earlier. Perhaps Mr. Winter had soothed a few of her separate hysterias. She accepted a bowl of soup and dandled the spoon above it, preparing her strategic remarks before beginning her meal. It's the spoon of Damocles, thought Lydia.

"I went across the river. No luck. Then I returned to the Vicarage. Ada is still gone," she said. "I didn't make a fuss as there was another medical moment going on. I'm surprised *you* aren't more distressed at your sister's continued absence."

"You don't know Alice very well."

Lydia was glad Mrs. Brummidge was collecting something from the larder, so missing this exchange; otherwise she'd have charged into this conversation. Lydia went on. "Alice lives in a queer no-man's-land, Miss Armstrong, as far as we can tell. She isn't capable of malice and she hasn't discovered deviousness. No doubt you're wise to become exercised over the disappearance of Ada. But for this household to do the same over Alice's adventures would be ill-advised. Alice will return when she does. Likely, Ada will be with her. I think you are rather overwrought today."

"It's hardly your place to say so," snapped Miss Armstrong. Still, she was a guest here, and Lydia was as much as the Croft could boast in the way of a proper hostess, so Miss Armstrong scooped some soup as a gesture of closure. When she had swallowed the first mouthful she continued.

"Mr. Winter waited with me while the boatman finished his lunch. Until Mr. Winter felt he must return to attend Mr. Darwin, I learned a great deal about the new work Darwin is considering."

"I see," said Lydia, who saw mostly that Miss Armstrong now seemed alert to the significance of Mr. Darwin. But Lydia took little interest in questions of natural history. Mrs. Brummidge, having returned to the kitchen, went about her business, ears cocked.

"At home in Kent, Mr. Darwin showed Mr. Winter a most peculiar orchid. It was sent the great naturalist from an island off the coast of Africa. I forget which coast and which island. Geography is a sore mystery to me. In any event, the nectary of this amazing plant, according to Mr. Winter, is an eleven-inch tube. Surely no insect flies around, even in darkest Africa, with an eleven-inch proboscis. Such would be ungainly. Yet Darwin imagines a moth possessed of a rolling proboscis, like an uncoiling snake, that could collect the nectar. Such a moth could retract his implement and propagate the species by visiting a sister plant. I don't think such a strategy is likely. But just imagine the mind that can imagine such a thing."

"You are flushed with the effort of imagining it," observed Mrs. Brummidge.

"It's known as the Star of Bethlehem orchid," said Miss Armstrong with complacency, as if biblical allusion must deter any unsavory associations.

"And the insect would be a variety of the species *magi*, in that it comes bearing gifts," said Lydia.

"Malarkey and confustication," said Mrs. Brummidge, trying not to laugh. "Rhoda, pay no mind to nonsense."

"I hate to pester you with questions," said Lydia to Miss Armstrong, "but when you were returning here from the Vicarage, I don't suppose you caught sight of Mr. Winter's boy roaming about? He came back to the house with me but then scarpered off somewhere like a wagtail in the underbrush. Mr. Winter went in to dine without knowing where the boy has gone. And I understand the guests intend to take the mid-afternoon train back to London so Mr. Darwin can return to Down by nightfall. This is an arduous trip for a man with his set of conditions. Mr. Winter won't be able to postpone their departure just because his boy has gone larking about."

"I saw no sign of that child," returned the governess, "but when luncheon is over perhaps Mr. Winter and I can make another perambulation together and look for *both* our charges." She smiled at Lydia as if grateful the girl had scared Siam away. Oh no, you don't, thought Lydia. You're not making your jelly out of my jam.

"You people lose children the way scholars lose gloves," declared Mrs. Brummidge. "Lydia, I've had enough of keeping my place. After luncheon you'll go locate our Alice, and no chatter about it. Yes I know your casual confidence, but if only for my nerves. I can't take more of this, and I won't. My heart, you know."

"They'll all be found together, no doubt, playing a childhood game, Ada and Alice and Siam. The soup is quite strong, Mrs. Brummidge." Miss Armstrong's anxiety over Ada had quite settled itself, Lydia noted.

"It's my belief his interest in that boy is unseemly," said Mrs. Brummidge. She wouldn't elaborate upon the matter. Shortly thereafter Lydia spilled her bowl of soup toward Miss Armstrong's lap. Her aim was poor. Hardly a dozen drops landed where they could do the most good.

# CHAPTER 33

———— ✑ ————

$W$hen Siam was able to believe that he had come unto another new world—as different from England as England had been from Gwinnett County, Georgia—he tried to take note of what this world was. A name would be helpful, like Little Egypt. Which was what the plantation had been called, the one from which he'd come out under pain and suffering, like the Israelites into the desert. Names of places mattered. Little Egypt. Bellerive. Down House, the home of that kind, distracted old man that Mr. Josiah was courting. But if Siam could reckon no name for this place yet, he'd at least sort out a portfolio of impressions regarding what it was *like.*

He came to his senses, if these still were *his* senses, sprawled on his hands and knees in a patch of ferns. Falling through some sort of hearthside chute, he'd expected kitchens, a root-cellar, an ash-bin. Like any number of dank and spidery clinches in which he and Clem had been hidden. Or if he'd somehow been tipped outside the Croft, surely he'd be within sight of its narrow mullioned windows? But he found himself in a forest of some sort. Young trees with spindly trunks were established in sward smooth as felt, not thick with undergrowth like an American woods. As if woodland creatures cropped the grass here and kept it level.

He sat on his haunches. He rubbed the dirt and char from his face. With a little uncertainty, he stood up.

The tree trunks were regular, like slender columns of iron. The canopy above was brown with shadow. He saw no sign of sky. This forest was, in fact, as dark as the room into which he had climbed to escape—but he couldn't think of that person's name he was trying to avoid. The older girl with the blond—the blond whiskery business on top. Perhaps he had hit his head and he was still in that space? He wished he could walk to one side and push aside the—the hanging things that kept the light from coming in—coming in the glass—but he couldn't think of the name of the set of glass panes that let light in.

Must be shook up. That long fall. My words flown right out my head.

He turned around. In all directions the woods seemed to go on with sameness. It was impossible to tell which way to go in order to find his way back to—

What *was* his name, that rescuer, who had brought him all the way across the sink? No, not the sink . . . across the water, the big water?

A sound in the underbrush made Siam turn his head. A creature hurrying, pausing, sitting up, looking about, twitching its white whiskers, checking an item on a chain that came out of a pocket in its . . . cloth wrapping. The creature had funny ears covered with white fur, and a pouff of a tail. It said, "If only I could remember how to tell time, I'd know if I was late or not."

"I din't know time was something you could tell," said Siam.

"One can tell time to hurry up, to slow down, or to stop making such a dreadful racket," replied the thing, hopping a few feet closer and examining Siam with a placid expression. "One can tell time to be still. Two can tell it the same thing, only more forcibly, with the courage that comes from uniting voices in song. However, I seem to have forgotten how to tell it a thing, including to be sure to wipe its feet when it comes in from tramping about at all hours."

"Does time have feet?"

"You've heard of time dragging. What do you suppose it is dragging, its nose? Of course it drags its feet."

"I din't know it lugged itself about. I thought time flew."

"Ah, yes. The wings of time." At this the creature swung the object about on its chain and then let it go. It soared upward but didn't return. It had become lodged. "It's stuck on that protrusion," observed the creature. "I feel I should know what that is called, that lengthy thing with greenery clinging to its tips. Can you hear the tick-talk, tick-talk, that time is telling us?"

Siam listened carefully. Yes, just barely, he could make out a regular pulse from the dial at the end of the chain. "So time does fly," he said. "Does it fly back, too?"

"Oh, yes. Remember the poem. 'But at my back I always hear / Time's wingèd hat-rack hurrying near.' It's a bother to have a wingèd hat-rack always poking one in the back, but there's little else to be done if time is to return. Is that a hat-rack it is stuck upon, do you suppose?"

"This has a name," said Siam. He shook the trunk to see if he could jostle the moments loose. "Still, I can't remember if it a hat-rack or not." His labors were useful. The time-machine fell off. The creature caught it in a furry paw, and slipped it into a convenient slit in the cloth that was bracketing its middle.

"Shall we stroll together for a spell," asked the creature, "now that we have the time?"

Siam couldn't think why not. He was twice the size of this woodland animal. He might easily outrun it if it called the authorities. "You headed anywheres special?" he asked.

"Oh, very special indeed. Though I can't recall what it is called. Perhaps you might suggest a few special sites? I will choose from among them which is the nearest."

"Perhaps you are headed to . . ." Siam scratched his head. "To a shoemaker?"

The creature looked down at its unshod hindquarters. "Uncommonly rude of you to point out that sartorial impossibility for one of my appendages, not to mention the other one."

"Maybe you are headed to a headache factory?"

"That sounds peculiarly right, and yet: *no*. Any other ideas?"

Siam tried to think of wonderful destinations. He could

envision a fireside at night, and massive warm presences that gave off gusts of affection and protection. He could find no words for that sensation, though. "You hunting for a velveteen ladle? A hill conquered by a rocking chair?"

"You speak reams of nonsense. I don't understand a word you say." While they had been talking, and scratching their heads out of consternation, the path had meandered through some thickets of red berries and prickery leaves. At the other side of this growth the forest suddenly tapered off. They came out into a spill of sensible light.

"My goodness," said Siam. "You a White Rabbit, and you can speak."

"And you're a black child," said the White Rabbit. "I don't suppose we're twins who have lost our way in the Wood of No Names?"

"Is that where we were?"

The White Rabbit turned about and pointed. "Yes. And we've lost time in there, I'll warrant."

"No, we din't," said Siam, "it's in the pocket of your waistcoat." For suddenly he remembered *pocket* and *waistcoat*.

"Oh, my," said the White Rabbit, examining the watch and snapping its lid shut, "this will never do! I'm late for the *garden party*! She'll have my head, see if she doesn't!" At this, the White Rabbit tore off across the meadow, as if the hounds of a hunting party were on the scent and baying for blood. Siam remembered what that was like. In three shakes of its tail, the White Rabbit was out of sight.

I won't go backward, thought Siam, for I know little enough about where I am as it is. A forest that makes you forget the names of things is a dangerous place to hide. Odd that no one ever mentioned that animals could talk here. Perhaps that's why Mr. Winter was so eager to speak with Mr. Darwin. Evolution a mighty power, could it yield up creatures capable of argument.

Then again, thought Siam, what good did arguing ever do me?

He tried not to be alarmed. After all, the past few years had brought him dozens of surprises, many of them unpleasant, and yet here he was. But where *was* he?

Siam had a fine memory. He pictured the page of the book that a kindly New England matron had opened upon a table. She had picked up his hand and run it across the letters. She'd made him say the words that the letters were spelling. She had thought she was teaching him to read, but she was really only feeding his memory bucket, slowly and carefully. He moved his hand in the air before himself. He felt the words in their kinky, obstinate shapes. He said their sounds aloud:

*The Pilgrim's Progress,*
*from This World to That Which Is to Come;*
*Delivered under the Similitude of a Dream.*

That he could carry such a memory still, even after he'd spent some time in the Wood of No Names, gave him a boost of courage not unlike a draft of ale. He straightened up his spine and went forward, whistling.

# CHAPTER 34

———— ✤ ————

Lydia decided to sabotage Miss Armstrong's plan of waylaying Mr. Winter for another private walk. Lydia said, "Since Mrs. Brummidge insists I find Alice, I'll go look, and return with Alice *and* Siam. Mr. Winter will be *so* pleased."

"I'll have your head for a doorstop if you don't bring Alice in," swore Mrs. Brummidge. "I'd go hunt her myself did we not have Mr. Himself to dine."

"I'll come with you, Lydia," said Miss Armstrong promptly, as Lydia had gambled she would. Better Lydia should suffer the company of this sycophant than that the governess should prey upon Mr. Winter while Lydia was out-of-doors. Miss Armstrong continued. "Before the men finish their meal, let us put this hide-and-seek routine to an end. Those children are having us as fools, I fear. It is the age-old gambit of the young against the adults. No doubt you played it in your time. I am certain I did."

Lydia couldn't decide if she had ever engaged in such a campaign, and if so, whether or not she had finished. She was only aware of confusions, which might be the same thing. Resenting Mr. Winter his chivalry toward the governess, resenting Miss Armstrong's menacing solicitude about him. Lydia was also aware of a throb of guilt about Siam's hiding from her. Still, wherever Siam might be, it was his fault, not hers. *She* hadn't pocketed a game-piece. And from a room more mausoleum than anything else. Lydia found herself becoming indignant all over again.

It's not easy to be half of anything. Half-adult/half-child is a state with no reliable signposts.

She left her soup half uneaten. She ignored the brown slices on the bread tray. She rose from the table. "If Siam isn't found soon, do you suppose Mr. Winter will send Mr. Darwin home on his own? So the American can stay here to search for his lost boy?"

"I believe Mr. Darwin's needs take precedence." Miss Armstrong's air of propriety about Mr. Winter's obligations, thought Lydia, was nothing short of insolent. "Mr. Winter told me that the old scholar hasn't left his home in months. People come to him. Whenever he *does* venture up to London, he lets no one know, or he'd be bedeviled with invitations. Your father must be a very honored friend of Mr. Darwin's for the man to travel so. He is feeling the stress of this trip. Nothing would induce Mr. Winter to abandon him. Mr. Winter has his own petition to make of Mr. Darwin, you see."

"The gentleman went around the world on the *Beagle*, and it took five bloody years," intoned Mrs. Brummidge. "If he can't get from Oxford to London on his own, he needs to grow a new pair of flippers." She made vaguely *arfing* noises under her breath for the next several minutes.

Lydia and Miss Armstrong went to the garden. Love-in-a-mist, sweet sultan, bachelor's buttons. Hardy annuals. "The children are *not* in the house," said Lydia. "I am sure of this. It's true, Alice can be silent as a corpse when she is in one of her dream games. I found her once lying under the bed staring up at the mattress ticking. I sensed her presence, there's no other word for it. She'd been there all day."

"Which room?" asked Miss Armstrong.

"Does it matter?"

"Perhaps not."

In fact, the bed in question had been the bed that Mama had died in. Lydia had yanked Alice out by her elbow and by the hem of her skirt. Lydia had had to slap Alice, twice, to make her blink her eyes and notice where she was.

But though one child, an Alice-like child, could pretend to marble, three together would give themselves away in whispers and giggles. The children must be underfoot, hiding somewhere obvious. It was a matter of thinking where to look. Of becoming like unto a child again. Of yielding to that paradox: that the least powerful among us are privileged with the greatest exposure to feeling. The greatest susceptibility to impression.

"When Ada has come to visit before, the children have played in the garden," said Miss Armstrong, looking about. "Shall we leave no stone unturned?"

"They won't be under a stone," said Lydia.

The property of the Croft consisted of a small orchard (four trees), a kitchen garden with a hen run, and a misshapen apron of grass across which Dinah sometimes stalked with stiff swiveling legs, and her kittens pounced, black and white against the green. The garden had been Mrs. Clowd's domain. Much flourished now that ought not to do: stands of weed, frotheries of vine that had not been cut back in the appropriate season. No shortage of blinds for hide-and-seek. In ten minutes Lydia and Miss Armstrong had made a thorough circuit, even peering into the chicken house. No stowaways could be found.

"We've *been* back and forth across the river path and the nearer meadows," complained Miss Armstrong. "Does Alice often go far afield on her own?" She spoke with a minimum of disapproval, for which Lydia was grateful.

"Not very far. She's too young."

"We all grow up." This, a bulletin from the front, courtesy of the five or six years Miss Armstrong could claim against Lydia. Lydia despised her all over again. "On my way here after checking at the Vicarage, I called out to the Trillings' gardener, who was passing by in a rowboat. He hadn't seen the girls. I didn't ask him about Siam, but I suspect he'd have mentioned if he'd seen a displaced child of that variety. Are you *quite* certain the children aren't hiding in the Croft? You've examined all its crannies and particulars? You've been to the attics? Have you remembered the basements?"

"I've been all about, but not to the crawl space," said Lydia. "It is too wet to keep anything there but spiders. In any case Pater minds the keys. No, Alice is not at home, Miss

Armstrong; I've said that already. And I insist she wouldn't venture into town. She's given to silence and solitary play. She doesn't seek out company. She avoids it generally. And in among the colleges and the market there is nothing *but* company. Even in the long vac, when the streets are quieter than in term, there'd be too much fuss made over her."

"I can't see that Alice deserves much fuss."

"She's become a motherless child, Miss Armstrong. That type of creature calls forth a response from all, whether Alice requires it or not. Though she abhors the stickiness of sentiment. She's too brave for that."

"Then there's nothing for it; Alice and Ada must have put their wicked heads together and decided to light out farther afield along the riverside than we've thought. If we find them, we'll find Siam in tow, I hope. He'll have caught up with them. They've had a good start and might have gone a distance. Shall we push on beyond the University Parks? It gives us something to do, anyway, while the men are finishing their meal."

Miss Armstrong plunged forward across the fields to the river path. She was a land-borne ship in full sail, the large violet and ivory oblongs upon her plaid skirting a semaphore of maidenly distress. The fabric billowed and luffed about her. Lydia had to grip her own skirts in her fists and run to keep up.

When they'd settled to a more sensible pace along the path, heading south, the governess said, "I've always approved of Ada's friendship with Alice. Ada Boyce is frail and speculative where Alice is decisive. I fret for what life will deliver unto poor Ada, with that distortion in her skeletal structure."

"It has never seemed all that dreadful to me," said Lydia.

"The appliances that she wears perform adequately. But no one will have a young woman with a stoop and a gimp. No one respectable. I think it quite fine of Alice to overlook Ada's shortcomings so nobly." She glared this way and that, tendentiously. "We all have our shortcomings, it seems, though some are less visible than others."

About Miss Armstrong's opinions of Lydia's shortcomings, Lydia didn't enquire. They fell into a silence more companionable than either of them expected. Something about the lull of the long noontime pulled them along the riverbank without further negotiation. They angled along Longwall Street and crossed the High. At the Botanic Gardens Lydia lunged in and peered, walked until she had seen the whole outlay and listened for give-away sounds of laughter, and then returned. The two of them then kept a brisk pace into Christ Church Meadows. Only when a bell sounded again marking some quarter hour—Lydia had lost track of where in the day they were—only then did they pull up and reconsider. Were they going to walk all the way to London?

"I suppose we must start back," said Miss Armstrong. "But despite your protestations about Alice's meekness, let us go out to St. Aldate's and return through town. Perhaps the girls have emboldened each other to venture in that direction. Oh, Ada will get a good thrashing from her father if he ever catches wind of such impertinence! And *your* father will

have to reconsider what is to be done about Alice. A convent
school in France, perhaps."

Lydia was about to say that she herself was perfectly com-
petent to tend to Alice, but then she'd been the one to lose
sight of her. So, meekly, Lydia allowed herself to be pulled
along toward the bulk of Christ Church College, hulking
as it did beyond the meadows like a great stone creature in
repose, possibly in senescence.

As they neared the back of it, they saw a door swung ajar
in a high garden wall. "Do you think the girls might have
ventured there?" asked Lydia.

"The colleges are not open to children, and most especially not to girl children."

"Alice is not one to notice prohibitions even when they're
posted. We may as well have a quick look." Before Miss Armstrong could squawk, Lydia darted forward. She put her
head into a small pretty cloister of a space, the sort where an
afternoon garden party with croquet and lemonade might
be held. Foxgloves and larkspur poked and swayed in abun-
dance. A serene male sort of calm obtained. Then Lydia saw
a fellow in a corner by a ground-floor window. Its lower sash
was flung up. He was patting a contraption of some sort as
if to tame it. He was looking at his pocket-watch with some
distress. He caught sight of Lydia. He said, "Oh, heaven provides! Miss, M-miss, might I ask you to perform m-me a small
favor?"

"You may not go in there, Miss Lydia," said Miss Armstrong, reaching the door in the wall.

"It's between t-t-terms and no one is about, and only for a m-moment," said the man. He was a student or a young fellow of some sort, agitated and twitchy. He made an arabesque in the air next to his equipment, which on closer inspection seemed to be a camera on legs. "I was set up to take a p-portrait, you see, and my companion m-must be detained. And the light is . . ." He mumbled. Had he said "delightful"?

"We were looking for my sister," said Lydia, cordially enough.

"Come, whi-which of you?—It is to be a self-p-portrait, only I cannot release the shutter. H-he was to do it and I cannot say where he has disappeared to."

"Half the world has gone missing today," said Miss Armstrong. She entered the garden as if stepping into a tepid footbath, gingerly.

"Show me," said Lydia.

The young man beckoned to the black fabric arranged on an armature of wires. A portable cloth cave set up in the middle of midsummer luxuriance. "Miss Lydia, you don't dare," said Miss Armstrong, but she was not Lydia's governess. Lydia did indeed dare. She ducked into the black tent with the stammering student. It was warm and close. The mechanics of the camera looked faintly menacing, as if intended for the use of a surgeon.

"You just look here, you see. I will call out when I am ready. You must press this b-button all the way down, and stay qu-quite still and do not jostle the delicate thing. All will-will—well, it just will," he concluded. Lydia followed the instructions well enough. There was nothing thrilling about being in close quarters with him. He had all the electrical excitement of a suit of clothes upon a dressmaker's armature. She had somehow hoped for more.

There he went, out of the black envelope and across the lawn to the half-opened window. He perched himself against the frame, his buttocks slightly elevated on the stone sill, one leg gently uplifted. He might have been climbing into the window, or just perhaps leaving. In the square in which she peered, he looked tentative. Sweetly alert, and trembling. If he was after an expression of sobriety and scholarship, he was well wide of the mark. He looked as if he had just been slapped and perhaps had felt a rush of confused pleasure in the aftershock.

"If you w-would be so kind," he said, "just now."

Huddled under the black cape, the misbegotten midnight, she saw him in the aperture, and pressed the button. A click and a whirr, and time seemed to stand still. He froze in his place, bland innocence masquerading as a young man. Perhaps into the room behind him someone had opened a door, for an imprecise glow briefly backlit a corner of the otherwise black glass. Against such correct rectitude it took the look of a hastening creature not intended to be caught by such a tool. The blur of a swift Siamese cat, perhaps, or an Angora rabbit.

# CHAPTER 35

———— ❧ ————

Lydia waited. He was caught now, but unless he stayed still for a full minute the effect would be compromised. She wasn't to budge an inch for fear of jostling the box. The black tent was, for a moment, a shroud. She wondered if, for the dead, the life they had left behind seemed to them frozen the way this young scholar was frozen. The dead could no longer intervene, regardless of the need. But they could study, perhaps, the frozen past from which they'd been exiled. Look at the creases of the skin beside his eyes, the hesitant light in his face. Look at the creases in circumstance. Press up against everything that has happened exactly the way it had. Reconsider how forces actually work, and how one thing leads to another, until it is frozen, and all that is left is the intelligence of it, but not the living nub.

"Highly irregular," said Miss Armstrong, when they were done. The scholar stammered and apologized and was grateful. "The colleges are not arranged so that young women

might be entrapped in the garden," said Miss Armstrong fe-
rociously. She turned on the young man as if she thought he
must be lying when he said he had not seen Ada or Alice or
Siam. Then all at once it occurred to her that she, too, was
trespassing upon precincts forbidden her. She pulled Lydia
away.

Along St. Aldate's, Miss Armstrong pressed Lydia on
what it had been like to be cloistered in the dark with that
student, as if there was a secret to be learned about huddling
under a cloth with a young man. Lydia demurred.

# CHAPTER 36

The White Queen and Ada continued along the path. They couldn't step sideways, for the lawn edging prevented them from straying. Neither could they retreat, for when they looked back, they saw that the gravel path had retracted and formed a little loop like the eye of a needle. Should they bother to retrace their steps, they'd only be marching forward again in a moment.

Ada was perturbed. "Let's *try* to reverse ourselves—"

"Hard to do that without a looking-glass," interrupted the White Queen. "And why bother?"

"Because," Ada continued, "as far as we can see, this path only goes forward across the meadows, while the Sheep and the Lion and the Unicorn flew off in the opposite direction. They were going to the garden party, back that way, and we will be wanting to get there before long."

"*You* may want that," said the White Queen. "*I* want peace among all nations. Either that or a lemon drop, I can't decide." Still, she fed her arm through Ada's. They began to traipse along the return path, which curved neatly to join up with where they'd been. The exercise had taken a quarter of a minute, but it had been so much fun, or so little trouble, that they started out again along the loop. The White Queen said, "Who is this Alice about whom you keep chattering about who is the girl about whom you keep mentioning?"

"Everyone knows Alice, it seems," said Ada. "She's been all through these parts. Yet we're having *such* a time catching up with her."

"I don't know the girl of whom you refer, referring that is to the girl about whom you keep referring. Whom I don't know."

"Do you feel quite all right? Is this making you dizzy?" Ada asked the White Queen as they began their fourth circuit. "We could stop if you like. There's no need to continue."

"To whom much is given, much is expected of those to whom much is given," replied the White Queen uncertainly. "I expect."

"You're talking in circles," said Ada. "Let's go on."

But the path seemed to have so enjoyed their company that it now limited itself to no more than this single loop around a small hummock of grass. There was no backward or forward, no horizon of past or future, just a circle around.

"We *are* in a zoo," said Ada. "Look, we're caged in a pen, with the open world all around us, a temptation and a paradise, but forbidden."

"No, that's the zoo." The White Queen pointed. "That enclosed circle of grass, around which we are now tottering around, and around, and around which we round with nearly tottering competence with which we totter around." She looked ill.

Ada patted her alabaster elbow. "You hush now and save your breath. We may be on this road quite some time. I shall tell you about Alice, since you asked. She is a friend of mine. Well, in actual fact she is my only friend."

"Why—is that why is that? Why?"

"I have not been lucky in my limbs," said Ada. "They are not frisky enough. I frighten the other little girls. They run away."

"Who who who who who who?" The White Queen's eyes were wide and dreadful, filled with terror either at the collapse of her power of speech or at the thought that Ada scared little children.

"Everyone except Alice," said Ada. At once the thought of sensible, stoic Alice filled her heart and her breast to bursting. How queer that inscrutable child was. How beloved of so many. For the first time since slipping into the hole in the riverbank, Ada felt alarmed. *Would* she be stuck in this wonderland forever, always chasing after Alice, never catching up? And *was* Alice all right? Ada began to cry. She was well-bred enough to know that crying was undignified. She tried to hide it from the White Queen, but the old creature noticed.

"Now, then," said the White Queen with great effort. "Now, then, now, then, now, then. There, there. There there there there there. Now, then now, then now. Now." Though her face was rigid with stress, the White Queen leaned down. She creaked out a crooked smile. The old potentate was carved of ivory crazed all over with *craquelure*. Her expression, a rictus of caring concern, might have seemed a caricature of senile dementia. But Ada responded with brave gratitude. At least in her regard for a young companion, the White Queen is like Miss Armstrong Headstrong, she thought. If not half so highly strung.

"It's all right," Ada managed. "Alice, you see, is the reason I am here."

"Hear, hear," said the White Queen, or maybe that was "Here, here."

"She's the only one who—who—" Ada didn't know if she was stuttering from sudden emotion or if they had been around the loop so often that she was going loopy, too. "Who—"

"Who," said a voice that was not Ada's or the White Queen's.

The girl and the White Queen looked up. The mound around which they'd been walking had turned into a mushroom, and upon this spongy fungus lounged a Caterpillar, one distinguished by a vigorous ugliness. "Who," said the Caterpillar, "are you?"

"Well, that's easy enough to answer, now that you ask it, and it's high time somebody did," jabbered the White Queen. She hopped up and down with joy, relieved of her verbal paralysis. The white pedestal upon which she stood made impressions in the gravel. "I am the White Queen, of course, any fool can see that—"

"I am no fool," replied the Caterpillar, "and so it follows that *I* cannot see any such thing. You a White Queen? You appear to be a migrating finial afflicted by a poor conversational technique. In any case I wasn't speaking to you. I was addressing the slug-like child at your side. Who," he said again, drawing out the syllable like an elocution master, "are *you?*"

"Well, I'm Ada Boyce, if you please," said Ada, "and I hate to rush matters along, but—"

"And if I don't please?" asked the Caterpillar, puffing upon a pipe of Oriental workmanship. "Who are you then?"

"I'm still Ada," said the child. "Whether I please you or not, I'm still Ada. Even if you run away from me like some I know, I'm still Ada."

"Caterpillars seldom run," he replied loftily, "unless pressed by the clamor of a devoted public. You were asking after Alice?"

"Well, I hadn't done that yet," said Ada.

"You said to rush matters along, so I am anticipating. If you would like to ask *before* Alice, you are too late. She has come and gone."

"Was she quite all right?" asked her friend.

"It seemed to me she had some growing up to do," replied the Caterpillar. "Or some growing down. I can't remember. Memory is unreliable, anyway."

The White Queen said, "I have a fine memory myself. I can remember when I licked an envelope to seal it. The envelope stuck to my tongue. I had to walk the envelope all the way to the Queen of Hearts myself. I was replying affirmatively to her kind invitation."

"Her kind invitation?" asked the creature. "What kind of invitation?"

"A garden party, as it happens."

"And that is where Alice is going," said the Caterpillar. "Perhaps she has already arrived and been sentenced to death. If you want to catch the fun, I shouldn't linger here. In fact, I want to see the proceedings, and *I* shouldn't linger here. And I shan't." At this, he turned into a butterfly. Ada hadn't known butterflies could manage to be so ugly. The Caterpillar lifted from the mushroom cap like an angel of death off an ottoman. It whisked itself away with a speed and a sense of destination hitherto unknown to its species. Just as it disappeared, it called, "Don't eat the mushroom. You don't know if it is poisonous!"

"Do *you* know?" called the White Queen, but the insect had disappeared.

"Look," said Ada, "the garden path has vanished. We're free."

"It's dangerous to stray from the garden path, they say, but when the garden path itself takes to straying, that's horticultural mutiny," replied the White Queen. "Look, bits of this mushroom have teeth marks in them. It can't be poisonous or the ground would be littered with corpses." She reached up and broke off two pieces the size of dinner plates just as a voice cried out in alarm. It was neither the Caterpillar's voice nor the Sheep's, nor, in fact, was it much like any other of the peculiar characters Ada had met so far. The girl turned.

A boy came stumbling out of the woods. He waved his arms to dissuade them. He looked like the boy in the Sunday lesson book, from the page about Afric's pagan interior.

"Might do you harm," he panted. "A mushroom that virile. Best take no chances."

"Who," said Ada, imitating the vowels of the departed Caterpillar, "are you?"

"You sound a big old hoot owl," he said. "I'm Siam, I am."

"I'm Ada," she replied. She turned to introduce the White Queen. But it was too late. The White Queen had taken a mouthful of mushroom. She had frozen into a statue of herself. At least her expression looked pleased, as if her last meal had met with her approval.

# CHAPTER 37

⁂

The shadow of Tom Tower had retracted from St. Aldate's. It was concentrated solely upon the cool tunnel of Tom Gate below it. The doors stood open as if, in a grand parade, scouts were about to march through with buckets and brooms, six dozen strong. Through the blue tunnel could be seen a fountain and a still, green lake of lawn. Various distracted dons and a few gentlemen wafted about as if by the strengthening breeze, apparently so lost in labyrinths of their own scholastic minds as not to have noticed that Trinity term had already concluded. Otherwise the streets were emptying. "Does it seem that a storm is coming?" asked Miss Armstrong.

"I wouldn't know."

"Whatever might the time be?" One of Oxford's unhurried bells rang the half hour obligingly, but of which hour was it the half? The city seemed to have become unmoored. "Did you know that at night Great Tom rings five minutes

later than the hour in London? Oxford being that degree
west of Greenwich?"

"Does that mean that at night it takes longer to get from
London to Oxford than it does to get from Oxford to London?
Or shorter?"

"Oxford is the beginning and the end of all nonsense.
Don't be foolish," said Miss Armstrong. "I don't know what
it means, I'm just jabbering." On they pressed, toward Corn-
market. In the heat, the Saturday morning market was already disbanding. The streets were emptying as luncheons
were being laid, cheese slapped upon the boards, shutters
going up for an afternoon break and perhaps a slumber in
the back room or a little something nicer if the wife felt overheated enough to remove her skirts. A dog padded across the
junction at Carfax with all the insouciance of a gypsy tinker
at the gates of a bishop's palace.

They turned into the Broad. In the light and dust the
street looked as if lined by buildings made from skillfully
carved oat bread. The spirits of Miss Armstrong and Lydia
Clowd lifted at the sight of two girls emerging from Black-
well's, but those girls started to run away. "Oh, Ada could
never lift her limbs like that," said Miss Armstrong. She
slackened the pace that had quickened in hope. An older
woman, a grandmother sort, next emerged from the shop.
Her squawkeries were lost in the breeze. The girls paid no
heed. They rushed on, laughing merrily.

Miss Armstrong and Lydia Clowd pushed east. The colleges, barricaded against the two females in favor of faith and
reason, stood stolid in the strengthening wind. A squidge of

something got into Miss Armstrong's eye, or so she said. She dabbed at her face with a cloth. Lydia turned to examine the reddening eye with a gallows mercy. "A bit of grit, a midge, a fly, a plank, a mote, what does it matter?" Miss Armstrong snapped at Lydia.

"Whatever it is, blink quickly to flush it out, for if I'm not mistaken—"

Lydia was not mistaken. The Vicar was bearing down upon them from across the Broad. He was heading in the same direction they were, but faster. Miss Armstrong flinched. "Reverend Boyce, sir," she began as they seemed about to collide upon the pavement.

"You're far afield, Miss Armstrong, but I daren't stop to pass the time. The doctor has sent me to collect a new bromide suitable for the infant. We expected you back to help when you'd collected Miss Ada from the Croft. Have you given yourself leave for a perambulation? It won't do, Miss Armstrong! And in this heat! Watch out, weather's coming. Or, forgive me, perhaps you are on an errand for Mrs. Boyce, did she send you out for—?" The Vicar caught himself in time. Family secrets stayed within the household. He pivoted. "Good day to *you*, Miss Lydia. I hope you and your family are keeping as well as can be expected in this season of sorrow." He didn't pause to see if his hopes were being met; he cannonaded away. The various demands of Mrs. Boyce and the Baby Boykin got the better of him. Apparently he didn't know that his clumsy Ada was lumbering about God's good creation without the benefit of a chaperone. Lydia elected not to summon him back to clarify. For this she received a wordless moue of gratitude from the beleaguered governess. In a moment the Vicar had disappeared beyond where the Broad became Holywell.

In a low voice, Miss Armstrong said, "Oh, what are we failing to consider, Miss Lydia? Where can they *be*? If they are lost, I am lost, too. I shall never get a position supervising children again. I shall have to go below-stairs."

"How sad for you," said Lydia. "And of course, *they* may be dead. That's even more below-stairs than household staff."

"You are cruel and then you are kind and then you are cruel beyond compare. I do not understand you, but there is no time to try. I ought to have told the Vicar. But he sends me into such a tizzy. He doesn't know the half of it!"

"Which half does he know? That you are incompetent, or that you are sentimentally excitable? Or is there a third half buried in there somewhere that even I can't detect?"

"Who taught you to bruit words about like a barrister? It is unnatural and unbecoming in any female. In a girl of your slender years it is demonic." Was that a spatter of rain, or drops from a mop shook out an upper window? "I do not put my heart onto a table in the operating theatre so that a young *voyeuse* like you can dissect it and see how it works or fails to thrive."

Lydia fell silent. Not wanting to follow the Vicar, they took an alternate route, and turned into the Parks Road. Before long the University Museum gathered its stone haunches in the distance and grew larger as they approached. "If you are let go, you could get a job dusting the bones of the great lizards dug up in the desert. Dinosaurs," said Lydia. "Those

creatures are already dead, so you could do them no harm."
But perhaps she had only thought those words, as Miss Arm-
strong did not rise to her own defense. Lydia tried again.
"Did you ever see that claw of a dodo, and the painting some
Dutch master made of it?"

"The Vicar does not approve of his household visiting
such a place. It only strengthens the temptation to doubt. I
understand the painting is famously vile, in any case. Such a
creature deserves to be extinct."

"Were ugliness the criterion for extinction, we'd be freed
of a great many matrons stopping to call and to console my
father. Dodos, the lot of them."

On they passed, across the University Parks, toward the
Cherwell, toward home, past Park Town, where the university's dons, forbidden marriage, were said to lodge their
female companions. Once or twice Lydia thought she saw
the hastening figure of the Vicar emerging from the plunging shadows of an elm, becoming faint in the light. But from
this distance that could be anyone hurrying home before the
storm.

Were a dark boy standing in those shadows, thought
Lydia, we might not even see him.

Then through the lane this time, hoping that the lagging
girls and the stray boy might have turned up under their own
authorities. But Lydia knew how everyone lingered under a
death sentence. Postponing it with prayers and promises was
as ineffectual as pleading upon a star, or throwing a copper
into a wishing well. You lost your copper as well as your faith
in wishes, and prayers.

# CHAPTER 38

———— ❧ ————

$\mathrm{S}$iam," said Ada. "What sort of a name is that?"

"It is like Lazarus," said the boy.

"Biblical?" asked Ada. Not for nothing was her father a Vicar.

Siam didn't reply.

Ada didn't understand Siam's point. Had he been put in a grave, like Lazarus? Or raised up from one? "I always wondered if Lazarus *wanted* to be raised up from the grave," said Ada. "He had two sisters who were always arguing over whether to sit and listen to the Savior or whether to do the washing up. Martha and Mary, do you know about them? I always think there must have been a third sister, perhaps named Maggie, who didn't want to join either of her sisters in their worthy tasks, but preferred to get dressed up and go out dancing like a Jezebel. The noise in that house must have been ferocious. The sleep of the dead must have some advantage, don't you think?"

"Where are we at?"

Ada had been so accustomed to the peculiarity of her day that it took Siam's question to remind her of her circumstances. "I wonder. It's a very strange land, wherever we have strayed to. I assume you've just arrived, or you wouldn't be asking."

"We came by London," he said, "but so gritty and foul. Not like here."

"Are you alone?"

"Now I am," he said. Then he corrected himself. "Now I'm not."

They looked about themselves. The White Queen seemed to be made of salt. She was blunting and softening in the wind. A bit of salt made itself at home in Ada's eye. She had to blink. She liked the White Queen quite the best among all the denizens of this place, but the poor creature was eroding fast. Now she was like a spool and now like a spindle. Now she was a pile of white sand tracked in from a foreign strand. As the miniature dune changed shape in rising winds, shrank to a mere pile as from a broken hourglass, something like a scrap of palmetto leaf revealed itself.

"Why," said Ada, "I do believe I know what that is." She leaned down and plucked the item out of the salty sand or sandy salt. She shook it out.

"This is a cloak made of seaweed," she told Siam. "Come, let us try it on together."

"That's not permitted of me," he replied.

"Everyone else always makes the rules," she said. "Just now, no one else is here. Come in." She slipped the seaweed over her shoulders. "It's a capacious cape, with room for all. I have known it to be useful."

"It smells like the air from Boston Harbor to Portsmouth," he said, ducking under. "It smells like all beginnings."

As Ada began to draw the cloak closed over their heads, she looked about to see how the world had changed, for surely it had. It always did. She noted a perforated set of images coming through the cape. Glowing and insubstantial, as if thrown by a magic lantern, or several magic lanterns operating at once. She saw the mouse with the marmalade jar, and the great hall with the glass-topped table. She saw the seashore and the scraping roses. She saw the tired old Knight and the singing pig and the looping gravel walk and the troupe of liberated marionettes. The difficulty was in assembling such contrary information into coherence. Whenever she thought she might have begun to manage it, the images slid and shifted. The material meant something different. How very like a dream this all is, she finally said. Just like the song, merrily merrily, and so on. Like a boat on the Cherwell out for a summer picnic, and the Thames, and seeing what went past, and making up a tale that connected it all, while past it slid past it slid past. And life was just a dream.

Then darkness.

# CHAPTER 39

———— ❧ ————

Lydia and Miss Armstrong came onto the property of the Croft through the shortcut. The lone cow in her corner looked ruminatively at them, but offered no testimony about whom she may have seen pass, and in which direction. The main walkway led to the portico, though a path forked off around the side of the house. Lydia intended to lead Miss Armstrong that way, through the kitchen garden to the back door. Another spontaneous encounter between Mr. Winter and Miss Armstrong would only make Lydia feel more sour in herself, and unsettled. But the front door stood wide open. Voices were heard in the steep midday shadows within. The choice was taken from her.

Mrs. Brummidge was wringing her hands and wiping her eyes. Oh, no, they've been found, and it isn't good, thought Lydia. A sunk boat on the Isis, a rotting beam in some hayloft hideaway . . . The instinct toward panic, once experienced, cannot be unlearned. "What is it, Mrs. Brummidge?"

"It's the bloody Begum of Banbury Cross, that's what it is. I'm set to get what for, and no mistake," said Mrs. Brummidge.

"Whatever—?" Before Lydia could speak further, voices rose in the hall behind the cook.

"This is intolerable." Pater sounded pained. "Madame, I must insist that you take your leave at once."

A volley of musical syllables flew forward from the hallway. A woman's accented voice, an oboe descant originating in the mysterious flyspecked Raj. Cajoling, syrupy. She appeared at the door hauling a straw hamper of some sort. A veil of blue and gold angled across her brow. From beneath a respectable tartan shawl cascaded several contrapuntal swags of glorious and unreasonable skirting. The woman was slim though more full of figure than most of the good wives and maiden aunts that Lydia had ever met. And dark, dark of complexion, though in a different way from Siam—dark persimmon—and glamorous beyond contemplation. But she was a nuisance, clearly. Mr. Winter was obligingly seeing her out.

"The great man, his interest in the wide world, it must include my shells from the sea; it will finish his work," she was claiming, as near as Lydia could hope to understand.

"Mr. Darwin is in no condition to entertain impromptu guests. He came here under promise of privacy," explained Mr. Winter. "You've been misinformed, Miss Gurleen. Miss Mittal. Madame Gurleen Mittal, whatever is proper to call you, Mr. Darwin has no wherewithal to examine your collection."

"She's here to show more than her seashells," said Mrs. Brummidge, brazenly. "I ought never have opened the door to her. Off with you, milady, and tell your brother he has over-stepped, gossiping like that." She waved the exotic woman down the walk with a flap of her apron. Gurleen Mittal disappeared at an uneven gait, her parcel of seashells bumping against her thigh. The bland English air in the garden was, momentarily, stained with incense of sandalwood.

"*What* was all that about?" asked Miss Armstrong as Pater appeared beside Mr. Winter.

"It's my fault, sir," said Mrs. Brummidge, addressing both the gentlemen. "I made a misstep. I only barely hinted at the name of today's guest, you see, to my sister, in service in the buttery at Balliol, don't you know. She may have chirped it to someone who chirped it to someone else. And Miss Mittal has a brother stopping at Balliol over the summer months to do research in maths and suchlike. But I had no idea the hussy would hear of this. Any excuse, and there she is at the door again. Setting her ribbons to charm the widower. This time I take the blame." She lowered her head as if she fully expected to be struck, though Mr. Clowd would not strike the top of a table.

"She's been here before? Those people, they don't know their manners." Miss Armstrong fairly flashed outrage.

"They don't know our manners," corrected Pater quietly. "She may think she's doing a kindly thing for me, to appear with a basket of specimens and hope to lift the burden of conversation off my shoulders. I wish I'd never stepped up to help her brother find his materials in the Bodleian. But no matter now. She's gone. It's a mercy she didn't come earlier or our esteemed guest would have found us lacking in honor as well as hospitality. Mrs. Brummidge, we *did* promise him anonymity."

"Curse the day the Lord put a tongue in my mouth," mumbled the cook.

"Mr. Darwin requires to visit the facilities again before we set out," said Mr. Winter soothingly. "Mr. Clowd, would you kindly call for the carriage while I see to his needs? He's decided to stay in London tonight after all. He's too wrung out to get all the way to Down House in one day. Miss Lydia, Miss Armstrong, summon the boy, if you would. It is nearly time to go."

Lydia opened her mouth, but no words came out.

Miss Armstrong spoke to Mr. Winter's back as he headed inside. "If Siam hasn't returned, then we have no earthly idea where he is. The boy has fled this house and its surrounds." But Mr. Winter, hurrying down the passage, didn't catch her remark, what with his concern for Mr. Darwin.

"The young lad will be with Alice, no doubt," said Pater, peering along the lane with an expression that suggested he was afraid Miss Gurleen Mittal might be huddled in the hedges, ready to pounce. "Lydia, where is Alice?"

"Off with Ada," Lydia said, she hoped. She hadn't the heart to say more.

"Oh, Mr. Clowd," said Miss Armstrong. She swept upon the portico and caught his arm. "To be pestered by well-meaning townspeople of every stripe, common and exotic. Let us see your guests to their carriage without alarming them, if possible. Then, dear Mr. Clowd, I fear we shall have to send for the constable."

# CHAPTER 40

———— ❧ ————

The darkness in which Ada and Siam had stood was both close and echoing. There had been time, a lot of time, in which to characterize it, but Ada hadn't been inclined to sort out the wool from the warmth of it. A sort of sleepiness had come over her, a balmy complacency. It hadn't been so bad.

None of this occurred to her, really, until the husk of seaweed fell away from them. My, what was that, was really all she managed to think, before the insistent demands of *here* and *now* barked in her direction once again.

Siam was blinking in the light. Ada thought it was daylight, but then she realized that ever since she'd tumbled into the foyer of the rabbit warren, she'd found herself in a place with a light that was, somehow, not expressly sunlight. Shadows on the ground positioned what she was looking at, but they were insincere, sloppy things. They tended to wobble if she looked at them through the sides of her eyes. As if they were trying to get away with something. The sky was blue, but vapidly, evenly so. It didn't seem to thin at the edges or deepen at the apex. I wonder, thought Ada, if people ever see the overland sun in their dreams. *I don't believe I've noticed the actual sun once since my descent.*

"Where are we?" asked the boy.

"Well, a bit of here and there, it seems," said Ada. They were standing on a square lawn that had been recently rolled in very even stripes, back and forth. It resembled a checkerboard with lighter and darker squares. A thin and undernourished sort of woods grew up to the edges on three sides. Off center upon the lawn loomed that same old pedestal table with a glass top. And upon the tabletop was a key.

Where there was a key there must be a keyhole, thought Ada. Turning around, she realized that the fourth side of the forest-room was a high stone wall in the uneven colors of scones and fresh farm eggs. The wall had a familiar look, as if it might edge a cloistered walk or a Fellows' garden in Oxford. A painted door that could use some touching up was set directly in the wall. "I have a strange feeling I've seen this door before," said Ada.

"I never," said Siam. He picked up the seaweed cloak. He began to fold it up. When it was the size of a Cornish pasty he handed it to Ada. She didn't want to eat it.

And to put it in her pinafore pocket might look like stealing. So she slipped it in the heel of her left shoe. It wedged there without complaint.

"A keyhole," he said. "In the door. But I don't see no key."

"There's a key on the table," said Ada, "though this is a table for a dreadfully lofty member of society."

"We never do climb that mast." Siam put his hands on his hips and leaned far back. "It's a forbidding sky." He meant the glass tabletop.

It is, thought Ada. As she looked, it seemed that reflections of something else steered and slid across the top surface. There was movement up there, soundless alarum of some sort represented in pale flickering shapes. But there was no way to tell what it might pretend to mean.

"The key, up there," he said, pointing.

"I see it. Will it work in this door, do you think?"

"I known some keys and their habits." He cocked his head toward the door. Through it, sounds of merriment and abandon. It was the brightest garden party of the season. It was where everyone would be. Ada guessed that she hadn't been invited because of her deformity. But maybe, now that she was not alone, Siam might find a way in. He was clever.

For a while they took turns peering through the keyhole at a festive affair neither could quite bring into focus. Ada thought she spied a recumbent Cat floating through the air, though perhaps that was a superior cloud in a feline formation. Then she imagined she saw Alice, at last, but a buxom grandee in a tortured headdress swept up and grabbed the child by the arm and concealed her from view. What Siam saw, when it was his turn, Ada could not say, for he didn't tell her.

"We want in there." He said it neutrally. Perhaps he meant it as a question.

"I *do*," Ada replied. "I've been searching for my friend Alice since I got here, and everyone says she was inclining toward a garden party. Have you been looking for anyone?" she continued, remembering her manners just in time.

"No one to look for," he mumbled. "No one left."

Ada had a hard time being sure what he meant. "If they didn't leave, then they must be here," she said encouragingly. "Maybe in there."

"Won't be. So it don't matter none. But we get in if you want to." He looked at the key. Because the glass was invisible, the key appeared to float in the sky. "Can't climb that big old table but I do maybe break the glass." He hunted around for something to throw. He found a few small white rocks. When he tossed them they turned into blackbirds and flew over the garden wall. "Contrary stones," he said.

"How about your boot?"

He took it off. He pitched it as hard as he could. It banged against the underside of the glass tabletop, quite hard. The key danced, making a sound like tin thunder. The glass was resolute. The shoe fell down. It hit Siam on the head.

"Must be something to use. Some stone or other thing to throw. Nothing's unbreakable," he told her. He went about on his hands and knees feeling in the grass. "Hell's doorbell, what's this?"

"Show me."

He opened up his hand. It was a small black game piece, perhaps from a chess set. "Let me see," she said, looking at it more closely. Then she said, "Siam. What happened to your hands?"

He pocketed the item and put his hands behind his back. She said, "Show me. Tell me." He did not want to do that.

She would not let it go. Finally he opened his palms again. The skin on the inside of his hands was paler than the rest of him, a private sort of color one might keep to one's self, for it looked vulnerable to Ada. But that was not what she needed to see. There were round marks on his hand, red and raw, all the same size, some of them overlapping. Each one about the circumference of a grape.

The sounds of the party on the other side of the wall may have carried on and they may have gone away; she was no longer listening. There was a terrible feeling in her insides. "I want to know," she said.

He relented at last. "Back when we was all together still, they play a game one night. They planning to take us upcountry for loaning to another overseer, for the otherly cotton was ready and they needed hands. They'd some liquor the night before we was to leave." She reached out and held his hands. "It nothing worth saying now." After a long pause: "So, they tell us young ones iffen we want to buy our freedom, come on here. I din't like it but—" Another pause. "—but our own said, Maybe this your chance, it only gets worser when you get on in years. Maybe they knowed what going to happen to them somehow. Maybe they could see into days ahead. I put myself up for freedom. The bosses say it cost a dollar and I says I ain't had money paid me afore. We give it to you, they go. You collect a hunderd pennies in one minute by Master's timepiece and you bought yourself free. Then they shakes a jar of coppers onto the belly of a shovel and holds it over the campfire long time. When they think it fun enough, they say, get yourself ready, and now you go, boy. The pennies go in the dirt around the fire and I got to pick them up and keep hold on them."

"Oh," said Ada, with a sound like a kind of punch in the air, or out of it.

"I gets forty-two hot cents before that minute up," he said, holding out his hands again. "Here's the proof."

"Oh," she said. "And no freedom."

"Nothing next, but that we left," he said. "One by one, and not on the same path, turns out."

"And here you are."

"And wherever this be, I don't know. Some mystery or t'other."

She lifted her shoulders and dropped them. "Well. With me I suppose."

# CHAPTER 41

⸺ ❧ ⸺

They heard an intrusion of thunder. They looked at the glass sky but the key above it lay there undisturbed. The indeterminate shapes above, those hints of a separate reality, scudded and shifted shapes, none of them nameable. Ada said, "I know that noise, it's been following me. They called it the Jabberwock I think."

"I know that noise, too," said Siam. His face was grey as paste. "We got to get us into that garden and hide us-selves there." He went up to the door and felt it. A metal plate, in very small letters, said

KEEP OUT.

"Not too friendly," he said.

"All doors say that, when they're closed," said Ada. "An advertisement to go away. But so what?"

"Use the key," said the Cat, appearing at the top of the wall. It was flicking its tail dangerously, like a civet cat.

"We can't reach." Ada pointed to the glass tabletop. "Can you get it for us?"

"Cats do favors for no one," it replied. "Not to mention that it's the wrong key for right now."

"Somehow that does not startle me," asked Ada. "Little that has happened today has proven advantageous."

"Try your pockets," suggested the Cat, beginning to fade in the air, like wood-smoke.

"I have nothing left. I've given away the marmalade already."

"Maybe I gots something," said Siam, and dove his scarred hands therein. He came up with that characterless figure on a pediment, nicely turned in ebony. "I took it," said Siam, "but I gave it back."

"Maybe it *wants* to be lost," said Ada. "Is this a key in any way, do you think?" She turned to raise an eyebrow at the Cat, but it was gone.

Siam put it up to the keyhole, which seemed now to be little more than a bung hole. The head of the figure fit neatly in the aperture. They heard no click, turned no knob. Regardless, the door in the garden wall swung inward.

They walked through, hand in hand, and the air instantly seemed warmer, though still there was no sun to speak of, only a bland differentiation in color and shadow upon the flowering borders. "Well," said someone, "I never thought to see you here. I didn't think you properly brought up. Walking about on your own, no chaperone, like an urchin." It took Ada a moment to realize that the nearby rose-tree was addressing her.

"Rosa Rugosa," said Ada. "You survived being transplanted."

"Few do," said Rosa Rugosa, "but I always had a desire to grace the court. So here I am, doing my bit for beauty."

"You look lovely."

"They wanted to paint me white but I objected," said Rosa Rugosa. She gave Siam a glance. "I make no further comment."

"There's a great deal going on here," said Ada. "Have you seen a girl called Alice?"

"I wouldn't say. I don't interview the madding throng. Though every type and token seems to be invited. The Queen of Hearts has a wide circle of admirers."

"They look abject," said Ada, scanning the bewildering assortment of guests.

"Well, the Queen is hot-tempered, and is constantly sentencing them to death. It tends to cast a pall on the chitchat. There she is now."

From around a stand of violet larkspur came a ferocious-looking creature cut along the lines of a Queen printed upon a playing card. "It is time for the entertainment, and where has that troupe of barmpots got to? You!" she barked at Ada and Siam. "Are you the marionettes? Tie your strings on and get to work."

"Begging your pardon, Your Highness, we are not," said

Ada. She didn't expect to be able to manage a curtsey but perhaps the seaweed inserted in the heel of her shoe gave her a rare balance. She dipped and swayed and returned without falling over, or even threatening to do so.

"Hmmmmpph. I don't recall your names on the guest list. I don't recall your names at all, come to think of it. Who are you? Where is the Master of the Household? Why am I shouting? Heed!" she bellowed.

"I'm Ada, and this is Siam," said Ada.

The White Rabbit scurried forward and adjusted his spectacles. He carried a long trailing scroll of paper in which many holes had been cut. "Your Highness," he said. "At your service."

"Check the guest list, and tell me if Ada and Siam are upon it."

The White Rabbit peered with grave intent. After a few moments he said, "Ah, yes. Here they are."

"Well, take them off," she said. At this the White Rabbit pulled a pair of sewing scissors from a pocket and made two little holes. The paper scraps went into another pocket, which was stuffed with earlier excisions.

"You're not to be found on the guest list," said the Queen of Hearts darkly. "I have half a mind to take off your heads, now I've eliminated your names, but I need to work up to it."

"If you please, Your Loudness, we're looking for a little girl named Alice," said Ada.

"The place is crawling with objectionable creatures," came the reply. "I'm sure you'll find something nasty to take home as a door prize." She reached out and plucked Rosa

Rugosa with her bare hands. Ada caught sight of the rose's startled horror. Whatever had suffused her with character faded. She was no more than a limp crown of petals upon a torn stem. "Here, this can be Alice. Now you can go."

Before Ada could speak again, in another part of the garden a tawdry and hysterical brass fanfare sounded. It seemed to be summoning guests to the theatricale, as the Queen of Hearts was rushed away on the arm of the White Rabbit.

"My," said Ada, laying the dead rose upon the peaty moss. "Life is a very cheap thing here."

"Cheap and dear all at once," said the Rose from her grave. "That's the thing. You'll figure it out sooner or later."

# CHAPTER 42

M r. Clowd looked at his older daughter and then at the cowering Miss Armstrong. "Whatever can you mean?"

"The children have run off, all of them," said Miss Armstrong. "Our Ada, and your Alice, and Mr. Winter's Siam. They are having a pretend adventure and have forgotten the time, perhaps. Or they are in some sort of distress. We've been searching for them."

"Lydia, how can this be? I thought you were looking after Alice?"

"Papa, you know our Alice." Lydia made a dismissive wave of her hand, pretending an insouciance she didn't feel. "All hours are the same to her. No doubt she's bullied the other children into going along on one of her games. I only worry about Siam, for Mr. Winter seems about to depart."

"We can't alarm Mr. Darwin. He's been upset enough by the incursion of that uninvited Hindoo lady."

"Oh, for shame." Miss Armstrong was sympathy itself. "I'll tell Mr. Winter what is happening. Leave it to me, Mr. Clowd."

"But you were to be watching Alice," said Mr. Clowd to Lydia, weakly.

"She slips in and out of sight," replied Lydia, in her own defense. A poor choice of words, perhaps. Mr. Clowd turned pale. But even moments of dread are interrupted by creaking dailiness. A noise in the road, and Alfred was drawing up the carriage. Mr. Darwin was emerging from the Croft and plopping a wide-awake upon his head. Mr. Winter held his elbow as the intrepid naturalist steadied himself in the portico. Mrs. Brummidge and Rhoda hung back in the shadows, an honor guard of domestic sentinels observing the passage of the great man.

"We'll get to the station ahead of the rain, I'll warrant," said Alfred, tipping his hat.

"It wouldn't rain today," said Mr. Darwin without glancing upward. "It wouldn't have the nerve. Mr. Clowd: I regret not having seen your other daughter, but the young have escapades of their own. My own little Annie, before she died at the age of ten, was always in a state of ambition and espionage. The comings and goings! Hold on to her, Mr. Clowd." He bowed to include Lydia. "Hold on to them both. In time you'll find children the greatest comfort you can imagine. Indeed, they prove to be the only possible distraction from the unanswerable question of *why*."

"You have been too good," said Mr. Clowd, miserably.

"Not good enough to answer your question of *why*. Each

must await his cataphany in his own turn and time. In any case, no one can be too good; and I have merely returned sympathy to a sympathetic soul. Good day, my dear Mr. Clowd."

"We are shy of Siam. Call him forward," said Mr. Winter.

"I haven't found him," said Lydia. "It's as simple as that. He wasn't upstairs nor down, nor about the water-meadows. We went as far as Carfax and the Broad."

Mr. Winter's brow contorted; he blinked in disbelief. But Mr. Darwin was hobbling with evident distress. He was minding his feet upon the paving stones and wheezing a pulmonary étude in a minor key. He needed his young friend's assistance. He seemed not to notice the consternation stirred up on the walk behind him, though Mr. Winter kept turning his head at Lydia.

"What can you have done with him?" hissed Mr. Winter, *sotto voce.* "He's been glued to me since we left Rowes Wharf in Boston Harbor."

"Here we are then, sir," said Alfred, taking over and assisting Mr. Darwin.

As Mr. Clowd presided upon the step of the Croft and the staff peeped from the shadows, Mr. Winter turned back to Lydia. He wore the look of a hawk at hunt. He frightened her. But now Miss Armstrong, of all unlikely barristers, came to Lydia's defense. "Your Siam has come unstuck," she said coolly. "Perhaps in the presence of real children, he's remembered how to play."

Lydia was emboldened to add, "I wonder if the cost of your saving him from menace was the denying of his other liberties." A tone of accusation rose in the way she slapped

her words in place. She found her regard for Mr. Winter turning to something like suspicion—though notice how often we
lower suspicion upon others to avoid putting ourselves under
scrutiny.

Now Miss Armstrong grabbed at Lydia's arm and linked
it with her own. "There is no need to fret, Mr. Winter. See
to Mr. Darwin as far as he needs, all the way to Down House
however long it takes. Return to Oxford tomorrow or the next
day. The boy is larking about with the girls, no doubt. He can
wait at the Vicarage with the Boyces till you return."

"Nonsense, not with the new infant wreaking havoc in
that family," said Mr. Clowd affably. "Siam can stop here. Mr.
Winter, I agree with Miss Armstrong. She talks good sense.
From what you've said, the child hasn't had a childlike day in
most of his life. Let him roam and see what freedom means
in England. No one will accost him. He'll turn up with our
Alice and with Ada Boyce. We'll tell him he's to wait with us
until you return for him. He can trust us."

Mr. Winter managed only, "Siam is not adept at trust."

"We'll woo him with our confidence. Or we will force
him." Miss Armstrong gave a brittle smile. She squeezed
Lydia's arm cheerily. The girl hadn't asked Miss Armstrong
to step forward, but she wasn't unhappy for the unforeseen
alliance. She stared beyond the trembling Mr. Winter at Mr.
Darwin, now settled in the carriage and leaning forward to
see what the delay was. The white beard captivated her. He
was like an image of the Ancient of Days.

"We're off then," said Alfred from up top. Mr. Winter
had no choice but to depart.

Miss Armstrong dropped Lydia's arm the moment the carriage had cleared the property wall. "And now it is time to call upon the constable," she said. "Mr. Clowd, will we go together?"

"Midsummer evenings are long. I'm certain the children have merely lost track of time," replied Lydia's father. "Surely we have another hour before we need to become concerned. Alice will come home when the shadows lengthen at last. Would you care to take refuge from the sun, Miss Armstrong? The good Mrs. Brummidge could fix us a pot of tea."

Lydia followed them. Her grip on the moment was uncertain. She was demoted to a mute member of this noxious tableau. She was a sallow adolescent girl, no more than that. Her thoughts were seized within her, words carved immemorially upon an upright grey tablet. *Miss Armstrong has already given up on Ada. Miss Armstrong apprehends that her tenure at the Boyce household is done. Miss Armstrong is tendering a kindly attention to my father.*

# CHAPTER 43

⸺ ❧ ⸺

$A$da thought, It's as if a botanical display and an athletic contest and a gypsy circus have all set themselves up in a hippodrome of some sort. Creatures and things bobbed and weaved this way and that, like cottage farmers and housewives on market day. If there were a central commotion amidst the sideshow specimens, it came from beyond a tall stand of ornamental rushes. The entertainment, perhaps, accompanied by hasty ragged music and cheers. "I think since we don't see Alice on the lawns, she's joined the throng to watch the marionettes," said Ada. "Let us make our way there."

"That Queenie told us we wasn't invited," replied Siam, though he didn't seem perturbed by that.

"It's too varied a crowd for us to be noticed. We'll skulk," said Ada. "I've never skulked before, as it requires a talent for slinking and sloping. But I'm up to trying it now."

"I can learn you skulking. Let's go."

A hooded figure meandered by. He was made out of papier-mâché, colored all over with dark paint, with a prominent jawline and protuberant eyes. He was studying a pamphlet. "Pardon me, has the spectacle begun, then?" asked Ada. "It's begun, and then some," replied the character. "The program seems to be a very good one today." He took a bite of it and chewed carefully. "I do approve. A nicely varied offering, with body, heft, character, and nuance. I believe they are almost up to the trial. I don't have any lines, but I'm trying to digest the proceedings before I'm called to do my work."

"What work is that?"

"Why, I'm the executioner, of course."

"And what do you execute?" asked Ada politely. But he had begun to run a bone-like finger along the margins. He was no longer listening. He veered away from them. He got his papier-mâché axe caught in the low branches of a hornbeam tree.

"I suppose I'm late," said another voice behind them. "The baby was such a pig today."

Ada turned to see a fiercely ugly old woman tottering along in a headdress of stupendous proportions. It split in two as if it meant to disguise disfiguring horns growing out of her head. "You don't know where they're all gathering, do you?" she growled at them.

"If you're looking for the marionettes," said Ada, "I suspect they're over there behind the sedge-grass."

"I'm looking for the trial. I believe I'm wanted as a witness."

"Who is on trial?" asked Ada.

"The marionettes will be if they don't perform up to snuff. Though I couldn't be bothered about who is the defendant. I'm trying to stay out of court. Aren't you dreadfully nosy for a little girl. Then again, it seems a day for it. It'll end in tears, see if it doesn't."

"I thought you said you were wanted as a witness?"

"What made you think that?"

"You just said so."

The wizened old creature frowned. "Yes, they wanted me, but I didn't want *them*. A Duchess has better things to do than make a spectacle of herself."

"Off with her head!" bellowed the voice of the Queen of Hearts.

"Oh, my, I hope they're not talking about Alice," said Ada. "We must hurry."

"Do you know Alice?" said the Duchess. "She was by my house earlier today. A right proper pill she is, too."

"She's not," said Ada.

"She is so. She taught the baby to scream."

"A baby knows how to scream all by itself."

"That's impossible. I was a baby once, and *I* never screamed. I was precocious. Though I was a mere abbreviation of what I would become, I was already brittle, loathsome, and fatuous."

"A brittle baby?"

"That's a contraction for *brilliant* and *little*, of course."

"But surely you couldn't have been a loathsome child," said Ada, glancing up and down at the loathsome adult.

"Of course I was. *Loathsome* is a contraction for *loquacious* and *thoroughly toothsome*."

"And *fatuous* is a contraction, then?"

"*Fat* and *fabulous*. I was simply adorable."

"What does *adorable* mean?"

"Dull." The Duchess fanned herself with a program folded into pleats, not unlike the one the executioner had been devouring. "You haven't seen my Cheshire Cat or my kitchen maid, have you? They're conspiring against me, no doubt. Sidling up to the prosecution and whispering all sorts of innuendo."

"Off with her head!" roared the Queen of Hearts.

"My, the trial is proceeding at quite the clip today, or perhaps they've moved on to pudding," said the Duchess. "I daren't loiter or I'll be called as a witness, and the only thing to which I can reliably attest is that, as a witness, I am nothing if not unreliable."

"Should I trust anything you say?"

"Not all babies are brittle, loathsome, and fatuous. The ones who are deserve extra kisses. Remind me to kiss my own baby the next time he lifts his snout from the trough." With this she gripped her skirts with hammy, washerwoman fingers. She lit out across the lawns as if wolves were after her.

"I don't care to go before no judge," said Siam. "Mercy in short supply here and everywhere."

"We must find Alice," said Ada, "or I must. Do you want to wait here for me?"

"There ain't no waiting," he said sadly. "You leave, you don't come back."

He looked as if he knew what he meant better than Ada knew. She didn't want to pause. She didn't want to be unkind. But it seemed that in his life Siam had seen a sort of sadness that Alice had not. Alice was younger. Untried. Alice, Ada decided, needed her more. "You can trust me," she said to him, and reached out to his hand. But he pulled back as if she might burn him.

All of life hinges on what one does next, until finally one makes the wrong choice. But was this that moment? "Alice, I'm coming."

# CHAPTER 44

Rhoda brought the tea. Lydia chose to sit at a distance. She pretended not to notice that her father indicated that she should pour. The governess took up the teapot with vigor.

"Was the visit with Mr. Darwin what you would have hoped?" asked Miss Armstrong.

Mr. Clowd slid his head peculiarly, describing with his chin a sort of S-curve that had fallen into italics. It resembled neither a nod nor a negative shaking. Or perhaps it was meant to be both at once. The governess continued. "You are a brave man, Mr. Clowd."

"Bravery has nothing to do with times like this," he replied. "One gets on with it. Mr. Darwin is circumspect in his remarks. But it's clear he can't reconcile the instability of the species—transmutation, or evolution, as it's now being called—with the faith of his fathers. I believe he can no longer conceive of a benign Godhead who could allow his daughter Annie such suffering. He tried with great delicacy not to go this far in his consoling words, but I'm not a fool."

"If it is spiritual solace you seek, you might turn to Vicar Boyce."

"He *is* a fool."

Miss Armstrong tolerated this attack upon her beloved employer with alarming equanimity. Lydia sank in her chair, curving her spine in a way that would have elicited a correction from her mother.

Miss Armstrong stirred her tea. "You must rely on your own instincts, Mr. Clowd. As the American, Emerson, wrote in his First Series, 'Character is centrality, the impossibility of being displaced or overset.'"

"I did not imagine a governess might read Emerson's *Essays*."

"She might do. But the essayist's point is about the urgency of not being dislodged from one's deepest beliefs. No matter how beset one might be."

"Perhaps Emerson's comment is wrong. Perhaps we are meant and made to shift our beliefs. If it is a choice between being consistent or being willfully blind . . ."

"If we are 'made' or 'meant,' then someone must have made or meant us. But in any case, if you abandon the faith you shared with your dear departed wife, where does that leave her?"

"It leaves her wherever she is," he admitted, looking at the carpet. "Missing. Unaccounted for in heaven and no longer registered upon the earth."

This was intolerable. Lydia said, "I have no use for tea,

after all. My mother died, Miss Armstrong. She is, conse-
quently, dead. She had a big head like mine and Alice's and
it's my opinion that it simply exploded."

"For shame," said Miss Armstrong, but mildly. It was not
her place.

Lydia's father said, "You aren't welcome, Lydia, if you're
inclined to be discourteous. Go locate Alice as you ought
to have done earlier. And that boy, too. It's time they were
home." When Lydia didn't arise, Mr. Clowd turned back to
Miss Armstrong. "Darwin found Siam charming. Darwin
told us that one of his first friends at Edinburgh was a black
man, a former slave, who taught him how to stuff and mount
birds. I believe Darwin's deep aversion to slavery must date
from this time. He had a falling-out with the master of the
*Beagle* over a difference of opinion on the subject, as I've
been told."

"It seems inconceivable to me that there can be more
than one opinion on the matter."

"Mr. Winter wouldn't have had to rescue that child if everyone agreed with you. Mr. Winter's hope in visiting Mr.
Darwin was to solicit a testimony from the great man in support of Negro emancipation."

"I don't know the American mind, but I should imagine
that the remarks of the prophet of evolution would not be
persuasive to those in the disassociated southern states."

"Perhaps not. Still, as Americans go, he seems a kind
young gentleman, that Mr. Winter."

"I wouldn't have had the chance to notice."

What a liar you are, thought Lydia. The room fell silent as

the adults sipped their tea. Mrs. Brummidge or Rhoda must have gone to the garden well. The sound of the flywheel muttered into the windows like the whirrings of a mechanical insect out there in the slackening sunlight.

Mr. Clowd observed, "Darwin's professor, a certain Mr. Sedgwick at Cambridge, wrote him to say he feared that the popularization of his notions would serve to 'brutalize humanity.' I think those were the words."

"We are quite brutal enough, I fear." Miss Armstrong hefted up the tray of scones and proffered it to her host. "Had Ada done her job, there'd be nice fresh marmalade for these."

Mr. Clowd shook his head as if to clear away evidence of the futility of human affairs. "How is Ada coming along, then? I haven't laid eyes on her since the services."

"Frankly, I don't hold that the iron corset and brace will succeed in correcting her posture, nor promote elegance of movement. Thus improving, eventually one must allow, her hopes for marriage and its subsequent rewards." Miss Armstrong flushed a tempered pink at the mention of marital satisfactions. She sat a bit more upright upon her cushion, perhaps without being aware that it looked as if she were taking pride in the architecture of her own uncorrupted spine.

"She's an odd little clod, from what I've seen."

"The arrival in the Vicar's household of a beloved infant boy has, I fear, delighted the Vicar and exhausted his inattentive wife to the point that correct governance of Ada has gone into arrears. I have spoken too freely, perhaps."

"I thought it was your job to govern Ada."

"Indeed it is." Miss Armstrong settled her teacup. "I have allowed myself to be delayed out of respect for your grief, Mr. Clowd. No opportunity to acknowledge your loss had hitherto presented itself to me. I am indeed a governess. I shall be off at once. Perhaps we might walk together, Miss Lydia?" She stood. Mr. Clowd stood. They both turned to Lydia Clowd.

"I'm not walking with a governess, I have no need of one, *myself*," said Lydia with a doomy and suggestive intonation meant to wound, and wound it did. But Mr. Clowd put his hand out to comfort Miss Armstrong's elbow. "Oh, is there no end to the bonnyclabber of it all?" asked Lydia. Expecting no answer, she proceeded out the door of the parlor, leaving her father inappropriately alone with the governess of the Boyce household, and to Hell with them both.

# CHAPTER 45

———— ✑ ————

$W$ ithout Siam, Ada hurried around a
stand of creamy viburnum. The sound of the assembly grew
faint. It became distant, screened off, the way the sound of
the sea at Sandown was hushed when Miss Armstrong closed
a window, complaining of the breeze. Ada felt as if a great
glass box had descended from the sky to muffle the proceedings of the trial, if trial it were. Or the performance. Or, she
thought, to muffle her.

A great glass box upon her! Ada noted that lately her
thinking had gone colorful.

The viburnum formed a sort of closed grove. A wind
turned itself over in the canes. The flowers lifted and settled in succession, as if they were whitecaps churning upon
a shore. Poking out from them was a beached bathing machine, its steps descending to the grass. A figure in great
black robes was sitting on the top step looking disagreeable.
Ada knew at once who it must be, but she had no idea how

Her Majesty might have got here. She was far too substantial to fall down any hole.

"We are lost," said Queen Victoria. "Wherever we meant to be, we are not there."

"I beg your pardon, Your Majesty. Is there any way I might help?"

The Queen of England said, "We doubt it very much indeed. Go away. Come back. Where is the Solent, do you suppose?"

"I'm not very good at maps, Your Majesty."

"We find our-self in a garden among a set of lunatics and one-offs. Amusing, and novel to be sure, but we are disturbed by the diversion from protocol. Have you a sweetie?"

Ada had nothing to offer the Queen. "This is a garden party, not a bathing strand. Still, I believe you would find something to eat shortly if you came down."

"We don't hunt for food like commoners. Food is brought us. Though perhaps we ought not to partake, for fear this is an underworld of some sort and we should be detained for seven years, or at least until springtime. We are like unto Persephone. We don't suppose—that is, it would be too much to hope for—you haven't by any chance seen the Prince Consort among this rabble?" To herself she mumbled, "We should be very cross indeed to find the Prince Consort had condescended to join this motley host."

Ada knew that Prince Albert was dead, and the widowed Queen was steeped in mourning. "I have no reason to think that dead people are at large," said the girl cautiously. "That is to say, I haven't seen any. Unless you're dead yourself."

"We never would. We have obligations. We carry on."
The Queen's rolled shoulders were like balls of yeasty bread
that wanted punching down. Her intelligent eyes in their
pouches regarded Ada warily. "We imagine we are indulging
in some regrettable dream, provoked perhaps by a suspicious
element in last night's prawn bisque."

"I don't believe this is a dream," said Ada, "but if it is,
you'd hardly be in *my* dream. I don't even know you. Shall I
try to go find the Hatter? Perhaps he managed to cadge some
cakes from the table after all, and he'd be willing to share."

"We saw some mad creature go by arm in arm with a
rangy hare. We would care for no confections discovered in
those pockets. But what have you in *your* pinafore pockets?"

Ada was glad she had put the seaweed packet in her shoe.
"My pockets are empty," she said truthfully.

The Queen sighed, and then brightened up. "But did
you see the Tweedle twins, Dum and Dee? Oh, they made us
laugh. We *were* amused."

"I haven't had the pleasure." Ada didn't want to be rude,
but the need to intercept Alice seemed to be more urgent
with every moment that she dallied. "Would you excuse me?"

Queen Victoria put one elbow on her knee and rested
her set of chins in her fist. She looked every inch the potentate in her waxy black bathing skirts, a crown of diamonds
and pearls pinned into her greying tresses so it wouldn't float
away in the event of a surprise submersion. She was thoughtful and sad. "I had no childhood," she said to Ada. "I was
groomed to be Queen from the time I was five. No one read
stories to me, only tracts of English history. I sometimes have

the urge to go back and study childhood from inside it, so that I might be a better mother to the younger ones. Now the Prince of Wales has grown into a man, and I didn't know so much as a patty-cake rhyme to teach him. No one had taught it to me."

"I could teach you that. It's a quick one, and very satisfying." Ada climbed upon the lower wooden step and took hold of Her Majesty's hands, which were clammy and not quite as clean as she would have imagined. Ada said, "Repeat after me."

"Repeat after me," said Queen Victoria obediently.

> *"Patty Cake, Patty Cake,*
> *Baker's Man;*
> *That I will Master*
> *As fast I can;*
> *Prick it and prick it*
> *And mark it with a V—"*

(Ada edited as she went, in deference to the Crown of England.)

> *"And there will be enough for Her Royal Majesty Queen of England, Supreme Governor of the Church of England, Defender of the Faith, and so on and so on, and me."*

"You?" said the Queen. "I wasn't imagining I would share. I have become hungrier than ever." She shook her head. Ada could hear the wattles on her cheeks softly wuffing. "Even in our dreams, it seems, the Prince Consort is gone. What satisfaction is left to us?" She stood up with determination and effort. "We shall retire into private life even in our dreams."

"You have your nation to govern. And your children to raise. And it's not too late to read the books you missed in childhood," said Ada.

"Have you anything to recommend?"

Ada considered *The History of the Fairchild Family.* Unrewarding and macabre. What about those uplifting tales of child martyrs that her father was always pressing upon her? Perhaps not for a widow. "You want something nonsensical," said Ada. "Keep looking. It will come along."

"We need something to return our stolen childhood to us," said Queen Victoria sadly. "We do hope it is not too late for that."

"It's very late," said the White Rabbit, appearing just then by the wheels of the bathing carriage and looking at his watch. "You've missed the marionettes entirely. They've all been executed and are pausing for a refreshment before the second show. But the trial is about to start, and I must be there, as I have important evidence."

Ada did not know if he was addressing the Queen of England or herself, but the Queen had disappeared into the cabin. The sound of soft snores had begun to issue out on little clouds that smelled like prawn bisque. "Take me with you," Ada said, and grabbed his proffered paw.

# CHAPTER 46

It did not seem as if they ran at all, but merely that the leafy viburnum parted. The white blooms fluttered away like moths. They stood at the back of a paneled hall. It must be the one that had turned into a forest and back again, as to the left of the judge's bench stood the pedestal of the overgrown glass-topped table. Ada craned to see if the key was still there. It was, farther away than ever. Whatever advantage *this* key promised—a key to all understandings or a key to the larder—it was still out of reach. The table was a living thing and its central post was a tree trunk, growing by inches like Jack's beanstalk. Soon the key would be out of sight in the clouds above her head, and Ada would never escape. "I am required at the bench," said the White Rabbit. "If you need me, shout and scream and jump up and down. I may not deign to notice you, mind. You've become common."

"According to Miss Armstrong, I'm ungovernable," said Ada. "But I won't shout and scream, thank you very much. I've learned not to follow advice."

"Very sensible, too," said the White Rabbit. "I never would." He looked her over with a twitch of his whiskers. "I think I like Alice better than you."

"I do, too," she said, "but I'm not on trial, am I?"

"Not yet," he said. He bounded away.

Now, at last, over the shoulders of various animals and other creatures, Ada caught sight of Alice. She was standing before the bench in a very Alice-like way. Her elbows were neatly drawn in at her waist. Her hands were calmly cupped, one in the other. She seemed neither alarmed nor bored, just attentive. Ada wanted to wave and catch her friend's attention, but she didn't dare.

The judge was the King of Hearts. The Queen of Hearts was marching back and forth in front of the members of the jury, hitting each one on the head with a flamingo. The flamingo and its chosen victim both squawked upon impact. Perhaps Ada could sidle around the various raucous creatures and collect Alice quietly, when no one was looking? Then they might make their escape.

The only thing that stopped Ada was the presence of Siam back in the garden. If she stood just so, she could still see the door in the wall, which was now the *door not a door*, but ajar. The light inside the garden was glamorous and fresh. Siam was waiting, somewhere. If she could only position Siam within her sight, she might manage to apprehend both Siam and Alice at once. Though what they three might do when joined together against the world!—for all the education this day had afforded, she could not yet imagine.

"Call the first witness," said the King of Hearts.

"First witness," shrilled the White Rabbit.

The White Queen's head emerged from a pile of chattering oysters near Ada. "Oh, my, you're alive," said Ada gratefully. She reached over and helped the White Queen climb out of the *mêlée*.

"It's nearly time to get back to the Duchess's kitchen," said the White Queen. "I imagine the baby has turned into quite the little hog by now. It will need its hoofs trimmed. Babies want tending, you know. And there's supper to put on."

"Would you like your cloak back?"

"You need it more than I do, dearie. Save it as a souvenir, if you get out of here alive."

"Oh, I'll manage that," said Ada. "I do think using it as a lift in my heel has evened me up. I feel quite the new person."

"So do I. I think I may be a Lady Clothilde, or perhaps a cockle vendor named Mopsy Maeve." The White Queen shook Ada's hand with formality and feeling. "I *never* give advice, but were I you, I should go through the ceiling." She didn't lift her head but just pointed with one ivory finger. "It's the only way out of this madhouse, you know. Coming, I'm coming," she called to the White Rabbit when he'd begun to shriek for her. "And I have testimony that is going to blow the lid off this affair, believe me." She shook the last remaining oysters from the folds in her garments. She walked forward, a little bit of unorthodox regency. Very sure of herself, and content because of it.

"Good-bye," whispered Ada. She imagined, if she did manage to escape, that the ones she would miss were the White Queen and the White Knight. Generally adults were a failure, but these two managed failure well.

But should she find a way to take the Queen's advice, when advice around here was regularly unreliable? In any event, it seemed that the chances to escape were drawing in. She must find Siam and urge him to come with her.

She ducked through the door into the garden. The place was still and beautiful, but the only life it had was of the inanimate sort. No caterpillar upon the rose made nasty comment, no rose replied. The sunless shadows were deepening. The trees had grown extra boughs. Great drooping swaths of greenery, like theatre curtains, came folding in. Nothing could be heard from the courtroom behind her, though the door was still open; it had not yet swung closed. All was as still and silent as the world in the slowed growth in a photograph. Though the leaves swayed, they made no rustling.

"Siam," she said, almost frightened to break the silence. "It's time to go."

He was there beside her. At first he looked at the ground. "I ain't going," he said in a mumbly voice.

"You can't stay here, Siam, because I can't stay. I have to get Alice back to her father. He would suffer so if she didn't return. He's had too much to bear already this year. You must come with me, or you'll be left here all alone. I mean, with them."

"They cain't hurt me any strength. I been hurt enough elsewhere." His chin poked up, his eyes were guarded and brave. "Whatever mind I got, it made up."

"You'll miss the world."

"Little left to miss."

"Your memories, though. Siam! They'll haunt you."

"Thought of that. I don't want those memories. I going back to the Wood of No Names. I do make myself a hut in there, I know the how-to."

Ada didn't feel she could do everything that needed to be done. Who was she, anyway, to say that he was wrong? But she had no time to argue. "I must return to the courtroom, if it hasn't drifted away already. Siam. If you change your mind, come through the door."

His expression was wry and unreadable. Maybe if she were an adult she might interpret it. She couldn't grow up on command though, finish the job while he stood there looking like—like that. It was getting late.

"I won't say good-bye, in the hopes you'll have a change of heart."

"Change of mind, change of heart. What I need, change of skin."

She threw her arms around him, wordlessly. She ducked away.

For once the transmuting world had not revised itself, at least in no way Ada could tell. She tiptoed behind a tea-cart piled high with celery and boot-laces. She peered about. A pack of playing cards was assembling at the front of the room. At the bench, the King of Hearts was trying to win at noughts and crosses, using a salamander as a pen and a slice of bread as a paper. He poked the salamander's tail in a vaguely familiar pot of marmalade, but the salamander kept twisting about and licking the juicy compote off its tail before the King could make a mark on the bread. "Very tricky game, this," he was muttering to himself, "but I'll master it yet."

"I've so enjoyed myself, we must do it again sometime," the White Queen was saying to the King of Hearts. "I especially enjoyed the recitation and the Highland Fling. I never saw a Highland flung so far as that! Now, if you'll excuse me, I have one very tired little piggy at home who needs some mash slung his way. It's not his fault, you know. That he is such a little brute. Being birthed is hard work."

"So is being dead," replied the King of Hearts.

"Call the next witness," whispered the Queen of Hearts to the White Rabbit.

"Alice!" cried the White Rabbit.

"If you please," said Alice. "I won't come. I have nothing to say today."

"But you must," said the King of Hearts, absentmindedly sucking the tip of the salamander's tail. "Otherwise we're all at sixteens and sevens."

"That's sixes and sevens, I do believe," Alice corrected him.

"No, we left the sixes in the larder, and we brought the sixteens by mistake. Nothing adds up. Do you see what I am up against? Now come here and take your place like a good girl, and do as you're told."

"I'll come," said Alice, "but I can't promise to be useful."

"Little girls often lie," said the King of Hearts helpfully. "You may be useful despite yourself."

Ada found herself thinking, Alice, don't fuss; just go there and do their bidding. No one can pay attention for more than a few moments in this place.

"Do as he says, or your head will spin," roared the Queen of Hearts.

"Stuff and nonsense," said Alice with what, to Ada, seemed uncharacteristic insolence. But who knew what sort of a day *she* had had?

The Queen of Hearts turned crimson. "Hold your tongue!"

"I won't," said Alice.

"Off with her head!" shouted the Queen.

"Who cares for you?" asked Alice. "You're nothing but a pack of cards."

An upheaval, a commotion, a seism shuddered the room. The standing army brought several suits against Alice. Ada watched Alice raise her arm to her eyes to fend them off. She fell backward against a marble statue of a dodo. She slumped against it, limp, rag-like. Her eyes were closed and didn't open.

"Call the next witness!" said the White Rabbit to himself, and did so. "The Jabberwock!"

# CHAPTER 47

Miss Armstrong reclaimed her gloves from the table in the passage. It was time to put folly behind her. She had taken a false step somewhere early in the day, and she would pay for it for the rest of her life. She only hoped it would not come to pass that someone had seen her pursuing Ada, catching up with her, and tumbling the girl into deep water. If Miss Armstrong had done that—had acted on her dreadful fantasy—she could not recall it, and that much was true. The amnesia of the hysteric. She would say so to the magistrate, or the warden of the gaol at Oxford Castle. For now, there was nothing left awaiting her in the benighted Vicarage but the accusations and recriminations of a hard-lived day. Another one. She left the Croft by the front door, unable to imagine she might return, and soon.

Lydia wandered out, too, through the kitchen garden. Darwin had been right; there would be no downpour. The afternoon was pulsing with the last energy of daylight, which had turned dry and flecked. It was the time of year when English evening can take three hours being absorbed into night-time. But dusk was out there, ferrying in from Low Countries, halting and hovering off the coast of Essex, picking up strength from dark waters, gathering its moods and forces.

For the first time Lydia began to wonder, seriously, if she should be frightened for Alice. It would be a novel exercise, both because Lydia's capacity for raw emotion had been so overwhelmed in recent months that, until today, she'd imagined she could never feel anything deeply ever again; and also because, well. Alice.

Alice was immortal. Alice was immortal in a way their mother had not been. It had to do with Alice's strange gravitas, her unerring solidity. Death wouldn't come near her. It wouldn't dare. And mind, this was not the immortality that children demonstrate, blindly, children who, because they do not know they will die, behave as if it cannot happen. Sooner or later we grow into deserving our own deaths, somehow.

Alice was different. She was rectitude and curiosity and bravery; she was stubbornness and tolerance. Something of her childhood always seemed to slip out of her— as if through permeable membranes—as if she were one of Darwin's anomalous specimens. Alice was an ordinary child whose unordinary childhood seemed an infectious condition to those who came near. Lydia often felt like a bit player, a common sort of business, her own existence merely some adumbration ornamenting the life of her weird sister. The spider under the table at the Last Supper, the cat who looked

at a King. The King is history; where the cat went next is not
recorded.

And yet—Lydia had been pacing along the path as she
mused, and now she had reached the place on the riverbank where she had stopped earlier that day. Look, she'd
dropped her book of commentary on Shakespeare's midsummer dream, and she'd never noticed: There it still lay in the
meadow-grass—and yet, and yet. Who else to play the part of
a bit player in the life of a child? What is a parent but a sort
of valet to the royalty of innocent youth? With Mrs. Clowd
gone, and Mr. Clowd lost in grief, Alice had no one else. And
Lydia was all she had, and not enough.

Lydia paused and sat down, and leaned against the tree.
She put her hands to her face. She didn't care to think about
her mother. She wasn't ready. Unwelcome, indeed forbidden,
a memory rose up through the flooring of the day, a memory
of Jane Clowd. Lydia tried to resist it but memories are anarchic.

Some winter morning. A few years ago. Jane Clowd had
come back from London. A visit to a surgery in Harley Street.
Alighting from the carriage onto the glossy, ice-slicked cob-
bles of the lane. Leaning to thank the driver and turning to
greet her girls. Her hair had fallen out of its pins on one side.
The bonnet was askew. Forsaking their December wear, the
girls had pummeled down the path from the Croft, meaning
to throw themselves in her arms. Against the cold, one hand
was still immersed in a white muff of rabbit fur. The other
hand, gloveless, was reaching toward her girls.

# CHAPTER 48

———— ✺ ————

$A$da began to lunge toward Alice, to make sure she was not badly hurt, but a sound behind her made her turn. Everyone else was swiveling and pulling back at the same time. The playing cards built themselves into a kind of pyramid. The Queen of Hearts flew to the top, claiming the advantage. The Tin Ballerina and the Tin Bear tossed their kites into the air, and climbed the ascending strings like circus roustabouts. The Cheshire Cat allowed his tail to appear, flicking viciously and offering no doubt as to its owner's disapproval. The White Queen was gone, having retired into domestic service. The Duchess was trying to hide behind a fan made of a splayed hand of Clubs, a royal flush, who were objecting though to no avail. Having hopped upon the bench of the King of Hearts, the White Rabbit circled madly, crying, "Beware the Jabberwock, my son!" No one in the room, as far as Ada could tell, had a son or was a father.

All told, this seemed a rather parentless set of circumstances. So she couldn't imagine whom he might be addressing.

Indeed, the only person not contorting or shrieking in alarm was Alice, because she was insensate against the plinth of the marble dodo.

"I do hope you don't mind," said Ada to the White Knight, who had risen creakily to his feet. "I would like to climb upon your shoulders."

"Fancy serving the likes of you. Mind your bony knees, sir. But be my guest."

She scrabbled up and peered over the heads of various hedgehogs, lollygagging sarsen stones, gossiping potatoes, a walrus, and some roses that looked vaguely familiar but turned snootily away. The back of the room, as if unable to shake off a habit of recidivism, had returned to forest. The wall was junglefied, hung with vines, lurid with unseemly fruits and lascivious flowers. Shrieking gibbons and toucans conversed in an unfamiliar patois. The floor of the forest remained tiled in black and white squares, but those tiles were being tossed forward like flotsam on a storm-hurried tidal surge. Soil from beneath the floor spat up. The Jabberwock was approaching from below.

"An underworld beneath this one?" said Ada to the White Knight. "Has it no shame?"

He answered, "Did you seriously believe you would ever understand all that there is to be known?"

Then a roar shook the room. It was like the collapse of a textile mill into a dry riverbed. The King of Hearts replied, "Silence!" in the most timid, mouse-like voice he could manage. "If you please." The Jabberwock, sandy dirt streaming from its iron jaws, clawed its way up from some unimaginable tomb.

"Oh, you," said Ada. "I might have known."

"You are on speaking terms with this monstrous threat?" cried the Queen of Hearts.

"In a manner of speaking. I mean, in a manner of non-speaking."

The Jabberwock finished dragging its clawed grips from below. It stood flexing its skeletal wings. There was rather little head, so one had to be impressed that it could manage to roar at all. The circlet of neck brace, which buckled in front, seemed to serve as the mouth, for as it contorted in slits and ovals, an assortment of enraged industrial sounds was heard. The rib cage had grown iron extensions. They unfolded into pinions, like the skeleton of a bird. Where its knuckled, prehensile feet had come from, Ada could not imagine. They looked something like bundles of fish forks.

"*You've* had yourself quite the adventure, I see," said Ada.

The Jabberwock developed a couple of grommets on its upper brow and blinked them at her. She wondered if it would recognize her now it had grown so grand.

"I'm afraid the excursion is over," she told it. "It's time we returned."

"If you mean to take your little pet home, now would be the proper moment," said the King of Hearts, quaveringly.

"Off with its head," added the Queen of Hearts, though

without conviction, as it really didn't have much of a head.

The Jabberwock flexed its wings and circled above the crowd in the courtroom, snatching at a sleeping dormouse. It deposited the dormouse into its open maw, but the dormouse simply dropped through and landed into a barrister's starched wig, snoring all the while. Ada thought, Is that all that happens by walking into the mouth of doom?

"For a creature with a magnificent wingspan, it doesn't seem to be able to attain any useful altitude," said the King of Hearts, diving flat upon the judge's bench to avoid being taken for a ride.

"Naturally," said the Tin Ballerina. "Its wings are merely an armature. The air goes right through them, providing no lift. It needs skin, it needs an area of resistance. Like the cloth of a kite."

"I have just the thing," said Ada. She took off her shoe and removed the seaweed cloak. It was none the worse for compression. As Ada began to unfold the triangle of material, she said, "Come here and behave; it's time for you to knuckle down and accept correction. It's for your own good, mark my words. You'll never be much, but you can be better than you are now." The sentiment wasn't hers but Miss Armstrong's, retailed of a morning after shucking Ada of her nightgown and submitting her to a brisk scrub. Hateful words, but they came in use now. The Jabberwock settled docilely enough upon the head of Humpty Dumpty, who held still and kept his eyes squeezed shut, pleading that the iron claws did not clench, or the yolk would be on him.

"I'm fried," he whimpered. "This is it. I'm finally cracking up. All the King's horses and all the King's men won't be able to put me back together again."

"Shhh," said Ada. "Don't worry. Why the King's horses and men? I'm sure the Queen's attendants are much more capable when it comes to managing eggs, but no one ever mentions *them*." She nimbled upon the helmet of the White Knight and flung wide the unfolded cloak.

"This will only take a moment," she said to the Jabberwock. "There. That's much better, don't you agree?"

The Jabberwock turned its head this way and that to regard its wings, newly fledged with seaweed. It fit perfectly, as if it were custom cut by a Parisian seamstress. Oysters in a crate began to shriek in joy and beg to be taken for a ride.

"We've no time for that now," she told the oysters. "Come, now, Jabberwock; we must be off."

"Must you leave so soon?" asked the White Rabbit. "Can't you leave sooner?"

"It'll be as if I was never here at all," promised Ada. She stood still. The Jabberwock came forward and settled itself around her. Ada buckled the strap about her neck and another about her waist. She fit her arms into the rings that clamped tight in her armpits. The Jabberwock had grown, but so had she, it seemed. The fit was even keener than it had been this morning. Of course, Ada was accustomed to being shucked into the apparatus below her clothing, and now it was overlaid, and public, like a suit of armor, but she had no intention of stripping to her smalls in a court of law, however deranged the audience.

When she was properly corrected, she said to the White Rabbit, "You're the time-keeper here. What time is it?"

He looked at his pocket-watch. "It's very late indeed."

"Then there is no time like the present to say good-bye." With this Ada flexed her new wings and pushed her way to the front of the room. Humpty Dumpty exhaled sulfurously. Ada knelt below the bust of the marble dodo. "Alice, my dear, it's time to go home."

Her friend was breathing nicely enough. She didn't stir. She was lost in some dream-world. With the strength allowed by iron reinforcement, Ada reached down and collected Alice beneath her armpits. She hugged her close, as if she were a tender mother, or even an older sister, and Alice a child who had fallen asleep under the dining room table.

Rising, Ada cast a glance toward the door to the garden, but the door was closed now, Siam behind it, and the sign that had said

KEEP OUT.

now said

KEEP IN.

and there was no longer a keyhole.

Those who are roped into bed at night often fall into delusions of flight. Though usually a dreamer of commonplace notions, once in a while Ada had enjoyed dreams of flying. So she was hardly surprised to find herself not only capable but skilled at this exercise. The wings of her iron cage flexed mightily. She moved upward in a spiral, leaving behind without regret all those creatures, their idiocies and affections. She disobeyed earlier advice and looked up rather than down. She could see in the underside of the glass tabletop a reflection of the impossible wonderland, a looking-glass simulacrum that could entice without either endangering or offering reward. On the other side, above the glass, which had widened to roof all of this underworld, rested the key. If she could leave with the key she could, perhaps, come back someday and rescue Siam. When he was ready to allow it.

As she was pumping her iron wings to batter against the glass ceiling and claim the key for once and for all, a hoary old tench drifted above this world. He waggled his brown fins at her. He swallowed up the key, tag and all. He swam away.

She felt a sudden rage. The ascent of the human creature — one has to fight to be born, after all. She bashed against the glass with every ounce of her might. She would break through, she would. So she did, being a child with more force of intention that she'd previously allowed herself to acknowledge. The tabletop split with a jagged line. The glass shattered. An ocean of water rolled over Ada and Alice. Whatever was below the wave was lost to view. Anything that might be above it could not be imagined. There is a limit to the nonsense even a dream can attempt.

# CHAPTER 49

———— ❧ ————

$G$asping for air, Ada pulled Alice safely
into the shallows. The bank was low. Though Alice was limp
and heavy, Ada felt in herself the strength that accompanies
terror. She saw Lydia still sitting by the tree, though the light
had shifted across horizons, and the air had lost its morning
warmth. Lydia had nodded off over a boring text. Good. The
tracks of a few tears showed on her cheek. Ada was able to
hoist Alice the several feet to the trunk of the tree. Alice
murmured something that Ada couldn't quite make out, but
Alice's voice even in nonsense syllables sounded like herself.
Ada believed she would be all right.

She turned to look in the river to see if she could find
that damnable tench. If he was in there, taunting her, she
would come back another day with a fishing pole and a handful of bait stolen from the larder. She'd go to work to rescue
Siam. There was always a key somewhere. One only needed
to know where to start looking.

For a moment the river seemed to cease its endless motion. Perhaps Ada was having a dizzy spell of some sort. She leaned over the surface, which was as still as a waxed tabletop. She caught sight of her bemused face. Her hair was drenched and bedraggled. She had lost the perfect form of the ringlets that Miss Armstrong always tortured into her hair. But a fierce light rain was beginning to fall (no matter what Darwin had predicted). Ada would seem only to have got caught in a downburst.

She glanced back. Alice was already beginning to stir. She had crawled nearer and placed her head in her sister's lap, and murmured her sister's name. In her own somnolence, Lydia had let her hand fall over Alice's outrageous brow, comforting.

Ada looked back at her reflection again, to see if she could find on her face any trace of what she had been through, the details of which were beginning to fade. She could not. All she could see, drifting in the water now like the wreck of a dressmaker's dummy, were the struts and buckles of her closest companion, drowned for good. If it had once worn a seaweed skin, all that was dissolved away.

She left it there. She straightened up—straighter than she'd ever managed before—and wondered which way in this fantastic world to turn.

A girl, even a clumsy one, who had managed to rescue her best friend might prove qualified to serve as a big sister.

A white rabbit hopped out from a stand of grass. It was that hour when rabbits feed, though they don't often come out in the damp. It twitched at something appealing, but then turned to look at Ada. It had no waistcoat or pocket-watch. Still, it stood upright, as if a lone member of some honor guard. Then, without possible doubt, the rabbit pointed at the path toward Alice's home.

So Ada gave a curtsey, the first real curtsey she'd ever managed in her life, and set off at a startling clip to surprise Mr. Clowd and Mrs. Brummidge, and whomever else might be lingering at the Croft of a summer evening, and to apologize for having lost a gift of marmalade, somehow, along the way.

# CHAPTER 50

— ✦ —

Darwin had nodded off at the rocking of the train. When he woke up, he guessed they were nearing Paddington. London was purple in the midsummer gloaming, so its lamplights, just being lit, made a fever rash of amber sparks. He glanced at Josiah Winter, the only other traveler in the cabin. The American was distraught, picking at his nails. Darwin knew about fretfulness as well as he knew about anything else. To distract the poor fellow from whatever he was suffering, Darwin made a remark. The noise of the train wheels muffled it.

"I beg your pardon? Did you refer to a catastrophe?" asked Mr. Winter. "Or epiphany?—I misheard."

"I was musing on the notion of a cataphany."

"I don't understand."

"Cataphany. My own word, from the Greek *cata*, meaning down, and *phantazein*, to make visible. Also the root of *fantasy*, don't you know. Cataphany: an insight, a revelation of underness. The findings of Odysseus in Hades, interviewing the shade of Achilles. Or Gilgamesh, hunting Enkidu. Or even, meaning no disrespect, the Christ arising after three days in Hell. What sort of revelation can occur in perfect dark? What would Eurydice tell us if Orpheus had been able to bring her back?"

Winter gave a shrug, looked away. A sequence of lights and darks played across his shuttered face. He shuffled a few ha'pence in one hand. A sound like small jangling keys, or the links of a slack chain falling upon one another.

The elderly man continued, out of mercy and out of curiosity, for that was what he was like. "Let me put it more scientifically. If separate species develop skills that help them survive, and if those attributes are favored which best benefit the individual and its native population, to what possible end might we suppose has arisen, Mr. Winter, that particular capacity of the human being known as the imagination?"

*—finis—*

# C. S. FRIEDMAN

# DREAMSEEKER

Book Two of
*The Dreamwalker Chronicles*

**DAW BOOKS, INC.**
DONALD A. WOLLHEIM, FOUNDER
375 Hudson Street, New York, NY 10014

ELIZABETH R. WOLLHEIM
SHEILA E. GILBERT
PUBLISHERS
www.dawbooks.com

DAW Books Collector's No. 1695.

Published by DAW Books, Inc.
375 Hudson Street, New York, NY 10014.

First Paperback Printing, August 2016
1  2  3  4  5  6  7  8  9

FOR TANITH LEE
WHO TAUGHT US ALL HOW EXQUISITE
THE MARRIAGE OF BEAUTY AND DARKNESS
COULD BE

# Acknowledgments

Thanks once more to my beta team for all their moral support and creative input: David Walddon, Zsuzsy Sanford, Carl Cipra, and Jennifer Hina. Also to Kim Dobson and Larry Friedman, whose story suggestions led to some delightfully evil plot twists. Bradley Beaulieu gave me some timely and very insightful feedback, for which I am also grateful. (His newest book is amazing, btw, and you all should read it.)

Thanks to Brandon Lovell for his help with Farsi. 'Cause undead Persian necromancers don't just name themselves.

Last, but not least—never least!—special thanks to my agent, Russ Galen, and my editor-goddess, Betsy Wollheim. Betsy's creative input was invaluable, as always; I couldn't imagine writing books without her.

# PROLOGUE

VICTORIA FOREST
VIRGINIA PRIME

SEBASTIAN HAYES

**B**ACKLIT BY A BLAZING ORANGE SUNSET, the floating rabbit was an eerie sight. The dappled forest shadows made the snare almost invisible, so that it looked as if the small body was levitating of its own accord, and as it swayed back and forth in the breeze it appeared more ghostly than real.

With a quick and practiced motion, the wanderer known as the Green Man freed the dead rabbit and tucked it into his game pouch. Then he reset his snare.

It was Sebastian's third catch of the night. All had been young animals, without much meat on their bones, but that was to be expected this time of year. Summer's offspring were so busy exulting in their new existence that they rarely saw the snare's fine line strung across their path. The older ones tended to be more circumspect.

With a sigh he settled the strap of the game pouch on

his shoulder, ready to return home. The pressure of the thick leather band across his chest conjured an unexpected sensory memory, from a time when the pouch at his hip had contained not freshly killed meat, but black powder cartridges arranged in neat rows. He remembered how their newsprint wrappings had tasted as he used his teeth to tear them open, spitting out bits of blackened paper as he fed explosive powder into the mouth of his musket. A ravenous beast, that weapon. Always wanting more.

Memories from another world, another time.

The hike back to his new base camp was a long one, and by the time he reached it the sunlight was nearly gone.

*I should have gone to Shadowcrest with them,* he thought.

Not a night passed that he didn't think about the three young people from his homeworld, or regret that he had sent them to face the Shadows alone. Yes, it had seemed the logical choice to make at the time—the only rational choice, one might argue—but that didn't make it any easier to accept. Once, long ago, he had failed to protect his own child, and she had died as a result. Now these young people had needed him, and he had abandoned them.

*I was a prisoner in Shadowcrest once,* he reminded himself. *There are wards all over the place that no doubt are still attuned to my presence. Had I remained with Jessica and her friends, I would have triggered those alarms. The only chance they had to sneak past the Shadows' security was to go in without me.*

Such a thing might indeed be true. But guilt was a visceral torment, not so easily banished.

What happened to the teens from Terra Colonna after he had parted company with them? He knew that the Blue Ridge Gate had been destroyed—even the

Shadows couldn't keep something that big a secret—but his informants had been unable to bring him any specifics on the matter. Had Jessica and her friends made it back to their own world, or remained trapped in this one? Or worse yet, had they become lost in that place between the worlds that all sane men feared? He might have been trapped in that nightmare realm himself, had he tried to cross over with them.

As he approached his camp the trees began to thin out, and the dirt beneath his feet gave way to patches of naked stone, windswept and lifeless. From here he could see the opening of the crevice he now called home, a deep black gash in the mountainside. The cave that he'd located halfway up one of its walls wasn't the most luxurious shelter, but these days caution trumped comfort. He didn't think the Colonnans would tell anyone about him, but the local boy they'd been travelling with was a wild card. And if Jessica and her friends were taken prisoner, their willingness to talk would cease to be a significant factor. Both the Seers and the Domitors had the means of squeezing secrets from a human mind, and if the Shadows decided to question the teens, their methods did not bear thinking about.

He had almost been at the receiving end of those methods, once.

Almost.

What was the name of the local boy who'd been travelling with them? Isaac? So pale, that one. So haunted. The edge in the boy's voice when he'd asked Sebastian about a murdered Shadowlord had been unmistakable, but what exactly was Isaac's connection to that secretive Guild? Clearly he was not a Shadow himself: no one born to that Guild would have been allowed to wander the world without supervision as he was doing. But his family might have business ties to a Shadowlord, or perhaps some sort of political alliance, that gave Isaac a

vested interest in the undead. So did he seek out the
Shadows after he left Sebastian, and tell them what he'd
learned about the Green Man? Did he tell them that the
possible murderer of a Shadowlord was hiding out in
Victoria Forest, and might be located by following the
trail of dead vegetation he left in his wake?

It wasn't the truth, exactly. But Sebastian doubted
that would matter to the Shadowlords.

*I should have killed the boy when I had the chance,* he
thought. But even in the midst of war he'd had no stomach for killing innocents, and the boy had done nothing
to harm him. Not to mention Isaac had helped the three
Colonnans escape from the Warrens, so that Sebastian
could meet them. That deserved a better answer than
death.

*I saved his life as well as theirs,* he reminded himself.
*Hopefully that will earn his silence.*

There were just too many variables in play. Even for
a man who thrived on mysteries, it was an uncomfortable situation. So he had broken camp after they left
and moved to a place that was naturally barren, where
his curse would not give him away. It was a desolate, unpleasant location, but its inherent lifelessness would
mask his presence.

*Maybe I should leave this forest altogether.*

How long had he been here, anyway? Ten years?
More? True, Victoria Forest was only a base of
operations—his endless search for information kept him
constantly on the move—but there was danger in remaining anywhere too long. Maybe it was time to move on.

Suddenly he saw something on the ground ahead of
him, a mark imprinted in a narrow strip of soil. The fading sunlight made it hard to see, so he had to squat down
low to be able to make out its details.

A paw print. Wolf sign.

Larger than any natural paw print should be.

He drew out his knife and quickly rose to his feet—but it was already too late. Something massive burst from the forest with unnatural speed and barreled into him from behind, sending him crashing to the ground. Only by thrusting both hands out in front of him could he keep from smashing his head into bare rock, but in doing that he lost hold of his knife. Now he had only his hands, his wits, and a thick leather coat to protect him from the beast's assault.

He could feel the great wolf's jaws closing around his neck, trying to crush his windpipe, and he barely managed to evade them; dagger-like teeth pierced the heavy collar of his coat, coming within a hair's breadth of tearing out a chunk of his neck. The beast jerked back with a growl of rage, ready to try again. But this time Sebastian was ready. He twisted around and elbowed it on the side of its head, hard enough to stun it for a second, then managed to reach out and grab his knife: long and sharp and tempered in the blood of bears and mountain lions and men, it had never failed him.

Now they both were armed.

The wolf lunged for his throat again but he twisted lithely out of its way, and all it got this time was a mouthful of coat lapel. It jerked its head back and forth wildly, tearing at the garment as if it was raw flesh. Sebastian's fettered brooches broke loose and flew in every direction while he thrust at the creature, aiming for its gut, but the wolf's wild movements skewed his aim, and he sliced into its shoulder instead. As the beast's hot blood splattered everywhere Sebastian yanked his blade free, bracing himself for the next attack.

Then he looked into the wolf's eyes, sensed the cold human intelligence behind them, and he knew that this was more than a simple attack.

He stabbed at the animal again, but instead of renewing its attack the wolf backed away, leaving Sebastian's blade to slice through empty air. He had misjudged the thing: it didn't want to kill him, only force him to the ground and scatter his protective fetters beyond reach. Dark figures rushed in from all sides—four? six? eight?—and though they were human in shape they were bestial in their ferocity. Sebastian struggled to get to his feet before they had a chance to engage him, but there was no time. No time. The fetters that might have helped him escape glittered on the ground surrounding them, reflecting the last of the sunlight in tiny points of fire. Even the nearest ones were hopelessly out of reach.

The ambush had been well planned.

Ingrained reflexes took over as the shadowy figures fell upon him. He moved automatically, channeling combat instinct from his soldiering days, kicking out sideways to sweep the legs of the first man out from under him. Then another assailant moved in and Sebastian rolled deftly away from him, grabbing the arm of a third who was swinging a weapon at his head. He used that man's own momentum to yank him off his feet and send him sprawling to the ground. He tried to send him straight into one of the other attackers, but he wasn't as agile as he had been in his youth—nor as strong—and the maneuver fell short. Then some kind of impact weapon struck him from behind, between his shoulder blades, and for a moment the whole world was awash in crimson. Half blinded from pain, he kicked out wildly in the direction the blow had come from, hoping to drive his attacker back just long enough for him to recover his bearings.

But there were just too many of them, and now that they had him surrounded even a soldier in his prime would have been hard pressed to prevail against such numbers. And he was not that, by a long shot. Usually he had fetters to bolster his strength or sharpen his reflexes, but they were out of reach, and though he fought with the ferocity of a cornered animal, he knew that a single hunting knife was not enough to save him.

He was going to die tonight. After so many years of tempting fate, of walking a tightrope between treacherous patrons and powerful enemies, his time had finally come. A terrible sadness filled his heart, but also determination. Very well. If these were the men who would remove the Green Man from Terra Prime, he'd give them scars to remember him by. Maybe even take one or two of them out before he died.

But then something struck him on the side of the head with numbing force, and the world began to spin wildly about him. Vomit surged into his throat and he swallowed it back with effort, knowing that surrendering to sickness meant surrendering to death. And he wasn't ready to die yet.

Blackness was closing in from the corners of his vision, and a terrible keening sound filled his ears, drowning out the ruckus of combat. He shook his head to clear it, and instantly regretted the move. Spears of pain shot through his skull. The world was growing darker each second.

Drawing in one final breath, he braced himself for the death blow that was sure to come.

But then hands grabbed him by the upper arms and hauled him to his feet. Someone jerked his knife from his hand, and he was helpless to stop them. Spears of agony lanced through his shoulders as his arms were pulled roughly behind his back, but the pain was a strangely distant thing, as if it belonged to someone else. His wrists were being bound behind his back. A stranger's wrists.

These men hadn't come to kill him. Whoever had sent them here wanted the Green Man taken alive.

It was his last thought as darkness claimed him.

||||||||||||

Light. Too much light. It made his eyes hurt.

But pain was good. Pain meant that he was still alive.

He squinted, trying to bring the world into focus. His head throbbed, as did his neck, his chest, and every other part of his body. But it wasn't the kind of sharp pain one would expect from shattered bones and torn flesh. That pain was gone; this was only its memory.

Someone must have healed him.

Slowly his surroundings came into focus. He was in a small room, dimly lit by a single glow lamp; once his eyes adjusted he found it a comfortable illumination. He was lying on some kind of bed or couch, and there were two people standing over him, armed men dressed in uniforms he didn't recognize. Had they been among those who attacked him in the woods? He tried to move, and discovered to his relief that he wasn't bound. As he sat up, the guards made no effort to restrain him.

He discovered he'd been lying on an opulent couch, deep crimson velvet with coordinated brocade pillows. The room looked like some kind of study, with bookcases and a desk of dark wood, polished to a glassy shine. He was hardly ungrateful to find himself in such benign surroundings, but where in God's name was he? Who would assault him in the woods like that, then heal him and bring him here? It made no sense.

A door at the far end of the room suddenly opened. The woman who entered was dressed entirely in white; in the dim room she seemed to give off a light of her own.

"Leave us," she said to the soldiers.

They seemed surprised by the command, and one began to protest, "But your Ladyship—"

"*Leave us.*"

Her tone allowed for no argument. They bowed in unison and left without a word.

The woman in white looked at Sebastian. "Do you know who I am?"

He could guess her identity from descriptions he'd heard, though he'd never seen her in person. "Lady Alia Morgana, Guildmistress of Seers." It was rumored she was more than that—much more—but even hinting at such knowledge was likely to get him killed. There were secrets he was sure she would kill to protect.

She nodded. "And you are Sebastian Hayes, who served as a private in the Ninth Virginia Regiment during the Colonial Insurrection." A cold, dry smile curled her lips. "Do I have it right?"

He couldn't remember a time when he'd shared that much of his background with anyone. The Shadows knew, of course, as they knew every other detail of his history. But Sebastian understood enough about how the Guilds functioned to know that any cooperation between the Shadows and the Seers was strictly superficial; at best they were fierce rivals to one another, and at worst, something much darker. He couldn't think of any reason why the Shadows would share his personal information with Morgana.

Which meant she'd discovered it on her own.

Impressive.

"We called it the War of Independence, but otherwise you have it right." America had never won its independence in this world.

"Do you know why you're here, Private Hayes?"

"I presume you ordered your men to bring me in."

Her pale eyes glittered. They were mostly grey, he noted, the color of fog, smoky crystal, the sky before a storm. Subtle blues and greens played in their depths as she moved. "Ah, but those were not my men who attacked you."

"Whose, then?"

"Think, Private Hayes. Whose authority have you

repeatedly defied? Who might have reason to suspect that you played a part in the death of one of their leaders?"

There was no safe way to respond to that, so he said nothing.

"Apparently the Shadows heard rumor that you assassinated one of their own. It's easier for them to interrogate a bound spirit than a living man, so no doubt that's what Lord Virilian intended. However, you're of more use to *me* alive than dead—for now—so I'm forced to disappoint him." She paused "You understand, it's no small thing for me to frustrate the plans of such a powerful man. I would expect my efforts to be ... appreciated."

For a moment Sebastian said nothing. She was asking him to serve as her agent. And perhaps much more. He'd heard whispers about a secret consortium that sought to gain through conspiracy the kind of power that could not be obtained otherwise. Morgana was rumored to be a member of it. Which meant that if he became indebted to her, he would effectively become a pawn of that group.

Their agenda was unknown. For all his sources, he had been unable to verify their membership.

"Or I could just deliver you to Lord Virilian," she said affably. "I'm sure he would be generous in his gratitude, after I stepped in to capture you when his own men failed."

*I have no choice,* he thought. Some debts could not be denied. "I owe you my life," he said quietly.

"Excellent!" The pale eyes glittered; something in their depths made him shudder. "Then we do understand each other. I'm sure we're going to have a most productive relationship."

She withdrew a handful of items from a pocket of her silk slacks and held them out to him. He hesitated, then put his own hand out beneath hers, palm open. Slowly she dropped his fetters into his hand, one by one. All except the last. She held that one up to the light, so she could see it better.

"Fetters from the Guild of Obfuscates are very rare," she mused. "It's almost unheard of for a Grey to share his Gift with an outsider." She looked at him. "You must have done something quite remarkable to earn this one."

He shrugged stiffly. The motion hurt. "Simply a trade of information, your Grace. In this case regarding an assassination plot against a high ranking Master of the Greys. He was grateful for my warning."

He continued to hold his hand out. After a moment she dropped the last fetter into it. "I have sufficient influence to turn the Shadow's attention away from you," she said. "For now."

"I would be most grateful if you did that."

"You would be well advised to keep a low profile for a while."

"I understand."

His heart skipped a beat. *Low profile* suggested he would not be kept a prisoner here, that he would be allowed to go about his own business again. At least until she needed him. His hand closed around the Grey fetter. All he needed was a moment when she wasn't looking directly at him and he could use it to escape from this place.

He nodded. "I believe I can manage that."

"Good. I may have a task for you soon. In the meantime, I trust that if you come across any information that would be of interest to me . . ."

He bowed his head ever so slightly. "It would be my honor to share it with you."

"Excellent. Rest here for as long as you like, then. My people will bring you whatever refreshment you require, and will see you out when you're ready to leave."

"Thank you, Your Grace."

She walked toward the door, the fine white silk of her garments rippling like water. But at the threshold she paused, then turned back to look at him. "Did you really kill Guildmaster Durand?"

The words were more than a question, he knew. They were a test of his commitment, and perhaps of his value. He chose his own words carefully. "Durand was killed by a rival Shadow, who slit his throat with a sacrificial knife. There were so many death-impressions on the blade already that no one could draw forth from it any useful information. Hence the killer remained undetected. Rather clever, actually." He paused. "Of course, I have no idea what sort of information Durand's rival might have come across, that convinced him such drastic action was necessary."

For a long moment she just looked at him. One corner of her mouth twitched slightly; he could not tell whether it indicated disapproval or amusement. Perhaps both.

Without further word, she left him to his thoughts.

# 1

BERKELEY SPRINGS
WEST VIRGINIA

JESSE

**T**HE BLACK PLAIN feels unsteady tonight.

Normally I have better control over my dreams than this. Normally I can force the energy under my feet to take whatever shape I want it to. It's only an illusion, after all. The space that lies between the worlds is a realm of utter chaos, with no real physical substance; it's hardly the sort of thing one can walk on. But in my dreams I can make it take whatever form I want. If I want the primal chaos that separates the worlds to look like a sheet of black glass, a field of obsidian gravel, or even a dusty linoleum floor, that's my choice.

It's always black, though. I've tried a thousand times to give it color, but I can't.

Tonight the dreamscape seems unsteady. Energy shivers beneath my bare feet as I walk, squelching up between my toes like mud on a beach. Is there some special meaning to that? Should I worry about it? Or is the dreamscape just harder to control some nights than others? I look behind me and see my path marked in thin lines of golden fire on the plain, as always. And as always, I take a moment to memorize its pattern, in case I need that information in the future.

I'm only now beginning to learn the rules of the place. And of my own abilities.

The doors scattered across the black plain look like cavern entrances tonight. Not naturally shaped caverns, but gaping, surreal mouths with crystal teeth jutting inward, like something out of a grade B horror movie. Waiting to swallow me whole. That's what the Gate in Mystic Caverns looked like, before we destroyed it. Now it's what all my dream doors look like, every night. Apparently that image has been burned into my brain, and no conscious effort can banish it.

But tonight the openings seem different, somehow. I can't put my finger on how, but it makes me uneasy.

I pass the nearest doors without looking inside. I already know what's behind them. Each archway allows me to gaze into a parallel world, and the closest ones will be similar to my own. Maybe a universe where my brother got an A in History instead of a C-, or Mom decorated the living room a little differently, or *Star Wars* bombed on opening night. Little changes. Such worlds have nothing to teach me, and peering into them, I have learned, is a waste of time.

I still don't know if those worlds are real or not. Oh, parallel worlds do exist—I've still got a nasty scar across my belly from the last one I visited—but whether my dreams give me access to the real thing or just show me the kinds of worlds that might exist, is something I haven't figured out yet.

As I walk along the black plain, crystal maws gaping on all sides of me, I suddenly feel a chill. Something is

wrong, very wrong. I sense the wrongness without knowing its cause, and I feel the sudden urge to run.

But no. The world of the black plain is mine, I tell
myself. My dream, under my control. Nothing can hurt
me here, because nothing can exist here without my
consent. So I have no need to flee.

That calms me a bit, and I start to look around, seeking the source of my unease. When I find it at last, the
shock is so great that for a moment I can hardly think,
much less absorb what I'm seeing.

She's standing maybe ten yards away from me, a slender young girl with wind-mussed hair and enormous
eyes. Or maybe it's a boy; the lean body offers no clear
sign of gender. Complex geometric patterns flow across
her body, sketched in golden light, and they change
when I try to look directly at them. It's as if my brain
can't decide exactly what the patterns are supposed to
be, so it keeps trying different ones.

A stranger. In my dream!

I can sense the otherness in her, and I know instinctively that she senses it in me. This isn't just some image
my mind has created, but an alien presence invading the
landscape of my sleeping mind. An intruder, where no
intruder should be.

I open my mouth to speak, but words never have a
chance to get out.

She turns.

She runs.

I hesitate for a moment, then begin to run after her.
But her legs are longer than mine, and she seems to know
the twists and turns of the dreamscape better than I do;
I'm hard pressed not to lose her. Several times she makes
a sharp turn to pass behind one of the crystal arches, and
I have to slow down to keep from impaling myself.

What will I do if I catch her? Block her path? Tackle
her to the ground?

"Hey!" I call out. "Stop! I just want to talk to you!"

She glances back at me for a second but doesn't stop running. Now we're approaching a place where the spiked arches are clustered together so tightly that it's hard to make out any space between them, but she's not slowing down at all. I can't see how she's going to make it through that tight maze, so I brace myself for whatever evasive maneuver she's about to come up with. But instead of avoiding the arches, she heads straight toward one of them. Then into it.

And she's gone, swallowed by the darkness of another world.

I skid to a stop in front of that arch, and for a moment I just stand there, struggling to absorb what I've just seen. I've been dreaming about these doors for years—though I didn't understand what they represented until recently—but never, ever, have I been able to pass through one of them. Yet beyond this arch I can see the misty shadows of another world, and I know that the girl I've been chasing is out there now, somewhere on the other side of the gate.

Holy crap.

Slowly, warily, I reach out a hand, trying to extend it through the arch. Always before, such efforts have failed.

It fails this time as well.

Standing in the middle of the black plain, I experience a kind of fear I never felt before. This dreamscape is my territory. MINE. How can someone else enter it? Why would this invader be able to enter a doorway that was conjured by my dreaming mind, while I, its creator, am stuck at the threshold?

It matters. I know that instinctively. This is more than just a dream.

But I don't have a clue how to make sense of it.

||||||||||||||

When I first woke up, it took me a moment to remember where I was. The ceiling overhead was unfamiliar, with thick crown molding where none should have been, and an antique lamp of painted glass hanging from its center, now dark. The furniture was weathered pine with dark brass fittings, wholly unfamiliar. The cotton quilt I had thrown off while tossing and turning was country calico, not something I would ever have chosen for myself.

Then I remembered.

I shut my eyes for a moment, trying to come to terms with the recent changes in my life. Mom, Tommy, and I were living in Berkeley Springs now, in the home of Rose and Julian Bergen, distant relatives who we'd been told to call Aunt and Uncle. They'd generously taken Mom in after our house had burned down, and when Tommy and I returned to this world we'd joined her there. Their house was a rambling, century-old creation with period gingerbread details adorning its wraparound porch, and plenty of guest rooms for visitors. It was packed to the brim with antiques, and original works by local artists hung on every wall. A museum curator would have been envious. Normally it was the kind of house I would have enjoyed visiting, and I could have spent many days exploring its nooks and crannies, but given the circumstances that had brought us here, it was hard to take pleasure in anything.

I reached out to the nightstand and took up the sketchpad I kept next to it. I knew from experience that I had to record my dream as soon as I woke up or the details would fade from mind. Each time I returned from the black plain I recorded the path I had walked through the dreamscape, along with notes about any doors I had opened. Their patterns reminded me of the glowing lines that had appeared inside the Shadows' Gate just before we crossed through it, as well as the codex that I'd activated later to get us home. They were all maps, I understood now, only they charted meta-physical currents instead of roads. Maybe if I studied enough of them I could learn how to read them—or even design them—and then I could—

Do what? Travel between the worlds again?

The mere thought of it made me shiver.

"Jesse!" Aunt Rose's voice resounded up the stair-case and through my bedroom door. "Breakfast!"

I glanced at the window. There was light seeping in around the edges of the heavy shade. I'd slept longer than usual.

"Jesse?"

"I hear you!" I yelled. "I'll be right down."

I tried to do a quick sketch of the girl (boy?) I had seen in my dream, but my drawing came out looking like a cartoon. Try as I might to capture the patterns that had flowed across her body, they were already fading from memory, angles and lines slithering from my mental grasp before I could commit them to paper.

*Start without me,* I wanted to yell down to her, but I knew that she would never do that. Food was more than physical nourishment to Aunt Rose, it was a vehicle of emotional bonding. Which meant that family meals had existential significance, and she wouldn't start this one until all of us were present.

With a sigh I finally closed the sketchbook, slipped on a robe, and turned the lamp off. Then, with the pad tucked under my arm, I headed downstairs to join my family.

||||||||||||||

Coming home.

It should feel good, shouldn't it? Especially after spending time in a parallel universe as terrifying as the one called Terra Prime, being hunted by shapechangers and angry undead. Home was familiar. Home was safe.

Home was the one place where you could relax and be yourself.

That was the theory, anyway.

But the home that I'd known all my life was gone. The house I'd grown up in was ash. A lifetime of artwork, into which I'd poured my very soul, ash. My journal, my computer, my schoolbooks, my jewelry, the dolls that I'd kept since childhood because they brought back special memories . . . all of it gone forever. You didn't appreciate how much those things kept you grounded until you lost them all.

Tommy was still around, and in some ways we were closer than ever, but he wasn't the same kid he'd been before. We both slept with kitchen knives under our pillows now, and I knew he wouldn't hesitate to use his if he had to. Granted, some of the nasty things that might come calling were not flesh and blood, but at least we'd be prepared to face those that were.

He told me that late at night he sometimes heard voices. As if people were whispering by his bedside, too softly for him to make out the words. He said they sounded like the ghosts in Shadowcrest, so these were probably ghosts as well. But were they local spirits, drawn to the strange boy who could sense their presence, or something more ominous? Shadowlord spies, perhaps. Spirits of the dead who had followed Tommy home from his prison cell in Shadowcrest.

Neither of us sleep much these days.

As for Mom, she was alive, but her spirit was sorely wounded. The night our house burned down she'd managed to escape the flames, but not before inhaling more smoke than human lungs were meant to contain. She'd stopped breathing altogether on the way to the hospital (the EMTs told us later) and though they managed to bring her back to life, apparently something in her brain had gotten damaged in the process.

*Don't be discouraged,* the doctors told us. *She may get better over time.* But it was clear from the way they talked to us that they didn't really believe that.

Some days weren't too bad. Some days she seemed almost normal. Other days she might not remember who we were staying with, or the names of her own children. It was heartbreaking to witness, and I couldn't help but feel that I was responsible. I was the one with the forbidden Gift, who had drawn the Shadows' attention to us. I was the one whose dreams had caused the Greys to kidnap my brother, thinking he might be a Dreamwalker, and burn our house to hide the evidence of their visit. If I'd just been a normal kid, with normal dreams, none of this ever would have happened.

And then there was Rita. I still didn't know if my former traveling companion was dead, or a prisoner on Terra Prime, or trapped between the worlds. If not for me, she would still be safe at home.

Breakfast that morning was pretty stressful. Not because the food was bad. Aunt Rose made killer french toast, and the mere sight of it made my mouth water. And not because the company was lacking. She and her husband Julian were genuinely warm people, hospitable to an extreme. They'd taken in our whole family when we were homeless, hadn't they? And they were both pleasantly quirky. Rose was an accomplished ceramics artist, and her husband . . . well, hunting wasn't my thing, but Julian had taken me out target shooting once and taught me how to clean, load, and shoot a variety of guns, which might be a useful skill someday.

No, everything about breakfast was just fine, except that my brain was still buzzing with details of my strange dream, and what I really wanted was to show Tommy my drawings and see what he thought about them. Sometimes he had insights that a person more firmly rooted in reality might not. But first the ritual of breakfast had to be satisfied, so I put my sketchbook beside my plate, and after a moment's homage to the pile of luscious french toast in the middle of the table, went to the pantry to fetch my second favorite breakfast, toaster strudel. I didn't want to risk having all that syrup around my drawings.

Of course, as soon as Rose saw the sketchpad she asked what I was working on. I said I was drawing a character for Tommy, an illustration for one of his games. Of course she asked to see it. So I opened the pad to my drawing of the dream visitor and showed her that. My brother played along, leaning over to look at my work and murmuring, "Yeah. Yeah. That's it!" I could sense how curious he was, but he didn't ask me any questions.

We'd become well practiced at hiding the truth from family.

Then Rose reminded me about her booth at a local art gallery, and how I really should display some of my work there. We had that conversation pretty much every morning. Berkeley Springs was a haven for local artists, and there was a converted mill on the outskirts of town where people could rent booths and sell their work. Rose had a table for her pottery, and she kept trying to convince me to display some of my drawings there. She seemed to think it would help with my emotional healing, though she never said that directly. Truth was, under normal circumstances I would have jumped at the chance to display my artwork in a real gallery setting. But all my pieces had burned in the house fire, so I had nothing to display. Unfazed, Rose pointed out (again) that I could always paint something new, and she offered (again) to buy me any supplies I needed.

Art heals, right?

Finally breakfast wound down and it was possible to take my leave of the family. As I left the room I heard

Tommy follow suit. He walked behind me in silence through the house, holding back any questions he had until we could find a place to talk privately.

As we passed by the front parlor I saw Uncle Julian's gun cabinet, which had been adapted from a 1930s wardrobe. It now had shatterproof glass in the front and a modern lock on the bottom drawer. He'd told me it was a compromise between his desire to have a gun rack on the wall and his wife's demand that weapons be stored under lock and key. Of course he explained to me during my shooting lesson that you would never fire a rifle in the house, for fear of the bullet going through a wall and killing someone in the next room. I didn't bother to argue that if the servants of the undead came for you in the middle of the night, you might deem it worth the risk. I just studied the cabinet when he wasn't around, noted that the back of it wasn't as solidly constructed as the front, and stashed a crowbar behind the cushions of a nearby couch, just in case.

Past the parlor was the front door. As we left the house I looked around the porch to make sure that no one else was outside, then sat down in one of several squeaky metal chairs and handed Tommy the sketch pad. He settled onto a nearby wooden bench and whistled softly under his breath as he flipped through my latest drawings. He stopped when he got to my picture of the girl. "This is from a dream?"

"Someone I saw in a dream. I think she came from outside it."

He looked up at me, eyes wide. "No shit?"

I nodded solemnly. "No shit."

I told him the whole story. I tried not to sound too anxious, but once I started putting the experience into words, I realized just how truly bizarre—and threatening—the situation really was.

Tommy looked over my drawings while I talked, and

when I was done he turned back to my portrait of the intruder. "This looks like anime."

Startled, I realized that he was right. I wasn't a big fan of Japanese animation, but Tommy was, and I'd caught sight of enough brief snatches while he was watching to recognize the general artistic style. And yes, the over-sized eyes, wildly spiked hair, and other subtle details of disproportion did indeed suggest that genre. Did that mean my dream invader was some kind of Japanese cartoon character? From a style of media I didn't even watch? What kind of sense did that make?

"Could be an avatar," Tommy mused.

"An avatar?"

"You know. Like in a computer game. It's an image that you use to represent yourself in a fantasy universe."

"I know what an avatar is," I said sharply. "What makes you think this is one?"

He shrugged. "Young androgynous figure with strange magical effects floating around it . . . pretty common design elements, really. The anime crowd loves that kind of thing."

I was silent for a moment, trying to wrap my brain around this new concept. "So . . . you think the avatar's owner wasn't really in my dream? He or she was just projecting a fantasy image into it?"

"*You* weren't in your dream either," he reminded me. "It's like when you play a computer game. You create a fictional identity that allows you to interact with it, and its image is visible, walking around inside the game universe like a real person, but you're not really *there* in any physical sense." He paused. "Maybe someone did the same kind of thing with your dream. Treating your brain like a multi-player platform."

"If that was the case, wouldn't I have had complete control over the programming?"

"You'd think," he agreed.

But what if I was just imagining the whole thing? Dreamwalkers were supposed to go insane over time. Maybe an early symptom was that you thought strangers were invading your dreams.

It was an unnerving concept.

Just then my phone vibrated. Pulling it out of my pocket, I saw that I had a text message from Devon. I continued talking as I went to read it. "If so, then the next question is—"

I stopped. And stared at the phone. I could feel all the color drain from my face.

"Jesse?" Tommy was immediately on high alert. "What is it?"

Slowly I turned the phone so he could see it. The message was only two words, but as he read it I saw his eyes go wide in astonishment.

"Holy crap," he muttered.

*Rita's back,* it said.

# 2

**T**HE ELEVATOR'S CAGE carried Isaac smoothly down into the earth, its lamp revealing rough-hewn rock walls pressing in on every side. Two years ago Isaac might have found the closeness unsettling, but compared to the dank, lightless tunnels of the Warrens, he now found it downright inviting.

Besides, he had bigger things to worry about.

He practiced breathing steadily as the elevator passed through level after level of Shadowcrest's underground complex, offering fleeting glimpses of the floors where the Guild's most secretive business took place. He tried not to fidget. Real Shadows didn't fidget. They didn't shift their weight nervously from foot to foot, or pace from one side of the steel cage to the other, working off their nervous energy. They certainly didn't crush a letter from their father in sweaty hands until it looked more like a crumpled wad of toilet paper than a meaningful communication.

Swallowing dryly, Isaac unwadded the short note and read it one last time. It offered no more insight into his father's intentions than the last ten readings.

*Well of Souls*
*Midnight*
*Lord Leonid Antonin, Umbra Maja*

He hadn't even known that his father was back in Virginia Prime until that note arrived. The elder Antonin had been attending to business in another sphere for the last few weeks—some kind of probability survey in the Sauran Cluster—and Isaac had been stuck in limbo, waiting for his judgment. Oh, his mother had welcomed him home right away, and had championed his cause among the other Antonin elders, encouraging them to accept him back into the fold despite the fact that he'd run away for two years. But she was still alive, an *umbra mina,* so her influence among the Shadows was limited. Not until his father returned would Isaac's fate be decided.

And now there was this note. With no explanation.

Isaac had no clue what to expect from his father. The days when human affection might have impacted the Shadowlord's actions were long past, and whatever undead emotions coursed through his heart now were shadowy and mysterious things, beyond the understanding of a mere teenager. Leonid Antonin had accepted First Communion—the transformative Shadow ritual—soon after Isaac's birth, so his son had no memory of him that didn't involve moaning soul shards and eerie whispers from other worlds. Not exactly the kind of father it was easy to bond with.

And then of course there were all the other souls that

gazed out at him from his father's eyes. One never got used to that.

With a sigh Isaac shoved the crumpled note back into his pocket and wiped his sweaty palms on his jeans to dry them. At least he was alone in the elevator. Displaying this much agitation in front of an *umbra maja* would have reflected poorly on his entire family and probably doomed any chance of earning his father's approval. Assuming that was still possible.

The Well of Souls was a level of Shadowcrest that apprentices usually didn't enter, so Isaac had no clue why his father wanted to meet him there. It was where the darkest and most secretive rituals of the Guild were performed and, normally neophytes were not privy to such things. If he'd been just a little more paranoid, or a little more ignorant, he might have feared that his father intended to force him to submit to First Communion. But any schoolchild knew that one had to submit willingly to the transformation for there to be any hope of success.

Isaac drew in a deep breath as the elevator finally slowed and stopped; a section of steel grate moved aside to reveal a large, dimly lit chamber. As he stepped out, he saw that everything in the place was black. Black floor, black walls, black pillars supporting a black vaulted ceiling. The only hints of color were polished gold sconces affixed to the pillars, with tiny glow lamps inside, though what little light they exuded was sucked in and devoured as soon as it hit one of those merciless black surfaces. In such little light Isaac could neither see any details of the chamber, nor even be sure how large it was.

There were spirits present, of course, whispering indecipherable secrets into the darkness. Any place the Shadowlords frequented drew the dead to it like flies to rotting meat. Many of the spirits here were probably just soul shards, fragments of identity incapable of independent thought or motive, but there might be a few bound souls as well, serving as guardians of this place. Isaac had heard rumors about the ritual used to create such servants, and even by the dark standards of his Guild they sounded unusually gruesome.

Then the tenor of the whispering changed. New voices were approaching, whose cadences were familiar to Isaac; these were the spirits that were bound to serve his father. Drawing in a deep breath for courage, he turned to face their master.

Leonid Antonin was a tall man, stoic and dignified, and the long formal robes of an *umbra maja* fell from his shoulders in crisp, precise folds. He seemed more solid than most of his kind, with only the outermost edges of his form fading out into darkness, but for some reason that made his presence even more disturbing. Black, hollow eyes fixed on Isaac, cold and dispassionate; it was impossible to meet that gaze without shivering.

*This is what they want me to become*, Isaac thought, suddenly remembering why he'd run away from home in the first place. "Father," he said, bowing his head respectfully.

For a moment his father studied him in silence. Isaac dared not meet his eyes, for fear of the condemnation he might find there.

"Come," the Shadowlord commanded at last. He turned away and began to walk. Isaac followed, jogging slightly to keep up with his father's longer stride. Across the chamber and through a narrow archway they went, moving quickly, into a long corridor dressed entirely in black marble. Glow lamps in the ceiling sparked to life as they approached, illuminating white veins in the polished stone; the lamps extinguished after they passed, creating the illusion of an island of light that moved down the hallway with them. Isaac caught sight of doors marked with mysterious symbols to either side, but his father was leading him forward too quickly for him to get a good look at anything. One door was open, and there was just enough light for him to make out the shape of a vaulted chamber beyond it, with some kind of large table in the center. He thought he saw shackles lying on top of it.

He shuddered.

At the end of the long hallway they came to a pair of ornately carved doors, twice as high as a man. They reminded Isaac of the ones at the entrance to Lord Virilian's audience chamber, but these were grander in scale, and the carvings were much more complex. Images of men, beasts, skeletons, and demons had been rendered with such depth of detail that they seemed about to burst from the door's black lacquered surface. Subtle gilt highlights only increased the illusion. The artwork was beautiful but morbid, and Isaac could feel his skin crawl as he studied it.

"Images from the Lost Worlds," his father said. "Meant to remind us of the burden of responsibility that we bear, in our duty as Shadows."

*The Lost Worlds.* Those were human civilizations that had been destroyed by the coming of the Shadows. Some had been unable to handle the sudden influx of alien germs and parasites that outworlders brought with them, some had been raided so often by slave traders that their gene pool fell below the threshold required for species survival, and some simply could not face the revelation that they were no longer masters of their own fate, and died a slow spiritual death.

And then there were those rare worlds that needed to be Cleansed, because the Shadows decided they were a threat to interworld commerce. That might mean destroying the underpinnings of local technology, so that society collapsed into barbarism, or taking actions more directly destructive.

Now Isaac understood why the doors here were black. Why this whole place was black. The path to a Shadow's duty was paved in death: this was their reminder of it.

He watched as his father took hold of the ornate lever that served as a door handle and turned it to the right. Nothing happened. Then a prickling at the back of Isaac's neck alerted him to the approach of a new spirit, whose presence was far more powerful than that of the others. He could sense it approaching the door, perhaps touching it—and then the lock snicked open.

Of course, he thought. Since no one but an *umbra maja* could command spirits, any lock that required the touch of both the living and the dead would be impassable to other Guild members. It was a simple but effective security.

"Come," his father repeated as the great doors swung open—seemingly of their own accord—and Isaac followed him into a vast, shadowy chamber with tiny golden lights hanging in mid-air as far as the eye could see. Like stars in a night sky. As his eyes adjusted he could see that each light was in fact set atop a marble pedestal, and that there were walkways running around the chamber at several heights, each with its own row of pedestals, evenly spaced.

His father gestured toward one of the nearest pedestals, indicating he should approach it.

There was just enough light for Isaac to make out the shape of a golden sphere with symbols inscribed in it, protected by a glass dome. He recognized the mark of the Weavers on the glass; there were others he didn't recognize.

"We call these soul fetters," his father said, coming up behind him, "but they're not really that, you understand. Simply recording devices that store the memories of former Guild members."

Suddenly Isaac realized what he was looking at, and a wave of nausea came over him, fear so thick in his throat he could hardly breathe. This *thing* was the source of Communion, the mechanism used to pour the soul of one Shadow into another. He had to fight the urge not to back away from it, and though he managed to keep his expression calm, his heart was beating so wildly it made his chest shake. Had he been wrong about his father's intentions? Had the Shadowlord discovered a way to initiate an unwilling candidate into the ranks of the undead? Why else would he have brought Isaac down here?

But his father made no move toward him, and after a few seconds Isaac found himself able to breathe again. Turning his attention to the pedestal itself, he saw a column of small brass memorial plaques with names and dates on them. Three dates each. There was also a narrow shelf with a thick leather-bound journal on it, and as his father reached out to remove the book, his arm brushed against his son's, sucking all the heat from his flesh. Isaac tried not to flinch.

"The names on the plaques are those who contributed their memories to this particular fetter," the Shadowlord explained. "Some of the earliest date all the way back to the Dream Wars. Most are more recent. Communion didn't become common practice until centuries after that." He placed the book on the pedestal in front of Isaac and opened it. "These are the histories contained in this fetter."

Isaac looked up at him. "I thought Communion only transferred a single set of memories."

"In a technical sense, yes. But each man's input includes the memory of his own Communion. So when you accept the memories of one Shadowlord, you inherit echoes of all the others."

*Good God,* Isaac thought. That meant that a Shadow

who accepted Communion one time would absorb the memories of what, dozens of other men, hundreds? How could anyone maintain his sense of identity in the face of all that?

*Not everyone succeeds,* he reminded himself. Though it had been a long time since any Antonin had been driven insane by First Communion, the lesser bloodlines lost people regularly. Initiation into the ranks of the *umbra maja* was a high-risk enterprise, and only the strongest survived. "It sounds . . . chaotic."

"The memories of a Shadowlord fade in clarity over the centuries. A few generations down the line, only the most intense fragments remain," his father said. "But, yes." A faint, cold smile was briefly visible. "The experience can be quite disconcerting."

Isaac reached out to the book and slowly turned the pages. The paper felt ancient beneath his fingertips, and the pages made a soft rustling noise as they moved. There were handwritten notes in a variety of scripts, some of them noting major historical events, others more personal details. Every few pages he saw a new name and a set of three dates: Birth, undeath, and true death.

"These are the histories of the Shadowlords whose memories are contained in this particular fetter," his father told him. "The elders try to match each candidate to an appropriate fetter. Compatible Shadows stand a much better chance of successful Communion."

Isaac looked up at him. "So . . . you get to choose whose memories you absorb?" That certainly wasn't something they'd taught him in school.

But his father shook his head. "The living don't know enough to make an informed choice. So that decision must be made for them. But our family is ancient and highly respected, and rest assured, I would allow no outsider to dictate who *my son* was to bond with."

There was pride in his words, but also admonishment;

the combination brought a lump to Isaac's throat. He looked back at the book, unwilling to meet his father's gaze.

"So," his father said softly. "Is this what you feared so desperately? Enough to compromise your family's honor by fleeing the Guild like a frightened colt?"

The words left his mouth before he could stop them. "Shouldn't I be afraid?"

For a moment there was silence. Then: "Yes. This is a place worthy of fear."

Isaac hesitated. Normally he would never ask his father a personal question, but this was hardly a normal moment. The Shadowlord clearly wanted Isaac to understand how Communion worked; wasn't the man's own experience part of that picture?

"Were you afraid?" he asked. "When they handed you your first fetter, when you had to open your mind to the memories of so many Shadowlords? Didn't that frighten you?"

"I was terrified," his father admitted. "And any Shadowlord who claims that he wasn't, is lying. But I understood that my family's honor was at stake, which was far more important to me than my own fleeting pleasure."

Isaac said nothing.

"There is beauty in the change," his father told him. The ghosts around him had grown strangely quiet; perhaps they, too, were listening. "The pleasures of the living world are but pale shadows of it. To step beyond the boundaries of one's birth world and plunge into the chaos that lies *between,* to feel one's soul resonate with the music of the spheres, to know with utter certainty that any world which can exist, does exist, and that we — and *we alone* — have the power of free passage between them . . . What earthly pursuit can rival that?"

Isaac had never heard his father talk that way before. He had never heard any Shadowlord talk that way before.

For a moment he was at a loss for words. "Aren't we supposed to not feel passion?" he stammered. "For anything? I mean, that's what they keep telling me."

His father chuckled; it was a disconcertingly human sound. "The passions of the living are forbidden to us, my son. As are the passions of the dead—though those are so bizarre that few men are tempted by them. To cling to either world too closely threatens the balance of spirit that we need to survive. But there are passions unique to our kind, more intense than anything you can imagine. There is a kind of beauty that only the *umbrae majae* can see, senses that a man gains access to only when he is willing to leave his life behind forever. And of course there are the memories—centuries of knowledge and experience that attend one's every thought." He paused. "Shadows may fear their First Communion, but none regret it afterward."

Isaac looked back at the fetter. "Is there one of these that contains your memories? Or don't they make one of those until after you die?"

"I have a soul fetter, though it's not stored here. Right now it's functioning as a recording device. Nothing more. Not until I die will my memories be available to someone else." A corner of his mouth twitched. "It would be quite confusing otherwise."

"But if all a soul fetter does is give you knowledge, how does it transform you?"

A faint smile ghosted across his father's face; he seemed pleased by the question. "It doesn't. Communion simply grants a man knowledge of how to join the ranks of the *umbra majae*. He must embrace the change on his own."

"So . . . you could undergo First Communion without becoming a Shadowlord?"

For a moment, there was silence. "No man who has gained such knowledge has ever chosen that course."

"But you *could,*" Isaac persisted. "In theory, at least. Right? You could absorb all those memories, all that knowledge, and remain a living man. Couldn't you?"

His father's gaze was solemn. "In theory. But the memories you absorb come from men who chose to walk the line between life and death. Your mind would contain all the reasons they did so, the force of their commitment, their satisfaction with the results. Resisting such influence would be like swimming against a rip tide. And what would the point be? Higher knowledge is wasted on the *umbrae minae.* Only by embracing the change can one map the currents of the universe."

"What is it you want from me?" Isaac asked suddenly. "Why did you bring me here?"

If his bluntness displeased his father, the Shadowlord showed no sign of it. "I simply wish to advise you to keep your options open. If you resume your training to be an *umbra maja,* all paths will remain open to you. But if you surrender that honor, and commit to a more lowly rank instead, doors will be shut in your face. Your education will be restricted to the things that living men are allowed to learn. And your status in the Guild will be severely constrained. All for what purpose? So you can make a public show of rejecting an Antonin's duty? What will it gain you?"

Isaac said nothing. No words were safe.

"You can undergo the training of an *umbra maja* without setting a date for your First Communion. Perhaps in twenty or thirty years you will feel differently than you do now. Perhaps you will hunger to join your father in exploring unknown worlds, to bring honor to your family. There is no need to close that door forever, Isaac."

He said nothing.

"Do not shame the family name unless there is need for it," his father said quietly. There was an edge of harshness to his tone now, but delicately sheathed, like a knife in a velvet scabbard.

*So that's it then,* Isaac thought bitterly. *I'm free to follow another path, so long as no one finds out about it. And what if I don't play along? Will you cast me out of the family? Or is this just a test, to see how much I really want to come back?*

But he couldn't deny that his father's suggestion had appeal. As a Shadowlord in training Isaac would have access to documents and artifacts that no *umbra mina* would ever be allowed to see. He would study the true history of the Guild, taught by men who had witnessed those events. Or rather, men who had absorbed the memories of others who had witnessed them.

But he would be living a lie. Pretending to be something he was not.

For his family's sake.

Isaac observed how the edges of his father's body faded out into the darkness. He felt the unearthly chill that enveloped the man like a shroud. He heard the whispering of the dead souls who never left his father's side; invisible harpies who never fell silent. Maybe in twenty years Isaac might be willing to transform into a creature like that, but it didn't seem likely. Still, all his father was asking was for him to keep his options open. To pretend there was a chance that someday he would change his mind. Couldn't he manage that, if it was the price of acceptance?

Isaac looked back down at the book, now open to the first page. *Twice-decorated Grand Crusader in the Final War between the Shadows and the Dreamwalkers,* it said. Hell, Isaac hadn't even known there *was* a war between Shadowlords and Dreamwalkers. All he'd been told was that the Guilds had banded together to hunt the dreamers down, to save the human worlds from destruction.

This fleeting reference hinted at centuries of history he knew nothing about.

Jesse had asked about the dreaming Gift, he remembered suddenly. Had she done that because her brother was suspected of dreamwalking, or for some more personal reason? These records might hold answers for both of them.

"I see no reason to choose my path now." He formed his words carefully, trying to echo his father's formal tone. "There'll be time enough later, when I understand the situation better. I acted rashly when I fled, for which I humbly seek your forgiveness and the forgiveness of my family. I will resume my former course of study immediately, if the Guildmaster sanctions it."

A cold hand fell upon his shoulder. He tried to ignore the icy burning sensation where it touched him, to focus on the warmth that the gesture was meant to communicate. Or maybe it was just meant to be cold approval. Who knew what a Shadowlord was feeling?

"I accept your apology," his father said, "and I am sure His Grace will approve your petition." For the first time since Isaac's return there was pride in the man's voice. "Welcome back, my son."

# 3

## BERKELEY SPRINGS
## WEST VIRGINIA

### JESSE

**B**Y THE NEXT MORNING I was so brimming with nervous energy that I felt like I was about to explode. There was no way to give it safe outlet indoors, so I went outside and started pacing the length of the porch. Back and forth, back and forth . . . It helped a little, but it also left my mind free to worry. Tommy came out and sat down on one of the metal chairs to watch me. He had as much invested in this as I did, and I could tell he was equally nervous.

Devon had been disturbingly uncommunicative since Rita's return. Normally he texted me as often and as casually as most people breathed, but after his first mind-blowing announcement of her arrival he'd sent only a few sparse messages, maddeningly uninformative.

*Time dilation maybe,* he'd texted. *Will drive up 2morrow we can talk.*

*How did u find her?* I asked.

*Later. Will leave here after breakfast. Promise.*

After that there was only silence.

"You think he'll be here soon?" my brother asked.

"It's a two-hour trip," I pointed out. Suddenly I realized I didn't know if Devon was a morning person or not. What time did he eat breakfast? We could be waiting for a while.

Tommy asked, "You think he showed his dad the fetter?"

"I don't know," I said. It was frustrating to have no answers for him. "We'll find out when he gets here."

Devon had wanted to tell his Dad the truth about what happened to us in the other world, so I'd given him the glow lamp. The alien tech with its thought-sensitive light would at least bear witness to the fact that he wasn't making the whole story up, though what Dr. Tilford would deduce beyond that was anyone's guess. What if he decided that Devon's story was just too crazy to believe, tech or no tech? What if he became concerned about his son's mental stability, and thought that maybe my influence had caused him to start raving about shapechangers and world gates and undead necromancers? If so, he might never let me see Devon again.

I couldn't handle that. Devon and Tommy had become vital psychological anchors for me, my only two confidants in a world gone mad. Who else could I confide in, when I feared that my Gift was unhinging my mind? Mom had always served as my rock—and I hungered to tell her the truth about Terra Prime now—but I knew she wasn't strong enough to handle this stuff. She was having a difficult enough time dealing with one world, without my throwing parallel universes at her.

I needed Devon.

*He's coming up here,* I told myself as I paced. *Which*

*means his father gave him the car. So he's okay with Devon seeing me. That's a good sign, right?*

I looked at my watch for the hundredth time. The small hand hadn't moved significantly since my last check.

I'd dreamed about Rita the night before. I dreamed about her every night, guilt-drenched nightmares from which I woke up sweating and trembling. But this last dream wasn't a regular nightmare. Nor was it a symbolic dream full of mystical doors and arcane symbols, and a sense that the universe was a puzzle I must solve immediately or terrible things would happen to me. This one was simply a memory, like a movie playing out in my brain.

I witnessed our flight from Shadowcrest and our descent to the crystal Gate that controlled passage between the worlds. I relived the moment when the Greys jumped us and all hell broke loose. I felt blood splattering my face as I stabbed a Grey in the neck with a ball point pen, to free my brother. I saw how we ran back to the Gate, grabbing hold of each other as we dove into the unknown darkness between the worlds. Rita had gripped my arm so tightly that her fingernails dug into my flesh; I still had the marks. So what had gone wrong? How did we get separated? Even in my dream I couldn't identify the moment it happened. One minute she was hanging on to me for dear life, and the next minute I was immersed in the chaos between the worlds. Then Devon, Tommy and I arrived in Mystic Caverns without her. Had she lagged a split-second behind the rest of us, and been trapped in Terra Prime when the Gate collapsed? Or had she entered the archway with us, but lost her grip on me afterward, and gotten lost in that terrible place? Try as I might, I couldn't remember.

At least I knew now that she wasn't dead. That eased the burden of guilt a little. And time dilation could explain why she'd arrived here a week later than the rest of us, though it still didn't answer the question of why that phenomenon had affected her, and not Devon or Tommy or me. But soon she would be here. Then I would learn what had happened to her.

IIIIIIIIIIIIIIIIII

Shortly before noon, Dr. Tilford's Lexus drove up the gravel road leading to the house. The sight of the car stirred such powerful memories that for a moment I flashed back to the night we had abandoned it in the woods—that awful night which began in one universe and ended in another. By the time it pulled into the driveway and stopped, my heart was pounding.

The motor shut off. Three doors opened.

Three?

The first to get out was Devon's dad. I guess I shouldn't have been surprised that he came along, all things considered. Devon must have told him *something*. But was he here to support his son, or to confront the bad influences that were misleading him? Then Devon disembarked from the passenger side. I wanted to run to him, to throw my arms around him and hug him until his ribs hurt . . . but with his father there, such a display was out of the question. So I just stood at the head of the stairs, waving and smiling, my heart pounding, waiting for him to come to me at his own pace.

Then Rita got out, and when I saw the condition she was in my stomach tightened and the joy I'd felt a moment before vanished in an instant. She moved with the stiffness of someone injured, her face was cut in several places, and there was an angry purple bruise covering most of one cheek. Tommy and I had looked pretty bad when we first came home, but a week's time had muted our bruises to dull gold and our bodily aches to memory; her damage looked much more recent, and the bright purple hue of her wounds made my own fading bruises throb in sympathy. She was wearing long sleeves, I noted, and given how hot the day was, that suggested there were marks on her arms as well. I wondered if Dr. Tilford had seen them.

"Well, hello!" Aunt Rose's sudden voice exploding behind my shoulder made me jump. "You must be Jesse's friends!"

The greeting was so mundane under the circumstances that it seemed almost surreal, but Dr. Tilford just took it in stride, smiling and coming up the stairs to shake her hand as if this was a normal, everyday visit. And then my uncle came out and was introduced, and Rose asked Dr. Tilford how his trip was, and he said that it had been lovely, thank you, this part of the country was lovely, and by the way, so was her house. She beamed. The banal irrelevance of their chatter made my head spin, but there wasn't much I could do about it. I knew my aunt well enough by now to recognize that she wasn't going to leave us alone to talk about anything substantial until basic social amenities had been taken care of.

She had lunch ready and waiting for the newcomers, of course. Mom joined us there, and she offered her hand to Dr. Tilford as he entered, as if greeting a stranger. "So nice to meet you. I'm Jesse and Tommy's mom." I felt my heart sink, and I could see a shadow of concern in Dr. Tilford's eyes, but he responded graciously and shook her hand like nothing was wrong. They'd met before, of course. He was the one who had brought us back to Manassas after we'd escaped from the Shadows' prison, and driven Tommy and me home to meet my mother. So this moment was a painful reminder of how much memory she had lost.

Rose began to chatter as she set out chicken salad sandwiches and lemonade, filling what could otherwise have been an uncomfortable silence. The Fourth of July celebrations were this weekend, with a big cookout during the day and fireworks at night, so it was a pity our visitors wouldn't be here for that. Of course if they wanted to stay for it, they were welcome to, though someone might have to sleep on a couch. And the local gallery was open on the weekend, so if they wanted to stay that long, she could show them her work there. Speaking of which, she was really hoping that I would display something at her booth. Maybe the newcomers would help talk me into it?

I caught Julian looking at Rita, and sometimes Rose's eyes fixed on her a bit longer than they should have; clearly they were wondering about her bruises. But no one asked any questions about them, at least during lunch.

One small thing to be grateful for.

Not until all the food was eaten, and the social chit-chat had gone on for so long I was ready to scream, were we finally able to get away from the adults. Devon, Rita, Tommy and I headed up to Tommy's room in the attic to talk. It was a narrow room that ran the length of the house, and we figured it would offer us decent privacy. A small cot and chest of drawers had been fitted into one tight corner, and there were boxes everywhere, many with a film of dust on them. Makeshift accommodations at best, but as soon as Tommy saw the space he declared this was where he wanted to sleep, and I totally understood why. With two dormer windows offering direct access to the roof, he had a quick and easy escape route should aliens come calling.

As soon as we were alone, I turned and hugged Rita like the world was about to end. I'd spent a week thinking she was dead—or worse—and blaming myself. Now she was here, in the flesh, and not only was I glad to see her, but the guilt that had been my constant companion since our return was finally easing its death grip on my soul.

"Hey, girl. I do need to breathe." She chuckled as I let her go, but I saw the glimmer of tears in her eyes, and there were some in mine as well. It was a pretty overwhelming moment.

"What the hell happened?" I asked her. "How did you get separated from us?"

She shook her head. "No clue. One moment I was right there next to you, then next . . . well, everything was gone. I mean, *everything*. The Gate, the cave, all of you guys, even the world we had just come from, completely gone. I was so terrified. I just couldn't move, couldn't breathe. I couldn't even think. Then suddenly I felt myself falling, and I landed on something hard. It was totally dark. I yelled for you guys, but no one answered. I didn't know if you'd been lost between the worlds, or killed back at the arch, or . . . or what. I didn't even know where I was, but when I felt around all I could find was rubble. Oh God, Jesse, I was so scared."

I reached out and rubbed her shoulder. It seemed to steady her a bit.

"I fumbled for my flashlight, then realized it had been taken by the Shadows. I had no light. It was so dark." She shivered. "The place smelled damp, like a cave, so I guessed I was back in Mystic Caverns. But the room the Gate was in had been enormous, and this place . . . When I called out your names the echo didn't sound right for that. So I reached out over my head and I . . ." Her voice broke for a moment. I saw her tremble as she fought to pull herself together. "There was rock only a few feet above me. It was like I was sealed in a tomb."

"Shhh," Devon said. He put a hand on her other shoulder and squeezed gently. "You're here now, okay? You're safe."

"I just lay there," she whispered. "Overwhelmed. I knew that I needed to do *something*, not just lay there and wait to die. But what? I didn't even know which way was out, and crawling randomly in the dark wasn't going to get me anywhere. I never felt so helpless in my life.

"But then as my eyes started to adjust to the darkness, I realized that there was a faint light off to one side. Really faint, barely enough to see by, but at least it was something." She drew in a deep, shaky breath. "I can't even tell you what that moment was like. Like something inside me was coming back to life, and it wanted to live. It wanted desperately to live. So I began to scrabble toward the light, mostly by feel. It seemed hopeless, there were mounds of rubble in my way, and I had no idea where I was going, but I just kept crawling toward the light."

God. I couldn't even imagine what that must have been like. When Devon and Tommy and I had arrived back home Mystic Caverns was in the process of collapsing, and it was hard to believe any of the chambers had survived intact. If Rita arrived after we did, which was what it sounded like, it was a miracle she'd found any space big enough to crawl through.

"Slowly the light grew brighter," Rita continued "and eventually I got to a place where there was an opening overhead, and I could see stars through it. And that's . . ." her voice broke for a moment, "that's when I lost it," she whispered. "Just laid there and cried like a baby."

Suddenly it hit me how recent all this was for her. Devon and Tommy and I'd had a week to recover from our ordeal in Shadowcrest—and to heal our wounds—but if Rita had just arrived, then for her all that had happened yesterday. I reached out and hugged her again, oh so tightly, and she just held me, while Devon rubbed her shoulder sympathetically and even Tommy offered her a fleeting touch of reassurance. "I must have arrived pretty close to the surface," she whispered. "I don't know how that happened. Maybe without its Gate, a portal can't stay anchored right. And we destroyed the Gate that controlled this one." She laughed weakly. "Maybe I owe my life to a malfunction."

"Whatever the reason," Devon said, "you're damn lucky. The lower levels are a wreck. Police couldn't get down there at all."

Rita shut her eyes and sighed heavily. "When I finally climbed out, that's when I saw the scraps of yellow police tape all over the place. The wind had torn it loose in a few places, so I figured it had been put up a while ago. That was when I realized that you guys must have arrived before I did. That you might be safe." She opened her eyes again. "I managed to find my way to a nearby house, slipped in an open window, ate some food, and borrowed some clean clothes. They had a landline phone, so I used it to call Devon, to see if he'd gotten home safely. His dad answered." She looked at Devon. "He didn't have a clue who I was."

"We couldn't tell anyone about you," he said. "If you never came back . . ."

She nodded. "People would keep looking for me, even after you guys came home, and there would have been more media attention. Don't worry, I get it."

Devon looked at me. "Since our cover story was that we'd been kidnapped, I told Dad that someone we'd met in our captivity had turned up, but was hurt. He didn't ask any questions, just drove us out there to pick Rita up. I texted you on the way, but when you started asking questions, I didn't have any other information to give you . . . I'm so sorry, Jesse."

" 'It's okay," I said softly. "I understand."

"Once we got back, and Rita was all cleaned up, Dad gave her something to help her relax." He drew in a deep breath. "I told him about Terra Prime, and what really happened to us. Maybe it wasn't the best time for that conversation, but with Rita back, I couldn't put it off any more."

"How'd it go?" Tommy asked.

Devon hesitated. "He didn't accuse me of being crazy, or of getting into his drug cabinet or anything. So I guess you could say it went well. I had given him the glow lamp a few days earlier, figuring if he looked it over before we talked that might help. But he didn't say anything about it. Just listened to me without saying a word, and then said we needed to come up here together, so all of us could talk."

I opened my mouth to say something, but a call from downstairs came first.

"Jessica!" It was Julian. "Tommy!"

We looked at each other, then Tommy yelled back, "What is it?"

"Dr. Tilford wants to talk to the four of you. Can you all come down to the parlor, please?"

I looked at Devon. His face was ashen.

"It'll be all right," I told him. "He's seen the glow lamp. He'll come to the right conclusions."

I could see how much effort it took for him to force a smile to his face. "Yeah. And the fact that he knows from those earlier tests that our DNA doesn't match, so I'm not really his son . . . it won't affect his reaction at all, right?"

There was nothing I could say to that, so we headed downstairs to talk to Dr. Tilford.

||||||||||||

The glow lamp on the coffee table appeared as bland and uninteresting as an object could possibly be. If you looked closely enough you could make out the Weaver's etched sigil etched into the small fetter, but it was subtle—like a watermark—and easy to miss. Other than that, the thing was featureless. A child who was shopping for a glass marble would probably pass it by in favor of something more interesting.

Dr. Tilford gestured for us to take seats around the table, which we did. He was a handsome man, with skin the color of dark chocolate and the long, lean features of East Africa. Given that Devon wasn't really his son, the resemblance between them was remarkable. But his expression was that of a statue right now, rigid and unreadable. Even his eyes, as he looked us over one by one, revealed nothing of his thoughts. At least with the other adults gone we could talk freely.

"You understand," he said, once we were all seated, "I was limited in what tests I could run. I didn't want to show this item to anyone else, lest word get back to the government that there was an object of unknown tech in the neighborhood. Trust me when I tell you, that wouldn't be good."

Devon nodded solemnly. I got the impression his father was referencing a specific past incident and Devon knew what it was.

"The object appears to be made of quartz crystal," Dr. Tilford continued, "albeit a more perfect specimen than we usually see in nature. I could detect no structural or chemical variation of any kind, which suggests there isn't a physical mechanism. Regarding electromagnetic energy, there's nothing detectable when the item is dormant, but there's a brief spike when it's activated. The lamp appears to require the electromagnetic charge of human skin to activate it. I was able to trigger it with my bare finger and with a conductive stylus, but not with an insulating object." He stared at it for a moment, his eyes narrowing slightly. "The necessity of *intent* defies all my analysis. How one's desire to have the lamp activate figures into the trigger mechanism, I still don't know, but given my other findings, my guess is that it's some sort of electromagnetic signal." His lips tightened. "That's all my tests could tell me—enough to raise new questions, but not enough to answer the one that matters most."

He reached out to the lamp and touched it. There was a strange hesitancy to the gesture, almost a sense of awe. The light flickered on briefly, then off again. The blue glow was dimmer than before. Whatever energy source powered the thing was clearly starting to run out.

"No one has published any articles hinting at this kind of tech," he said quietly. "Not even speculating that something of this nature could be produced. I suppose it's possible someone has been working on a completely new type of technology, and not a whisper of it has gotten out . . . but secrets on that scale are hard to keep." He shook his head, clearly frustrated by his inability to solve this puzzle.

Devon leaned forward slightly. "So you believe it could be from another world?" Another question, unvoiced, hung in the air, edged with silent desperation: *You believe what I told you about our experiences?*

For a long moment Dr. Tilford stared at the marble. I found I was holding my breath. "Are you familiar with Clarke's Law?" he said at last.

Tommy spoke up first. "Any technology sufficiently advanced is indistinguishable from magic." When I looked at him in surprise, he said, "What? I read science fiction."

A faint smile flickered across Dr. Tilford's lips. "Our army has developed a pain ray for crowd control. Point it at a target and he or she will feel pain, without actually being harmed. Just like in science fiction. Scientists have isolated the force required for a functional tractor beam, so we may see that in our lifetimes. A 3D printer has been used to replicate pizza. The speed of light has been altered in a laboratory." He shook his head. "So many things done today that would have been considered impossible a mere decade ago. Ten years from now the world will be so far advanced that aspects of it would seem magical to us today . . . but the seeds of that future technology are all around us. No unearthly source is required to explain them." With a deep sadness in his eyes, he looked at his son. "I'm sorry, Devon. What you're asking me to believe . . . this artifact alone isn't proof of it."

The crestfallen look in Devon's eyes made my heart ache. "I understand," he whispered.

Dr. Tilford looked around at all of us. "The four of you were held prisoner for a week, isolated from the world. God alone knows what you experienced. Your captors appear to have drugged you with something in the Rohypnol class, which makes all memories suspect." He looked back at his son. "So, I'm sorry, Devon. I do think you genuinely believe what you told me, but that doesn't mean it really happened."

Devon lowered his head. All he had to do was indicate he wanted help, and Rita and Tommy and I would back him up. If the four of us reported the same events, wouldn't that be convincing? Rohypnol didn't cause *mass* hallucinations, did it? But Devon just sighed and shook his head. He knew his father better than we did, and maybe he sensed that whatever story we told, Dr. Tilford would just explain it away like he had done with the glow lamp. And if his explanation cast the rest of us in a bad light, he might forbid Devon from seeing us.

Dr. Tilford turned to me, and the look in his eyes became gentle. "Devon told me what happened to your mother. I'm so sorry."

I looked down at my hands. I was grateful for a change of subject, but wished he'd chosen something else to talk about. "The doctors say there's not much hope."

"The brain is a remarkably resilient organ. When one part of it ceases to function, another sometimes take over its duties. Usually that involves vital processes: speech, physical movement, things a person needs to function. But medical science is full of surprises. Don't give up hope yet, Jesse."

I blinked away tears that were coming to my eyes. "Thanks," I whispered. Why did a cool, rational guy like him offering sympathy affect me so deeply?

Dr. Tilford looked back to Devon. "Could I keep the lamp, to study it further?" His tone was quiet, even casual, but you could sense the intense hunger behind it. He was a scientist. The lamp was a mystery. He wanted it.

Devon hesitated. "It was given to all of us. So everyone would have to agree."

My first impulse was to say yes. The lamp was clearly running out of power, and soon wouldn't be useful to anyone. Why not let him study it further? But it wasn't that easy to give up an alien artifact, especially when it was the only proof you had been to another world. "Could we maybe have some time to talk about it?"

"Of course." He nodded. "Let me leave you to that, then." As he stood up to take his leave, his eyes never left the fetter; you could tell how much he wanted to pick it up and take it with him. He walked around the table, heading toward the door, then paused beside his son. He looked down at Devon for a moment, then put his hand on his shoulder. Briefly. Silently. Just a fleeting touch, but it spoke volumes.

Then he was gone.

Devon fell back in his chair with a weary sigh. He reached up a hand to rub the bridge of his nose, as if the spot pained him.

"Could have been worse," Rita said gently. "He could have thought you were crazy."

"He may still think that," Devon said. "Granted, I

hadn't really expected him to believe me, but damn it, I'd hoped . . ." He shook his head as his words trailed off into silence.

"Sorry about the Rohypnol," Tommy muttered.

I blinked. "Say what?"

"It was my idea to add that to our cover story, so that we didn't have to explain too much about our disappearance. Only now, Devon's dad won't believe him because of it."

"That's not the only reason," Devon assured him. "And if you hadn't come up with that idea, we'd still be in the police station answering questions about what happened to us the week we were gone. Sooner or later one of us would have gotten the story wrong, and then all hell would have broken loose. So don't you *ever* regret that suggestion. Ever."

Tommy bit his lip and whispered, " 'Kay."

Rita turned to me. "I'm really sorry about your mom, Jesse. Didn't get a chance to say that before."

I sighed. "Yeah. Not much hope on that front, though Dr. Tilford was nice to pretend that there was."

She hesitated. "Jesse . . . you know . . . there might be Healers who could help."

I stiffened. "You mean from Terra Prime?"

Eyes wide, she nodded.

I leaned back in my chair and shut my eyes for a moment. Yes, there were Healers in the other world. Sebastian had used a fetter to heal my leg, and fetters were created by binding someone's Gift to an object, which meant that there were Healers in Terra Prime, probably a whole Guild full of them. Could someone with that kind of Gift help my mother? Possibly. But w*ould* one of them help her? That was a much bigger question, and one that Tommy and Devon and I had been debating all week.

The mere thought of dealing with someone from that

world filled me with dread. It would be best for all of us if Terra Prime just forgot we existed. But if there was someone who could help Mom? I sighed. "Even if a Healer was able to help, why would she? It's pretty clear that Guilds don't give two squats about outworlders. And how would I even find one to ask? It's not like a Google search will turn up 'Healers from Terra Prime.' "

Rita shrugged. "No clue how to find them, but once we do, the rest isn't a big mystery. They sell their Gifts, remember? There were fetters for sale all over the place in the other Luray. All we would need is money."

"I've got some savings," I mused. "But who's to say that would be enough?"

"I'll chip in," Devon offered.

"I'll throw in what little I've got," Tommy agreed.

Rita snorted lightly. "I think you can guess the state of my finances. If I had anything, you know I'd offer it."

I was so moved by their generosity that it took me a moment to find my voice. "Even if that added up to enough, we're still left with the problem of finding someone. I can't just go the Greys and ask for help in hiring a Healer, not after what we did to their Gate. They don't strike me as the forgiving type. And they work for the Shadows, who we *really* need to avoid."

"Well," Rita said, "forgive me if you've already discussed this—I'm playing catch-up here—but what about Miriam Seyer?" She raised a hand to forestall my objection. "Yeah, I know you don't trust her. I don't either. But all you need is someone to set up a meeting, right? Can't you use her for that?"

For a long time I said nothing. In my mind's eye I could see my house burning, that black-haired Seer standing across the street and watching it. Just watching it. What had brought Seyer to my home, just in time to witness the fire? It couldn't have been coincidence. Later, when I overheard her talking to Morgana in the

Seers' garden, it sounded like the two of them wanted me to be safe. But they also talked about controlling my movements, and my being part of some mysterious project they were running. Games within games within games. Every instinct in my soul warned me to keep away from her—far, far away—but Rita's suggestion had merit, there was no denying that. Seyer was one link between the worlds that did not involve Greys or Shadows. Perhaps the only one.

"Why would she help?" I asked at last. "She doesn't give a damn what happens to Mom. And her Guild seemed pretty affluent; I doubt the kind of money we could offer would tempt her."

"But you have something else she wants," Tommy said. "Your paintings, remember? She wanted to buy one. Well, now all your art is gone, so there's nothing she can buy from you, or even steal, unless you paint something new."

The thought of giving one of my paintings to Seyer made my skin crawl; it bothered me that I didn't know why. *Easy, girl. It's just a painting. Not like you're selling her your soul.* "Even if I did that, how would she find out about it? She saw my work the first time because it was in a show at the school."

Rita said, "What about the gallery your aunt was talking about? Could you put something on display there?"

"Yeah, but what are the chances Seyer would wander through on the day it happened to be there? I just don't see that happening."

"Maybe if there was some kind of publicity?" Devon suggested.

Tommy pulled out his cell phone and start scrolling through web pages. I couldn't read the text from where I was sitting, but I saw a picture of Berkeley Springs Castle flash by. Then: "Bingo!" he announced, and he turned

the phone to face us. The text was too small to read, so I
took it from him, read what he'd found, and then passed
it on to the others. The web page was *www.bsoldmillgal
lery.com.*

*Vendor list for the Independence Day Show,* it said.
Aunt Rose's name was on it. So were dozens of others.

"Of course," Tommy said, "Getting on that list would
only help if Seyer was still keeping tabs on you online."

A chill crept up my spine. "You think she's doing that?"

"Don't you?" he asked.

I wanted to say no. I wanted to believe that when we
left Terra Prime, that was the end of our involvement
with that dreadful world. But Alia Morgana had referred
to me as her *project,* which meant she probably had people keeping tabs on me. And since we knew that there
were Greys who used the internet for surveillance—
that's how they'd found out about Tommy's alleged
dreams—we'd be fools not to expect the same level of
expertise from Morgana's people.

She was watching me. The thought of it made my skin
crawl, but I knew in my gut it was true. "Only three days
away," I muttered. "Not a lot of time to paint a masterpiece."

"It doesn't have to be a masterpiece," Devon said
reasonably. "Just good enough to pique her interest."

I shut my eyes for a moment. I could see Seyer standing in front of me, her eyes glowing yellow, like a serpent's, reflecting the flames from my house. Like a
demon from Dante's Inferno.

*It's for Mom,* I told myself. Gritting my teeth, I forced
the ominous image out of my mind. *Do it for Mom.*

"All right," I muttered. "I'll talk to Aunt Rose about
painting something for the show." I shook my head.
"She'll be ecstatic about that, anyway." I handed Tommy
back his phone. "Let's see if we can't draw the serpent
out of her den."

# 4

## BERKELEY SPRINGS
## VIRGINIA

## JESSE

**I**'M NOT ALONE.

I look around, but no one else is visible in the black dreamscape. I listen as carefully as I can, but I hear nothing out of the ordinary.

No, that's not quite accurate. There's music surrounding me, a ghostly orchestral hum like you sometimes hear in the middle of the night, conjured by the vibrations of the air conditioner. Maybe real music, maybe imagined. Almost subliminal.

That's new. And on another night I might have paid more attention to it, perhaps even tried to trace it to its source. But tonight I have bigger things to worry about. The sense of someone watching me is so strong that it gives me goosebumps. Is it the avatar girl again? The mere thought that a stranger might enter my dream is so unnerving that my spirit wavers briefly, and for a moment I'm tempted to wake myself up, to flee the dream-scape. But my hunger for knowledge is greater than my fear. I need to understand how other people can enter a world that my mind created, and what they can do to it once they're here. Not to mention the sheer stubbornness factor: I'm damned if I'm about to be driven out of my own dream.

Slowly I begin to walk, but my attention is less on the doors this time, and more on the darkness surrounding them. As I come to each door the ghostly music seems to get a bit louder, then it fades again. The melody is changing each time, very subtly. Like each door has its own musical theme. Weird.

Suddenly I see a flash of movement off to one side. I turn toward it and see the avatar girl standing there, watching me. Why didn't I see her before, when I looked in this direction?

As soon as my eyes meet hers she turns away and starts walking.

"Wait!" I cry out. "Just for a minute! I want to talk to you."

She shows no sign of having heard me. She's walking quickly, speeding up bit by bit but not running outright, moving off into the darkness. I follow her, mirroring her pace, not wanting to close the distance between us (because what would I do next, tackle her to the ground?) but hoping that if she realizes I'm not a threat to her she'll slow down and talk to me. I have questions that only she can answer, and I'm not going to let her out of my sight before I get a chance to ask them.

The music seems louder, now that I'm focused on her. Maybe that's just an illusion. Or maybe it's easier to hear such things when you're not paying attention to them. The arches are changing shape as she passes them, too. Crystal spines vanish in a puff of glittering smoke. Stone arches stretch upward, sides thinning out, rounded tops transforming into a graceful point. The new shapes, tall and peaked, remind me of an Arabian palace.

It's a shape that has meaning to her, rather than to me.

The implications are chilling, but I continue on. The only thing worse than having a stranger mess with your dream, is having that happen and not knowing how they did it. Or why.

As we approach a dense cluster of archways she breaks into a run. With a start I realize that the pattern of these arches is familiar: this is the cluster where she lost me the last time, when I couldn't follow her through an arch. I can see from the way her body is tensing for one last burst of speed that she's about to try the same trick again.

Not on my watch.

Her final dash is sudden, but I'm right behind her, and I'm ready for it. As she enters the arch I launch myself at her, closing the gap between us with all the reckless ferocity of a baseball player sliding into home plate, grabbing hold of her so that she can no longer pass through the arch alone. The force of my momentum knocks us both off our feet—and then suddenly we're falling through the archway together, and we hit the ground on the far side with enough force to drive the breath from my body.

Fear and elation flood my soul: I made it!

But to where?

Thick grey fog surrounds us, so I can't see much of anything. While I struggle to get my bearings the girl breaks away from me and gets to her feet. I see a flash of fear in her eyes; clearly she didn't think I could follow her here. Then she's running again, full speed this time, and by the time I can get to my feet the fog has swallowed her whole.

I look up at the shadows looming over me, tall and

thin, their crowns spreading into a dark mass overhead. Trees? Am I in some kind of forest? There are long black streamers trailing down from unseen branches, and I fervently hope they're just some kind of hanging moss. The ground beneath me is soft and damp, and it takes impressions well; I realize that I can see her footprints clearly.

I start to follow her. The fog changes as I do, shifting in color from bluish gray to a dull green, then to brownish mauve. It's still thick enough to hide her from my sight, so I'm forced to run blind. The trees are also changing, shrinking in both girth and height, and there is less and less of the black stuff hanging from their branches. All in all the place doesn't look as threatening as before, but I'm not reassured. I'm chasing a girl who invaded my dreams. The rest of this is just window dressing.

Finally the fog thins out, and I see that the last of the trees are gone. There's an open plain ahead, and my quarry is visible in the distance. She must sense my approach, because she glances back nervously over her shoulder to see where I am. Too close for her comfort, apparently. She starts running even faster, and I sense desperation in the effort. This time I'm hard-pressed to keep up. But all of that only increases my determination: I'm not going to let this strange creature get away from me until I find out how—and why—she's invaded my dreamscape.

Now the entire world is changing around me, far more dramatically than before. First I'm running on a field of plain dirt, then it's a field of grass, then it's poppies stretching out as far as the eye can see. Overhead the sun is yellow, then white, then red and swollen, filling half the sky. Then yellow again. Whatever dream world we've entered, it appears to be totally unstable.

There's a wide hill ahead of us, and she's starting up

its slope. It's not very high, but once she goes over the top I won't be able to see her any more. I try to run even faster, but I'm already going at top speed, and my legs are starting to get tired. How long have I been chasing her? I thought it was only a few minutes, but now it feels like an eternity. Dream time.

But if this is a dream, then I can control it, right? Thus far I've been too busy running to think about strategy, but surely I can leverage that to my advantage. As I continue running I try to detach my mind from the pounding rhythm of the chase, focusing my attention on the hill itself, trying to unmake it. God knows, this dream is volatile enough that doing so should be easy, but to my surprise the alien landscape rejects my efforts. I try to make other changes, but nothing responds to me. I can't make a single poppy wilt or a butterfly leave its perch, much less flatten a multi-ton mound of soil.

She's nearing the summit now. I'm getting tired. Any minute now I'll lose sight of her, perhaps for good. And all the answers she might provide will be lost.

I can't let that happen.

I try again to alter the dreamscape, drawing upon the force of my frustration as a kind of fuel. And after what seems like an eternity the dreamscape finally responds. I see a tiny bit of soil come loose from the top of the hill and roll down the slope, breaking up as it does so, and I know that I caused that. But it's all I can do. Part of me is elated to have managed even that much, but part of me wants to scream in frustration, because I can't seem to do anything useful. This unstable world shows amazing tenacity when I'm the one who wants to change it.

I focus all my attention back on running, not wanting to lose her. But by the time I reach the base of the hill she's already at the top. The slope turns out to be much steeper than I expected, and covered with loose rocks that shift underfoot, forcing me to concentrate on each step. Progress is agonizingly slow. By the time I reach the top she's long out of sight, and I just pray that from that vantage point I can spot her again.

I pause for a moment at the top to catch my breath and take stock of the situation.

The view on the other side of the hill looks like it's from a completely different dream. There's a vast lake stretching out to the horizon in all directions, its water so still that the surface is like a mirror. The sun (still yellow) reflects from it with such painful intensity that I'm forced to squint to see things clearly. I can make out a narrow tongue of land extending into the lake, from the base of the hill, but it's not made of regular earth, rather some kind of black sand. I can see the girl's footprints in it, though not as clearly as in the forest soil. Her trail leads down the hillside, along the length of the peninsula, then out into the lake itself.

Or rather, onto the lake.

She's running on top of it.

At first I figure maybe there are stepping stones right under the surface—the mirrored water could hide anything—but her feet aren't splashing when they hit the lake, as they would if that were the case. Anyway, there's no reason dream-water can't support a human being, if the dreamer wants it to.

In the distance an island of black rock juts up from the lake; stark and jagged, it's her obvious destination. There's a tall building perched on its peak, and at first glance it looks like a castle of some kind. But then I blink and it looks more like a cathedral. Another blink turns it into a ziggurat, only with lines of windows instead of ledges running around the outside in a spiral. It's like the building itself can't decide what it wants to be. The only thing that remains constant through all the transformations is the shape of the windows: narrow and peaked, just like the new arches that appeared in my black plain. Through them I can see flickering movement, but though I'm too far away to make out details, I get the sense that no two windows look in on the same interior.

The avatar girl is halfway to the island.

With renewed energy I start down the hill after her, half running, half stumbling. The sight of the strange island has energized me, and even if she manages to lose me now, I might be able to find some answers there. Soon I'm racing down the length of the narrow peninsula, bracing myself to step out onto the lake's surface, just like she did. Because the same rules should hold for both of us, yes?

No such luck.

My first step splashes down into ice-cold water and I land on something loose and slippery. I lose my balance and go flying forward, landing face first in the frigid stuff with a force that sends up gouts of white spray in all directions. Ripples spread out from me like the concentric circles of a great target. When I surface, coughing, it takes me a few seconds to find a section of the lake bed stable enough to stand on. The stones underwater are slick, and like glass marbles they shift beneath my feet with every movement.

Jesus. How am I supposed to follow the girl now? This water is too cold for me to even contemplate swimming, and there's no way I can walk any distance on such unstable ground. I look up, and the sight of her walking so easily across the surface of the lake fills me with frustration and anger. Why can she control this dreamscape so easily, while I have to strain to dislodge a single clump of earth? It shouldn't be that way. A stranger shouldn't be able to control my own dream better than I can.

Unless, I think suddenly, it isn't my dream at all.

The mere thought sends a shiver down my spine, but there's no denying that all the evidence points to that. If I were the true invader here, someone who burst into her world—her mindscape—without invitation, then control of this setting would come naturally to her, and I would be powerless to change things. Which seems to be exactly what's happening.

No, I remind myself. I'm not completely powerless. I did change this landscape, albeit minimally. And maybe now that I understand the rules of the place I'll be able to do more.

Reaching down into the water with all the force of my mind, I attempt to reshape the lake bed. It would be foolish to try to make the water itself support me, like she's doing; one moment's inattention might get me dumped back into the frigid lake. But moving dirt from one place to another offers a more permanent solution. So, gritting my teeth from the strain of the effort, I try to mold this dream as I would one of my own, superimposing my preferred reality over the current one. The task should require no more than a concentrated thought, but even though I strain my utmost, there's no response. Then, just as I'm about to give up in frustration, a thin strip of earth begins to rise up from underneath the lake. Water falls back from its flanks as it breaches the surface, and a narrow land bridge takes shape. It's only a foot wide and a few yards in length, and it's so close to the water's surface that ripples lap over the edge of it, but as I climb up onto it I feel confident I can extend it all the way to the black island, and once I do that, it should stay in place even if I get distracted.

Finally I'm standing on it, swaying slightly on its wet, uneven surface, ready to get moving again. I look up to see if my quarry is still visible. She is.

She's watching me.

She's almost at the island, but she's not running any

more. She's just standing on the water's surface, her eyes, narrow and dark, fixed on me. The message in them is clear: *how DARE you try to take control of my dream!* Slowly she raises both her hands, like a conductor signaling an orchestra to start, and I know in my gut that something very bad is about to happen. Is she going to try to unmake my land bridge? I prepare to defend it (however on earth you'd do that), but to my surprise, the dream-construct remains steady beneath my feet. That's not her target. The water surrounding me is beginning to move, however, and slowly it draws back from the shoreline, revealing the lake bottom. Fish are flopping helplessly in tiny pools as the receding tide leaves them stranded—

Oh, shit. I've seen too many disaster movies to not know what's happening. Or, more precisely, what's about to happen.

Desperately I look around for high ground. Or something I can climb. Or even something to hang on to, before the great wave that she's summoning hits me like a giant flyswatter. But there's only the one low hill behind me, and even a small tsunami would sweep right over that.

No trees in sight.

No protection anywhere.

The water in the center of the lake is starting to rise up now, and a foam-capped ridge is taking shape that stretches from horizon to horizon, blocking the girl from my sight. I can't be sure of its position, but I can measure its rise as window after window of the strange citadel is hidden from my sight. The ground beneath my feet has started to tremble, and a cold wind gusts across my face. It's coming fast.

For one brief, crazy instant I want to stand my ground. I want her to see that her dream can't scare me off, no matter how scary she makes it. Maybe she'd respect such an effort and tell me what's going on.

Yeah. Right.

I need to wake myself up. Now.

Turning my attention inward, I reach out with my mind, trying to reconnect to the reality of my sleeping body. Waking up should be easy once that's done. But even as I begin to concentrate, the wave starts to transform. Color bleeds from it, the stormy blue water becomes a dull grey. The foam turns to white mist, then to smoke, then it's carried away on the wind. The wave itself starts to collapse, and row after row of windows become visible again as it falls back into the lake that spawned it.

Stunned, I hesitate.

I can see the girl now, and her expression is one of pure horror. She's staring at a point directly above the collapsed wave, where a wraith-like shadow has suddenly appeared. It's darker than any natural shadow would be, and its presence is so cold that even from where I stand I feel its chill. I sense that it has no substance in the normal meaning of the word, but rather is a void, a gaping wound in the dreamscape into which all reality is draining.

It's heading straight toward her.

With a cry of terror, the girl begins to run to the island. She's hasn't got far to go, but the shadow-wraith is moving quickly, and in its wake the entire dream world seems to be dissolving. Beams of sunlight fade as if the wraith passes through them, the shining surface of the water grows dull beneath it, color bleeds from the sky and the clouds overhead, and even the sun dims as the wraith passes in front of it, its bright golden surface dulled to a muddy brown, its brilliant light all but extinguished.

I need to leave this nightmare now, before the horrific thing notices me. But hard as I try, I can't seem to wake myself up. That's really frightening. Ever since my visit to the other world I've been able to end my dreams at will, just by shifting my awareness to my sleeping body. The fact that I can't do so now suggests that the rules I've come to take for granted don't operate here.

I turn back the way I came and start running. Hopefully if I can get closer to the arch—closer to my own dreamscape—I'll be able to escape this nightmare.

But as I turn, it seems to notice me. And in that instant, as it pauses in mid-air deciding who to go after, I can sense the full scope of its horrific nature.

It is Death. It is Pain.

And it is hungry.

I flee from the terrible thing as an animal would flee, blind in my panic. All thoughts of exhaustion are gone now, all muscular weakness forgotten. I will run till the last ounce of strength leaves my body and I collapse, rather than let this thing touch me.

It's following me now. I know that because the world is transforming around me, reflecting its horrific nature. I run through a field of poppies, but all the flowers are dead, motionless insects strewn like black snow across their browning petals. I run through an open meadow, but the grass has been eaten away to stumps, and corpses of fallen birds litter the ground as far as the eye can see. I run into a forest, but the ground is buried in fallen branches and rotting leaves, and the place is so putrid with the stench of decay that I can barely breathe.

The arch must be here somewhere. It must be! I have to find it before that thing catches up with me.

Suddenly my foot catches on something underneath the dead leaves. I'm falling—falling!—and I cry out in fear as I hit the ground. Color is draining out of the whole world now, leaving only shades of murky gray, which means the creature is close, very close. I roll over onto my back so that I can defend myself—but how does one defend against an incarnation of Death?

It's closer than I'd imagined, and though I can see nothing but shadow when I look directly at it, I can sense vast black wings spreading over me, blotting out the last vestiges of sunlight. Instinctively I raise up my arm to guard my eyes, and something sharp and cold rakes across it. The pain is like nothing I have ever felt before. I hear myself crying out in terror, and I try again to wake myself up. No luck. I'm trapped here.

A ghostly voice cries out my name in the distance. My mind is so paralyzed by fear that at first the sound doesn't register. The death-wraith is lunging at me again, and I roll to one side. The frigid claws pass so close to my face my cheek feels numb. What will happen to my waking mind if this thing kills me here? Will I ever wake up again?

*Jesse!*

This time I recognize the voice, and I feel a spark of hope. I focus myself body and soul on my brother's voice, using it as a lifeline to connect me to the world of living things. Even as the death-wraith attacks me again I reach out for Tommy with all the strength that is left in my soul, trying to absorb his perspective into myself as he stands over my sleeping body—

‖‖‖‖‖‖‖‖‖‖

"Jesse!"

I awoke gasping. My body was shaking violently, and I was sick from terror. But I was also home again, and that meant the creature was gone. Thank God.

My brother was kneeling on the bed, his hands on my shoulders. He'd been shaking me, trying to wake me up, and not until my eyes were fully open did he stop. "Are you okay?"

For a moment I had no words. I just lay there, drinking in reality. "Yeah," I rasped at last. "I think so."

"You were moaning in your sleep. I figured whatever dream was causing that, you'd want to wake up."

I whispered, "Good instinct." Then I asked, "Did anyone else hear me?"

He shook his head. "They're all asleep. I wasn't." He paused. "It wasn't that loud, just . . . damn scary-sounding."

"Damn right," I muttered. "Thanks."

What would have happened to me if my brother hadn't tried to wake me up? Would I have been trapped in that dream forever? I remembered the death-wraith, and I shuddered. At least it lacked the power to follow me here. The waking world was my refuge.

I tried to lever myself up to a sitting position. My muscles were sore, like I'd really been running for hours, and the upper part of my left arm stung fiercely. I winced and used my other arm to push myself upright. The sensations were just echoes of my dream, I knew, and they should fade soon.

"So what scared you so badly?" Tommy asked. "Can you talk about it?"

I sighed. I didn't feel up to telling the whole story right then, but he deserved at least the bare bones of it. He might well have saved my life. "I ran into the avatar again. This time I followed her through a door, which led me into another dream, not one of mine . . . I think maybe it was her dream. Then a death-wraith appeared and the whole dream fell apart. It was attacking me when you woke me up." I put my hand on my arm where the claws had torn my flesh—

And I froze.

"Jesse?"

There was pain in that spot. Way too much pain for a mere dream memory. The sleeve of my sleep shirt was warm and wet.

*It was a dream,* I told myself. *Just a dream. I probably banged my arm against a bedpost while I was trying to wake up. Or something.*

Slowly I pushed my sleeve up my arm, not wanting to see what was under it, but knowing I had to. The source of the blood turned out to be a jagged slash that ran diagonally across my arm. It wasn't deep, but blood was oozing out of it, and the surrounding flesh was red and swollen.

I think I was more afraid in that moment than I had been while the wraith was actually attacking me. Because however frightening that had been, it was just a dream. This . . . this was *real*.

It was my brother who found his voice first, and with it the perfect words for that moment.

"Holy crap," he muttered.

# 5

**R**ITA ACCEPTED MY AUNT'S INVITATION to stay with us a few days, and I was grateful for the company. She and I might come from different backgrounds, and have few interests in common, but once you faced death together those things didn't matter as much. And it was good to have another confidant in the house, who could look at my wound and hear the tale of how I got it, and reassure me that somehow everything would be okay. Yeah, Tommy was doing that, but it helped to hear it in stereo. Devon wasn't able to stay, but we convinced Dr. Tilford that the two of them should come back up for the show, in part by telling him we wouldn't be able to give him the glow lamp until then. Then Aunt Rose talked Dr. Tilford into staying the night, so that we could all watch the fireworks together without his having to drive for hours afterward.

So for a brief time, the world-travelers were reunited.

Rose's gallery was at the north end of town, in a converted 18th century mill. It had a waterwheel on one side, a millstone and grinding mechanism in the center of two open floors, and a vast expanse of parkland outside. According to the tourist pamphlets, the mill had been grinding wheat back when George Washington came to soak in the town's famous hot springs, and I saw no reason to doubt that. These days there was no grain being processed, of course, but a different kind of harvest was being celebrated, that of local artists and craftsmen. Every weekend they displayed their work in small open spaces which were (for reasons that were a mystery to me) called "booths." This weekend the place would be packed, every inch of it filled with paintings and pottery and hand-dyed silks and wood carvings . . . and my new painting.

Of course we had argued about who would be in Rose's booth with me, while we waited to see if Seyer would show up. Rita and Devon both wanted to be there for our meeting, and truth be told, it would have steadied my nerves to have them there. But I was afraid that too much of a crowd might scare Seyer off, and I didn't want to take any chances. In the end they had to settle for wandering around the old mill, perusing art displays with poorly feigned interest as they tried to look like legitimate tourists. Probably they wouldn't fool anyone, but at least it gave me room to breathe. As for Tommy, his coming to the show simply wasn't an option. If he really was hearing ghosts, I told him, the last thing he needed was to be in the presence of a Seer, whose job it was to identify kids with interesting powers and kidnap them for Terra Prime. He sulked a bit, but he didn't argue the point. He knew I was right.

My aunt was actually a talented potter, and her impressive work was displayed on wooden bookshelves six feet high, arranged to mark out the periphery of her booth on the second floor. She moved one bookshelf back a bit to make room for my display easel, but it was still a pretty tight fit. I hoped that when Seyer showed up we would be able to talk without Rose listening in on us.

*If* Seyer showed up.

What was I going to say to her if she did? I'd tried to anticipate every possible avenue of conversation, as a mental exercise, but things like this never went the way you expected. I was just going to have to wing it.

The mill didn't have central air conditioning, so the exhibit space got warm pretty fast. I'd worn a long sleeved shirt to hide my dream-wound from Rose and Julian, so I was pretty damned uncomfortable. But at least the wound was healing normally. Despite Tommy's fears that I had become infected with death-wraith essence, and would slowly transform into a creature of darkness, that didn't seem to be happening. I joked with him about it—"This isn't *Lord of the Rings*, you know"—but in truth, I was pretty damned relieved.

Then Seyer arrived.

It was noon, and the place was a madhouse; I almost missed her. Devon spotted her first, and he signaled me from across the floor to draw my attention to her. She was dressed in her usual goth black, which was so out of place amidst the frothy summer crowd that once you noticed, she stood out like a sore thumb. My heart pounded as I watched her approach Rose's booth, but she was apparently in no hurry. At every booth she would stop to peruse its offerings, handling every glass necklace and walnut tissue box and raku vase as if it were a precious museum piece, whose every detail had to be studied before she could put it down. It was maddening, and no doubt quite deliberate. She was sending me a message: *Don't think that because I answered your summons, you are the one in control here.* What could I do? I tried to breathe deeply and pretend I didn't care if she came to Rose's booth or not. Let that be my message to her: *You can play whatever games you want, it's not going to shake me.*

Finally she arrived at Rose's booth, and of course she studied every piece of pottery before coming to look at my painting. For a while she just stood there, gazing at the dark loops and whorls, and the temptation for me to say something was overwhelming. But I just waited. Let her make the first move.

My painting had two round shapes, one smaller than the other, that were woven together into a single mandala-like composition. Tentacle-like rays splayed out from the larger one, that divided again and again until the whole canvas was filled with tiny curling lines. At first glance the painting appeared more chaotic than my usual work—no neat fractals in this one—but if you relaxed while viewing it, and didn't try to impose an artificial order upon it, you could sense a greater pattern underlying the chaos. You realized that the dual figure was reaching outward to surround all the other elements on the canvas, as if trying to ensnare them. Disturbingly, the ends of some of the tentacles were unclear, so that you couldn't be sure exactly where they ended, or whether or not they had made contact. A deadly net.

It was a fate portrait of Alia Morgana.

At last Seyer spoke. "It's darker than your previous work."

I shrugged stiffly. "I've been into some dark stuff lately."

She looked around the edges of the canvas. "I don't see a price tag. Or a 'not for sale' notice." She looked at me. "Does that mean you aren't sure if you want to sell it?"

"For the right buyer, I'd consider it."

She glanced over at Rose, probably to assess how

much privacy we had. But my aunt was busy with her customers at the moment, explaining the intricacies of raku pottery to a pair of tourists in Hawaiian shirts and Bermuda shorts. No one within ten feet was paying any attention to us.

Seyer turned back to me. As always, her thick black eyeliner and Cleopatra-style haircut lent her gaze an Egyptian flavor, like something you would see painted on the wall of a Pharaoh's tomb. "I'm guessing it's not money you're after." She spoke very quietly.

I nodded. "Good guess."

"Name your price, then."

I could feel my hands trembling, and I put them behind my back where she couldn't see them. *Everything rides on this moment,* I thought. From across the room Rita and Devon were watching, having abandoned their pretense of being interested in art. I wondered if Seyer was aware of them.

Finally I said quietly, but with strength: "I want a Healer for my mother."

Her eyes narrowed slightly. "For the damage she suffered from the fire?"

I kept my voice steady. "Yes."

She sighed deeply. "I'm afraid you're asking for something I can't give you, Jessica."

My heart sank. "Why not? I'm sure you have the connections needed to find a Healer. There are probably some on your Guild's payroll. Are you telling me—what?—that they won't Heal someone from my world? Is that it?"

I saw my aunt glance in our direction, and realized that my voice was rising in volume. I nodded reassuringly at her and drew in a deep breath, willing myself to be calm.

"It's not that simple," Seyer said softly.

"Then explain it to me."

She glanced at Rose again, then nodded toward the staircase. "Come. Walk outside with me."

I hesitated, then told Rose I was going to leave for a few minutes to buy some apple fritters from a food truck outdoors. She asked me to bring her back a lemonade, and gave me money for both orders. Then she turned back to regale her customers with glorious tales about raku glazing, and we headed toward the stairs.

"Your mother isn't sick," Seyer said as we walked. "She's *damaged*. There's a difference. A Healer works in harmony with the body, prompting it to do what it does naturally, only better. Their Gift can make bones knit faster, stimulate bone marrow to produce more blood, or even prompt the immune system to attack a cancerous tumor. Anything that a body has the natural capacity to do, a Healer can improve on. But your mother's brain has been damaged, Jessica. Neurons have died. That kind of cell doesn't regenerate naturally, which means that a Healer can't prompt it to do so." As we reached the bottom of the staircase she stopped walking and looked at me; there was sympathy in her eyes. "I'm sorry."

I felt like I'd been struck in the face. "You're lying," I whispered.

"What reason would I have to do that? You have something that I want to purchase—something *her Grace* wants to purchase. I could bring in a Healer for you, and take your painting home with me in return, and leave you to discover the truth after I was gone. Consider it a sign of respect that I'm being honest." There was pity in her eyes now, and I hated her for it. "I'm really sorry, Jessica."

We were heading outside now, to the area where the food vendors were hawking their wares. The smells of greasy meat, popcorn, and fritters breezed across the lawn. "So what now?" I had to fight to keep my voice steady. "Are you telling me there's no hope? That there's a whole universe full of people with fancy mental Gifts, and not one of them can help my mother?"

"Ah. I didn't say that. In fact there is one Guild that might be able to help you. But they're reclusive, pricey, and don't generally travel to other worlds doing favors for people."

"Who?"

"We call them Potters. Fleshcrafters. Unlike Healers, they can force living flesh to do things it wouldn't do naturally. Sometimes that allows them to repair things that can't be healed."

My breath caught in my throat. "They can cure my Mom?"

"*That* I can't promise. Few outside their Guild know exactly how their Gift works, or what its limits are. But I've heard about them taking on cases like this, so let's say . . . , it might be possible."

"Okay." I nodded. "Okay. Then let's call that my price."

"For the painting?" She smiled slightly.

"That's right."

"You do value your work rather highly."

"No, I don't. But *you* do, or you wouldn't be here." When she didn't respond I pressed, "Am I wrong?"

She looked at me in silence, taking my measure. I tried to meet her gaze confidently, even though deep inside I felt the opposite of confident. Finally she said, "The Potters don't just hire out for odd jobs, Jessica. And there's nothing you possess that they would value in barter. You would need someone with enough personal influence to call in a favor from them, on your behalf. And given that you're talking about one of them travelling offworld, which they don't like to do, it would be a significant favor." She shook her head. "I just don't have that kind of influence. I'm sorry."

I felt my heart sinking. No. No. I refused to give up. To be so close to an answer and yet have no way to make it happen ... I refused to accept that. There had to be a way.

Suddenly I realized who could help me. Not that she *would* help me, necessarily. Or that I wanted to ask her for help. In fact, the mere thought of dealing with her made my blood run cold.

Alia Morgana.

She was the one who had ordered Seyer to spy on me. And had put Tommy's life in danger by lying to the Greys about him, telling them he was the Dreamwalker they were looking for. She was the type of person one should do everything possible to avoid. But what if she had the kind influence Seyer was talking about? What if she could help me hire a Fleshcrafter?

It took effort to force out the words. "What about Morgana?"

Seyer raised an eyebrow. "An intriguing suggestion. She's the one who's interested in your art, you know; I'm just her purchasing agent. And I suppose if anyone had enough sway with the Potters to do what you want, she does. But that would have its own price, you know. Apart from your painting." She nodded back toward the building. "And she's not going to come to Terra Colonna just so you can bargain with her. You would need to go to her."

*Go back to Terra Prime.* A wave of vertigo came over me, like I was standing on the edge of an abyss, gazing down into a bottomless darkness, while the dirt beneath my feet crumbled away. But was the idea truly untenable? Seyer had once referred to me as Morgana's *project,* which suggested that the Guildmistress wanted something from me. I didn't know what it was yet, but maybe if I was face to face with her I could figure it out. Maybe I could leverage it for the favor I needed. Maybe I could do that and get home safely again.

Maybe.

"So," I said slowly, "if in return for my painting I wanted passage to and from your Guild headquarters—*safe* passage, door to door, with all the proper documents and clearances—and an audience with your Guildmistress . . . would that be a reasonable price?"

She smiled slightly. "I believe that would be within my budget."

"And if I wanted to bring someone with me?"

Her expression darkened slightly. "I'll cover expenses for the ones who were with you before. No one else."

We took a few minutes to buy fritters and lemonade and then started back. As we headed up the stairs, Seyer opened her purse and took out a business card, which she handed to me. "I'll be leaving tomorrow morning for Terra Prime. You can travel with me if you want. Give me a call tonight, and we'll discuss the details. You can deliver the painting yourself when you arrive." As we neared the pottery booth she instructed, "Introduce me to your aunt as an old family friend, so we can arrange for the proper cover story. The fact that your mother doesn't really know me won't be an issue, given the current state of her memory. No doubt she has forgotten a lot of other friends."

My heart clenched at the callous reminder of my mom's incapacity, but as we delivered Rose's lemonade, I did as Seyer had suggested, and marveled at how easily she slipped into a new role, playing the part of an old family friend to perfection. Truly, she was a social chameleon of impressive skill. I listened as she told Rose about a cabin she had in the mountains, and how she would love to invite me out there for a week. It would be restful, she said. Good for my soul. Rose said she wasn't sure this was a good time for me to part from my family, given recent events, but Seyer said she'd stop by in the morning to discuss it with Mom, and that was good enough for now.

"Pack for overnight," she said in a low voice, as Rose turned her attention to her customers. "And leave your electronics behind. I don't want trouble with Customs."

"But Mom hasn't agreed yet—"

She put a finger to her lips, cautioning me to silence. "She will. I promise. So will everyone else. Trust me."

When she left I was far too agitated to hang out with Rose, and besides, I needed to fill my friends in on what had happened. So I said goodbye to my aunt, and gestured for Devon and Rita to follow me outside the building. There, at least, people wouldn't be breathing down our necks as we talked about aliens and mind-readers.

As we descended the worn wooden stairs of the mill, I wondered if I had just done something very clever, or very stupid.

||||||||||||

"You're *what?*" Rita's tone left no room for doubt about what she thought of my bargain with Seyer.

"I'm going back to Terra Prime." I tried to say it casually, like you might talk about taking a train to visit Philadelphia. Maybe if I could keep myself sounding calm, the fear swirling in my stomach would settle down. "Round trip tickets compliments of Ms. Seyer."

"You *trust* her?" Devon asked sharply.

"No," I said, equally sharply, "and I trust Morgana even less. But what else am I supposed to do, Devon? Sit home and watch Mom fade away little by little, knowing there are people in that world who could help her?" *It's my fault she's sick,* I wanted to say. *So it's my responsibility to heal her.*

Rita was silent for a moment, just staring at me. Finally she muttered, "You shouldn't do this alone, you know that. I'll go with you."

I'd been praying she would say that—hence the

relevant clause in my bargain with Seyer—but I couldn't accept it without challenge. "You just got back from there. You've still got bruises—"

"And you shouldn't be alone with those people. Least of all in a place where if something happened to you, no one back home would know about it." She raised up a hand to silence me. "Don't even argue with me, Jesse. I'm coming."

Relief washed over me. "I would like the company," I admitted.

"Provided Seyer makes proper arrangements for us to cross over, of course. And protects us from the Shadows while we're there. Assuming she—or anyone—can do that." How quickly and easily Rita committed herself to that other world again! I remembered what she told me, the last time we talked about going through a Gate. *I've got nowhere better to go.* With no family or home she cared about, Rita could pick up and leave at will. And while I'd never asked about the intimate details of her upbringing, I knew she came from a challenging environment, and wasn't the kind of person who expected life to be easy or safe on a normal day.

The thought that I would have her by my side in Terra Prime did a lot to steady my nerves.

Devon shook his head, clearly frustrated. "I wish I could say the same, but it's not as easy to walk away when you've got a parent watching you like a hawk. My dad was pretty shaken by our 'kidnapping,' and he's determined not to let me out of his sight for a while. Just in case any of our assailants survived. I'm so sorry, Jesse. I'd go with you otherwise."

"Seyer said she could convince my family to let me go. She sounded pretty confident that she could deal with all their objections. Maybe she could do the same with your Dad as well."

God, it would be good to have him with me. Good to

have both of them with me. The mere thought of us going to Terra Prime all together bolstered my spirit considerably.

Hopefully we would all come home together.

|||||||||||||

Filling Tommy in on my plans didn't go quite as smoothly as I'd hoped.

"I'm going with you," he said, folding his arms defiantly over his chest.

I shook my head. "You can't, Tommy."

"Why? Do you think I can't handle myself there? I tricked the Shadows into keeping me alive," he reminded me. "I kept them thinking that I was the one they were interested in, so they wouldn't go after you. I even fooled one of them into making their ghost guards leave me alone. Isn't that enough to prove I can take care of myself?" He threw up his hands in exasperation. "What more do you want?"

I sighed. *You're my 13-year-old brother. The 'brother' part of that means I'm supposed to protect you, not drag you into danger. And the 13-year-old part matters. I'm sorry, but it does.* Yes, Tommy was a hellishly resourceful kid, and with his background in fantasy gaming he was probably more qualified to explore an alien world than the rest of us put together. But we weren't going there to explore. We were going to negotiate with dangerous and powerful people, and having Tommy play fly-on-the-wall would only complicate that meeting.

None of which would matter to the kid standing in front of me, of course. All he would hear if I said that was that his sister was going to visit an alien world and not allowing him to come. "I have as much right to go there as you do," he said between gritted teeth.

But he didn't. That was the key point. I'd been born in Terra Prime, Devon and Rita also. Discovering that our DNA didn't match that of our parents had been the first step in that discovery. Tommy was a child of this world, and though that might not matter to us, it mattered a hell of a lot to the people we would be bargaining with. And they were the ones responsible for our safety. I'd already seen how they treated children from their own world, and I didn't want to think about how they would treat Tommy, who had no intrinsic right to be in their territory.

With a sigh I took him by the arms and drew him near to where I was sitting on my bed. I held him like that for a moment, just gazing into his eyes, wishing I had some words to offer that would make this easier. "What about Mom?" I asked gently. "What if I don't make it back—or at least, don't make it back in the right time frame? Because you know that's a possibility, no matter how well we plan. Losing one kid would be hard enough on her. How would she take it if both of us disappeared, and she never found out what happened to us?" I paused. "It would kill her, Tommy."

He stared at me for a moment. "Aw, crap," he muttered. He jerked out of my grip. "Crap!"

"You know I'm right," I pressed.

He turned from me and stomped melodramatically out of the room, slamming the door shut behind him. I shut my eyes and sighed deeply. It was not the way I'd wanted to end this conversation, but at least he seemed to accept the inevitable. One hurdle down.

The rest would be dealt with in the morning.

||||||||||||||||

We watched the fireworks from the roof of the house that night, Devon and Rita and Tommy and I, four world-travelers strung out in a line along the gritty shingles, while a backyard full of adults with beer cans in their hands watched from the property below. The night was misty and warm and the park was near enough to the house that, as each rocket exploded, it blossomed overhead, lighting up the sky from horizon to horizon. It was an amazing sight, invigorating to watch.

But it was also saddening. I couldn't help but think about Sebastian, who'd fought in the war we were now celebrating. I wished there was some way to bring him home to Terra Colonna, so that he could see the whole country lit up like a field of stars, honoring his victory.

Devon caught sight of a tear forming in my eye and put his hand over mine. We stayed that way until the last of the lights were gone from the sky, and the mist faded into darkness. Then we climbed back in through the attic window to go join the others.

# 6

## SEER GUILDHOUSE IN LURAY
## VIRGINIA PRIME

## ALIA MORGANA

**T**HE SAFETY LAMPS CAME ON as Morgana entered the underground chamber, providing just enough light for her to make her way to the large circular table at its center. A dozen velvet-upholstered chairs were visible surrounding it, but the rest of the chamber was shrouded in shadow.

Fewer distractions that way.

Morgana walked to the table and put down the two things she was carrying: a golden mask with a length of striped cloth attached, and an elaborately carved box. The mask was in the style of ancient Egypt, regal and elegant, the kind one would expect to find in the tomb of a queen. The box, when opened, revealed a large quartz crystal cut neatly into slices, nested in folds of velvet. Morgana lifted out one of the slices, looked at the Guild sign etched into its polished surface, and then put it back. Not the one she wanted. She inspected other slices, one by one, placing the ones she needed on the table as she found them. Elemental, Fleshcrafter, Obfuscate, Domitor, Healer, Soulrider, Weaver, and of course Seer. Eight Guild sigils in all.

"Brighter," she commanded, and the fetter lamps obediently increased their illumination. Now patterns etched into the table's surface were visible, a series of stars radiating out from its center, each with a different number of points. The resulting design was somewhat chaotic, and it took her a moment to isolate the star she wanted. Eight points. Using it as a guideline, she placed her crystal slices at the ends of the rays, so that they were perfectly spaced around the edge of the table. Then she sat down in front of the Seer sigil and checked the time. There were still a few minutes left to go.

It was rare these days that she experienced quiet. Rare for her to be so far away from other people that the incessant buzz of their thoughts and emotions was dulled to a murmur, little more than soft background music. She'd built this chamber far beneath the Guildhouse so that the earth would provide her with privacy—as much as was possible for a master Seer—and now, as she waited for her meeting to begin, she drank in the silence with relish.

A few minutes later her fetter watch vibrated gently. She took up the golden mask and fitted it to her face, smoothing the striped cloth back over her head until her hair was completely covered. Then she reached out and placed her hand on the Seers' crystal. As soon as she did, ghostly figures began to take shape around the table. Each one was masked, and like her, had its hand upon the crystal fetter corresponding to its Guild.

The first to appear was a Healer, a man wearing a mask of polished silver with a jeweled eye set in the center of the forehead. Right after that a Domitor appeared, a short and stocky man whose fierce red-and-black mask reminded Morgana of a Kabuki demon. Next came an Elemental, whose mask appeared to be carved from ice and crowned in flickering fire. Though the flames danced realistically about her head they brought no heat to the room, and the light they cast did not extend more than a few feet past her fetter. Next, an Obfuscate and a Weaver appeared simultaneously. The Grey was a small man whose mask had a mirrored surface; as he looked around at each of the others, their own faces were reflected back at them, distorted as if by a funhouse mirror. It was more than a little disturbing. The Weaver's mask was an intricate tapestry with arcane symbols woven into it and more designs embroidered on top of that; despite her exhaustive knowledge of symbology, Morgana didn't recognize all of them. Next a Soulrider arrived, a tall, lanky man in a wolf mask, and right behind him came a Fleshcrafter. The latter's mask was colorful, a bright carnival design that was elegantly human on the right side and twisted and bestial on the left. Morgana wondered which side better represented her true nature.

They all knew each other, of course, but given that their consortium sometimes acted against the interests of the Shadows, it was best to make sure that any spirits who might spy on them wouldn't recognize the participants. "I'm glad to see everyone could make it," Morgana said. "Master Grey, would you be so good as to update us on the situation with Luray's Gate?"

The Grey's mask hid his expression, but from his posture Morgana guessed that he was surprised to be the first one addressed. He was relatively new to the group, and of lower Guild rank than the rest of them; it was possible he felt a bit intimidated in this company. If so, that was something he would have to get used to. He was too valuable to the group to be cast out for simple social awkwardness.

He cleared his throat. "Things are moving at a good pace, but we've still got tons of rubble to move before we can allow access to the main chamber. The Lord Governor has crews working day and night on it, and the Elementals have provided terramancers, but it's still a monumental task. I estimate another week before we can send someone down to evaluate the condition of the portal. If we find that it's collapsed or become so unstable it's beyond practical use ..." he hesitated. "Then there's no point in clearing out any more rocks, is there?"

The Weaver spoke quietly. "The Luray portal existed for centuries before the Gate was built to stabilize it. It's hard to believe a simple explosion would damage it."

"That explosion took place on the Gate's threshold," the Grey reminded her, "and thus did far more damage than an explosion in the chamber would have. We already know that it resonated in other spheres; we can't ignore the possibility that the portal itself has been damaged."

The Domitor shook his head. "Bad news for Luray if the Gate is gone for good." He was one of the few members of the group who didn't live in or near the city, but he sounded like he would take a perverse pleasure in Luray's being humbled. Morgana made a mental note of it. "What's this I hear about lawsuits on the horizon?"

Morgana answered him. "Every day the Gate remains nonfunctional means our merchants have to route their goods and people through distant cities. That costs time and money. People will expect compensation for it: it's human nature. And Luray is a hub of interworld commerce, so the compensation will be sizeable."

"Who are they planning to sue? Or, to put it in plainer English: Who's getting blamed for all this?"

The Grey reached up nervously to rub his forehead and seemed startled when his fingers encountered the mask. Such disguises were a necessary precaution, but it took time to get used to wearing one. "Lord Virilian has informed the governor that my Guild was responsible for the Gate's security, hence this was our failing. Which is bullshit," he muttered. "We're facilitators for his Guild, nothing more. Don't they keep telling us that? The ultimate responsibility for this mess lies with them. But who wants to drag a Shadowlord into court? It's much easier to target us."

"This will go all the way to the top," the Healer mused. "And if it turns out the portal can't be made functional, someone big is going to go down for it. Possibly even a Guildmaster."

"Let's hope it's Virilian," the Weaver offered, "and not the Grey's Garret."

The Grey turned to glare at her. Even through his mask one could sense the intensity of his gaze. "Lady, I spent ten years in a hellhole in the Sauran Cluster because of one spoiled aristo brat who suffered a week's time displacement and missed a final exam. When his family demanded that someone be punished for that, Guildmaster Garret decided that I was the ideal scapegoat. Do you know what it's like to milk a six-foot centipede for venom? No? Because I do. It's not fun. It's even less fun when you have to do it for eight years straight. So either Virilian or Guildmaster Garret can go to hell for all I care."

"Easy, brother." Morgana's tone was sympathetic but firm. "You're among friends now."

The Domitor nodded. "The fall of your Guildmaster, pleasing though it might be, won't help us achieve our goals. We need to make sure this incident serves our greater purpose."

The Grey lowered his eyes and said nothing more. Like a child being admonished, Morgana thought. Such a gesture of submission wasn't necessary in this company — or appropriate — but the Grey wasn't a political player by

nature, and he didn't yet understand all the fine points of
the game he had been dragged into.

*We'll have to keep an eye on him,* Morgana thought.
*See that he makes no mistakes while he's learning.*

Normally they would never have invited someone so
inexperienced to join their conspiracy, but it was hard to
find any Grey who was willing to act against his undead
masters, and the opportunity could not be wasted. Never
mind that this one had just returned from exile and had
neither influence nor authority among his fellow Greys.
For Morgana and her allies to have eyes and ears inside
the Guild of Obfuscates had value in its own right.

*He needs training,* she thought. *Someone to take him
under wing and see that he becomes what we need him to
be.*

"Virilian isn't the most stable of Shadowlords on a
good day," the Fleshcrafter noted. "If he gets hit with
the blame for this, things could get interesting. And not
in a good way."

The Elemental snorted, "I'm not sure 'stable' is an
adjective one can apply to any Shadowlord."

"They're all pretty crazy," the Healer agreed.

"But some more than most," the Grey warned them.

All eyes turned to him.

Startled to have suddenly become the focus of attention, the Grey needed a few seconds to find his voice.
"There are dark souls in our Guild. Monsters who
should have been left in their graves, but whose spirits
were preserved for future Shadowlords to Commune
with. Only the strongest ones can take them in without
going insane ... or so I'm told, anyway. But as the Lady
Elemental pointed out, how many of the undead are
sane to start with?"

The Domitor breathed in sharply. "Are you telling us
that Virilian is host to one of these—what did you call
them—dark souls?"

The Grey hesitated. "It's rumored that he is. No one knows for sure."

"So the psychopathic Guildmaster may be host to an even bigger psychopath?" The Weaver shook her head in exasperation. "That's just great."

"It won't change our plans if he is," Morgana said evenly. She bowed her head respectfully to the Grey. "Thank you for that information." *Which no one but a Grey could have provided,* she thought with satisfaction. *You are as close as we will ever come to having a spy among the Shadows.*

The Healer looked at Morgana. "You said you had a tool that might prove useful to us, something you were testing. Can you give us an update on that?"

"I wish I could," Morgana answered, her voice tinged with regret. Fortunately she was the only one in the room who could sense when a person was lying. "But at this point I need to keep the details quiet, so my testing environment won't be compromised. When I have results worth talking about, you'll all know it. I promise."

The Domitor stared at her for a moment in obvious displeasure, then snorted. "Well then, there's not much point in going on with this meeting, is there? Because we can't discuss future plans without knowing the status of the portal. And some people clearly aren't willing to talk about their existing plans." He glared at Morgana.

"There's no reason for you to share in the risk of my work until I've confirmed its value," she said steadily.

Before the Domitor could respond the Healer clapped his hands, putting an end to the exchange. "All right. What say we close this meeting now and reconvene next week for an update? I'm sure there will be more to report then." He looked pointedly at Morgana.

"I second that," the Weaver said.

"Any objections?"

There were none.

The Elemental was the first to remove her hand from her fetter; the minute she did so her image vanished. One by one the others followed suit, until the Soulrider's image was the only one left in the room.

Before the wolf-masked figure could break the connection, Morgana gestured for him to wait.

"A moment, Hunter."

The Soulrider looked at her.

"I need a favor from you. And I'm afraid it's a somewhat challenging one."

"Challenges temper the soul, Lady Seer. What is it?"

"Four changelings from Terra Colonna crossed into our world a short while ago. They're back on their adoptive world now, but I expect some of them to return here. When they do, I need time to observe them ... without interference."

It took the Soulrider a minute to realize what she was driving at; when he did, he breathed in sharply. "You think one of my Guild will be tasked with hunting them down?"

"They angered Virilian. He's a notoriously vengeful creature. If he learns they're back on Terra Prime, there's a good chance he'll go after them, if only for personal satisfaction. And his Soulrider already knows their scent."

He nodded. "Rhegar is a skilled tracker, and he's fiercely loyal to Virilian. I doubt he would refuse to hunt someone if the Guildmaster asked him to."

"He doesn't have to refuse the request," she said quietly. "He just has to fail at it."

For a moment the Hunter stared at her in silence. Then he shook his head. "You weren't kidding about the *challenging* part, were you? Rhegar's as proud—and as stubborn—as his undead master. Asking him to feign a hunt would be like asking a champion prizefighter to throw a match."

"But sometimes prizefighters do that, when the price is right. So the issue is not *whether* it can be done but *how*." When the Hunter said nothing she pressed, "Can you arrange it?"

He considered for a moment before answering. "My Guildmaster trusts my counsel. I could probably convince him to give the right orders. But I'd have to come up with a damn good reason for him to comply. Our Guild is less involved with the Shadows than yours is, but defying the will of a Shadowlord is still no small thing. Especially that particular Shadowlord." He cocked his head to one side, a move that was oddly canine. "So are you going to give me a story to offer him? Or do I need to come up with something on my own?"

She spread her hands. "I don't know the inner workings of your Guild well enough to know what would convince him. So I'm afraid I would need to leave that in your hands."

"And is this part of your secret experiment?"

A practiced wave of Morgana's hand casually dismissed the thought. "If you must know the truth, my Guild assessed the potential of these changelings when they were born, and sent them into exile on Terra Colonna. Now they're back. When's the last time you heard about a changeling finding his way home like that? It's a once in a lifetime opportunity for us to see what these children are capable of, when isolated from Gifted influence."

"Do you think they may be Gifted themselves?"

"I've seen no signs of that yet," she lied easily. "But if it turns out that one of them is, that would mean a Seer failed in his duty when he evaluated them. . . . so you understand why it's something I would need to investigate. Discreetly."

The Hunter sighed. "I understand, Lady. I'll do the best I can to keep Rhegar off their tail."

"Thank you, my friend."

The ghostly figure lifted his hand from his fetter and then he, too, was gone.

For a few minutes Morgana sat alone in the dimly lit room, wondering if she had told the Hunter too much. Or perhaps too little? She didn't dare let the others know why she was really watching Jessica, but she had to tell them something. Which meant that the closer her plan came to fruition, the more dangerous it would become.

*I've risked everything for this experiment,* she thought. *Let's hope the girl proves worth it.*

# 7

JESSE

THE SOUND OF GLASS SHATTERING woke me up.

For a moment I lay there in the darkness, not sure if it was something I'd dreamed or something real. Then I heard a heavy thud downstairs, like a body hitting the floor. Reflexively I reached under my pillow for my knife, just in case trouble came calling. These days it was reflex.

As I got up and moved toward the bedroom door I could hear people stirring in the hall outside; it sounded like the noise had awakened everyone in the house. I opened my door and saw my aunt and uncle rushing down the stairs, Rita and Tommy behind them. My brother had his knife in hand, which was probably why he was keeping to the rear of the pack: there was less chance of someone noticing that way.

I followed the flood of people down the stairs.

The ruckus was apparently coming from the kitchen. Dr. Tilford was already there. Devon was crouched on the floor, his back against a cabinet, wrapped in a trembling ball with his arms around his knees and his head down. Fragments of glass and pottery were scattered all around him, as well as pieces of what had once been a sandwich. He must have come down here to make himself a midnight snack.

As Rose and Julian rushed to his side. I looked around the room for anyone or anything that might have hurt him—perhaps oddities in the room that the others might not notice—but the only people there were known to me, and no objects looked out of place save for the mess on the floor. That didn't necessarily mean there was no one else present; I'd learned the hard way that there were aliens who were skilled at going unseen. But for now, at least, this seemed to be a mundane accident.

Devon's father knelt by his side, and as we all pressed in close to see what was going on he looked up and said, "Give him room, please." I could sense fear coming off Devon in waves, like heat off the summer pavement. Dr. Tilford seemed calm and collected on the outside, but I guessed that was just a facade. A good doctor knew how to keep his patient from sensing how worried he was.

"I'll call an ambulance," Uncle Julian said.

"Already did," Dr. Tilford told him. Then he turned back to his son. "You'll be fine. Try to take deep, slow breaths."

Devon didn't respond to him. His breathing was rapid and shallow, like a dog's panting, and his body vibrated with tremors every few seconds.

Aunt Rose asked, "What happened?"

"He's having trouble with his balance," Dr. Tilford said without looking up. "No idea why, yet."

"Is there anything we can do?"

Lips tight, he shook his head. "Not at the moment."

My aunt crouched down and started to clean up the pieces of shattered crockery. It wasn't what I would have worried about at a time like this, but maybe she needed the distraction.

Devon whispered hoarsely, "It's worse when I move my head."

"I know," his father said. "Just sit still for now. Help is on the way."

I could hear sirens now, moving toward us at a fast clip. That was one benefit of living in a small town; there were no traffic snarls to slow down an ambulance.

Devon looked up at me for an instant . . . or tried to. One of his eyes was twitching wildly back and forth, and I got the impression he couldn't see anything clearly. Then he shut his eyes again, leaned his head back against the wall, and shuddered. I was so terribly afraid for him, and also frustrated. There's nothing worse than seeing a friend in pain and not being able to help. I looked at Rita and Tommy and saw similar emotions in their eyes. None of us knew what to do, or even what to think.

When the ambulance finally arrived Rose met the paramedics at the door and led them to the kitchen. Dr. Tilford identified himself and gave them a quick rundown on Devon's condition. Mostly medical jargon, but some phrases were recognizable. *Sudden loss of balance. Disorientation. Severe nausea.* He displayed such an air of medical authority that I felt somewhat reassured; clearly he was on top of this.

With his hand on Devon's shoulder he asked, "Can you move?"

"I'm not sure." His son's voice was barely audible, and he winced when he spoke, as if even the slight movement of his jaw made him feel sicker.

Then the paramedics took him by his arms and helped him get to his feet. He was swaying like a drunk, and at one point it looked like he was about to throw up. Two more paramedics had brought in a stretcher, and they helped ease him onto it while Dr. Tilford watched in obvious torment. I could taste how much he wanted to step in and help, but that wasn't the protocol, and he knew it.

When Devon was finally lying down he shut his eyes, sighing deeply as they strapped him in, as if relieved that he would not have to move for a while. His color was ghastly. The paramedics wheeled him out with Dr. Tilford close behind; the rest of us followed in their wake, down the hallway, through the entrance foyer, and out onto the front porch. From there we huddled together and watched as they slid the stretcher into the back of the ambulance. Dr. Tilford exchanged a few words with the head paramedic, then the two of them climbed inside the back, and the heavy doors swung shut behind them.

Suddenly I realized that we weren't alone. Neighbors had come out onto their porches to see what all the commotion was about, and a few people in robes and pajamas were standing in the roadway across from our house. For one sickening moment I had a flashback to the pajama-clad crowd that had surrounded my house when it burned down. I tried to shut them out of my head as I looked back at the ambulance.

Someone grabbed my hand and squeezed it briefly. Rose? Tommy? I didn't want look away long enough to find out.

Finally the ambulance began to move out. Sirens pierced the night as brightly colored lights began to strobe from its roof. I felt tears start to gather in the corner of one eye, born of fear and frustration. I felt helpless not being able to help the friend who had been such comfort to me in my own need.

"C'mon." Uncle Julian's strong hand gripped my shoulder. "Get some clothes on, we'll take the SUV."

||||||||||||||

The emergency room was sleek and clean and mostly empty. In one corner was a middle-aged woman who was knitting nervously; every few minutes she would glance at the double doors that led to the hospital's interior, a look of concern on her face, then she would turn back to her yarn and knit even more furiously. Other than her, we were the only non-nurses there.

A woman in scrubs showed up to tell us that Devon was being cared for and that for now he seemed to be okay, but she wouldn't give us any more details. We weren't family.

Eventually Dr. Tilford came out. His normally stoic façade was clearly being strained to the breaking point.

"Devon is suffering from an acute attack of vertigo," he told us. "They don't know the cause yet, but they've ruled out some major concerns. He seems stable for now." He turned back toward the double doors. "I'll let you know if anything changes."

Before he could leave I asked, "Is he going to be okay?"

He hesitated. "We're doing everything we can to make sure of it."

He didn't wait around for any more questions, so I pulled out my phone and looked up vertigo. *Extreme dizziness*, Wikipedia said. *Sometimes comes on without warning.*

Not a big help.

Time crept by after that with agonizing slowness. Tommy had stayed at the house to monitor the internet channels, searching for any sign that other changelings were getting sick. It wasn't so long ago that someone had been killing them off one by one, and if that was starting up again, we needed to know. But he said he hadn't found anything to suggest that was the case. One bit of good news, anyway.

Finally Rita and I were allowed to see Devon.

He was sitting in a hospital bed, in a small enclosure with curtains for walls. He seemed to be aware of us when we entered the room, but he didn't open his eyes.

"Hey," I said.

"Hey," he whispered weakly.

"You okay?"

"If I don't move. Or try to look at anything." He paused. "Or breathe too hard."

He barely moved as he spoke to us. His hands were gripping the rails of the bed as if he was afraid of falling out of it. I placed my hand gently on top of one of them. His skin was clammy, and I felt him trembling.

Dr. Tilford came into the enclosure. "Tests all negative so far," he told Devon.

"Is that good?" I asked.

"Well, it doesn't tell us what's wrong, but some rather serious possibilities have been ruled out, so that's good. Sometimes this kind of thing just comes out of the blue. We may never know the cause."

A nurse entered the enclosure, took Devon's blood pressure, and gave him some medication. Then Dr. Tilford left for a minute to go talk to the doctors. And the three of us were alone together.

Devon whispered, "Do you think *they* did this?"

Neither Rita nor I had to ask what he meant. Was it possible that people from Terra Prime were responsible for his sudden illness? I couldn't recall a case where any changelings had been struck down exactly like this, but that didn't mean much. There were probably dozens of changeling deaths we didn't know anything about. Tommy's online research suggested that none of the others were being assaulted, but the three of us might be a special case. We were the only changelings who knew the truth about where we were from. The only ones who had crossed into the world of our birth and destroyed a major transportation hub on our way out. The Shadows might want revenge for that. The Greys might want revenge for that. Hell, a dozen other Guilds whose Gifts we'd never heard of might want revenge for that.

*But they could have killed Devon if they'd wanted to*, I reminded myself. *This was just a warning shot.* "They have people who can heal. I suppose they have people who can un-heal." I spoke softly, so no one outside the curtain would hear me. "Maybe they're trying to scare us off."

"To keep us from going back to Terra Prime?" Rita asked.

I nodded.

She folded her arms over her chest, a gesture that managed to be both defensive and aggressive at the same time. "So what, then? Are we supposed to give up, just like that? What about your mom?"

I looked down at Devon. His coffee-colored skin was filmed in sweat. "We can wait a few days, until Devon gets better. I can talk to Seyer—"

"No," Devon rasped. "No. You two have to go. Now. Don't wait for me."

"Why?" I asked.

"Because if you're right, and they're trying to scare us off, what will happen when they figure out you're just delaying the trip, not cancelling it? They might do something worse than this, to drive the message home. Maybe go after Rita next time . . . or even you. But once you cross over, there'll be no point in threats anymore; they'll have lost that battle."

"Shit," Rita muttered. "He's right."

"And second . . ." He sighed. "I'm sorry, Seyer's Gift may be terrifying and powerful and utterly beyond my comprehension, but nothing short of a direct message from God Himself is likely to convince my father I should go with you. I mean, it was nice to dream, but. . . ." His words trailed off into a pained silence.

For a moment no one said anything. I wondered if Dr. Tilford was rethinking his response to the story Devon had told him. No one on our world could cause sickness like this, but Devon had described a world where people could. Was Dr. Tilford wondering now if he'd dismissed his son's tale too quickly? Was he wondering if the maker of our alien artifact might want to hurt his son? Or was he ascribing the timing of this to mere coincidence?

"I don't want to go without you," I murmured.

He sighed. "Yeah, and I don't want to lie in a hospital bed worrying about whether you're both safe or not. But we don't always get what we want." He attempted to shake his head, but winced as soon as the motion began. "I wish I could go with you too, Jesse."

Something about the way he said my name made my heart lurch in my chest. I leaned down and kissed him gently on the forehead. His skin was cool and salty against my lips. At least he had no fever. That was good, right?

He opened his eyes and looked at me. His left eye was twitching less than it had in Rose's kitchen. "Come home in the right time frame," he whispered. "Even if you have to stay there a while to figure out how to do it right. Don't end up like Sebastian, coming home after everyone you love is long dead." *Including me,* his eyes pleaded.

"We will," I told him, and Rita said, "We promise."

Dr. Tilford came back then, so I let go of Devon's hand. The doctor told us he was going to spend the night by Devon's side, and promised to text us if anything changed. So we left them both there. What else could we do? Whoever had struck Devon down had played his hand well.

One third of our team was lying helpless in a hospital bed, we hadn't even left home yet.

As omens went, it was a pretty lousy one.

# 8

## BERKELEY SPRINGS
## WEST VIRGINIA

### JESSE

SEYER SHOWED UP IN THE MORNING, right on
schedule. My mother hadn't been all that happy
about our plans, when we'd discussed them the night before, and with Devon's midnight emergency having
shaken us all pretty badly, she was even less happy about
them now. Despite our assurances that Seyer had once
been "an old family friend," Mom said she didn't know
her *now*, and that was what mattered. As Seyer drove up
she stood on the porch with her arms folded across her
chest, and it looked like we weren't going to be traveling
anywhere.

Seyer had brought a young girl with her, a thin waif
in a flowered sundress, who she introduced as Samantha. The girl stuck by Miriam's side, her wide blue eyes
taking in the scene as Seyer explained to my mother
how good it would be for me to get away for a while. A

kind of vacation. It all sounded pretty lame to me (vacation from what?) but within minutes Mom was nodding and smiling, and saying yes, yes, it might be good for me to get away, and she was glad that Seyer was giving me the opportunity to do so. She agreed that while it would be nice if Seyer's mountain retreat had good cell phone reception, so she could keep in touch with us, of course in the mountains of West Virginia, service might be spotty and she understood that. Ten minutes later I had her permission to go, and even Rose—who had been more wary of the trip than Mom was—beamed as she gave us a tin of chocolate chip cookies to take with us. So Rita and I fetched the bags we'd packed for the trip, including a large black portfolio with the painting in it, and she climbed into the car while I said goodbye to Mom.

As we hugged I pressed my cheek against hers, drinking in her scent, her warmth, and her affection, trembling as I tried not to think about all the things that might keep me from returning to her. True, I was only going to Terra Prime to talk to someone, and Miriam Seyer had promised to bring us home right after that, but neither Rita nor I was so naïve as to think that it would all go off exactly as planned. The universe just didn't work like that. Terra Prime was a frightening and unpredictable world, and we barely knew a fraction of its rules. When we left our own world behind, we had to accept that there was a small chance we might never come home again.

*I will come back to you, Mom.* I buried my face in her neck so that no one could see the tears forming in my eyes. *I'll find a way to heal you, and I'll come home to you. I promise.*

Finally it was time to leave. I threw my backpack into the car, waved a final farewell to Tommy, and climbed into the back seat, next to Rita.

It wasn't until Seyer's SUV pulled onto the main road that she formally introduced us to her companion: *Samantha Cassidy, Journeyman of the Domitors.* It didn't take a degree in Latin to figure out the nature of Cassidy's Gift. Suddenly my family's unexpected change in attitude made total sense, as did a few other things, considerably darker in nature. I remembered how many of the other changelings had died because they'd made foolish choices. One had gone surfing in hurricane waters, I recalled, and another had dived into a concrete pool at the wrong angle. And one person with a bee allergy had walked right into an angry hive. Back when we'd first heard about those deaths we couldn't imagine how an outside agency could have caused all that, but if there was a Gift that allowed one to nudge people's thoughts in a particular direction, quieting the inner voice that normally kept them from doing stupid things, maybe it wasn't so great a mystery after all.

I wondered if Samantha had been involved in any of those killings.

Since the Gate in Luray was now buried under tons of rubble, Seyer said she was going to take us north, to something she called an E-Gate. Apparently the 'E' stood for *ephemeral.* Unlike the portal in Luray, this one hadn't been around for centuries, but was a fleeting phenomenon, like the rift Sebastian had run into at the North River. Seyer assured us that the Greys had stabilized it for now, but you didn't have to be a rocket scientist to figure out that something named *ephemeral* was probably temporary in nature. Did that mean that the portal might vanish at any moment? Maybe while we were passing through it?

*The Greys are experts at this stuff,* I told myself. *Surely they wouldn't let people enter the Gate if it was dangerous.*

We drove for a while without anyone talking. Not

that there weren't a thousand and one questions I wanted to ask Seyer, but the situation with Devon had left me badly shaken, and his absence hung like a dank cloud over our journey. Rita spent most of the trip leaning against the window of Seyer's SUV, staring out at the passing landscape in silence, so she must have felt it, too. It was strange for the two of us to be going to Terra Prime without him. Like leaving part of your own body behind.

Just before hitting the main highway, Seyer pulled over for gas. There was a nearby convenience store, and the Domitor took some money from the glove compartment and headed inside to buy us all drinks. When she was gone, I turned to Seyer and asked, "How long were you watching me?"

She raised an eyebrow slightly, said nothing.

"I know that you scoped my house one day, before I met you. Tommy saw you there. So, was that the first time you spied on me? Or is this something that's been going on for a while?"

She didn't say anything. She just looked at me for a moment longer, smiled slightly, then got out of the car and went to where the squeegees were stored. A minute later she was cleaning the windshield. A faint smile creased her lips, maybe part amusement, maybe something else. Something darker.

She never answered me.

Damn her.

⁜

If you'd asked me a year ago what I thought the portal to another world would look like, the last thing I would have said was *The Department of Motor Vehicles*.

Life is full of surprises.

After a couple of hours on the highway, Seyer turned off onto a narrow dirt road. At the end of it was a large open field surrounded by a primitive stone wall, and a weathered barn at the far end that had seen better days. The field was full of vehicles, not all of them neatly parked: cars, vans, pickup trucks, even one eighteen wheeler. Some looked brand new, others like they had just come from a demolition derby. Seyer parked at the end of the last row and then told us we would have to leave our cell phones in her glove compartment for safekeeping, as we couldn't bring electronic devices through the Gate. I noted that she took it for granted that we both had our phones with us, which of course we did. I couldn't answer for Rita's motives, but I figured if we wound up returning to Terra Colonna in some unexpected time or place, I wanted my phone with me. With a sigh I checked to make sure my phone was locked, then turned it off and stowed it in the glove compartment alongside Rita's and Seyer's.

I had far worse contraband in my backpack, but of course I wasn't going to tell her that.

It turned out the barn wasn't an old building at all, just a big stage set. What had appeared from a distance to be mildew turned out to be speckled green paint, and a power sander had clearly been used to grind off some of the color in strategic spots, I could see little dents where someone had beaten the wood with a chain to make it look weatherworn. *Shabby chic alien portal.*

Inside was a small foyer, where a pleasant looking woman with nondescript features greeted us politely from behind a cheap Formica counter. "Good afternoon," she said in a quasi-British accent (modified by a Southern twang). "How may I help you?" Wordlessly Seyer removed three small black booklets from her purse and handed them to her; the Domitor apparently had her own. As the woman flipped through the booklets I saw my picture in one of them and Rita's in another. Some kind of passport? The clerk gave each one a cursory glance, compared our names to those on a list on her clipboard, then handed them back to us.

"Departure in twenty-three minutes," she said pleasantly. "Any special dispensations?"

"No," Seyer responded.

"Customs declarations and waivers are over there." She indicated a shelf I hadn't noticed before, also cheap Formica, a narrow ledge running the length of the wall. There were papers stacked neatly in bins and pens in little black cups, the universal symbol for *Hey, you need to fill something out.* "We have lockers for contraband, if you need one."

"Thank you," Seyer said, and she ushered us toward the shelf.

There were two documents there, and Seyer told us to sign them using the names in our passbooks, and date them. The first had a bold heading that read CONTRABAND DECLARATION, and below that a statement in smaller type: *I, _____ verify that I am not carrying on my person, nor will I attempt to bring through the Gate, any of the following items.* Below that was a list of items the folks of Terra Prime didn't want in their world. Some of them we already knew about—*electronic devices of any kind* topped the list—but some were surprising, and a few were just plain weird. Seriously, how much would it threaten their world if someone brought a pack of chewing gum? I reviewed the list, then got to the part where I had to initial a box to verify that I'd read and agreed to it. I glanced at Rita. Did she also have something in her backpack that was less than kosher, or was she playing it straight? Her expression offered me no clue. Finally I sighed, checked the box, and then looked in my passbook to see what alias Seyer had assigned to me. Jennifer Dolan. I signed on the dotted line, thus establishing that my first official act in traveling to Morgana's world was to lie to authorities.

The other document was a legal disclaimer. *I,
_____, hereby acknowledge that the portal I
am about to enter is a natural phenomenon, neither created for or by, nor controlled by, the Guild of Obfuscates.
I acknowledge that while the Guild has established a
Gate to help facilitate safe passage, minor temporal dis-
turbances are still possible, which the Guild may not be
able to predict or nullify. I verify that I am choosing to
enter the Gate fully cognizant of these risks, and will not
hold the Guild liable for any temporal disturbance I may
suffer, or for any other adverse effect attending my passage.*

It was more than a little chilling, but I figured we
were already past the point of no return, so I signed that
one, too.

Once we handed in our paperwork we were allowed
to proceed to the main room, which was so utterly mundane in appearance that I felt like I'd walked into the
DMV. It was a large room with a counter running along
one wall, rows of molded plastic chairs in the middle,
and a big sign overhead that proclaimed in capital letters, SERVING NEXT: E43. Surely any minute now we
would hear an announcement about where to go to get
a photograph taken for our portal-crossing license.
Thank God Seyer had all our papers in order, so we
didn't have to wait in any lines. It was only a short wait
before we ushered through a door at the far end of
the room, along with a dozen other people.

Having only seen the Gate in Luray, I'd assumed that
the other ones looked much the same: mysterious archways hidden deep underground, flanked by rows of insensate bodies ready to be used as transportation tools.
But this arch was a much less imposing structure, smaller
and simpler than its Luray counterpart, and without the
layered crystals that had lent the other such a fantastic
air. Still, I felt my heart flutter with fear as I looked at it.

I still remembered the icy breath of the void that lay beyond that Gate and had no desire to ever experience it again.

Suddenly the space inside the arch began to shimmer. A golden pattern began to take shape line by line, in its center. The design wasn't something I saw with my eyes but rather with my mind. Faint strains of music wafted toward me, as if floating on an unseen breeze. Random chords, haunting and somber, as if an orchestra worlds away was fine-tuning its instruments, and we were hearing their echoes.

Then a Shadowlord stepped through. His sudden presence was like a blast of icy wind, and the hair on the back of my neck pricked upright as I stared at him, mesmerized by the unearthly quality of his appearance. Bloodless skin, empty black eyes, a body whose edges shifted and faded even as I tried to focus on him . . . the sight of him stirred a visceral fear deep within me, and I instinctively stepped back from him. A few of the locals did the same, though more discreetly than I did. Apparently even people who were used to ghosts and shapechangers didn't want to get too close to his kind.

*What if this Shadow knows who I am?* I thought suddenly. *What if he recognizes me as one of the Colonnans connected to the destruction of the Gate in Luray?* The Shadows might not have considered it worth their time to hunt me down back home, but now I was re-entering their world—their territory—and the rules might change. Every survival instinct in my soul was urging me to turn and run out of here, to get as far away from this unnatural creature as I possibly could. If I could make it outside, into the sunlight, he wouldn't follow me there. Shadowlords hated the sun as much as vampires did.

But the Shadow didn't spare a glance for me, or for any of the tourists; he just spoke briefly to the Grey in charge, then turned back to the arch and addressed . . .

well, empty air. Out of the corner of my eye I thought I saw a shadow that might or might not be in the shape of a man, but it disappeared as soon as I tried to look directly at it. A ghost, perhaps? The Shadowlord gestured toward the Gate, and I saw the wispy shape move toward the portal. All right, that made sense. Passage between the worlds required precise coordination, and since there was no cell phone service spanning the distance, someone had to carry messages back and forth. And since spirits of the dead were immune to the negative side effects of crossing, they were the obvious candidates. I was witnessing the very service that had made Shadowlords the undisputed masters of the multiverse. Without them, individual worlds like mine were isolated islands in a vast and angry sea, their wealth—raw materials, slave species, children with valuable Gifts—hopelessly out of reach. It was the Gift of the Shadows that allowed Terra Prime to rape all the other worlds of everything from dinosaurs to artwork to infant psychics in their cradles. Whatever other worlds had that was valuable, the Shadows enabled Terra Prime to claim it.

A gentle prod between my shoulder blades nudged me forward. Travelers were queuing up to go through the gate, their order dictated by a Grey reading names from a clipboard, and when my name—my fake name— was called, I took my place in line. I tried not to think about the realm of formless chaos that we were about to enter. This passage would be different than the others; the chaos of *between* was no threat to me.

But I remembered the terms of the waiver I had signed, and I shuddered.

A new pattern was beginning to take shape in the center of the Gate now, that reminded me of some of my dream designs, and also of the codex that Sebastian had given us, the symbolic map that had helped us find our way home. I concentrated on memorizing its twists and turns so that I could reproduce the pattern later. Then the line of travelers began to move, person after person stepping through the Gate and disappearing into darkness. As each one crossed the threshold, a different person emerged from the arch to take his place, similar to him in size and shape. The exchange was perfectly synchronized, a dance of almost-twins set to the music of the Gate. I knew enough about how portals worked to understand that these people were here to balance our passage, so that the delicate equilibrium of energy required to keep the Gate stable could be maintained. But given that the last such people I'd seen were wheeled across on morgue gurneys, I was startled to see these walking under their own power. I looked back at Seyer, a question in my eyes, but she just smiled that maddening smile of hers and nodded for me to move me forward.

Into the darkness between the worlds.

Passage lasted no more than a split second this time—apparently it was faster when proper procedures were followed—but that brief moment was almost more than I could handle. I understood the nature of the realm we were passing through in a way these other travelers never would, and even a split-second reminder of that formless chaos, and the visceral terror it inspired, was nearly more than I could handle. By the time I stepped out into Terra Prime my whole body was shaking, and after Rita and Seyer came through, we couldn't get out of the building fast enough for my liking.

Outside there was sunlight: golden-bright, summer-warm, its heat carried to us by fresh mountain breezes. Gradually I relaxed, and my trembling subsided. Seyer arranged for a horse-drawn cab to take us to a nearby train. She'd booked a private cabin for us, she said. The trip to Luray would be long, so it might as well be comfortable. She and Samantha chatted on the way, but it was the kind of small talk that goes in one ear and out the other. Universal custom. I didn't feel like talking to these people, or to anyone.

When we got to the train an attendant in uniform led us to our cabin, and I sank down gratefully onto one of the thickly padded benches. Now that the horror of the Gate was behind us, the exhaustion of the last few days was catching up with me. How long had it been since I'd had a good night's sleep? I was so upset by the attack on Devon that sleep was impossible, and the nights before that had been filled with tossing and turning, as fear of the dream-wraith's return possessed me each time I sank into a dreaming state. Now . . . the leather seats were soft and deep, the rhythm of the train was mesmerizing, and though I didn't trust Seyer and her people worth a damn, I suspected the dream-wraith wouldn't visit me while I was in her presence.

I did ask Seyer about the people who'd balanced our crossing. I didn't expect her to answer, but to my surprise she did, explaining that there were many different ways of managing the exchange, and keeping bodies in stasis so they could be sent across was just one of them. It was more expensive to hire an unending stream of people to make the crossing, but this far from a major population center, harvesting local material was difficult. The big cities were full of people no one cared about, but in a small town, people tended to notice when their neighbors went missing.

*Harvest. Material. Bodies in stasis.* That's all the people of my world were to Seyer and her kind. The un-Gifted had no value save to be used as tools, as commerce, as sport, or as servants. Hell, my world treated dogs better than her world treated people.

With a sigh I leaned back in the seat. My eyes began to slide shut of their own accord, and I lacked the strength—or the desire—to keep them open. I needed to be fresh for my meeting with Morgana, right? Surely it would be far worse to nod off in her presence than to do so now, when I was—in a relative sense, at least—safe.

My last thought as I drifted off to sleep was: *God help me if I ever become as callous as these people.*

# 9

JESSE

IT FELT STRANGE entering the Seers' estate through the front entrance, like a legitimate visitor. Strange to be waved in by the guards like a visiting dignitary and helped down from our coach by liveried servants who bowed to us, albeit more deeply to Seyer.

Viewed from the front walk (as opposed to my previous experience of peering through a hedge), the Guildhouse seemed twice as imposing as before. On my first visit I'd taken note of the Egyptian frieze over the doorway and statues of Bast, the cat god, flanking the staircase, but now that I was closer I could see just how pervasive that ancient cultural influence was. Decorative carvings surrounding the base of each column might have looked like simple geometric designs to most people, but I recognized them as stylized lotus blossoms, a common Egyptian motif. The sconces flanking the front doors were in the form of papyrus stalks, and a matching pattern was carved into each door. Was there an actual connection between the Guild of Seers and the ancient Egyptians, or had the architect who designed this place just liked the style?

There was one element that wasn't Egyptian, a geometric symbol etched into a bronze plaque, right over the door. I remembered seeing it on a banner at the fair we'd visited the first time we came to this world. A small circle nestled inside an oblong shape, framed by an equilateral triangle: the sigil of the Guild of Seers. Now that I had a chance to look at it in a calmer setting, without the ruckus of the fair distracting me, it seemed oddly familiar, as if I knew the design from somewhere before. Maybe in my own world? Try though I might, I couldn't place it.

Inside the building, a shadowy entrance foyer with a high vaulted ceiling offered relief from the summer heat. The polished marble floor was inlaid with an intricate mandala-like pattern, at the center of which the Guild sigil was repeated. Our footsteps echoed eerily in the chamber as we crossed it, like footsteps in a tomb, and an abbie stepped forward to meet us. The small slave hominid was dressed in a loose white shift with a gold-and-silver belt, and her hair had been neatly braided and coiled around her head. She was the first abbie I'd ever seen who was nicely dressed. Maybe her species was treated better here.

Seyer told us, "I'll need to brief her Grace before I introduce you. Meanwhile, Sarai will bring you whatever refreshments you would like." She indicated the abbie, who bowed her head submissively and did not look up again until Seyer was gone. In truth I was too distracted to care about eating, but the day was hot and a cold drink would be pleasant, so I asked if she had iced tea. Rita said that any cold drink would do. The abbie bowed again, then left us alone in the echo chamber. I don't think either Rita or I was really thirsty, but I wanted to send the hominid away so we could talk freely.

Suddenly I realized that we'd never heard any of the abbies speak. They'd made animal-like sounds when we spied on them in the woods, but every other time we'd seen them, they were submissively silent. Did they lack the physical capacity for human speech, or had they just decided that silence was the best mode for a slave to operate in? At what point in human evolution did language first appear?

When she was finally gone I looked at Rita. "Does it seem strange to you that Seyer would be briefing Morgana?" I whispered.

She raised an eyebrow. "How so?"

"Well, she knew for a whole day that we would be coming here. Wouldn't you expect her to have contacted Morgana before this? So everything was prepared for our arrival?" I was turning puzzle pieces over in my mind, trying to see how they all fit together. "But that would have required a messenger, either living or dead . . . and the Shadows control the dead."

"She could have just sent a normal person with a message." Rita rolled her eyes slightly. "Assuming anyone could be considered 'normal' here."

"But that messenger would still have to go through a Gate to get to Morgana, and the Shadows control the Gates." I paused. "Maybe Seyer was afraid they would ask too many questions about her business. Or about us."

"Jeez, Jesse." Rita shook her head in mock dismay. "You're seriously overthinking this stuff."

"Says the girl who doesn't have a Gift that people would kill you for," I pointed out. How did the old saying go? *It's not paranoia if people are really out to get you.*

I returned my attention to the pattern at my feet, trying to place where I'd seen it before. I didn't even hear when the abbie came back, and Rita had to nudge my shoulder to get my attention.

The iced tea was good, if a little too sweet for my taste. Sipping it, I suddenly realized why the pattern looked so familiar. Resting my portfolio against my legs, I handed my drink to Rita, then slid my bag from my shoulder and rummaged inside it. My wallet was in a zippered compartment at the bottom, not easy to open without emptying the whole bag. But eventually my questing fingers found the wallet, and I pulled a single bill out of it. One American dollar. I studied it, turned it over, and felt my heart skip a beat as I saw it. Right there. Just like I'd remembered it.

"What?" Rita demanded. "What is it?"

I held it over the symbol on the floor and invited Rita to compare the two. She did, and her eyes went wide. "Holy crap."

On the back of the bill was an unfinished pyramid glowing with light, with a human eye above it. If you reduced that image to a simple line drawing, it would look similar to the design on the floor.

No. Not similar. It would look *exactly* like the design on the floor.

So what did that mean? That the Guild of Seers had designed our currency? My head was spinning from trying to make sense of it all.

Footsteps could be heard now, coming toward us. Probably Seyer returning. I stuffed the bill into my pocket so she wouldn't see it, shouldered my bag again, and took my drink back from Rita.

All my life I'd disdained conspiracy theorists, especially when they talked about secret organizations that manipulated human history for shadowy purposes. But maybe I shouldn't have been so quick to dismiss them. I remembered how easily the Domitor had convinced my family to do what she wanted, in a way that no observer would remark upon. A powerful woman like Morgana, with all the Gifts of this world at her disposal, could easily nudge human history in whatever direction she wanted it to go, and no one would be the wiser. Doubtless there were Shadows and the Greys who could do the same. Psychics and undead and aliens, secretly guiding our world. Maybe the conspiracy junkies weren't so crazy after all.

Seyer looked calm and collected as she rejoined us; clearly her meeting with Morgana had gone well. She called for the abbie to take away our glasses, and Rita took one last sip before handing hers over. This time I noted that the hominid kept her eyes averted while she interacted with Seyer, though whether that was from fear of her, or simply ritual submission, it was impossible to say.

"Come," Seyer told us. "Her Grace will see you now."

|||||||||||||||||

The library where Alia Morgana received us was a traditional Victorian style study, with dark wooden bookshelves, thickly upholstered chairs, and a polished mahogany reading table. Positioned between the bookshelves were narrow glass-fronted cabinets that contained mixed assortments of small artifacts, all of which looked ancient. Music was playing softly in the background—something classical—and Rita and I both looked around for speakers, wondering what manner of non-electronic device was broadcasting it. But nothing was visible.

"Beethoven's Eleventh." The voice came from behind us: smooth, sophisticated, emotionless. I turned and found myself facing the woman I'd seen with Seyer at the assessment fair. She was still wearing white, and the sculpted curls of her golden hair were arranged around her head like a halo. In the midst of all the dark Victorian wood she glowed with light, like an angel. Or perhaps like something darker, that wanted to pass for an angel.

"A bit reminiscent of the Fourth Symphony," she continued. "Although I find his later works more mature."

I had promised myself that no matter what Morgana said or did I wouldn't act surprised. I knew that I needed to exude confidence if I was going to negotiate with her, and gaping like a backwater rube every time she made some reference to Terra Prime technology was not the way to accomplish that. But for all our talk about visiting parallel worlds, I'd never really considered all the artistic implications of that. What masterpieces might Van Gogh have produced if he hadn't died young? Or Mozart? Or John Lennon? Somewhere there were worlds where those people had survived. Where they had continued creating works of genius until they died of old age, resulting in a wealth of art and music that my world would never see. Morgana and her kind harvested those works for their private pleasure, while the rest of us were left in the dark. *They're vultures,* I thought. *Fashionable, well-spoken vultures, feeding off the carrion of other worlds.*

Speaking of vultures, there was a tall birdcage in one corner of the room, with a creature inside that was both like and unlike a bird. It had colorful feathers arranged in clusters at the ends of its wings and tail, but the body was lizard-like in shape, and when it squawked at me I saw rows of needle-sharp teeth in its mouth.

"Your Grace." Seyer bowed her head respectfully to her mistress. "Allow me to introduce Miss Jessica Drake and Miss Rita Morales, of Terra Colonna."

"Of Terra Prime," Morgana corrected her gently. "They do acknowledge their birthright, do they not?"

Seyer flushed. "Of course, your Grace. My apologies."

The Guildmistress smiled at us. Her expression was polished and perfect, and so clearly rehearsed that it lacked even a hint of sincerity. If she'd been holding a knife behind her back and thinking about how to stab us, she probably wouldn't have looked any different.

"I'm glad to have a chance to finally meet you," she said, "though I admit, the last thing I expected was for you to return to Terra Prime." She looked me over as she spoke, and suddenly I felt very exposed. Was she able to read my thoughts? My emotions? What did a Seer's Gift do, exactly?

She noted the portfolio tucked under my arm. "I understand you have something for me?"

Not trusting myself to speak, I simply nodded.

She gestured toward the reading table. I walked over to it and set the stiff black folder down, but before I could open the zipper Rita put a hand on my arm, stopping me.

"Just so we're clear," she said to Morgana, "the price for this painting includes an audience with her Grace, then safe passage home for both of us. *Safe* passage. You agreed to that, right?"

It was Seyer who responded. "Her Grace is aware of the terms of our bargain," she said acidly. "All the conditions we discussed will be honored."

Rita continued staring at Morgana; clearly Seyer's assurance was not enough for her. After a moment Morgana chuckled softly and said, "All your terms are acceptable, Miss Morales. I shall see you delivered home like royalty."

Rita let go of my arm. I unzipped the portfolio and spread it open on the table so that my painting was exposed. As I stood back and tried to see my work through Morgana's eyes, I realized that the bright colors that had seemed so harmonious at the brightly lit mill looked a bit garish in this dark setting. But that was okay; the goal had been to create a work rich in meaning, not subtlety.

Morgana studied the painting in silence for a minute and then reached out to touch it. When her finger made contact with the canvas I felt a faint cold prickling along my skin, as if she were touching me instead of my work. As she ran her fingers along the ridges of my paint strokes I had to fight the urge to cross my arms in front of my body, to cover myself.

"Not as complex as some of your earlier work," she murmured. Finally her hand fell away from the piece. "The emotional energy is a bit . . . erratic. Had you devoted more time to it, the resonance probably would have been more stable. But the composition is interesting."

"Glad you like it," I muttered.

"I do. Which means you've earned your time with me." Her eyes were an odd mix of blue, green, and grey, I noted, and they shifted color as she moved. Disconcerting. "So what business of yours is so pressing that you think it merits this audience?"

I was pretty sure Seyer had explained to her about my mother's situation, so I just reviewed the highlights. She listened in silence. I couldn't tell from her expression what she was thinking.

When I was done she said, "Mistress Seyer has explained why no Healer can help your mother?"

I nodded. "She has, Your Grace." The title felt strange on my modern American tongue.

"A Fleshcrafter might be able to do something for her, but it would be a chancy operation at best. And they're an insular lot, the Potters. Outside of their work in prepping changelings for adoption they generally keep to themselves, and they don't welcome commissions from outsiders. It would take more than a handful of coin to convince one of them to travel to another world, to help save a woman who, by the measure of our society, is of no consequence."

I bit back on the sharp comment I wanted to make. I knew from our last visit that she considered my little brother expendable, so it came as no surprise to hear that the rest of my family meant nothing to her. But *I* was not nothing to her. I was part of some project she was planning, which meant that someday she might need my cooperation. If she left my mother to suffer now, when she had the ability to save her, she could kiss that cooperation goodbye.

None of which had to be said out loud, I was sure.

In my best negotiating voice I said, "I was hoping that you might be willing to help me cut a deal with them. Maybe there's something I could offer you in return for that?" I glanced pointedly at the painting.

She followed my gaze and chuckled. "You would bargain for my assistance without knowing anything about me, or even why I have such an interest in your art? At least you don't lack for audacity." I blushed slightly but otherwise didn't respond to her; now was not a moment to display weakness. She sighed. "I suppose it's time you understood what's behind that interest. Not that it will be a gentle lesson, I warn you. There is knowledge that has the power to alter a human soul, and once you embrace it, you can't go back." Her lips pursed as she studied me. "Do you want to risk being altered thus? Or go home now, and take comfort in your ignorance?"

The warning was scary (if a bit melodramatic), but I hadn't come here to play it safe. "I want to know what this is all about," I told her.

She nodded solemnly, then walked over to one of the display cabinets, took a key from her pocket, and unlocked it. On the top shelf was a large leather-bound volume, which she handled with extreme care, taking it down and laying it on the table beside my painting. Its surface was stained and worn, and I could see places where the leather had dried and cracked; clearly it was an ancient item. As she opened it, I saw that it wasn't a regular book, but a collection of individual papers of different shapes and sizes, that someone had bound loosely together. She leafed through the pages too quickly for me see what was on any of them, then found what she was looking for, smoothed the book open, and gestured for me to come closer so I could see it.

I did so. And my heart stopped beating for an instant.

On the page was a drawing done in charcoal, clearly rendered hastily by a hand that had little artistic skill. But despite its aesthetic shortcomings, there was no mistaking what the drawing represented, and a shiver ran down my spine as I gazed at it.

It was a fate map.

Each twist and angle represented a choice someone would have to make, a potential future. The sizes and relative position of the elements suggested the possibility that a particular event would take place, while smaller lines splayed off from the main elements like branches of a tree, representing possible consequences. I had no clue who or what had inspired the painting, so I could guess what all the shapes referred to, but not the overall pattern. This was the same symbolic language that I had developed for my own art, which—until this moment—I had believed was uniquely my own.

The paper felt brittle between my fingers as I turned the page, like it might crumble to dust at any moment. The next drawing in the collection was in color, done in a different style than the first one; the quality of the paper suggested it was a more recent work. My hand trembled as I looked at it.

Also a fate map.

I turned more pages, and found more fate maps. Some even had patterns that looked like ones I had trailed behind me when I wandered through my dream-scape. Like someone had been watching me there. I found a few representational works as well, including a watercolor rendering of a mountainous landscape with a disembodied door suspended several feet above the ground. That one really shook me. I glanced up at Morgana to see if she guessed the significance of the image, but she was looking at me, not the book, and I couldn't read her expression at all. I turned another page—and saw something so startling that I backed away reflex-ively, banging my knee into a chair.

No. No. Not that. Not here.

"Jesse?" Rita sounded alarmed. "What's wrong?"

The drawing was done in ink, and it depicted a ghostly figure reaching out toward a cowering victim. Darkness billowed from the spirit's shoulders like vast wings, and its black body was painted so thickly that the ink had caused the paper to buckle. How did one capture the essence of a soulless void with mere pen and paper? The landscape behind the creature was meticu-lously detailed near the edges of the page, but the closer you got to the center of the picture the blurrier and more confused the details got . . . as if the ghastly crea-ture was erasing its surroundings.

Or devouring them.

It was the same death-wraith I had seen in my dream. There was no mistaking it. "What . . . what is that thing?" I struggled to keep my voice steady, even as my fear provided its own answers:

*It is death incarnate. It eats dreams. It wants to eat you.*

"No one knows," Morgana said. "It appears in several of the drawings, and since they were all sketched by dif-ferent artists, that suggests it isn't just a figment of one person's imagination. Something real probably inspired all these artists, but what it might have been, I haven't yet determined."

*It's real, all right.* I had to fight the urge to rub my arm where the wraith had clawed me. "Who made these drawings? Where did you get them?"

"They're from young people, mostly. From dozens of different worlds. They have nothing in common save for these images." She paused, and; I could feel her eyes fix on me. "There's no predicting when or where the dreamer's Gift will surface, you know."

My heart skipped a beat. My hand fell back from the page. "You are saying . . . these were drawn by Dreamwalkers?"

"Not exactly. Oh, some of them might have become that, had they lived. But people who are born with the dreamer's Gift these days rarely manifest more than a faint echo of the ancient power. Most likely these artists would have gone through life tormented by strange dreams, and nothing more. However," the grey/green/blue eyes fixed on me with disturbing intensity, "we do need to err on the side of caution."

Was she threatening me? Or warning me? I was suddenly aware of how out of my depth I was. "Is that what you think my art means? That I'm. . . . what . . . one of these Dreamwalkers?" I tried to sound like the idea seemed utterly crazy, rather than something I'd been obsessing about for weeks now.

For a moment she was silent. What if it was her custom to collect Dreamwalker drawings and then kill the artists? That would certainly explain the collection she'd just shown me. If so, I had walked right into the spider's web. A cold sweat was forming on my palms. I fought the urge to wipe them on my jeans.

"I think you're a sensitive young woman," she said at last, "and your dreams are clearly influenced by outside forces. Dreams do occasionally bleed from one world to another, you know; many of humanity's great oracles drew their inspiration from other spheres, without ever knowing it. Are you sensitive to such things, as they were? Clearly so. Does that mean you are a true Dream-walker, capable of altering the dreams of others?" She paused. "If I believed that, I would be honor bound to destroy you. That is the law of the land, and the duty of my Guild in particular." A pause. "You understand me?"

"I do," I said quietly. But in fact I was more confused than ever. It sounded like she had figured out what I was, and was teaching me how to explain it away so that others wouldn't find out. But why would she do that? What was in it for her? From what little I knew about Alia Morgana, I doubted she had an altruistic bone in her body.

"Now, my dear, you see why I've been so interested in your art. And in you." She walked to the other side of the reading table and sat down in a thickly tufted leather chair. Her golden hair glowed against the deep green leather, waves of it rippling like water as she moved. "As for your request . . ." She tapped a polished fingernail on the arm of the chair. "What you've asked for would re-quire me to call in a personal favor from the Potters. That's not the kind of service I'd be willing to provide in return for more artwork, I'm sorry. No matter how in-teresting that artwork might be."

Frustration welled up inside me, and also anger. Had I come all this way for nothing? Was I only standing here so that she could toy with me? "What else can I offer you? There's got to be something."

Her regretful smile was maddeningly insincere. I had a sudden urge to pick up my painting and smash it over her head. "There are few things of value in this world—or any other—that I don't already possess." She nodded back toward the cabinet filled with ancient relics. "What do you have that you think would be of value to me?"

I tried to think of something—anything—but it was

hopeless, and we both knew it. A woman of Morgana's wealth and power, with access to all the human worlds, probably lacked for nothing. What could I possibly offer her?

Then Rita spoke up. "Maybe some kind of service?"

We both looked at her.

"Well, you said Jesse was sensitive to dreams, right? It sounds like that's not a common talent here. Is there something she could do for you, maybe, using that ability?"

Butterflies of dread fluttered in my stomach. Did Rita understand what she was suggesting? If Morgana learned how much of the Dreamwalker Gift I really possessed, she might reconsider her decision to spare my life. But what other option was there, besides just giving up and going home? I held my breath as Morgana considered Rita's suggestion, not sure what outcome I was hoping for.

Finally Morgana got up and walked over to another bookcase. This one was unlocked, and there was a stack of papers on the top shelf, from which she withdrew a large brown envelope. She hesitated a moment, as if considering her next move, then handed it to me. I opened the clasp and peered inside. There was a single piece of paper, folded in half, marked with a webwork of shadowy folds that suggested it had once been stuffed unceremoniously in a pocket or purse. I drew it out and opened it. There was a line drawing, with repetitive geometric forms radiating out from a central point, like a Tibetan mandala. It looked vaguely familiar, but my life was so full of weird, vaguely familiar designs these days, that didn't necessarily mean anything.

I blinked and looked up at her. "Am I supposed to know what this is?"

"One of my Seers drew it while meditating. He believes it is somehow associated with the ancient dreamers.

He also saw a vision of a location nearby, that appears to be connected to it. We believe there may be an artifact of historical significance there."

"That sounds kind of vague," I said doubtfully.

"Our Gift is often cryptic," she agreed.

"So . . . you want to get hold of this thing? But you know where it is, right? Can't you just send your people out there to look for it?"

"I did. Several times. They failed to find it."

"Even the Seer who originally had the vision? Can't he just, like, tune in on it, or something?" As the words left my mouth it occurred to me that a technological metaphor might not be appropriate here, but she seemed to understand what I meant.

"Our Gift doesn't work that way. The images that come to us in our trances arrive without invitation and are beyond our conscious control." She paused. "You may be more sensitive to the influence of such an artifact than my people are."

I drew in a deep breath. "So, let me make sure I'm understanding this right: You're looking for an item that has something to do with Dreamwalkers, and you want me to help you find it? So that you can . . . what? Hunt them better? Why on earth would I help you do that?"

She smiled as she closed the book of drawings. It was a cold expression. "We know very little about their kind, outside of a few dark legends and these cryptic drawings." She tapped the book with a gilded nail. "Perhaps understanding them better would enable us to save them, rather than destroy them."

*Yeah. I'm sure that's your real motive, saving lives.* "What is it exactly that you want me to do?"

"You're more sensitive to dreams than my Seers are. If you went to the location in question, perhaps your own visions would offer you insight into what this pattern signifies. Locate its source, bring the artifact back to me, and I'll arrange for a Fleshcrafter to tend to your mother."

Before I could respond Rita demanded, "Where is this place? And would you supply transportation? And how long do you expect this to take?"

"It's in a *shallow*, several hours west of here." She raised a hand, forestalling Rita's response. "That's a place where the barrier between worlds is naturally thin, though not physically passable. Native shamans used such locations for meditation, and for ritual purposes. We believe this one may have served as an Indian burial ground at one point. And yes, I'll take care of all the travel arrangements. The last leg of it would have to be managed on foot or by horseback. Your choice. I'll supply you with whatever equipment you need, including a fetter to hold wildlife at bay. It's bear country. And of course Mistress Seyer will accompany you, for security purposes."

"And petty cash?" Rita asked, adding quickly, "Just in case something unexpected comes up."

Morgana's mouth twitched slightly. "And petty cash."

Despite the momentum of the conversation, I still wasn't convinced this was a good idea. "If your Seer picked up on a vision from another world, there might not be any artifact in this world for us to find."

"Then bring me back information on what the pattern represents, and that will satisfy the terms of our bargain."

It was all happening too fast. I needed time to think. God knew, the last thing in the world I wanted was to get more involved with Morgana than I already was. Every instinct in my soul was warning me that the woman was more deadly than a pit viper, and if she was asking me to go somewhere, I should expect that path to be a treacherous one. But there was no denying that her offer tempted me, and not just because it might win me a

Fleshcrafter's service. If there was some secret artifact related to the Dreamwalkers, I wanted to know what it was. And I wanted to see it before Morgana did. Yeah, she would eventually find it with or without me—of that I had little doubt—but if I got to it first, maybe I could do something to minimize the danger it posed to my kind. Or even destroy it, if that was the only way to assure their safety.

I looked at Rita. She hesitated, then nodded, so slightly that Morgana probably didn't see it. Her meaning was clear: She didn't like the situation, but if I chose to go, she would go with me.

"All right," I told Morgana. Sealing my fate. "I'll go there and look for this thing."

"Excellent. I'll have my people gather the necessary supplies for you. Meanwhile, Mistress Seyer will show you to rooms where you can relax until dinner, and afterward get a good night's sleep, so that you can start fresh in the morning."

"We'll share a room," Rita said quickly. Clearly she meant to follow through on her promise of not leaving me alone with these people. God, I was grateful to have her with me. This world was like a mine field, and I couldn't imagine navigating it without her.

"As you wish," Morgana said, smiling slightly. Rita's caution seemed to amuse her.

Seyer moved toward the door, gesturing for us to follow. I nodded respectfully to the Guildmistress and did so, Rita falling in behind me. But as Seyer opened the door, Rita paused, then turned back to face Morgana. "What if the legends are wrong?" she demanded. "What if a Dreamwalker was able to evade your murder squad long enough for his Gift to manifest, and it turned out nothing like what you expected? What if he didn't go crazy—and no one around him went crazy—and all those other assumptions that people have been making about Dreamwalkers being dangerous turned out to be just so much bullshit? So that you've been killing them for no good reason?"

Morgana smiled slightly. If Rita's challenge disturbed her at all, it didn't show. "Then the rules of the game would change, wouldn't they?"

She waved us toward the door in dismissal, and Seyer led us out.

|||||||||||||

"We're being played," I muttered.

Rita paused in her perusal of a garnet-and-sterling bracelet. "What makes you think that?"

She was rummaging through jewelry I'd purchased for our trip, trying on bracelets and rings, turning her hand so that one piece after another caught the light. We'd agreed it would be foolish for us to travel without emergency funds, but since the currency of our world was worthless in Terra Prime, we had no choice but to buy things we could sell or pawn once we got here. I'd withdrawn a good chunk of money from my savings account to bankroll that effort; so much for buying a car after graduation. Now that Rita had convinced Morgana to supply us with cash, of course, it seemed a wasted effort. Well, mostly a wasted effort. I still had one thing of value with me, that no local money could buy.

"I don't know," I said. "Maybe the fact that she accepted your suggestion so quickly. Didn't that seem strange to you? It was as if she had that envelope all ready for us." I paused. "Maybe she already knows what this artifact is, and there's some other reason she wants me to go out there. But what? I can't figure it out."

Alia Morgana had made it clear she could kill me with a word. So was I supposed to be afraid of her now, or grateful, or what? I felt like a pawn on a chessboard, surrounded by lethal pieces on every side, trusting a powerful chessmaster to maneuver me safely through all the deathtraps. But what was her end game? My survival might well depend upon figuring that out.

*A pawn isn't a piece you protect forever,* I reminded myself. *It's something you sacrifice to keep more important pieces on the board.*

Rita put down the jewelry. "Do you want to go home, Jesse? Because we still can do that. Our transportation costs were covered when you gave Morgana the painting, and she hasn't done any other favors for us yet. We don't owe her anything. Do you want to get out of here now, while that's still easy to do?"

Did I? On a purely visceral level, it was tempting. But any hope I had of helping Mom would be shot to hell if I left. And who was to say Morgana would allow me to quit the game? If she'd been planning this deal from the start—as I suspected—she wasn't going to let me just walk away from it. I had no idea why she'd chosen to protect me this long, but if I walked out on her now, I could kiss that protection goodbye.

I had no choice in this. Not really.

"I've come this far to help Mom," I murmured. "I'm not going home empty-handed." Never mind that it wasn't my only reason for staying. Rita didn't need to hear every dark thought that was churning in my head.

With a nod she pulled off the rings one by one and dropped them back into their storage pouch, followed by the bracelets. "Then let's just deal with the task at hand, and not drive ourselves crazy trying to guess at Morgana's motives. Okay? I doubt the devil himself could figure that woman out." She pulled over my backpack to return the pouch to its zippered compartment, but as she did she seemed to discover something. "What's this. . . . ?"

I realized what she must have found. "Don't take it out, Rita—"

But she did, and she held it up in disbelief. "A Kindle?" She blinked. "They told you not to bring any electronic devices with you, and you packed a *Kindle*?"

I tried to grab it away from her, but she held the device high, out of my reach. "Say it a little louder," I muttered. "I don't think people in the next county heard you yet."

"I doubt they'll hear anything over the tussle we're about to have. Or are you going to let me look at this thing without a fight? Because sooner or later I will look at it, you know that."

Exhaling noisily, I gave up and sat back. She opened the cover and activated the device. "Oh look, no Wi-Fi signal available. Who'da thought?"

I sighed. "Can you at least look at it without being snarky?"

I watched her swipe the screen as she went through the index item by item, checking to see what books I had downloaded. Slowly her expression grew more serious. When she was done she looked up at me. "This is for Sebastian," she said softly.

"Very insightful." I took the Kindle from her and shut it off.

"Does this mean you're planning to contact him?"

I sighed. "I'm not *planning* anything. I just thought that if we needed help while we were here, he was the only person outside Morgana's circle that we knew well enough to turn to. And he's a mercenary, so I brought something to pay him with." I pulled my backpack to me and tucked the Kindle deep, deep into it, hiding it beneath folds of clothing. "I wouldn't know how to contact him even if I wanted to."

She was about to respond when we heard someone approach the door. Both of us froze.

A soft knock sounded. "Dinner's being served." It was a woman's voice. "You're welcome to join us in the common room if you'd like, or else we can have something sent up here for you."

Rita and I looked at each other. I suddenly realized that I was clutching my backpack to my chest so tightly that anyone who came in would surely wonder what was in it. I forced my grip to relax.

"We'll eat up here," Rita called out. "Please." After a moment she added, "Thank you."

The footsteps padded away.

"We need to be careful," I whispered.

"I wish you'd told me about the Kindle." Then she sighed. "No, I don't wish you'd told me. In fact, I wish I still didn't know about it."

I closed the pack and padlocked the main zipper shut. Normally I didn't bother with locking it, but I was feeling particularly paranoid at the moment. "How about, 'Don't look in other people's bags if you don't want to know what's in them'?"

She ignored my sarcastic tone. "Are you going to warn Sebastian that he has to read everything in there before the battery runs out? 'Cause he'd have to come back to Terra Colonna to plug in the adapter."

A knowing smile crossed my face. I patted the bottom of the pack. "Portable solar charger. Size of a cell phone."

"Damn!" She shook her head and laughed. "I underestimated you, Jesse."

"Good." I stowed the pack under my bed, wedging it in tightly, so anyone who tried to pull it out would shake the frame and wake me up. "Now let's hope Morgana does the same."

# 10

## SHADOWCREST
## VIRGINIA PRIME

### ISAAC

**"IT'S TIME."**

Isaac shut his eyes for a minute, then nodded.

The journeyman who had come for him was a distant relative, someone Isaac barely knew. Giovan Antonin was dressed in formal Guild attire similar to what Isaac was wearing: a long robe the color of smoke, with a silk stola—a long, narrow band of fabric—hanging down both sides of his chest. It was the kind of outfit you had to practice walking in, especially when going up stairs, lest the stola get caught underfoot. Isaac had learned that the hard way. Giovan's stola was gray, a shade lighter than his robe—a journeyman's color—and symbols of his achievements had been embroidered down both sides. By contrast, Isaac's stola was white—the color of a blank page—and the only decoration on it was the crest of House Antonin embroidered on one end. Not until he had earned a journeyman's status would he be allowed to advertise his accomplishments.

Not that he had any accomplishments to advertise. At least not ones the Shadows would celebrate.

"I'm ready," he told his cousin. A half-truth. While part of him was genuinely curious to witness the secret rites of his Guild, another part wished he were miles away from Shadowcrest right now. The fact that his father had pulled strings to get him invited to this event only reinforced the lie that Isaac had been living, and he was sick of pretending that he was interested in following in the man's footsteps. But he'd promised that he would pursue a Shadowlord's education, so sooner or later he would have to attend their rituals. Apprentices were rarely invited to witness a Binding of the Dead, so the fact that he had been invited to this one was a high honor. Or maybe just a measure of how many strings his prestigious father could pull within the Guild. By bringing his son to this ritual, Leonid proclaimed his own power.

Isaac followed Giovan silently through Shadowcrest to the elevator, and together they descended to the Well of Souls. There were so many spirits present this time that the effect was physically claustrophobic, and for a few seconds Isaac found it hard to breathe. What must this place be like for the Shadowlords, to whom the voices of the dead were not muted whispers, but full-volumed cries? He shuddered to think about it.

The chamber Giovan led him to was the one he had passed while walking with his father. Now it was filled with Shadowlords and their ghostly retinues. The black stolas of the *umbrae majae* were embroidered with elaborate heraldic crests, representing dead Shadowlords whose memories the wearers had consumed. Some displayed dozens of such crests, which was a dizzying number when you considered what each one represented.

How someone could absorb the memories of a dozen other people and remain sane was a mystery to Isaac.

Not that anyone had ever accused the *umbrae majae* of being sane.

A few journeymen were standing in a far corner of the room, trying to stay out of the way of their betters, and Giovan led Isaac over to them and quietly made introductions. Several of the younger ones scowled at Isaac, clearly disapproving of his presence. *They'd* had to earn their journeyman rank before being invited to this prestigious ritual, so why should Isaac be exempt from that requirement? Did the same rules not hold for Leonid Antonin's son as for everyone else? They were all polite to him, in a superficial way, but the undercurrent of resentment was unmistakable.

*Great way to start out*, Isaac thought bitterly.

His father was in the chamber, but he was focused on Shadowlord business and didn't seem to notice that Isaac had entered the room. Just as well. If he paid any special attention to Isaac right now, it would only make things worse.

From where Isaac was standing he had a clear view of the stone table at the center of the room, and he could now see that there were deep channels incised in its surface, as well as the chains and shackles he had noted previously. Several of the *umbrae majae* were arranging the latter so that they lay open and waiting, and Isaac noted that the surface of the table was canted slightly, so that whatever fluid pooled in the channels would flow to the lower end, where a wide brass bowl was waiting to receive it. Isaac felt a knot form in his gut at the sight of it. When his father had invited him to witness the Binding of the Dead, he had assumed that it would be performed on . . . well, the dead. But clearly that was not the case.

The Shadowlords suddenly fell silent, and they began

to move back from the table, forming a wide circle around it. Isaac hadn't heard any kind of signal, but maybe it had been voiced by one of the many wraiths present. The journeymen took their cue from Shadowlords, and Giovan nudged Isaac into position in the circle. Isaac could sense the spirits in the room growing agitated. Though his fledgling Gift allowed him to detect their emotional state, he couldn't make out what they were saying, but it took no great skill to guess what the trouble was. Those for whom death had been a traumatic experience hated to witness the death of others.

A pair of doors at the far end of the room swung open and two *umbrae minae* entered, dragging a young boy between them. He had been stripped to the waist and his skin was slick with sweat. He was obviously drugged, and at one point fell to his knees, so that his escorts had to lift him to his feet again, forcing him to walk toward the gruesome altar. The fact that he appeared to be Isaac's age, or very close to it, made the spectacle doubly disturbing. Where had the Shadows gotten this boy? Had they purchased him from his parents, perhaps, after a Seers' evaluation had declared him unGifted? Or harvested him from the ranks of some orphan gang that was wandering the streets of the city? Or maybe captured him in a raid like the one that had decimated the Warrens? There were a dozen different ways that one might obtain unwanted children for ritual purposes, most of which made Isaac's blood curdle.

Then the boy turned toward him, and Isaac's heart stopped beating in his chest.

He knew this boy.

He *knew* him.

Shaken, he watched as the two *umbrae minae* lifted the boy up onto the stone slab, trying to gather his thoughts enough to remember the boy's name. Jason? No, Jacob. A regular visitor at the Warrens, who often snuck out of the orphanage he lived in for a few hours of secret midnight freedom. Isaac had gone on thieving expeditions with him, and had found him to be a skilled pickpocket, agile in both his hands and his wit.

Now he was here, trussed like a sheep for slaughter.

Isaac felt sick.

As they started to bind the boy down, the full horror of his situation finally broke through his drugged stupor, and he began to struggle wildly. But whatever drug they had given him had sapped all the strength from his limbs, and with practiced efficiency one of the men held him down while the other fastened shackles about his wrists and ankles. Then chains were stretched across his body and hooked in place, binding him down so tightly to the cold stone surface that he could do little more than twitch desperately. Only his head could move freely, and he whipped it back and forth as he searched the room for . . . what, exactly? Sympathy? Hope? There was no mercy to be found in this crowd.

*Don't look at me,* Isaac thought, drawing back into the shadows. *Please, please, don't look at me.*

The *umbrae minae* bowed respectfully to the assembled Shadowlords and took their leave. They might be Masters of the Guild in their own right, but they were not undead, nor planning to become undead, so they had no place here. As soon as the doors shut behind them, two of the Shadowlords stepped forward to take over. One of them, a women robed in deep crimson, took up station on one side of the sacrificial altar. The other, a man in black robes, stood across from her. In his hand was a knife whose long blade appeared to have been carved from obsidian, and the curved facets of its flaked edge glinted in the light as he moved, reflecting fireflies on the walls.

The woman began to chant in a tongue that Isaac did not understand. It sounded ancient. The man in black raised up the knife and presented it to her over the boy's bound body. Seeing the blade, the boy began to struggle even more desperately, looking feverishly around the room, desperate for anything that could save him—

And his eyes met Isaac's.

The boy's sudden recognition of him struck Isaac like a physical blow, and he had to ball his hands into fists in the folds of his robe, struggling to suppress any visible response. Fingernails digging into his palms hard enough to draw blood, he tried to focus on the pain rather than the horrific tableau before him. The one thing he could not afford to do now was display any emotion . . . least of all sympathy. But the boy's eyes were pleading with him, and their message pierced Isaac's soul. *Help me,* Jacob begged silently. *You're my only hope. Don't let them kill me!* Isaac's hands trembled in the folds of his robe, and he knew he should look away, but he couldn't. He couldn't bring himself to move. The boy's terror had transfixed him.

Then the crimson Shadowlord took the knife from her assistant and cut deeply into Jacob's arm. He whimpered in pain and jerked against his chains, but his eyes never left Isaac's. It was as though there was a connection between the two of them, an umbilical cord of pain binding their souls together. The woman cut his other arm. Then his chest. Then his thighs. He cried out anew with each cut, but his eyes remained fixed upon Isaac. *Help me*, they begged. *Help me Help me Help me.* Heart pounding, Isaac finally dared to respond, shaking his head from side to side, a gesture so slight that he hoped no one else would notice it. *I can't*, it said. *I'm sorry. I don't have the power to change this.* Even that much sympathy would be condemned as inappropriate passion if anyone noticed it, but everyone else was focused on the ritual, watching with vampiric delight as cut after cut was made, until every inch of the boy's flesh was lacerated, bright scarlet streamers running down from his flesh to the table beneath him, and from there to the brass collection bowl at his feet. Still Jacob's eyes remained fixed on Isaac, as he desperately grasped the one shred of sympathy he'd been offered to keep from drowning in utter madness.

*This is why we are taught not to feel,* Isaac thought miserably. Maybe if he'd been more attentive to his lessons he would be able to look away. Maybe it wouldn't feel as though every cut was slicing through his own flesh as well as the boy's.

Now the chanting changed to English, and Isaac heard poetic promises about how the boy's soul would find refuge in eternal service, would have this Shadowlord's undying protection, how death was a blessing. Pure bullshit. The Shadowlords didn't give a damn about whether their slave spirits were happy.

Jacob's eyelids began to droop as the last of his life drained out of his veins. The Shadowlord in black retrieved the collection bowl from the end of the table and handed it to the woman. The blood within it contained the spark of the boy's life, Isaac knew, and at the moment of death it could be used to bind his spirit. Isaac was no longer trying to look away from Jacob, but willingly held his gaze for as long as the bloodshot eyes were still open. At least he could give him that much, so that he didn't have to die alone. The contact seemed to steady the boy a bit . . . or perhaps he was simply too weak to struggle any more. Then the woman sipped from the bowl of blood, and Isaac could sense a connection being established between the two of them. When the boy's spirit left its body it would discover it was tethered to this woman, unable to leave her side for as long as that blood was in her system. If she could establish mental control over him before it was gone, he would never be able to leave her.

That's what all the torture was about, Isaac realized. To shatter the boy's mind, so that once he died it would be easier for a Shadowlord to take control of him.

Finally Jacob's eyes closed. Isaac's Gift was just strong enough for him to sense the moment of death, which was also the moment of birth: a new wraith coming into existence. It was the first time Isaac had ever witnessed such a thing, and he strained his fledgling senses to witness what was going on. Death was a kind of creation, he'd been taught, and Shadowlords were masters of the process. But when he heard the boy's ghost cry out in terror at its birth pangs, he wondered if anything could justify such practices.

The chamber was silent. The boy's body lay still, relieved at last of its struggles. The new ghost's cries faded in volume as spiritual exhaustion overwhelmed it. It was said that such bound spirits were insane, and now Isaac understood why. Who wouldn't be driven mad by such an experience?

The ritual was over at last. The circle was breaking up, Shadowlords coming up to the woman in red to congratulate her on a successful Binding. With a start, Isaac realized that his father was approaching him. As always, he could hear the moaning of spirits that surrounded the man, just as he could hear the voices of every other Shadowlord's retinue. Now, for the first time in his life, he understood what prompted those sounds, and it sickened him. How many people had his father murdered, tormenting them to the edge of insanity so their ghosts could be dominated more easily? How many of the hundreds of spirits in this room had been initiated into servitude in the same way?

Bile rose up in the back of Isaac's throat as he looked at his father. Surely the Shadowlord had known about him and Jacob. Surely he knew that forcing him to watch the death of someone he knew would be like twisting a knife in his gut. That was why he'd invited him here. To test him. To torment him. To force him to be strong, in the way that only a madman should be strong.

*I don't belong here,* Isaac thought bitterly. *I never will.*

A cold hand settled on his shoulder. "You did well, my son."

He bit his lip to keep from responding in anger. "I know what's expected of me."

His father's finger touched the underside of his chin, turning his head until their eyes met. Isaac gazed into the black eyes of his undead father—haunted eyes, chilling eyes—and tried not to shudder.

*You were human once,* he thought. *When did that change? If I continue in this training, will human compassion drain from me slowly, like the blood did from that boy? Or does First Communion cut it out of you suddenly, like a surgeon's scalpel excising a malignant growth?*

"I'd like to go home now," Isaac muttered. "Unless you have more to show me."

His father stepped back, clearing a path between him and the exit. Isaac headed toward it. He walked past the journeymen, who were chattering about how much they looked forward to mastering the mysteries of life and death. Past the Shadowlords and their retinues of wraiths. Whispers of pain surrounded him, soft moaning, an occasional cry of anguish . . . now he understood why the dead sounded like that. Now he knew what it really meant to be a Shadowlord.

He managed to find a private spot, away from all the others, before he threw up.

# 11

## BLACKWATER MOUNTAINS
## VIRGINIA PRIME

### JESSE

**T**HE LEAVES ON THE TREES were green.

The underbrush was scraggly.

The soil was brown.

It was, on the whole, the most mundane, uninteresting stretch of woodland I'd ever seen.

"So let me make sure I've got this right," Rita said. "Morgana wants you to go to a creepy place and take a nap, and if something creepy happens to you during that nap, you tell her about it. Then we get to go home?"

"Well, except for the fact that this place doesn't seem very creepy . . . and we're supposed to bring back whatever is causing the creepiness . . . yeah, that's pretty much it."

"Okay. Just so we're clear on the goal here."

I wasn't sure what I'd expected to see at the site of an ancient Indian burial ground. Gravestones? Symbols carved into the ground? Restless spirits haunting the place, half-visible in the forest shadows? Whatever had been here in the past was long gone now, and had left no visible sign for tourists like us to discover.

I sighed and thought, *This isn't going to be easy.*

We'd left Seyer behind at the last small town we'd passed through, a few miles back. She hadn't wanted to split up, but I was resolute. There was no way I was going to test the limits of my dreaming Gift with a Seer watching me. In the end she'd reluctantly agreed, and gave me a fetter that would allow me to signal her when we were ready to leave. Which meant that Morgana had anticipated my request all along.

Damn her.

I had a pretty good sense of how to handle myself in the woods, the result of growing up with a regional forest in my backyard. And Morgana had given us a map of local landmarks, including a long mountain ridge that we could follow back to civilization if we had to, so I wasn't worried about getting lost. Now, after a brisk morning hike, we were here, alone in the woods, able to do whatever we needed to do to search for Morgana's mysterious object without being observed ... with no clue how to start.

"Let's set up camp," Rita suggested.

So we did that, and since neither of us were experienced woodsmen (woodspeople?), it took a while. Then we searched the *shallow* again, looking for anything out of the ordinary. But there was nothing. Finally we gave up and came back to the camp to light a fire and break out the rations Morgana had given us.

"Too bad Sebastian's not here," Rita said. "I bet he'd know all about shallows."

*I bet he wouldn't want to go near one,* I thought. *A place where he might hear echoes from his birthworld, near enough to be audible but forever out of reach. It would be torture.*

When it finally got dark I lay down on my bedroll and tried to go to sleep, but it was still too early for that, as far as my body was concerned. Fine by me. The fact that I'd agreed to open my mind to whatever powers were active here didn't mean I was comfortable with the concept. Morgana wouldn't have agreed to our price if she thought this task would be painless. Or safe.

So I watched as stars crept slowly across the heavens and a slender moon appeared in the east, rising up against the black dome of the sky with agonizing reluctance. And I struggled to ignore the feeling of dread that was slowly consuming me, until finally—just when I thought I would go crazy if I had to stay awake one more minute—my body surrendered to the inevitable.

I slept.

||||||||||||

**The dreamscape is calm tonight, but ominously so. I can sense destructive energy seething behind it, masked by an illusion of peace.**

**I envision the design that Morgana showed me, forcing my mind's eye to see it in lines of gold against the black ground. I sense that it should connect to something—that it *wants* to connect to something—but the thing it seeks is not to be found here. The longer I study the pattern, the more I'm sure.**

**We're in the wrong place.**

**I let the pattern fade from my mind and look around me, to see if the avatar girl is present. But she's nowhere to be seen. Maybe I frightened her so badly when I took control of her dream that she won't ever come back. Or maybe the dream-wraiths got to her after I left. My blood runs cold at the mere memory of them, and the wound on my arm starts to twitch. Whatever those horrific creatures are, they're not subject to the normal limits of dreaming, and I pray I'll never have to see one of**

them again. Especially now, when I'm trapped in a foreign world, with no brother to wake me up if things go bad.

A wave of homesickness suddenly comes over me. The distance between me and my loved ones is so vast it might as well be infinite. My tie to my family, such a strong anchor during my first visit here, has been robbed of its power by my knowledge that in my current reality they don't exist. Yes, somewhere in this vast ocean of probability there is a world where Tommy and Evelyn Drake are going about their daily lives, waiting for me to come home. But in this world, right here, right now, they are unreachable. My heart aches to connect with them, if only for a moment—

Suddenly I'm standing in front of an archway, with no memory of how I got there. I sense that it's meaningful, but I don't know why. I put my hand on the arch, feeling its sharp crystal spines prick my fingertips. The doors in my dreams are usually impassable; only when I tackled the avatar girl was I able to cross through one of them. Could I enter this one, if I wanted to? It would be a dangerous thing to do, when I have no idea how or why I was summoned here, but I have to try, if only to learn more about how my Gift works.

Warily I extend a hand into the arch, bracing myself for the moment when a metaphysical barrier will stop me. But nothing does. Trembling slightly, I extend my arm full length and wiggle my fingers a bit. My hand feels cool and my fingers look misty and insubstantial, as if viewed through frosted glass. Have I reached into another world? Am I now half in one dream, half in another? Or is there some less exotic explanation for what I'm seeing?

There's only one way to find out.

I concentrate long enough to manifest a large hunting knife. The weapon feels comfortable in my hand, reassuring. I manifest a gun as well, modeled on one of Uncle Julian's pistols, but I leave it holstered for now. I'm not that sure I could hit a moving target, but I figure it's good to have it with me just in case.

Looking around one last time to make sure I'm still alone, I step forward.

There's no sense of transition; one moment I'm standing on the black plain, and the next, I'm on a windswept path running along the edge of a deep ravine. The sky overhead is a blue so intense it's unreal, like the cobalt glow of a PC error message. In the distance I can see clouds gathering, and even as I watch lightning flashes suddenly, flooding the entire sky with blinding light. Thunder follows in its wake, rumbling overhead like angry surf. However far away the storm is, it's a powerful one.

As the afterimage of the lightning slowly fades, I can see that there's a figure riding toward me, mounted on a white horse. Nervously, I glance back to make sure the arch is right behind me, just in case I need to make a run for it. It is. I can sense the same otherness in the rider that I did in the avatar girl, and I know instinctively that he is not part of my dreamscape, but from some place outside it. As he comes closer I can see that he's a massive creature, heavily armored, with a sword as tall as a man harnessed across his back and an oversized crossbow clipped to his saddle. His mount isn't a horse at all, but some kind of animal with two spiral horns jutting out of its head and glowing red embers in the place of eyes. If there's a stable in Hell, this is what the Devil's horses surely look like.

As the monster warrior approaches me he draws his greatsword from its sheath, raising it high overhead, preparing to strike. Its edge flares molten white as lightning strikes again, and the long hair that flows out from underneath his helmet is white as well, unnaturally glossy.

I should flee this place. Now. Every cell in my body is screaming for me to do that. But I find myself mesmerized, frozen in place by raw curiosity. In dreams I've looked in on hundreds of different worlds—thousands, perhaps—but all of them were similar to my own universe. Even the avatar's dream-world started off looking normal. This place, on the other hand, is truly alien. I've never seen anything like it before.

I want to understand where I am.

I *need* to understand where I am.

But suddenly he's coming within striking range and my fascination gives way to pure survival instinct. I start back toward the portal—

And he pulls up short. His mount squeals in frustration (definitely not an equine sound) and some gravel that was knocked loose by its hooves plummets down into the ravine. It falls for several long seconds before hitting bottom. Then there's silence. My heart is pounding so hard the knife in my hand shakes, but I stand my ground. Waiting.

One second. Two.

The rider pushes up his visor. His face is pure white, unnaturally translucent, as if carved from alabaster. In the place of his eyes are glowing red embers, like those of his mount. There's no way to read that inhuman expression.

He stares at me for a moment, then says, "Jesse?"

I open my mouth, but find that I'm speechless. Because the voice coming out of that ember-eyed demon is my little brother's. That alabaster hulk is Tommy.

"What's going on?" he asks. "You don't play this game."

Is it possible I'm really in my brother's dream? True, I entered the avatar's dream once—or at least I think I did—but that was different. I'd followed her from the black plain and used her to cross into her world. The concept that I might wind up in someone else's dream without meaning to—and without someone leading me there—is both exhilarating and terrifying.

*This may not really be Tommy,* I remind myself. *I might just be dreaming that he's in front of me.*

Whatever he is, he's staring at me, waiting for my answer. He thinks this whole scene is real, I realize. I've gotten so used to lucid dreaming that I take it for granted. How do I get him to see that this setting isn't real, and that he can control it? If you tell someone in a dream that he's dreaming, is that enough to make him self-aware? It's worth a try.

"We're in a dream," I tell him.

His eyes widen. "Seriously?"

"Seriously."

"You mean, like, I'm really asleep in bed? Just making crap up in my head?"

I nod. "That's the idea."

"So, did I make you up, too? Or are you really here?"

*Isn't that the question?* Can Tommy and I really occupy the same dreamscape? Our bodies are in different worlds, and supposedly nothing can cross between the worlds but ghosts and Shadows—

And dreams.

Was it Isaac who talked about that, or Sebastian? Which one of them described to me how dreams can bleed from one world into the next, giving a sleeper access to sounds and images from another universe? Does that mean that in this dream state I can contact people in another world? The concept is dizzying in its implications. But how can you test such a thing? I shut my eyes for a moment, struggling to come up with an idea. Maybe if I share information with Tommy that he couldn't possibly know otherwise, he can confirm it when he wakes up and know that our meeting was real. It won't help me verify things at my end, but it's a start.

"You remember the flowered chair in the front room?" I ask him. "The one with the high back?"

"Yeah. What about it?"

"Go there when you wake up. Reach under the cushion, all the way to the back. There's a crowbar I stashed there. No one else knows about it."

The glowing eyes blink. "Why on earth would you hide a crowbar under the chair?"

"In case we need to break into Uncle Julian's gun cabinet, of course." I shrug, smiling slightly. "I figured something could happen where we might not have time to ask him for the key."

Suddenly I catch sight of something odd in the sky behind him. A small patch of blue is losing its color, turning from a bright shade to muddy grey. Like something is sucking the color right out of the sky.

Panic floods my world. Everything else is forgotten.

"You need to wake up!" Surely he can hear the fear in my voice and will do what I say. "RIGHT NOW! Don't argue, don't question me, just trust me and do it."

How far away is the dream-wraith? How fast can it move? I don't want to stay here long enough to find out, but I can't leave until I know Tommy is safe.

He twists around in his saddle and looks at the grey patch in the sky. "Shit," he mutters. "That's not good."

The patch is getting closer now. The wraith is moving fast.

He turns back to face me. The glowing embers are gone now; my brother's eyes stare out at me, very human and very scared.

"Your first aid kit," he says. "Look in it when you wake up."

And then he's gone.

At which point his dream vanishes.

And so do I.

When I first awoke I was so disoriented I didn't know where I was. I watched the sky in terror for what seemed like an eternity, waiting for the wraith to show up, but it never came. Slowly, very slowly, my heart quieted, and my breathing steadied. I remembered where I was, and I knew that I was awake and safe. At least for the moment.

I got up as quietly as I could, not wanting to wake Rita. Crossing the campsite, I retrieved my backpack and moved off into the woods a bit, so I'd be less likely to wake her when I rummaged through it. When I looked back at her for the last time she was snoring gently, her eyelids twitching as she explored some dream of her own.

The first aid kit was in the bottom of the bag, a small plastic box with a snap lid. My hand trembled as I took it out and popped it open. From fear? From excitement? My emotions were so mixed up at that moment I wasn't sure what I was feeling.

Under the bandages, next to the tube of antibiotic cream, was a flat item in a plastic wrapper. I held my breath as I pulled it out. Even in the near darkness I knew what it was: A toaster strudel.

There was a note fastened to it with a rubber band. I didn't have enough light to read by, so I took out the small flashlight from Dr. Tilford that we had charged earlier and turned my back to Rita so its bright beam wouldn't wake her up. The last thing I wanted to deal with right now was her questions.

I turned on the flashlight, unfolded the note and read it.

*I thought if you had to open this kit you might need some cheering up.*
*Be strong.*
*Tommy*

For a long, long time I just stared at that toaster strudel. Couldn't think clearly. Just stared at it.

*I talked to him. I really talked to him. Across the worlds.*

The concept was so stunning that I had to reach out to a nearby tree to steady myself. I was shaking like a leaf and had to fumble to turn the flashlight off, so its beam would stop jerking all over the place.

Everything in Terra Prime revolved around the fact that no one could communicate between worlds. Even the spirits of the dead, who crossed freely back and forth to carry messages, couldn't exist in one reality and converse with ghosts in another. It just wasn't possible. And the power of the Guild of Shadows was rooted in that fact, because they controlled the passage of messengers. The power of the Greys derived from theirs. Other Guilds were rooted in that system as well, all of them networking together to exploit that scientific fact for their advantage.

But if it turned out their science was wrong, and messengers weren't needed after all—that the Shadows weren't needed—it would be like yanking the cornerstone out from under a tower. The whole vast construct could come crashing down. That was why they wanted the Dreamwalkers dead, I realized suddenly. All the other reasons I'd been given were bullshit. *This* was why they'd wiped us all out centuries ago, and why they'd established rules about hunting down any new Dreamwalkers who were born. But did the people who were hunting us today know why they were doing it? Or had centuries of propaganda and misdirection obscured the true story, so that even the most fanatical Shadows didn't remember why they wanted us dead? From the few things people had told me about the ancient dreamers—or not told me—it sounded like that might be the case.

I looked back at Rita. Her eyes had stopped twitching, and she was sleeping so soundly now. So peacefully. I couldn't tell her about this yet. I couldn't tell anyone about it.

I needed time to think first.

I looked down at the toaster strudel that was still in my hand—now crushed beyond recognition—and I suddenly started laughing and crying, all at once. This was my symbol of revelation: a ruined breakfast cake. How appropriate.

*Thank you, little brother. You have no idea what you gave me tonight. Thank you.*

# 12

## Shadowcrest
## Virginia Prime

### Isaac

THE DEAD WERE RESTLESS.

Lying in his bed in the darkness, Isaac could sense them in his bedroom. Moans and cries and whispers echoed just below the threshold of his hearing, and whenever a spirit drew close he could feel its presence, like prickly pressure on his skin. Sometimes there were so many of them surrounding him that he felt claustrophobic.

He was starting to be able to sense their emotions. Not that the dead were supposed to have real emotions. The Shadowlords taught that ghosts were merely echoes of human souls, that death robbed a man not only of his physical substance but also of his capacity for passion. But Isaac wasn't buying it. Sometimes he could sense the emotions of the spirits that were near him, and they felt totally human. Rage, despair, frustration, resentment . . . it was a dark and disturbing—but utterly human—repertoire.

Besides, if they had no feelings, why did one hear sounds of human suffering whenever they were nearby? His teachers said it was just a reflex, like when you cut the tentacles off an octopus, and they kept on twitching. The wailing of the dead was like that. Postmortem twitching. Yes, it was hard to accept now, when his Gift was still immature, but they assured him that once he underwent First Communion he'd see that it was true. Until then, he would just have to take it on faith.

Tonight the dead were thick as flies in his room, and he pulled the blanket over his head, even though he knew it would do nothing to shut them out. The sounds of the spirit world weren't physical in nature, and merely blocking his ears wouldn't stop him from hearing them. They seemed unusually agitated tonight. Maybe the Shadowlords had committed some new atrocity that upset them. Isaac thought back to the ritual he had witnessed and shuddered. The look in Jacob's eyes as he died was seared into Isaac's brain. He would do anything to forget it.

Suddenly, unexpectedly, the ghostly murmuring ceased. Startled, he came out from under the blanket and looked around. He couldn't see anything, but he could sense that spirits nearest him had drawn back. The space around his bed felt empty now.

Why?

The temperature in the room dropped slightly as a new spirit entered. This one was more substantial than the others, a complete human soul rather than a mere fragment of consciousness. It was rare for that type of spirit to be wandering around Shadowcrest, Isaac knew. The bound servants of the Shadows generally stayed close by their masters, while free spirits avoided this place like the plague.

Isaac stiffened as the spirit approached the bed. In theory it couldn't do him physical harm, but as a mere apprentice he had limited power to banish the dead, so he was wary. But the spirit came to the foot of his bed and just stopped there. Maybe it was making some attempt to communicate, that he couldn't hear. Maybe it was just watching him.

The situation made his skin crawl.

"Who are you?" he demanded. "What do you want?" That's how one was supposed to deal with spirits: firmly and authoritatively. Death robbed a soul of initiative and left it highly suggestible. If you gave it an order in a forceful manner it was likely to obey you.

The spirit made no sound. It didn't move.

"Why are you here?" Isaac pressed.

A cold breeze gusted across his face. He could sense the ghost reaching out to him, as if to make physical contact. Instinctively he drew back from it, until the headboard behind him put a stop to his retreat.

Then the spirit began to speak. Isaac could make out a few scattered words but not enough to figure out what it was saying. That was the curse of his immature Gift: to sense the speech of the dead but not be able to hear it clearly. If he concentrated hard enough, could he do better? It was worth a try. Gathering all his mental energy, he focused his concentration on the spirit. He knew the technique that was required, and tried to envision the spirit standing before him, to give it substance in his mind. He channeled all his strength of will into the effort—

—And suddenly he saw *those* eyes again, the terrified bloodshot eyes of a young boy in the process of being slaughtered. No body was visible—just the eyes—but Isaac could smell Jacob's blood as it flowed across the granite altar, he could smell the stink of sweat and the fear that filled the room, he could hear the chanting of the Shadowlord who held the knife—

Gasping, he jerked backward, slamming into the headboard. The vision dispersed, but the sense of fear in the room remained. He was trembling now, and it was hard for him to force the words out. "You're . . . you're . . . Why are you here? What do you want?"

But if there was any answer, he lacked the ability to understand it. Maybe Jacob had come to find out why Isaac had done nothing to save him. "I had no power to change anything," he offered. "They just brought me there to watch." Would he have saved the boy if he could have? He'd never asked himself the question before. Until tonight it hadn't seemed to matter.

The chill that had accompanied the spirit's arrival began to fade, and with a start Isaac realized that the boy's ghost was leaving the room. Why? Had Isaac told him what he wanted to know, or was the wraith just giving up in frustration now that it understood the limits of Isaac's Gift? Maybe it had expected him to be able to communicate with it like the Shadowlords did.

He remembered how the boy had locked eyes with him while dying. Was it possible the connection between them had compromised the ritual somehow, so that the bond between this newly created spirit and its mistress wasn't all that it should be? If so, did that mean the boy's spirit was a free agent? Or just poorly bound? Isaac wished he knew enough about how the ritual worked to guess at the answer. Frustrated, he stared into the darkness as the spirit withdrew, cursing the weakness of his Gift. He tried to invoke some kind of vision again, but whatever spark had made that possible the first time was gone.

And then the spirit was gone.

All that remained in the room were questions.

# 13

JESSE

THE RACCOON SHOWED UP shortly after midnight. At first only its eyes were visible, two tiny spots of reflected moonlight glinting at me from among the trees. They were low to the ground, so at first I just figured they belonged to some small animal, and I wasn't worried. But when it saw me looking back at it, the raccoon turned and scampered into the woodland shadows. Its bushy ringed tail twitched into the moonlight just long enough for me to identify its species. For a moment— one sweet innocent moment—I thought it was a raccoon, and only a raccoon.

Then I realized the truth.

I went over to Rita and nudged her. "Hey. Hey. Get up."

The urgency in my voice must have triggered her innate survival instinct, because as soon as her eyes opened she was sitting upright with knife in hand, looking around the clearing for something to stab. "What? What is it?"

"I saw a raccoon."

She looked at me as if I had just announced I was from Mars. "A raccoon? Seriously?" The hand holding the knife lowered, and she snorted. "Hardly nature's great killing machine, Jess."

I took out the fetter that Seyer had given me and showed it to her. I'd strung it on a cord so I could wear it like a necklace. It was a copper disk with a symbol on one side that looked like a hashtag, only at right angles and with four bars running in each direction. A crudely etched wolf was on the other side.

When she still didn't make the connection I said, "Wards off wildlife, remember?"

Somewhere there was a person whose Gift allowed him to influence the minds of animals. A Weaver had bound a trace of his mental energy to this item, so that for as long as we had it with us, beasts would not approach. Any and all animal brains would be affected.

*Animal* brains.

"Shit!" Suddenly Rita got it, and from the way she stared intently into the woods I knew that she was thinking the same thing I was. We weren't equipped to deal with Soulriders. "Shit."

"We'll have to sleep in shifts from now on," I said. Not like that would help us much if Hunters attacked in force.

She looked up at me. "Does that mean you want to sleep now? 'Cause I can take a turn at watch if you want."

"No." I sighed. "I'm way too wound up for that. I just wanted you to know what was going on, so if I did have to wake you up to deal with this you'd be prepared." I looked in the direction the raccoon had fled, but there was no motion visible. Even the night breeze was still. "It isn't here," I said quietly.

"What?" Rita looked confused. "Oh . . . you mean Morgana's artifact? Did you dream about where it was?"

"I dreamed where it wasn't." I sighed heavily. "We're in the wrong place, Rita."

She exhaled in a hiss. "So what, then? This whole trip was a waste?"

I looked out over the forest. We were high on a hillside, and the moonlight provided a clear view of miles of wooded land, all of it looking pretty much the same. The Seers' Gift allowed them to pick up impressions from people's minds, right? So if something was emanating Dreamwalker energy so strongly that Morgana's people had sensed it from halfway across the state, maybe the source wasn't an artifact. Maybe it was human, and we should search for clues where there was human activity. To the south it was possible to see a faint light in the distance, if you squinted just right. A pale blue glow peeking out between the trees. "What's down there?"

She peered in that direction. "Not sure. Let me get out my tourist guide . . . oh, wait, that's right, I don't have one."

*Smartass.* "I think we should look down there."

"Like, right now?"

"Like, when there's enough light to see by. Duh."

"We'll have to signal Seyer that we're planning to spend another day in the field."

We were supposed to use the fetter Seyer had given me to signal her once a day, to let her know we were still okay, and that we were staying in the forest of our own free will. But we didn't have to tell her why we were staying, or what we planned to do, just let her know we were still all right.

Thank God I told my family I'd be gone for a whole

week. We still had time before anyone back home started worrying.

Seyer was the one who had suggested that, I realized suddenly. She must have known back on Terra Colonna that Morgana was planning to send us on this quest. It was all contrived, from the start. Damn. Was this how a pawn felt when it first realized it was standing on a chessboard? Did it look down at the squares surrounding it and think, *Shit, now I'm really in for it?*

Rita lay back down again. "I'm going to try to get some more sleep, if that's possible." She shut her eyes for a moment, then said, "It could just be that the fetter's not working. In which case, the only thing we need to worry about are bears."

"Yeah," I muttered. "Got that." I'd rather deal with bears than Hunters, any day.

I kept watch till dawn, but the raccoon never came back.

‖‖‖‖‖‖‖‖‖‖

Our maps indicated there was a chasm nearby, heading in the right direction, so we decided to follow it by way of a landmark. I marked a few trees as we hiked, as backup, but that turned out not to be necessary. Soon we came across a packed dirt road with a ribbon of scrub down its center; clearly a carriage trail. It was heading toward the area we wanted to explore, probably connecting it to the main road that ran along the ridgetop to our west. We followed it downhill, alert for any sounds of people approaching. But the one time someone came our way, the clopping of hooves and the creaking of carriage springs warned us in plenty of time, and we were able to hide in the brush before they reached us.

Eventually we got to a place where we could see that the road ended a short distance ahead, with an open plain beyond. There seemed to be buildings there, and maybe a fence, but we didn't want to get too close while we were out in the open. So we headed back into the deep woods and crept carefully toward it. When we got to the place where the underbrush gave way to open land we lay full length upon the ground and let the vegetation close over our heads, parting the leaves with our hands just enough to peer between them.

The area ahead of us was large, treeless, and bounded by a tall chain link fence with barbed wire at the top. Short, scraggly grass covered most of the ground, with a small stand of trees in its center. There were a few wooden cabins at one end of the enclosure—including two large ones with barred windows—and a big cinderblock structure at the other. Tables and benches of weathered wood were strewn about the enclosure, more like an afterthought than a decorating feature, and in the far corner was a long building that looked like a stable, with a small carriage parked in front of it.

Inside the fenced enclosure were children. Lots of children. Boys and girls of all ages, wearing loose clothes of unpatterned cotton and simple canvas sandals that made them look interchangeable. All of them had their hair cropped close to their heads, and they looked dazed and listless. Some were sitting on the grass or on the benches, unnaturally still, just staring into space. Others were walking around with no clear purpose or destination, shuffling along with the kind of spiritless resignation I'd once seen in animals in a small zoo, where cramped, featureless cages had sucked the life out of them.

To say that the place made my skin crawl would be an understatement.

"Not exactly high security," Rita whispered.

"Huh?"

"No sentry post. No observation platform. The lock

on the main gate looks pretty basic. Probably easy to jimmy." She pointed to the only guard in sight, a middle-aged man who looked more bored than dangerous. "Rent-a-cop. Token presence."

"There's barbed wire," I pointed out.

"To discourage people from climbing out. Maybe to keep animals from climbing in. It looks more like an animal pen than a prison."

That was uncomfortably close to my own thoughts. "You think maybe they're patients of some kind?"

"Hospitals don't have bars on the windows," she pointed out.

"Some mental hospitals do."

Suddenly I saw a figure I recognized, at the far end of the enclosure. Startled, I squinted to bring her into focus. She'd been a small and wiry child when Rita and I first met her, and she'd worn her blond hair cropped close to her head even then, so she hadn't changed much. As soon as she turned my way I knew who it was.

"Moth," I whispered.

Rita followed my gaze; her eyes grew wide as she spotted the girl. "From the Warrens?"

The last we'd heard about the children living in Luray's sewer system, city officials had been planning to raid the place, and we'd assumed they intended to exterminate them. But this was a world where homeless children had market value, and Moth's presence here suggested that some of the orphans might have been rounded up for sale, rather than killed. Sold to cover the cost of the raid.

So what was Moth doing here? What was this place? She was wandering aimlessly, her eyes downcast, moving slowly toward the fence on the far side of the enclosure. I watched for a minute, then slipped out of the straps of my backpack, "I'm going to talk to her."

It took me forever to scrunch and crawl my way

around the compound without being seen, but Rita had been right about the security. No one inside the compound was paying attention to anything going on outside. I managed to locate a spot with good cover near the fence and laid down in it, waiting for Moth to come close enough that I could risk talking to her. At last, when she was only a few yards away, I whispered, "Psst! Moth!"

Startled, she turned in my direction. I raised up my head just far enough for her to see who I was, then ducked down into the shrubbery again. "Look away," I whispered sharply. "Pretend there's no one here."

I could see a tiny spark of life come into her eyes, and it made my heart ache. I remembered the feisty little blond who challenged us so boldly when we'd first arrived on Terra Prime. It was hard to imagine what kind of misery could have turned such a firebrand into the listless creature I saw now. But hiding from people was second nature to her, and as she slowly approached the fence she pretended to be watching the other children. It was very convincing. Finally she sat crosslegged with her back to the fence and started playing with the grass, absently picking one long blade after another to chew on. It disguised the movement of her lips as she whispered to me. "Jesse? Is that really you?"

"Sure is."

You could sense how much she wanted to turn around and look at me. "What are you doing here?"

"At the moment, I'm trying to figure out what you're doing here."

She sighed; a terrible sadness bowed her small body. "They caught me in the Warrens. They kept me in some kind of holding cell for a few days, then they brought me here."

"Are any of the others here?"

She shook her head. "Ethan and Kurt were sent to a

labor camp. I heard a rumor that Maysie wound up in a pleasure house in Front Royal, but I don't know if that's true or not. A lot of kids died in the raid, only a few were taken alive."

"Moth," I asked it gently: "What is this place?"

"Hell," she whispered bitterly.

I lowered my head and waited respectfully for more.

"It's run by the Weavers. There's some kind of laboratory in the brick building over there." She nodded slightly toward the cinderblock structure. "I think they're trying to use us to charge fetters, but you need Gifted people for that, don't you?"

"No one here is Gifted?"

"Just the Weavers. The kids are all deadheads. Like me." She raised up a finger slightly, her hand in her lap, so that only I could see her pointing. "That woman over there is Mistress Tennant. She told me we all had *trace essence*, whatever that means, and that's why we're here. I think she's in charge. She talks about this place like it's some kind of experiment."

The woman she was pointing at looked to be in her forties, a short brunette with an air of concentrated energy about her. I stared at the woman intently, memorizing her appearance so I would recognize her later. "What do they use you for?"

For a moment she didn't speak. Then: "They bring us into the lab one by one and strap us down and do Weaver things to us. Sometimes it hurts. Sometimes it feels like a hand is reaching into you and ripping out your insides. But your body is never damaged." Her voice wavered for a moment. "I heard that they never let anyone leave here, they just drain a kid till he dies and then replace him. There was a boy who died last week, just wasted away after weeks in a coma. Someone told me that while he was still walking around, all he talked about was how much he wanted to die. He said he had someplace to go, a castle that looked different every time he saw it, and once he let go of his body he would be free to go there."

My heart skipped a beat. "Tell me about the castle."

She shrugged. "I don't know any more than that, other than it was something he dreamed about. The others didn't pay much attention to him when he rambled on about his dreams, they just thought he was crazy. Which maybe he was." She drew in a deep breath. "Jesse . . . you came to get me out of here, right?" Her voice was pitiful, like the whine of a wounded puppy.

It was a few seconds before I could speak. "I'll try to figure out a way, Moth."

"Please," she begged. A universe of pain was in that one word.

"I promise."

I reached into my pocket and pulled out the drawing Morgana had given me. Scrunching forward, I slid it along the ground until it reached the fence. Moth looked around to make sure no one was watching, then took it. She opened it in her lap where no one could see. "What is it?" she whispered.

"I was going to ask you the same question. Have you ever seen anything like it?"

She shook her head a tiny bit.

"No designs of this type at all?"

"No. Sorry. Nothing." She looked around again and then slid it back to me. The gesture reminded me of a kid passing notes in class.

"What about dreams?" I asked. "Anyone else here talk about strange dreams?"

"Just that boy and his castle. Otherwise, we dream pretty much what you'd expect in a place like this. Nightmares, mostly." She paused then said softly, "Sometimes I dream how I'll get out of here someday."

I lowered my head to the ground for a moment,

grateful that Moth couldn't see my expression. "Did they try to make a fetter from that boy's energy?" I asked.

"I assume. They try with everybody." She nodded slightly toward the cinderblock building. "There's a safe inside the lab where the experimental stuff is kept. They keep the fetters locked up in a safe because they're dangerous. I heard one of the Weavers talk about how they're not *tempered* yet, whatever that means."

I opened my mouth to ask another question, but just then a loud clanging filled the compound. Moth jumped.

"That's lunch. I have to go. They'll notice if I don't." She dared to look back at me. "I'll see you again, right? You won't just forget about me?" *I helped keep you safe when you first came to this world,* her eyes seemed to be pleading. *You owe me.*

A sudden knot in my throat made it hard to breathe. "I won't forget about you. I promise."

The guard was looking our way now. Moth hurriedly got to her feet. "I'll walk by here every hour or so," she whispered behind her hand. "They won't notice, so long as it isn't meal time."

"I'll get back to you when I can," I whispered.

She headed toward the largest cabin, where all the children were gathering. It seemed to me there was a hint of newfound vivacity in her stride, but maybe that was just my wishful thinking. Once she entered what I assumed was the mess hall I started the long scrunch-crawl back to Rita. By the time I got to her, all the children had disappeared into the building, and most of the adults had disappeared as well. During mealtimes the yard was nearly empty. Something to remember.

"Well?" Rita asked impatiently.

I hesitated. I needed a few minutes to sort things out in my head . . . and to figure out how to talk about the situation without tears coming to my eyes. Was Moth staring out at the woods even now, wondering if we would really come through for her? Or was the concept of abandonment something she just took for granted? "Let's go find a safe place to talk. I'll fill you in then."

We headed back into the woods to find a suitable place to stow our gear, eat, and make plans.

|||||||||||||||||

We found a place that suited our purposes, a small clearing near a stream, far enough from the compound that we could talk safely. As we set out a sparse picnic of bread, cheese, and dried meat, I told Rita most of what Moth had said. I didn't tell her about the castle the boy had described. It sounded like it might be the same building my dream-avatar had fled toward, perched on a black island in the center of a mirrored lake. If so, that was a connection I wasn't ready to share with anyone.

"I'm guessing it was the boy's presence the Seers sensed," I told her. "He's been dead for a week, but Morgana didn't tell us how old her information was, so maybe they gathered it while he was still alive."

"Or it's connected to the fetters somehow."

It seemed the obvious conclusion. But getting to the fetters would require passing through the main gate and into the lab, then breaking into a safe, all without being seen. Rita assured me she could take care of the lock on the gate, no problem, and we could probably dodge the rent-a-cop without too much trouble, but she didn't have any experience with safecracking, and neither did I. So unless we could figure out a time when the safe would be open, there was no point in trying to get to it.

And then there was Moth. It was only a few weeks ago that she and her friends had rescued us from the streets of Luray Prime, and started us on the path that eventually got us home. We owed her. But how were we supposed to get her out of there? And if we came up with a way to rescue her, did that mean we should free all the other children, too? Where would they go, if we did that?

We decided to spend the rest of the day observing the compound, getting a sense of its people and work rhythms. I spent much of my time watching the Weaver who Moth had said was in charge. If I had dreams about this place, I wanted them to include her.

I wondered if I could get into a Weaver's head, the way I had gotten into Tommy's.

# 14

## BLACKWATER MOUNTAINS
## VIRGINIA PRIME

### JESSE

**T**HE SUN IS JUST BEGINNING TO SET when Master Weaver Marjorie Tennant begins her final rounds. The lights in the compound come on one by one as she walks past them, filling the courtyard with a soft blue glow. It has been a long day, but a rewarding one. The product from one subject is particularly promising, and she suspects that when the girl's fetter is properly tempered it will accept a Gifted imprint.

Project Beta is her creation, her pride and joy, and she loves her work dearly, even if she does not love where the Guild requires her to do it. But their caution is understandable. An untempered fetter is a dangerous thing under the best circumstances, and two dozen wild children producing sparks of energy with no structure or focus is hardly a recipe for stable power. No one has ever tried to collect and store the emanations of the unGifted before, so no one knows exactly where the process might backfire. Which is why her Guild dictated that if she undertook this dangerous experiment, she had to do so in the middle of nowhere.

But imagine if she is successful! No longer will Weavers have to pay exorbitant prices for the other Guilds to empower their fetters. Raw energy can be harvested from the unGifted, and other Guilds will only be needed to imprint that energy with purpose. Which means her Guild will be able to produce ten times as many fetters as they do now — a hundred times as many, a thousand! — and while the market price will inevitably drop, the lesser cost of production will more than make up for it. Net profits will skyrocket in the long run.

And imagine the social implications of it! There can be enough Gifted tech for every household to enjoy, at prices even the lower classes can afford. Imagine what it will be like when every family can have a house full of fetters — even the working classes — without having to go into debt for them. And the new system can provide employment for thousands of unskilled laborers, whose unGifted energy can be bound to empower the new tech. No, she tells herself, Project Beta isn't just about increasing the wealth and influence of the Weavers' Guild — though that is certainly a consideration — but about bettering the entire world.

As she walks the grounds, she notes that everything seems to be in order. The horses sound a little nervous, but they might be responding to the smell of a bear in the distance. Otherwise everything seems peaceful enough. A few of the children are still wandering about, mostly younger ones — they seem to be more resilient than the others — but soon they will retire to the dormitory so they can be locked in for the night. Not because Tennant fears they'll try to break out of the facility, but simply to keep them from disturbing the lab. Some of them are no longer connected to reality as much as they should be, and they often wander where they shouldn't.

A guard nods to her as she passes. What a boring job this must be for him! The closest thing to a threat that Project Beta ever faces is when a forest animal tries to get over the fence. Once a small bear made it halfway up, and the guards and Weavers placed bets on whether it would give up before hitting the barbed wire. And once a large bird got tangled in the wire, and a guard had to climb up to cut it free. They bet on the guard's climb, that time, and later enjoyed owl cutlets for dinner. Which tasted like stringy chicken.

As she heads toward the lab for a final security check, something catches her eye in the distance. Far to the north a faint light can be seen rising from the forest, casting a ruddy glow on the underbellies of the clouds. For a moment she thinks that it's probably just the last few beams of sunlight shining upward from the horizon . . . but no, it's in the wrong part of the sky for that. She stares at it for a moment, noting how the clouds seem to pulse slightly, as if the source of the light is unsteady. Suddenly she realizes what is causing it—what must be causing it—and panic sets in.

Wildfire.

The compound has an alarm bell for such events, but it's rusty from disuse, and fallen leaves have jammed the mechanism; she has to yank on the lever a few times before it becomes unstuck. When it finally sounds people come pouring out of the buildings, startled and confused. Her staff has never faced a real fire before, and though they know what's expected of them in theory, they lack any instinctive grasp of the situation. She even sees several of them look at the distant glow in the northern sky and relax, thinking that if the fire is far away they have plenty of time. But she's seen wildfires before, and she knows how fast they can move. And while it's possible that one of the neighboring towns will have an Elemental on call who can turn the flames aside, she can't bet the welfare of her people on that. Besides, few people in the area know Project Beta is out here, so an attempt to divert the fire from nearby towns could wind up sending it their way even faster.

They have to evacuate. Now.

She gives the necessary orders, and people rush to obey. As the horses are led from the stables they whinny nervously, responding to the atmosphere of fear in the compound. Or maybe they can smell the distant fire. But there's something inside the compound that's far more dangerous than any fire, and Tennant knows that if she doesn't secure it properly, more than the compound may be at risk.

"Bring the dolly," she orders her assistant, as she pulls out the keys to the lab and starts running toward the cinderblock building. She fumbles with the lock for a moment, her hands unsteady, then gets the door open and heads inside, several Weavers following.

The lab itself doesn't matter, she knows. Equipment can be replaced. Tennant's lab notes have been copied to Guild headquarters on a regular basis, so even if all her notebooks burn, no important data will be lost. But there's one thing they dare not leave behind, something so unstable that the intense heat of a forest fire might set it off, even if its steel container keeps it from burning.

"Let's get the safe out of here," she orders.

She can hear the jangle of tack outside as a horse-drawn wagon is brought to the front door, and a ramp moved into place. Inside the building, her people are struggling to move the safe onto a reinforced dolly, but it's a heavy piece, and sweat is running down their faces by the time they finally get it settled. As they start to roll it outside, Tennant can see that a carriage and a second wagon are waiting for them, ready to go. There aren't a lot of vehicles in the compound, and she'll be hard pressed to get everyone out of here in time, but all Tennant has to do is get them to the nearest town, and then they will be protected by whatever defense local Elementals provide.

The safe rolls smoothly toward the door and

"Get the safe out of here," she orders.

She can hear the jangle of tack outside as a horse-drawn wagon is brought to the front door, and a ramp moved into place. Inside the building, her people are struggling to move the safe onto a reinforced dolly, but it's a heavy piece, and sweat is running down their faces by the time they finally get it settled. But as soon as they started moving the dolly the Weaver can see that it's damaged. It moves only a few feet before one of the wheels splits off from the base with a sound like the crack of gunfire. A corner of the frame slams down onto the floor, and the safe skids in that direction until part of it slides off the dolly entirely, striking the wooden planks of the floor with enough force to gouge deeply into them.

Frustrated, Tennant stares at the wreckage. Clearly the dolly isn't going anywhere now; the only way they can get the safe out of the building is to push it along the floor, or maybe lift it. She considers the dynamics of the two options, then orders one of her people, "Go get some more help. We'll carry the damn thing out of here if we

As soon as they start moving the dolly Tennant can see that it's damaged. It only goes a few feet before one of the wheels splits off from the base with a sound like the crack of gunfire. A corner of the frame slams down onto the floor and the safe careens in that direction, hitting the wooden planks so hard that two of them split. Now the safe is wedged corner-first into a jagged hole in the floor, with cracks fanning out from it in every direction.

Appalled, Tennant stares at the wreckage. The safe isn't going anywhere. "We'll have to unload it," she says decisively. Her people run to gather the boxes and packing materials she'll need, as she works her way slowly across the floor, easing carefully from one broken plank to the next. Wood creaks beneath her weight, and once she hears an ominous cracking sound, but the floor holds, barely. When she finally reaches the safe she crouches down in front of it and begins to dial the combination. God willing, she'll have time to unload the fetters with the care they require, and then get everyone out of the compound before the fire cuts off their escape route and

‖‖‖‖‖‖‖‖‖‖‖

I awoke to pain, and an exhaustion so overwhelming I could barely muster the strength to open my eyes. Every muscle in my body burned, as if had just run a twenty-mile marathon and then topped it off by doing a hundred pushups. When I tried to move one arm it spasmed painfully, and my other limbs followed suit, until my entire body was knotted in a shivering ball of agony. I tried to cry out to Rita for help, but my chest muscles had spasmed so tightly it was hard to draw breath, and my voice came out little more than a choked whisper.

After what seemed like an eternity, the pain receded. One by one my muscles began to relax, and I stretched them out as best I could, gasping for breath as I did so. I had a pretty good guess about what had caused all that pain, and it wasn't happy news. Apparently taking control of a stranger's dream was much harder than just chatting with my brother. Getting into the Weaver's head had required herculean effort, and every tiny change I'd made to her dreamscape had required more exertion than the last.

This was the price of my success.

I don't know how long I lay there, so exhausted I could barely muster the strength to draw air into my lungs. I was surprised that Rita didn't come over to see what was wrong. She was supposed to be on watch, wasn't she? When I finally felt I had enough strength to do more than gasp for breath, I lifted myself up on one elbow and looked around for her.

She wasn't anywhere in sight.

Struggling to my feet, I used a nearby tree to steady myself. My legs were still so weak I couldn't stand without support. "Rita?"

She wasn't anywhere to be seen. Not in the camp, not on the nearby hill we'd chosen as a sentry point, not down by the stream. For a moment I wondered if she might have ducked behind some bushes to take care of private business, but if so, she should still be close enough to hear me call her name. I couldn't call out too loudly, for fear that someone in the compound might pick up on it—sound travelled far at night—but if she was anywhere near our camp she should have heard me.

There was no response.

Surely Rita wouldn't have just left me alone, I thought. The whole point of us sleeping in shifts was to make sure no Hunters could sneak up on us, and I couldn't imagine her walking off and leaving me unguarded. But if someone had attacked her, and either killed her or dragged her away, why would that person have left me untouched?

Walking unsteadily to where I'd left my flashlight, I thought I saw a faint light in the woods. It took me a few seconds to be sure it wasn't just moonlight shining down through the canopy, but no, the light was perfectly still, unaffected by the wind-stirred branches overhead the way moonlight would have been. And it didn't look like the color of moonlight, either. I began to make my way toward the light source. The moonlight was barely enough to see by, and my legs were still pretty weak, but I wanted to observe the source of that light, so I kept my flashlight turned off. Once or twice I had to stop to catch my breath, but soon I could hear a voice from up ahead, pitched low to avoid detection. Heart pounding, I crouched low and inched toward it, finally settling behind a fallen tree that was covered in brush. No one looking this way in the darkness would see me there.

The voice was Rita's.

She was standing with her back to me, and at first I thought she was talking to empty air, but as my eyes adjusted I could make out a ghostly image hovering in front of her. A woman's face. I squinted, trying to bring its features into focus, but with Rita in the way I couldn't get a clear view of it. Not until I heard the woman's voice did I realize who she was . . . and when I did the shock was so great I had to grab hold of the tree trunk to steady myself.

"You told me there would be no Hunters," Rita said.

"I said I would do my best to hold them at bay," Alia Morgana responded. "You knew there was risk."

Morgana. She was talking to Morgana. What the hell—?

Rita exhaled in a soft hiss. "Well, they haven't attacked us so far."

"Then they're probably not Virilian's people," Morgana pointed out. "They're certainly not mine. Perhaps some locals are curious about you."

Rita had betrayed me. She was working for Morgana. The revelation was so mortifying that I could barely absorb it. All her friendship, all her support, even her seeming ignorance of the ways of this world, as we traveled side by side . . . it had all been a sham. We had guessed that there was a spy among us, and everyone had thought it was Isaac. But of course it wasn't Isaac. A Shadow would have no reason to serve the Seers like that. Rita must have been the one reporting to Morgana all along, informing her of our every move, nudging us in whatever direction the Guildmistress wanted us to go. Thanks to her, we never made a move or had a conversation that Morgana did not know about.

I suddenly felt nauseous.

"Jesse's planning some kind of disruption at the Weaver compound," said the traitor who had once been my friend. "Do you want me to talk her out of it?"

I'd trusted her. In Berkeley Springs she'd been like a sister to me. Hot tears trickled down my cheeks, burning them like acid.

Morgana's eyes narrowed. "I want you to keep your cover. I want you to let her take the lead. Those have been your orders since the day you entered my service, and they will not change. If the Weavers suffer a loss . . ." She shrugged. "I will light a candle for them. What about Jesse's dreams? Have you learned anything new?"

Rita shook her head. "She sensed at the shallow that we were in the wrong place, but she said that was just a feeling she got while she was half-asleep. Nothing that a regular Seer might not have picked up on."

"All right. Don't press her for more. It will come when it comes. The single most important thing now is for you to maintain her trust, so that if she does show signs of the Gift we seek, she will want to confide in you."

"I don't think that will be a problem." Rita's smugness was like a knife plunging into my heart.

"For now, no more calls to me. I understand that you were worried about the Hunters, so this time it was justified, but I don't want you contacting me from the field again, unless lives are at stake. It's too risky. Understood?"

It sounded like they were beginning to wrap up their conversation, so I started to edge away from my hiding place, moving off to one side so that if Rita headed back to the camp she wouldn't bump into me. I was shaking so badly that I couldn't take a step without something to hold onto. How long had Rita been working for Morgana? Was she on the Seer's payroll when I first met her, that day in the IHOP with Devon? Before that? Events I hadn't paid much attention to at the time suddenly took on terrible significance. I started remembering comments Rita had made, things she had done; the way Morgana and Seyer had stopped by the fair at exactly the right moment for us to see them ... Rita must have told them we were coming. And she had been the one to suggest that I get in touch with Seyer, which had set this whole trip in motion. Oh my God, it was staged, it was all staged, every minute of it was staged. . . .

Suddenly I remembered how Rita had come to me the night my house burned down, arriving in my bedroom just in time to save me. Her explanation for that had always seemed lame, but what other reason made sense at the time? Seyer had been standing outside the house, watching the fire. Had they been working together all along, trying to get me out of my house in time? That would suggest that they'd known about the arson in advance. My God, what if she'd actually *set* the fire, so that her people could make a show of rescuing me from it?

Tears were pouring freely from my eyes now, and I made no effort to wipe them away. All the pain of my family's suffering was in those tears, all my agony at seeing my mother's spirit wither away, all my rage at the time I had wasted worrying about Rita after our return home, thinking I had killed her, when in fact she was probably just hanging out at Morgana's place having tea and biscuits. It was more than any soul could contain. The best I could do was try to stifle the noise of my sobbing, burying my face in my shirt as my body shook from the force of my sorrow. Was Morgana the one who had orchestrated Devon's sickness? So that the only person traveling with me would be someone who answered to her? Sickness welled up inside me as I realized how thoroughly I had been manipulated. I leaned over and vomited, violently and wretchedly, but the fit offered a perverse cleansing for my soul, so I gave myself over to it. Wave after wave of sickness coursed through me, until my stomach was finally emptied of misery and all that was left was dry heaving.

"Jesse?"

Startled, I looked up. The call had come from the direction of our camp. Rita had gone back and was looking for me. Probably she heard all the noise I just made.

Crap.

With trembling hands I used the front of my shirt to wipe my face dry. There were a few bits of vomit left on my shirt, and on the back of my hand where I'd wiped my mouth, but I left them there. Vomit would be easier to explain to her than tears. "Yeah," I rasped. My throat was so raw I could barely get sound out. "I'm coming."

Thank God I had moved away from my original path when I started back. As I headed back to the camp I circled around even further away from the place where she had betrayed me, and I stumbled noisily through the woods, like someone who didn't know how to move quietly. If she heard me coming from another direction, she wouldn't suspect that I had overheard her treachery.

When she saw me stagger into camp, her eyes went wide. "Holy crap, girl. What happened to you?"

*I learned what you are. And I'm so filled with disgust*

*that I can hardly bear to look at you.* "I was sick as hell when I got up," I whispered. "Didn't want to throw up on top of our supplies." I waved vaguely toward the woods. "I think I'm okay now."

"Something you ate?"

I hesitated. We'd eaten the same food, so that story might not stand up to close inspection. My mind raced to come up with another excuse. "I had a nightmare. Really awful one. Left me feeling sick when I woke up."

"What kind of nightmare?"

Instantly I realized my mistake. Morgana had ordered her to report on my dreams, so there was no way Rita was going to let this one pass without explanation. I was going to have to make something up, with enough gruesome detail in it that the Guildmistress would think it was genuine. So I told Rita about a nightmare in which we broke into the Weaver's camp, only to find that Tommy was there, and that he'd been put through the same torture that Moth had talked about, but in a much more literal way. Halfway through my description of my little brother's body turned inside-out on a gurney, organs pulsing outside his skin, Rita decided she's had enough. Looking a little green around the gills, she waved the recitation short. My alibi was credible.

*Analyze that one, Morgana.*

I did manage to sneak the information about the safe combination into my fiction. There was no way to avoid Rita finding out about that—we couldn't break into the compound without it—but I sure as hell wasn't going to tell her that I'd altered the Weaver's dream to trick her into revealing it. I just told Rita that at the end of my nightmare I had seen three numbers appear, and I thought they might be the combination we needed.

Even a Seer could dream that much, right?

After I finished my story, Rita came over to me and put an arm around my shoulders, gently pulling me close to her. At any other time such a hug would have been comforting, but now that I knew the truth I had to swallow back on my revulsion to let her touch me. Hopefully if she sensed me drawing away from her, she would ascribe it to the aftermath of my nightmare. I had to keep up the illusion of friendship for now, no matter how painful it was. Rita and I were dependent on each other in this wilderness setting, and nothing good would come of our splitting up. As for later ... I would have to play that by ear. It might be useful to be able to feed false information to Morgana, through her spy, but that would only work if Rita believed we were still best buddies.

I offered to take a turn at sentry duty so Rita could get some sleep, and I changed to a fresh T-shirt while she stretched out on top of her blankets. Then I climbed up the embankment and settled down on the large rock that had become our sentry post. Wrapping my arms around myself, I rocked gently back and forth, trying to comfort myself. If a horde of rabid raccoons had come running by at that moment, I doubt I would have noticed them.

I wanted to go to sleep again. I wanted to visit my brother in his dreams, or maybe Devon. Or maybe even my mother, though she wouldn't understand what was happening. I wanted to hug them so tightly they couldn't breathe, and tell them how friggin' scared I was, and how the one person I'd trusted most had turned out to be a traitor. How everyone around me seemed to be allied to either the Shadows or Morgana, and I was no longer sure which of those I should fear more.

Tears began to trickle down my cheeks again, but they were quiet tears, and Rita slept right through them.

Never in all my life had I felt more alone.

# 15

## SHADOWCREST
## VIRGINIA PRIME

### ISAAC

IF ISAAC HAD BEEN ASKED to name all the things in
the world he didn't want to do, meeting with Guildmaster Virilian would have been number one on the list.

*Yet here I am,* he thought unhappily, as he walked the
length of the corridor leading to the Shadowlord's audience chamber. The last time he'd come here it was to
beg for reinstatement in the Guild. Now all that was
done with, but he was being called back, and he could
not think of a single good reason why that would happen. Ordinary business would be handled by his father—now that they were speaking again—or perhaps a
teacher. A Shadowlord of Master Virilian's rank didn't
schedule a private audience with a mere apprentice unless something was very wrong.

Maybe Isaac's father had sensed how repelled his son
was by the binding ritual, and was having second

thoughts about Isaac's membership in the Guild. Or maybe others had complained about Isaac's attending that ritual, in breach of normal protocol. Or maybe there was some other offense involved. Isaac couldn't begin to guess, so he just braced himself for the worst as he approached the great doors. One of the men standing guard outside cracked a door open and slipped inside, probably to announce him. Wiping the nervous sweat from his palms in that precious moment of privacy, he waited.

The man reappeared. "You may enter."

The doors were opened just wide enough for Isaac to pass through, and they closed behind him as soon as he was inside. The vast audience chamber was filled with an unusual number of ghosts, more moans and screams echoing through the cavernous room than he remembered from his last visit. Or perhaps he was just more sensitive to them. Now that he knew he was hearing the terror of souls that Virilian had murdered, they were harder to ignore.

The Shadowlord was waiting for him at the far end of the chamber, seated on his black throne. The closer Isaac came to him, the louder the voices in the room seemed to become. Within ten paces of the throne he could almost make out words.

His Gift was growing stronger.

When he had come as close as seemed appropriate he stopped and bowed. He held the position for a few seconds, not just out of respect, but because it allowed him to put off the interview a tiny bit longer.

"Apprentice Antonin."

He stood up straight. "Your Lordship summoned me?"

Virilian's black eyes studied Isaac from head to toe. "Your family has taken you back, I see."

Isaac nodded. "My father was most gracious in his acceptance."

"He sees great promise in you."

The concept that Isaac's father might have praised him to the Guildmaster, after all their disagreements, was a startling one. That Virilian would tell him about it was even more so.

*But even if my father said good things about me, that doesn't mean they're true.* If Leonid Antonin believed that his family interests would be best served by the Guildmaster thinking that he was pleased with his son, then that was the story he would tell. Briefly, Isaac wondered what it was like to be part of a family where relationships were less complicated. Or more honest.

"I hope to serve my family faithfully and well," he said evenly.

The thin, bloodless mouth twitched slightly. "And your Guild, of course."

"Of course, your Grace."

Virilian leaned back in his throne and steepled his hands in front of his chest; It seemed an oddly human gesture for such an inhuman creature. "An apprentice's duty is to serve this Guild without hesitation or reserve. So if I asked you for information regarding your recent ... adventures ... you would of course provide it?"

Fear fluttered in his heart. The last thing he wanted to do was talk to Virilian about the details of his two-year walkabout. There were some memories too private to share. But he bowed his head and said, "Of course," because no other response was acceptable.

He wished he were anywhere but here.

"You know what happened to our Gate." It was a question.

"I heard that it was destroyed," he said carefully. "Not much more than that."

The Guildmaster nodded. "The Greys have kept the details of it quiet, at my request. Only a handful of people know the whole story."

Isaac's heart sank. Did Virilian suspect him of having played a part in the Gate's destruction? Or think that maybe Isaac had known the Colonnans were planning it? A thin film of nervous sweat began to gather on his forehead, but he didn't dare wipe it away for fear of drawing the Guildmaster's attention to it.

"It seems," the Shadowlord said, "our visitors had a codex. Presumably one keyed to Terra Colonna, though that has not been officially confirmed. They smashed it against the arch as they passed through, and the resulting explosion was powerful enough to destroy the Gate, along with its counterparts on more than a dozen worlds. The facility on Terra Colonna itself was completely destroyed. Though apparently they made it safely through before that happened."

"But a codex can't—" Isaac began. He bit his tongue and stopped.

"Yes?"

"Forgive me," he murmured. He lowered his eyes in formal humility. "I didn't mean to question you."

"But you should, Apprentice. Because what I just described to you should not be possible. A codex is a recording device, nothing more. It has no special mechanism or power that would enable it to destroy a Gate, much less devastate the surrounding landscape as it did so."

Startled, Isaac looked up at him.

"The Greys believe that some other power was fettered to it," Virilian told him. "They're not sure what, just yet, or who might have done the weaving. Investigation is ongoing." The steepled fingers twitched slightly. "I was hoping you could help shed some light on the matter."

Isaac's mouth was suddenly so dry it was hard to force words out. "I . . . I didn't even know they had a codex. Much less who might have created it."

"No doubt if you had known, you would have told us about it as soon as you returned."

"Of course," he said quickly. If Isaac had known about the codex and not informed his Guild about it, that would have been a mortal offense. He remembered how the boy in the binding ritual had died and he shuddered; with a single word, Virilian could consign him to the same fate.

"You were with the Colonnans while they were here. For how long?"

Suddenly he was very aware of how intently the Guildmaster was watching him. The fact that the Shadowlord had forsworn human emotion in himself didn't mean that he couldn't detect it in others. Isaac needed to choose his words with care. "I met them the week before I returned to Shadowcrest. I believe they had just recently arrived."

"And you taught them about us." The Guildmaster's voice was deathly cold. "Do I have that right?"

Isaac's heart skipped a beat. "Grade school basics, your Grace. The stuff every commoner is taught. Nothing about the Shadows. Certainly nothing about codexes."

The Guildmaster's expression was unreadable. "Go on."

"I travelled with them for a while after that. But they didn't trust me enough to tell me their plans. They didn't trust anyone from this world, to be honest."

The subtle lift of an eyebrow warned Isaac that he might be saying too much. *Don't talk about your relationship with them,* he told himself. *Even if your words reveal nothing, he may sense the emotion behind them.* "We split up as soon as we got back to Luray. They dropped me off at the south docks. I don't know where they went after that." He paused. "They could have gotten the codex from someone in the city."

*Or from Sebastian,* he thought suddenly.

He suddenly remembered what the Green Man had told them of his history, specifically his past conflict with the Shadowlords. Remembered the look in Sebastian's eyes when Isaac had asked about the death of Guildmaster Durand. Remembered all the fetters on Sebastian's coat, dozens of them, some of which manifested powers Isaac had never seen before. A man who knew how to obtain such fetters would know how to have a codex altered. And he would have the contacts necessary to do it.

"You remember something," Virilian said quietly.

Isaac hesitated. God knows, he owed Sebastian no particular loyalty. The Green Man had made a show of saving his life in the Warrens, but there had never been any real threat to Isaac; all he ever had to do was let the raiders know who and what he was, and they would bend over backward to get him home safely. Sebastian had done nothing more than protect Isaac's masquerade.

A loyal Shadow would tell the Guildmaster everything he knew about the Green Man, right now. A loyal Shadow would be pleased when Hunters brought Sebastian in for questioning, and proud to witness the ritual wherein Sebastian was murdered, his spirit bound to slavery, forced to serve the Guild he despised. A Shadow would be pleased that an enemy of the Shadows had been neutralized. But the man who had tried to save Isaac's life in the Warrens deserved better than that. Hell, *anyone* deserved better than that.

Virilian was waiting. Isaac had to say something.

"I took them to the Assessment Fair." Isaac gazed off into the distance as he spoke, partly so he'd look as if he was trying to access an elusive memory, but mostly so he didn't have to look into Virilian's eyes. "They went off on their own for a while. Someone might have contacted them then. Maybe word of their arrival had gotten out, and someone thought they might serve as a useful tool. I don't know. Why would someone want to destroy the Gate, anyway? Surely they know we could just rebuild it. I mean, I can understand why the Colonnans would have wanted to destroy the Gate behind them, to keep people from following them through it, but why would someone here help them do that? What would they have to gain from it?"

The Guildmaster stared at Isaac for a long moment. "Our Guild has its enemies," he said at last. "As do the Greys, and the Potters, and every other Guild whose livelihood depends upon interworld commerce. What better way to strike at us all than to destroy a Gate we depend upon, then sit back and watch while we blame each other for its loss?" He paused. "Now you understand why it's so important for us to find out where that codex came from."

"Of course," he said evenly. "And I'm sorry I can't help more."

"But you will help in the future, if you can. Yes? You will bring me any new information you find. And bring it directly to me, not entrusting it to servants or messengers?"

"I . . . yes, your Grace. If that's what you want."

"It is," he said curtly. He stared at Isaac for another long moment, then gestured toward the exit. "That's all for now, Apprentice Antonin. You may leave."

Heart pounding, Isaac bowed deeply to the Guildmaster, then backed out of the chamber without looking up. It was an apprentice's gesture of humility, a statement of innocence: *Behold, I am nothing but a servant of my Guild, with no higher goal than to serve your will humbly and faithfully*. But inside his mind was churning. Had his answers been good enough to satisfy the Shadowlord? Did the Guildmaster really think he'd been involved in the Gate's destruction, or was he hinting at that just to keep Isaac off balance, so that maybe he would slip up and reveal other secrets?

If the Shadowlord wanted answers badly enough he had ways to get them, Isaac knew that. The binding ritual that he'd witnessed was a nearly perfect interrogation tool; any man the Guild was willing to kill could be forced to reveal all his secrets . . . at least the secrets that survived the mental trauma of the ritual.

*My father would never let that happen to me,* he thought. *No matter how much I frustrated him—or even angered him—He would never let Virilian do that to a member of his family.*

But the thought was cold comfort as he walked back to his quarters, and it was a long time before his heartbeat settled down to its accustomed pace.

# 16

## BLACKWATER MOUNTAINS
## VIRGINIA PRIME

### JESSE

THE MOON WAS LOW IN THE SKY, half-hidden by the trees, so lighting was minimal, making it hard to see obstacles. More than once we had to work ourselves loose from a particularly aggressive vine or thorn bush, making way too much noise in the process. No one inside the compound seemed to notice—probably they just assumed that local wildlife was making a lot of noise—but it wreaked hell on my nerves.

We had observed three types of people in the compound—Weavers, guards, and experimental subjects—and had decided that it would be best if we looked like members of the first group, in case someone spotted us. Most of the Weavers were dressed casually, so hopefully anyone who saw us from a distance would assume we were members of the staff. Of course that illusion would fall to pieces if someone looked at us too closely—in a facility this small everyone probably knew each other. The three guards were big men whose uniforms wouldn't fit us even if we could get hold of some, and if we dressed like the kids we'd set off alarm bells just being outdoors at night. There really was no other choice. So we brushed the leaves out of our hair, smoothed out the worst of our camping wrinkles and hid our bulkier supplies in deep brush not too far from the compound. None of the Weavers were wearing backpacks.

We knew that whichever guard was on duty could be counted on to make a slow and leisurely round of the compound every couple of hours. Moth had told us that all three guards followed the same routine, and we'd timed the circuit a few times, so we knew when we would have the best window of opportunity to cross the compound. Once we got to the lab building we would climb in through the rear window—Rita assured me she could get us in without breaking any glass—and then search the place for any sign of Morgana's mandala pattern. When that was done, we would set the place on fire. Which—according to the Weaver's dream—would bring everyone running to fight the flames. Hopefully that would clear a path to the kids' dorm, which we would unlock, and then they could flee during the ruckus.

Was it a risky plan? Hell yeah, on at least a dozen counts. But there weren't any guard dogs in the compound, and no one seemed to be carrying firearms, so as long as we kept our exit path open we should be okay. We strung some ropes between trees just outside the fence, to trip up anyone who tried to follow us. I was praying that wouldn't be necessary. Dodging pursuit in the depths of the forest in the middle of the night was a sure recipe for disaster.

As for Moth and the other children . . . maybe it was a questionable mercy to release them into the forest, when we had no way to get them to safety. But Moth had made it clear that she would rather risk death in the woods than spend one more day as a test animal, and she said the others felt the same way. At least they could follow the carriage trail to the main road, which would lead them to nearby towns. And the weather was good, there was water nearby, and Moth was going to organize the children to sneak food out of the mess hall, so they would have supplies to take with them. A few days' hike would bring them to more populated cities, the kind of setting a girl from the Warrens was used to. They would all make it, I told myself. Moth was a plucky kid. She would lead the others to safety.

"You ready?" Rita whispered.

"No."

She grinned. "Good to go, then."

How loyal and brave she looked, as she prepared to follow a friend into danger! I wondered how much hazard pay she was getting for this trip.

From our hiding place we watched as the guard shifted his weight from leg to leg, trying to keep his mind occupied in the absence of emergencies. He looked like he was humming to himself. Every few minutes he checked his watch, and when 3 A.M finally rolled around he looked pleased to have something to do. Slowly he strolled toward the dining hall and checked its front door. Then he walked around the back of the building to check things there. We knew his next stop would be the area behind a row of small cabins, which meant we would be out of his line of sight for several minutes.

"Now," Rita whispered.

We moved through the brush quickly and were soon at the gate. Rita already had a small leather case in her hand, and as soon as we stopped she pulled out two small tools. The handles were mother of pearl, far more ornate lock picks than I would have expected Rita to possess. Probably gifts from Morgana.

She placed an L-shaped tool in the keyhole and pressed it to the side with one finger, then inserted a tool with a curved zigzag shape at the end. She moved the second one around a bit, mostly in a sawing motion, angling the end up or down in response to things she was feeling inside the lock. I heard a few soft clicks, and then the L-shaped lever turned slightly, and the lock snapped open. Just like that. Maybe five seconds from start to finish.

She saw my expression and grinned. "Hey, it's not that hard. I'll teach you sometime."

Jeez. Lessons in breaking and entering from Rita. No comment on that.

She released the bolt, and I took out the wad of glue we had painstakingly scraped from the back of our duct tape and pushed it into the space around it with my fingernail. Then I pushed the bolt back in, released it . . . and it held. No one was going to be locking this gate any time soon.

We slipped inside the compound and Rita quietly shut the gate behind us. The main area was empty right now, but we knew that any minute the guard would come back into view, so we sprinted toward the lab building as fast as we could and managed to slip behind it before he appeared again.

I plastered myself against the wall beside Rita as we took a moment to catch our breath. My heart was pounding wildly, but it was more from exhilaration than fear.

Rita looked at me. "Calm is good," she whispered. "Calm is your friend."

The back of the lab overlooked a drainage ditch, and once we skirted the building and slid down into that, we would no longer be visible from the center of the compound. I looked up at the one window high on the wall overhead and suddenly had my doubts about this phase of our endeavor. The window hadn't looked quite that high when we'd reconned it.

Rita's hand on my shoulder startled me. "It's all good," she whispered.

I nodded and braced myself on the only piece of solid ground, a slab of concrete half-buried in the wall of the ditch. Then I offered Rita my cupped hands and helped vault her up toward the window. It took three tries for her to grab the edge of the frame, and then a few awkward seconds for her to settle her feet on my shoulders. Then I held tightly onto her ankles as she cut through the caulking around a pane of glass. Once the pane was removed she was able to reach in and unlock the window, slide it open, and climb inside. A few seconds later a rope with knotted loops fell down to me, and I was able to climb up to the window and crawl inside.

We'd landed in a washroom, and for a few seconds we both crouched silently, listening for any other activity in the building. But it sounded as empty as it had looked. Rita eased the door open, and we moved into the main area of the building. We didn't want to use our flashlights for fear the light would be seen from outside, but I took out the small glow lamp, which had lost so much power by now that it was hardly brighter than a night light. I cupped it in my hand to direct the beam, and we could see by its light that we were in the lab Moth had told us about.

We were there. We had made it. The sensation of triumph that I felt was so powerful it made me giddy.

*Easy, girl,* I warned myself. *That was only the first step. Lots to do yet.*

The lab was bigger than I'd expected. A few steel tables with leather straps on them dominated the center of the room, and metal trolleys filled with tools were arranged along the walls. I remembered Moth's gruesome description of the Weavers' experiments, and I shuddered. There were also some filing cabinets, a small desk, shelves filled with tools and boxes, all neatly arranged, and a large industrial sink in the corner. A faint oily smell hung in the air; not unpleasant, but odd.

"Over there," Rita whispered, pointing to an alcove across from us with a small shadowy shape in it. I knew where the safe was located, thanks to the Weaver's dream, but I couldn't reveal that to Rita, so I let her take credit for its discovery. Carefully we moved through the room, trying to avoid all the tables and trays that would make noise if we bumped into them, until we got to the alcove, and yes, that shadowy shape was the safe. Rita grinned and looked at me expectantly.

Suddenly I felt my confidence waver. What if I hadn't really contacted the Weaver, but only dreamed that I had? In that case the combination I had seen her use would be useless. Or what if the dream had been true, but I'd gotten the numbers wrong? By the time the woman had opened the safe in her dream I'd been so exhausted I could barely see straight.

*The world won't end even if you screw this up,* I told myself sternly. *We'll just sneak back to camp and come up with a new plan. Nothing's happened yet that would keep us from trying again.*

The thought that my input might not matter as much as I'd thought was oddly comforting. Steadier now, I crouched down by the safe door and began to turn the dial, setting the numbers that I'd been repeating to myself ever since I'd woke up. Fourteen right. A whole circuit to the left, then twenty-three. Four right. Drawing in a deep breath, I took hold of the handle and pulled it back.

The door didn't budge.

Shit.

Rita muttered, "It would really suck if you got the combination wrong."

I cursed her silently and shut my eyes, struggling to concentrate. I needed to replay the Weaver's dream in my head, exactly the way I'd seen it, so that I could make sure I had all the numbers right. It turned out to be harder than I expected. The exhaustion I'd experienced while crafting that dream came back to me, as strong as when I'd first felt it; it was as if I was trying to affect the Weaver's mind again, rather than just remember a few details. And the dream itself was hazier this time, like viewing it through a veil of static. I could see the Weaver kneel down by the safe and start turning the dial, but I couldn't get the numbers into clear focus.

*Come on, girl. You can do this.*

Squinting into the static, I finally managed to bring the dial into focus, and I watched her open the safe again. *Fourteen right. Twenty-three left. Four right.*

So I had remembered the numbers correctly. That was comforting, but not at all helpful. I stared at the safe again, frustrated beyond words. My exhaustion had faded when the dream did, but in its place now was the sharp bite of despair. What if we had come all this way for nothing? Over and over, I replayed the opening of the safe in my mind, over and over. Finally I realized that the Weaver had spun the dial a few times before starting the combination and maybe that mattered.

I turned the dial clockwise a few times, then counterclockwise, then clockwise again—just to make sure—and then I tried the combination. I dialed each number with meticulous care, making sure it was perfectly positioned before moving on to the next. When the whole sequence had been set I took a deep breath, reached for the handle, and tried the safe door.

It opened.

We were in.

"Well, damn." Rita muttered. I could hear awe in her voice.

Inside the safe were three shelves with several wooden boxes on each one. They looked like recipe files, only, instead of printed cards being inside them, there were thin metal plates. Experimental fetters? I pulled one out to inspect and I saw that the surface was inscribed with data, mostly in alpha-numeric codes I didn't recognize.

"Shit," Rita said, looking over my shoulder. "How are we supposed to find the one we need?"

I took Morgana's paper out of my pocket and set it down beside the safe so that I could refer to it easily. "Maybe one of them is marked with this sign."

"Yeah, but there must be hundreds . . ."

I looked up at her. "You have somewhere to be?"

She looked pointedly at her watch. But though it felt like an eternity had passed since we'd snuck through the main gate, apparently, in real time, it wasn't that long. When Rita saw that we still had plenty of time, she sighed and nodded.

I turned back to the fetters. "Why don't I go through these to see if Morgana's symbol matches anything, while you check out the rest of the place? 'Cause we don't know for a fact that what she's looking for is in here." *Anything that keeps you from looming over me like a vulture while I search for Dreamwalker artifacts.* "I'll let you know if I find anything."

Her mouth tightened, but my suggestion was perfectly reasonable, so she moved off to explore the rest of the facility. Which left me alone to flip through the metal plates one by one, looking for any markings that might indicate whose fetters they were. There were several lines of information inscribed on each plate, but aside from a date at the top, it was all rendered in mysterious codes. It soon became clear that nothing like Morgana's mandala design was going to be found here, but that didn't mean there weren't other things I could search for. The fetters were arranged chronologically, so I started looking for ones that had been made while the coma boy was still alive. If I was right about his being the presence the Seers had sensed, then those were the fetters I needed to see.

"Any luck?" Rita whispered loudly from across the room.

I shook my head. "Nothing yet."

I finally found fetters from the right time frame, but they looked no different than any of the others. Clearly this method of searching was not going to help me. With a sigh I leaned back on my heels and tried to think of a new angle. The fetters were supposed to have mental energy bound to them. So if the boy's energy contained a hint of the Dreamwalker Gift, could that be used to identify it? It was worth a try. Risky as hell, since the kid had been a basket case when the fetter was made, but worth a try.

Drawing in a deep breath, I laid my hand on the first fetter and thought: *C'mon, fetter, do your stuff. Let's see what you've got.* Dr. Tilford had said that the glow lamp required both touch and intent to operate, so I offered it both. *Do something.*

Nothing happened.

I tried a few more fetters, and it soon became clear that a general invocation was not going to trigger any of them. Which actually made my search much easier. If each fetter responded to a specific type of command, I wasn't going to set any of them off accidentally.

Drawing in a deep breath, I spread my hands out over the fetters so that my skin would make contact with as many of the fetters as possible. I had to lean forward to use my forearms as well, but once I did that I was able to make contact with the fetters in two of the boxes, all at once.

*Give me your dreams,* I thought. My command wasn't

in words this time; rather, I was calling to the fettered energy with my own Gift: soul to soul. I was willing it to respond to me, to commune with me, to reveal its true nature to me ... whatever that turned out to be.

Still nothing happened.

Muttering a curse in frustration, I moved into position to test the next batch. Maybe this whole trip was a fool's errand. Maybe experimental fetters couldn't be activated by just anyone. Maybe you needed the Weaver's Gift to do it, otherwise they would just stay inert strips of metal.

*Steady, girl. Keep it together.*

Carefully I laid my arms and hands across the next two rows of fetters, shut my eyes, and tried to summon whatever residual bit of dream-power one of them might contain.

*The castle is tall beyond measure, and shadowy figures can be glimpsed through its windows, each one of which reveals a different time and place....*

*The tower looms overheard, the signatures of thousands of travelers spiraling around it, leading the eye upward, upward....*

*The mausoleum is vast, grey and cold. So cold! Tier after tier of stone crypts stack up into the windswept sky, a plaque on each one identifying its occupant. The names are all different, but the same word is carved beneath each name, in identical letters: Dreamwalker....*

With a gasp I fell back from the fetters, the image of the Dreamwalker tomb seared into my brain. Was that the same shape-changing structure I had seen in the avatar's dream? If so, it had taken on a pretty dark aspect this time.

"Jesse!" Rita's voice was a hiss. "You okay?"

"Uh ... I cut myself," I muttered. I shook my hand

and sucked at a fingertip, to lend the fiction weight. "These things have sharp edges."

I waited until Rita had turned her attention back to her search before reaching out to touch the fetters again. Slowly I ran my fingers down the first row of plates, touching them one by one, attempting to summon back the vision that I had experienced so briefly. And I tried to lock my body in a rigid position, because I knew that if I moved suddenly or made a suspicious sound when I found the thing, Rita would be on me in a heartbeat. And this time she'd want more than a lame story about a non-existent wound.

Fetter by fetter, my fingertips slowly caressed the stack, and I fixed the position of each one in my mind so that I would not forget which I was in contact with when—

*Color bleeds from the sky, from the trees, from the ground. The world is dissolving into thick black muck, and it traps his legs like quicksand so he cannot run, he cannot run! Darkness rushes down from the sky as he struggles to envision the pattern he needs to escape this world, the maps that will open a gateway for him. Desperately he sketches out its shape in his mind's eye, but it's not coming out right, the darkness is skewing his brain, it's not good enough! So he tries another—and another and another and another—and the patterns start overlapping, details running into one another until all he can see is a vast mandala that contains all the patterns he needs, but gives access to none. Then the darkness closes in on him and he hears himself screaming, because he senses what it can do. The taste of death fills his nose and mouth as memories start to rush out of him, every thought and hope and fear and love that he ever knew, sucked out of him into the void and devoured until there is nothing left . . .*

\*          \*          \*

Suddenly the images were gone. Maybe I banished them. Maybe when you saw a vision so horrifying that your soul begged for it to end, the fetter interpreted that as an "off" switch. Or maybe there was nothing left to be seen. Maybe the boy's emanations ended when the dream-wraith devoured his soul, and that was why he became catatonic. His body had gone on living, but his soul was dead.

Tears threatened to come to my eyes as I removed the dream fetter from the box, keeping my movements as small as possible so that Rita wouldn't notice what I was doing. No one but a Dreamwalker should possess such a fetter. I would take it home with me, and I would explore its mysteries, and maybe learn more about the strange castle which seemed to have such significance to my kind. And I would mourn this boy who had slipped through the Seer's net because they thought his Gift was not strong enough to manifest, who had left me this precious inheritance.

Suddenly my reverie was broken by what was, in our current context, a truly terrifying sound: a key turning in the lock.

"Shit!" Rita muttered.

Desperately we both looked around for cover. The room's interior door was too far away for us to get to it in time, and there were few hiding places nearby. Rita flattened herself against the wall behind a filing cabinet, scrunching down a bit to make sure her head couldn't be seen from the front door, but as soon as someone walked past the filing cabinet she'd be in plain view. I dove for cover under the desk, then realized that I'd left the safe door open, so I nudged it closed with my foot even as the doorknob began to turn. I tried to fit myself completely under the desk, but the space was too shallow for that, and my legs were stuck out the back. Like

Rita, I would be vulnerable to discovery as soon as someone walked past my hiding place.

Things were not looking good.

Heart pounding, I peered under the desk's lower edge to see who entered. My view was limited to six inches above the floor, and all I could see was that the newcomer was wearing black shoes—nicely polished but with mud on them—and blue uniform pants. A guard, most likely. But why was he here? The guards didn't enter this building as part of their regular rounds. Our whole operation centered around that premise. Had someone seen us cross the compound, or heard us moving around inside the lab?

It could be my fault, I realized. I'd spent half the night crafting dreams for the head Weaver, in which her precious lab was threatened with destruction. She might well have felt uneasy when she woke up, and asked her guards to check in here, just to be safe. If so, it was a frightening lesson in the consequences of screwing with someone's dreams. If I survived this, I should learn from it.

The feet had stopped moving, and just in time; two more steps and he would have passed Rita's hiding place. Thank God I'd thought to close the safe. I glanced back at it—and froze. Morgana's mandala drawing was lying on the floor beside it, in plain view. In my panic I'd forgotten about it.

I slid the dream fetter into my back pocket as I waited to see if the guard would come any closer, and I took out my knife, though I wasn't sure I could bring myself to use it on him. This wasn't some creepy servant of the undead, a monster who had helped kidnap my brother, maim my mother, and destroy the house I'd grown up in. This was just some working class guy trying to earn a living, at a low wage job in the middle of nowhere. Maybe Rita could stab somebody like that, but I didn't think that I could.

Maybe he wouldn't notice the paper. Maybe he'd just make a cursory check of the premises and leave without ever seeing us.

A beam of bluish light swept across the floor. It worked its way around the room, then stopped when it hit the safe. And paused there. It was centered on Morgana's drawing.

Shit.

The guard began to move forward—and then suddenly there was a sickening thud and he fell to his knees, stunned. As I scrambled out from under the desk I saw Rita cast aside the metal lamp she'd struck him with, and lunge for the back of his neck. She didn't have her knife out, so I wasn't sure what she meant to do. Tear his throat out with her teeth? My own preference would have been to try to talk our way out of this situation, but that option was off the table now, so I rushed in to help.

Rita was a small girl, no match for the guard's six feet of beefy weight, but she was quick on her feet, and her surprise attack had gained her a few seconds to act. The guard was still struggling to get his bearings when she grabbed him from behind, wrapping her arm around his throat in a chokehold that pressed in on his windpipe, cutting off his air supply. That woke him out of his daze pretty fast. He reached up to try to break her grip, but she was squeezing so tightly he couldn't pry her loose.

Suddenly he lurched backward, slamming Rita into the filing cabinet with a crash. She held on tight, so he tried it again, pounding her back against the thing as hard as he could. But he was rapidly losing strength, and as I ran to help her, he collapsed to his knees. I saw him fumbling for the nightstick he'd dropped when Rita first attacked, and I tried to kick it out of the way. But he was faster than I was and he grabbed it first. The next thing I knew the heavy black rod slammed into my side with stunning force. Pain shot through my ribs, and then I was on the floor, struggling to get my bearings. He resumed his assault on Rita, so I stumbled to my feet and tried to help her, but it was no longer necessary. Lack of blood and air had drained him of strength, and even as I watched, his struggles ceased, and he closed his eyes and slumped down to the floor. Rita still held on.

"It's done," I gasped. "Don't kill him."

She didn't let go. Her expression was cold.

"*Don't kill him,*" I ordered.

Muttering a curse under her breath, she let go of him. I went to shut the front door and set the lock. If someone came to investigate what all the noise was about, it would buy us a moment's time.

"You okay?" I asked Rita.

"Yeah. You?"

The pain in my side was sharp but not unbearable. My ribs were bruised, but probably not broken. "I think so."

She looked around the room, exhaling sharply in exasperation. "What now?"

Our original plan had been to set fire to the place, then exit out the back window and use the drainage ditch to get away. But we couldn't lower the guard's six foot body out that window. And I wasn't going to leave him here to burn to death.

For a moment we just stood there, looking around at the body, the safe, the door, and not saying anything. Time was running out.

"You go out the back," I said. "I'll drag him out the front."

She blinked. "Say *what*?"

There were voices outside now, coming our way. Clearly our struggle had been heard, and people were trying to figure out which building the noise had come from. Any minute now they would test our door.

"I'll make a show of rescuing one of their people," I

said. "My back will be to most of them, and the others will be paying attention to the fire, not me—"

"Jeez, are you *crazy*? You can't just walk out there—"

"So what the hell do you suggest we do?" I demanded. "We can't get his body out through the back window, and I'm certainly not going to leave him here to burn. We need that fire to cover our exit, which means we need to get him out of here. Do you know another way? Because if you do, I'm listening."

She stared at me for a moment. "You've got balls, girl."

"No," I said sharply. "What I've got is no other choice. Now, get the damn fire started while I drag this guy's body over to the door."

I checked his neck first to make sure there was a pulse. There was. Then I started to drag him across the floor, positioning him right in front of the door. It would have been easier if Rita had been helping me, but we needed to get our diversion started, fast. She was grabbing up handfuls of paper from the filing cabinet and cast them across the floor, creating a line of flammable refuse that stretched across the room. If we'd been able to follow our original plan to set the fire in secret, it could have grown to strength before anyone even realized what was going on. But any minute now someone could walk in the door, ready to beat out a small fire. So it had to spread fast.

"Here." I pulled the guard's keys from his belt and threw them to Rita. "Get the kids out of the compound if you can. If not, at least get yourself out."

For a moment she looked like she was about to argue with me, then she just shook her head grimly and pulled out her lighter. Kneeling down, she set fire to the paper in one spot, then another. As the flames began to spread she grabbed up Morgana's drawing and started to back away. It startled me at first that she would save the thing, then I realized she had no clue we had already found what we came for.

The fires spread quickly, joining together to separate us. There was no denying the bone-deep, visceral dread I felt at the sight of it, as memories of my own house in flames flooded my mind. I had to fight to stay focused on the present moment. "Good luck," I heard her say, and then she disappeared into the back of the house.

Muttering a prayer under my breath, I pulled the front door open. There were people right outside, all of whom turned to look at me. Heart pounding, I took hold of the guard's arms and began to drag him through the door, my back to the crowd outside. "He's hurt!" I yelled. "Someone help me!" The panic in my voice wasn't feigned, and within seconds people were at my side, helping me drag the man out of the building. Flames were now visible through the doorway, and I could hear frightened voices coming from every direction. "What's happening?" "Oh my God!" "The lab's burning!" Then the alarm sounded. It was much louder in real life than in the Weaver's dream, and it made my head ring. "The fetters!" someone yelled. "Save the fetters!" To say that nobody was paying attention to me was an understatement.

Once we were clear of the doorway, two sturdy men leaned down to pick up the guard and carry him away. I stayed with the body, pretending to help, using it to shield myself from view. The crowd parted for us, and soon we were past the frightened throng and rushing across open ground. The next few minutes were so wild—and so terrifying—that I lost any sense of where I was in the compound. But then I saw the stand of trees nearby, and I figured that was as good a place as any to make my exit. As we passed by it I broke off from my group, and headed toward the shadows of the tree. No one noticed. No one cared. The men carrying the body were focused on pulling their comrade to safety, and behind us fire was pouring out the doors and windows of the lab, and people were rushing around trying to deal with it. In the chaos that now filled the compound, I was a mere shadow.

I ducked behind the trunk of a massive forked oak and leaned back against it for a moment, trying to catch my breath. People were shouting, water was splashing, and I could hear the spurt of what must be fire extinguishers. Whatever they were doing to fight the fire must not be working very well, because the compound was filled with blazing light, and I could feel the radiant heat of it even from where I stood.

Fetters would melt. Lab notes would burn. Test tubes would shatter. The whole damn place with its history of torture would soon be nothing but ash, like my home was ash. The image was deeply and primitively satisfying.

A hand fell on my shoulder; I nearly jumped out of my skin.

"Easy," Rita whispered. "Just me."

The rush of relief I felt to have her there was undeniable. "Did you get the kids out?"

"Couldn't. Take a look." She pointed toward the center of the compound.

While most of the Weavers were now fighting the fire, a small group of people stood halfway between the lab and the cabins, just watching. I hadn't expected that. In the Weaver's dream everyone had rushed to help out, each person in the compound having a specific role to play. Like cogs in a well-oiled machine. Granted, the dream had depicted an evacuation, not an actual fire, but still, it spoke to how the place was organized —

No, I realized. It spoke to the way the woman in charge *imagined* it was organized.

*Damn.* Lesson two in how relying on dream knowledge could screw things up.

The spectators were positioned so that no one could leave the compound without being seen. Rita and I could probably have gotten out, since we were dressed like Weavers, but a horde of children in their trademark scrubs could never pull it off.

"There's nothing we can do for Moth now," Rita murmured. "I'm sorry, but that's the truth. We need to get out of here while we can."

"I'm not leaving her," I snapped.

But I had no idea how to get those people to move out of the way. What we needed was a new distraction, something that would jar them out of spectator mode and send them running elsewhere. Anywhere. I tried to think of a way to do that, but I couldn't come up with any ideas, other than an explosion. And we didn't have the materials needed to produce one of those. I inventoried our supplies in my head, hoping that something would spark an insight, but the only things we had with us were stuff we'd packed for the break-in. Nothing useful.

I thought of Moth sitting miserably against the fence during our second secret chat, whispering to me how she would rather die than stay in this place one more day, and my heart clenched in sympathy. I couldn't just abandon her. I couldn't.

Then I remembered something else I had on me. Something that hadn't been stored with our regular supplies. Slowly a plan took shape in my head, and yeah, it was a bit crazy, but it might work. And I wouldn't have to fight with armed guards or stand inside a burning building to pull it off.

"Watch the dorm," I ordered Rita. "As soon as you can break the kids out, do it, and lead them out of here. I'll catch up with you later."

"What—" she began.

But I was already gone, sprinting toward the stables.

The horses were upwind of the fire, and they had no direct view of the lab, so though they'd heard the commotion and smelled the smoke, they hadn't gone into panic mode yet. A few were whinnying nervously, but grooms were working to calm them down, and thus far everything was under control.

As I approached the building I slowed to a walk, dropping behind it so no one would see me. It seemed to me the nervous whinnying increased slightly in volume. Now I could hear the grooms talking, trying their best to instill calm in their charges. "Whoa girl, easy now . . ." "It's okay, don't worry, we won't let anything hurt you. . . ."

I moved a bit closer. The volume of the equine protests increased. There was a loud bang. Someone cursed.

Closer.

The horses started to buck and thrash in their stalls. High pitched squeals split the night. I heard objects crashing loudly to the ground, wood splitting, grooms yelling. A wave of guilt sickened me, but I stood my ground. The horses weren't being hurt, they were just scared. Their fear would fade as soon as its cause left the vicinity.

Or so I hoped.

The ruckus in the stable had become loud enough now to draw attention, and some of the Weavers came running to see what the trouble was. Unlike the fire, this catastrophe wasn't playing out in the open, which meant that anyone who wanted to know what was going on had to head this way. And the spectators came. They came. Not all of them, but enough to clear the way to the gate.

I looked over to the dormitory and saw Rita standing in front of it, keys in hand. *What the fuck?* she mouthed, when she saw that I was looking at her. I lifted the wildlife fetter out of my shirt just far enough for her to see it, then pointed toward the dormitory. As long as I was close to the horses, they would try to get away. She looked at me a moment longer, nodded her approval, then turned her attention to the key ring.

As I started to run toward her, the ground trembled. It only lasted a second, but that was enough to awaken memories of Mystic Caverns collapsing around me. I focused all my attention on Rita, trying to shut the memories out. She tried a few keys, with no success, then decided to kick in the door instead. She struck it right beside the doorknob, with enough force that the frame began to split. Then she kicked again and it gave way, bits of shattered wood flying everywhere as the door slammed open.

Lightning struck nearby with a deafening crack; it was so close that I could feel the electricity prickle my scalp. What the hell was going on? The weather had been calm when we'd entered the compound. Then the ground began to buck and heave, so violently that I lost my footing and fell to my hands and knees. Gasping, I looked at the dormitory, hoping that Rita was doing better than I was. There were children pouring out of the door now, headed toward the gate, many of them clutching food in their arms. Rita herself was staring at something in my direction, unable to move. I followed her gaze to the tops of the trees right behind me, and saw to my wonder—and horror—that they were all sprouting leaves, fresh green leaves, that grew to full size as we watched, then turned red or orange or yellow and fell to the ground, making way for new ones.

She looked at me, then at the mutating treetops, then back at me. There was fear in her eyes.

What the hell was happening?

I struggled back to my feet, and as I started to run toward her, rain began to fall from the cloudless sky. Not normal rain, but a dark, viscous liquid, that looked and smelled like blood. Suddenly I remembered the fetters we'd left behind, now in the heart of the blazing fire. Had the flames somehow triggered them, so that all the energy they contained was pouring into the compound? Lightning cracked again, and I saw a white-hot bolt strike one of the trees, splitting its trunk in two. A massive limb came crashing down right next to me, and I slipped in a puddle of the sticky red rain, almost going down again. As I grabbed at a branch to steady myself I could feel the bark crawling beneath my fingertips, and I let go of it quickly. The whole world had gone mad, and nothing within it was stable or solid any more.

Rita met me at the base of the dormitory stairs. Her face was streaked with red from the unnatural rain, and the terror in her eyes reflected what was in my heart. She grabbed me by the arm and we started to run. By now the ground was muddy—a thick, unnatural mud, that clung to our feet like glue—and the earth heaved repeatedly beneath our feet, as if we were running across the stomach of a living creature.

What had we done?

The gate was standing open when Rita and I reached it. Most of the children had passed through it ahead of us, but a few of the smaller ones were huddled together in fear just inside it. Rita grabbed up the smallest one and yelled for the others to get moving. The plan was for them to follow the road as long as they could, and abandon it only when forced to by pursuit . . . but there would be no pursuit tonight.

Suddenly I heard a horse screaming. I glanced toward the stable and saw that several animals had broken out into the pasture. As I watched, two of them fell to their knees, then collapsed full length upon the ground. I knew in my gut they were dying—they were all dying—and I had caused it. Insects began to swarm into the compound, wasps and bees pouring out of their hives, flying madly through the bloody rain, all sense of direction gone, a whirlwind of wings and buzzing and venom-tipped stings that swept through the compound like a twister.

"Jesse!" Rita grabbed me by the arm. "We have to go!"

Shuddering, I started to turn away from the horror that the compound had become, but out of the corner of my eye I saw something that chilled me to my core, and I turned to look at it. Against a sky seared white by lightning, a single spot of darkness had appeared, a terrible black void that sucked in all light, and it was slowly expanding, taking on the shape of a man—

*No! No! Please, God, not that!*

There was no mistaking it now: this was the creature from my dreams, the void-wraith, devourer of dreams, whose wound I still bore on my arm. Somehow, the terrible forces we'd unleashed had enabled it to cross into the real world, and now it hovered over the compound, feeding on the chaos. Its presence was an icy wind that sucked all the heat from the world, and I could see a film of frost spreading across the treetops beneath it, the leaves curling and dying as a glistening white shroud enveloped them.

Then the wraith looked at me. I wasn't sure how I knew that, when it had no eyes, but I could feel its scrutiny in every fiber of my being. "Run!" I screamed. But a crack of thunder split the night, drowning out my warning. I could see children strung out along the length of the road, the frontmost ones lost in shadow as they fled for safety. But not fast enough. If I ran in that direction too, following them, the dream-wraith would come after me, and then they would be vulnerable. I thought of the trees behind me, now sheathed in ice, and shuddered. Even if the thing didn't attack the children outright, its mere proximity to them might cause damage. I needed to flee in a different direction, and that meant only one thing: into the woods. I wouldn't be able to run as fast there, but at least I would be running alone, and if the wraith followed me, the children would be safe from it.

So I turned to the north and ran by the side of the fence until I passed the end of the compound, then I dove into the forest and kept running. I had left the fire behind, and the moonlight coming through the trees was minimal, so I ran in near darkness. I tripped and stumbled over various obstacles, struggling to keep on my feet. Lightning struck and for a moment everything was starkly visible, trees looming overhead like hostile aliens—and then that light was gone, too, and in its wake I was left blinded, and had to stumble through the darkness based on the memory of what I had just seen, until my vision cleared.

The wraith was getting closer, its presence a chill wind, each gust colder than the last. I dared to look up when the tree cover thinned, and I saw it looming overhead, its unnatural darkness devouring the stars. Despair gripped me. Where was I running to? What kind of refuge could protect me? This wasn't just a dream, like the last time; I couldn't just wake myself up to make it end. No little brother would hear my screams, shake me by the shoulders, and banish this thing. Sooner or later it *was* going to catch up with me, and not all the running in the world could save me.

Suddenly the trees were gone, and I was sprinting across open ground. I dared another glance overhead; the wraith was so large it looked like it had devoured half the sky, and it was bearing down on me. I turned back just in time to see the ground fall away before me, and I skidded to a stop, desperately trying to save myself. But the earth was too soft, and I couldn't get traction. Dirt crumbled away beneath me and I fell, landing with half my body on solid earth and half of it dangling over a chasm. It was probably the same crevice we'd followed on the way here, but in the darkness it looked ten times as deep. Desperately I grabbed onto an exposed tree root and tried to pull myself back to safety before the wraith fell upon me. Somehow I managed to get back onto solid ground, and as I did so I felt something sharp stab me in the butt. The fetter in my pocket.

The *dream* fetter in my pocket.

The whole world was losing heat now, and frost began to coat the treetops surrounding me. I couldn't see the wraith any more, only a terrible blackness in place of the sky. Why was it coming after me? It had only done that before when I used my dream Gift. It never showed up in my regular dreams. So why was it hunting me now, when I was awake?

I dug the dream fetter out of my pocket. It looked like a piece of inert metal, but I knew the power that was in it. I had seen the wild energies of the other fetters crackling through the air of the compound, warping the very forces of nature. Maybe the wraith was responding to the energy in this one. Maybe it could sense the Dreamwalker's essence in it, the same way Morgana's Seers had.

Twisting around, I tried not to think about all that this fetter could have taught me, all the mysteries it could have revealed, all the powers it might have unlocked. None of that would do me any good if I was dead. With a cry of anguish I threw the thing as far I possibly could, and I watched it arc high over the chasm and then begin to fall. Lightning flashed, turning the smooth piece of metal into blazing fire, just for an instant. Then a dark and terrible presence rushed down into the chasm, passing so close to me that it left a film of frost on my hair. Ice formed along the edges of the crevice as it swept down its length, until it reached the falling fetter and enveloped it. Then the darkness began to draw into itself, blackness folding in upon blackness like some hellish origami. And an instant later it was gone. Half-blinded by the lightning, I couldn't identify the exact moment it vanished from the waking world, but I could feel the frigid weight of its presence lifting from the universe, and overhead the stars returned.

And then there was silence. I waited, breath held, to see what would come next.

Melting icicles tinkled softly overhead. A patch of frost broke from the chasm's rim, crumbling as it fell to the bottom, landing gently.

Nothing else.

Numbly I lowered my head to my arms, and I wept. I wept for the dead horses and the terrified children and even for the Weavers who had just lost all their work, because that was my doing. But most of all I wept for myself, for the loss of that precious hope I had enjoyed so briefly, when the key to knowledge was in my hand, and the future had appeared to be within my control. Now gone.

I was not consciously aware of the moment when this world gave way to the next, nightmares of the solid world morphing into nightmares of an imaginary one. But Rita found me shortly after dawn and woke me up, so sometime during the night that moment must have come.

Sometimes it is merciful not to know.

# 17

## SHADOWCREST
## VIRGINIA PRIME

### ISAAC

**I**SAAC WAS ASLEEP when the spirit returned. He sensed it in his dream first: a presence in the shadows that was not quite visible, an unnatural breeze that chilled his skin whenever he looked in a particular direction. By the time he was fully awake, he knew that the event he'd been preparing for was finally at hand.

He squinted as he peered into the corner of the room where the spirit seemed to be. Struggling to see it. His teachers said his Gift was too weak to allow true death vision, but as he was beginning to discover, not everything his teachers taught him was correct. Whether they were deliberately hedging the truth to make him behave in a certain way, or just doing the best they could with the limited information they had, he didn't know, but the end result of both paths was the same: the only sure way for him to discover what his limits were to test them.

He'd spent the last few days researching the techniques that the *umbrae majae* used to bolster their Gift, and now, as he peered into the darkness, he whispered the spirit's name over and over again, envisioning a ritual design he'd discovered in one of his father's books, something called a *death codex*. Concentrating on it was supposed to help open a window into the world of the dead. *Jacob Dockhart,* he chanted mentally. *Jacob Dockhart. Jacob Dockhart.* He tried to visualize the boy's face, superimposing it over the shifting shadow that was in front of him, but it proved surprisingly difficult. The last time Isaac had seen Jacob, the boy's face had been contorted into a mask of pure horror; it was not the kind of image the mind naturally wanted to recall.

But slowly the darkness in the room seemed to coalesce, until there was a single human-sized shadow. While it lacked any color or detail, and there was only emptiness where its face should have been, it was vaguely human in shape, and Isaac felt a rush of pride at having managed that much. Most apprentices could not conjure a vision of the dead at all.

"Jacob Dockhart." He spoke the spirit's name firmly, because it was important for the dead to know who was in charge. "Why are you here?"

He sensed that the spirit was responding to him, but the ritual that had allowed him to see it did not help him make any sense of its speech. Shutting his eyes for a moment, he envisioned another codex he'd found, which supposedly would open his mind to the voices of the dead. It was a dangerous pattern to invoke, especially for a mere apprentice. If some malevolent spirit decided to take advantage of the fact that he was now opening his mind to the influence of the dead, there was little he could do to stop it. Only a Shadowlord had the power to cast out a possessing spirit.

But no spirit tried to take control of him, and after a few moments of concentration he found that he could make out fragments of the spirit's speech. It wasn't that he heard actual words, so much as he sensed their meaning. The tide of ghostly sounds chilled his skin, it stirred his blood, it made his eyes burn and left a strange taste in his mouth. And in the wake of that came understanding. There was no real sound.

*Help me*, the spirit seemed to be saying. Isaac's skin prickled as he absorbed the words, not just through his ears but through every cell in his body. Even for a boy who was accustomed to the presence of the dead, the sensation was eerie.

*Help me.*

"I can't," he said quietly. His voice was pitched low so that no one outside the room would hear him. "You've been bound to a Shadowlord. There's no way I can undo that, I'm sorry."

Again he sensed, rather than heard, the ghost's question. *Forever?*

Isaac hesitated. He knew that such slaves often became free when their masters died, but he also knew that Shadowlords who accepted Communion could claim the bound spirits of their predecessors. He didn't know enough about the process to give the boy's ghost any kind of definitive answer. "Why are you here?" he demanded.

For a moment there was silence. The air around him began to take on weight and substance; he felt as if the darkness were pressing in on him. Fear fluttered in his stomach, and for a moment he was tempted to try to banish his visitor—though God alone knew if he was capable of that. But instead he drew in a deep breath and waited.

After a few seconds the sensation eased a bit. *Unfin-*

*ished,* came the ghostly flesh-whisper. A bit clearer this time. *Help me.*

"Do you mean, you left something unfinished? From your mortal life? Is that it?"

The spirit's affirmation was a wordless sensation that raised the hairs on the back of his neck. But what sense did that make? The dead couldn't remember their former lives in any meaningful way. Details from that time were just disjointed shards, devoid of the neural connections that were needed to stir living passion. A physical brain was required to make any kind of emotional connection. Wasn't that what they taught in his *Introduction to Necromancy* class? Wasn't the whole point of the Shadows' wretched training program to teach their children how to live without passion, so they could be closer to the dead in their mindset?

*Mae.* The name was a whisper of ice, of fire. Terrible frostbite yearning.

"You left her behind?" Isaac asked. "Is that it?" He hesitated. "You can't be with her again. I'm sorry, it doesn't work that way."

As the next words were spoken the sensation of pressure returned, twice as suffocating as before. *Three steps from our mark.* A vision of a rising sun flashed in Isaac's mind. Or perhaps a setting sun? The image came and went so quickly he couldn't be sure. *Please,* the ghost begged. *Tell her.*

Then the pressure eased. The spirit fell silent.

Isaac didn't know what to say. This situation was so bizarre that he didn't know how to respond to it. The spirit in his room wasn't just an ordinary ghost, it was a bound spirit, theoretically incapable of independent thought or action. It shouldn't be in his room at all, much less be reminiscing about lost loves and asking him for favors. That was so out of line with everything he'd been taught about spirits that if he told his teachers about Jacob's visitation they would tell him he was imagining things.

But what if his intense concentration on the boy during ritual had screwed things up? Maybe this spirit was not only bound to the Shadowlady in red, but had some kind of connection to Isaac as well. If so, his father would be pretty damn angry when he heard about it.

But his father didn't know about this yet. And neither did anyone else.

Best to keep it that way.

"Where would I find her?" he asked.

The spirit's gratitude rushed over him like hot burning ashes; for a moment he found it hard to breathe. *Where I died*, the ghost said. *Soul death. Not flesh death.*

The death of the boy's flesh had taken place at the ritual, but what did *soul death* mean? Maybe he was referring to the moment when they'd fed him drugs to render him helpless, and he'd lost his last hope of freedom. No, it couldn't be that, because no outsider would have been present. Maybe this Mae was someone he'd known at the orphanage—someone he'd loved—and when he was sold to the Shadows, and separated from her forever, that was a kind of death. The moment at which his former life ended, and he lost control of his fate.

Clearly the trail began at the orphanage. But did Isaac want to follow it? The fact that this spirit retained enough living memory to yearn for closure was all very well and good, but a Shadow was under no obligation to indulge the dead in their last whims. In time—probably very little time—Jacob's final memory of Mae would fade on its own.

But.

Whatever ritual bond had been established between Isaac and the ghost, it seemed to make his Gift stronger.

And that had value to him. So did having a spirit indebted to him. As an *umbra mina* Isaac couldn't bind a
spirit to him with one of the normal rituals, but that
didn't mean he couldn't control one by other means. If
the ghost of Jacob Dockhart was coherent enough to
beg for closure, it was coherent enough to owe Isaac a
favor. A damned big one.

"Do you think she's still there?" he asked.

But the boy's ghost was no longer in the room.
Maybe its mistress had summoned it, to do whatever
slave spirits did when they weren't visiting other Shadows. Maybe it had just communicated all that it could
and felt no more need to manifest.

*Jacob's ghost doesn't belong to me,* he reminded himself. *There are rules about this kind of thing. My father
would never approve.*

For the first time in his life, he wondered how much
that really mattered.

iiiiiiiiiiiiii

The orphanage was a few miles outside of Luray, two
train stops south of the place where Jesse and her
friends had dropped Isaac off on their way into town.
That day he'd had trouble finding a ride, and had wound
up tucked between baskets of smelly produce on a cart
heading to Luray's central market. Now he was wearing
the robes of an apprentice Shadow, and that changed
everything. People fought for the honor of transporting
him, taxi-drivers jostling each other as they tried to get
his attention. Whether that was out of respect for his
Guild or fear of a Shadow's displeasure, or simply because they assumed that a member of such a rich and
prestigious Guild would tip them well, was anyone's
guess.

No one questioned his presence at the orphanage.
The minimum-wage security guard standing duty at the

gate looked pointedly at the sigil of the Shadows embroidered on his robe and waved him through, then went back to reading his dog-eared novel. Isaac caught sight of the title as he passed: *Seven Guildmasters in Hell.*

He probably could have gone to the main office and asked for help finding Mae, but that would increase the odds of this visit being reported to the Shadows, who would ask why the girl mattered to him. He wouldn't take such a step unless he had to.

He skirted the office complex and headed to where two large, featureless dorms were located. Most of the orphans worked during the day, in factories and workshops elsewhere on the property, so if he found someone to talk to there shouldn't be dozens of other people listening in. After walking around a bit he spotted a couple of skinny boys mowing the grass, and he approached them.

"Your Lordship!" The nearer of the two boys made an awkward gesture that was probably intended as a bow, but he stumbled doing it, and there was no mistaking the edge of fear in his voice. "How can we help you?"

His use of the wrong title wasn't worth the trouble of correcting. "I'm looking for a girl named Mae," he said. "Do you know her?"

The boy looked back at his companion. Whatever silent communication passed between them, it was clear they were both suspicious of the request.

"I just want to talk to her," Isaac said. He shouldn't have to give them any kind of explanation, but their fear was rational, and he respected it.

The younger boy hesitated, then pointed east. In the distance, Isaac saw a low building with smokestacks. "She's working at the mill."

He nodded curtly, thanked them for the informa-

tion—which seemed to surprise them both—and
headed that way. It was a bit of a hike, but long before
he got to the building he could smell it. Even diluted by
the open air, Its faint chemical odor was enough to
make his eyes sting. As he got closer, he could hear the
rumbling of machinery inside the building, probably
steam driven.

There was no security, only a heavy door with a lock
as big as his fist. He raised a hand to knock, then recon-
sidered and let himself in. There was no antechamber,
just a vast workroom with a row of steam-driven looms
running down each side. Some of the girls and boys running the machines were so young they had to stretch to
reach the controls, while the smallest children of all
darted underneath the machines, dodging shifting
combs and flying shuttles to retrieve fallen objects and
pull gobs of lint out of the machinery. It looked hellishly
dangerous.

The overseer spotted Isaac immediately and climbed
down from his elevated platform at the far end of the
workspace to talk to him. Though his manner was polite,
it was hardly welcoming; Isaac guessed he was suspicious about why a young Shadow would show up in his
mill. Or maybe the man was just territorial by nature,
and the arrival of any stranger in his workspace made
his fur bristle. "Your visit honors us, Sir. May I ask what
interest the illustrious Shadows have in our facility?"

"I've come to talk to one of the orphans here. Her
name is Mae."

The overseer's eyes narrowed suspiciously. "On what
business, may I ask?"

"Guild business," Isaac said shortly. He could tell that
the overseer wasn't satisfied by that answer, and for a moment the man just stared at Isaac, waiting for him to offer
more information. After a moment of silence the man
glared resentfully and gestured toward the machines.

"This way." He led Isaac to where a young girl was working, and she was so fixated on her work that when the overseer prodded her she jumped.

"This Shadow wants to talk to you." He nodded toward Isaac. "Ten minutes."

The girl was younger than he was, maybe fourteen, maybe less. The fear in her eyes was unmistakable.

"He just wants to talk," the overseer assured her. He looked at Isaac; his expression was a warning. "That right?"

"That's right."

Isaac turned toward the exit and gestured for her to follow. Another child scurried over to take her place, so that her loom never skipped a beat. Both children were like cogs in a vast machine, perfectly synchronized. Had Jacob worked here too? If so, then he had not been free even when he was alive.

Isaac led the girl out of the mill and a short distance away from the building, until the noise of the machinery was no longer distracting. Then he turned to her. "I bear a message from Jacob Dockhart."

The brown eyes widened in surprise. "Oh my God! Is he okay?" A tentative smile lit her face. "Where is he?"

He'd braced himself for a display of sorrow, but the spark of joy in her eyes was unexpected and surprisingly painful. "I'm a Shadow," he said gently. "Remember what our Gift is."

The smile vanished. The moment of joy faded from her eyes, and fear took its place. "You . . . you speak to the dead," she whispered.

He nodded. What pain there was in her expression now, what raw emotion! No one in Isaac's Guild would ever display their feelings like this, no matter how much they hurt inside. He stared at her in fascination, as if she were some kind of exotic animal.

"So he . . . he's gone?" Her small hands twisted in her skirt, her voice was trembling. "Dead?"

He nodded. "I am sorry."

"Why?" she begged. She started to reach out to him but pulled her hand back quickly. "*Why?*" she pleaded, as tears began to run down her face.

There was no good answer to that, so he didn't try to offer one. Better honest silence than a poorly constructed lie. "I came to bring you a message from his spirit. Do you want to hear it?"

Eyes wide, she nodded. "Yes," she whispered. "Please."

"He said to tell you, *three steps from your mark.*" When she looked confused he pressed, "Does that make sense to you? I believe he was referring to something that belonged to both of you."

Her eyes grew wide. "Oh," she breathed. "Maybe. . . ." The words trailed off into silence.

"You know what he was referring to?" he pressed.

Biting her lip nervously, she nodded. Then, with one last glance at the mill, she started walking. Away from the factory, toward an area dense with trees and underbrush. She gestured for him to follow her. As the trees closed in around him, his long robe caught on a thorned branch, and he had to yank it free. Soon it was no longer possible to see the mill through the trees, or any other part of the orphanage grounds. Then the girl stopped, and she reached out to touch the forked trunk of an aged oak, her fingers gently caressing its bark. At the juncture of its two main limbs a design had been carved. At first glance it looked like some kind of abstract symbol, but then Isaac realized it was in fact two initials intertwined: *M* and *J*.

Unfamiliar emotions stirred deep within him. Sympathy? Compassion? The feelings were exotic, intense, uncomfortable.

"Three paces from this," he said. The meaning of the rest of his vision was now falling into place. "Either due east or due west, directly from this point."

Three paces to the west there was a mass of underbrush with poison ivy woven into it, so thick that it was clear no one had tried to walk through it recently. Three paces to the east was another tree. Its gnarled roots sketched out a V on the ground, its mouth pointed directly at the spot where they were standing. He pointed to it. "Maybe there?"

She went to the tree, hesitated, then knelt in the soil and began to dig at the vertex of the V. The dirt was loose, Isaac noted, as it if had recently been disturbed. Beneath the top layer of soil was a layer of old leaves, easy to move aside. As she brushed them away, a small hole containing a worn wooden box was revealed. She glanced back at Isaac, then pulled out the box and rested it in front of her. From the look on her face it was clear she had no clue what it was.

She opened it and gasped.

Inside the box was money. Not a lot of it by Isaac's measure, but no doubt a fortune to one in her circumstances. There were small coins, large coins, and a thin wad of bills wrapped in string. There were a few pieces of jewelry as well, one of which Isaac thought he recognized from the Warrens stash. A pocket watch, a pendant, a silver brooch . . . the kinds of items one could pinch from a person in passing. Isaac had lived on the streets long enough to know how that worked.

"We were going to run away," she whispered. "He told me . . . Last time I saw him . . . he was almost ready. He said that he had everything we needed, and I could go with him. He said he would take care of both of us. Then the Shadows came, and took him away from me. . . ."

With a sob she lowered her head to her chest. The

sight of her struggling not to cry broke through all the
barriers that he had erected to guard himself from human emotion, and made his soul bleed.

*We caused this human misery,* he thought. *My Guild.
For no better purpose than our convenience.*

"You have the power to leave now." Isaac spoke quietly. "I'm guessing that's why it mattered so much for
him to make sure you got this. But you shouldn't do so
now. The masters of this place know that I came here,
and if you disappear right away they'll make the obvious connection. It will help them track you down. You
understand?"

"I understand," she whispered hoarsely. The tear-
streaked face looked up at him. "He's still around? You
can talk to him?"

Isaac shook his head. "An echo of his soul remains,
nothing more. Think of it as a recording of his last
thoughts, that I managed to hear. Now that their purpose has been satisfied, they, too, will fade. There's no
one for you to talk to." At least part of that was the
truth.

She lowered her head again and began to weep, this
time without trying to stifle the sound. Isaac watched
her for a moment, then turned and left. This was not the
sort of scene a Shadow had any business being part of.

Love. Fear. Loss. Mourning. There were so many
emotional energies swirling about him that it was overwhelming. Isaac wondered what it would be like to live
with such emotions every day, like people outside his
Guild did. To be at the mercy of those terrible tides each
time one suffered a loss. No wonder the boy's identity
had survived death, with so much emotion behind it.
Maybe when his spirit learned that its final wish had
been granted those emotions would fade, until all that
would be left was a mindless and purposeless ghost,
identical to every other slave spirit.

Or maybe this one would prove to be more than that, and with its help, Isaac could learn more about his own potential.

He looked back at the crying girl one last time, a strange pang of jealousy in his heart, then started down the path toward home.

# 18

## BLACKWATER MOUNTAINS
## VIRGINIA PRIME

## JESSE

**D**URING OUR RIDE BACK TO LURAY, I leaned my head against the train window and watched the scenery go by without really seeing it. The vibration of the glass against my forehead might have been soothing, had I been capable of being soothed. I wasn't.

"No one died," Seyer reminded me. "That's a good thing."

"No *people* died," I corrected her.

I was bone-weary, soul-weary, almost too tired to remember my name. I did remember part of a dream I'd had the night before, and it played out again in my mind's eye as I stared out the window. When had I dreamed it? Right after I collapsed, as I lay half-dead at the edge of the chasm? Just before dawn, when Rita found me? All I knew was that I'd escaped the horrors of the night in the only way I knew how, and in my dreams, sought out one of the few people I still trusted.

**The field of battle is still. The fallen bodies are gone now, but their imprints remain in the grass, along with their blood. The tang of black powder hangs in the air, mercifully masking whatever human smells might cling to this place. It's lonely here. No, more than that: it is the archetypal embodiment of loneliness.**

**I see a figure standing atop a hill, a soldier with bands of leather crisscrossing his chest. The fingertips on his right hand are black from gunpowder, his boots are coated in mud up to the calves, and his youthful face is splattered with blood. Not his. He looks young, so young. I never picture him that way.**

**I start toward him, but my body is so drained from my recent experiences I can barely walk. I stumble in the wet grass and go down on one knee.**

"When you talk to Her Grace—" Seyer began.

"I'm not talking to Her Grace." I raised up my head with monumental effort and looked at her. "What's the point? We never found the mandala. We never found anything that even hinted at Dreamwalker activity. All we found were rumors about some boy who slept all the time, and maybe he had something to do with the mandala, or maybe not, but he's dead now, so no one will ever know for sure. I'll tell her all that and then she'll say, I'm sorry, that's not good enough to earn a Potter's service, and I'll say, but what about my mother? And she'll say, it's all very sad, but it's not my problem." I leaned my head back against the glass and stared out at the landscape. "Might as well save myself the trouble."

Did I sound bitter enough for that speech to be convincing? The part about my mom was true enough, though the part about failing in my quest was pure fiction. But I needed Morgana to think I was avoiding her out of despair, not because I feared her ability to sense deception. It was easier to stare out a train window and lie to Seyer—and Rita—than it would be stare into Morgana's eyes and try the same thing. I needed to play my part well enough for Seyer to report to her mistress that the failure of our mission had left me so overcome by despair that there was no point in her meeting with me, so that she wouldn't question why I avoided her.

"Just give us the tickets home," I muttered miserably. "We'll find our own way."

**Private Sebastian Hayes is handsome in his youth, his hair still brown, his face still unlined. But his eyes ... they are ancient, and they will always be ancient, no matter what form his dream body takes. Clearly he's startled to find me here, in this setting from his past. I see him blink as he struggles to make sense of it. "Jessica?"**

**I try to get back on my feet, but my legs are unsteady—and then he is right there, raising me up, lending me strength, my one certain anchor in a world where everyone and everything else has failed me. "What is it?" he says. "What happened?"**

**So I tell him the story. All of it. The dreams, the discovery about Rita, the nightmare in the compound, all of it. My delivery is halting and at times not wholly coherent, but he seems to get the gist of it.**

**When I'm done he's very quiet. I can sense that he's struggling to digest it all, so I wait. Finally he looks out at the blood-soaked battlefield and says, "So this ... this is something my own mind created for me?" He looks back at me. "But you being here, in the midst of it, my dream ... is that real? Can you enter other people's dreams?"**

**I nod. It's unnerving to share that secret with anyone**

other than Tommy, but it's also liberating. A weight that has been suffocating me since the night of the toaster strudel eases ever so slightly. "I trust you," I tell him. "I know you would never hurt me."

A shadow passes over his face. "You shouldn't trust anyone on Terra Prime," he says quietly. "Even me."

I put a hand on his arm. "The children need help, Sebastian. They have some food and a general idea of where to go—and Moth has enough courage for a hundred children—but I'm worried for them. Please, can you help them? Bring them some supplies and point them in the right direction? It isn't that far from your own territory. I . . . I have the means to pay for it."

Those ancient eyes fix on me. So much pain in them. So much weariness. "There's no need to pay me," he says quietly. "I can't go myself, right now, but I know someone who might be able to do so. I'll talk to him."

"Thank you," I whisper. Another crushing weight lifts from my soul. "Thank you so much. . . ."

"What will you do about your mother now? Morgana's not likely to help you if you won't do her bidding. And if I were you I would have second thoughts about meeting with her again. It's rumored she can sense when people are lying, and you're keeping a lot of secrets these days."

I draw in a deep breath and look straight into his eyes. "I was hoping you could help me with the Flesh-crafters."

"Me?" He raises an eyebrow. "The Potters owe me no favors. Nothing that I can use on your behalf, anyway."

"No, but you have access to information. You can help me identify something they want, that I can get for them. Or do for them. Or . . . something." He doesn't answer me right away so I press, "Is that too crazy an idea?"

There is a long silence. "It's not crazy," he says at last. His expression is dark. "I do know something they want, and given what you've just told me about your Gift, it might be possible for you to obtain it. Maybe." He sighs. "You go back to Luray. I'll make what arrangements I can for the children and look into the Fleshcrafter issue. Try to get some rest tonight; you'll need your energy tomorrow. I'll meet you at noon, at the pier where we left Isaac. Hopefully I'll have information for you then."

I hesitate. "Sebastian . . . the creature that chased me . . . do you have any idea what it was?"

He shakes his head. "I've heard legends about a wraith that devours dreams, but little more than that. Even if such a creature did exist, none of the legends suggest it would be able to manifest in the real world. The Shadows are the ones who study the dead, so they might know more."

"Yeah. Like they're about to share their knowledge with me." I sighed heavily. "So . . . what? If it shows up again, I just run away?"

A faint smile flickers. "I would."

He leans over and kisses me on the forehead. There is warmth in the gesture but also tremendous sorrow, and I feel a lump rise in my throat. "Be careful, Jessica."

"I can't go home like this," I muttered into the window. My breath frosted the glass. "Going through the Gate brings back such terrible memories . . . I need some time to pull myself together before I have to go through that again." Maybe it was a weak excuse for delaying our return, but I could hardly tell them why I really wanted to stay in Terra Prime. Hopefully Rita would remember the agitated state I'd been in after our first crossing, and buy the excuse.

She looked at Seyer, "Maybe we could spend a night at the Guildhouse—"

"No," I said quickly. "That's not right. We failed in our mission, so we shouldn't be asking Morgana for favors. And I ..." I pretended to hesitate. "I really need some time alone, Rita. Just a few hours. I haven't had a minute to myself since we got here. I'm so sorry, it's got nothing to do with you. I just need to pull myself together."

"I understand," she said gently. "I've been feeling a little edgy myself. But where would you go?"

"We've got some cash, right? I guess I could just pay for a hotel room. Like a normal person."

Rita glanced at Seyer—for permission, no doubt— then dug into her backpack. Taking out the wad of petty cash Morgana had given us, she divided it in two and gave me half. The bills were crisp, multi-colored, and had the face of some unknown queen engraved on them. I flipped one over to look on the back and see if the little pyramid was there. It was, but without the eye in it. There were other symbols as well, that I didn't recognize.

Tucking the money into my jeans pocket, I rested my head on the glass again and let the vibrations of the train carry me away.

**"The horrors unleashed by your fetters may not be unique," Sebastian says. "I've heard tales of similar things happening out west, in a benighted region called the Badlands. People who try to enter the area generally don't come out, or if they do, they come out mad. Even zeppelins that fly over it are affected, and the last one to make the attempt drifted back into civilized space with nothing but corpses and madmen on board." He pauses. "In the days when travelers still tested themselves against the Badlands' borders, survivors spoke of unnatural rain, trembling earth, sickness that came out of nowhere ... and creatures out of nightmare coming to life."**

"You think they meant that literally? The last one?"

"Who knows? All I can tell you is that Gifts don't appear out of nowhere. They require a human source. And while no one ever associated the wild forces of the Badlands with human Gifts, the similarity to what you witnessed at the compound is unmistakable. And that had a human source."

"You think there are people living out there? That no one knows about?"

"It's one possibility."

"Maybe ... maybe Dreamwalkers? Because that's the only Gift that would manifest nightmares, right?"

The ancient eyes fix on me. So intense, that gaze. So enigmatic.

"Maybe Dreamwalkers," he agrees.

# 19

SHADOWCREST
VIRGINIA PRIME

ALASTAIR WELLS

**M**ASTER ALASTAIR WELLS took a deep breath before
entering Lord Virilian's audience chamber. The
fact that the Greys had sent someone of his rank to deliver their report, rather than the usual journeyman, was
a sad comment on how they expected that report to be
received. Virilian might lash out at a mere apprentice in
anger, they'd reasoned, but surely he would exhibit
more control with a Master of Obfuscates.

Surely.

Nodding to the guard, Wells reminded himself that
not *all* the news he brought was bad. Just the part that
would impact Virilian's personal fortune.

The doors opened, and he stepped forward with what
he hoped looked like confidence. Virilian, like a wolf,
could smell fear. The Shadowlord was seated on his
usual throne, with the usual clamor of dead souls sur-

rounding him. Wells had dealt with Shadowlords often enough to regard the latter as background music, albeit of an irritating variety. "Your Grace." He bowed his head respectfully.

The Guildmaster nodded. "Master Wells. You honor this Guild by your presence. I understand you have news for me?"

"Yes, your Lordship. Both good and bad, I'm afraid."

Virilian's eyes narrowed. "In whatever order you like, then."

"We reached the portal, and have evaluated it. I'm pleased to report it's still functional. A bit unstable, but once we restore the Gate we should be able to rectify that."

"That's excellent news. How long before it can return to full service?"

Wells hesitated.

"There's a problem?"

"Not here, your Grace. We cleared out the entrance, and once we put a new Gate in place our people should be able to come and go freely. At this end, at least."

Virilian raised an eyebrow. "But?"

"Our Gate wasn't the only one damaged. Reverberations from the explosion triggered earthquakes throughout our network, destroying the infrastructure on several worlds. Those Gates are still inaccessible."

For a moment there was silence. A spirit moaned softly behind Wells's left ear.

"So what you are saying is, our people can enter the portal safely from this side, and use it to gain access to other worlds, but the points of arrival on those worlds have been blocked, so it is, for all intents and purposes, useless."

"Only on certain worlds," Wells said quickly. "We're cataloging the extent of the damage. Gates outside the Terran Cluster are unaffected, and many of those within the cluster can be restored quickly. Long term, we estimate we can restore eighty to ninety percent of the original network."

"Long term," he mused darkly.

"Yes."

"That does little for us right now."

Wells bridled slightly. "We're working as fast as we can, your Grace. There are still other Gates available. No world has been cut off from contact with ours."

"But commerce must divert to other cities. And merchants may establish such connections there that, even when Luray is restored to full functioning, some will not return."

Wells said nothing. Virilian's personal power was rooted in his control of a major interworld trade hub. Devalue that hub, and his power was diminished. No words from a Grey would change that reality, or make the current situation more palatable.

"I want this addressed as quickly as possible," the Guildmaster said. "Hire whomever you need, Gifted or otherwise. My Guild will cover the cost of it for now . . . though your Guildmaster and I will need to have a conversation about that responsibility."

It took all Wells's self-control not to respond sharply. *Don't think you're going to saddle us with the cost of this mess*, he thought. *If you hadn't kidnapped that Colonnan boy, thinking he was a Dreamwalker, none of this would have happened.* "I'm sure our Master will be pleased to receive you." He reached into his frock coat and took out a thick envelope, which he offered to Virilian.

"What is this?"

"A full report on the explosion."

Virilian took the envelope from him. "Have you identified the nature of the Codex?"

He hesitated. "Not yet, Your Grace. We're still working on it."

"Very well. I'll take your report under advisement. Meanwhile, you will keep me informed of your progress on the Gate."

"Of course." He bowed his head respectfully. "And I will communicate to my Guild how important it is that we restore it to full function as quickly as possible."

*Like we didn't already know that,* he thought acidly. *Like we haven't been overseeing the Gates for centuries, and need you to tell us how to manage them.* But he kept a polite expression on his face, and just in case that wasn't convincing enough, activated his Gift to mask his irritation. Never let a Shadow know how you are really feeling. That was the first rule of Guild etiquette.

If this Shadow wasn't so damn obsessed with hunting Dreamwalkers, the Blue Ridge Gate would still be standing.

He wound up leaving with his head still on his shoulders and his mind intact. Which, given the circumstances, was all anyone could ask for.

# 20

LURAY
VIRGINIA PRIME

JESSE

L URAY'S LONG RIVER BANKS were host to a wide variety of docks—public, private, and commercial—
and getting a cab to take me to the one I wanted without
my being able to provide its name, or to offer better direction than "it's at the south end of town," wasted a
good chunk of my petty cash allotment. By the time we
found the right one the sun was setting, and I was hard-
pressed to find suitable lodging before it got dark.

The place where I'd booked a room was laid out like
a motel, though of course in a world without cars it
probably wasn't called that. Two U-shaped floors had
small rooms that opened directly onto a central courtyard, allowing guests to come and go without having to
pass through a lobby or office. That suited my desire for
privacy. It also suited other people who wanted to come
and go unseen, who, in this particular neighborhood,

were an unsavory lot. I was careful to lock my door once I was inside.

Despite hours of lying on top of the bedspread with my eyes closed, I'd gotten little rest the night before. Maybe sleep deprivation was what drove the ancient Dreamwalkers mad.

It felt strange to spend a night on this world like a normal person. Not hiding in the woods, not cringing in the sewers, and not lying awake at the Seers' headquarters wondering who was spying on my brain emanations. Just me, a rented bed, and enough tired whores and petty drug dealers to give the place atmosphere.

At noon I headed back to the pier, where Sebastian was waiting for me. He wasn't dressed in his usual attire, but in an outfit so mundane that at first I didn't recognize him. Yes, there was a slight period flavor to the collar of his white cotton shirt, and the leather bag slung over his shoulder did have a military air to it, but no stranger seeing him would think to look twice.

I couldn't see his expression as I approached, due to his broad-brimmed hat, but I did see him tense when he spotted me. It took me a moment to realize why he was reacting that way. I'd been living with the concept of visiting other peoples' dreams for long enough that I'd gotten used to the idea. He, on the other hand, had not known up until this moment whether the Jessica who visited him in his dream was real or not. This was his toaster strudel moment.

"It's really you," he breathed, as I approached. Wonder resonated in his voice. "God in Heaven, it's really you...."

Despite my generally somber mood, I couldn't help but smile. "It does take a little getting used to."

He opened his mouth to respond, but just then a couple of people walking along the shore started up the pier. Given the sensitivity of what we needed to discuss, they were getting too close for comfort. "Perhaps we should seek some privacy," he said. He nodded toward where his canoe was moored, a question in his eyes.

I looked across the river, noted that the people on the opposite shore weren't all that far away, and said, "Walls are better. I have a room nearby we can use."

There were only a couple of people hanging around the motel when we arrived, both of them women with smeared makeup and tousled hair, who looked more than a little hung over. They watched with blatant curiosity as I led Sebastian into my room. Probably they were wondering what I would charge a man three times my age for my services. It was not a good neighborhood.

I offered Sebastian the one chair in the room, but he chose to remain standing. I watched as he took stock of the small space, and I was reminded of Rita in IHOP, checking for exits. It was a more wary aspect than I'd seen in him before, and I wondered what had put him on edge.

"You said you had something for me," I prompted.

"So I did." A shadow crossed his face. "You asked me if I knew of a task that you might undertake for the Fleshcrafters. I do, but it would be a dangerous one, with no guarantee of success. Are you sure this is something you want to pursue? It won't be easy."

I shrugged. "Nothing on this world is ever easy." Maybe that sounded impossibly brave, but I had just spent a long and sleepless night resigning myself to the fact that anything the Potters wanted that was safe and easy to obtain, they'd have gotten for themselves long ago. Anything I offered them would have to involve a task so dark, dangerous, or difficult, that they hadn't done it themselves. "Tell me."

With a sigh he sat in the room's one chair; it creaked beneath him. "There's one piece of information that the Fleshcrafters want, and they want it badly. Their Guildmaster approached me about it some time ago, but I wasn't able to help him. Please note, it's rare that a secret is so perfectly guarded that my contacts can't unearth it, but in this case it was true. The commission he offered me is still open. If you were to deliver that information to Guildmaster Alexander, payment of some sort would be guaranteed. I'm sure you could negotiate for what you want."

I looked at him incredulously. "You think I can succeed at something where *you* failed?"

He said it quietly: "You have abilities that I don't, Jessica."

It took me a moment to realize what he meant. "My Gift. . . ."

He nodded.

"Jeez." I didn't know how to respond to that. "All it does is allow me to enter people's dreams. I can't read minds, Sebastian."

"But you *can* alter dreams. You told me how you tricked the Weaver into revealing her safe's combination. That's a formidable power, Jessica."

But the safe combination had been a minor secret, probably known to many within the compound, and the Weaver's mind had invested little energy in guarding it. Sebastian was talking about far more significant information, and a level of secrecy so intense that it would probably affect a dreamer's mind. What would the cost of such an effort be? I remembered the condition I was in after altering the Weaver's dream, and shuddered. Was it possible that I could pour so much energy into dream alterations that my body would be irreparably damaged when I returned? Or that I wouldn't be able to return at all?

I needed to know the details before deciding. "Tell me what the Fleshcrafters asked you for."

"Several years ago a high ranking Master of their

Guild disappeared. His people searched high and low for him, but to no avail. It was as if the earth had swallowed him whole. They asked me to help, but even my resources could provide no clues. If he was murdered—which his Guildmaster suspects—it was flawlessly managed. And whoever knows about it is not talking."

"I'm not seeing how my dreamwalking fits into this. Unless you're suggesting that I use it to look for him, and I don't see how that could possibly work."

"If he was killed, there is at least one person who knows what happened to him."

"You mean his murderer."

He nodded.

"If you're suggesting I invade his killer's dreams, you must have an idea who it is."

"I know whom the Fleshcrafters suspect."

Something about his expression made me shiver. "Who, Sebastian?"

"The missing Potter's last known appointment was with a Shadowlord."

For a moment I was speechless. "You're suggesting I invade the dreams of a *Shadowlord*? Do they even have normal dreams? And do you know which one the Potter met with? Or am I supposed to check them all until I find someone with guilty dreams?" I shook my head. "This is crazy, Sebastian."

"We don't know who he was meeting with. But if any Shadow murdered a ranking member of another Guild, their Guildmaster would surely know about it."

My eyes widened in astonishment. "Virilian? Is that who you're talking about? You want me to go into *his* dreams?"

"I don't 'want' anything," he said evenly. "You asked me if I knew a task you might perform for the Fleshcrafters, of sufficient value for them to heal your mother in exchange. This is the one thing I know of. If you can't do it—or won't do it—then there's your answer. I know of nothing else they need."

I looked away from him, struggling to wrap my brain around the concept. What was it Sebastian had told us about the Shadowlords? *There's madness at the core of them. Dozens of ancestral voices clamoring inside their heads every waking moment, each derived from a Shadow who was himself insane. Madness layered upon madness, all of it trapped within a soul that must walk the borderline between life and death, committed to neither .... Never forget what they are. Never forget that no matter how human they may appear to be, they ceased to be human long ago.* That was the kind of person whose dreamscape he was proposing I invade. It was a crazy idea from start to finish. Totally insane.

"I've never met him," I muttered. "Never even seen him. How the hell am I supposed to find his dream? It's not like there's a search engine for that kind of thing."

He reached into his satchel and removed several objects, laying them out one by one on the bed in front of me. The first was a large crescent-shaped brooch with a long pin attached, covered in an intricate knotwork pattern. It looked Viking in design, or maybe Celtic. "This belonged to Augustus Virilian when he walked among the living. He gave it to the Guildmaster of the Potters several years ago, as part of an exchange of gifts that accompanied the latter's appointment. It has never been worn by anyone else." He laid a ring beside it. "This belonged to Travis Bellefort, the missing Fleshcrafter." Beside the two objects he laid out several pictures. "These are photographs of both men. Virilian's was taken when he was alive, of course; the undead don't photograph well."

I looked up at him. "The Potters gave these to you when you were commissioned for this job?"

"The Potters gave them to me yesterday, when I

asked for them." He smiled slightly. "Will they make the task easier?"

I reached out and picked up the brooch; its surface was cool to my touch, but it revealed no special secrets. Morgana had been able to read my essence from my painting; might an item like this have similar emanations attached to it? So that I could use it to focus in on its owner's dream? Even if it did, I wouldn't have a clue how to activate them. "In the past I've needed an emotional connection to my targets." I ran my fingers over the intricate pattern as I spoke. "It was ten times harder to get into the Weaver's head than yours or my brother's, because I lacked a personal connection to her. I had to focus on her relationship with Moth, who I cared about, to make it work. So what would tie me to Virilian? I don't know the man. I've never even seen him."

"But he's the one who ordered the kidnapping of your brother. The one who would have killed Tommy, if you hadn't rescued the boy. Are you telling me you feel no emotion toward Virilian? That there's no connection between the two of you?"

I bit my lip as I considered it. His logic was compelling, but I wasn't sure about the mechanics of it. I was still struggling to figure out how my Gift worked, and everything was guesswork at this point. "So." I drew in a deep breath. "Is that your counsel, then? That I should try to enter Virilian's dreams to gather this information?"

"My counsel?" He laughed. "My *counsel* is that you go back to Terra Colonna, crawl into a warm bed far from any Shadowlords, and try to get a good night's sleep without wandering into other people's dreams. Try to come to terms with your mother's condition and make a new life for yourself, far away from Alia Morgana, Miriam Seyer, and all the other people who care nothing for you except as a pawn. Never think about this world again and never return here. That would be the *intelligent* thing to do." A corner of his mouth twitched. "But it's not what you're going to do, is it? You might be tempted for a while, if you're frightened enough, but in the end that won't make any difference. Dreamwalking will call to you."

His certainty irritated me. "Maybe you don't know me as well as you think."

"I may not know you, but I know the Gifted. I've spent half a lifetime on this God-forsaken world learning how to deal with them, and one thing has become very clear: their Gifts aren't just fancy mental powers. They're a kind of hunger. An obsession. A Seer will instinctively sample the emotions of everyone who walks by him. A Shadow will bind passing spirits to him without conscious thought. A Fleshcrafter will contort his own body into strange and inhuman shapes just because he can. They don't think about doing those things, they don't plan them, it's just part of who they are. So no, Jessica, I don't think you can spend a lifetime denying your Gift, any more than you can spend a lifetime not breathing. And I'm willing to bet that while part of you is terrified by the thought of going into Virilian's head, another part of you is hungry to try it. To find out if it's possible." He paused. "Am I wrong, Jessica?"

I flushed slightly and looked away. For a long time I didn't answer him. "You're not wrong," I muttered.

"Then let's figure out how we can make this as safe as possible. You told me that Tommy woke you up the first time the dream-wraith attacked, and that saved you. So I can stand guard over your body and do the same, if necessary. You need not fear being trapped in a dream. That was one of your biggest concerns, wasn't it?"

I nodded.

He indicated the brooch in my hand. "If these items can't help you establish a connection to Virilian, you'll lose nothing by trying. But if it turns out that you can, indeed, use material objects to invade the dreams of a Guildmaster, and twist his mind to your purpose . . . that would be a useful skill to know about, Jessica."

Something in his tone suddenly made me wary. What was his real interest in this? For decades he'd been a mortal enemy of the Shadows, and now he might have discovered a brand new weapon to use against them. My Gift. Was that why he'd brought me this information? Why he was tempting me to undertake this particular project? Was I just a pawn to him, like I was to so many other people in this damned world? Someone to be tricked and manipulated, so that I served his personal agenda?

*Don't trust anyone on Terra Prime*, he'd warned me. But I needed a friend on this world. I needed to be able to trust someone. And if the price of Sebastian's friendship was that I allowed him to dream of the day I would help him destroy the Shadows, that was a lot more benign than what others were asking of me.

"I want to try," I said at last. Voicing the words sent a chill down my spine, but he was right; I couldn't turn away from this.

"The Shadowlords generally sleep during the day. So if you need to invoke your Gift while he's in a dream state, that would be the time to try it."

"Tomorrow," I told him. "I have preparations to make first."

I needed to contact Isaac. Yes, that meant I would have to reveal my nature to him, but I needed information on the wraiths that only he could give me, and had no other way to reach him. I could only hope that the fragile bond we'd established would be enough to keep him from betraying me. If not . . . well, I would deal with the consequences of that when I had to. One emergency at a time.

The full magnitude of what I was planning was slowly sinking in. In a quiet voice I said, "Promise that if anything bad happens, you'll get word to my family. You don't have to tell them the truth. Just give them a story that's easier to accept than my disappearing without a trace. Give them some kind of path to closure."

He hesitated. "Jessica, you know I can't go back there—"

"But you can arrange for a message to get to them. Yes?"

"I can do that, yes."

"So promise me."

He said it softly. "I promise, Jessica."

I walked over to the small desk in the corner, took a pen and a piece of paper from the drawer, and wrote down my home address for him. As well as any other instructions I could think of, that he should have if I died.

Tomorrow, I told myself. Tomorrow I would test my Gift. Tomorrow I find out what I was truly capable of.

Or get killed trying.

# 21

THE WELL OF SOULS is silent and dark, empty of life, empty of unlife, empty even of death. As Isaac walks down the black corridor it echoes his footsteps back at him with the solemnity of a tomb; not even the passing whisper of a wraith breaks the eerie silence. There are doors on both sides of him, and now and then he tries one, but they are all locked. Human bones are scattered along the bases of the walls: skulls, femurs, dislocated vertebrae, random bones bleached white with age. The eye sockets of the skulls are turned toward him, as though their owners are watching. The atmosphere is chilling even by the standards of an apprentice Shadow, and he shivers as he walks down the hall, wishing he were anywhere but here.

Suddenly the corridor divides into two. Confused, he checks each direction, but beyond ten feet it's too dark to see anything. He doesn't remember this part of the level having forks in it, but now that he is facing one he must choose a course. After a moment's hesitation, he starts down the corridor on the right. It's empty of life and empty of ghosts, like its predecessor, but there are many more bones in this hallway. They're stacked against the walls in no particular order, a junkyard of bones.

Soon the hall divides again and he must make another choice. He continues on to the right; maybe consistency will help him keep his bearings. But the hall twists around, skewing his sense of direction, and then it divides again. And again. There are more bones on the floor each time, until he has to kick his way through piles of them just to walk. The entire level has transformed into a maze, he realizes, and he is hopelessly lost. Is this some kind of test? He calls out his father's name, but no one answers.

Suddenly he finds himself standing in front of the great double doors that lead to the Chamber of Souls. A wave of panic overwhelms him. No, test or no, he won't go in there again. He turns and starts to walk quickly back the way he came. The straight corridor leads to a sharp turn, then to a long curving stretch, then to a fork where he must choose his direction. . . . and suddenly he is back in front of the doors. He feels the sharp bite of fear, and he turns to flee. This time he runs through the corridors, but that only brings him back to the doors faster. Either he is circling back to them or they are transporting themselves in front of him. Try as he might, he can't get away.

There is nowhere to go but through them.

His heart filled with dread, he reaches out with a trembling hand to open the door, but it swings open of its own accord before he can touch it, and a cold breeze pushes him inside. As he enters the chamber he can see soul fetters gleaming like malevolent stars on all sides of him. Ghosts begin to appear, grouped around the soul fetters that belong to them, and they call out to him. Some try to cajole him, some threaten him with shame, some deride his lack of courage or loyalty or honor. All are trying to coerce him into submitting to Communion. Their voices merge into a din that fills the chamber and makes his head ring, while soul fetters swirl around him in dizzying patterns. He falls to his knees and instinctively shuts his eyes and covers his ears, even though he knows it won't do him any good. The ghosts are speaking directly to his soul.

Then, suddenly, the voices cease. The ghosts are gone.

Startled, he opens his eyes. There's only one person in the room now besides himself, and she's not a ghost, but flesh and blood. The last person he ever expected to see here.

"Jesse," he whispers.

She's dressed as he last saw her, in a slim tank top and close-fitting jeans. Her face is flushed red with life, her eyes bright with passion. She is warmth. She is energy. He wants to take her face in his hands and feel the heat of her skin against his fingertips, to drink it in like a precious elixir, along with her passion and her strength. After two weeks in Shadowcrest he is starved for humanity, and she is full of it. The desire is so powerful it leaves him breathless.

But what is she doing here? No outsider is permitted in this place.

She looks around the chamber curiously, studying each element in turn as she would artifacts in a museum: the golden fetters, the richly carved doors, the piles of bleached bones. The fetters have stopped their wild motion, and are hanging in mid-air surrounding them. Isaac struggles to think of something intelligent to say, but all he can come up with is, "There aren't usually bones here."

And that's when it hits him: the bones *shouldn't* be here. The corridor shouldn't be twisted into a maze. The doors shouldn't appear in front of him no matter where he runs, and *she* should not be here. So many things are wrong, and while he ignored them before, she is one wrong too many. Only one explanation is possible: He's dreaming.

With the revelation comes awareness. Suddenly he can sense his body lying on a distant bed, and he's aware of just how thin the veil of sleep is that's keeping him here. A single thought could breach that veil and banish everything he's looking at. In fact, he has to concentrate for a moment to hold the dream steady, to remain by the sheer force of his will in a nightmare that ten seconds ago he would have done anything to escape.

But none of that explains Jesse's presence.

How real she looks! He's never dreamed of anyone with this kind of depth and clarity before. Compared to her, the rest of this nightmare is like a cheap stage set, ready to collapse the instant the curtain comes down. But in the same way he knows that he's standing in a dream, and none of this is real, he knows that the Jessica standing in front of him isn't something his mind created. Her existence is independent of him, and when the curtain falls on his nightmare she will continue to exist. But there's only one way that could be possible—

His mind won't complete the thought. He wants to bask in her presence for a moment longer, before speaking the words that will make everything more complicated.

"This is a dark dream," she says. "Do you have it often?"

The casual conversational tone jars him out of his trance. "Every night, pretty much. Sometimes worse than others. I don't get much sleep these days." On impulse he reaches out a hand to touch her—but stops inches short of her skin, not daring to make contact. Part of him is afraid of what he might learn if he did. He remembers how she asked him about dreams the night they first met. How he told her about the Dreamwalkers, that they went insane and infected everyone around them, so they had to be destroyed on sight. That's what his elders had taught him, and at the time he simply accepted it, as he accepted all their teachings. But were they telling him the truth? He's come to question so much of Guild dogma that he's wary of taking anything at face value now. Maybe the Shadows have some other reason to hunt Dreamwalkers, that they wouldn't share with a mere apprentice. Or maybe they're just wrong.

One thing he knows: he could never betray Jesse to his Guild based on those lessons alone. Not when she hasn't done anything wrong, or shown any sign of insanity. He couldn't bear to see them do to her what they did to Jacob.

"Why are you here?" he asks. "Why are you trusting me like this? Yes, I helped you get away before, but this . . . this is . . ."

"So much more?" she asks quietly.

He nods.

A shadow passes over her face. She looks back over her shoulder, as if making sure that they're alone. "I need your help, Isaac. In all of Terra Prime you're the only one who can help me. So I took a chance." Her eyes are fixed on him now, studying his every response. "Was it a mistake?"

He remembers the touch of her lips on his cheek when she kissed him in the dungeon, and the sudden rush of heat to his loins makes him grateful for the loose robe he's wearing, which shields him from any potential embarrassment. "No." His voice is slightly hoarse, no doubt due to the lump rising his throat. "It wasn't a mistake. I don't know that I can help you, though. What is it you need?"

"I've run across something that Sebastian thinks is a ghost, but he can't tell me anything more about it. It keeps showing up in my dreams. The other day it crossed over into the waking world and almost killed me. I have to find out what it is, figure out how to fight it. Or at least how to avoid it."

Again she looks nervously over her shoulder. It's the ghost that she's looking for, he realizes; any minute now she expects it to appear. The thought sends an icy chill down his spine. "Describe it to me."

"It looks like a dark blotch in the sky at first, and then it spreads. Eventually it takes on human form, at least in its outline. It doesn't appear to have any physical substance, it's more like a void where nothing exists. As soon as it shows up in my dream it starts sucking all the color out of the landscape, like it was . . ." She drew in a shaky breath. "Like it was devouring the dream itself. The first time I saw it, it attacked me." She pushed up her sleeve and showed him a jagged gash on her arm, that was just beginning to heal. "I still had the wound when I woke up. That shouldn't be possible, right?"

"Go on," he says quietly.

"When it showed up in the real world it was . . . cold. It didn't just suck the color out of everything, but all the heat as well. All the life. Everything it passed by became coated in ice." Her voice is trembling now, her mask of confidence stressed to the breaking point by memories. "I can't just keep running from it, Isaac. Your Guild knows how to deal with the dead. Tell me what I can do to keep this one from killing me. Please."

He draws in a deep breath, trying to think. A dream-bound spirit that acts like a black hole? He's never been taught anything about that—not officially, anyway—but he's heard legends. Fearful legends, of creatures that even Shadows would be afraid of. "It may be a reaper," he says at last.

"What's that?"

"A type of spirit that's bound to the dream world. I don't know much about it. No one has seen one for ages. Most people think it's only a legend."

"But legends can reflect something real," she reminds him. "You were the one who told me that. Remember?"

He nods solemnly. "I remember."

"So where can I find more information? If I don't, it's just a question of time before this one gets me."

"I don't know, Jesse." He shakes his head. "I've read all the basic primers on spirit types, and nothing like this is described in them. The Masters of my Guild might know—"

"But you can't ask them," she says quickly.

"If you think this thing will hurt you otherwise—"

"I'm a *Dreamwalker*, Isaac. The minute they even suspect that, they'll move heaven and earth to hunt me down. You know they will." She shook her head emphatically. "You can't talk to anyone about this. Not even indirectly. Promise me."

"Okay." The edge of panic that's coming into her voice is unnerving. She seems to fear the Shadows more than she fears the reaper. "I won't talk to anyone. I'll just research it myself. I promise."

Suddenly she looks around the room again. The atmosphere in the chamber has changed subtly, becoming colder by a few degrees. Maybe a bit darker. "I have to go," she says quickly. "I'll get back to you later."

"When do you need this information?"

"Yesterday." She attempts to smile but it's a strained expression, without any humor in it. "There's bad shit going down soon. I need to know how to deal with this thing."

**"I'll do what I can—"**
**But she's already gone.**

||||||||||||||

There was nothing about reapers in the library.

Of course there was nothing.

He had expected there to be nothing.

That didn't mean the Guild had no information on them. On the contrary, the Masters' archives probably contained the information Isaac was looking for, in a neatly organized format. The only problem was that as a mere apprentice he had no access to that specialized collection. He didn't even know where in Shadowcrest it was located.

A Shadowlord could gather that information for him, and Isaac's father would probably do so if asked, pleased that his wayward son was taking an interest in necromancy. But if the reapers turned out to be connected to Dreamwalkers somehow, then the Shadowlords would know Isaac was interested in that forbidden Gift, and might start asking questions. No, Jesse was right, the risk was just too great.

He would have to research this on his own.

As for Jesse herself, the fact that she had appeared in his dream was no small secret. The Shadows had been at the forefront of the campaign to eradicate the Dreamwalkers, and any sign of the ancient curse reemerging should be reported to them immediately. But the longer he kept Jesse's visit a secret from his elders, the more he realized that it gave him a perverse thrill to defy them. After years of the *umbrae majae* telling him who he must be and what he must become, such an act of defiance was intoxicating. Yes, he'd tasted a bit of independence during his two-year walkabout, but in the end he'd done nothing more rebellious than miss some school and avoid talking to his parents. Even freeing

Jesse and her friends had been little more than a minor offense, since the Shadows were convinced by then that her brother wasn't the person they'd been looking for. This, though . . . this was a whole different magnitude of defiance. It was meaningful. It was dangerous. And it made him feel alive, in a way Shadows weren't supposed to feel alive.

He knew of a place where he might be able to find the information that Jesse wanted, but it would be risky to go there. There was no hard and fast rule forbidding it, but that was only because the Shadowlords didn't think that such rules were necessary. This was a resource that no one but the Shadowlords themselves could access.

Or so they believed.

Now was the time to call in favors, and see just how useful his new ally could be.

⸏⸏⸏⸏⸏⸏⸏⸏⸏⸏⸏

The Well of Souls was black and silent. If Isaac listened hard enough he could hear faint murmurs of the dead, but they sounded distant, as if spirits were passing through the place on their way to somewhere else. The only clear presence was that of Jacob Dockhart, who was staying as close to him as possible. The newly made ghost was clearly terrified of coming down here, but he had agreed to help, and that was all Isaac could ask of him. Without Jacob's assistance this expedition would not be possible.

"Watch out for guardian spirits," Isaac whispered to him. "We'll turn back right away if you see any sign of them."

Jacob's acknowledgement—and relief—prickled his skin.

Slowly they moved down the corridor, retracing the path Isaac had once walked with his father. But as they neared the entrance to the ritual room the ghost grew more and more agitated, and Isaac had to stop several times and whisper assurances to calm him down. It made sense that Jacob would have issues with returning to the place where he was so brutally murdered, and Isaac was annoyed at himself for not anticipating that. For a while it seemed like they would be unable to move past that point. But then Isaac reminded him that they were defying the will of the Shadowlords by coming down here, and that seemed to help.

Once they made it past the ritual room there were no further incidents, and soon they were standing in front of the massive gold doors that led to the Chamber of Souls. Once he crossed this threshold there would be no turning back; he would be in territory reserved for the Shadowlords, and if anyone caught him there, the consequences could be dire.

Assuming he was able to cross the threshold at all.

"I don't know how the lock works," he said in a low voice as he reached for the handle. "I just know you have to do something to help open it." The last time Isaac had been here his father had summoned a spirit to help with the door, but Isaac's Gift had been too primitive back then to observe what the ghost did. Hopefully Jacob would be able to figure it out.

He waited in silence, his heart pounding so hard that he could feel his pulse throb against the door handle. He could sense his ghost ally approaching the door, perhaps touching it, but his spirit sight allowed for no more knowledge than that. The seconds ticked by with agonizing slowness.

Finally the handle turned.

Breath held, Isaac unlatched the right-hand door and pushed it open. He waited a moment to see if Jacob would warn him about anything in the chamber, but all he got from the ghost was a general feeling of dread.

Finally he stepped inside. The place looked the same as when he'd visited it with his father, but since that day he'd returned to it so many times in his dreams, with fresh horrors added, that now it seemed strangely empty, unnaturally peaceful.

*It'll be anything but peaceful if I'm caught here*, he reminded himself. Quickly he walked to the fetter he'd examined when his father had first brought him here. The collection of biographies that accompanied it opened naturally to the first page, and he read the title underneath the first name again: *Twice-decorated Grand Crusader in the Final War Between the Shadows and the Dreamwalkers*. If there was some kind of spirit that existed only in dreams, he'd reasoned, it might have been active during that time, and hopefully there would be some reference to it. If not, he had no clue how to begin searching in this vast place for a single thread of information.

There was nothing in the Grand Crusader's biography about the reapers, but the names of several other Shadowlords were mentioned who also fought in the Dream Wars, so he located their fetters and started reading their biographies. Not all the entries were in English, but his education had included enough languages that he could pick his way through most of them. By harvesting a few facts from each biography, he was slowly able to piece together a picture of the conflict between the Shadows and the Dreamwalkers, which was far more complex—and confusing—than he'd imagined. Not only had the Shadows played a major role in eradicating the Dreamwalkers, but they had gone to great length to get the other Guilds to join in the slaughter. The biographies never explained why. Maybe the scribes who had assembled these records simply assumed that anyone reading them would understand their context. Certainly some of the *umbra majae*, who had absorbed the memories of Shadowlords from this time period, must know the Guild's early history. So why had Isaac never been taught it?

Hours passed as he worked his way through the fetter records one by one. Jacob disappeared several times, apparently summoned by his mistress to perform one task or another. He always came back, but the brief absences were hell on Isaac's nerves. Without Jacob as lookout he was terribly vulnerable in this place. That, and the effort required to decipher notes faded almost past recognition, written in dialects centuries old, drained Isaac of energy. He wanted nothing more than to quit for a time, to recoup his mental resources.

But he couldn't bring himself to stop reading. This project was about more than Jesse now. He was uncovering a history of the Guild that no apprentice had ever been taught, and he could not turn away.

At last he came to a fetter that made him uneasy, though he didn't know why. The first name on its pedestal was Persian—*Shekarchiyandar*—and the pedigree that followed was shorter than most. It took him a moment to figure out that what disturbed him was not the list of names, but the dates that went with them. Evidently the Shadowlords who first Communed with this fetter had survived only a few years afterward. And the ones who tried later were even less successful; the last person on the list had lasted only a few months. Whoever this Shekarchiyandar was, his memories appeared to be deadly, and no one had attempted to Commune with them in recent centuries. Yet the fetter was still here, displayed among the Guild's active offerings. So it must have great value.

Pulling out the book of notes stored in the pedestal, he looked around to see if Jacob was still standing guard. But the ghost was gone again, leaving him on his own. With a nervous sigh he opened the ancient volume and began to read. The original entry was in Farsi, which was frustrating, as his knowledge of that language was minimal. Slowly he worked his way through the faded and brittle pages, trying to make sense of the ancient script. Some of the words were so faded they were nearly impossible to read, and he had to make educated guesses as to their meaning. But in the end his effort was justified, because he had finally found the records he was searching for.

*... created the reapers in order to [bring/begin] battle to walkers of dreams in their [fort/citadel/home]. Originally twelve existed, later [winnowed? destroyed?] to seven during final war. After [exit?] of dream walkers from [awake? Living?] world the reapers were not seen again. [?]*

There was a note in English following that, the relative freshness of the ink suggesting that it had been added at a much later date: *Appearance in 1132 A.D. disputed.*

1132. It took him a minute to place the date.

It was the year recorded on the pedestal, of the last attempt to Commune with Shekarchiyandar's fetter.

Heart pounding, Isaac leafed through the book until he came to that entry. It was a short one, no more than a single paragraph, but at least it was in German, a language he could read fluently. Someone named Gunther the Black had attempted Communion with the fetter, but had gone insane in the months following the ritual. In his final moments, just before the other Shadowlords had to forcibly put him down, he screamed something about the reapers returning. Since no one else had seen any reapers around, the chronicler took that as a symptom of his madness. But Isaac wasn't so sure. If the reapers were only active in dreams, wasn't it possible they could appear to Gunther without anyone else seeing them? The same way that Jesse had come to him, without anyone else seeing her?

He was so close to the answers he thought that he could taste it.

He started to turn back to the earlier entries, when suddenly he heard a noise behind him: footsteps, heavy and solid, headed his way. He thought he could hear spirit voices as well, which meant that the visitor was a Shadowlord.

He couldn't afford to be discovered here.

Panicking, he shoved the ancient volume back into its storage slot and looked for somewhere to hide. But as his gaze passed over the entrance he realized to his horror that he'd left the door open. If the Shadowlord saw that, he would know instantly that something was wrong.

Desperately he sprinted across the floor, grabbed the door, and pushed it shut. He tried to hold it back at the last moment to keep it from making too much noise, but the momentum of the heavy panel carried it forward despite him, and he flinched as it slammed loudly shut. Hopefully whoever was coming would be too distracted by the voices of the his ghostly retinue to pay attention to such noise.

Isaac looked around for somewhere to hide, but the pedestals were too narrow for him to fit behind and there was no other furniture in the chamber. If he could climb the stairs to an upper level he might be able to get out of the sightline, but there was no time to do that. So he did the only thing he could think of, flattening himself against the wall beside the door, hoping that when it opened it would shield him from sight. A cold sweat broke out on his face as spirits began to enter the room, not newly made wraiths like Jacob, but the vanguard of a powerful Shadowlord. They didn't notice him right away, and he could always hope that when they did they wouldn't report him. Some of the dead who attended the Shadowlords were slave spirits, like Jacob, but others were independent wraiths caught up in the wake of the undead against their will, who owed the Shadows no love or loyalty.

Isaac held his breath as the door handle turned and the massive doors swung open. He put his hands out in front of his face to keep the heavy wood panel from smashing into him; hopefully the visitor wouldn't notice that the door had stopped short of the wall.

Footsteps entered the room. They passed Isaac's hiding place without pausing. So far so good.

Suddenly a cold wind swept behind the door, raising goosebumps on Isaac's skin. A powerful wraith circled him, prodding him with its essence. Then it moved away, heading back to its master. The game was over.

"What?" he heard a Shadowlord exclaim. "Where?"

There was no point in hiding any longer. Drawing in a deep breath to steady himself, Isaac stepped out from his hiding place.

The Shadowlord standing in the center of the chamber was one he didn't know, but the man's elder rank was immediately apparent, as was his displeasure at discovering that the trespasser his ghost had discovered was a mere apprentice. "Who are you?" the Shadowlord demanded. "How did you get in here?"

"Isaac," he stammered. He couldn't bring himself to state his family name. If news got out that an Antonin had offended against Guild custom, his father's rage would be beyond measure. And causing that kind of emotion in a Shadowlord was a far greater offense than merely trespassing. The other question he couldn't answer without revealing Jacob's role in the break-in, and he refused to do that. If the boy's spirit had been absent when the Shadowlord arrived, then he was safe for now; Isaac would not compromise him, even to save himself.

A spirit whispered something to the Shadowlord, too low for Isaac to hear. The *umbra maja* nodded sharply. "Go. Report it to him." Isaac flinched inside. Report to whom? His father? The Guildmaster? Any hope he might have had that he could keep this situation from getting out of hand had just vanished.

He shouldn't have come here. He knew that now. It had been an act of utter foolishness, sheer youthful arrogance, and the magnitude of the mess he was in was just starting to sink in.

The Shadowlord gestured toward the door. "You will follow me," he commanded.

Isaac nodded weakly and fell in behind the man as he left the room. They walked down the black corridor without speaking, Isaac following the Shadowlord like a whipped puppy, but this time the hallway was not silent. The Shadowlord's ghostly retinue filled it with scorn. *Foolish boy!* they whispered. *Doomed!* Isaac flinched as ghostly fingers prodded at him, mocking his despair.

The Shadowlord entered the elevator. Isaac joined him.

It started to go down.

Not up.

Down.

Isaac felt his heart sink as he realized where they were going. His offense must have been truly dire in the eyes of this elder. After a brief descent the elevator stopped, and the two left the cage and entered the prison level, where Jesse and her friends had once been locked up. As the Shadowlord directed Isaac toward one of the cells, they crossed the very spot where she had kissed him, and a wave of despair suddenly came over him, so powerful that he was forced to stop walking for a moment to pull himself together.

•

Emotion. He was displaying raw emotion in front of a Shadowlord. The shame of it doubled his misery.

Finally he entered one of the cells, and the *umbra maja* locked the door shut behind him. There was nothing inside the small space—no food, no water, not even a chamber pot. He could lick cave moisture off the stone wall if he got thirsty enough, but that was about it.

"Your father will be informed of this," the Shadowlord said. "He'll deal with you."

There was no point in responding to him. Isaac had gambled everything for the sake of knowledge, and he had lost. Protesting the consequences would only bring more shame upon his family and make his situation worse.

Assuming that it was possible for it to get any worse.

With a sigh he sat down on a stone protrusion and rested his back against the wall. Spiritual exhaustion enveloped his soul like a shroud, the long hours of tension finally taking their toll. Two years ago he had fled from this place to escape a Shadow's destiny, and this was the natural end of that journey. Whatever misery came after this, at least he would no longer have to pretend he was something he was not. In the midst of his despair, it was perversely comforting to know that he would face his final moments being true to himself.

He wondered if Jesse could reach him in this place. He had so much to tell her, but no idea how to establish contact. If he fell asleep, could she come to him again? Or must she wait for him to start dreaming on his own, before she could do that?

He was far too anxious to sleep but too exhausted not to. He lay back and closed his eyes, leaving the choice to destiny.

# 22

THE DAYS WERE GROWING LONGER AND LONGER, Morgana noted, in workload if not in hours. Each one seemed more complicated than the last, and more dangerous. Seeds that had been planted years ago were starting to bear fruit, and a decade of watching and hoping must now give way to a careful—and secretive— harvest. At her level of functioning there was no room for error.

Miriam Seyer knocked and entered. "Rita Morales is here, Your Grace."

A painted eyebrow arched upward. "Send her in."

She had not called Rita to her, but she wasn't surprised that she'd come. Miriam had already reported that Jesse had no intention of talking to the Seers, so there was little left for Rita to do, other than debrief.

Soon a quick, light stride could be heard approaching

the study. The footsteps paused at the door—perhaps uncertain, perhaps just respectful.

"Come in, Rita. Shut the door behind you."

The girl obeyed, taking up a respectful position before Morgana. The Guildmistress noted that she had not seen a Healer yet. Fresh scratches marked her face and arms in a dozen places; combined with the bruises from a week ago, it gave her skin a surreal aspect, like an abstract painting. The scratches were real injuries, of course, unlike the bruises which had been applied as part of her cover story. Not that voluntary bruises hurt any less than the real thing.

Morgana nodded brusquely to her. "I would say you did a good job, but in light of the chaos you left behind you in the Blackwaters, perhaps 'good' isn't an appropriate adjective. Nonetheless, you accomplished the task I set for you."

Rita bristled slightly. "I warned you what Jesse was planning. You told me not to interfere."

"So I did. Though, to be fair, your warning of a 'disruption' was a bit of an understatement. But that was my failing, not yours. You did well, Rita. As always."

The girl bowed her head slightly, a gesture that was respectful but not submissive. Rita was never submissive.

"Tell me more about her dreams," Morgana commanded.

Rita shrugged. "I already sent you a report about her nightmare. It didn't sound particularly significant, save for the appearance of the safe combination at the end. And that just appeared, without any kind of context or story. She seemed to be as mystified by it as I was."

"Do you think that was really the case?"

Rita's eyes narrowed slightly. "Are you asking, would she lie to me? I see no reason why she would. We've been in this together since day one. She told me once that she was coming to think of me like a sister."

"Yet she didn't want you with her today."

She shrugged. "She needs some time alone. I totally get that. And she wants to approach the Fleshcrafters by herself. I get that, too. This is about her mother, her security, her future. I'm just a sidekick."

"You did encourage her to meet with me before the two of you headed home, yes?"

"Yeah. She was pretty adamant about not doing that. You're not on her list of favorite people right now. No offense."

Morgana waved off any concern. "No doubt she wonders how well she can guard her secrets in my presence. A good sign. She's learning the game."

Rita opened her mouth, then appeared to have second thoughts and closed it again.

"You have something to say?"

"It's not important, your Grace."

"You're free to speak your thoughts to me when we're alone together. What is it?"

Rita bit her lip. "Are you planning to tell her who you really are? Because right now she wants nothing to do with you, ever. Maybe if she understood the reason you're so involved with her life . . ." She shrugged. "I don't know, it just seems like if you wait much longer to tell her the truth, you could drive her away for good."

In answer Morgana walked over to one of the bookshelves, pulled down a black leather-bound volume, and placed it on the reading table. "This book explains the process by which Dreamwalkers go mad. It details a five stage process, of which the first two are fairly benign. In the last stage, their madness is broadcast to every sleeping mind within a hundred miles. There's a description of a city that devolved into total chaos because of one Dreamwalker living in it." She pulled down another book and set it beside the first; this one was thinner and bound in faded brown pigskin. "This book explains how they drain strength from other people through their dreams. Perhaps the source of succubus legends." A third book was added. "This one explains how they drain the *life* of others through their dreams—a particularly horrific version." Another book. "This one details how they slowly transform into terrifying creatures, monsters of darkness that hunger to devour human souls."

"Like the thing we saw at the compound?"

"Perhaps." She tapped the top book with her fingertip. "The point is, I can pull a hundred books off my shelves, and each of them will say something different about what the Dreamwalker's Gift is, and how it will change Jessica. We don't lack information. Rather, we have so much information that it's all useless. If the darker predictions turn out to be true, she may wind up being hunted by the Guilds and could fall into the hands of people capable of stripping her mind bare of secrets. In which case, there's one piece of information she can't be allowed to possess." She paused, and a muscle along her jaw tightened briefly. "If that means that when she finally learns who I am she curses my name and walks out on me, so be it. She will still play the role she was destined to. I'll just have to guide her from a distance."

"I don't suppose you'd share with me what that destiny is all about?"

Ignoring the question, Morgana walked back to the leather chair behind the desk and sat down. "You will go back to Terra Colonna, and maintain your friendship with her. Don't press her too hard for information on her dreams; it will only make her suspicious. She'll confide in you when she's ready. As for Devon, I want you to keep that tie close, as well. She may confide things in him that she doesn't tell you, and I want him to trust you enough to share that information."

Rita snorted. "She thinks I'm interested in him."

"Then use that. Use whatever you have to. You are my eyes and ears in that world, Rita. Do what you must to stay informed." She leaned back in her chair, steepling her fingers as she thought. "I want you to keep an eye on the other changelings, also. Report to me immediately if any more of them die suspiciously. The Council of Guilds ordered Virilian to cease killing them and if he persists, proof of it would give me valuable leverage over him."

"I'm surprised the Council is showing so much mercy."

"It isn't mercy, merely expediency. Those murders were sloppy. They revealed the nature of our Gifts too openly, and threatened to draw the wrong kind of attention to us. The Greys are going to work on a short range strategy to distract the locals, while the Council considers more permanent solutions."

"Such as?"

Morgana said nothing.

"It would be nice to know what's coming, if you're going to send me back there."

"Let's just say that right now it's safe for you to return. If that changes, be assured I'll pull you out in time." She paused. "Terra Colonna is an unstable world. It may well destroy itself without our help."

Rita pressed her lips together tightly, but asked nothing further. The girl was a loyal agent, Morgana noted, but that might change if the Council decided to Cleanse a world she had connections to. Stronger alliances than this one had collapsed over such details. Morgana would have to watch her closely.

More and more worlds in the Terran cluster were developing sciences that were capable of revealing the changelings' true nature. Terra Colonna wasn't the first, and it wouldn't be the last. The Council of Guilds couldn't just destroy every world that learned how to decipher the double helix. They needed a better solution.

Rita asked, "Are you going to let her approach the Fleshcrafters on her own?"

"She's welcome to approach them. As for getting what she wants from them without my help, I've set things in motion to see that doesn't happen."

"She's stubborn," Rita warned. "And not likely to give up on something just because you made it difficult."

Morgana smiled faintly. "I'm counting on that." She leaned back in her chair. "You know the proper channels to use to report to me from Terra Colonna. Keep me informed."

Rita bowed her head respectfully. "Of course, Your Grace."

As the door closed behind her, Morgana wondered how long it would be before the existence of a true Dreamwalker became public knowledge. Sooner or later it must; there was no way to avoid it. God willing the pieces of Morgana's plan would have time to fall into place before that happened. If not, a lot of people were going to go down, Morgana first among them.

So many variables. So many unknowns. The game was growing more dangerous by the day.

But that was the kind of game she enjoyed most.

And played best.

# 23

**T**HE LANDSCAPE IS FRIGID AND LIFELESS, lush forest and majestic mountains draped in a glistening layer of ice that renders everything sterile. In some places the ice is coldly beautiful, like a frozen waterfall, but in most it is simply forbidding. Overhead, carrion birds circle impatiently, their black wings stark against the grey and sullen heavens as they wait for something to die.

They are waiting for him to die.

Shivering, Isaac tries to remember the morning he watched the sun rise over those same mountains, with Jesse by his side. No sun is visible now, and though he tries his best to summon a memory of what that dawn looked like, he can't. His soul is too desolate right now to recall such a moment of happiness.

Suddenly he hears her approaching, her footsteps crunching the surface of the ice. She comes to stand beside him, like she did that morning so long ago, although this time there is no joy in her, only concern. It's his sleeping mind that conjured this setting, and as she watches the vultures circling overhead, she must surely be wondering why it looks like this.

"Jesus," she says. "What happened?"

He shrugs stiffly. "I went somewhere I shouldn't have, and I got caught. In a lesser family that might have been a minor offense, but for an Antonin, who supports the honor of the Guild on his shoulders, like Atlas supports the globe, it was an unforgivable sin." He laughs bitterly. "Right now my body is locked in the same cell your brother was once in. It's a bit warmer than this place, and lacks the vultures, but otherwise it's equally cheery." He looks up at the birds and then adds quietly, "Or maybe we do have vultures there. Just not the kind with wings."

"I'm so sorry." The sympathy in her voice makes him ache with shame. No one should have to feel sorry for him. "Is there anything I can do to help?"

There is more color in her than in the rest of the landscape, he notes. The spark of her life defies the sterility of his dream setting. He longs to reach out and touch her, to connect with that spark. Instead he looks away. "I have the information you want. It's . . . it's not good news, Jesse."

"Tell me," she says quietly.

"The reapers are wraiths, bound by their creator to hunt Dreamwalkers. I don't know how he empowered them to enter dreams, as we don't have that kind of ability ourselves, but he did. They haunt the minds of dreamers, and when they find signs of the ancient Gift, then they attack." He pauses. "That's why no one has seen them for centuries. There's been nothing to hunt."

"Now they have me," she mutters. "You weren't kidding about the bad news."

He nods. "There were seven of them originally; I don't know how many are still around. I couldn't find any record of them appearing in the waking world unless their creator summoned them. With him dead, they're probably just running wild." He pushes back a lock of frosted hair from his forehead. "If someone were to Commune with his memories they might be able to take control of the reapers, but he was one crazy sociopathic bastard, even by our standards, so that's not likely to happen." Very quietly he says, "I'm sorry, Jesse. But it sounds like a reaper has your scent, metaphysically speaking, and judging from everything I've read, it won't let up until you're dead."

She bows her head. He waits silently, knowing that she's struggling to process all that he just told her. It's a burden he wouldn't wish on anyone. "So there's no hope?" she murmurs. "Nothing I can do about this?"

"I didn't say that."

Startled, she looks at him.

"They're just wraiths. They may have some fancy powers, but at the core they're still ghosts, subject to the laws that rule the dead. And the universe is full of necromancers. We harvest the most Gifted ones for our Guild, so that's where most of the power is concentrated, but you'll still find echoes of it in other places. Your own world has its share of mediums, and some of those may have traces of legitimate power. If you can find one who does, who knows how to bind and destroy spirits, maybe he can help you."

"I thought the Shadows' Gift was the ability to travel between worlds."

He shook his head. "Our control over the dead gives us the knowledge we need to do that, but it's a learned skill, not inherent in our Gift. All the strange practices that we're known for—transformation into the undead, Communion with the departed—those came late in the game. Near as I can tell, we didn't start doing those things until the end of the Dream Wars. Before that we were simply necromancers." He managed a weak smile. "Or so I've read recently."

"Dream Wars? What were those?"

"Some kind of all-out conflict between Shadows and Dreamwalkers. The other Guilds supported us, but it was really our campaign. Planned genocide." He hesitates. "I have no clue why my Guild wanted the Dreamwalkers dead so badly. That's what I was trying to figure out when I was caught."

She turns away from him. After a moment she says, very softly, "I have an idea of why."

He waits for her to say more, but she doesn't. Finally he offers, "I wish I could be more helpful."

A shadow of pain crosses her face. "You told me what I need to know. If I manage to survive this mess at all, it'll be because of you." She hesitates. "But now you're in danger because of me—"

"No. No. That's not true." He takes her hands in his. How warm they are! How full of life! "No one forced this fate on me. I hungered for a destiny other than the one I was born to, and that hunger betrayed me. But because of it I got to experience life—*real* life—and I'll never regret that."

She is about to respond when the world suddenly begins to shake. Ice shivers on the mountaintops and then begins to crack, shards of it raining down into the valley. The birds overhead screech and then fall from the sky one by one, and as they strike the earth it swallows them. The landscape around them begins to dissolve like smoke.

"It's time," she said, squeezing his hands. "Good luck, Isaac."

||||||||||||||

"Enough," a voice commanded.

The ghosts who had prodded Isaac to wakefulness withdrew, leaving him half-asleep and disoriented. It took him a moment to focus on the person standing outside the bars of his cell: His father.

"It's time we talked," the Shadowlord said.

Quickly Isaac got up, ran a hand through his hair to bring order to it, and smoothed the worst sleep wrinkles from his robe. The actions were reflexive; even in these dire circumstances he couldn't bear to look disheveled in front of his father.

The Shadowlord watched in silence as Isaac approached the bars. Normally his father's expression was unreadable, but today there was anger in his eyes. The magnitude of emotion that he must be feeling for it to bleed to the surface that way was unnerving. "You have long disdained the sanctity of our customs," he told Isaac. "For two years you denied this Guild and our family, indulging in common passion rather than accepting your duty. Now I'm told you were discovered in the Chamber of Souls, an offense against the authority of the *umbrae majae* and the customs of our Guild. By doing so you bring shame to our family and damage the reputation upon which other Antonin depend. And this time you did it in the heart of Shadowcrest, so that all know the details of your transgression." He paused. "Have you anything to say for yourself?"

Isaac considered apologizing, but he knew his father well enough to realize that they were well past the point when it would do any good. "No, Sir."

"Why did you go to the Chamber of Souls?"

*Keep it short,* Isaac warned himself. *Keep it simple. The more you say, the more likely it is he will come up with new questions to ask.* "I wanted to learn more about our history, Sir."

"You could have gone to your teachers for that."

"There are things they don't teach us."

"Perhaps there are reasons for that."

Isaac said nothing.

"At least you could have asked a Shadowlord to bring you there, so that your visit was properly sanctioned. You could have asked *me* to bring you there." Now anger was evident in his voice, the fury of wounded pride. The man's own son had been unwilling to come to him for assistance. That was his failing as well as Isaac's.

Isaac felt as if he was standing on a rock surrounded by quicksand; no matter what direction he walked in, the end would be the same. *At least I can keep from betraying Jesse's trust,* he thought. It would be miniscule victory in the face of disaster, but a victory nonetheless.

He said nothing.

The cold eyes fixed on him, taking the measure of his soul. "Is there any reason I shouldn't cast you out from the family, excising you from our ranks to protect those who would embrace their responsibility with more enthusiasm?"

Isaac hesitated. He could launch into a speech about how strong his Gift was likely to become, about all the experience he'd gained in the outside world, and how it would make him a better Shadow in the long run, about the thousand and one things he might do for his family in the future if allowed to stay, that would cast honor upon their House ... but that was all bullshit, and his father knew it. Isaac didn't belong here. His actions had proven it. No simple words could change that fact.

He said it humbly: "None that I know of, Sir."

"Very well, then." His father's expression was grim. "By the authority of the elders of House Antonin, I sentence you to be cast out of our House, and out of this Guild. All ties of blood and duty will be severed. You will be as one who was born in the outside world, who has no claim to loyalty, assistance, or affection within our ranks. You will no longer be family to us, or to me. Do you understand?"

He had to swallow back the lump in his throat in order to speak. "Yes, Father."

"The possibility that you might share our secrets with the outside world must be addressed. While a Domitor could remove them from your mind, that process would enable him to learn things he shouldn't, and your mind could end up so damaged that death would seem a mercy by comparison. Therefore it has been decided by the elders of the House that a Domitor will be brought in to alter your mind, so that any attempt to divulge Guild secrets, no matter how trivial, will cause you unspeakable agony. In this way your silence will be assured. Do you agree to this course?"

Isaac swallowed thickly. The question was not a rhetorical one; reworking the fabric of someone's mind on that scale required the cooperation—or at least the assent—of the subject. But what choice did he have? Virilian wouldn't allow the Antonin to exile him if there was even a chance Isaac might spill the Guild's secrets to outsiders. It would be far easier just to kill him and secure those secrets forever. Isaac's father was offering him a chance to leave this place alive, as something other than a walking vegetable. Only one answer was possible: "I agree."

"They have decided you will also bear the mark of shame, so that all who see you will know that our Guild cast you out in disgrace. Do you understand what this means?"

Isaac flinched, then nodded.

"Do you have any objections to voice, about any of this? It's your last chance."

*None that would matter to you*, he thought bitterly. "I do not."

"So be it, then. I'll make the necessary arrangements."

His father turned away and walked out without another word. Isaac stood there in silence, the full magnitude of the elders' judgment slowly sinking in. He had little doubt that he could handle exile—he'd lived on his own for two years already—but the mark of shame that his father had proposed was a brutal punishment, meant to identify those who were unworthy of a Guild's trust. Anyone connected with a Guild would consider it his duty to shun Isaac, while anyone not connected with a Guild would see the mark as the sign of a failed elitist, someone who'd been given opportunities they could only dream of, and pissed on them. Someone who deserved to be taken down a notch.

Or several notches.

At least he was going to live. He hadn't even considered that his Guild might sentence him to death for such a minor offense, but his father was right—the secrets of the Guild mattered more to its masters than a mere apprentice's life. Isaac could be replaced. The secrecy of the Guild could not be.

Shutting his eyes, he leaned back against the dank stone wall and sighed. *You wanted a different destiny,* he told himself. *Now you have it.*

# 24

## SHADOWCREST
## VIRGINIA PRIME

### JESSE

**T**HE BLACK PLAIN BENEATH MY FEET is unsteady tonight, its surface undulating like ocean waves, barely solid enough to walk on. The blackness laps over my toes, my feet disappearing from sight for a moment, as if blotted out of existence. Will I be able to keep walking, or will the plain give way like quicksand beneath my feet? What will happen to me if I am engulfed in it? The ancient Dreamwalkers were driven mad by their Gift, legends say. Was this what they saw in their final hours? Did the universe buckle and crack on all sides of them, until the primordial chaos broke through and swallowed them whole?

*Easy, girl. Easy.* I shut my eyes for a moment, trying to steady my nerves. *I'm only projecting my fears onto the landscape. Nothing more. If I can't accept that mechanism and deal with it, I should just wake myself up now and not try to go any further.*

Much as I'd like to turn back, it's not a real option. Yes, I could give up on this insane quest and go crawling back to Morgana to beg for help, choking on humiliation as she fastened her puppet strings firmly to my limbs. Or I could forget about healing Mom, and just go back to Terra Colonna and try to live a normal teenager's life. But then every day I would know that my mother was sick because of my cowardice. And Morgana would know me for easy prey, and it would only be a matter of time before she sent her minions to Terra Colonna to screw with me again.

Granted, she'll probably screw with me even if I succeed tonight; I have no illusions about that. But obtaining a Fleshcrafter's services on my own will at least demonstrate that I'm willing to defy her—that I'm *capable* of defying her—and maybe it will drive home the point that I deserve to be treated as something better than a mindless pawn.

One can only hope.

My efforts to pull myself together emotionally have visible effect; the black plain is merely rippling now, like lake water shimmying in the wind, and as long as I watch my footing I should be safe enough. A feeling of intense relief comes over me. If I can maintain my mental focus and not let my own fears consume me, surely I can manage this journey.

Now I just have to figure out where the hell I'm going.

The doors surrounding me are in the forms of caverns this time, their mouths narrow and ominous, barred like the cell doors in Shadowcrest. The heavy locks look like they've been rusted shut for centuries, and even if I had a key, I'm not sure I could get one open. But how would I even know which door to unlock? I look down at Virilian's brooch in my hand and try to focus my attention on it, my eyes tracing the intricate knotwork pattern, praying it will unlock some secret Dreamwalker knowledge that will enable me to find my target. But though I feel a sharp sense of anticipation, as if something is about to happen, nothing actually does. Frustrated, I think back to Sebastian's suggestion about establishing an emotional link through Tommy, and I close my eyes and picture him as he was when I found him, pale and hollow-eyed and terrified. Virilian is the man who did that to him. Virilian is the man who kidnapped him and starved him and assaulted him with ghosts. Virilian is his Abuser. I remember the anguish that I felt when I first realized my brother was missing, the helplessness I felt later when it seemed like we would never find him, the rage I felt when I learned what had been done to him. All of it Virilian's fault. Everything that was done to Tommy, and to me, was done by this Shadowlord's command.

Suddenly I'm standing in front of a barred door. There's an image engraved on the lock, of a crescent moon with a knotwork design on it. I look at Virilian's brooch in my hand, confirm that it matches, then take in a deep breath and push at the door. It swings open, but reveals only blackness. Whatever lies beyond this point, I won't be able to explore it until I commit myself to the unknown shadows of Lord Virilian's soul.

For a long time I stare into that darkness. Then, very carefully, I alter my dream body. The changes I make to my avatar aren't big ones, but they're enough to function as a disguise, so that if Virilian sees me in his dreamscape, that won't give him the power to recognize me in the waking world.

I take a moment to steady myself, then step across the threshold—

\*   \*   \*

A gust of frigid air blasts me in the face, sucking the heat out of my flesh. Reflexively I try to create a coat for myself, but though that would have been effortless a few seconds ago, it's almost impossible now. A bad omen. Altering small elements wasn't this difficult in anyone else's dream; clearly there's something in the Shadowlord's psyche that inhibits my Gift.

Concentrating as hard as I can, I manage to create a formless wrap for myself, that keeps out some of the wind. It's the best I can do.

The dreamscape I've entered is white: white snow underfoot, white ice coating the boulders near me, white frost encrusting the mountains in the distance, and a sky so pale one can hardly see where the land ends and the heavens begin. There are no people in sight, nor any kind of house or monument visible. Just snow. I look back to make sure the door is still there—it is—and then move forward cautiously, searching for whatever makes this place meaningful to Virilian.

Soon I come to a place where the ground drops away, giving me a bird's eye view of a narrow valley with steep mountain walls and a ribbon of flowing water at the bottom. A fjord? There's a village on the shore, whose long, windowless houses have holes in their roofs, through which smoke is rising. The people there are all wearing cloaks of fur or wool over primitive garments: tunics, leggings, shoes that look like simple pieces of hide wrapped around their feet. I see a few flashes of metal jewelry, including a pin like the one in my hand. Whatever this place is, it's clearly connected to Virilian's past.

Suddenly there's a scream at the far end of the village, so terrified in pitch that it raises the hackles on my neck. Everyone starts rushing in that direction to see what's happening, and I look around for a way to get closer without having to climb down into the village itself. There's little cover on the snow-covered slopes, and for a moment I'm tempted to alter the color of my clothing to a matching white, but given how much effort it took to create the thing in the first place, I decide against it. God alone knows what challenges still await me, and I need to preserve my energy. Carefully I make my way around the C-shaped escarpment surrounding the village, and yes, if anyone looks in my direction I'll probably be spotted, but I'm figuring I can get back to my door faster than anyone can climb the cliff to reach me. I need to see what kind of narrative Virilian's mind has crafted, so I can figure out how to take control of it.

Two men appear, dragging a third between them. It's the third one who's doing the screaming, as he convulses so wildly they can barely control him. Specks of froth are frozen in his beard, and there is a madness in his eyes so terrible that it makes him seem more demonic than human. The two men, though broad-shouldered and strong in their own right, can barely restrain him.

Then someone yells out a name—or maybe it's a title—in a language I don't recognize. A moment later a tall blond man comes out of one of the buildings, and as soon as I see him I know he's the creator of this dream, though he looks nothing like Sebastian's description of Virilian. Despite his hollow cheeks and sunken eyes and skin as pale as the snow surrounding him, he's clearly alive. One side of his face is scarred in a zigzag pattern, cutting through his left eye socket, and the eye is missing. The regularity of the wound suggests it was a deliberate disfigurement. People move out of his way as he approaches, and it's hard to tell if they are doing it out of respect or fear.

The screaming man is convulsing on the ground now, and I can see blood splattered on the snow around him. Another two men have come forward to help, so now there are four burly guys trying to pin the man down, one on each limb. The screamer twists and bites one of them on the cheek, leaving a scarlet gash. I hear what sounds like cursing.

The blond Virilian looms over the group like a vulture, watching the ruckus. I get the sense that it pleases him. Then, raising his hands to the heavens, he begins to speak. The people nearest him back away quickly, and a few men and women at the back of the throng flee from the scene completely, seeking shelter inside one of the longhouses. I can't make out what he's saying, but it seems to be some kind of invocation, and at one point I hear the name of Odin. Suddenly the convulsing man freezes in mid-spasm, his body painfully arched back, and a cold wind rushes outward from him, freezing the blood on the snow to scarlet crystals. Even from this far away I can sense how unnatural that wind is, and for a moment it's all I can do to stand my ground, and not turn and bolt for my dream door. I experienced this kind of cold once before, when the reaper pursued me outside the Weaver's camp, and I have no desire to face such a creature again.

But no color is bleeding from the dreamscape this time, so I wait, breath held, to see what will happen next. An icy fog starts to seep from the screaming man's mouth, nose, and ears, tendrils of white gathering over him. Slowly it takes on the shape of a man, his mouth open wide, frozen in the act of screaming. It's a ghost, I realize suddenly, banished from the man's body by the blond man's ritual. I've been watching an exorcism.

The villagers have all backed far away now, and even the four men who were pinning down the possessed one let go and clear the area. The foggy form is taking on more detail, clarifying bit by bit like a slow-loading graphics file. Suddenly its identity becomes clear, and I take a step back in my surprise, nearly stumbling in the snow.

The spirit's face is that of the necromancer.

Then the features collapse into themselves, the spirit becoming a simple cloud once more—which then explodes, glittering particles of frost rushing outward in every direction, as if blasted from a shotgun. Everyone the frost touches falls to the ground and begins to convulse like the first man did. They're being possessed, I realize, by spirits that wear the face of their exorcist. Who is trying to banish each wraith as it manifests, but there are too many of them. As soon as he gets rid of one, two more appear. I can sense the fear in him as the situation worsens, and I realize that any minute now his mind might prompt him to awaken, to escape this nightmare. If that happens, I'm back to square one. But do I have the ability to change this entire dream, to cut short the gruesome narrative so that he feels less threatened?

No. I don't. I may not understand all the ins and outs of my Gift yet, but that limitation seems clear. I can't change this dreamscape in any major way—

—but Virilian can.

I need to feed him some cue that will set off a chain of associations in his brain, so that his mind switches gears of its own accord, exchanging this narrative for another. But what kind of cue would work? It has to be something small, for me to be able to conjure it; my power here is sorely limited.

Cold wind gusts across my face, sucking the heat from my skin. Down in the valley it must be even colder. Suddenly I realize what I need to do. Summoning all my strength of will, I focus on the concept of *warmth*. The gust of hot air I create down in the valley is only a small one, but it hits Virilian in the face so hard that it's as if some vast, unseen dragon suddenly vomited fire on him. He looks shocked, and for a minute he doesn't move. He's got two conflicting realities now. Will his dreaming mind try to reconcile them by working the blast of heat into its current narrative, creating a fictional source for it? Or will it switch gears instead and change the setting to one where such warmth might exist? I hold my breath as I pray for the latter.

The bonfire blazes high—so high!—sparks filling the night, heat singing the eyebrows of the warriors who are dancing around it. Their skin is ruddy, their hair long and black, and their bodies decorated with streaks of paint: black, white, red, gold. Some of them have fresh wounds on their bodies, but they show no sign of weakness as they dance around the fire, their feet beating out a pounding rhythm on the earth. The dance is a show of strength.

On the other side of the fire is a cage made of tree limbs bound together, with men packed tightly inside. They're all wearing the clothing of an earlier era: 18th century, perhaps? I can't see their faces clearly through the flames, but I can hear them screaming in fear and rage, a chilling concert. They're pale-skinned, and clearly not of the same race as the dancers.

Where is Virilian in all this?

Suddenly two painted warriors appear, dragging between them a man in a bloodstained shirt. He's shorter than the Norse necromancer was, and his black hair is bound back in a ponytail, but there's no mistaking the fact that this, too, is Virilian. He's badly wounded, and is too weak to offer resistance as the men drag him toward the cage.

Suddenly a tall man with a necklace of animal bones blocks the way. The others stop dragging Virilian and wait.

"You are the one who speaks to spirits?" the tall man asks. He has a thick accent.

Virilian nods.

The tall man signals for his release. I'm relieved that he's safe now, as he's less likely to wake himself up to escape this scenario, but I'm also frustrated. I need a

Virilian who knows about Shadows and Guilds and missing Fleshcrafters, a creature of the modern world. What can I change in the dreamscape to make that version appear? It would have to be a small change; already I'm feeling the strain of past alterations, and I remember what a wreck I was after the Weaver's dream. And this is surely not the last alteration I'm going to have to work tonight.

I decide to create a whisper just behind Virilian's ear. Only three words, barely loud enough for him to hear. Hopefully it won't require too much energy.

*Inspect the Gate.*

He turns around to see who spoke to him, but of course there's no one there. Nor do the words belong in this setting, and his dreaming mind knows that. Suddenly the whole scene around us begins to fragment. I pray that it will give way to something I can use for my purpose.

In the last instant before the dreamscape vanishes, I get a clear view of the men in the cage.

They all have Virilian's face.

We're in the cavern where the Blue Ridge Gate is located, and the arch is intact, though it has no crystals. I can't tell from looking at it if this dream is taking place in the past, before the crystals formed, or after the arch was rebuilt. The whole scene is strangely out of focus, as if I'm looking at multiple versions of the same image layered on top of one another. Only two people are visible — Virilian and a Grey — but the chamber is filled with invisible chatter, voices all around me moaning and weeping and screaming. One is even yelling profanities. The result is deafening, and I put my hands over my ears, but it doesn't help at all; the sounds are in my head. It's a struggle just to think clearly.

Virilian is undead in this dream. That much I can see

clearly, even from behind him. So we're getting close to the time frame I need.

I'm standing in the middle of the chamber, in plain sight, but the two men are talking heatedly and thus far neither has noticed me. I need to find cover before they do. But the closest cave formations are across the chamber, and the few nearby gurneys are covered in sheets whose ends stop short of the ground, making it easy to see under them. I decide the latter is my only viable option, so I dive for the nearest gurney, praying I can duck down behind it before anyone sees me.

But as I move, a sudden wave of dizziness comes over me. I grab for the gurney, then remember at the last minute that it has wheels, and reach out to brace myself against the floor instead. My head is pounding, my mouth feels dry, and the room seems to be swimming around me. Whatever energy I've been drawing on to stay in Virilian's dreams is running out, and the multiple-exposure quality of the current dreamscape isn't helping things. If I collapse in Virilian's dreamscape, will my body disappear, or will he find me lying here, unconscious, still bound by the laws of his mental universe? If he kills me in his dreamscape, will my real body die as well?

The Grey is saying, "We should be operative within the week."

"Excellent." Virilian isn't acting like someone who just escaped a horde of angry ghosts and was beaten bloody by Indians. I wonder if he even remembers those scenes. "And my other request?"

The Grey hesitates. "The Council ordered us not to kill the changelings."

"I haven't asked you to kill them. Simply to encourage Terra Colonna in its natural course. It's an inherently unstable world; encouraging a few key leaders to make ill-advised choices wouldn't even be noticed."

The Grey blinks slowly. "You want Terra Colonna destroyed?"

"I want it to cease to be a problem. If it were to self-destruct, as so many high tech worlds do, that would satisfy my requirements."

There is silence for a moment, at least among the living. Ghosts continue to howl in my ears, but I'm no longer hearing them. Virilian wants my homeworld destroyed. He has the power and the resources to make it happen. And if all he does is hire Greys to tweak the thoughts of key political figures, then no one on Earth— my Earth—will ever suspect the truth.

*It's only a dream,* I remind myself sternly. *This conversation may not have taken place in the real world.*

But Virilian's dream reflects his desires. If he hasn't given such orders yet, he may well do so in the future.

This is the fate he intends for my world.

"You're talking about a lot of Domitor activity," the Grey is saying. "That isn't cheap."

"Do what you need to do and send me the bill," Virilian says coldly. "I'll pay for it out of my own pocket if necessary."

The ghosts should have noticed me by now, I realize. Why haven't they? There are voices coming from all around me, including behind me, so I know I should be visible to some of them. Why haven't they tipped Virilian off about my presence?

*Maybe they have,* I think, *and he just hasn't acted on it yet.*

Then another idea occurs to me. A stunning one: *Maybe they can't see me.*

This dream is Virilian's creation, right? Which means that every person in it is conjured by his mind, every event orchestrated by his unconscious. Nothing exists in this dreamscape that is independent of him, other than me. So if he doesn't know I'm here, maybe his creations can't respond to me.

He's turning to walk out of the chamber now. I need to follow him, or shift the dream to another venue, or . . . something. But I'll have to cross in front of the Grey to do that. Will I be invisible to him, as I seem to be invisible to the ghosts? There's only one way to find out. Heart pounding in fear, I force myself to rise up from behind the gurney. My legs are unsteady, though whether from weakness or trepidation, I don't know. At last I'm standing. The Grey is looking straight in my direction. Virilian's pet ghosts swirl around my head, moaning their endless misery. One second passes. Two.

No one sees me.

No one sees me!

Trembling, I cross right in front of the Grey. He just stands there motionless, like a mechanical doll that has wound down. Virilian is heading toward the tunnel that leads up to Shadowcrest, and as he enters it, the cavern I'm standing in begins to dissolve. I have to keep up with him, even though the tunnel will offer me no cover; if for any reason he turns around, he'll see me. And while he may not recognize me, surely he'll sense that I don't belong in his dream, the same way I did when the avatar girl entered mine. That's more knowledge than I want him to have.

I need to transform this setting into something that will serve my purpose. But my strength is fading, and it's getting hard to focus my thoughts. I don't have many alterations left in me.

Small change. I need a small change.

I try a whisper again. With the voices of the dead already filling this place he'll probably assume that one of them is talking to him, which at least will keep my presence here a secret. I form the words in my mind and hold them there for a minute, pouring my fading mental strength into them; then I release them into the dreams-cape. The whisper manifests right beside his ear, and even though I can't hear it myself, I see Virilian stop short when he hears it, startled.

*Travis Bellefort,* it says. The name of the missing Fleshcrafter.

Suddenly the tunnel is gone. We're in the woods now, in a small clearing with a slender moon overhead. The latter provides just enough light for me to see where the surrounding trees are. Or were. Or will be. Layers and layers of tree-images fill the air, overlapping in mad quantity—young trees, old trees, trees split by lightning and trees hollowed out by birds, all of them occupying the same space. Is this the same multiple-exposure qual-ity of Virilian's dreamscape that I noted in the cavern, only ten times worse? Or is my vision breaking down from the strain of so much dreamwalking?

Virilian's back is to me; I need to get out of sight be-fore he turns my way. I spot a cluster of trees that seems to be holding its shape better than most, and I take shel-ter behind them, flattening myself behind the largest tree in the group, struggling to breathe quietly. For the mo-ment, at least, I'm not visible to the creator of this dream.

"What news?" The Guildmaster demands. His tone is harsh.

The man standing before him is tall, gangly, and has two slender horns growing out of his forehead. I don't need to see the Guild sigil on his ring to guess what his Gift is.

"Bellefort knows," the horned man says.

"You're sure?"

The Potter nods.

"How much?"

"I'm not sure. He started talking to me about a Fleshcrafter who was executed recently in Richmond, for sharing Guild secrets with one of the Seers there.

The message seemed pretty clear. He was warning me against similar indiscretion. Which suggests he has a pretty good idea what's going on."

"You think he knows about our arrangement."

"Given the way he presented his warning, I certainly think he suspects."

"Do you think he would have shared that information with anyone else?"

The Potter hesitates, then shakes his head. "I don't think so. Our Guild is ruthless in matters like this. If anyone else suspected I was spying for you, I doubt I'd be alive to have this conversation."

There is a long silence. The ghostly voices surrounding us have quieted to a murmur, little louder than the chirping of crickets. Finally Virilian says, "You understand what needs to happen."

The horned man shuts his eyes for a moment. "There's no other option?"

"Not if you value your life."

The Potter flinches. "Then at least make it clean," he begs. "Please. For my sake. He's never done anything to harm you or your Guild."

"I have no reason to bind his spirit," Virilian says coldly. "If that's your concern."

"It is," he breathes. "Thank you."

"I'll need someone to take his shape afterward, to establish a false trail. It can't be known that his last act on earth was to meet with me."

"Of course. Of course. Just let me know when and where, I'll take care of it myself."

I've focused so intently on the conversation that it takes me a moment to realize that the color is starting to drain from the Potter's face. His clothes are turning grey as well. I look to the treetops overhead, and see that one by one the dark leaves, barely visible in the moonlight, are losing their color.

Panic grips my heart. I close my eyes and try to re-connect to my sleeping body, to wake myself up, but I can't. Nor can I make my flesh move in its sleep, even a twitch. Which means that I have no way to signal Sebastian that I need help. For as long my body is lying still on that bed, looking peaceful, he'll assume my soul is content.

I'm trapped here.

Clouds are starting to congeal blackly overhead, and something even darker than the night sky is taking shape within them. The spirits of the dead have fallen silent, and the very air is thick with dread. I look around desperately for any sign of the door that brought me here, but of course it's nowhere to be found. I've travelled through three different dreamscapes since arriving: God alone knows if the door even exists in this setting.

Virilian suddenly notices the activity overhead. There's no sign of fear in him, and I get the sense from his confident posture that he knows exactly what is happening. He raises his arms to the heavens and begins to chant. Wisps of golden light appear, circling the mass of clouds, and they join together, first in small geometric patterns then in larger ones. Soon a glowing net has been woven around the place where the reaper is manifesting, a complex web of fine golden lines that is beautiful in form, terrifying in its power.

Suddenly the reaper bursts into reality. Wing-like shapes of pure blackness beat at Virilian's golden web, thrashing wildly as the creature fights to break through, like a bird throwing itself against the bars of a cage. The sky trembles with every blow, and streaks of shadow spasm across the clearing as the creature blocks the moon in its struggles. But for now, at least, Virilian's binding pattern is holding it prisoner. The reaper isn't going anywhere.

The Fleshcrafter is staring at the ghastly display in astonishment and fear. "What the hell is that thing?"

Virilian doesn't answer him. He's studying the reaper, as if trying to figure out exactly what it's doing here. Suddenly I see his body stiffen, and with a sinking in my heart I realize he must have put two and two together. Reapers only appear in dreams, so Virilian knows he must be dreaming. And since there is only one reason for such a creature to manifest, he knows there must be a Dreamwalker nearby. I can sense the enlightenment blossoming within him like a putrid flower, and I realize to my horror that by drawing the reaper to this place, I've revealed to Virilian the very thing I most needed to keep secret.

He knows I'm here.

Frozen in dread, I watch as he lowers his hands; the golden patterns overhead begin to dissolve. "Go," he commands the wraith. "Do what you came to do." Suddenly the web breaks apart and dissolves into the night. The wraith howls in triumph, its voice splitting the night like a thousand nails screeching across a blackboard. The leaves on the trees nearest to it freeze, then shatter; brittle fragments fall to the earth like hail. The moon becomes bleached of its bluish hue, the grass in the clearing is sucked dry of color, and even the Potter's face turns completely grey. Only the Shadowlord remains unchanged—not because he is immune to the wraith's power, but because he is eternally colorless. He and the reaper are soul mates.

The wraith turns toward me then, and I know that it can sense me there, standing in the shadows, as easily as a cat can smell its prey hiding in the grass. Desperately I try once more to cast my mind back to my body, to flee to the safety of the waking world, but I can't make the connection necessary. It's as if my body doesn't even ex-

ist. Sebastian and I had discussed the risks of this journey before I left, but that had been a rational discussion,
performed in a world whose laws we understood and
trusted. Now I'm here, trapped in a madman's dream,
facing a creature out of my worst nightmares, and it's
hard to think clearly, much less remember what we said.
*Run!* an inner voice screams, primitive survival instinct
drowning out rational thought. *Run! Run! Run!* But
running from this thing won't save me. It can move
faster than I can, and even if I managed to outrun it, I'd
still be stuck in Virilian's dream. No, my only hope is to
stand my ground, and so I struggle to do that, even
though the primitive part of my soul is howling in terror,
my whole body shaking as I fight to control it.

I can't run from this thing. I certainly can't fight it.
But there is a third option, that Sebastian and I discussed before I left, and terrifying as it is, I have to try it.
Or so I tell myself as Death incarnate bears down on
me, its vast wings blotting out the moonlight overhead.
The entire world has been drained of color, and my
breath turns to fog as it leaves my lips, crystals of ice
clinging to my eyelashes, blurring my vision. I draw my
knife, bracing myself for the creature's attack. I doubt I
can hurt it, but that's not my goal.

I need it to hurt me.

Darkness engulfs me, and with it a cold so intense
that it fills my lungs with ice, turning every breath to agony. I stab wildly at the creature, trying to drive it away
from my lower body, so that it will strike me where I
need it to. It clawed me once in the past, so it must have
some kind of physical substance. But there is nothing
there—no flesh to slice, no body to bleed. Only Death.
Still I keep stabbing at it, my blade angled low, thrusting
out again and again and again. Maybe the sheer energy
of my assault will convince it to strike a higher target,

either my arms or my face . . . the only parts of my body that are not clothed in the waking world.

When the blow comes it is not the swipe of talon or claw like I expected, but from a whiplash of pure cold. It cuts across my face like a razor, and blood spurts out in a rain of scarlet crystal. Terror fills my heart, but also elation. Because right now, in that other world, the flesh that I can't see or control is suffering the same wound, and Sebastian will see that. He will know by the gash across my face that I need to wake up, and he will do what is necessary to make that happen.

It's my only hope of escape.

*Jesse!*

I can hear his voice now. The reaper is striking out at me again, but I focus on Sebastian's voice, using it as a lifeline, as I struggle to reconnect to the waking world. All I need is one moment of awareness, and I'm out of here. But bands of cold are whipping around my body, and wherever they make contact my flesh freezes, leaving behind strips of ice that encase me like mummy wrappings. The vitality is being sucked out of my soul, and my very thoughts are freezing inside my head. I can't connect to my sleeping body yet, but I have to keep trying. I bet my survival on this one crazy gambit, and if it fails now, I'm doomed.

*Jesse!*

Images begin to flash before my eyes, my brain bleeding out memories as the reaper begins to feast on my soul.

—*the thing we're looking for isn't here*—

—*go over there and kiss, you two*—

—*you're not Guild, are you?*—

Then water engulfs me, and suddenly I can't breathe. Icy liquid is filling my lungs, and I'm drowning, and I'm coughing, and all the memories are gone, and I'm trying to scream for help but I can't get any air into my lungs. Suddenly I can sense my body in the distance, and I reach out to it with my mind, clinging to it so I can shake off this nightmare and escape—

And then I see the changing castle.

It flashes before me as a memory, but it isn't a memory—not my memory, anyway. I never saw it with those turrets, those windows, those pennants flying. Nor did the boy in the Weavers' compound, whose visions I shared, see it that way. Nevertheless, I recognize it. And the shock of having it appear here, now, is so great that for a moment the precious lifeline of Sebastian's voice slips from my grasp. Or perhaps I choose to let go of it, to grasp at knowledge that is even more precious.

It's the reaper's memory.

I can sense the shattered remnants of emotions long forgotten, fragments of an ancient life now dust. I look in the windows of the dream-tower and see images changing there, and I know that the reaper devouring my soul was once in that place, and it understood what those images meant. And I know that it did not come as an invader, or as a destroyer, but as one who belonged there. One for whom that place was built. I see the castle standing in the sunlight—first a red sun, then a golden one, colors flickering across its facade as changing hues swirl overhead—and the reaper's memories are not dark or fearful, but they are buried beneath so much hate and pain I can hardly stand to share them.

*Jesse!*

How desperately I want to drink in more of this creature's knowledge! I may never have such an opportunity again. But I can feel my bodily organs starting to fail as the life is drained from them, and I know that if my flesh expires in this world I will die in that other one as well. So I force myself to turn away from the landscape of light and wonder, focusing once more on my sleeping body, centering my awareness on the voice that is calling me home—

\*        \*        \*

Pain came first, and with it the awareness that my body was soaking wet, my right cheek burning with pain. Then the sickness hit, wave after wave of it, and I could do little more than gasp for breath between bouts of vomiting. Sebastian held my hair out of the way like a father whose wayward child had got drunk for the first time. Then the convulsions started, and he took me by the shoulders and held me steady until they subsided.

Finally I lay back gasping on the bed, and he went to fetch some towels from the bathroom. I saw a pitcher lying by my side, and realized that he must have dumped its contents onto me to shock me awake. That must have been what all the drowning imagery was about.

He came back with a towel soaked in warm water and handed it to me. I draped it across my eyes for a moment, drinking in its delicious heat, then started to wipe the mixture of tears, blood, and vomit from my face. In my mind's eye I could see the changing castle, and it rotated like a 3-D computer image, its shape shifting as I studied it. Dreamwalkers knew about this place. The avatar girl had sought refuge there. And now it appeared that a reaper had once been welcome there.

The implications of that were staggering.

"Did you get what you need?" he asked.

Startled, I let the vision fade. It took me a moment to remember what the original purpose of my dream journey had been. Yes, I'd invaded the mind of a powerful Shadowlord, and I'd tricked him into dreaming about his secrets without revealing my true identity. The fine details of that dream might have been fictional, but the seeds of truth were surely in it. And I was confident I knew how to interpret them.

"I have it," I whispered.

Had the reaper been a Dreamwalker once? It was a mind-blowing concept, but not an impossible one. Supposedly our Gift turned its users into creatures of nightmare, driving them mad in the process. The reaper I'd seen could certainly fit that description. Did that mean I was fated to turn into the same kind of creature, a specter of Death who haunted the dreams of innocents? That would certainly explain why people had been so anxious to kill all the Dreamwalkers. No grand economic theories were required.

*The Shadows had a hand in this*, I reminded myself. *Whatever that creature was, it was not wholly natural.*

Perhaps the thought should have brought me some comfort.

But it didn't.

# 25

**W**E WERE MET AT THE ENTRANCE of the Potter's enclave by twin boys. They were slender and pretty,
with eyes of a shockingly bright violet, and skin so pale
you could see their veins through it. They also had long,
thin horns sprouting from their foreheads, which swept
back over their heads in graceful arcs, circling down and
around to end right in front of their ears. Like a ram's
horns, only more delicate. They were strangely beautiful
things, delicately spiraled with shades of brown and
black and a touch of purple, paler at the base and shad-
ing gradually to dark, almost-black tips.

I wondered if they used them to butt heads during
mating season.

The twins indicated that we should proceed to the
main building. I leaned on Sebastian's arm as we walked,
trying to look more steady than I felt. It was a long hike,

and I wasn't in great shape. If I could afford the luxury of spending a week in bed, that's where I'd be right now.

"It's all right to stare," he told me as we walked. "In this place, it's considered a compliment."

"Then why do they live out in the middle of nowhere?" I looked at the high wall surrounding the estate and the woods that were visible just beyond it; this wasn't the kind of place you chose to live if you wanted people to notice you. "All those twins would have to do is walk down Main Street and they could be stared at to their hearts' content."

"But as curiosities, not artists. Those who like to experiment with self-modification prefer the company of their own kind. And perhaps a few trusted associates." He pushed a hanging branch out of the way. "It's rare that any outsider is allowed to see them. You should regard our invitation here as an honor."

Maybe it was, but I was still too drained from my dreamwalking—and too spiritually sick from the revelation that followed it—to take pleasure in anything. At one point I became so dizzy that we had to pause for a moment, until I could get my bearings again. Was it too soon for me to be up and about? Should I have waited until I had my full strength back—and my spirit—before trekking through the woods to visit shapechangers? Maybe so, but Seyer had told my friends and family on Terra Colonna that we would be back in a week, and that time was almost up. If I didn't return home soon, my aunt and uncle would likely call out the National Guard to look for me. I had no time for a leisurely recovery. Or a leisurely anything.

Was I confident that the news I was bringing to the Potters was correct? Hell, no. And the closer we got to the Potter's headquarters, the more aware I was that all I had to go on was a madman's dream. There was no guarantee that any of its details reflected reality, or that the people and events Virilian had woven into his narrative could rightfully be implicated in Travis Bellefort's disappearance.

But it wasn't the details of the dream that mattered; it was the emotions behind it. Years of interpreting my own dreams had taught me that the mind was a free-association machine that would frequently substitute one person or object for another, so that a nightmare about your dog being hit by a car might really mean that you were worried about your best friend moving away, or filled with guilt over hurting someone. What linked dream and reality together was the emotional charge they had in common. Interpret that correctly, and you could glimpse a dream's true meaning.

Travis Bellefort had discovered something he wasn't supposed to, involving another member of his Guild. Virilian had killed him because of it. That much was likely to be true. Of course, if I turned out to be wrong, and the scene I'd witnessed was simply a meaningless fantasy—or represented something other than what I thought—I was about to bear false witness to one of the most powerful men in the region, accusing an innocent Potter of treachery. That wasn't likely to end well.

*Sebastian wouldn't be here if he doubted me,* I told myself. *He's too much of a survivor to put himself at risk like that.*

The building that the ram-twins had directed us to was large and ornate, with stylized human and semi-human figures carved into its stone face. As we approached, I saw that the pillars flanking the main door were made up of sculpted figures—human and animal—intricately twisted together. You couldn't tell where one creature began or ended. A slender man with green skin and pointed ears greeted us at the door, and despite Sebastian's reassurance about staring, my childhood training took over, and I did my best to look away as he opened the door for us. The woman who greeted us inside had long peacock feathers trailing behind her, and though at first I thought they were attached to the train of her gown, I could see when she stepped in front of us that they jutted out from the base of her spine. Since she didn't have eyes in the back of her head—that I was aware of—I stared at the feathers swaying behind her with unabashed curiosity. Childhood etiquette be damned.

She ushered us into a large room with golden walls and crystalline chandeliers. It was filled with such a variety of quasi-human creatures that it was hard to know where to look first. I saw a woman with the skin of a crocodile, another with the whiskers and patterned fur of a great cat, and a man with a Medusa-like crown of snakes coiling and uncoiling around his head. There was even a small girl with bat-like wings jutting from her shoulders, the delicate membranes rippling with rainbow colors like oil in the rain. Clothing seemed to be optional here, but eating was not; a vast buffet table stretched the length of one wall, with dishes and bowls and pitchers full of decadent foodstuffs covering every inch of it. Nearly everyone in the room had some kind of dessert item in hand, which they nibbled as they turned to watch us progress down the center of the room. The air was filled with the heady scents of honey and chocolate.

At the far end of the chamber was a large ornate chair, and the figure sitting in it looked more like a Hindu god than a mortal man. His slender body was the color of burnished gold, and each of his six arms rested on a different part of his throne. There were half a dozen people gathered around him, of various shapes and colors, including a naked woman covered in iridescent blue scales. She had a bright scarlet tongue that flicked in and out of her mouth as she watched us approach.

If staring was regarded as a compliment here, then they must have been very pleased by my reaction.

"Well. Green Man." The god-figure nodded to Sebastian. "I hardly expected you back so soon. Does this mean you have information for me?"

"I do, your Grace. But the nature of it would be better suited to a private recitation." He glanced back at the room full of Potters, most of whom were now watching us.

The golden figure looked at him curiously for a moment, then nodded. "Leave us," he commanded loudly. A sweeping gesture of one of his middle arms directed everyone in the room to obey. "All of you. Leave us alone."

Most of them filed out, some Fleshcrafters grabbing a last helping of bonbons or truffles. The ones crowding around the throne seemed reluctant to leave their master's side, but he waved them off as well, until finally only three of his people remained: the woman with the blue scales and two dragon-faced men in matching uniforms. The latter looked like bodyguards and were clearly wary of leaving him alone with outsiders, but the golden Fleshcrafter waved off their concerns. "All is good. You can go." The woman with the scarlet tongue remained by his side.

As the doors shut behind the guards, Sebastian nudged me forward. "Your Grace, permit me to introduce Miss Jennifer Dolan, of Terra Colonna." We'd decided to use the alias that was on my Terra Prime passport. "She has uncovered information pertinent to the matter we discussed." To me he said, "You stand before Master Tristan Alexander, regional Guildmaster of the Fleshcrafters."

The mundane name seemed an odd match to such an exotic creature. "I'm honored to meet you, Your Grace."

I wasn't sure if I should bow or curtsy, so I wound up doing something midway between the two, hoping it didn't look as awkward as it felt.

"I'm pleased to meet anyone who has information for me," the Guildmaster said. He leaned back in his throne. "Tell me what you've discovered."

Sebastian and I had discussed what I should say—and, more importantly, not say—so that I would not have to reveal the source of my information. I chose my words with care. "What I bring you comes from the conversation of two ranking Shadowlords, when they thought they were unobserved. Travis Bellefort was killed by a member of their Guild. Apparently he had discovered that another Fleshcrafter was reporting all your business to the Shadows, and they murdered Bellefort to protect their informant."

For several long seconds there was silence. The golden expression was impossible to read. "Do you know the identity of this informant?" he said at last.

I'd made a sketch of the Potter in Virilian's dream; I took it out now and offered it to him. "I don't know his name, but he was described by the same source who gave me this information. He said this was an accurate portrait." It all sounded suspiciously vague to me, but Sebastian said that everyone would expect me to protect my sources thus.

Alexander unfolded the drawing and studied it. Scowling, he showed it to the blue woman. "This is a serious accusation. How sure are you of your facts?"

Sebastian interjected, "I'll speak for the quality of her sources, your Grace. That said, any report based on hearsay should be verified before it's acted upon."

"That goes without saying." The Guildmaster looked at the blue woman. "Go get the Domitor who worked with us during the Landres affair. Make sure he knows this job is off the books." As she left his side and headed toward the exit, the Guildmaster turned to me again. "Was it a clean death?" he asked.

Sebastian had warned me to expect that question. "They made no attempt to bind his spirit, sir. It seems they just wanted to silence him."

"Good," he murmured, clearly relieved. It was a chilling reminder that I was now in a world where death was not the worst fate a man could suffer.

Sebastian took out the items that I had used to connect to Virilian and placed them on a small table beside the throne. "I thank you for these. They were most helpful."

He nodded. "You've done well, Green Man. Clearly your reputation is not exaggerated. Assuming this information checks out, you've more than earned your reward."

I must have bridled visibly, because Sebastian put a warning hand on my shoulder. "With respect, sir, that should go to the one who was responsible for gathering the information."

A golden eyebrow arched upward. "Indeed?" He looked at me. "Well, Miss Drake. What payment would you like for your services?"

Hearing those words at last, after all I had gone through to get to this point, was nigh on overwhelming. For a moment I couldn't speak. "A member of my family suffered brain damage in an accident, your Grace. I've been told that Healers can't help her, because neurons have to be replaced, but that maybe a Potter could. I don't understand all the technicalities of how that would work, but if one of your people could try, I'd be very grateful."

His eyes narrowed slightly. "That's a small price to ask, given the value of what you just delivered."

Sebastian said quietly, "The work would have to be done on Terra Colonna."

"Ah. Now I understand." He nodded slightly. "We don't like to travel offworld—for reasons that I assume are obvious—but you've done me a considerable service, Miss Drake. Assuming your information is verified, I see no reason why I couldn't assign a Master to such a task."

"Thank you," I whispered. I felt like crying. "Thank you."

"And you." He looked at Sebastian. "Nothing for the man who brought this marvel of investigative talent to me? No finder's fee?"

"To have your favor is sufficient," Sebastian said, bowing his head. He had explained to me some of the ins and outs of Guild negotiation, so I recognized his message for what it was: *I'd rather have you in debt to me.*

"Of course. But surely a small token of favor would be appropriate." He smiled knowingly. "I hear the Hunters are restless these days. Perhaps you would like your scent altered?" When Sebastian didn't respond he offered, "One of my apprentices could do the work."

The value of Guild service was determined by the rank of the person performing it, Sebastian had told me. By specifying an apprentice for his job, Guildmaster was indicating it would be a trivial favor, not sufficient to cancel out the larger debt.

The politics in this place were starting to make my head spin.

"That would be appreciated," Sebastian said graciously. "Thank you."

"Can I get in on that too?" I asked. Maybe I could have asked the question more diplomatically, but if he had a way to keep Hunters from tracking me, it was an opportunity I wasn't going to pass by.

The Guildmaster looked amused. "I see no reason why we can't include that in your payment. That is, assuming that your report checks out. We do need to verify it."

I bowed my head. "Of course, Your Grace."

"We can fix that as well, if you like." He gestured toward the gauze Sebastian had dressed my wound with. I reached up and felt warm wetness where a bit of blood had seeped out.

"Thank you," I said. "I'd like that very much."

Sebastian bowed and urged me to do the same. "Thank you, Your Grace. I look forward to serving you again." With a start, I realized that my first real negotiation with a Guildmaster (as opposed to my scripted sham of a meeting with Morgana) had reached its end. And I had succeeded. I'd wanted to obtain something from this world, and I'd done what was necessary to get it. Without Morgana's help. The sudden realization of that was intoxicating. And my mother was going to be healed! What had seemed an impossible dream a mere week ago was about to become reality. It all seemed unreal.

*Easy,* I warned myself. *Your information has to check out before he'll pay you anything.* But it would check out. Maybe it was just the intoxication of the moment, but I no longer doubted my conclusions. Virilian's true passions had shaped that dream, and a Domitor would confirm its content.

Hordes of hungry sycophants were allowed back into the throne room as we took our leave. I walked out by Sebastian's side, as an equal. That was how the Guildmaster of the Fleshcrafters had treated me. A fellow information broker.

As we walked past the transformed Potters, I stared at a few of them. They smiled at me, pleased by the attention. One of them offered me a truffle as I walked by. I took it from him and bit into it. The creamy chocolate was delicious, but not nearly as sweet as the taste of victory.

*Screw you, Morgana.*

# 26

## LURAY
## VIRGINIA PRIME

### ISAAC

THE WORLD WAS BRIGHT. So bright! Apparently two weeks in Shadowcrest had been enough to dull Isaac's memory of just how colorful the outside universe was. You could get drunk on this much color.

He stayed in the shadows for a while, watching locals go about their business from the entrance of a shuttered store, then finally steeled himself for the inevitable and stepped out into the street. The sheer intensity of the human energy surrounding him was dizzying. Had he felt this overwhelmed two years ago, when he'd left Shadowcrest the first time? Or was he just so exhausted from what he'd been through recently that everything seemed ten times as impactful?

The mark of shame that the Fleshcrafter had etched into his face was livid and unmistakable, a wine-colored streak that ran down the center of his forehead, too perfectly shaped to be natural. Such markings were rare, and Isaac had never seen one before, but apparently everyone in Luray knew what it meant. Crowds parted for him as if he was a plague carrier, and the few people who glanced his way avoided any eye contact. One little girl who clearly didn't know what the mark meant stared at him in frank curiosity, until her mother noticed and jerked her away. As she dragged the girl hurriedly down the street, away from Isaac, he heard her explaining why she should never, *ever* talk to someone whom the Guilds had chosen to shun.

If the mark had a been smaller thing he might have tried to hide it beneath a hat—as far as he knew there was no rule against that—but the bottom of it extended down onto the bridge of his nose, and no hat, bandana, or bandage would cover that. Until the weather was cold enough for him to wear a ski mask, anyone who looked at him would instantly know that his Guild had cast him out and that all civilized folks were encouraged to reject him.

In the sea of color and sound that was Luray, he was a bleak island, lifeless and alone.

*He walks through the Antonin home like a ghost, a throbbing ache where his heart should be. His father has given him an hour to collect his belongings, but what does he own that's worth packing? The mementos he collected during his walkabout period, that he'd stored in the Warrens, were all destroyed in the raid. Anything from before that time would reflect a life he is no longer part of, an identity he no longer has a right to. Better to let it all go.*

*He gathers together some pieces of clothing—the few he has that are not Guild issue—and packs them into a pillowcase. Then he wanders through the house without focus or direction, picking up useful things as he comes across them. He finds a few fetters in his father's office and takes them. Such things have street value, especially in the poorer districts, and he figures that his father owes him.*

*When he returns to his room, his mother is there.*

*How alive she looks! The flush of her cheeks is a painful reminder of how dead everyone else in this place is, how lifeless his world is. Is he supposed to respond to her presence or pretend she isn't here? The moment he was marked as an exile he became a non-entity to his Guild, and all Shadows, minae and majae, are expected to shun him. His father has even sent the servants away so that he won't cross their path while he packs. Apparently a passing glance from a housemaid is more than an exile is worthy of. But now here his mother is, standing in front of him, and he suddenly discovers that he doesn't know how to ignore her. Sorrow wells up inside him, and he can see the same emotion reflected in her eyes. It shames him to inspire such passion in her, when she has spent her whole life trying to resist strong passions.*

*She gestures toward a canvas backpack lying on his bed. "I thought you might need this."*

*He has a sudden urge to run to her, to hug her with all his might, to drink in her living warmth one last time and take fleeting comfort from it . . . but he can't. She's already compromised herself by coming here to his room, and whatever spirits are watching will surely report this scene to his father. He won't make things worse for her.*

*Slowly he walks over to the backpack and looks inside it. Fresh underwear. A hair brush. A black leather toiletries case. Items so mundane they make the moment seem surreal. He's leaving home forever, and this is what she thinks he needs most? "You'll make it," she says quietly, as he fingers the items. He doesn't dare meet her eyes. "I know it doesn't seem that way now, Isaac, but you will."*

*"Will you undergo Communion when I'm gone?" He*

*can't imagine his mother transformed, her eyes black and empty, her skin corpse-cold. But she is an Antonin, raised from birth to seek that terrible half-death. It is inevitable.*

*She sighs. "I told your father when you were born that I would walk among the living for as long as you needed me."*

*He feels tears coming to his eyes, and turns away so she won't see them. Technically there's no longer a need for him to hide his emotions—he's not pretending to be a Shadow any more—but the habit is deeply ingrained. "You shouldn't have come here," he mutters.*

*"I know. But I couldn't let your father's rage be the last thing you saw. Your final memory of us." He hears her come up behind him, and for a moment they both stand still and silent, a stone tableau of misery. "Someday you will understand why this had to happen," she whispers. Her hand touches his shoulder. It's a gentle touch, fleeting, that leaves trails of warmth on his skin even after her fingers are withdrawn. He can hear spirits murmuring in the shadows, probably commenting on the forbidden contact. Will they tell his father that she was here? That she touched him? Must she suffer the wrath of the Guild because she cared enough to say goodbye? "Be careful, my son."*

*He doesn't trust his ability to speak without breaking down, and that would shame them both, so he says nothing.*

*A moment later she is gone.*

It had been hours since his last meal—most of which wound up on the floor of the Guildmaster's audience chamber—and his stomach was starting to groan from hunger. Fingering the few bills in his pocket, he looked around for some place where he could purchase food with minimal human contact. There wasn't a grocery store within sight, but there was a food cart at the end of the street, so he headed toward that. As he got closer to it, the smells of sausage and cooked onions enveloped him, intensifying his hunger tenfold. Surely he would feel better when there was something in his stomach. And maybe then he'd have the energy to figure out what to do next.

He stopped a short distance from the cart and waited until all its customers dispersed before approaching.

The cart owner did not look up.

Isaac kept his eyes respectfully averted as he told the man what he wanted, hoping that would make the conversation less uncomfortable.

The cart owner did not respond.

A tremor of fear coursed through him. While it was customary for a Guild outcast to be shunned in social affairs, he hadn't expected the custom to extend to necessary, life-sustaining services. Was this man really going to refuse to sell him food? He asked once again, in a tone that he hoped would appeal to the man's better nature, and when that didn't work he tried appealing to the man's greed instead, offering to pay three times the normal price for his wares. But nothing worked. As far as the vendor was concerned, Isaac didn't exist.

The ache of hunger in his stomach was growing stronger by the minute. He needed to find a source of food where the need for human interaction was minimal, so that his presence would be tolerated. A place where he could take what he wanted, put his money down, and leave. Like maybe a grocery store?

He had to search for several blocks to find one. When he did, he observed it from the outside for a few minutes, then entered. The people in the store instinctively moved away from him, and whatever aisle he entered soon became empty. He gathered up a few staples as quickly as he could—a loaf of bread, some inexpensive cheese, a piece of fruit—and then headed to the checkout counter. The people there turned their faces away from him, but they didn't leave. That, at least, was hopeful.

But when it came his turn to pay for his food he found that he was a ghost to everyone here as well. The cashier wouldn't acknowledge him. The customer behind him pushed Isaac's items out of the way and put hers in their place. And when he finally gave up and was about to put some money on the counter and walk out, the cashier swept his items into a container for restocking, out of reach. He stared at her for a moment, then walked out in silence.

Numbed by despair, aching with hunger, he began to walk aimlessly, not caring where his feet took him. The prosperous townhouses and shops of the plaza district gradually gave way to more humble dwellings, and then to run-down shanties. He tried to purchase food at several markets, but no one would take his money, and when he tried putting it down on the counter just walking out with his purchases a pair of store clerks blocked his way until he relented, leaving it all behind. Eventually he gave up trying.

After a while he realized that he had instinctively returned to the territory he'd patrolled while living in the Warrens, where he'd scavenged for food to help feed the small underground community. A whisper of confidence came back to him, then. He knew this place. He knew how to survive here.

He chose a shop whose security he knew was lax, a small grocery with stands full of fruit lined up outside the front window. He waited until no one was looking in his direction, then walked past the store. Instinct took over, and he reached out with minimal motion to claim an orange, letting his hand fall casually back to his side so that the fruit was hidden from view. He knew from experience that if he just kept walking casually by, and acted as if nothing was out of place, people wouldn't notice the sleight-of-hand.

But someone did.

A hand grabbed his shoulder from behind, and he was whipped around to face a burly man with rage in his eyes. The orange went flying from Isaac's hand.

"You stay away from my wares," the man growled. "You got that, boy? Stay away from this whole damn block! We don't need your kind of trouble around here." He shoved Isaac into the street, hard enough that he stumbled and almost fell. As he righted himself, a carriage coming down the block suddenly veered in his direction, and he barely got back to the sidewalk in time.

*My skills are just rusty,* he thought. But he knew in his heart that wasn't the reason he'd been caught. In the past he'd been part of a nameless, faceless crew of homeless waifs, whose petty thefts were an accepted part of life here. Now, with the Guild's mark of shame blazoned across his face, he was conspicuous. People saw him coming. They watched him out of the corner of their eye even while they pretended that he didn't exist. By becoming socially invisible, he had lost the ability to move unseen.

Exhausted, hungry, and thoroughly disheartened, he wandered into a narrow alley filled with trash, and crouched with his back to the wall, his head bowed. What was he supposed to do now? How was he going to survive? Should he start breaking into houses to steal food? Or go into the woods to play hunter-gatherer? Anger welled up inside him, temporarily drowning out the hunger. How could his parents do this to him? Was there really no fate they could have offered him that was better than this, dying of starvation and neglect on the streets of Luray? All he'd done was break a few goddamn rules! Yes, they were important rules, but surely his father could have come up with a more suitable punishment than this.

*I didn't kill anyone,* he thought bitterly. *I didn't destroy Guild property, or sell the Shadows' secrets to an enemy. I just hurt the family pride. That's all. Hurt the goddamned family pride!* He wanted to take his father by his undead shoulders and shake him and scream at him at the top of his lungs, *How could you do this to me?*

Suddenly something touched his arm. Startled, he looked up, and saw an abbie standing over him, a small female with a wrinkled face and deeply hooded eyes. She was holding out an apple.

He didn't move.

She nudged him with the fruit, urging him to accept it. Finally he reached up and took it from her. The scent of it made his stomach lurch in hunger. "Thank you," he whispered, ashamed and grateful. "Thank you."

She nodded and went back to her errands, leaving him alone in the alley.

*Is this what you want for me, father? That I should sink so low that even the abbies pity me? Do you believe that's a just punishment for my offense?*

The flesh of the apple was sweet in his mouth, but the taste of it was bitter.

ıllıllıllıllıll

*"Tell the Domitor about the ritual you witnessed."*

*Confused, Isaac looks up at his father. His forehead still burns from the Fleshcrafter's work, and the Domitor's ministrations have left him disoriented; it's hard for him to think clearly. "Sir? I'm not sure I understand."*

*"You attended a ritual that no outsider should know about." His father gestures toward the Domitor. "Describe it to her."*

*Isaac slowly turns to face the woman who has just altered his brain. Beside her stands Virilian, the Guildmaster of the Shadows, utterly expressionless. A statue of judgment.*

*He draws in a deep breath and begins, "It took place on one of the lower levels of Shadowcrest, a place called—"*

*Nausea wells up inside him suddenly, choking off his voice. It's followed by a wave of pain so intense that he doubles over, then falls to his knees on the stone floor. His flesh feels as if it's being peeled back from his bones, and as he struggles not to cry out in pain, wave after wave of sickness surges through him. Helplessly he vomits, right onto the polished floor of Lord Virilian's audience chamber.*

*Then, suddenly, both the pain and the sickness are gone. Gasping for breath, Isaac wipes his mouth clean with his sleeve. His whole body is shaking.*

*The Domitor says, "Any time he tries to share the secrets of your Guild with outsiders, this will be the result. The harder he tries, the worse it will be."*

*His father looks at Lord Virilian. "Are you satisfied?"*

*The Guildmaster studies the boy for a moment. Trembling, Isaac can do nothing more than wait on his knees for judgment.*

*"Very well," Virilian says at last. "You have my permission to exile him."*

‖‖‖‖‖‖‖‖‖‖

The Warrens were empty of life—of human life, anyway—and filled with a fetid odor that was worse than anything Isaac remembered. Maybe some of the bodies from the raid had been left behind to rot. The place also seemed more cramped than he remembered, but it had been a refuge for him when he needed one the most, and there was dark comfort in returning to it, no matter how bad it smelled.

Oil lamp in hand, he walked through the familiar tunnels, reclaiming his memories. He passed the place where he had first talked to Jessica. She had asked him about the dreaming Gift that day. If he'd understood the significance of her question, would it have changed any of the choices he made after that? Eventually he came to the circular meeting room where everyone had stored their mementos, and he discovered that the Lord Governor's men had gone out of their way to wreck the place, crushing or stealing any items that looked particularly valuable. Nothing that Isaac cared about was still intact, but he picked up a few broken fragments that reminded him of particular people, and put them into his backpack. The children here had accepted him despite his aristo origins, and right now, acceptance seemed the most precious thing in the universe.

The Warrens inhabitants had stored their food in metal containers to keep the rats out, and hidden them in the darkest corners of the labyrinth so sewer workers passing through the area wouldn't find them. If those supplies were still intact they might provide Isaac with enough to keep him going for a while. Or so he hoped. But when he reached the first such cache—a rusty locker tucked underneath a maintenance platform—he discovered to his dismay that the raiders had gotten to it already. Packages of food that he'd helped steal from aboveground were all torn open, cans crushed and split, jars shattered. The rats must have had a field day.

Staring at the mess in utter despair, he felt the sharp bite of hunger in his gut. The food stores in the Warrens had been his last hope. If they all failed him, he had no idea what to do next.

The next two caches he visited were as useless to him as the first. Clearly the Lord Governor's men had wanted to send a message to anyone who survived the raid, that they shouldn't even think about coming back here. And the message had clearly been understood. In all his wandering, Isaac saw no sign of another human presence. The Warrens were like a tomb.

Finally, just as his last fragile strand of hope was about to give way, he found a cache where not everything had been destroyed. Maybe the raiders had gotten tired by the time they found it, so they didn't notice when a few cans rolled under a low-slung utility pipe. Trembling with hunger, Isaac squeezed under the pipe to retrieve them, then searched for something in his collection of household items to cut them open. By the time he finally managed to tear half the lid off a can of baked beans, his mouth was so dry he could barely swallow the contents. The cold beans were clammy and dreadful, but they seemed a veritable feast, more delicious than anything he'd ever tasted. In less than a minute the can was empty.

Leaning back against the pipe in exhaustion, he wiped his mouth with his sleeve. Right now he wanted nothing more than to open all the cans and feast—he wanted it desperately—but this was the last food he might find for a while, and he needed to ration it carefully. He reached for his bag so he could pack the unopened cans for later use—

—and suddenly he was aware of another presence in the tunnel. Maybe it had arrived while he was eating, and he just hadn't noticed it, but there was no mistaking it now. A soft, almost inaudible moaning filled the tunnel, rising and falling in volume like the breath of a dying animal. He didn't think the spirit making the noise was a high-order wraith, but it didn't feel like a mere soul shard, a fractured remnant of a human spirit too far gone to think or act on its own. It had a faint aura of volition about it, and Isaac wondered if it had been drawn to him because of his Gift, as the dead so often were, or if it was here for some other reason.

"Who are you?" he asked hoarsely.

The spirit didn't respond.

Probably he should banish the thing. Only the undead

could afford to let unidentified ghosts hang around them, and the ritual used to banish bothersome spirits was one of the first things an apprentice was taught. But Isaac lacked the energy to perform any rituals right now, and perhaps he also lacked the will. This ghost wasn't hurting him. Who was he to decide where it was or was not allowed to go? Maybe it was seeking refuge here, like he was. God knows, enough people had died down here recently; there was probably more than one spirit bound to this place. If the wraith left him in peace, then he would leave it in peace.

That decided, he leaned back against the pipe and shut his eyes, savoring the feeling of fullness in his belly. He was safer here than he was going to be anywhere else. Maybe he should take a few hours and sleep.

*Free.*

His eyes shot open.

*Free.*

The primitive thought seeped into his brain without words, but its tenor was jarringly familiar. He knew that spirit's voice.

*Free.*

"Jacob?" he asked.

Silence.

The presence felt like Jacob; there was no mistaking that. But the murdered boy had been a high-order spirit, capable of complex conversation, repeatedly trying to communicate with Isaac. It made no sense that he would be here now, further from Shadowcrest than any bound spirit was allowed to travel, and barely capable of voicing a single word.

Then suddenly Isaac realized what must have happened, and for one endless, horrified moment he could do nothing more than stare at the place where the ghost was standing, unable to speak. "No," he whispered at last. Forcing the words out. "Please, please, tell me they didn't do that to you . . ."

The Shadows must have discovered that Jacob had helped Isaac break into the Chamber of Souls. Any wraith who was capable of acting against his Mistress's interests was too dangerous to keep around, so they'd condemned him to final death, performing the ritual that was commonly used to destroy malevolent spirits. Normally that would tear an unwanted soul into so many pieces that not a single sentient fragment remained. But Jacob must have survived it somehow. Maybe it was his link to Isaac that enabled an echo of his identity to cling to the living world while his mind was ripped to pieces. Or maybe the boy had simply been stronger than the Shadowlords gave him credit for. Either way, he had paid a terrible price for his freedom. Even Isaac's apprentice-level Gift could sense that the entity standing in front of him was little more than a hollow shell, his mind so fragmented that he probably didn't even know his own name. The best such a ghost could hope for in the wild was to wander endlessly without language or purpose, driven by emotions he could no longer name, mourning the loss of an identity he no longer remembered. Truly, it was a fate worse than death.

The wraith spoke again, this time more strongly. *Free.*

The ritual must have shattered his binding along with his mind, Isaac realized. Whatever fragment of Jacob Dockhart had survived now owed allegiance to no one. Would the boy have chosen such a fate over eternal slavery, had he been given the choice? What mattered more, one's mind or one's freedom? Just asking the question made Isaac queasy. God willing he would never have to make such a choice himself.

"What a pair we make," he muttered. Though the

spirit was too mentally damaged to offer any meaningful companionship, talking to him made Isaac feel less alone. "Hiding in the sewers with no purpose, no future . . . true soul-mates."

The spirit said nothing.

With a sigh Isaac pulled his backpack toward him and untied the top flap. His scavenged items from the Warrens were on top, along with the things he'd taken from home. He took them out and put them aside. After a moment's consideration he also took his clothes out of the pack and the toiletries case, so that the heavy cans could be placed at the bottom of the bag.

But as he picked up the toiletries case he paused. It was smaller than he'd thought, and flatter. Maybe it wasn't what he had assumed. There was a zipper running around three sides of it, and he opened it carefully, not wanting anything to fall out.

Inside was money.

A lot of money.

Spreading the case open like a wallet revealed a thick stack of bills. He stared at them for a moment in disbelief, then took them out and started counting them. Half the bills were of small denominations, the kind of money one might use to buy small items in a shop, but the other half were larger than that. *Much* larger. All told, there must have been at least a thousand pounds in the case. It was a veritable fortune to someone in his circumstances, though God alone knew where he could spend it.

His mother must have put this in the backpack, but why? Money alone couldn't save him now. Surely she would have realized that. Was this merely a ritual gesture, meant to ease his parents' guilt as they cast Isaac to the wolves? Surely if they really cared about him they would have chosen a different punishment and not sent him away forever.

Tears came to his eyes and he blinked them away, not wanting to break down in front of someone. Even a ghost. As he did so, he noticed there was a photo in the case, tucked into a side pocket. Taking it out, he saw it was a family picture, of him and his mother and father standing in some sunlit place, all smiling. It must have been taken years ago, because his father was alive in the picture, and Isaac was just a child. He no longer had any memory of what his father looked like as a living man, so he stared at the image in fascination, startled to discover how much he resembled him.

"Why would they give me this?" he whispered hoarsely. "They threw me out. They cut all ties between us, forever. Why would they think I even wanted something like this? So that I could pretend I still had a family? So that I could remember what I lost and feel even more pain?" There was a murmur of curiosity from Jacob, so he turned the picture so the ghost could look at it—

—and he saw that something was written on the back of it. In his mother's hand.

Startled, he moved the note closer to the lamp so he could read her message.

*V wanted you killed.*

His hand trembled as he lowered the note.

*What?* the spirit pressed. *What? What? What?*

Why had Virilian wanted him dead? Because Isaac had broken the rules one too many times? Because he'd corrupted a spirit belonging to a powerful Shadowlord? Or maybe Virilian suspected that Isaac had played a part in the destruction of the Gate. Whatever the reason, if the Guildmaster condemned Isaac to death, no one in the Guild would dare challenge him. Isaac's fate would be sealed.

His father must have protested that judgment. No one of lesser status would have the standing—or motivation—to pull off something like that. Isaac tried to remember what Virilian had said to his father, when the Domitor finished her work. *You have my permission to exile him.* He'd thought at the time that his father wanted to get rid of him, but what if that wasn't the story at all? What if the Antonin patriarch had asked for permission to send Isaac away as an alternative to Virilian killing him? In order to save his son's life?

The Guildmaster would never have allowed that unless the pain of Isaac's banishment was so extreme that the boy would wish for death. Agreeing to anything less might have been viewed as an act of mercy, and a Guildmaster of Shadows was not supposed to be merciful.

"That's what this was all about," Isaac whispered, staring at his mother's note. "The lifetime banishment, the mark of shame . . . he was trying to be harsh enough that Virilian would agree to spare my life. That's what my mother was hinting at when she came to my room. She couldn't tell me outright, not with all the dead watching."

Tears were flowing down his face, and he couldn't stop them. He didn't want to stop them. The dam inside had finally crumbled and emotions were pouring out, all the feelings he'd been struggling to deny since leaving home. Pain, fear, hopelessness, despair . . . but no anger. Not anymore. Shadowlord Antonin had dared to challenge the Guildmaster himself to give his son a chance to survive. Even though the odds of that survival were slim to none. And even though it meant the Shadowlord would never see his son again. Because the alternative to that was death by Virilian's order.

Lowering his face into his hands, Isaac wept.

# 27

## BERKELEY SPRINGS
## WEST VIRGINIA

### JESSE

**H**OME. The word felt strange on my tongue, especially in reference to a house I had only lived in for a week. But it was good to be heading back in Berkeley Springs. The people that I loved were there, and I hungered to rejoin them.

Seyer offered to drive us home, and despite my desire to separate myself from everyone and everything connected to Alia Morgana, I did need a way back from Pennsylvania, so I accepted. So did Rita. I would be relieved when we finally parted company; the stress of feigning friendship with her was wearing thin. But the day might yet come when I would need someone with access to Morgana's circle—besides Seyer—so I did the best I could to make her believe that nothing was wrong, even while I fantasized about wringing her neck.

As soon as we got in the car I retrieved my cell phone

and started texting, first to let Tommy know we were on our way home, then to check up on Devon. Apparently he had recovered from his strange bout of illness. No big surprise, if its sole purpose had been to keep him from travelling with us. Rita was in the seat right behind me as I texted him, so I had to be careful what I typed, but I did manage to send a quick warning while she was looking out the window. *Rita was the spy. Details later.* I wanted to tell him what I suspected about the source of his illness, including the fact that Rita might have played a part in arranging it, but this wasn't the time or place for that discussion.

*Is she with u?* he texted.

*Yeah.*

*Still friends?*

Was he asking if I had decided to overlook the spy issue, or if I was pretending everything was okay? I waited until Rita looked out the window again, then texted, *She thinks so.*

*What about ur mom?*

*Healer coming,* I typed. *Family only. No friends allowed.* We hadn't discussed his coming back to witness the healing, but some things don't have to be said. *Potter rules,* I added. *Sorry, I tried.*

There was a long pause. *I understand.*

*Their call, not mine.*

*Keep me updated?*

*K*

As soon as Seyer pulled into the driveway, Tommy burst out of the house and bounded down the front stairs, yelling my name as if he'd never expected to see me alive again. When I got out of the car he hugged me so tightly that he squeezed all the air out of my lungs. For a long moment I just hugged him back, drinking in the essence of Terra Colonna through our contact. Then I saw Mom on the porch, and this time it was me who did the running. I hugged her like the world was about to end, and since she had no clue what I'd gone through the previous week, she was probably a bit confused by that. I buried my face in her hair so no one would see my face, knowing I could never explain to these people why coming home affected me so deeply. Not until I felt I had control of myself again did I let her go.

Seyer watched our reunion for a few minutes, then said she needed to leave. "It was a pleasure to have you as a guest," she told me, with a faint ironic smile. "If you ever want to visit again, you know how to reach me." I nodded politely and thanked her for the offer, and didn't tell her what I was really thinking, a scenario that involved flying pigs and snowballs in Hell. Then Rita said that she should probably check in with people back home, would Seyer mind giving her a lift to the bus station? And so that final problem was solved.

It was surprisingly hard to say goodbye to Rita. For all my anger about her betrayal, she'd been by my side through some pretty harrowing experiences, and that made for a bond that even rage couldn't banish entirely.

"Good luck with your mom," she whispered. Then she got into Seyer's car, and I watched as it pulled away, feeling a vast weight lift from my chest.

Of course Rose had to feed us all, and over a hearty lunch she made me tell her all sorts of stories about my imaginary week in the mountains. It was hard to make up enough stories to satisfy her, but eventually I was able to turn the conversation to my real business. I said that Seyer had introduced us to a healer who might be able to help Mom, and would they be willing to give that a try? I knew that Rose and Julian were New Age folks at heart, and the Fleshcrafter had coached me on how to present the matter to them. So when I explained that this was a New Age healer specializing in reiki massage, who thought that restoring the proper flow of qi to

Mom's brain might clear out some of her spiritual blockage, I was speaking their language. In truth I think they would have supported any activity that gave Mom a taste of hope, if only for an hour. As for Mom, she wasn't into that kind of stuff, but if everyone else thought this was a good idea, she was willing to give it a shot. What did we have to lose?

After lunch I was finally able to get some time alone with Tommy. I filled him in on what I'd *really* been up to the last week, which was damn refreshing after hours of lies. He listened with wide eyes, surprisingly subdued. "Wow," he said when I was done. "That's just . . . wow."

I sighed. It felt good to unburden myself to someone I trusted, but retelling the story just reminded me of how many things in my life still weren't resolved. Some of which involved people who wanted to kill me. "Yeah. I know."

"They're never gonna let up, are they? Not as long as they think there's a Dreamwalker out there. They may not know it's you, but they're gonna keep looking till they figure it out."

I remembered Virilian's reaction when the reaper appeared in his dream, and I could only imagine his rage once he realized that a Dreamwalker had been messing with his mind. "Yeah," I muttered. "I'm afraid so." Thank God I'd thought to disguise myself in that dream. It wouldn't protect me forever, but hopefully it would buy me time to come up with some kind of plan.

"So," Tommy said, "what can we do about that? I mean . . . there has to be *something* we can do, right?"

I sighed. *Real life isn't like a computer game,* I wanted to tell him. *There's no finite, predictable universe filled with puzzles that have neatly scripted solutions, where all you need to do to defeat a powerful enemy is to assemble the right team and arm them with magical weapons. Real life is messy, and it doesn't always have neat solutions.* "If

I could find other Dreamwalkers, they might be able to help. Maybe they would know how to destroy the reapers." But the only other Dreamwalker I knew about had spent her last moments casting a tsunami at me, and I didn't know if she was alive or dead right now. Even if others of my kind existed, how was I supposed to find them, when their lives depended on hiding their Gift?

The dream tower was the key, I thought. The coma boy had seen it. The avatar girl had run to it for safety. Even the reaper had been there at some point. The tower tied all of us together somehow, and maybe I could use it to find others of my kind. But how did you search for something that, by its very nature, did not exist in the real world? If I searched for it in my dreams I could wind up with all seven reapers coming after me.

It was too much to think about. I closed my eyes for a moment, sighing deeply.

"You okay, Jess?"

"Just tired," I muttered. "It's been one hell of a week."

Was it only a month ago that I'd been struggling to deal with normal teenage angst? Final exam stress, family issues, concern over finding a part-time job for the summer so that I could afford a car next year? It had seemed like so much to deal with, back then. Overwhelming. That was the one upside about being hunted by monsters, I thought dryly. It really put things in perspective.

"Hand me the phone," I told Tommy. "I'll tell the Fleshcrafter we're good to go."

॥॥॥॥॥॥॥॥

The Potter arrived at eight o'clock sharp. Whatever I'd expected our assigned Fleshcrafter to look like, the stocky, ruddy-cheeked senior citizen who showed up at our front door was not it. But apparently Selena Hearst was the perfect person to win my family's trust, and soon Rose was setting out tea for us all and asking about Eastern massage techniques. The Fleshcrafter was surprisingly patient and showed us a collection of river rocks that she used in her work. She said she'd collected them from spiritually significant waterways. Would Rose mind warming them in the oven a bit? They worked better that way. Oh, and Selena would like to brew a special herbal tea for my mother, would it be possible to get some hot water for that? I wasn't sure how much of her performance was real and how much was just cover for her real business, but I suspected it was strongly weighted toward the latter.

Finally we all retired to a back room with Mom, where a table had been laid out with a camping mattress on top of it. I'd asked Rose to get us a couple of boxes of donuts, as per the Potter's request, and they were waiting on the sideboard, their lids folded neatly back. The room smelled of confectioner's sugar.

The Fleshcrafter had Mom drink the tea and then lie down, and she made a show of arranging the newly warmed river stones around her in a pattern designed to channel her vital energies. Or so she explained to Rose and Julian as they watched. Soon Mom's eyes shut, and it looked like she'd fallen asleep. Selena requested politely that everyone but the children leave, as too many people in the room would make it hard for her to channel Mom's qi properly. My aunt and uncle didn't want to go, but clearly they respected Selena's expertise. Soon the four of us were alone.

As Selena reached for a donut I noticed a change in her body language. Gone was the aura of homey warmth that had so charmed my family, and in its place was a sharp and sparing manner, totally at odds with her physical appearance. I must have been staring at her, because when she finished her first donut she looked over at me and said, "No, I'm not really old. Not female, either. That simply seemed like the most effective way to deal with your family."

"It was," I agreed. I looked at Mom. "What did you give her?"

"Something to shut down non-essential mental activity. I can no more fleshcraft an active brain than a surgeon can operate on a moving body. Not safely, anyway."

She (he?) took another donut. "You understand, my goal here is to restore the neural network as it existed before the fire. Any cells which died left their mark on the surrounding tissue, so there are ingrained patterns for reference. I can prompt the body to create new cells exactly where the old ones were." She started inspecting Mom with her free hand as she talked, touching her gently at various points on her face and skull. "Neurotransmitters, on the other hand, are temporary in nature, reabsorbed after every use. I can't judge how effectively they functioned before the fire, so I can't adjust their strength now. The brain will do that naturally once the neural network is restored, seeking its original balance, but that will take time. You should expect a period of confusion, with intense and possibly disturbing dreams. None of which will have any medical significance, save as a sign that she is healing."

*Yeah, but it'll be hell to explain to my family, after I gave them a song and dance about how you would make Mom feel better.* "For how long?" I asked.

"She seems highly functional, which suggests that repairs will be minimal; I'd be optimistic about the time. A week, perhaps." She looked up at me. "We're in the primary Terran Cluster, correct? Only one moon?"

"Uh . . . yeah. One moon."

She nodded. "One month at most, then. If disorientation lasts longer than that, contact me."

"Will there be any pain?" Tommy asked.

"Usually there is. The human body doesn't surrender its birth-form without protest. But since brain tissue has no pain receptors, your mother should be fine."

She finished off the donut and waved us to silence. "No more questions now. I need to concentrate."

Tommy and I watched her fleshcraft. Or more accurately, we stared at a man in an old woman's body while she leaned over our sleeping mother and nothing visible happened. The Potter spread her fingers over Mom's face and skull, lowered her (his?) head until their foreheads nearly touched, then closed her eyes and seemed to go into a trance. Periodically she would awaken from it long enough to get another donut, study Mom as she ate it, then return to her trance. Eight donuts in all. It was a long time to wait for something to happen. At one point I saw Tommy take out his phone and text somebody. Later I took paper from the nearby desk and started sketching the shapechanging castle that I'd seen through the reaper, angling my work so that even if the Potter looked in my direction she wouldn't see it. But the building defied my best attempts to capture it on paper; it was as if it existed only in the world of imagination and couldn't be translated into materials as mundane as pencil and paper. After several tries I gave up, closed the drawing pad, and waited in silence.

Finally the Potter drew back from the table. My mother was beginning to stir now, moving her head from side to side, whispering things that didn't sound like English. I felt a knot form in my stomach. What if this process skewed her brain so badly that she appeared even sicker than before? My aunt and uncle would take her to a hospital for testing, and God alone knew what would come of that. Would tests of her newly restored brain match the ones from before this operation? What would the doctors make of it if they didn't?

Suddenly her eyes opened. I held my breath as she stared at the ceiling for several seconds, then slowly looked around the room. Her eyes were wide. "The colors . . ." she whispered. "So different."

The Potter helped her to a sitting position on the table. Mom seemed very weak, but that might just have been from the drugged tea. "Tell me what you see."

"The colors . . . look brighter. Everything. Brighter. Like I'd been seeing the world through a grey veil before, but didn't know it. Now suddenly it's gone." She laughed softly, a sound of wonder and delight. "My God, I don't know the right words to describe it."

"I understand what you mean," the Potter said softy.

Mom turned to me then, and I went to her and held her, and this time I let the tears come. So did Tommy, I think. He hid his face so we wouldn't see them, but I saw his shoulders tremble.

Finally we disentangled from the three-way hug. Mom looked at the Potter. "Thank you," she whispered. "Whatever you did, it feels like something is better. Thank you so much."

The elderly female face smiled sweetly. "I'm glad to be able to help."

Mom slid her feet down to the floor, tested her weight on them, then pushed herself away from the table. "Even the pressure on my feet feels different," she whispered. "More . . . more detailed."

"The spiritual channels within you are fully open," the Potter said, in her best New Age voice. "Your qi is flowing freely again, and all your senses are coming back to life. It's part of the natural healing process."

Mom looked around the room. "Where are Rose and Julian?"

"In the kitchen, I believe. I asked them to give us privacy. They've been most patient."

Tears glimmering in her eyes, Mom hugged us both

again, then headed off to find the rest of the family. We watched as she walked down the hall, staring at every piece of furniture she passed as though seeing its color for the first time. Soon she was out of sight.

"Was that a normal response?" Tommy whispered.

"Not uncommon. It's a good sign." The Potter looked at her watch, then at me. "We'll give your family some time to absorb the news and express their gratitude, then you and I should retire to somewhere more private for your own alteration. You won't want to be seen right afterward."

I had been so focused on Mom, it took me a moment to realize what she was referring to: my own scent change. "We can use my room," I said. I felt a bit queasy that someone was about to reshape my body, no matter how minimal that change might be.

A few minutes later Rose and Julian and Mom jöined us, and the atmosphere was downright festive. Everyone told the Potter how grateful they were for her help, and Julian tried to offer her payment for her services, but she refused, saying that she'd done it as a favor to Miriam Seyer, not to worry about it. So Rose said that if there was ever anything they could do for her, ever, she had but to ask, and Mom said that went double for her. The Potter accepted their gratitude in a friendly old-woman way, and once more I was struck by the ease with which she switched roles depending on circumstances. Finally she said that Tommy and I had asked about her crystal work, and if it was okay with everyone she'd like to go off with us and teach us some things about the energies of semi-precious stones. And of course it was okay, though Rose did make me promise to share the information with her later.

There was a tremor of fear in my stomach as we headed up the stairs to my room, adult laughter fading behind us. But you gotta do what you gotta do.

||||||||||||

My transformation hurt. A lot. When it was finally done I felt like I'd spent a day on the beach without sunblock, then rubbed sandpaper into my skin until it was raw, then taken a bath in lemon juice. And I looked like a boiled lobster.

But if this was what it took to get my body to exude a new cocktail of oils and gasses, so that my scent was no longer recognizable to the Hunters who'd smelled me in the past, it was worth every minute of the five-donut operation.

Tommy perched by my side during all of it, clearly wanting to be helpful but not knowing how. At one point when I was struggling not to cry out in pain he reminded me of the *Mythbusters* episode where they demonstrated that yelling profanities improved pain tolerance. The information didn't do me much good—I couldn't yell anything without my whole family bursting in to see what was wrong—but it got the Potter's attention, and when she was done turning me into a lobster she asked Tommy to describe the experiment in detail. Apparently no one on Terra Prime had ever thought to ask whether screaming "oh, fuck!" at the top of your lungs would really make something hurt less. Maybe you needed an American mindset to come up with that.

The look on Tommy's face during that conversation was something to see. For a few precious minutes he wasn't a little kid, or a silent spectator, or even an ignorant Colonnan. He had knowledge that this powerful alien Fleshcrafter wanted, and she respected him for it. By the end of the conversation he was glowing so brightly from pride that you could have used him to light a room.

I understood just how he felt.

The Potter remained with us until the worst of my

pain had faded then declared the operation a success. As she packed up her crystals and river stones, she told me my unnatural redness should fade within the hour, and recommended I avoid the rest of the family until I looked more normal. She also told me to wash all my clothing and my bedding, and throw out any garments that weren't washable, as they still had my old scent on them. I hadn't thought about that.

I could travel on Terra Prime now, I realized—or any world—and the Hunters who'd tracked me before wouldn't recognize my scent trail. That was a heady concept. The Potter gave me a card with her contact information on it, and told me to get in touch with her if I had any concerns about her work. The name on the card was *Reginald Harrington III, Master of the Guild of Potters,* and the contact point was an office of the Guild of Greys. My hand trembled slightly as I noted that. Yeah, I understood that interworld mail deliveries normally went through the Greys, but servants of the Shadows were the last people I wanted to have knowledge of my business. At least I had the alias that Seyer had given me, so I wouldn't have to give them my real name.

It seemed like all our business was done, but as she turned to leave Tommy suddenly asked her, "What's with the donuts?"

We both turned to look at him—the Potter startled, me aghast.

"You've eaten fourteen of them since you got here," he pressed. "Not like I'm counting or anything. Jesse obviously knew you were going to do that, since she's the one who asked Aunt Rose to get them. So. . . . are you like, hypoglycemic? Or is it something more interesting than that?"

I was glad that my skin was already red so the Potter wouldn't see me blush. "Tommy, please, don't be rude—"

But she seemed more amused than insulted and

waved off my concern. "It's quite all right." To Tommy she said, "Aside from the energy expenditure required by fleshcrafting—which is considerable—our Gift has certain limits. I can force my flesh to take any shape I please, but I can't create flesh where none exists."

"So you can change your body shape, but not your mass."

"Correct."

"So if you wanted to make your body bigger than it is right now, you'd have to put on weight like a normal person first. Right?" His face had taken on the same solemn expression as when he was reviewing a new game system. I guess, to his mind, he was doing just that.

She smiled. "Precisely."

"So how much weight will you have to put on to go back to your regular shape? The male one, I mean."

She looked down at her stocky form and chuckled. "The bodies are roughly commensurate in mass. Deliberately so."

I suddenly remembered how small the Guildmaster's body had been, independent of his extra arms. And many of the Potters in his grand hall had likewise been slender of build. The girl with the wings had been downright tiny. All of that made perfect sense, if a Potter who wanted to create extra appendages had to reassign existing flesh to do so.

Leave it to my little brother to connect that to their chocolate fetish.

Finally Tommy ran out of questions, and the Potter was allowed to leave. With a weary sigh I fell back on the bed, so tired in body and soul that I felt like I was bleeding into the mattress. Which was a good thing. Any sensation other than pain was a good thing.

For a moment I lay there with my eyes closed, enjoying the silence.

The total silence.

Without the sound of footsteps leaving my room.

I cracked open one eye. Tommy was standing by the bed looking down at me. His expression was solemn.

"What's up?" I asked.

He shook his head and made a tsk-tsk noise.

I opened my other eye. "What? Is something wrong? What is it?"

A spark of amusement glittered in his eyes. "You didn't tell me there was a junk food Gift."

I picked up a pillow and threw it at him. It felt good. Normal, even. I was home.

For now.

# 28

SEER GUILDHOUSE IN LURAY
VIRGINIA PRIME

ALIA MORGANA

**M**ORGANA WAS IN HER STUDY when her organizer
chimed, alerting her to an incoming call. Taking out
the appropriate harmonie, she placed it in the holder on
her desk and activated it. The image that took shape before her was of a woman wearing a mask that was half
human and half bestial. Morgana nodded a greeting.
"Well met on a hot summer day, Lady Fleshcrafter."

"I prefer cool summer nights," the woman responded.

Morgana nodded her acceptance of the coded greeting. One could never be too careful with Fleshcrafters,
as any skilled member of that Guild could sculpt his or
her flesh to look like any other. Not to mention the
caller was wearing her consortium mask, which could
transform anyone. An identity check was the first order
of business in any such conversation. "You have news
for me?"

"You told me to let you know if the Colonnan girl showed up."

A delicate eyebrow lifted slightly. "She approached you?"

"She came to barter information with His Grace. She was spoken for by one whose word he valued, so she was granted an audience."

Morgana's eyebrow rose slightly. "The Green Man?"

"Indeed."

*That one is playing a dangerous game,* Morgana mused. *I may need to stage another attack on him soon, to remind him of his duty.* "And the information she offered to His Grace?"

"That's Guild business, and it doesn't pertain to the favor you asked of me so, with respect, I would prefer not to discuss it."

"As you wish." Normally the Fleshcrafter wasn't so evasive, which suggested that the information Jessica brought them had been unusually sensitive. Something Morgana would have to look into. "I trust you were diplomatic in turning her down?"

"On the contrary. His Grace approved her petition. A Master Fleshcrafter has been assigned to help her."

Morgana's eyes narrowed. "I asked you to keep her from closing a deal with your people." There was an edge to her voice now, razor-sharp. "Are you telling me you failed?"

"Alexander may value my counsel, but I can't give him orders. Least of all with no explanation. The girl arranged to fulfill an existing commission, for which he'd already promised payment. If I'd tried to convince him not to honor his own contract, he would surely have questioned my motives. Something that would not be good for either of us." A pause. The sculpted mask was impassive, but something about the eyes made Morgana think she was smiling. "I do believe she outplayed you, Alia."

"Apparently so," Morgana muttered.

"Is that going to be a problem?"

She tapped her fingers on the table, a drumbeat of irritation. "I would have preferred to control the exchange. I prefer to control everything around me, you know that. But if she's strong-willed enough to fight for independence, and clever enough to earn it . . . well, we'll just have to see where that path leads her."

"You have big plans for her."

"That's hardly a secret."

"Is she part of the experiment you've been hinting about?"

"That part *is* a secret." Morgana chuckled softly. "Have patience, Lady Fleshcrafter. All will be revealed in its proper time."

There was nothing more for them to discuss, so the masked Potter took her leave and deactivated the connection. As her image faded, the Seer leaned back in her chair. A cold smile spread across her face.

*Well played, my daughter. Keep this up and you may yet survive what lies ahead of you.*

# EPILOGUE

SHADOWCREST
VIRGINIA PRIME

AUGUSTUS VIRILIAN

**C**ANDLES BURNED ALL ALONG the periphery of the ritual chamber in the Well of Souls, their flames reflected in the polished black stone with such perfection that it was impossible to tell how many there were. Maybe a dozen, maybe a hundred, maybe a thousand. The Shadowlords who filled the room stood silent, and even the ghosts who attended them were unusually still. Tonight's business was somber even by the standards of the undead.

The door to the chamber opened, and the Guildmaster entered followed by a lanky Shadowlord named Caleb Aster. In Aster's hands was a golden box, its surface carved with the images of tormented souls. Reflected candlelight sparked along the edges of the figures as he walked, lending them an illusion of movement.

The Shadowlords gave way before them, forming a

circle three deep around the altar in the center of the room. There were more chains on the altar than usual, and the new ones were padded in leather. Ancient leather, stained with ancient blood. The Guildmaster took up position on the far side of the table, Aster facing him.

"Banish the dead," Virilian commanded.

Whispers filled the room as each Shadowlord present banished the spirits that attended him. Soon only soul shards remained, mindless ghost-fragments that lacked the ability to comprehend such orders. One of the Shadowlords picked up a candle and performed the ritual that would banish those as well, sketching out patterns with the flame. A brief afterimage of each pattern hung in the air for a few seconds before being swallowed by darkness; by the time the last one faded the soul shards were gone.

Virilian parted his robe and let it fall to the ground. Now he wore only a sleeveless linen shirt with ties down the front, and a pair of close-fitting breeches. As a Shadowlord came forward to gather up the robe, Virilian lay down upon the altar, placing his arms and legs into the positions indicated by the waiting shackles. His flesh was as pale as a corpse's, and the indigo blood that coursed visibly just beneath his skin looked more like embalming fluid than a life-giving substance.

Two Shadowlords stepped forward and began to fasten the chains across his body, until every limb was fixed in place, every joint immobilized. The chains were tight, and the leather coverings cut deeply into the pale skin. Movement was all but impossible.

When that was done, Shadowlord Aster took up position by the side of the table. He held the golden box out, over Virilian's heart, presenting it to him. "Augustus Virilian, Master Shadowlord, Guildmaster of Shadows. Do you come here tonight of your own free will?"

"I do," Virilian said.

"Is it your desire to Commune with the soul of a departed Shadowlord?"

"It is."

"Do you acknowledge and accept that if this process fails, the cost will be your true death? That if you cannot make peace with the soul you have chosen to subsume, and all the souls that reside within it, you will not be allowed to leave this chamber alive?"

"I acknowledge and accept it," Virilian said.

"Are you prepared to renounce your worldly ties, human and material, so that there will be nothing to distract you from this union? So that you enter into Communion as an infant enters the world, without title, honor, or obligations?"

"I hereby relinquish my title of Guildmaster and all the duties and honors that go with it. Let the Guild recognize Shadowlord Caleb Aster as its leader, until such time as I am restored to my rank by his word."

A second Shadowlord stepped forward to take the box from Aster, and he held it open for him as the new Guildmaster reached inside and removed a small golden object. Slowly, reverently, he raised it up so that all could see it. The glowing fetter throbbed in his hands like a living thing, and the power that emanated from it filled the room with light, eclipsing the candle flames.

"Behold the essence of Gunther the Black, who ordered the Cleansing of Terra Lorche. Behold the essence of Roland of Acre, who commanded the souls of fallen Crusaders. Behold the essence of Farbjodir, who banished the dead of Lindesfarne. Behold the essence of Shekarchiyandar, he who was called the Lord of Hunters, who slaughtered Dreamwalkers on a thousand worlds, and brought us victory against their kind."

He looked down at Virilian. "These are the souls of warriors, hunters, and destroyers. Their union is dark, even by our standards, and more than one Shadowlord has fallen to madness after Communing with this fetter." He paused. "Is this the union you seek?"

"It is."

"The risk of failure is high. The cost of failure is death. I ask you again: Is this the Communion you seek?"

"It is."

Aster held the fetter over Virilian's heart and addressed the assembly. "Witness, Shadows, that this man seeks Communion of his own free will, naming the fetter of his choice. By my rank as Guildmaster of the Shadows, I hereby grant his petition." He looked at Virilian. "Make ready."

An assistant reached forward and untied the front of Virilian's shirt, spreading it open to bare his chest. Softly changing incantations, Aster lowered the fetter slowly toward Virilian's chest, paused, and then touched it to the flesh above his heart. Virilian shut his eyes for a moment, willing it to activate—and then screamed, more like the wailing of a tormented ghost than a living man. It echoed from the cold stone walls until the whole chamber was filled with it, deafening all who heard it. Virilian's body began to buck against its bonds, struggling wildly to break free, but the iron-and-leather shackles were too strong. The straps cut into his flesh as he strained against them, layering fresh blood over the old, and spasms coursed up and down his limbs, his hands and feet clenching spastically as his body writhed in its bondage. His fingers dug into the stone table so hard that his fingernails split, smearing blood on the table, and he started to moan strange words in an unknown language, biting his tongue after each syllable, until it, too, bled.

The Shadowlords watched in silence.

The unknown words became language, garbled

fragments of different languages cascading from the bleeding tongue in rapid succession, with no clear pattern or purpose. Latin, French, Arabic, Old English, Ancient Norse: the sounds overlapped, producing a torrent of sound whose meaning—if any—was indecipherable.

The Shadowlords watched in silence.

Finally the terrible spasms began to subside. One by one Virilian's arms and legs went limp, as if the muscles within them had dissolved. Slowly his eyes fell shut, and he lay motionless, like one who was truly dead.

The Shadowlords watched in silence.

"Who are you?" The Guildmaster demanded.

For a moment there was no response. Then Virilian's eyes slowly opened. "I am Master Augustus Virilian, former leader of the Guild of Shadows. And I am host to the souls of Gunther, Roland, Farbjodir and Shekarchiyandar, and all the other souls that were in their keeping."

The new Guildmaster studied him for a moment, then finally nodded his approval and placed the fetter back in its box. "I hereby return to you the title that you bestowed upon me, and all the duties and honors of that rank." He nodded to the Shadows who had bound Virilian. "Release the Guildmaster."

One by one they removed the straps, setting him free. He lay still for a minute, gathering his strength, then rose to a sitting position. His body was marked with welts from the leather straps, and blood streaked his flesh and clothing. Brushing aside any offer of assistance, he slid down from the table and stood barefoot on the cold stone floor. The Shadow who had been holding his robe stepped forward and helped him into it. The folds of thick grey fabric hid the blood and injuries of his Communion, restoring him to an aspect of regal dignity.

Guildmaster Augustus Virilian looked around the room. "Allow the dead to return," he commanded.

The ritualist nodded and circled the room once more,

tracing the patterns that would undo their banishment.
Spirits began to flow back into the room, their agitated
murmurs tainted with fear. Most kept their distance
from Virilian.

Raising up his arms, the Guildmaster shut his eyes
for a moment, focusing his Gift. Then he cried out,
"Come to me, servants of Shekarchiyandar. Your creator walks the earth again, and he has need of you."

A shadow began to shape before him, that was the
size and shape of a man, but not a man. It had the aspect
of a spirit, but it was not a spirit. Ribbons of emptiness
coiled about it like serpents, momentarily obscuring the
terrifying Void that was its very core. When the manifestation was complete, a second shadow began to take
shape beside it. And then a third. Seven appeared in all,
and the force of their combined presence was so compelling that some of the Shadowlords instinctively
backed away, sensing in these wraiths something darker
than they could ever hope to control.

"Welcome, my reapers." Shekarchiyandar smiled
coldly. "We have work to do."

Coming soon from DAW,
the thrilling conclusion to
*The Dreamwalker Chronicles*:

# DREAMWEAVER

Read on for a special preview.

**O**N THE WORLD THAT HAS NO NAME.

Atop a mountain of black stone.

The skeleton waits.

Its bones are granite and mortar, scoured clean by the wind and sun. Its ribs are tall, vaulted windows, their glass long gone, their peaked arches crumbling. Amidst the ruins a single narrow tower stands, nearly intact, rising from the black earth as if the arm of some long-buried creature is struggling to reach the sun. Its turrets are jagged and broken, and where there are breaches in the walls one can see that the interior is streaked with soot from an ancient fire.

Surrounding the ruins is a field of tall crimson grass, and beyond that a forest of black thorn trees, their branches so intertwined that it is impossible to tell where one tree ends and the next begins. There are animals present: one can hear predators moving through the grass in search of prey, and catch a glimpse of birds amidst the tangled branches, dodging thorns as long as a man's hand. But there is little life on the mountain itself. A few patches of moss cling to the base of the broken walls. A single foolhardy vine has managed to climb halfway up the tower. The leaves of the latter stir in the breeze, giving the tower the illusion of breath. As if the ancient fortress that once stood here is just asleep, rather than dead.

A shadow passes in front of the sun.

A three-headed dog looks up from its hiding place in the tall grass, suddenly alert. A lizard with the wings of a bat crawls out upon a thorned branch so it can see better. A cluster of rats with their tails knotted together peers out from a burrow, its hundred eyes moving in unison as it nervously scans the sky.

The shadow is growing larger now, though there are no clouds in the sky to explain its existence. The leaves of the ivy curl in upon themselves, as if trying to draw away from it. The sky surrounding the shadow begins to lose its color, fading from bright blue to a more muted shade.

One of the dog's three heads whimpers.

The shadow begins to coalesce over the tower, taking on the shape of a man. Its body is not made of flesh, but a darkness so absolute that all light and heat from the surrounding landscape are sucked into it. The sky surrounding it turns grey. The leaves of the ivy begin to fall. Frost forms along the ancient turrets.

The winged lizard hisses in terror and disappears into the hollow of a tree.

The rats dart back into their burrow, tripping over each other in their flight.

Another shadow is beginning to form, identical to the first. It is followed by another. Seven wraiths appear in all, their substance darker than midnight, and the tower grows dim as they circle it restlessly, as if searching for something. Then, suddenly, the first one begins to howl. It is a cry of pure anguish—unbearable fury—and one by one the other shadow wraiths join in. The unnatural sound resonates across the landscape, and it awakens memories of loss in all who hear it. The three-headed dog remembers the mournful night its mate was killed. The lizard relives that terrible day when it returned to its nest to find that its eggs had been devoured. The king rat recalls what it was like to run free in the fields, alone and unencumbered, and whimpers.

And then, as suddenly as it began, the unnatural howling ceases. The shadows circle a few minutes longer in silence, then begin to dissipate. One after another they slowly fade into the greyness of the sky, until they can no longer be seen. The first to arrive is the last to leave.

Not until the last one is completely gone does color return to the world.

# C.S. Friedman
## *The Coldfire Trilogy*

"A feast for those who like their fantasies dark, and as
emotionally heady as a rich red wine." —*Locus*

Centuries after being stranded on the planet Erna,
humans have achieved an uneasy stalemate with the
fae, a terrifying natural force with the power to prey
upon people's minds. Damien Vryce, the warrior
priest, and Gerald Tarrant, the undead sorcerer must
join together in an uneasy alliance confront a power
that threatens the very essence of the human spirit, in
a battle which could cost them not only their lives, but
the soul of all mankind.

BLACK SUN RISING      978-0-88677-527-8
WHEN TRUE NIGHT FALLS   978-0-88677-615-2
CROWN OF SHADOWS     978-0-88677-717-3

To Order Call: 1-800-788-6262
www.dawbooks.com

DAW 18

# C.S. Friedman
## The *Magister* Trilogy

"Powerful, intricate plotting and gripping characters
distinguish a book in which ethical dilemmas
are essential and engrossing."
—*Booklist*
"Imaginative, deftly plotted fantasy...
Readers will eagerly await the next installment."
—*Publishers Weekly*

## FEAST OF SOULS
978-0-7564-0463-5

## WINGS OF WRATH
978-0-7564-0594-6

## LEGACY OF KINGS
978-0-7564-0748-3

To Order Call: 1-800-788-6262
www.dawbooks.com

DAW 121

## *And then he kissed her.*

Knightly. Kissing. Her.

Annabelle felt the heat first, of his lips upon hers. Of him being near.

She felt sparks, she felt fireworks. Her first kiss. A once in a lifetime kiss. With the man she loved.

She had waited for this. She had *fought* for this. She *earned* this. She was going to enjoy every exquisite second of it.

And then it became something else entirely.

*Romances by* Maya Rodale

SEDUCING MR. KNIGHTLY
THE TATTOOED DUKE
A TALE OF TWO LOVERS
A GROOM OF ONE'S OWN
THE HEIR AND THE SPARE
THE ROGUE AND THE RIVAL

# MAYA RODALE

# Seducing Mr. Knightly

AVON

*An Imprint of HarperCollinsPublishers*

AVON BOOKS
*An Imprint of* HarperCollins*Publishers*
195 Broadway
New York, NY 10007

Copyright © 2012 by Maya Rodale
ISBN 978-0-06-208894-9
**www.avonromance.com**

First Avon Books mass market printing: November 2012

Avon Trademark Reg. U.S. Pat. Off. and in Other Countries, Marca Registrada, Hecho en U.S.A.
HarperCollins® is a registered trademark of HarperCollins Publishers.

Printed in the U.S.A.

10 9 8 7 6 5 4 3

*For my sister Eve*
*May you always have the gumption*
*to go after what you want.*

*For my readers*
*Thank you for making this romance-*
*writing dream job possible.*

*For Tony*
*For always noticing me even though I*
*stand below your line of vision.*

# Seducing
# Mr. Knightly

# Prologue

## Young Rogue Crashes Earl's Funeral

### OBITUARY

*Today England mourns the loss of Lord Charles Peregrine Fincher, sixth Earl of Harrowby and one of its finest citizens.*

*The Morning Post*

*St. George's Church*
*London, 1808*

**D**EREK Knightly had not been invited to his father's funeral. Nevertheless, he rode hell for leather from his first term at Cambridge to be there. The service had already commenced when he stalked across the threshold dressed in unrelenting black, still dusty from the road. To remove him would cause a scene.

If there was anything his father's family had loathed—other than him—it was a scene.

The late Earl of Harrowby had expired unexpectedly of an apoplexy, leaving behind his countess, his heir, and one daughter. He was also succeeded by his beloved mistress of over twenty years, and their son.

Delilah Knightly hadn't wanted to attend; her son tried to persuade her.

"We have every right to be there," he said forcefully. He might not be the heir or even have his father's name, but Derek Knightly was the earl's firstborn and beloved son.

"My grief will not be fodder for gossips, Derek, and if we attend it shall cause a massive scene. Besides, the Harrowby family will be upset. We shall mark his passing privately, just the two of us," she said, patting his hand in a weak consolation. Delilah Knightly, exuberant darling of the London stage, had become a forlorn shell of her former self.

In grief, Knightly couldn't find the words to explain his desperate need to hear the hymns sung in low mournful tones by the congregation, or to throw a handful of cool dirt on the coffin as they lowered it into the earth. The rituals would make it real, otherwise he'd always live with the faint expectation that his father might come 'round again.

He needed to say goodbye.

Most of all, Derek desperately wanted a bond to his father's other life—including the haute ton where the earl had spent his days and some nights, the younger brother Derek never had adventures with and a younger sister he never teased—so it might not seem like the man was gone entirely and forever.

Whenever young Knightly had asked questions about the other family, the earl would offer sparse details: another son who dutifully learned his lessons and not much else, a sister fond of tea parties with her vast collection of dolls. There was the country estate in Kent that Knightly felt he knew if only by all the vivid stories told to him at night before bed. His father described the inner workings of Parliament over the breakfast table. But mostly the earl wanted to step aside from his proper role and public life to enjoy the woman he loved and his favored child—and forget the rest.

Knightly went to the funeral. Alone.

The doors had been closed. He opened them.

The service had begun. Knightly disrupted it. Hundreds of sadly bowed heads turned back to look at this intruder. He straightened his spine and dared them to oppose his presence with a fierce look from his piercing blue eyes.

He had every right to be here. He belonged here.

Derek caught the eye of the New Earl, held it, and grew hot with fury. Daniel Peregrine Fincher, now Lord Harrowby, just sixteen years of age, was a mere two years younger than his bastard half brother who had dared to intrude in polite company. He stood, drawing himself up to his full height, a full six inches less than Derek, and declared in a loud, reedy voice:

"Throw the bastard out. He doesn't belong here."

# Chapter 1

## A Writing Girl in Distress

*Dear Annabelle,*
  *I desperately need your advice . . .*
    *Sincerely,*
    *Lonely in London*
    *The London Weekly*

Miss Annabelle Swift's attic bedroom
London, 1825

**S**OME things are simply true: the earth rotates around the sun, Monday follows Sunday, and Miss Annabelle Swift loves Mr. Derek Knightly with a passion and purity that would be breathtaking were it not for one other simple truth—Mr. Derek Knightly pays no attention to Miss Annabelle Swift.

It was love at first sight exactly three years, six months, three weeks, and two days ago, upon Annabelle's first foray into the offices of *The London Weekly*. She was the new advice columnist—the lucky girl who had won a contest and the position of Writing Girl number four. She was a shy, unassuming miss—still was, truth be told.

He was the dashing and wickedly handsome editor and owner of the paper. Absolutely still was, truth be told.

In those three years, six months, three weeks, and two days, Knightly seemed utterly unaware of Annabelle's undying affection. She sighed every time he entered the room. Gazed longingly. Blushed furiously should he happen to speak to her. She displayed all the signs of love, and by all accounts, these did not register for him.

By all accounts, it seemed an unwritten law of nature that Mr. Derek Knightly didn't spare a thought for Miss Annabelle Swift. At all. Ever.

And yet, she hoped.

*Why* did she love him?

To be fair, she did ask herself this from time to time.

Knightly was handsome, of course, breathtakingly and heart-stoppingly so. His hair was dark, like midnight, and he was in the habit of rakishly running his fingers through it, which made him seem faintly disreputable. His eyes were a piercing blue, and looked at the world with an intelligent, brutally honest gaze. His high, slanting cheekbones were like cliffs a girl might throw herself off in a fit of despair.

The man himself was single-minded, ruthless, and obsessed when it came to his newspaper business. He could turn on the charm, if he decided it was worth the bother. He was wealthy beyond imagination.

As an avid reader of romantic novels, Annabelle knew a hero when she saw one. The dark good looks. The power. The wealth. The intensity with which he might love a woman—her—if only he *would*.

But the real reason for her deep and abiding love had nothing to do with his wealth, power, appearance, or even the way he leaned against a table or the way he swaggered into a room. Though who knew the way a man leaned or swaggered could be so . . . *inspiring*?

Derek Knightly was a man who gave a young woman of no consequence a chance to be *something*. Something great. Something special. Something *more*. It went without saying that opportunities for women were not numerous, especially for ones with no connections, like Annabelle. If it weren't for Knightly, she'd be a plain old Spinster Auntie or maybe married to Mr. Nathan Smythe who owned the bakery up the road.

Knightly gave her a chance when no one ever did. He believed in her when she didn't even believe in herself. That was why she loved him.

So the years and weeks and days passed by and Annabelle waited for him to really notice her, even as the facts added up to the heartbreaking truth that he had a blind spot where she was concerned.

Or worse: perhaps he did notice and did not return her affection in the slightest.

A lesser girl might have given up long ago and married the first sensible person who asked. In all honesty, Annabelle had considered encouraging young Mr. Nathan Smythe of the bakery up the road. She at least could have enjoyed a lifetime supply of freshly baked pastries and warm bread.

But she had made her choice to wait for true love. And so she couldn't marry Mr. Smythe and his baked goods as long as she stayed up late reading novels of grand passions, great adventures, and true love, above all. She could not settle for less. She could not marry Mr. Nathan Smythe or anyone else, other than Derek Knightly, because she had given her heart to Knightly three years, six months, three weeks, and two days ago.

And now she lay dying. Unloved. A spinster. A *virgin*.

Her cheeks burned. Was it mortification? Remorse? Or the fever?

She was laying ill in her brother's home in Bloomsbury, London. Downstairs, her brother Thomas meekly hid in his library (it was a sad fact that Swifts were not known for backbone) while his wife, Blanche, shrieked at their children: Watson, Mason, and Fleur. None of them had come to inquire after her health, however. Watson had come to request her help with his sums, Mason asked where she had misplaced his Latin primer, and Fleur had woken Annabelle from a nap to borrow a hair ribbon.

Annabelle lay in her bed, dying, another victim of unrequited love. It was tragic, tragic! In her slim fingers she held a letter from Knightly, blotted with her tears.

Very well, she was not at death's door, merely suffering a wretched head cold. She did have a letter from Knightly but it was hardly the stuff of a young woman's dreams. It read:

*Miss Swift*—

Annabelle stopped there to scowl. *Everyone* addressed their letters to her as "Dear Annabelle," which was the name of her advice column. Thus, she was the recipient of dozens—hundreds—of letters each week that all began with "Dear Annabelle." To be cheeky and amusing, everyone else in the world had adopted this salutation. Tradesmen sent their bills to her addressed as such.

But not Mr. Knightly! Miss Swift indeed. The rest—the scant rest of it—was worse.

> *Miss Swift—*
>     *Your column is late. Please remedy this with all due haste.*
>     *D.K.*

Annabelle possessed the gift of a prodigious imagination. (Or curse. Sometimes it felt like a curse.) But even she could not spin magic from this letter.

She was never late with her column either, because she knew all the people it would inconvenience: Knightly and the other editors, the printers, the deliverymen, the news agents, all the loyal readers of *The London Weekly*.

She loathed bothering people—ever since she'd been a mere thirteen years old and Blanche decreed to Thomas on their wedding day that "they could keep his orphaned sister so long as she wasn't a nuisance." Stricken with terror at the prospect of being left to the workhouse or the streets, Annabelle bent over backward to be helpful. She acted as governess to her brother's children, assisted Cook with the meal preparation, could be counted on for a favor when anyone asked.

But she was ill! For the first time, she simply didn't have the strength to be concerned with the trials and vexations of others. The exhaustion went bone deep. Perhaps deeper. Perhaps it had reached her soul.

There was a stack of letters on her writing desk across the room, all requesting her help.

Belinda from High Holburn wanted to know how one addressed a duke, should she ever be so lucky to meet one. Marcus wished to know how fast it took to travel from London to Gretna Green "for reasons he couldn't specify." Susie requested a complexion remedy, Nigel asked for advice on how to propose to one sister when he had already been courting the other for six months.

"Annabelle!" Blanche shrieked from the bottom of the stairs leading to her attic bedroom.

She shrunk down and pulled the covers over her head.

"Annabelle, Mason broke a glass, Watson pierced himself and requires a remedy, and Fleur needs her hair curled. Do come at once instead of lazing abed all day!"

"Yes, Blanche," she said faintly.

Annabelle sneezed, and then tears stung at her eyes and she was in quite the mood for a good, well-deserved cry. But then there was that letter from Knightly. Miss Swift, indeed! And the problems of Belinda, Marcus, Susie and Nigel. And Mason, Watson and Fleur. All of which required her help.

What about me?

The selfish question occurred to her, unbidden. Given her bedridden status, she could not escape it either. She could not dust, or sweep or rearrange her hair ribbons, or read a novel or any other such task she engaged in when she wished to avoid thinking about something unpleasant.

Stubbornly, the nagging question wouldn't leave until it had an answer.

She mulled it over. *What about me?*

"What about me?" She tested the thought with a hoarse whisper.

She was a good person. A kind person. A generous, thoughtful, and helpful person. But here she was, ill and alone, forgotten by the world, dying of unrequited love, a virgin . . .

Well, maybe it was time for others to help Dear Annabelle with her problems!

"Hmmph," she said to no one in particular.

The Swifts were not known for the force of their will, or their gumption. So when the feeling struck, she ran with it before the second-guessing could begin. Metaphorically, of course, given that she was bedridden with illness.

Annabelle dashed off the following column, for print in the most popular newspaper in town:

*To the readers of* The London Weekly,

*For nearly four years now I have faithfully answered your inquiries on matters great and small. I have advised to the best of my abilities and with goodness in my heart.*

*Now I find myself in need of your help. For the past few years I have loved a man from afar, and I fear he has taken no notice of me at all. I know not how to attract his attention and affection. Dear readers, please advise!*

*Your humble servant,*
*Dear Annabelle*

Before she could think twice about it, she sealed the letter and addressed it to:

Mr. Derek Knightly
c/o *The London Weekly*
57 Fleet Street
London, England

SEDUCING MR. KNIGHTLY 11.

Mr. Derek Knightly
c/o The London Weekly
57 Fleet Street,
London, En...

# Chapter 2

## Lovelorn Female Vows to Catch a Rogue

THE MAN ABOUT TOWN
*No man knows more about London than Mr. Derek Knightly, infamous proprietor of this newspaper's rival publication. And no one in London knows one whit about him.*

*The London Times*

*Offices of* The London Weekly
*57 Fleet Street, London*

**D**EREK KNIGHTLY swore by three truths. The first: *Scandal equals sales.*

Guided by this principle, he used his inheritance to acquire a second-rate news rag, which he transformed into the most popular, influential newspaper in London, avidly read by both high and lowborn alike.

The second: *Drama was for the page.* Specifically the printed, stamp-taxed pages of *The London Weekly*, which were filled to the brim with salacious gossip from the ton, theater reviews, domestic and foreign intelligence, and the usual assortment of articles and advertisements. He himself did not partake in the aforementioned scandal or drama. There were days were he hardly existed beyond the pages he edited and published.

The third: *Be beholden to no one*. Whether business or pleasure, Knightly owned—he was not owned. Unlike other newspapers, *The London Weekly* was not paid for by Parliament or political parties. Nor did theaters pay for favorable reviews. He wasn't above taking suppression fees for gossip, depending upon the rumors. He'd fought duels in defense of *The Weekly*'s contents. He'd already taken one bullet for his beloved newspaper and would do so again unblinkingly.

When it came to women—well, suffice it to say his heart belonged to the newspaper and he was intent that no woman should capture it.

These three truths had taken him from being the scandal-borne son of an earl and his actress-mistress to one of London's most infamous, influential, and wealthiest men.

Half of everything he'd ever wanted.

For an infinitesimal second Knight paused, hand on the polished brass doorknob. On the other side of the wooden door, his writers waited for their weekly meeting in which they compared and discussed the stories for the forthcoming issue. He thought about scandal, and sales, and other people's drama. Because, given the news he'd just heard—a *London Times* reporter caught where he shouldn't be—London was about to face the scandal of the year . . . one that threatened to decimate the entire newspaper industry, including *The London Weekly*.

Where others often saw disaster, Knightly saw opportunity. But the emerging facts made him pause to note a feeling of impending doom. The victims in this case were too important, the deception beyond the pale. Someone would pay for it.

With a short exhalation and a square of his shoulders, Knightly pushed opened the door and stepped before his team of writers.

"Ladies first," he said, grinning, as always.

The Writing Girls. His second greatest creation. It had been an impulsive decision to hire Sophie and Julianna to start, later rounded out by Eliza and Annabelle. But the guiding rational was: *Scandal equals sales.*

Women writing were scandalous.

Therefore . . .

His hunch had been correct. The gamble paid off in spades.

*The London Weekly* was a highbrow meets lowbrow newspaper read by everyone, but the Writing Girls set it apart from all the other news rags by making it especially captivating to the women in London, and particularly attractive to the men.

To his left, Miss Annabelle Swift, advice columnist, sighed. Next to her, Eliza—now the Duchess of Wycliff—gave him a sly glance. Sophie, the Duchess of Brandon—a disgraced country girl when he first met her—propped her chin on her palm and smiled at him. Lady Roxbury brazenly took him on with her clear, focused gaze.

"What's on this week, writers?" he asked.

Lady Julianna Roxbury, known in print as the Lady of Distinction and author of the salacious gossip column "Fashionable Intelligence," clearly had News. "There are rumors," she began excitedly, "of Lady Lydia Marsden's prolonged absence from the ton. Lady Marsden is newly returned to town after she missed what ought to have been her second season. I am investigating."

By investigating, she likely meant all manner of gossip and skulking about, but that was what *Weekly* writers did. Like the writers at *The Times*, but without getting caught.

No one else in the room seemed to care for the significance of a debutante's whereabouts. Knightly barely did, he knew only that it would sell well to the ton. If the news covered one of their own, they talked about it more, which meant that more copies were sold just so people could understand conversations at parties.

To his right, good old Grenville grumbled under his breath. His irritation with the Writing Girls was never far from the surface. If it wasn't the deep, dark inner workings of Parliament, then Grenville wasn't interested.

"Annabelle has quite the update," Sophie interjected excitedly. "Much more interesting than my usual news on weddings."

Knightly turned his attention to Annabelle, the quiet one.

"My column this week has received more letters than any other," she said softly. She held his gaze for a quick second before looking down at the thick stack of correspondence on the table and a sack on the floor at her feet.

He wracked his brain but couldn't remember what she had submitted—oh, it had been late so he quickly reviewed it for errors of grammar and spelling before rushing it straight to the printers. Her work never required much by way of editing. Not like the epics Grenville submitted or the libel Lady Roxbury often handed in.

"Remind me the topic again?" he said. Clearly, it had resonated with the readers, so he ought to be aware of it.

She blinked her big blue eyes a few times. Perplexed.

There was a beat of hard silence in the room. Like he had said something wrong. So he gave the room A Look tinged with impatience to remind them that he was an extremely busy man and couldn't possibly be expected to remember the contents of each article submitted the previous week for a sixteen-page-long newspaper.

But he could feel the gazes of the crew drilling into him—Owens shaking his head, Julianna's eyebrows arched quite high. Even Grenville frowned.

Annabelle fixed her gaze upon him and said, "How to attract a man's attention."

That was just the sort of thing *Weekly* readers would love—and that could lead to a discussion of feelings—so Knightly gave a nod and said, "Good," and inquired about Damien Owens's police reports and other domestic intelligence. The conversation moved on.

"Before we go," Knightly said at the end, "I heard a rumor that a reporter for *The London Times* has been arrested after having been caught impersonating a physician to the aristocracy."

Shocked gasps ricocheted around the room from one writer to another as the implications dawned. The information this rogue reporter must have gathered from the bedrooms of London's most powerful class . . . the fortune in suppression fees he must have raked in . . . If information was power, suddenly this reporter and this newspaper held all the cards.

There was no way the ton would stand for it.

"That could explain so much . . ." Julianna murmured thoughtfully, her brow knit in concentration. "The broken Dawkins betrothal, Miss Bradley's removal to a convent in France . . ."

This only supported Knightly's suspicions that there would soon be hell to pay. Not just by *The London Times* either.

"Why are you all looking at me?" Eliza Fielding, now the Duchess of Wycliff, inquired.

"Because you were just famously disguised as a servant in a duke's household," Alistair Grey, theater reviewer said, with obvious delight. Eliza grinned wickedly.

"I'm married to him now, so that must grant me some immunity. And I am not the only reporter here who has gone undercover for a story. What about Mr. Owens's report on the Bow Street Runners?"

"That was weeks ago," Owens said dismissively.

"You were impersonating an officer," Eliza persisted.

"Well, has anyone asked Grenville how he obtains access to Parliament?" Owens questioned hotly. All heads swiveled in the direction of the grouchy old writer with the hound dog face.

"I don't pretend anything, if that's what you're suggesting," Grenville stiffly protested. "I sit in the gallery, like the other reporters."

"And after that?" Owens questioned. "Getting 'lost' in the halls like a 'senile old man'? Bribes for access to Parliament members?"

"We all do what needs to be done for a story," cut in Lady Roxbury, who had once disguised herself as a boy and snuck into White's, the most exclusive and *male* enclave in the world. "We're all potentially on the line if authorities start looking into the matter. But they cannot possibly because then every newspaper would be out of business and we'd all be locked up."

"Except for Miss Swift. She would be safe, for she never does anything wicked," Owens added. Everyone laughed. Even Knightly. He'd wager that Dear Annabelle was the last woman in the world to cause trouble.

# Chapter 3

## What to Wear When Attracting a Rogue

**I**F there had been the *slightest* doubt in Annabelle's mind about the dire need to enact her campaign for Knightly's attention, this afternoon's events had dispelled it. Even if she'd been quaking with regrets, consumed by doubts, and feverishly in a panic about her mad scheme, her exchange with Knightly would have cleared her head and confirmed her course of action.

*Mission: Attract Knightly* must now commence, with every weapon at her disposal. It was either that or resolve herself to a lifetime of spinsterhood. The prospect did not enthrall.

The rest of the staff had quit the room; the Writing Girls stayed. Annabelle remained paralyzed in her place.

"He hadn't read my column," she said, shocked. Still.

She needed to say the wretched truth aloud. If she needed any confirmation of what Knightly thought of her—or didn't—this was all the information she needed. Her own editor, *a man paid to look at her work*, didn't even read it. If it weren't for the thick stack of letters from readers, she might have flung herself off the London Bridge, that was how lonely it felt.

Lord above, it was mortifying, too. Everyone else knew why she sighed when Knightly walked in the room. She was sure they all knew about her inner heartache during her brief exchange with him. How could Knightly not see?

*He hadn't read her column, and it had been about him!*

"Annabelle, it wasn't that terrible. I'm sure he doesn't read all of our work either," Sophie said consolingly. "Certainly not my reports on weddings."

"It's not just that," Annabelle said glumly. "No one thinks I am wicked."

Julianna, who was very daring and wicked, grinned broadly. "So they shall be all the more speechless when it turns out you are! I loved your column on Saturday. Knightly may not have read it, but the rest of the town did. Your next course of action is being fiercely debated in drawing rooms all over town."

"Indeed?" It was strange to think of strangers debating her innermost vexations.

"There seems to be two schools of thought," Sophie replied. "One suggests that you simply confess to him your feelings."

"I am terrified at the thought," Annabelle replied.

"Then you may be interested in the other method . . ." Sophie paused dramatically. "Seduction."

"I couldn't possibly," Annabelle scoffed. "That would be wicked, and you heard Owens; I never act thusly."

"He's an ass," Julianna retorted.

Usually Annabelle would have admonished her friend's coarse language. Instead, she said, "No, he's right. I am Good. Therefore, I am not interesting. Why should Knightly take notice of me? There is nothing to notice!"

Wasn't that the plain old truth!

The mirror dared to suggest she was pretty, but all Annabelle saw was a riot of curls that were best restrained in a tight, spinsterish bun atop her head. She did have lovely blue eyes, but more often than not kept her gaze averted lest she draw attention to herself. Furthermore, her wardrobe consisted entirely of brownish-gray dresses made of remnant fabric from her brother's cloth-importing business. To say the cut was flattering or fashionable was to be a liar of the first order.

She might dare think people would see beyond her disastrous hair and hideous dresses. Most of the time she couldn't.

"Oh, Annabelle. You are rather pretty—so pretty that he, like any red-blooded male, should notice you. Unless he's not . . ."

"See, I am blushing at your mere suggestion!" Annabelle squeaked.

"We do have work to do," Julianna murmured.

"What do your letters say?" Sophie asked, picking one up.

Annabelle scowled and grabbed the first one, reading it aloud.

" 'Dear Annabelle, in my humble opinion a low bodice never fails to get a man's eye. It plays to their rutting instincts, which we all know they are slaves to . . . Betsy from Bloomsbury.' "

"A trip to the modiste! I love it." Sophie clapped her hands with glee. But Annabelle frowned. Beggars ought not be choosers, yet . . .

"I want him to notice me for *me*; who I am as a person. Not just bits of me."

"You have to start with certain parts. Then he'll attend to the rest," Julianna replied. "Come, let's go get you a new dress."

"You must wear it for my party later this week," Sophie said, then adding the most crucial detail: "Knightly has been invited."

The opportunity dangled before her like the carrot and the horse. Never mind that the analogy made her a horse. The facts were plain:

There was something she might try (thank you, Betsy from Bloomsbury) and an opportunity at which she might do so (thank you, Sophie, hostess extraordinaire).

She had made that promise to her readers, and it would be dreadful to let them down. She did so despise disappointing people.

Annabelle twirled one errant curl around her finger and mulled it over (Swifts were not known for their quick decisions). She supposed there were worse things than a new gown and a fancy ball. For her readers, she would do this.

Not one hour later, Annabelle was standing in the dressing room of Madame Auteuil's shop. A previous customer had returned a lovely pink gown after a change of heart, and Annabelle wore it now as the seamstresses took measurements for a few alterations.

"I don't think it quite fits," she said. It wasn't the size per se, for she knew it would be tailored to her measurements. It was the dress itself.

It was silk. She never wore silk.

It was pink, like a peony or a rosebud or her cheeks when Knightly spoke to her. She never wore pink.

The pink silk was ruched and cinched and draped in a way that seemed to enhance her every curve and transform her from some gangly girl into a luscious woman.

Annabelle wore simply cut dresses made of boring old wool or cotton. Usually in shades of brown or gray or occasionally even taupe.

The Swift family owned a fabric importing business, which dealt exclusively in plain and serviceable cottons and wools guided by the rational that everyone required those, but so few indulged in silks and satins. Blanche generously provided Annabelle with last season's remnants for the construction of her wardrobe.

This silk, though, was lovely. A crimson silk sash cinched around her waist, enhancing what could only be described as an hourglass figure. It was a wicked color, that crimson.

Madame Auteuil stepped back, folded her arms and appraised her subject with a furrow of her brow and a frown on her lips. She had pins in her mouth and Annabelle worried for her.

"She needs a proper corset," the modiste finally

declared. "I cannot work without the lady in the right undergarments."

"A proper corset fixes everything," Sophie concurred.

"And lovely underthings . . ." Julianna smiled with a naughty gleam in her eye.

Annabelle began to do math in her head. Living as glorified household help for her brother and his sister meant that her *Weekly* wages went to her subscription at the circulating library and a few other inconsequential trinkets, and then the rest went into her secret account that Sophie's husband had helped her arrange. It had been her one small act of rebellion.

"I'm not sure that underthings are necessary . . ." Annabelle began to protest. Silk underthings sounded expensive and no one would see them, so how could she justify the expense when she could have a few delicious novels instead?

"Do you have the money?" Eliza asked softly. She was a duchess now, but she'd had anything but an aristocratic upbringing or connections. She understood economies.

"Well, yes. But I feel that I should save," Annabelle said frankly.

"For what?" Eliza asked.

"Something," Annabelle said. Something, someday. She was always waiting and preparing for an event that never came—or had she missed it, given that she didn't know what she was waiting for?

"Annabelle, this is that something," Sophie said grandly. "You want Knightly to notice you, do you not?"

"And you have an occasion to wear it," Eliza said, adding a dose of practicality.

"But he won't see my unmentionables. Those needn't be—"

"Well he might, if you are lucky," Julianna said frankly. And lud, didn't that make her cheeks burn! The thought made her entire body feel feverish, in a not altogether unpleasant way.

"Annabelle," Sophie began, "you must think of fashion as an investment in your future happiness! That is not some silk dress, but a declaration that you are a new woman, a young, beautiful woman interested in life! And love!"

"But the underthings?" Annabelle questioned.

"I promise you will love them," Sophie vowed. "You'll see . . ."

In the end, Annabelle was persuaded to purchase one pink silk dress, one blue day dress, one corset that enhanced her person in ways that seemed to violate natural laws, and some pale pink silk unmentionables that were promptly stashed in the back of her armoire.

# Chapter 4

## Misadventures in the Ballroom

Town Talk

*One is hard pressed to determine who is the more perfect specimen of an English gentleman: Lord Marsden or Lord Harrowby. Both are widely regarded as the catch of the season. Again.*

The Morning Post

*Ballroom of Hamilton House*

**O**N the terrace, Derek Knightly leaned against the balustrade, gazing at the party raging within. This morning he had been in the warehouse hauling and tossing reams of paper upon which the next issue would be printed until his hands were filthy with dirt, dust, and ink and until his muscles ached from the exertion and his skin was damped by sweat. Damn, it felt good.

This evening he wore a perfectly fitted, exquisitely expensive set of evening clothes, made by Gieves & Hawkes, his tailor on Saville Row. He sipped the fine French brandy—the only thing the

French were good for—and noted that it was a rare and excellent vintage.

His newspaper empire had brought him a fortune, and with it a taste for finer things, as well as the connections he had always aspired to. Here he was, a guest at the home of the Duke and Duchess of Brandon. They were friends.

Not bad for an earl's by-blow who had sullied his hands in trade.

Yet those damning words still taunted him: *Throw the bastard out. He doesn't belong here.*

Knightly lifted his head higher, damned proud of himself. His Writing Girls stood near the French doors leading to the terrace. He watched them chattering animatedly.

Annabelle glanced his way and he caught her eye. She quickly turned away. Shy, that one. He allowed his gaze to linger. Something seemed different about her. She just seemed a bit . . . *more*. It was probably because instead of meeting at the newspaper offices in the afternoon as usual, they were at a ball and midnight was drawing near. And the brandy was taking effect.

His gaze drifted back to Annabelle. More? Yes, definitely *more*.

Knightly took another measured sip of his drink and watched the party progress from his vantage point on the terrace, alone. A guest, yet an outsider all the same.

Tonight they were worse than usual. He was often tolerated, lest one risk insulting the host who had invited him. With those rumors, however . . . he saw the fear in their eyes as he wove his way through the ballroom. They wondered what he knew, what he would extort from them to keep the information private, or what he would print for all their family, friends, businessmen to see.

With just a few lines of movable type, he could reverse fortunes and ruin reputations. Aye, that explained the wary glances and averted gazes.

The New Earl was here tonight. Even after all these years, Knightly still referred to him in his head as the New Earl. *Harrowby* was his father, not this pompous oaf who still refused to acknowledge his half brother. Refused to even meet his eye, the coward. Upon occasions when they both attended the same function, Knightly made a sport of catching his eye, or even nodding, and watching the New Earl redden.

His fortune had not earned the man's notice. Neither did his ever-growing influence over the London ton due to his immensely popular paper. Nor did the New Earl seem to notice that he never printed anything remotely damaging about him in the pages of *The Weekly*. Nor did his friendships with dukes, plural. Which brought Knightly to the last point in his plan:

An aristocratic wife would make it impossible for the New Earl to ignore and snub him without conferring the same disregard upon a member of the haute ton. Which he would not—could not—do to one of his fellow peers.

It was, for reasons Knightly did not deeply examine, imperative that the earl recognize him publicly.

Most of the ton did not want to associate with him, but unlike his brother, so many could not afford to ignore him. That was also part of the plan.

Case in point: Lord Marsden, cigar and brandy in hand, who now ambled over to where he stood. They were of the same age, approximately. In spite of his young age, Marsden was immensely respected in Parliament—in part from the legacy of his late father, and in part because of his own talents, for the man had been born to the role in more ways than one.

Marsden was a charmer who cultivated a vast array of relationships at every opportunity. He flirted with women—young, old, debutante or spinster, married or widowed. One could often find him in the card room, smoking, laughing, and wagering with his fellow peers. He peppered his conversation with stock tips, minor gossip, compliments, and he listened attentively to one's problems. Far too attentively. He was good, Knightly had to give him that.

The marquis was forever seeking *The London Weekly*'s support for his various causes and political initiatives, given that the paper served such a large audience. Yet Knightly knew those readers flocked to his paper because it was beholden to no one, so the marquis was forever disappointed.

Nevertheless, the men were on familiar terms. It served them both well.

"I'm sure you have heard the news," Marsden said, and when Derek deliberately did not reply, he continued, "About *The London Times* reporter. He's in Newgate after impersonating a physician."

"I did hear rumors to that effect," Knightly allowed.

"Revolting, isn't it? The haute ton is terrified. Or they will be," Marsden said with a ruthless smile. Knightly understood how this would work: in his every conversation, the marquis would stir the pot, disseminating carefully selected bits of information designed to enrage and appall until the Upper Orders become a raging mob, hungry for the blood of newspaper magnates like him.

"I am considering how to portray this story in *The Weekly*," Knightly remarked.

Marsden had a wide circle of friends, connections. But Knightly had power of his own: each week thousands of Londoners read his newspaper full of information that he selected, edited, and presented. And then they discussed the contents with family, friends, the news agent, the butcher, their maids . . . Marsden might wish to stir the pot, but Knightly knew he could blow the whole thing up.

"There will likely be an inquiry," Marsden added casually, tipping the ash off his cigar. He spoke casually, but his words were always deliberately chosen and directed. This was a warning.

Translation: *Heads are about to roll.*

"I'd find that very interesting," Knightly remarked.

Meaning: *Tell me everything.*

"Indeed, I shall keep you informed," Marsden said. And then he changed the subject—or seemed to. "I am here with my sister this evening. This marriage mart business . . ." Marsden heaved a weary sigh, as if Lady Lydia was the last in a long line of troublesome sisters to foist off to the parson's mousetrap. In fact, she was his only sister. And she had missed her second season, mysteriously. Knightly declined to mention this. For the moment.

"You must be eager for her to marry," he said, testing Marsden's suggestion. Among bachelors, marriage wasn't a subject to be broached without an ulterior motive.

"As long as it's a match I approve of. A man who is able to provide for her in a manner that she is accustomed to." Marsden punctuated this with a heavy stare. Knightly's fortune was no secret. Reports of Marsden's declining coffers had made their way to Knightly's desk.

"A suitor whose business interests don't take a turn for the worse, perhaps," Knightly suggested, leveling a stare.

Marsden's eyes narrowed. He pulled on the cigar, then tapped it so the ash tumbled to the ground. Knightly did not look away.

"I am glad we understand each other," Marsden said, blowing a curl of blue-gray smoke into the night air.

It was one hell of an offer: *You protect* The London Weekly *and I will marry your sister.*

ANNABELLE was always aware of him, and so she knew that he was just there, on the terrace. It was a useless sixth sense. But how could she not sneak one glance after another as he leaned against the balustrade? For the hundredth time she wondered how the simple act of leaning could be so . . . so . . . arresting. Compelling. He appeared at ease but she knew he wasn't; he was aware of everything and ready for anything.

She, who never felt quite comfortable in her own skin, envied him that.

As she stood in conversation with her fellow Writing Girls, she kept trying to angle herself so that she might display her new gown to its best advantage.

The front. The very low bodice made her feel utterly naked. Perhaps even a bit wicked. Whatever it was, she barely recognized herself in this pink silk gown that slinked against her skin in a soft and sensual way.

It was just a dress, she reprimanded herself. Except that it wasn't—for better or for worse, this gown gave her a confidence she didn't usually possess. Annabelle caught herself standing up straighter, no longer awkward about her height but eager to show off her dress to the best effect. She smiled more because she felt pretty.

It wasn't just a dress; it was courage in the silken form.

She stole another glance. He was conversing with another gentleman, a handsome one.

She wracked her brain for a reason to go out on the terrace alone. A "Wallflower in Mayfair" had written: "Romantic stuff always happens on terraces at balls, everyone knows that."

She just needed an excuse. *I need air. I feel like trouble. Perhaps I'd like to try smoking a cigar. I'd like to be compromised. I can't breathe in this stifling corset that defies laws of gravity.*

"Oh, here comes Knightly," Eliza whispered to Annabelle, who already knew. She stood up straighter. Butterflies took flight. Her heartbeat quickened.

Knightly's gaze locked with hers. His eyes were so blue and contrasted so intensely with his black hair. Tonight he wore a black jacket and a dark blue silk waistcoat.

*Do not blush. Do not blush. Smile, Annabelle. Stand up straight.*

But the commands were lost between her head and her heart and the rest of her. Knightly nodded in greeting, and likely received a startled doe expression from Annabelle. She watched as he strolled purposely through the ballroom until he was lost in the crowds.

"Oh, look, if it isn't Lord Marsden," Sophie said flirtatiously to a handsome man walking by; the very one Knightly had been speaking with on the terrace.

The man in question stopped and gave the duchess a delicious smile. Annabelle recalled a mention of his name from Grenville's parliamentary reports (the man was apparently a born leader) and from Julianna's gossip columns (the man was widely regarded as an eminently eligible bachelor). She knew he worked closely with the Duke of Brandon, Sophie's husband, on parliamentary matters.

"If it isn't the lovely duchess," Marsden replied with an easy smile and kissing Sophie's outstretched hand.

"Don't flirt with me, Marsden," Sophie admonished. "Please meet my friend, Miss Swift. You may know her as Dear Annabelle."

"From the pages of *The Weekly*?" This, Marsden inquired with brow lifted. It was not an unexpected question, given that it was well known that Sophie wrote for the paper and alternately covered society weddings and the latest fashions.

"The very one," she replied.

Annabelle noted that this Lord Marsden was so classically, perfectly handsome that she found herself reluctantly searching for some flaw. His hair was blond, and brushed back from his perfectly chiseled cheekbones. If anything, he wore a dash too much pomade. But his eyes were warm and brown and they focused upon her.

Most importantly, he knew of her writing. She liked him immediately.

"You have a gift, Miss Swift," he said, and she found herself smiling. "I have often remarked at how gently you advise and rebuke people, whereas I would be sorely tempted to write something along the lines of 'You are a nodcock. Cease at once.' Tell me, did you ever consider it?"

"Everybody deserves sensitivity and a genuine—" She stopped when he arranged his handsome features into a look of utter skepticism. "Oh, very well, yes!" she said, laughter escaping her.

"If you do ever call someone a nodcock in print, it would please me immeasurably," Lord Marsden said, grinning.

Annabelle laughed. Then she caught a glimpse of Knightly speaking with a beautiful woman, decked in diamonds.

"I can foresee an instance when I might," Annabelle remarked coyly. When did she ever say anything coyly? Goodness. It must be those silky underthings she dared to wear this evening, making her bold. Or the warmth and encouragement in Marsden's expression.

"Would you like to waltz, Dear Annabelle?" Lord Marsden asked, offering his arm. She linked hers in his and allowed him to lead her to join the other dancers. It was only after the first steps of the waltz that she realized Sophie had quietly slipped away. And that she had lost sight of Knightly because she'd ceased to pay attention to his every movement. And that she didn't know how to waltz. And that she was quite excited to try with Lord Marsden.

She thought the evening couldn't possibly improve, however . . .

# Chapter 5

### The Dangers of Dimly Lit Corridors

DEAR ANNABELLE

*If one wishes for romantic encounters, one ought to abandon the ballroom and venture to places more secluded and dimly lit, such as the terrace, or corridors . . . But do so at your own risk!*

*Yours Fondly,*
*A Rakish Rogue*
*The London Weekly*

*A dimly lit corridor*

ANNABELLE swayed on her feet, light-headed and breathless.

The hour was late and her senses had been dulled by the pleasant fatigue of waltzing and two glasses of finely sparkling champagne. Happily, she hummed a tune under her breath and imagined Knightly asking her to waltz as she made her way back to the ballroom through a dimly lit corridor.

And then she walked straight into a gentleman. Or he barreled right into her. One might say they collided. The result was, Annabelle swayed on her feet, and breathlessly uttered a single, unfortunate syllable: "Oof."

Then her senses started to focus and she noticed she had crashed into a very fine wool jacket, a crisp white linen shirt, and a dark silk waistcoat, all of which covered a rather firm and broad male chest.

Had she known it was Knightly, she might have lingered to breathe in the scent of him (a combination of wool, faint cigar smoke, brandy, and *him*) or savor the feel of him under her palms (and not just the quality of his wool jacket either). She certainly wouldn't have said "Oof" like a barnyard animal.

Two warm, bare hands grasped her arms to hold her steady.

"Oh, I beg your pardon," she had said, stepping back and tilting her head up to see who owned this firm chest that positively radiated heat and impelled her to curl up against it. Her eyes adjusted to light and then widened considerably when she saw whom she had collided with: Knightly, the man of her dreams, the King of her heart, the object of her affections . . .

"Miss Swift," Knightly said, with a nod in greeting. "My apologies, I hadn't seen you."

Of course he didn't. He never did. But that was just the way of things. Also the way of things was her unfortunate tendency to either go mute in his presence or ramble excessively. She had yet to manage a normal conversation with the man.

"Mr. Knightly. Good evening. I'm sorry, I was not attending to my surroundings . . ." Annabelle rambled. To her horror, the words kept coming, oblivious to her fervent wishes to stop. "Obviously, I had not seen you. For if I had seen you, I certainly wouldn't have barreled headlong into you."

Surely some reader was bound to suggest the very tactic.

"So I gathered. Are you all right?" He inquired politely.

"Yes, quite. Though your chest is rather hard," Annabelle said. Then she closed her eyes and groaned. Had she *really* just said that? Was it too much to ask that she not make a complete nitwit of herself all the time?

"Thank you," he replied, ever so gentlemanly. But there was enough light to see that he was amused.

"My apologies. A lady ought not attend to such things, or mention them aloud. Rest assured I would never advise a reader to—" She was babbling. She couldn't stop.

And yet, through the mortification a sweet truth dawned. She was alone with Knightly. And she was dressed for the occasion. Even better, she had felt the firm strength of his chest for one extraordinarily exquisite second that she wished to repeat (albeit in a far more seductive manner).

"I'm sure that would be scandalous, if you did tell a reader to compliment a man thusly. However, I can't imagine any man would be bothered by it," Knightly said, a faint grin on his lips, which was his way of saying it was fine. She exhaled in relief.

"But I do apologize that I wasn't attending to my surroundings. I was quite distracted."

"Something on your mind?" Knightly inquired. And then he folded his arms over his very hard chest and leaned against the wall. He gazed down at her.

That was all it took for the world to shift on its axis, right under her feet.

Because Knightly had asked her a question. About herself. About her *mind.*

How to answer *that*?

"Oh, just enjoying the evening. And you?" she replied, hoping to sound as if she chatted with dashing gentleman all the time and wasn't beset with nerves. Even though every nerve in her body with tingling pleasantly. For here she was in a dark, secluded place having *an actual conversation* with Knightly.

More to the point, it was a conversation that was not about the newspaper.

"This evening has been . . . interesting," he replied.

"How so?" Annabelle asked, still breathless, but now for an altogether different reason.

"Life takes a strange turn upon occasion, does it not?" he remarked, and she didn't quite know what he was referring to, only that it fit her moment perfectly.

"Oh, yes," she replied. What gods had conspired to bring about this fortuitous occurrence of circumstances, Annabelle knew not. But she was happy. And hopeful. And proud of herself for trying; this had to be her reward.

Now if only she could prolong the moment . . .

"The duchess has outdone herself this evening," Knightly said. "We'd better return before—"

"Someone notices that we are missing," Annabelle said, perhaps a touch too eagerly. Not that she would mind being caught in a compromising position with him. Not at all.

"Or before someone else with less noble intentions accosts you in the dark hallway. Can't have any danger befall my Writing Girls," he said, gently pressing his palm to her elbow, guiding them both to the ballroom.

Annabelle only smiled faintly and wondered if it was wrong to wish a gentleman's intentions were less than noble.

# Chapter 6

### The London Coffeehouse:
### Meeting Place of "Gentlemen"

**G**ALLOWAY'S coffeehouse was full of men, high- and lowborn alike, sipping coffee and delving into the assortment of periodicals offered. Everything from literary publications to periodicals devoted to sport. The air was full of men's conversations both serious and bawdy, cigar smoke, the heavy fragrance of coffee, and the shuffling of pages.

Knightly was in the habit of meeting at Galloway's every Saturday, joined by Peter Drummond, a playwright and theater owner—who had been his comrade in trouble since Cambridge—and their scoundrel of a friend, Julian Gage, a renowned stage actor who was better known for his disastrous romantic entanglements than the quality of his acting.

After all, it's not like White's would admit the likes of them as members. They hadn't the birth, status, wealth, or connections required for access to that exclusive enclave. Galloway's was their club instead.

"Women never bloody listen to me," Drummond muttered into his newspaper. He grasped a handful of his salt and pepper hair in utter vexation. "I vow, I could tell a lass to get out of a sinking boat and she'd protest."

"Is that in reference to something specific or the general lament that women don't take the advice of a man who makes up stories for a living?" Knightly asked casually. A copy of *Cobott's Weekly Register* lay before him.

"It's playwriting. And your mother would have your head to hear you dismiss the theater like that. If you must know, I am grumbling about your Dear Annabelle," Drummond answered. He punctuated this with a frustrated shake of the newspaper.

Knightly coolly lifted one brow. The conversation had suddenly turned toward the unexpected and possibly unfathomable.

"She took my advice!" Julian grinned triumphantly in spite of Drummond's vicious glare.

Knightly frowned at his friends. Both usually read the theater reviews, gossip column, and naught much else. Julian, in particular, usually read only articles that were about him.

They certainly never read the advice column in the back, next to the advertisements for hats, corsets, and miracle cures of all kinds. It was women's stuff, presided over by the Dear Annabelle column in which Miss Swift, who was sweetness and innocence personified, doled out advice to the lovelorn, socially unsure, etc, etc. He tried to recall her last column and why she would be in search of advice, especially from these idiots.

"Oi!" Drummond shouted when Knightly snatched the paper from his hands. He found her column on page seventeen and began to read with annoyance (because something in his paper had escaped his notice) and intrigue (because it was Annabelle. What could she be writing about?):

### DEAR ANNABELLE

*This author was humbled and heart-warmed by the outpouring of advice from her loyal readers in response to last week's solicitation for desperately needed advice on how I might attract a particular man's attention.*

*Never has this author received so many letters! One reader wrote that I ought to steal into the gentleman's bed at the midnight hour as a wicked surprise. I fear that is too bold, but we shall see what desperate acts I am driven to. Nancy suggested perfume "delicately applied to my décolletage" and a gentleman named Peregrine offered to compose love sonnets that I might dramatically recite, thus captivating the object of my affections with his verse. Dozens of letters advised me to lower the bodices on my gowns. My friends greatly encouraged this endeavor and I found myself at the modiste before I knew it.*

*Readers, I know not if it was the dress itself, the ample display of my person, or the confidence I possessed from such fine garments, but I daresay this worked! While it failed to attract the object of my*

*affections (that nodcock!), I certainly basked in the*
*attentions of other charming gentlemen. This week I*
*shall alter the rest of my wardrobe accordingly. But as*
*I shall settle for nothing less than true love, I suspect I*
*require more schemes to enact. Your suggestions are*
*welcome and will be put to the test!*

Miss Swift requesting love advice from all of London?

This was not the Annabelle he knew. This was not the work of a shy girl who spoke softly, if at all. The girl who usually wore her hair in a bun and dresses in the style best described as Spinster Auntie. The girl who had rambled quite charmingly when they bumped into each other the other night and who hadn't once made him think of her as a Spinster Auntie during that darkened interlude.

Quite the contrary. It seemed Annabelle possessed the sort of luscious curves best kept for sin. It wasn't an altogether unpleasant discovery, even though nothing would come of it.

He had thought there was something different about her, something *more*. His suspicions were confirmed. It seemed a lot of things were different with Annabelle all of a sudden.

She usually advised the masses on proper manners, or offered practical household tips, or consulted, gently, on the love lives of readers.

Annabelle did not use words like "nodcock."

Thus it was the damnedest thing to read this column from a girl, so sweet and fair, publicly pursuing a man with advice from strangers. Annabelle didn't know any of these people she was courting information from!

They could be like . . .

Drummond and Gage. Drummond, who had three broken engagements in his past, and Gage, who had a tempestuous relationship with Jocelyn Kemble, the famous actress, and who never refused female company when offered. As a popular actor, it was offered to him. Often.

Heaven help them all, Annabelle especially.

"I thought she ought to send him an anonymous letter. Perfumed. Romantic like," Drummond explained. "There is nothing like the power of the written word to seduce the mind, and the heart will follow."

Knightly snorted. What romantic rubbish.

"That's pathetic. My advice was better, which was why she followed it," Gage replied arrogantly with a smug smile.

"Lower her bodice?" Drummond scoffed. "Like that's original."

"Annabelle doesn't want original, she wants what works," Gage said, and Knightly frowned at this lout referring to one of *his* Writing Girls so intimately. Gage didn't notice and barreled on. "Since time immemorial, women have flaunted their figures and men have been slaves to their baser natures."

Case in point, Knightly thought. Idiots.

And yet . . .

Was that what was different about Annabelle at the ball? He'd seen her chatting with the Writing Girls, and then waltzing with some young buck. He'd connected intimately with her person for just a second, but it had been enough to discover she had a figure for sin.

But he had not really noticed her lowered bodice.

Why? Was he ill? No, there was nothing the matter with him. He just wasn't in the habit of looking at his female employees In That Way. From the start he had treated his female writers the same as the men; it was just easier.

Should he have noticed?

He should have noticed. If it concerned his business then the answer was yes.

This concerned his business. Thus, he would make a point to look when he saw her next. For the sake of his business. No other reason, such as a dawning intrigue.

"We don't even know what Annabelle looks like," Drummond mused, sipping from a steamy mug of coffee. "For some women, amply displaying their bosoms is ill advised."

"That's true. If they're too small. Or too old," Gage concurred, pulling a face.

"One does wonder about Dear Annabelle. We know nothing about her, except that she hasn't been able to get the attentions of some bloke for *years*." Drummond continued his dissection of Annabelle's situation with the same seriousness with which he examined *Hamlet*.

"She could be a grandmother," Gage whispered, aghast. Color drained from his face. "I might have just written a letter to someone's grandmother telling her to show off her you know whats."

"Oh for God's sake," Knightly cut in. "Annabelle is young and pretty."

"Why hasn't this nodcock noticed her, then?" Gage challenged.

"Damned if I know," Knightly said with a shrug. He had no idea who this bloke was and nor did he care, so long as Annabelle's quest sold issues of the paper. It seemed like it was well poised to do so if these corkbrains were so fascinated with it. "She's very quiet."

"Young. Pretty. Quiet. I think I'm in love," Drummond said dreamily.

"You don't even know her," Knightly said, bringing a dose of much-needed logic to the conversation. One did not fall in love with strangers. Although, his father had fallen in love with his mother at first sight. But that was rare. And neither Drummond or Gage had even *seen* Annabelle.

"I've heard enough. My next suggestion to her will be to forget that nodcock and marry me," Drummond said with a grin.

# Chapter 7

### The Dangers of Sultry Gazes

FASHIONABLE INTELLIGENCE BY A LADY OF DISTINCTION
*There are two questions burning on the lips of every Londoner: Who is the Nodcock and what will Dear Annabelle do next?*
*The London Weekly*

*Offices of* The London Weekly

**A**NNABELLE'S heart pounded. Any second now Knightly would stroll through that door and the butterflies in her belly would take flight.

He would flash them all a devilish grin, and she couldn't help but imagine him grinning at her like that, just before he kissed her under a starry, moonlit sky. Without fail, a blush would suffuse her cheeks.

Then Knightly would say "Ladies first" and she would sigh, a world of longing, desire, and frustration contained in that little exhalation.

This routine occurred like clockwork every Wednesday afternoon at precisely two o'clock when Knightly met with the writers of *The London Weekly*.

But this week things would be different. Of that, she was certain. She had a plan.

"Annabelle, I adored your column this week, and it is the topic du jour in all the drawing rooms," Julianna said as she sashayed into the room and took a seat next to Annabelle, who had arrived early.

Previously, her reason for arriving a good quarter of an hour prior to everyone else had to do with a terror of arriving late, interrupting everyone and finding herself the center of unwanted attention. But lately she thought not of that potential embarrassment, but the potential magic that might arise should she find herself with Knightly, alone.

Sophie and Eliza followed right behind Julianna and took their seats. The rest of the writers began to file in, talking amongst themselves.

"Lord Marsden liked it as well," Annabelle said, and could not hide her smile.

"He's such a charming rake," Sophie said, smiling. "Almost *too* charming."

"That charming and attentive rake that actually reads my column," Annabelle corrected gleefully. "He sent flowers on Saturday afternoon because he was so pleased I had obliged him by using the term 'nodcock' in my column. Can you believe I used such a word? I have shocked myself."

"You might be wicked after all," Julianna replied.

"Let's not get ahead of ourselves," Annabelle cautioned.

"And let's not forget that the gentleman sent you flowers!" Eliza said.

"Pink roses. Blanche and her awful friend Mrs. Underwood couldn't let that pass without an array of snide comments. She couldn't fathom they were for me, and then she wondered what sort of shenanigans I had engaged in to oblige a man to send these to me, and then she said they would look very fine in Fleur's bedroom."

"Fleur is such a whimsical name. I'm quite surprised by it . . ." Sophie said.

"Indeed, coming from my brother and his wife," Annabelle said. "They suffer terribly from a lack of imagination. Fleur's fancy name is the one thing that gives me hope. I later stole them out of Fleur's bedroom and put them in mine. I'm certain I'll find them in Blanche's chamber when I return."

"But you have received flowers. From a gentleman. A very eligible and marriageable one," Julianna said, smiling.

Annabelle beamed. She had also spent hours with a needle and thread to lower the bodices on her dreary old gowns. When Blanche saw what she was doing, she asked why Annabelle wished to look like a dockside harpy. *Because a dockside harpy can attract the attentions of men. So I can marry and move out of this suffocating household.*

If only Blanche knew about her silky underthings and her phenomenal corset—which she wore now, of course, for confidence, along with the pretty blue day dress she'd ordered on that wonderful life-altering trip to the modiste. Sophie had been so very right about the dresses and the underthings, although Annabelle knew she was not yet wicked enough to mention her unmentionables in mixed company.

Ever since that fateful day, she had entertained that wicked thought, "Why me," and life in the Swift household had become more stifling. And after she wore that silk dress, waltzed with a marquis, received a bouquet of pink roses from an eligible gentleman, and had an actual conversation with Knightly, she started to think less about Old Annabelle who did Blanche's bidding and more about New Annabelle who might do anything.

"But what does this mean for you know who?" Eliza asked in a conspiratorial whisper.

"Oh, I have more tricks up my sleeve, thanks to my readers," Annabelle replied in a hushed voice. As per the instructions of "A Courtesan in Mayfair," she had spent hours before the looking glass, as she practiced lifting and lowering her lashes and gazing smolderingly.

Today, Annabelle was armed and ready in a fetching new dress with a remarkably low bodice and sultry glances for her beloved Mr. Knightly.

The clock struck two. First the pounding heart. Next, the butterflies. And then, the sigh.

KNIGHTLY strolled into the room and began the meeting as he'd begun every other one, with a grin and a cheeky nod to the Writing Girls.

His gaze was immediately drawn to Annabelle. To be exact, specific parts of Annabelle. The conversation in the coffeehouse came galloping back to mind. Lowered bodices. Advice from idiots. Young. Pretty. Quiet. Significantly lowered bodices that revealed . . . a handful. A mouthful. A woman.

He cleared his throat.

"Ladies first," he said, hoping not to sound . . . distracted.

Julianna launched into the ton's latest scandal and Knightly didn't listen to a word of it. His gaze kept shifting one seat to her left, to Annabelle. When he managed to wrench his focus away from her very low bodice and up, he saw a dreamy expression on her face. Her blue eyes were focused on something far off and far away. Her full pink lips were curved into the slightest trace of a smile. Annabelle was daydreaming.

In a meeting.

Which he was leading. He would not be ignored.

"Miss Swift, you and your column were the topic of conversation in the coffeehouse Saturday last," he said briskly. He fought to keep his expression neutral as he recalled that bedeviling conversation with Drummond and Gage. He'd be damned if his staff saw that he was affected by her. It was bad enough to mention this topic of her bodice in a room of mixed company, in a professional setting, however indirectly.

He wanted to look. He could . . . not . . . look.

"Oh? It was?" Jolted from her reverie, she fixed those big blue eyes upon him, the force of which stunned him for a second. Then she lowered her lids and lifted them again. And pouted her lips, almost as if she were sucking on a lemon. Was she unwell?

"I urge you to take care with the advice you elect to follow. I'm not sure if indelicate or idiotic is the right word for some of these bloke's suggestions," he lectured. In the back of his mind, he wondered when he'd become so stuffy.

Her eyes seemed bluer today. Why was he noticing her eyes? Was it her blue dress? Didn't she always wear brownish-grayish dresses? His gaze dropped to Annabelle's dress, and he did not take note of the color at all. He saw creamy white skin rising in tantalizing swells above an extremely low bodice.

"With all due respect, Mr. Knightly, it seems to be working." She said it softly, with a hint of defiance mingling with deference. Her mouth reminded him of an angel's pout—sulky, sweet, mysterious and mischievous.

The kind of mouth a man thought of kissing.

And thoughts like that were exactly why women were not oft employed with men. Damned distracting.

"Annabelle's column has taken the ton by storm," Sophie said.

To Knightly's surprise, Owens—the most promising young rogue reporter who covered all manner of sordid stories—spoke up. "My mum and sisters keep yammering on about it. Miss Swift, they are of the opinion that you should try a different manner of styling your hair. I told 'em blokes don't notice that sort of thing. Instead what they really notice is—"

"That's enough, Owens," Knightly said sharply. If that cad mentioned anything below Annabelle's neck . . .

Knightly snuck another glance.

*Damn.*

She had caught his eye and then closed her eyes for a second or two, slowly lifting her lashes, fluttering them, and then sort of pouting again. How odd. Truly strange.

"Is this more rubbish about attracting a gentleman's attentions?" Grenville muttered. "Because the word in Parliament is that an inquiry is being formed to examine journalistic practices in light of *The London Times* reporter's arrest and subsequent imprisonment. I for one am concerned about what this means for our own publication."

Knightly offered a prayer of thanks to Grenville for ending the conversation about Annabelle's . . . charms. And for sitting on the far side of the room so that he could focus on Grenville and turn his back to her . . . charms.

"Will that parliamentary inquiry be focused on *The London Times*, specifically, or other publications, generally?" Owens asked. "Rumors are flying. I heard every periodical will have to submit to a government review before publication. A footman was fired from Lord Milford's employ after it was suspected he sold secrets to the press."

"Oh, it's worse than that," Julianna added gravely. "I heard Lord Milford gave the poor footman quite a thrashing before turning him out on the streets. To quote Lord Marsden, 'One is appalled at the peddling of aristocratic secrets for the profit and amusement of the lower classes.' Many are in agreement with him."

The room fell silent. The faces of his writers peered at him expectantly. Of course they would assume he would have a strategy or a scheme to exploit public opinion to their advantage or to otherwise ensure that *The London Weekly* was triumphant—and that their livelihoods and reputations were secure.

This thing with *The London Times* might be another newspaper's problem, or it could explode into an industrywide scandal and investigation. It looked like Marsden had a taste for blood, and intended more than the ruination of one reporter, or one newspaper.

The question was, how would *The London Weekly* fare in the midst of this crusade?

His writers routinely risked everything and anything for stories that had made *The London Weekly* great. Eliza had done numerous dangerous undercover stints, including disguising herself as a maid in a duke's household—the very exploits that had the ton riled up and calling for blood. Julianna routinely put her reputation on the line by exposing the scandals and foibles of her peers. Owens never met an assignment he didn't risk a stint in prison for, and no person or thing was too sacred for his ruthless investigating. What would become of Alistair or Grenville if they didn't have an outlet for their wit and discerning writing?

Knightly knew that he might own the newspaper, but it would be worthless without them. He couldn't let this scandal blow out of control, and definitely couldn't let his faithful and talented writers be sent to Newgate for their work, which served a city, both informing and entertaining the population.

He hadn't given much thought to Marsden's offer until this moment when it seemed he was the only thing standing between safety and disaster for the people he owed *everything* to.

Though the marquis dangled something he wanted very badly—entrée into high society with a strategic marriage—it conflicted with truth number three: *Be beholden to no one.*

But if it would protect his newspaper and his writers—while assuring his prominence in London society—hell, it was an offer worth entertaining. The New Earl would never be able to snub the man so connected to such a prominent marquis. This inquiry would turn a blind eye to his scandalous newspaper and the exploits of its writers.

It was an offer worth taking. Knightly made decisions quickly, and then abided by them. On the spot, he made up his mind to court Lady Lydia and probably marry her. He would take Marsden up on his offer to protect his paper and his writers.

"Rest assured, I'm doing everything in my power to ensure the authorities don't turn their attentions to *The Weekly*," Knightly said confidently. He could see them all visibly relax at the pronouncement, and he knew he'd made the right choice.

But speaking of turning one's attentions . . .

Knightly's eyes reluctantly flicked back to Annabelle. She did that strange thing with her very blue eyes again. Her lips were pursed into a pout that verged precariously on the side of ridiculous, and yet was strangely tempting all the same.

Grenville mercifully carried on about other, duller matters of government, and Damien Owens regaled everyone with that week's news of robberies, fires, murders, ridiculous wagers, and notable court cases. Knightly rushed everyone through, eager to conclude the meeting so that he might further investigate the burgeoning scandal with *The London Times*. And, frankly, so he could escape the distraction that Annabelle had suddenly, inexplicably, become.

He could kill Gage for suggesting the lowered bodice. But he suspected that damned actor wasn't the only one to send in that advice, and for good reason: it worked. Yea gods, it worked. Knightly couldn't stop looking—Annabelle and her décolletage was a sight to behold. That he'd forbidden himself made it all the more alluring.

She caught his eye again, and shyly looked down at her lap. He watched her lips murmur something incomprehensible, and then she glanced back at him. Eyelashes batting at a rapid pace. Lips pushed out. What the devil was she doing?

"Miss Swift, is there something in your eye?" he asked when he could restrain his curiosity no more.

"I am perfectly fine," she replied as a flush crept into her cheeks.

"Ah, it seemed you had something in your eye," he remarked, quizzically.

"No, nothing. I'm fine. Just fine." There was a hollow note in her voice. But he couldn't puzzle over that. Not when his empire was possibly under attack and it was up to him to protect it.

# Chapter 8

## A Writing Girl, Writing

**DEAR ANNABELLE**

*In reply to Embarrassed in East End, I suggest fleeing
to America, praying fervently for the floorboards to
open up and swallow you whole, or do your best to
pretend the mortifying incident never occurred.*

*—Annabelle, who has herself addressed many
prayers to the floorboards and even investigated
the price of a one-way ticket to America*
*The London Weekly*

*Annabelle's attic bedroom*

**A**NNABELLE sat frozen at her writing desk, still
paralyzed with mortification hours after the Awful
Incident. Never in her entire life had she been more
embarrassed, including the occasion in her twelfth
year when she had unwittingly tucked her petti-
coats and skirts into her unmentionables and proceeded to church. Thomas had paid attention to her
then, and laughed heartily despite the chastising of
their parents.

The Awful Incident was even more horrifying than the time she accidentally sat on a freshly painted brown park bench whilst daydreaming . . . and en route to a weekly writers meeting. It was the only time she'd ever been thankful for her grayish dresses, though the paint was still visible. In attempting to keep her backside from view of anyone, particularly Knightly, she tripped over a chair and fell sprawled to the floor.

Annabelle groaned and replayed the worst of the Awful Incident again in her mind. The thrill of Knightly fixing his attentions upon her. The devastating realization of why. *Miss Swift, is there something in your eye?*

Her attempts to appear seductive were an unmitigated failure. If she couldn't even look at the man seductively, how was she to make him love her? After the success of the lowered bodice, she thought a sultry gaze would spark his interest, and perhaps he would start to fall in love with the mysterious Writing Girl in his midst. Intrigued, he would begin to seduce her and she would prettily resist his advances for the appropriate amount of time, at which point . . .

She sighed as the truth sunk in: it seemed she would have to seduce Mr. Knightly and that it would require a few more tricks from her readers.

Annabelle crossed the room to the mirror and tried her sultry gaze once more. Lowered eyelashes. Pouting lips. Smoldering thoughts. Oh very well, she did look ridiculous! In a fit of despair and humiliation, she flung herself on her bed.

She had gotten his attention, at least. But for looking like a fool of the first water! In her head she heard his voice echoing over and over, asking that wretched question: *Miss Swift, is there something in your eye? Miss Swift, is there something in your eye? Miss Swift, is there something in your eye?*

She groaned and flung an arm over her eyes.

Not even the pink roses from Lord Marsden could console her. Very well, they did, slightly. Annabelle lifted her arm and looked at the gorgeous, fragrant bouquet sitting proudly and so *pinkly* on her writing desk, reminding her that a gentleman, *a marquis*, paid attention to her and read her column and shared private jokes with her.

Not all hope was lost, sultry gazes notwithstanding.

No man had ever sent her flowers before. She bolted upright, needing advice. Was she to write a thank-you note? If so, what did one say? She was an advice columnist and thus she ought to know these things.

Oh, but what a problem to have! Annabelle smiled proudly and, Lord help her, a giggle escaped her lips. She was not so disconsolate that she couldn't appreciate such a lovely problem: whether or not to pen a thank-you note for an exquisite bouquet of hothouse flowers from an eligible gentleman.

Not like, say, the man of your dreams asking if you have something in your eye when you are attempting to throw sultry glances his way.

Best not try sultry glances on Lord Marsden. Or anyone she might ever wish to pursue.

It was now her noble duty to alert the female population of London not to heed the well-intentioned advice of a "Courtesan from Mayfair." Annabelle returned to her writing desk, this time with more focus. After another heavenly inhalation of the roses, she began to write her next column.

> *Ladies of London, beware! A Courtesan from May-fair suggested that this author delivery sultry glances to the object of her affection. My attempts resulted in utter mortification! He—henceforth known as the Nodcock—merely inquired if I had something in my eye.*

Here Annabelle paused, and tapped the quill against her cheek as she thought about Knightly reading these very words. In an instant he would know that she had concocted a massive scheme involving the ten thousand regular readers of *The London Weekly* in a desperate attempt to gain his attention.

And that she called him a nodcock.

That was not acceptable. True, but unpublishable.

Her quill was poised above *nodcock*, ready to strike it out, when she meanly thought that Knightly wouldn't even read the column at all! The Nodcock.

However, it would do to make it just a touch more vague, because if she were to examine the contents of her heart and soul—as she was doing, in an effort to procrastinate, as one is wont to do—she would see that she wasn't ready to give up the jig just yet. In spite of the Awful Incident, she had made progress.

Her wardrobe had improved, and with it her confidence. A man had sent her flowers. She had managed a conversation with Knightly. Readers were responding with great favor to her column and to her quest. A New Annabelle was emerging; one who had adventures and flirtations to go along with Awful Incidences.

New Annabelle had much more fun than Old Annabelle, and being in possession of a great imagination and curiosity, she wondered where it would all lead. She wanted to know. She *could* know, so long as she did not allow one little Awful Incident to set her back. And as long as she composed her column to be vague enough so that Knightly might not put two and two together straight away.

Annabelle wanted his heart and she wanted his attention. But not from some slip of the pen. She wanted him to be drawn to her, interested in her, desperately in love with her. If she had to become a better version of herself, so be it. Frankly, it was much more exciting.

And so she rewrote the column to be a touch more vague, just in case Knightly did read it, and had a mind to place himself in it.

Then she rummaged through her assortment of reader letters for questions to answer, advice to dole out, and tricks to try to gain Knightly's attention.

"Ah, this one is perfect," she murmured. "Excellent idea, Sneaky From Southwark."

# Chapter 9

## Newspaper Proprietor Seeks Aristocratic Bride

### Dear Annabelle

*I was eager to attempt to "seduce a man with naught but the smoldering intensity of my love, revealed wordlessly in a sultry gaze," as per the advice of a Courtesan in Mayfair. Alas, dear readers, this led to a mortifying disaster! Rather than succumb to the fervor in my gaze, more than one person inquired if I had something stuck in my eye.*

*The London Weekly*

*Home of Mrs. Delilah Knightly, Russell Square*

"**W**ELL if it isn't my favorite son," Delilah Knightly remarked with a laugh as Derek Knightly strolled into the breakfast room unannounced. He was in the habit of calling on his mother every Saturday morning, like the good progeny that he was. Also, her cook made the best breakfast biscuits and refused to share the recipe with his cook. Never mind that he paid for them both.

"I'm your only son." This correction came with a slight grin.

"That's what I said. You're so literal, Derek. How did that happen?" she asked. Her voice was loud—all the better to carry to the back of the theater—and there was always a note of mirth in her tone, whether she was scolding her young child or requesting more tea from a servant. No matter what, life was terribly amusing to Delilah Knightly.

"I believe you possess all the acting ability and inclination to fantasy in this family," he said. She was a renowned stage actress, and one of his guiding principles was to avoid drama, unless it was on the stage or the printed page. "I'm as straightforward as they come."

"I know, I'm you're mother," she said with a broad smile, pushing a basket of freshly baked biscuits in his direction. "How are you, my dear?"

"Business is good." He took a seat and poured himself a cup of steaming hot coffee.

"Which means that everything is good. Such devotion to your work!" She paused, smiled wickedly, and said: "I wish you'd employ some of that infamous work ethic of yours on providing me with grandbabies."

"Mother." The word was a statement, a protest, and an answer. She loved to vex him with the topic and he refused to react. He didn't see why she bothered bringing it up.

"Oh for Lord's sake, Derek, I can't help my natural inclinations. Tell me, how is Annabelle faring?"

"Annabelle?" This caught him off guard. So much so that it took a moment before he realized whom she was referring to. Dear Annabelle of the lowered bodices and sultry gazes who was on a quest to win the heart of some nodcock.

That his mother was mentioning this topic did not bode well.

Why the devil would his mother give a whit about one of his Writing Girls? Granted, she was tremendously proud of those girls and was known to say that hiring them was the best damn thing he'd ever done. Made your mum, proud, she'd say.

Which isn't why he did it. The chits were good for business.

And how had Annabelle—a chit he never gave much of a passing thought to—suddenly intruded upon his every thought and conversation? He brooded over this, sipping his coffee, as his mother explained.

" 'Dear Annabelle.' The gal with the advice column. The one who is soliciting tips from readers on how to attract a man. You're really onto something with that one. I hadn't laughed so hard in an *age*." She chuckled again just thinking about it.

"Actually, I'm sure you have," he replied patiently. "You find humor in everything."

"It's an important life skill. But regardless, that girl is a doll. What is she really like?" His mum sipped her tea and then fixed her full attention upon him. The hair on the back of his neck stuck up in warning. When his mother took an interest in something . . . Things Happened.

"Annabelle?" He repeated her name in an effort to stall. And why was everyone asking him what Annabelle was like? He made a note to himself to read her columns more closely in the future.

His mother gave him a look that distinctly communicated *you dolt*.

"She's young. Pretty. Nice." The answer was deliberately evasive. The same answer he'd given to Drummond and Gage, and for the same reason. If Annabelle and this column didn't come across as too interesting, his mother might lose interest. Like playing dead to avoid a dog attack.

She yawned. Dramatically.

"You should include a picture with her column. One of those illustrations." Knightly thought about what the blokes in the coffeehouse had talked about. Was she pretty? Were they advising a grandma to show more cleavage? Some protective instinct flared; he did not want those louts looking upon Annabelle's beauty. In some way, she belonged to him, in that he had hired her and given her this platform to enact her romantic schemes.

But a portrait of her would be damn good for business. Pretty girls sold so well.

"That's a fine idea. Randolph can have it done in an afternoon," he answered, and made a mental note to make the request when he returned to the office later.

"What did you think of her column? Wasn't it hysterical?" his mother asked. "Is she unwell? What a nodcock! Ha!"

It was not hysterical. He felt like an ass. She wrote of her failed attempts to employ a sultry gaze and that numerous people inquired if she had something in her eye. He took consolation in the fact that he was not the only one to ask. But still—he felt like an ass.

She must have been idly practicing in the meeting, or the man she was after was on staff. Definitely not Grenville. She was set up for heartache if it were Alistair. It had to be Owens. It mattered not to him.

But really, *Owens*? The man was young and talented but hotheaded, and with a habit of frequenting gaming hells and embarking on the most dangerous schemes to get stories. He spent most of his hours chasing down murders, investigating fires, and impersonating footmen and officers. When would he have time to court Annabelle? Or perhaps that was the point of her escapades.

"It was amusing," Knightly answered carefully. His mother's eyes narrowed. Bloody hell. She suspected something.

"You were one of the men to ask if she was unwell, were you not?" she asked, her eyes narrowing further. Damned intuition of mothers. Why they were not employed by the Bow Street Runners was a mystery to him.

She sighed heavily. "Oh, Derek, I do worry about you, taking everything so seriously. So literally. Then again, I do tend to the dramatic—"

"Overdramatic?"

"Oh, hush you," she said playfully and swatting at his hand. "Speaking of my flair for drama, I have a new show opening. I play the wicked fairy-godmother-like character. I love it."

"Sounds perfect for you," he said, grinning. "I shall be there opening night."

"You are a good son. A Great Son would bring that theater-reviewing employee of his. The one with the brilliantly colored waistcoats. If he gives me a bad review, you mustn't print it."

"I wouldn't dare. And I won't worry about it because you'll be fantastic," he said. And she would. For all her dramatics off the stage, Delilah Knightly had a gift and was a supremely talented actress.

"What will you do with the rest of your day? Back to the office?" his mother inquired, sipping her tea.

"Actually, I must pay a visit. Lord and Lady Marsden," Knightly said, sipping his coffee. Once he decided something, he acted. And he had decided to accept Marsden's offer. Thus, he would court Lady Marsden.

"Still angling to marry into the ton? I really don't know why," his mother said dismissively. It was an argument they'd had often over the years, ever since October 4, 1808, when he'd been forcibly ejected from his father's funeral. *Throw the bastard out. He doesn't belong here.*

But he did belong. And he would prove it.

She carried on with her condemnation of the ton, as she tended to do: "The lot of them are stiff and stuffy old bores with naught to do but make up silly rules and gossip viciously when they are broken. Except for your dear departed father, of course."

His father, the Earl of Harrowby, an esteemed member of Parliament and the ton. Respected peer of the realm. Beloved father.

There was a moment where they both fell silent, both thinking the same thing. There was someone missing from this scene. Even after all these years, *decades*, there was still a vague sense of incompletion. Like all the i's hadn't been dotted and the t's hadn't been crossed.

Her lover. His father. The late Earl of Harrow.

They had been *almost* the picture perfect family. Knightly remembered a home filled with warmth and laughter. His parents would dance around the drawing room to songs his mother would sing.

And inevitably his father would return to his other

family. The proper family. The family that wanted no part of the bastard by-blow. The brother that shared his blood but wouldn't look him in the eye.

"I am not cultivating this connection for amusement. Merely for business," Knightly answered curtly. The business of claiming what he deserved. What he had spent every moment since the funeral pursuing. He would not lose everything now.

"Oh, business! It's always business with you, Derek," his mother said with a huff and a pout.

How could he explain that amusement and work were one and the same for him? That everything he had ever wanted involved acceptance from the one person who wasn't alive to give it to him, and the next best thing was his half brother and the society that had claimed the late earl as one of its own.

And then there was his newspaper, which Knightly protected as if it were his own newborn. He couldn't explain these things; the words always died in his throat, if he was even able to articulate them in his mind at all. Funny, that being a man of words, there were so many unavailable to him.

*Berkeley Square*

KNIGHTLY discovered that the Marsden residence possessed many of the traits typical to an old ancestral home: it was drafty and vast with many wood paneled rooms and the air of being gently worn after a century of use. Marsden had invited Knightly to call upon him when Knightly sent a note indicating interest in discussing ways in which they might collaborate on the Inquiry, as it had become known.

From ballrooms to the coffeehouses it was fervently discussed in hushed whispers. What had the reporter uncovered? The rumors ranged from the benign to the horrific. What was to become of the newspapers?

Livelihoods were at stake. Knowledge, power, and wealth, too.

For Knightly, it was a simple matter of having everything he ever wanted: the success of *The Weekly* in addition to the aristocratic marriage that would assure him a prominent place in the high society that had rejected him.

Or risk it all . . . for what? There were too many livelihoods on the line, from his writers to the unfortunate boys selling newspapers on street corners. The more he thought about it—and sipped excellent brandy and enjoyed Marsden's conversation—the more saying no became unthinkable.

"Ah, Lydia, there you are," Marsden said as his younger sister appeared in the doorway a short while after her brother had sent a maid to fetch her.

She was beautiful not because of her features or her figure—both of which were admirable—but because Lady Lydia moved with a perfect grace. Where others might walk, she would glide. Her every movement, whether the incline of her head for a nod or the gentle waver of her fan in a heated ballroom, was a demonstration of perfect elegance. Her hair was dark and sleekly curled. Her eyes were dark and expressive. Her attire—from her sage green silk day gown to the ruby ear bobs—announced her status as A Person of Consequence.

She would look perfect on his arm. Save for the petulant pout. She was not pleased to have his company.

"We were just talking about the scandal at *The Times*," Marsden said.

"That's no surprise," she remarked dryly. The gentlemen stood as she strolled leisurely across the carpet. She was in no hurry to make his acquaintance. Knightly kept his emotions in check and reminded himself of the facts: she was the subject of gossip, and he was an infamous and influential newspaperman. Also, she was the sister to a marquis and he was a bastard. Literally.

"I'd like to introduce you to Mr. Knightly, of *The London Weekly*," Marsden said. "He's a new friend of mine."

"I recall that you've been singing his praises. Good afternoon, Mr. Knightly." She offered her hand languidly. The action was polite, and yet there was a stunning lack of interest motivating her. Knightly was intrigued.

"Pleased to meet you, Lady Marsden."

"Are you here for a story? Will we read about this in the gossip columns?" she inquired in the voice of a polite hostess, and yet there was an icy undercurrent not to be missed.

"Lydia—" Marsden said in a tone of lethal warning.

"It's a fair question, given the newspaper's *interest* in us," she said, gracefully lowering herself to sit upon the settee.

"I am pleased to let you know Knightly is on our side," Marsden said, with a glance at Knightly, who nodded to confirm that their understanding was in effect. Knightly would marry Lady Lydia, and Marsden's Inquiry wouldn't look too closely at the daring, questionable practices of *The London Weekly*.

"Really," she said, her voice dripping with disbelief. She stared hard at her brother.

"Really," Marsden said firmly, returning her stare.

Knightly sipped his drink and wondered if this was a typical sibling rivalry or if something else was afoot. He wouldn't know . . .

"The weather is very fine today. Would you care to walk with me, Lady Marsden?" Knightly offered, thinking he'd have better luck with her if he was not in the middle of some sibling battle. Also, should the New Earl happen upon the sight of him with Lady Lydia, the earl would be rankled and he would be pleased. Sibling rivalry was in full effect even if they'd never met.

"What a capital idea," Marsden said, clapping his hands. "It'll afford you both the opportunity to become better acquainted, and to perhaps see if you'll suit."

# Chapter 10

## An "Accidental" Encounter

TOWN TALK

*We hear that a certain marquis with a scandalous sister has been rather short on funds of late. We wonder: how does one lose a centuries-old fortune in under a year?*

*The Morning Post*

IN order to attempt the advice offered by Sneaky from Southwark, Annabelle enlisted the assistance of her own devious, meddlesome, and well-connected friends.

The tip: orchestrate an "accidental" encounter.

The trick: discovering when and where one might accidentally encounter Knightly. As far as anyone knew, he traveled from his home to *The Weekly* offices and back again—very early in the morning and very late at night.

However, thanks to Sophie and Julianna's machinations, the Writing Girls learned that he planned to visit Lord Marsden, probably to discuss the parliamentary inquiry into newspaper practices. The marquis conveniently lived near Sophie, between her house (which might more aptly be described as a castle, it was so massive) and Hyde Park.

The sun was shining. The birds were singing. Yes, they had snooped in Bryson's schedule for Knightly, but it was for the noble purpose of true love. Annabelle happily strolled along the neat streets of Mayfair with Sophie. Their pace was that of snails. The better to enjoy the atmosphere, of course.

"We have arrived at the park," Annabelle stated. Yet they had not encountered their quarry. This was not proceeding according to plan.

In her imagination, Annabelle would have seen Knightly as he strolled out the Marsdens' front door. They would laugh together at the marvel of meeting thusly. Then Knightly would suggest they take advantage of the fine day to stroll along the tree-lined paths of the park. They would stroll arm in arm, and at some point Sophie would discreetly vanish, leaving them alone. Perhaps a thunderous storm cloud would arise and they would seek shelter in an abandoned gazebo and he would gather her in his arms and say something devastatingly romantic, like—

"Come to think of it, I cannot believe I did not bring my parasol. I fear freckles," Sophie remarked, apropos of nothing.

"Since when do you care about freckles?" Annabelle asked, puzzled.

"I think we ought to return to the house for my parasol before we walk through the park," Sophie insisted. But Annabelle did not wish to spend a minute indoors, where they would certainly not see Knightly.

"You have your bonnet," Annabelle pointed out.

"I fear it may not be sufficient, and I'll be a social pariah if I get freckles," Sophie refuted.

"You're a duchess . . ." Not only that, she was extremely well regarded. She'd have to do a lot worse than freckles if society were to cut her.

"Oh, Annabelle," Sophie said with a giggle.

"Oh. That was just an excuse to walk past the Marsden home again, wasn't it? How silly of me. I'm just hopelessly distracted," Annabelle said as Sophie's intentions crystallized. She'd been so swept up in her imagined scene.

"Ah, young love," Sophie remarked lightly.

They continued their stroll. Annabelle began to marvel that what had seemed so simple on paper might be difficult to manage. At the very least, a stroll with her friend through the elegant cobblestone streets of Mayfair was vastly preferable to her usual afternoon activities of mending worn-out shirts, leading the children in their mathematics lessons, or writing her column solving everyone else's problems.

Sophie's exclamation jolted her from her thoughts.

"Mr. Knightly! What a coincidence!"

*It's really working!* It was Annabelle's first thought. Then, second: *She is not supposed to be here.* Her brain registered a woman on Knightly's arm, and further cognitive function ground to a halt. Sneaky in Southwark hadn't mentioned that she might interrupt Mr. Knightly with another women. More to the point, a beautiful, graceful, elegant lady who made Annabelle feel like the most provincial spinster auntie, even in her fetching new day dress.

"May I present Lady Lydia Marsden," Knightly

said, and the perfect woman on his arm inclined her head ever so slightly. "These are two of the infamous Writing Girls, The Duchess of Brandon and Miss Annabelle Swift."

There was a flicker of recognition on Lady Lydia's perfect features.

"My brother has been quite taken with you, Dear Annabelle. Did you enjoy the roses he sent?" Lady Lydia asked, much to Annabelle's surprise. She glanced up at Knightly and saw him peering at her, intrigued.

Her pulse quickened with a feeling that could only be akin to triumph, for Knightly was now curious to know that she was desirable, for other gentlemen—marquises—had sent her roses.

She felt a surge of affection for Lady Lydia.

"Oh, they were absolutely beautiful," Annabelle replied. "Although I am surprised your brother finds my column of interest. He must have so many greater concerns."

"He likes to know everything, however great or small. Like a terrier with a rat, he is," Lady Lydia said. "I myself don't bother much with the newspapers these days. I abhor the gossip columns."

Knightly grinned at Annabelle, and she smiled in return, knowing the same thought had crossed their minds: *Thank goodness Julianna isn't here!*

It was such a small thing, that knowing smile. But she of the overlooked sighs and unrequited longing was now sharing a private joke with Mr. Knightly during an encounter of her own orchestration.

A heady rush of pleasure stole over Annabelle, and it was as much Knightly's smile as it was the sunshine warming her skin. Most of all it was that she had made this moment occur. Fate had nothing on her.

"It's a lovely day for a walk, is it not?" Sophie said.

"Indeed," Lady Lydia replied. "We were just returning from a walk in Hyde Park."

Annabelle's hopes started to fade.

"There are matters at the office I must attend to after I see Lady Lydia home," Knightly added.

After politely wishing them a lovely afternoon, Sophie and Annabelle walked along in silence, until a safe distance had elapsed.

"Perhaps he is merely digging for gossip for Julianna," Sophie said. "She is like a hound at a fox-hunt when it comes to that particular rumor of Lady Lydia's missing season."

"Ah yes, the missing second season. What are they saying?" Annabelle asked. Her pleasure in the exchange was starting to fade as she watched Knightly and Lady Lydia stroll off together.

"There are only three reasons a woman would miss her season," Sophie explained "A death in the family, which we know is not the case, or illness, or a baby."

"What does it matter?" Annabelle asked.

"It probably doesn't in the grand scheme of things. But everyone is desperate to know," Sophie said. "The ton does love their gossip."

"Do you think Knightly is courting her?" Annabelle asked, with a prayer the answer was no.

"It would appear to be so. Gentlemen generally do not escort marriageable misses for walks in the park if they are not considering something more," Sophie explained. She didn't need to add that it was doubly true for a man like Knightly, who did nothing that wouldn't ultimately benefit himself, his paper, or his empire.

"You do know what this means, Annabelle. It seems you have competition and must try a more ambitious scheme."

# Chapter 11

### Every Rogue Needs a Rival

*Offices of* The London Weekly, *late*

THIS was madness. This was dangerous. The suggestion of Careless in Camden Town had seemed clever and simple when it was just the few lines of a letter. Leave something behind. Return for it later. Find herself alone with Knightly. Allow romance to ensue.

Simple, no?

It had seemed imperative to Annabelle that she try something more daring after learning she had competition: Lady Lydia Marsden. It wasn't just the walk in the park. Julianna had learned that Lord Marsden was encouraging the courtship. They would have more walks in the park until they walked down the aisle.

Unless she managed to win his heart . . .

At the moment, however, Annabelle was having second thoughts about her quest, and in particular, this latest scheme. But it was too late to turn back, for she had already arrived at the offices of *The Weekly* after hours.

At the end of this week's staff meeting, Annabelle had left behind her shawl. Her nicest shawl, to add credence for her subsequent return for it. For the expedition, she wore her newly purchased day dress cut in a style that flattered her figure and in a shade of pale blue that enhanced her eyes. At the very least, she looked her best for this poorly planned adventure.

At home, Blanche would be wondering where she'd gotten off to—after realizing that the children hadn't had their lessons and fires hadn't been lit.

How was she to explain herself? She hadn't thought every aspect of this mad scheme all the way through because if she had, Old Annabelle would have concocted a million things that could go wrong and a million other reasons why she ought to stay home, safe.

New Annabelle prevailed.

And if anyone asked why she didn't wait until next week's writers' gathering, she had no good answer other than that dusk was much more romantic than daylight, and romance was more likely to occur in solitude rather than with the editorial staff of *The London Weekly* looking on.

Plus, she had a column due. She needed something to write about.

Thus, Annabelle slipped into the offices at the end of the day.

Knightly was still here, thank goodness, but he

wasn't alone. She lingered in the shadows outside of his office, waffling over her course of action but ultimately settling upon eavesdropping. Julianna would have her head if she didn't.

"What have you found out?" Knightly asked. She recognized the impatient tone of his voice. As if the earth didn't spin fast enough for him.

"Brinsley had kept up the ruse of doctor for months and ventured into many a proper woman's bedchamber," another man said.

Annabelle recognized the voice as belonging to Damien Owens. If Knightly had an heir to his empire, it would be Owens—young, brash, ruthless, and quite the charmer.

They could only be talking about the scandal with *The London Times*. Brinsley must be the reporter who had been arrested and now languished in Newgate.

"Bloody hell," Knightly swore. "What he must know . . ."

"My thoughts exactly," Owens agreed.

Annabelle dared to peek around the corner, glancing into Knightly's office, for the door remained ajar. She saw him pacing, hands clasped behind his back and brow furrowed in thought.

She bit back a sigh.

There was an intensity, depth, and energy about him that awed her and captivated her attentions. She noted the lock of hair that fell rakishly into his eyes, which he ruthlessly shoved back. How she wanted to run her own fingers through his hair . . .

His mouth was pressed into a hard line; she thought only of softening it by pressing her own lips to his.

"I want to talk to Brinsley," Knightly said briskly. "Our best angle is to portray it as a crime of one rogue reporter, not endemic of the entire newspaper industry," he added confidently.

"Understood, sir," Damien said.

She, too, understood that numerous articles would soon appear suggesting exactly that, then rumors to that effect would circulate. It was only a matter of time before Londoners believed it as the gospel—and marveled how *The London Weekly* was always so in tune with the heart of the city.

The conversation ended and Owens stepped out of the office, bumping right into Annabelle.

"Oof," she said. Again. For goodness sakes.

"Miss Swift! What are you doing here?" Owens asked, looking at her curiously.

"My shawl," she said. She became aware of Knightly glancing at them through the open door. "I had forgotten it here. It's my best one."

"You probably left it in the writers' room. I'll go look with you," Owens offered. Then he linked his arm with hers and led her along.

"What are you—" Annabelle started to ask in a hushed whisper, but Owens cut her off.

"Lovely weather today," he remarked. What did that have to do with anything? And didn't the man realize he ought to make his exit, leaving her alone with Knightly?

Owens followed her into the writer's room and then he *closed the door*, effectively shutting them alone, together.

"What are you doing?" she hissed, reaching for the doorknob.

Owens blocked her access by stepping in front of the doorway. For the first time, she noticed that he was quite tall, and his shoulders were rather broad.

His torso was flat and underneath his jacket he was probably well muscled from all of his dangerous exploits.

Her eyes locked with his. Dark brown. Long lashes. She had never noticed.

Annabelle's mind reeled. This was not what she had planned. What on earth was occurring?

"Is this one of your schemes?" Owens asked, a slight grin playing on his lips. There was no escaping and avoiding the question.

He leaned against the door. Lord save her from men who leaned.

"Whatever do you mean?" she asked. She didn't want to answer the question. She didn't quite know what was happening.

"Oh, come off it, Miss Swift. We're not all as dense as he is," Owens replied.

"So what if it is?" she asked, a bit miffed. "If so, you are standing in the way of my . . . story. My work. For the paper."

*Of true love,* she wanted to add. Instead, for emphasis, she uttered a certain three words for the first time in her life. "How dare you."

Owens laughed. "It's a good trick, Annabelle, leaving something behind. Classic. But how are you going to write about this without him discovering everything? He isn't stupid."

That was a good question. One she didn't have an answer for. Especially since Owens was right: she couldn't write about this without giving herself away. Again she realized that she hadn't thought this through. She blamed deadlines for her hasty actions. And the sad fact that if she thought about something too much, then she'd never do it.

"I'll come up with something," she replied. The room felt small all of a sudden. And warm. Owens peered down at her with dark, velvety brown eyes.

His response was unexpected.

"You're welcome," he said bluntly.

"I beg your pardon?" she asked, aghast. He was ruining her plans with every moment that he stood blocking the door with his tall and strong self and every second that he kept them mysteriously ensconced in this room. Together. Alone.

"Look, Annabelle, here is some free advice. Men thrive on rivalry. On the chase. On the challenge. And for the sake of your column, you need to raise some suspicions in his mind. If he's certain that he's the Nodcock, then it's too easy. But if it might be me," Owens let his voice trail off as the suggestion sank in.

Annabelle paused, allowing the words to sink in.

Making Knightly doubt would give her the liberty to write freely, without fear of betraying herself. It would make for better copy, which would make for better sales. And if there was one thing that caught Knightly's eye like nothing else, it was stellar sales.

People had written her letters suggesting that she encourage a rival and competition, but she'd dismissed it as impossible, for who would play such a part with her?

Owens, that's who. Owens who, she was now noticing, was a rather handsome young man.

"I see your point," she conceded. "But why would you do this to help me?"

"Because the sooner he gets married and starts having a life outside of this office, the sooner I get a promotion," Owens explained, as if it should have been obvious. "He's not the only one with ambitions around here."

"How does this work?" she asked.

"It's already working. Because now you can write about this and he'll wonder if you're after me or him. It'll make you interesting."

"Are you saying I'm dull?" she asked, aghast. Again.

"Not anymore, Annabelle," Owens said, grinning. "Not anymore."

"I'm not quite sure how to take that," she muttered, brow furrowing.

"I'm being helpful, Annabelle. And really, do something else with your hair," he said.

"Whatever do you mean?" she asked, aghast. Again. But her hands reached up to that tight bun held fast by a ribbon and pins.

"Allow me," Owens said softly, and reached out to expertly remove a hairpin or two, thus freeing a few wavy strands that fell softly around her cheeks. She watched him watching her. His gaze was warm and she saw something like wonder in his expression.

"Much better," he murmured. Her lips parted but no sound emerged. Something was happening— something far more than the removal of a few hairpins. Annabelle, always one to shy away from things, took a step back.

And promptly tripped over a chair.

She started to fall, but Owens moved quickly to catch her in his arms.

At that moment Knightly happened to open the door, discovering her in the arms of another man with her hair tussled and her lips parted. She knew it could only mean one thing to him: that she and Owens were up to something wicked.

"Is something amiss?" Knightly inquired.

"I forgot my shawl," Annabelle blurted out, which didn't explain anything, really.

Owens helped her to her feet and stood by her side. "I was assisting Miss Swift," he said smoothly.

It wasn't exactly a lie. Owens deviously let those words hang in the air, allowing Knightly to make assumptions. Annabelle watched Knightly process the scene with narrowed eyes and clenched jaw. Was Owens right? Was a rival just what she needed?

"I was just leaving to see about that thing we discussed," Owens said, affectionately touching Annabelle on the elbow before quitting the room, leaving her alone with Knightly.

Knightly leaned against the doorjamb. She bit back a sigh. She did so love it when he leaned.

"That must be quite the shawl," Knightly remarked.

"It's my best one," she replied, wrapping the blue cashmere around her even though she wasn't cold in the slightest. Quite the contrary, in fact.

"Is there a particular event you require it for?" he asked politely. Too politely. As if he suspected that she was up to her neck in some sort of scheme. She told herself she was oversensitive.

"Church on Sunday, of course," she said. But then she didn't stop there, as she ought to have done. Nerves got the better of her. Rambling Annabelle took over: "Which will come before our next weekly staff meeting, and I didn't dare risk forgetting to come another time. I must have my best shawl for church as it's the only one that matches my best dress and of course I have to wear my best dress to church. Do you attend church?"

"No," Knightly said flatly. "Not unless you count this."

By "this" she presumed he meant *The London Weekly*.

"Oh," Annabelle replied. She did not know if that counted. Didn't know how quite to reply, really. She loosened the shawl, for she was now quite hot. They really ought to open a window.

Knightly smiled at her in a way that made her heart race. Like he had a secret. Like they had a private joke. Like he knew she was up to something.

"I'm glad that you have your shawl," he said. "Given that it's June."

"Oh, you know the weather in England . . . so very fickle," Annabelle managed to reply.

"A second best shawl just wouldn't do," Knightly persisted, wickedly having fun at her expense, she was sure of it. This was not how this was supposed to go. And yet she was alone, with Knightly, when otherwise she would be sitting at home while her brother read the newspapers and Blanche read improving literature aloud to the family. Such was the unexciting life of Old Annabelle.

This was wicked good fun, and New Annabelle would enjoy it and play along.

"What makes you think I have a second best shawl?" She tried to sound perfectly natural, and thought she did an all right job of it.

"Your family owns a cloth importing business. If there is one thing you are lacking in, I would not put my money on it being shawls," Knightly replied as her mouth parted slightly in shock.

Some days she had wondered if he even knew her name, and yet he was aware of her family's business? Her jaw might have dropped open.

"How did you know that?"

"Miss Swift, it is my business to know," Knightly replied. Then, pushing off the doorjamb, he stood tall and said, "Come, let's take you home."

"Oh I couldn't impossibly intrude." The words—stupid words refusing such a coveted invitation—were off her tongue before she could stop them because she knew her home was impossibly out of the way.

That's what happened when one made a habit of being deferential and always thinking of others first. It became an automatic behavior that, in spite of her every effort, she still occasionally defaulted to.

"I couldn't call myself a gentleman and allow you to go off into the London night. Alone," Knightly said. She had come alone, for Spinster Aunties such as herself didn't have chaperones, they were chaperones.

"Well if you insist," Annabelle replied, quite possibly sounding coy for the first time in her life.

# Chapter 12

## Carriage Rides Ought to Be Chaperoned

**DEAR ANNABELLE**

*Some gentlemen are N.S.I.C. (Not Safe in Carriages). I
hope your nodcock is one them.*
*Frisky on Farringdon Road*
*The London Weekly*

**K**NIGHTLY couldn't say *why*, but the prospect of
this journey with Miss Swift intrigued him. Possibly because she was the last female in the world he
expected to find himself alone with, like this. Shy,
quiet, pretty, unassuming Annabelle. Seated nervously across from him in the dim, velvet interior
of his carriage.

She was a woman whom he'd barely given any
thought to for four years, and now she constantly
intruded upon his thoughts and conversations. Everyone, it seemed, was talking about Annabelle.

She was also a woman who by all accounts had
no romantic entanglements until just this week,
when he could link her to two unlikely prospects.

Lord Marsden, a bloody marquis and a notoriously charming one, sending her roses.

And then there was *something* between her and

Damien Owens. How else to explain her tussled hair, pink cheeks, and the fact that she was in his arms?

More irritating was why the thought of them together bothered him. So much so that he'd left his desk to investigate their lengthy silence behind a closed door. And when he opened it? The sight before him sent a surge of jealously, and a desire to plant a facer on Owens.

And now here he was, alone, with Annabelle.

"Where to, Miss Swift?" he asked once they were settled into his carriage. It was a very fine carriage, if he did say so himself: the newest design, comfortable forest green velvet seats, black lacquer detailing. He did enjoy the trappings of success: a stately home, the finest tailoring, and the best of anything money could buy.

"One hundred fifty Montague Street, Bloomsbury," she answered. "Or did you already know that?"

"I already knew. But it seemed prudent to confirm your destination in the event you planned to go elsewhere," Knightly said. *Like Lord Marsden's residence. Or Owens's flat.* The thought caused a knot to form in his gut.

"That is very considerate of you," she replied, and then paused, obviously debating whether to say what was on her mind. In the habit of snap decisions himself, it was intriguing to watch this internal debate.

"What else do you know about me?" Annabelle decided to ask. He watched her straighten her spine as she did, as if it required such determination to do so.

"You are six and twenty years of age," he answered.

"It's not polite to mention that," she replied, inadvertently confirming it.

"You live with your brother, the cloth merchant, and his wife. You have doled out advice to the curious, lovelorn, and unfortunate for about three years," Knightly told her.

It was an easy matter to accumulate basic facts about people, which often proved useful to have in hand.

Some other newly discovered facts would go unmentioned: Annabelle looked angelic with her tussled golden curls free of the knot she usually kept her hair in. And yet her mouth—all plump and red—hinted of sin. When she smiled, there was a slight dimple in her left cheek. She was prone to blushes and sighs, and he thought it fascinating that one should be able to feel so passionately and to show it.

He never could. But that was a woman for you. Most of them never had a thought or feeling they didn't share.

"I'm curious what you know of me," he said, turning the tables on her. She smiled, and thought for a moment, as if debating where to begin.

"I know that you are five and thirty years of age, that your mother is an actress, you have a town house in Mayfair, and your handwriting is an impossible scrawl," she replied pertly.

"And that my chest is firm," Knightly couldn't resist adding.

Annabelle only groaned in response. He couldn't quite see in the dim light of the carriage, but he would wager that a blush was creeping into her cheeks.

"You embarrass easily," he said, adding to his list of Facts About Annabelle.

"Did you know that already or are you only just discovering it?" she asked with a laugh.

"I'm learning," he said. He knew less about her than the other Writing Girls mainly because the others were in the habit of barging into his office, giving him a piece of their mind, and generally raising hell and causing trouble.

In fact, this might have been the longest conversation he and Annabelle had to date. Funny, that.

"I also know that your column has been the talk of the town," he added. Besides Drummond, Gage, and his mother, everyone seemed to be talking about Dear Annabelle's quest to win the Nodcock. (Owens? Or Marsden?) In every meeting he took, be it with a writer or fellow businessmen, they were discussing the matter. He'd even overheard his valet and butler in a heated discussion over just how low a woman's bodice should go.

"What do you think of my column lately?" she asked.

"It has been immensely popular," Knightly said. "You even have the blokes in the coffeehouses devoted to it. You should keep up the ruse as long as possible, because readers love it." Annabelle's Adventures in Love made for a great story. Great stories equaled great sales.

Also, the continuation of the ruse meant delayed satisfaction for Owens. Or was it Marsden? One of the two was surely the infamous Nodcock.

"I see," she said softly, and idly stroked the velvet

of the carriage seat. She looked out the window for a moment. It was as if a cloud passed over, for she suddenly was just a bit less vivacious. It was as if he'd said the wrong thing, which was confusing, as he had intended a compliment.

"The mail clerks have been complaining to me about the volume of letters you are receiving," he said, hoping that a mention of her popularity would bring back some brightness.

"They always complain about that," Annabelle said with a smile. "People do love to send their problems to me."

"You must have a knack for solving them. And giving good advice," he said idly. Her shawl had slipped off her shoulders, exposing her first trick in attracting that nodcock. Knightly was suddenly aware that he desired her, and that they were alone.

"I must have? Do you not *know*?" she asked, peering up at him with those big blue eyes of hers. He'd lost track of the conversation, distracted as he'd been by the swells of her breasts and a dawning awareness of his desire for Annabelle.

"I don't know how your readers fare after your suggestions. Or what constitutes good advice, which is why you won't see me penning your column. I have three truths I live by, that is all." And really, did a man need more? No.

"Scandal equals sales," Annabelle said, predictably sounding bored, as all the writers did when reciting that particular phrase. Yet it worked like a charm. They shared a grin over the shared knowledge.

"What is the next one?" she asked.

"Drama is for the page," he told her. Even though

he never actually said these truths aloud and he especially didn't talk about them. But with Dear Annabelle it felt safe to do so.

"Funny, given that your mother is an actress," Annabelle remarked.

"Or precisely because my mother is an actress," he countered.

"More drama *off* the page would be greatly welcomed by me," Annabelle said wistfully. "Of course, it must be different for men. There is very little adventure and excitement available to us unmarried females."

"Doesn't this count?" he asked. It was just a carriage ride. But there was nothing to stop him from tugging her into his lap and ravishing her completely. Nothing, that is, save for his self-restraint, which seemed to be eroding with every moment.

*It was just Annabelle,* or so he tried to tell himself. But it wasn't. He was discovering, slowly but surely, that Annabelle possessed a mouth he wished to taste, pale skin he wanted to touch, and breasts that—oh God, the wicked thoughts she inspired. How had he not noticed her all these years?

In his defense, she hadn't been wearing these revealing dresses until lately. She pulled the shawl up closer around her shoulders. Her best shawl, she had said. Or a ruse to meet privately with Owens?

"Oh, yes, this might count as an adventure," she replied with a smile that might actually be described as wicked. "Fortunately for you, I am not a Person of Consequence. Nor will my relatives ask you to declare your intentions."

"Why is that?" Knightly asked, because that was a deuced unusual attitude for relatives of unmarried females. Usually they were keen to foist off their sisters and daughters as early and as soon as possible. Look at Marsden, for instance.

"That would mean losing their free household help," Annabelle said. She forced a laughed that stabbed at his heart. She tried to be light about it but came just short of succeeding. "Blanche has actually done the math . . ."

Knightly assumed Blanche was her brother's wife, and that she must be horrid. The impulse to rescue Annabelle from this wretched situation stole over him; he chalked it up to some notion of ingrained gentlemanly behavior. Or too many hours at the theater.

*Drama is for the page. Repeat. Drama is for the page.*

"No wonder you crave adventure," he said, steering the conversation away from the apparently awful Swift household.

While the words still hung in the air a huge thud and a jolt rocked the carriage, sending Annabelle flying into his lap and bringing the vehicle to a halt. A loud commotion ensued just outside of the carriage. They must have collided with another vehicle.

He ought to go see what happened.

Knightly remained inside and discovered new things about Annabelle. She was warm. He knew this because he was suddenly, incredibly overheated. And she was luscious. He'd instinctively wrapped his arms around her to keep her steady. He felt the curve of her hips, the curve of her bottom, the curve of her breasts.

Fact: Annabelle was a tempting armful of woman. It wasn't just her mouth that tempted a man to sin. The rest of her, too.

Tempting as sin, that Angelic Annabelle.

How had he not discovered this about her before?

For one thing, he hadn't held her in his arms before. He certainly hadn't done so for longer than was necessary or proper.

Knightly also discovered that his body very much liked Annabelle on his lap. In fact, certain portions of his anatomy strained to display its fondness. It was positively indecent how much he liked it.

"I should go see what happened," he said, though it was another moment before either made an attempt to move.

As they disentangled themselves, he might have accidentally been less than concerned about the proper placement of his hands and might have unintentionally brushed his hand against certain round portions of her person.

He was a man, after all.

But it was wrong. She worked for him. Worked . . . for . . . him.

To play there would be to take unfair advantage. And it would be just a dalliance, given his impending betrothal to Lady Marsden. All of which would inevitably lead to hurt feelings, awkwardness, issues of pride, etc., etc., and the loss of one of his writers who was currently writing an increasingly popular column.

Annabelle was Off Limits.

As Knightly stepped out into the crisp evening air, his first thought had nothing to do with the melee before him. His first thought was: *Good thing Annabelle has her shawl.*

And then he focused on the situation at hand.

A collision had occurred between two carriages. One of them, unfortunately, belonged to him. The cattle were fine, thank God. No one was injured, save for some minor damage to his conveyance. The occupants of the offending vehicle were hollering and blustering and it took some time before Knightly's cool demeanor calmed them down, sorted out the mess, and sent everyone on their way.

Meanwhile, he was aware of Annabelle watching from the carriage windows. Which is why he did not take a swing at the man who accused his driver of ineptitude and hurled curses at everyone in vicinity. It was the reason why Knightly was in such a hurry to have the matter resolved. Not that he would have ever been inclined for a drawn-out scene, but knowing Annabelle waited in the dim confines of his carriage lent an urgency to the situation.

"There will be an article advocating traffic laws, will there not?" she asked when he finally rejoined her.

"Absolutely," he said with a grin. "And one lamenting other people's deplorable driving skills."

"It must be quite fun having your own newspaper to tell the world just what you think," she mused. "It must be wonderful to have so many people read it and agree with you. Is that why you work so much, Mr. Knightly?"

"I love the work. I love the success and what comes with it," Knightly replied frankly. He loved the challenge, and the chase, and the pride that came from his success. And all of the wealth and influence he had accumulated would soon deliver his ultimate goal.

*Throw the bastard out. He doesn't belong here.*

Oh, but he did. And they would soon have to accept him as one of their own.

"I can imagine. This is a very nice carriage," Annabelle remarked, sliding her hands along the plush velvet seat.

"It was a lot nicer an hour ago," he said, and Annabelle laughed.

Knightly added *Annabelle has a lovely laugh* to the list of things he knew about her.

"We are nearly there," she said, after a glance out the window. "Thank you very much for seeing me home. I hope I didn't keep you from anything important."

"Can't let my star columnist go gallivanting off in the night unescorted," Knightly said with a grin.

"Because this carriage ride with you wasn't dangerous or improper at all," she replied, smiling.

It wasn't. Nothing untoward had occurred . . . and yet now that he had this new knowledge of Annabelle, it felt dangerous for some reason.

When the carriage rolled to a stop before a neat little town house, the thought of taking Annabelle in his arms and tasting that sinful mouth of hers crossed his mind. He noted that she was thinking about it, too. How else to explain the nervousness in her pretty blue eyes? Or the flush across her cheeks? Or the way she nibbled at her plump lower lip.

*Why not kiss her?* The devil on his shoulder wanted to know.

*Why not, indeed,* logic countered, withering.

Because she worked for him. Had he not declared her Off Limits just a quarter hour ago? Clearly, he needed to remind himself why she was Off Limits.

Because she had her heart set on either Owens or Marsden. Because she had to keep up her quest to win one of those blockheads. Her column was the talk of the town, and if everyone was discussing Annabelle's adventures in love, they were not sparing a thought for the looming, sordid scandal brewing thanks to that damned inquiry. He'd like to keep it that way.

Because he would be courting and marrying Lady Lydia, because her hand in marriage would deliver him everything he'd always wanted: acceptance from the haute ton and protection for his newspapers. For his writers.

Because Annabelle was a sweet, innocent woman. And he was a ruthless, cold man who cared for nothing but his business and social climbing, as uncouth as that sounded. He didn't want to break the heart of a girl like her.

"You should go," he said. His voice was more hoarse than he would have liked.

# Chapter 13

### A Writing Girl's Lamentable Household

FASHIONABLE INTELLIGENCE BY A LADY OF DISTINCTION
*'Tis a small crowd in London that does not read* The
London Weekly. *What curious creatures.*

The London Weekly

*The Swift Household*

BLANCHE descended upon Annabelle the moment
she stepped into the drawing room. Blanche's bosom
friend Mrs. Underwood, who Annabelle suspected
might be a witch, hovered just behind Blanche. Privately, Annabelle thought they were both ghastly,
though she felt pained to do so because she always
made an effort to find the good in each person.

"How kind of you to grace us with your presence, Annabelle," Blanche remarked snidely. From
the first, the woman had taken a dislike to her, and
no amount of sweetness or helpfulness or anything
else could dissuade her. Thomas had defended Annabelle once, when he declared his new wife would
not cast out his thirteen-year-old sibling. Ever since,
Annabelle had been left to manage her wicked

sister-in-law on her own. For years Annabelle had tried to make Blanche happy with her choice to keep her on. Lately, she only tried to be at peace with her situation.

Blanche turned to her husband, who took refuge behind a newspaper. "Thomas, ask your sister where she has been this whole day.'"

"Where have you been, Annabelle?" Dear brother Thomas did not even lower his newspaper. It was *The Daily Financial Register*, and a duller publication Annabelle had never read. She didn't blame him for hiding behind it, given the company.

"I have spent the afternoon busy with charity work," Annabelle said, relying on her usual excuse. "And visiting some friends," she added, in the event that they saw Knightly's carriage and inquired about it.

Her family did not know about "Dear Annabelle." Her family did not read *The London Weekly* and must have been the only people in London not to do so. This suited Annabelle just fine.

Her family labored under the impression that she dedicated her time to a vast array of charitable works and committees, which explained her Wednesday outings and friendship with the other Writing Girls (who she might have declined to mention happened to be duchesses and a countess).

*The London Weekly* and the Writing Girls were her secret life. They were the only things that belong to her, and her alone. Well, other than those wicked silky unmentionables (she'd ordered more) and two fine dresses.

"I personally believe that charity starts at home," Blanche said stiffly. "Which reminds me, Cook may have set something aside for you. Or perhaps she was too vexed not to have your assistance in the kitchen this evening. You may go see for yourself."

"You're too kind, Blanche," Mrs. Underwood praised, and the two old birds clucked over their generosity. Annabelle was in too fine a mood to scowl or snort or otherwise express her disbelief.

Eat? She lived on love alone. Finally she had more than crumbs to sustain her. She sent up a silent prayer of thanks to Careless in Camden Town for such a brilliant suggestion. It was all she could do not to waltz across the foyer or burst into song.

What an adventure she'd had this afternoon!

"What, pray tell, is so amusing, Annabelle?" Blanche inquired.

For a second Annabelle considered telling her the truth. But why, when Blanche would not believe it? No, this would be her secret pleasure.

"There must be a man in the picture," Mrs. Underwood said.

"Hmm," Thomas murmured from behind his newspaper.

"That explains the prolonged absences. The flowers. The dresses like a dockside harpy." Blanche ticked these items off on her short fingers, much like the way she added up the accounts for the cloth business.

"Today I met with the Society for the Advancement of Female Literacy," Annabelle replied, which was her code for *The Weekly* staff meetings. Blanche, as the businesswoman behind the man, could not disagree with it.

"But you do not deny that there is a man in the picture," Mrs. Underwood said gleefully, as if this were a trial and she'd inadvertently made Annabelle confess to some heinous crime punishable by years of hard labor.

"Well let me inform you now that should you find yourself in a state of disgrace," Blanche lectured, "you won't darken this door with your presence. I shan't abide such an example in front of my children."

Watson, Mason, and Fleur, ages nine, seven, and five. They were miniature replicas of their parents and thus no friends of Annabelle's, no matter that she'd functioned as their nanny and governess for their whole lives.

"Do you not agree, Thomas? We cannot have your sister setting a poor example for our children," Blanche said loudly, as if he were deaf or as if newsprint effectively blocked sound.

"Yes, dear," he replied.

Old Annabelle would have blinked back tears to have her brother, her own flesh and blood, agree so blindly to his wife's cruelty. New Annabelle, however, knew that he likely hadn't been listening to the conversation and had no idea what he'd just agreed to.

New Annabelle was also overwhelmed by the urge to waltz around her bedroom and revel in raptures of delight.

Because some people—like Owens and Careless in Camden Town, and even A Courtesan in Mayfair—cared to help her. She'd been lonely until she worked up the courage (or desperation) to ask for help and discovered that people were more than willing to oblige.

Because this scheme had been the greatest risk of her life so far, and it was proving to be a success.

Because she had a carriage ride with Knightly. Alone. At dusk. It was the stuff Old Annabelle dreamed about late at night. New Annabelle lived it.

Because she had managed an entire conversation with Knightly, instead of her usual tendency to ramble or lose the ability to construct sentences—and even after tumbling awkwardly into his lap. (Although she had ceased to think, only to feel a million exquisite new sensations when that had happened.)

Because she had an adventure with Knightly.

Because Knightly had been about to kiss her, she just knew it.

Because New Annabelle was wicked good fun.

# Chapter 14

## A Lady's Lesson in Flirting

PARLIAMENTARY INTELLIGENCE

*London newspapers, beware! Lord Marsden's Inquiry
is gathering information and testimonies, all because
of the nefarious actions of* The London Times's *rogue
reporter, Jack Brinsley, who is festering in Newgate,
awaiting trial.*

The London Weekly

*Offices of* The London Weekly

**W**EDNESDAYS had long been Annabelle's favorite day of the week. But this one made her smile a little more broadly, made her heart beat a little more quickly. The sky seemed bluer, the birdsong more pleasing. She herself was becoming a little more . . . alive or awake or in bloom or something lovely like that.

Knightly was no longer a remote figure with whom she'd never really conversed. She now knew the firmness of his chest (if only for one, exquisite and accidental instance) and what it felt like to have his arms around her (if only for one exquisite, accidental tumble in a carriage accident). She knew the truths he lived by, although it had occurred to her after their carriage ride that he'd only mentioned two of the three. She resolved to discover the third.

Yet it was Owens, not Knightly, who immediately sought her out upon her early arrival. She liked to allow for the possibility of drama or adventure to occur.

"Good afternoon, Miss Swift." Somehow Owens had managed to make it sound like he was saying something else entirely. Something very naughty. He affectionately touched her arm. It was lovely, that.

"Good afternoon, Mr. Owens," Annabelle said sweetly.

Heads turned in their direction. The other Writing Girls came up the stairs and looked at her very curiously as they passed by. Something about her company and her and Mr. Owens's pose must have told them not to interrupt.

Owens paid them no mind and leaned against the wall next to her, just outside of Knightly's office. Then a slow, lazy smile dawned upon his mouth and he took a slow, lazy, absolutely rakish look at her person. Her lips parted, slightly aghast. Her heartbeat quickened with the pressure to perform.

Owens was acting rakishly with her. Owens, who had said she'd never be wicked, was now looking at her as if she'd been very wicked *with* him. It was appalling. It was also part of the ruse and the sort of high jinks New Annabelle engaged in.

"I trust you are enjoying this fine weather, Miss Swift. With such warm temperatures, you needn't worry about leaving your shawl behind," Owens said with a knowing nod and wink of his velvety brown eyes. What unfairly long lashes the man possessed.

"It was so kind of you to help me . . . find my shawl," Annabelle replied. "I could never have done it without you." She hoped that sounded appropriately *something*.

"I live to serve—especially a beautiful girl like you, Miss Swift." Owens smiled at her again. She smiled back.

"I thought we were talking about the weather? And my shawl?" she asked in a whisper. Owens leaned in close to whisper directly in her ear.

"We are flirting," he explained.

"Oh," she gasped. She was so silly, needing to have a man explain flirting to her. And Owens of all the men in the world, too. She couldn't help it, she giggled.

"Don't giggle. Nothing terrifies men more," Owens said, fear creeping into his expression. "Men thrive on competition. And you need a rival, remember?"

"Oh, I remember," she said, and it even sounded a bit naughty.

"That's my girl. Now after you, Miss Swift." As they walked off toward the meeting, Owens placed his palm lightly, fleetingly, on the small of her back. She just happened to glance over her shoulder in the direction of Knightly's office. Just happened to see him looking her way with a dark expression.

"Dear Annabelle, do explain," Sophie said the second Annabelle took her seat. The other Writing Girls turned to give the full force of their attentions to her.

"Owens and I have an understanding," Annabelle said, and she didn't try to hush her voice. Across the room, she caught his eye and he flashed a grin and nodded in encouragement. He was rather boyishly handsome.

"What sort of understanding?" Julianna inquired.

"According to Owens, men thrive on rivalry. And that I ought to make Knightly wonder just whom I am writing about. Otherwise, how can I write freely about my exploits?"

"He does have a point," Eliza agreed. "I found it extraordinarily challenging to write about Wycliff without revealing my housemaid disguise."

"But do you not want Knightly to discover your feelings for him?" Sophie asked. It was a fair question.

"I want him to discover *me*. And fall in love with *me*. I don't wish for him to simply figure out whom I'm writing about because of a slip of the pen," Annabelle said. Then she added determinedly, "Besides, I am having more fun than I ever have and . . . *It's working.*"

It wasn't just that she was now on speaking terms with Knightly, but that she felt like a new person. One who was daring, adventurous, wore pretty dresses and wicked, silky undergarments. She liked New Annabelle.

The conversation then devolved into a flurry of whispers in which Annabelle related the lost shawl adventures. With their four heads bowed together, she almost didn't notice when Knightly arrived. Almost, for he was never far from her mind.

HE had caught them at it again—Miss Swift and *Owens*, of all the young, brash bucks in London. He saw them flirting. He saw Annabelle giggling. He did not miss the winks and smiles.

He couldn't say why it bothered him. Just that it did.

Next, he caught the Writing Girls with their heads bent together in some hushed conversation. Did they discuss his own innocent, gentlemanly carriage ride with Annabelle? But he couldn't very well let her go off into the London night alone, risking life and limb for her shawl.

He had done the right thing. The gentlemanly thing. He just hadn't felt remotely gentlemanly about it at the time, or since. The idea of ravishing Annabelle had begun to intrude on his thoughts with a stunning regularity.

"Ladies first," Knightly said as he strolled in. But instead of smiling, he scowled. What the devil did he care if Annabelle and Owens flirted and courted and married? He didn't care at all. They just should not engage in such behavior on work time.

But there they were, making eyes at each other across the room. Revolting.

"I have gossip," Julianna announced.

"I should hope so," he said dryly.

"It's about Lady Marsden's missing season," she said. Across the room, Grenville sighed. Knightly scowled at him, too, because he was intrigued by this, especially after making the acquaintance of the lady in question. During their walk, he'd learned that she despised newspapers, wished to leave London, and her favorite pastime was dancing.

They would be a horrible match. Nevertheless, he'd pursue her. For *The Weekly*. So he could quiet those damned words that haunted his every action: *Throw the bastard out. He doesn't belong here.*

"I have made inquiries, discreetly, of course," Julianna continued. "The official line is that she had been ill. But many are saying she had taken a lover—a scandalous one. It seems that her brother found a packet of love letters. He was livid. Positively outraged! He locked her in her room for a whole year."

"Who is her lover?" Sophie asked, a bit breathless in her eagerness to know.

"She still has not revealed his identity," Julianna replied dramatically.

"And yet she has been released from captivity," Eliza said, as dramatically.

"*If* he actually locked her in her bedchamber for a year," Knightly interjected. But this was dismissed by the group as not being as interesting.

"I suppose Lord Marsden gave up and decided the next best course of action was to marry her off," Julianna said. "Thus the whole matter would become another man's problem." She shrugged lightly. Clearly, she had not uncovered his discreet agreement with Marsden.

Another man's problem indeed. This shed new light on the matter, but did not change the fact that she was the sister to a powerful marquis, and ladies of such high standing were not exactly lining up to marry an illegitimate man who engaged in trade . . . fortune or not.

"Nothing like secret lovers, now is there?" Owens said from the other side of the room. And then he winked—*winked*—at Annabelle, who fluttered her lashes in his direction.

Sickening stuff. Truly. This was a place of business.

"One point to consider," Knightly said sharply, "is that Lord Marsden is leading the parliamentary inquiry into *The London Times* scandal. I would hate for him to have reason to turn his attentions to *The Weekly*."

"Oh, but the ton can speak of nothing else!" Julianna said passionately. "I have a feeling this scandal is going to explode."

"I don't care," he said. He especially wouldn't give a damn when his paper was shut down. Plus, Lady Lydia obviously held a particular loathing for newspapermen, and it would not help his suit if his own paper were printing salacious gossip about her.

"You would not believe the lengths I went to in order to obtain this information," Julianna argued. Knightly just shrugged.

"I'm quite sure that I don't want to know," he said. "When your husband finds out and comes storming in here in a rage, again, I would like to honestly say that I know nothing."

"Very well. Perhaps I shall just allude to it . . ." Lady Julianna pressed on, as she was wont to do.

"There should be no mention of the Marsdens in this paper," Knightly declared sharply. This elicited an audible gasp of shock from Julianna and an uncomfortable silence from the rest of the writers. He'd just violated one of the founding principles of the paper: *Everything and everyone was fodder.*

To hell with the lot of them, Knightly thought. But Annabelle's expression tugged hard at his heart. Some combination of dismay and betrayal was the only way he could describe the look in her big blue eyes. But he didn't want to know more. He'd made his decisions and now all that remained was following through.

Besides, she had Owens and his winks and smiles and all manner of romantic expressions and sickeningly sweet glances flying between them.

"Speaking of mystery lovers, Miss Swift, an update on your column this week, please," Knightly said dryly.

Bloody hell, had he just said *mystery lovers*? Bloody hell, he was getting soft. Except with Annabelle around, he wasn't soft at all. What the devil was happening?

"The letters keep pouring in, as you can see," she said, gesturing to another large stack before her. Letters full of inane suggestions from the likes of his friends Drummond and Gage. Letters full of dangerous suggestions like lowering her bodice to be positively distracting . . . and the devil only knew what else. He didn't want to know.

"I have seen in an increase in sales, not to mention all the talk about your column," he said. Annabelle was wearing another one of those low-cut bodices, and it took every ounce of his considerable willpower to lift his gaze a few inches higher. "Which means we have a good thing going, so draw this one out as long as you can."

Even if it killed him. Even if it slowly, excruciatingly tortured him. And then killed him. But he would endure, especially if it delayed and thwarted and slowed the budding romance between her and Owens, or perhaps Marsden, which he did not care about. Not at all.

No matter how many times he told himself that, however, the thought wouldn't stick.

"Yes, Mr. Knightly," Annabelle agreed softly.

He couldn't stop himself; he snuck one last glance at her bodice, and the generous swells of milky white skin rising just above the fabric. His mouth went dry. Where was her damn shawl when she really needed it?

THIS really was the happiest hour of her week, Annabelle thought. She propped her chin on her palm and just enjoyed being in the same room as Knightly. And her friends. And even her pretend-beau.

She battered her lashes at Owens for good measure. She even considered treating him to one of her sultry glances that were anything but seductive.

Knightly was in a terrible mood today. She wondered why, and if it was wrong that she thought the dark and broody look suited him.

Was it something with the newspaper, or another matter?

And what was this business with Lady Marsden? First, he'd been calling upon her and walking with her on sunny afternoons. And now he had banned her name from the pages of the newspaper. *It is probably nothing*, she told herself. She hoped it was naught but a strategic business decision that had nothing to do with his heart.

But still, it meant competition.

For the moment, though, there was nothing to do but enjoy this brooding version of Knightly in which he scowled, gazed darkly at his writers, raked his fingers through his hair and paced like some magnificent caged beast.

His gruff demeanor made her want to soothe his temper and smooth the rough edges. She wished to run her fingers through his hair, cradle his cheeks in her palms. Press her lips to his and kiss away that scowl . . .

Was it wrong that she wasn't paying attention in the slightest? It was. A Good Newspaper Woman would attend to the conversation.

"So let's get this straight," Owens said, brow furrowed. "A reporter for *The London Times* was caught impersonating a physician. Now he's imprisoned in Newgate, and Parliament and this parliamentary inquiry is looking into . . . what?"

"What exactly is the crime that merits such a massive investigation?" Eliza asked, puzzled. The methods of investigating were immoral, Annabelle thought. But it did seem like an isolated incident, as Knightly had said. It didn't seem to merit an investigation of the entire newspaper business.

"Why impersonate a physician anyway? That's an awful lot of risk and work," Grenville grumbled, and Annabelle quietly agreed with him.

"To get the story, of course," Eliza said, who thought nothing of adopting all manner of disguises for a story.

"What story?" Annabelle asked. The words were out of her mouth before she thought to censor them. And oh, she wished she had.

The room felt silent. Pin-drop silence. Pin drop on plush pile of sheepskin silence. Pin drop on plush sheepskin a country mile away.

The blush crept high onto her cheeks. Knightly focused on her intently. Had she thought his brooding stares were attractive? Because she could feel herself wilting under the intensity of his focus.

Would she *ever* stop humiliating herself in front of Knightly?

"What you're suggesting, Miss Swift, is that Brinsley didn't just wake up and decide to impersonate a doctor for amusement. He adopted that ruse because it enabled him to gain access and information to the *real* story."

"Just a means to an end," Owens added, thoughtful.

"Something like that," Annabelle mumbled.

"Brilliant," Knightly said, his voice rich with awe. Annabelle felt the warm heady rush of a rare, exquisite feeling: pride. She had impressed Knightly! "Miss Swift is right. What is the real story here?"

"Can we publish it if we uncover it?" Julianna dared to ask. "Given that Parliament is mucking into the practices of journalists . . ."

"Publish and be damned," Knightly said, with a grin that spoke of daring and danger.

# Chapter 15

## Newspapermen in Newgate

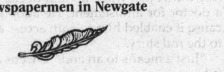

ACCIDENTS & OFFENSE

*A fire at the offices of* The London Times *was deemed suspicious. A source informs that the editors were burning compromising files gathered by rogue reporter Jack Brinsley before Lord Marsden's Inquiry could collect them.*

The London Weekly

*Newgate*

**B**RIBERY was wonderful. Some men had compunctions about sort of thing, but not Knightly. He valued accomplishments and efficiency. Especially when one was at Newgate. It was not the sort of place where one wished to linger.

He was here because of Annabelle and her brilliant insight.

"It was only a matter of time before you showed up." Jack Brinsley, reporter and "physician" said gruffly upon Knightly's arrival. "At least one newspaper editor isn't afraid to show his face."

"Hardwicke has not visited?" Knightly inquired about the editor of *The London Times*.

"That patsy?" Brinsley spat on the floor.

"You have caused quite a scandal, you know," Knightly told him.

"You're welcome," Brinsley said with a smirk.

"It occurs to me that there's more to your story than the gossip or the paltry information I receive from the parliamentary inquiry." Knightly caught himself about to lean against the walls and then thought better of it.

"And I'm just supposed to tell you it, am I? I'm supposed to just tell-all to the rival newspaper," Brinsley said with a bemused expression.

"Aye, the rival newspaper that isn't turning its back on you," Knightly said pointedly. "Do you have a minute to talk?"

Brinsley snorted. Of course he had time, being in prison. He would talk. They always did with the hangman's noose swaying in the not-too-far future.

"Tell me about the day you woke up and thought 'I know! I'll pretend to be a physician to the aristocracy.'"

Brinsley took a long pause before answering: "It was a Tuesday. Foggy."

Knightly gave him A Look.

"I heard rumors about a particular lady. Hardwicke gave me orders to confirm them. And I thought, how the devil could I manage to confirm rumors about a pregnancy? Before anyone else did, that is."

"By impersonating a physician," Knightly surmised. Annabelle was right. Brinsley wasn't pulling this stunt on a lark, there had been a reason.

"Assisting one," Brinsley corrected. "But then the old blighter took ill himself and sent me on his calls. It proved to be rather informative. Lucrative, if you understand me."

It was a mad, genius scheme that definitely went beyond the pale, even for Knightly's bold tastes. He'd never support a reporter going to such *personal* lengths for a story.

But Damn, how lucrative it must have been. All newspapers made a small fortune in suppression fees when they obtained information the person in question did not wish to see in print. In this instance, it could be details of pregnancies or the pox or the devil only knew what else.

Some might say collecting those suppression fees was akin to blackmail. Others might say that's the newspaper publishing business. This was probably first on Marsden's list of practices to attack. One had to wonder, though, why he suddenly cared so much about an age-old practice?

"Whatever happened to bribing a housemaid?" Knightly mused.

"Child's play. Can't compete with *The Weekly* with those simpleton methods," Brinsley retorted.

"And the woman with the pregnancy rumors. Who was she?" Knightly asked. He had his suspicions.

"You're not stupid, Knightly, I'll give you that," Brinsley replied. "You're the only one to suspect I had a reason for this scheme. That I was after a lead and not just on a lark."

The credit was for Annabelle. He'd been as obtuse as the rest. But a more urgent matter persisted:

"Who is she?"

"I'm not just going to *tell* you," Brinsley said in an obvious play for cash. Knightly did love bribery. But he abhorred wasting money.

"Suit yourself. I'm confident I can discover it with a little sleuthing. I'm sure the ton will be riveted. Especially now that you and *The London Times* have so kindly set us up to reveal the details of such a riveting scandal."

"You're not going to publish this, are you?" Brinsley asked, jaw hanging open.

"I am," Knightly said. Publish and be damned.

"I take it back. You're not stupid. But damn, you are insane."

# Chapter 16

### Drama Is Not Just on the Stage

#### DEAR ANNABELLE

*Let the Nodcock know you care by a simple affection-*
*ate touch on his hand.*

> *Affectionate from All Saints Road*
> *The London Weekly*

*Covent Garden Theater*

**B**Y the end of Act One, Annabelle's cheeks were as red as her crimson sash and she was thinking some very uncharitable thoughts about Affectionate from All Saints Road, whose well-meaning suggestion that a delicate caress or an affectionate gesture would somehow make Knightly notice her, desire her, love her.

This hint of affection was supposed to be a suggestion of *more*.

Who could predict that such a simple action would be so fraught with peril?

First, she practiced upon Alistair Grey, who had brought her as his guest to the opening night of *Once Upon a Time*, featuring Delilah Knightly.

"Knightly's exact words to me were, 'My mother receives rave reviews or I find a new theater reviewer.' I understood this to mean I should attend," Alistair told her. "Of course, I always bring a guest. Given your situation and the assurance that you-know-who would attend, I thought to extend the invitation to you, Dear Annabelle. I expect a public display of gratitude in your next column."

"But of course," Annabelle replied, lightly touching her gloved hand to Alistair's forearm, clad in a deep mauve wool that set off his violet silk waistcoat to great effect.

Alistair did not take much notice of the gesture, but more importantly, he did not laugh or mock or ask her what the devil she was doing touching him thusly. *She could do this.*

She mustered her courage, straightened her spine, and quite nearly lost her nerve when Knightly arrived at the box appearing impossibly handsome in the stark black and white of his evening clothes.

If he was surprised to see her, he didn't show it. His eyes were as blue and focused as ever and his expression as aloof and inscrutable. She couldn't help it, a little sigh of longing and desire escaped her lips.

After greeting Alistair, Knightly took the seat beside her.

"How are you this evening, Annabelle?" he asked, leaning in toward her so his low voice might be heard over the din of the audience chattering before the start.

"Fine, thank you. And how are you?" Then she dared to brush her fingertips along the soft wool covering his arm, just for a second before snatching her hand away. Meanwhile, she kept her gaze upon him, so riveted was she by his blue eyes. That, and she was attempting to discern if that light touch had any effect upon him.

"I'm very well, thank you. Prepared for an evening of theatrics."

"Drama is for the page. Or the stage," she remarked, drawing a slight smile of recognition from him. She recognized an opportunity to seek an answer to a question that had been vexing her ever since their carriage ride. "Mr. Knightly, I don't think you ever mentioned your third truth."

Annabelle dared to punctuate this by placing her gloved hand upon his arm. In her head, she counted to three. Did he feel the warmth, the shivers? She felt positively electrified by the touch, however slight, and however much fabric separated his bare skin from hers.

Knightly leaned in closer. Her heart started to pound. She was sure her bosoms were heaving in anticipation, but in the dim light of the theater she couldn't tell if Knightly dared a glance or not.

"Be beholden to no one," he said in a low, heartbreaking voice.

"Oh," she replied, withdrawing her hand. That was the mantra of a man who refused love or attachment. The sort of man a woman ought not waste her time upon. That was a declaration of "Abandon all hope, ye who venture here."

But then she did catch Knightly glancing at her. And her bodice. She would swear that she felt his gaze like a caress. Her skin warmed. With the rush of pleasure from his attention was the satisfaction of knowing she had dared, she had achieved some small triumph.

The lights dimmed further. The audience hushed. The thick red velvet curtains were drawn apart, revealing a stage set to reveal a bedroom and a brightly dressed cast of characters ready to play.

The play was excellent, but couldn't fully capture her attention. Beside her, Knightly shifted and his soft wool coat brushed against her bare arms like the gentlest caress. She bit her lip, craving more.

Oh, it was just the brush of wool against her skin. It ought to have been nothing. But it was a tactile indication of all the affection she'd been lacking and all of her longing. It was an indication of how far she'd come, how close she was.

Old Annabelle never had moments like these, alone in the dark with Knightly, close enough to touch.

Throughout the performance, she'd kept her hands folded in her lap. But then she thought perhaps . . . perhaps she ought to try a little more.

She slid her hands across the pink silk of her skirts, over to the edge of her velvet chair just to where her fingers brushed with Knightly's, interlocking and then releasing for one exquisite and all-too-fleeting second.

In the middle of the first act Knightly leaned over to whisper in her ear some remark about the play. His voice was low, whisper quiet, and her attentions were distracted.

"What was that?" she asked at the exact moment when, as per the instructions of Affectionate from All Saints Road, she reached over intending just a brief gesture of affection on his arm, or his hand.

But he had shifted and she accidentally brushed her hand across a more personal and intimate and decidedly male portion of his anatomy. At the precise moment she had asked *What was that?*

Dear God, he would think—

That wasn't what she meant!

She just hadn't heard him!

All the words and explanations stuck in her throat. With cheeks flaming, Annabelle clasped her hands firmly on her lap and spent the second act regretting deeply the advice of Affectionate from All Saints Road and praying that she might disappear.

KNIGHTLY sincerely hoped that Alistair had paid excellent attention to the performance and planned to write an extensive, thorough, and meticulously detailed review, for he had not paid attention at all.

No, he'd been too damned distracted by Annabelle. First, it was those little flirtatious touches during their polite conversation, which fortunately consisted of just small talk. He'd had the devil of a time concentrating and instead wondered if Annabelle was *flirting* with him and if so, since when did Annabelle flirt?

It was probably for her column and probably practice for Owens or Marsden. But it tortured him all the same.

Especially when she had inadvertently touched him on a certain portion of his anatomy, which was far too pleased by it, given the circumstances. Such as a crowd of hundreds preventing him from *more*.

"Would you care for a glass of champagne?" Knightly asked Annabelle. Alistair had gone off to interview the actors backstage, leaving the two of them alone. He needed a drink, badly.

"Yes, *please*," she replied, averting her gaze. Her cheeks were pink.

"Shall we?" He offered his arm and she entwined hers. It was the gentlemanly thing to do. But after all those little, taunting touches he wanted to feel more of her, feel her against him. With the slightest caress, she had started a craving.

With her tucked against him, he noticed Annabelle was taller than he expected—her head was just above his shoulder, and he towered over most men. He also noted that if he glanced down discreetly he was treated to a marvelous view of her breasts rising above the cut of her gown. God damn—or God bless?—that damn Gage and all the rest who made the suggestion that she lower her bodice. He hadn't been able to think of much other than Annabelle's breasts since.

He also noted that she gazed up at him with those wide blue eyes and caught him looking. She smiled shyly. Her cheeks were still pink.

They obtained the desperately needed glasses of champagne without further incident and sought refuge from the crowds in a private alcove near the lobby.

"Something is different about you, Annabelle," he remarked. It wasn't just the new dress or, now that he looked closely, a new way of wearing her hair that allowed a few golden curls to fall tantalizingly, gently, on her face.

"You noticed?" Her voice was soft and her blue eyes widened as she peered up at him.

"It's been hard not to, Annabelle." Every time

he saw her, there was something else to note. Even when she wasn't around, she managed to infiltrate his every conversation—and thoughts, and dreams. When he ought to have been planning his marriage to Lady Lydia, he instead thought of discovering Annabelle, inch by inch.

"Oh. I'm sorry—" she stammered, flustered, and he realized she must have thought he was referring to the, ahem, incident in Act One. What he couldn't tell her was that it worked. Or rather, he wouldn't tell her for it would only mortify her more (as adorable as that sight was, he couldn't torture her thus). And if he were practice for Owens or Marsden, then he took a perverse pleasure in denying them the pleasure of Annabelle's touch. However unintentional, however fleeting.

"No, don't be sorry," he said. For once he allowed himself a long, leisurely look at her, discovering all the tempting curves of Dear Annabelle, from the soft gold ringlets of her hair to the plump mouth, as if ripe for a kiss. The swell of her breasts, the narrow tapering of her waist, and the seductive flare of her lips made his mouth go dry.

Knightly was struck with the urge to claim her mouth with a kiss. He took another sip of his champagne instead.

"I don't know what inspired you, Annabelle. But I'm having the devil of a time watching your transformation." All that loveliness had been hidden away before. Idly he wondered, why now?

"In a good way, I hope," she ventured, nibbling her lower lip. Tempting. Knightly took a long swallow of his champagne, but it did nothing to quench his desire to taste her.

"Definitely in a good way," he told her. Good, yes. And also in an intriguing, tempting, beguiling, tormenting kind of way. In an interrupting-dreams-and-waking-thoughts kind of way. Annabelle was starting to happen, and for some reason, he was the lucky bastard who got to watch this bewitching transformation unfold.

She smiled, shyly. She gazed up at him like he was the whole damn world—sun, moon, and stars included. He stepped farther back into the shadows, drawing her close with the slightest grasp of her wrist. Kissing Annabelle suddenly became a necessity.

She tilted her head up. He lowered his mouth to hers.

Then Alistair interrupted, and Knightly thought of firing him for the offense.

# Chapter 17

## Writing Girls' Gossip

### THE MAN ABOUT TOWN

*The White's betting book is full of wagers on when Mr. London Weekly will propose to Lady "Missing Second Season" Marsden. All agree a betrothal announcement is imminent. He's been reported to call upon her regularly, and they have waltzed twice at each of the three balls they attended together this week.*

*The London Times*

**O**N Sunday afternoon Annabelle often volunteered her time with the Society for the Advancement of Female Literacy. Meaning, of course, that she escaped the domestic drudgery and dull company at home so that she might spend a few hours in the company of her fellow Writing Girls.

They most often gathered at Sophie's massive house to read periodicals, indulge in tea and cakes, and gossip shamelessly.

Sundays were definitely her second favorite part of the week, Annabelle thought as she curled up on the mulberry-colored upholstered settee in Sophie's drawing room. Last night at the theater, however, was certainly the highlight.

If she were not mistaken, it seemed that last night, Knightly noticed her. Was it her new hairstyle, thanks to Owens's strategic removal of a few hairpins? Or was it the silk dress that felt like a caress? Or the way those wicked silk underthings emboldened her?

Or was it the mortifying encounter with her hand and Knightly's anatomy?

At the thought, her cheeks flamed. But she took a deep breath and reminded herself that not only did Knightly notice her now, he had said so. And he had been about to kiss her, she was certain of it. If only Alistair hadn't interrupted.

"Annabelle, enough with the woolgathering," Eliza said. "We are desperately curious to know what has you lost in thought."

"And the reason for that dreamy smile and your blush," Sophie added.

Annabelle sighed, but this sign was one of utter delight. In spite of the most mortifying three seconds of her life, all was well. Funny, the power of an almost kiss. She went breathless imagining how it would feel to actually kiss him.

"I do believe that Knightly is beginning to notice me!" she exclaimed, in spite of all her efforts to be coy or demure or restrained. She saw the way he looked at her last night, as if it were the first time.

God bless Careless in Camden Town and even Affectionate from All Saints Road, and all the others who had written to her.

"Sophie, you were absolutely right about the dresses and the silky underthings. You have my everlasting gratitude," Annabelle vowed. "I daresay they have given me a new confidence."

"You are very welcome. In return, please tell that to Brandon when my modiste bills arrive," Sophie replied.

"Speaking of noticing you, Annabelle," Julianna, ever the gossip, said, "Knightly is not the only one, it seems. There is also Owens. And Marsden."

"You had said Owens was a ruse," Eliza added after a sip of tea. "But he seems genuine."

"He came up with the idea during the Forgotten Shawl Incident," Annabelle said. He'd also been extraordinarily attentive to her and affectionate. It might have begun as a ruse, but it was starting to feel like a friendship.

"A remarkably good idea and experiment," Eliza replied. "I daresay Knightly glowered every time Owens glanced in your direction during last week's meeting."

"Is that why he was scowling? I noticed he was brooding. Then my mind drifted, " Annabelle admitted with a sheepish smile. And she had been spending half of her attention on winks and smiles for Owens—even a sultry glance or two, for his amusement.

"Speaking of Knightly," Sophie said delicately, as she intently examined the lace trim on her dress sleeve, "they say that he is courting Lady Lydia. The Man About Town reported on it this morning."

"And that explains why Knightly forbade me to write about the Marsdens," Julianna grumbled. "I loathe when I am scooped by the Man About Town."

"It was just that one afternoon walk, was it not?" Annabelle asked. "Remember, Sophie?" One walk did not a courtship make. He couldn't possibly be courting another woman, not now. Not when she was finally coming out of her shell. Not after three years, seven months, and two days in which she languished in the shadows, only to emerge when it was too late.

"It's more than that, I'm afraid," Sophie said, wincing. Annabelle glanced from Sophie to Eliza to Julianna. Three dear faces with expressions of concern and anguish and worry, and even traces of pity.

"He's visited her on at least three other occasions," Julianna said. "Furthermore, they have waltzed twice at the Winthrop soiree."

Given that Knightly was not known to spend much time outside of *The Weekly*, three visits, two waltzes, and one afternoon walk were significant indicators of a courtship. Even Annabelle, ever the optimist in possession of an inventive imagination, could not see any other excuse. The truth left her breathless. A knot formed in her stomach. That warm glow of pleasure faded, leaving her cold.

She felt her shoulders rounding. She felt that familiar bleak hollowness as she contemplated a life without love; a life under the same roof as her brother and Blanche. A life just off to the side, in the shadows, forever handing props or whispering lines to the actors on stage.

"That is an interesting turn of events," Eliza said thoughtfully. "Perhaps it has nothing to do with the woman herself and everything to do with strengthening the relationship with Marsden and his blasted Inquiry looming over all of us."

"Are you suggesting it's some noble sacrifice to protect *The Weekly*?" Julianna asked.

"He would do that . . ." Annabelle said softly. "But Lady Lydia is also beautiful. And titled. And probably a lovely person."

"I've heard her dowry is paltry," Sophie said. "The Marsdens have recently fallen on hard times."

"Knightly has a fortune of his own," Julianna said. "He has no need of a wealthy bride. Though it sounds like she needs a wealthy husband."

"What she has is an immensely powerful brother," Sophie said. "Brandon works with him frequently in Parliament. Given this Inquiry, and the practices of *The Weekly*, Knightly needs all the allies he can get. Marsden is stirring up many, many supporters. He is so popular, and charming, and righteously outraged over the matter, no one is able to refuse pledging their support to his cause."

"And then there are the rumors," Julianna said, with such relish that Annabelle felt a spark of hope after the sinking feeling in her stomach following Sophie's appraisal of the situation.

"Have you discovered her mystery lover yet?" Eliza asked, leaning forward, intrigued.

"No. But the latest *on dit* is that her illness was the sort that lasts only nine months," Julianna shared, pausing for effect and to sip her tea.

"Knightly probably doesn't care one whit about the rumors," Sophie said with a shrug. One should never believe in rumors, especially disparaging ones. How many times had Annabelle counseled her readers thusly?

"She is quite the competition," she said softly. A battle of tug of war erupted in her soul. *Give up*, Old Annabelle whispered. *Fight for him*, New Annabelle urged. The conflict made her stomach ache. "I did not realize that he had set his cap for someone else when I started my campaign to win him."

"So what if he has?" Julianna asked, shrugging. "What does that have to do with anything?" Not for the first time, Annabelle wished she possessed some of her friend's brazen spirit. Or her ability to *not* consider the contents of Lady Lydia's heart or her lifelong happiness when considering what to do.

"I shouldn't want to steal him," Annabelle said softly. "Or make anyone unhappy." That was the thing about always seeking the good in everyone, and doling out advice for years. Her point of view always focused on how to make everyone else happy.

It pleased her to do so. Truly. How could she even enjoy Knightly's love if it came at the expense of another woman's happiness?

"It's not 'stealing,'" Eliza said. "He would be exercising his free will."

"Annabelle, you have loved him for years—" Sophie began.

"Three years, seven months, and two days. Give or take," Annabelle replied. She gave a shrug of her shoulders as if to suggest it mattered not. But it did. Her heart had beat just for him for all those days . . . and all those nights.

"Precisely. You have loved him for quite some time, and now, finally, he is showing signs of returning your affections," Sophie pointed out, bolstering Annabelle's confidence.

"He is beginning to notice me. I know he is," she said fiercely. But she now realized that noticing was only the first step. She wanted his love. She wanted his undying devotion and eternal passion. She had wanted it for three years, seven months, and two days.

"Until a few weeks ago, you'd never quite had a conversation with him," Eliza pointed out, "and now you two are gallivanting all over town in a closed carriage and sipping champagne together at the theater. You cannot give up now."

"But how can I compete with Lady Lydia?" Annabelle cried.

The woman was a formidable opponent. Lady Lydia owned numerous gorgeous gowns, all in the first stare of fashion, whilst she had only two nice dresses and a wardrobe that demonstrated the different shades of brown and gray.

Lady Lydia's every movement was elegance itself. Annabelle had, in an attempt to be flirtatious and affectionate, placed her hand where no lady would dare, while asking, "What was that?"

Lady Lydia indulged in the social whirl, and she was oft found busying herself with other people's problems.

Lady Lydia's brother held the fate of *The London Weekly* in his hands. Annabelle's brother never looked up from his newspaper and didn't even read *The Weekly*.

The competition was fierce. Swifts were not known for being fierce.

"Just be you, Annabelle. Or the you that you are becoming," Sophie urged gently.

"If he doesn't notice and fall madly in love, then to hell with him," Julianna declared.

What she wouldn't give to possess Julianna's fiery streak. Or Sophie's confidence. Or Eliza's daring.

The words "to hell with him" didn't just stick

in Annabelle's throat, she couldn't fathom uttering such a phrase. Not for Knightly. Not for love.

"What have your readers suggested you try next?" Eliza asked, slightly changing the subject.

"Oh . . ." Annabelle sighed evasively. That was another issue. She had tried all the easy things. Each week the suggestions grew more and more outrageous.

"Annabelle, what do the heroines of the novels you like to read do?" Sophie asked.

"That's just the thing, you see. The most compelling suggestion from a reader is to faint into Knightly's arms, but no heroine worth her smelling salts would ever *faint*."

And that was precisely what Swooning on Seymour Street had advised her to do: feign a faint and hope the man who never noticed her would catch her when she fell.

# Chapter 18

## Impossible Advice

DEAR ANNABELLE
*Fetch the smelling salts!*
*The London Weekly*

*Annabelle's attic bedchamber*

**O**F all the letters Annabelle had received in her years as an advice columnist, of those hundreds upon thousands of questions and pleas, not one had tugged at her conscious, tormented soul or broke her heart quite like this one.

It quite took her breath away, this letter. Squeezed the air right out of her lungs.

It came from Lady Lydia Marsden. Not that she signed her name; Annabelle recognized the crest on the sealing wax. It was the same crest that accompanied the note that had been tucked into the bouquet of pink roses her brother sent. This little slip revealed oh so much more than the author intended.

If Annabelle hadn't noticed that detail, she would have easily composed a reply urging one to pursue true love at all costs. But Annabelle had noticed, and thought twice about encouraging her rival to increase her efforts to ensnare the man she herself loved.

After she finally completed her domestic drudgery for the day—tending to the children's bedtime routine, dusting Blanche's collection of breakable porcelain shepherdesses with a scrap of white flannel, mending her brother's shirts—Annabelle returned to her bedchamber to practice fainting, along with reading her letters and drafting her next column.

Now she actually did feel faint, thanks to this letter. Who needed air, anyway? Who needed to breathe when her heart was torn in two?

Where were the smelling salts when a girl needed them?

The letter began *Dear Annabelle*, as all letters to her did. It read:

> *I am in love with an unsuitable man, for his station is far below mine. My brother wishes me to marry another. Surely you, Dear Annabelle, believe in the love match! My dear brother will listen to you. Perhaps you might advocate for true love as the primary consideration in marriage?*
> *Scandalously in Love in Mayfair*

Annabelle understood, plain as day: Lady Lydia had fallen in love with Knightly. Given that she was the sister of a marquis and he was the son of an actress . . . of course they could not be together.

How on earth was she to advise Lady Lydia without compromising her own ideals (true love!) or without compromising her own aims (Knightly!)?

Annabelle believed in love the way the Pope believed in the holy trinity or physicists believed in gravity. She could not, in good conscience, advise Lydia *not* to pursue true love. Yet to encourage Lady Lydia was to thwart her own aims. Could she so willingly thwart herself?

A heroine would fight for her love, Annabelle thought as she tucked the letter into her copy of *Belinda* and stuck the novel high on the shelf.

A heroine would also never be so lily-livered as to faint, and certainly not deliberately. And yet . . .

Annabelle stood next to her bed for a soft landing. She wavered on her feet. The waver had to be essential, so that Knightly would have a moment to, oh, notice she was unsteady and prepare to catch her. For dramatic effect, she tenderly draped the back of her hand across her brow.

And then she let go . . .

Let herself simply collapse . . .

No more strained effort to keep her spine straight and proud. No more tense muscles, awaiting some kiss or heated gaze that never came her way. She allowed her knees to be weak (for that happened to heroines all the time). She allowed herself to stop trying so darned hard to be still and strong in a world with all odds stacked high against her.

She fell softly on her feather mattress. Her breath escaped in a whoosh.

She had let go and landed unharmed.

She stood again, and closed her eyes this time. She released all of the problems that came her way—those of her readers, Lady Lydia's, and those of her own creation. Just let them, let herself, go.

This time when she faux fainted she let her arms

splay out. Her hair started to escape from its confines and it felt so pleasant to be so unrestrained. She thought of Owens, and that he was right to risk such an intimate gesture to loosen those hairpins. To let her hair down. To let herself go.

Again and again Annabelle practiced her swoon. Again and again she discovered the pleasure of letting go.

# Chapter 19

### A Lady's Guide to Feigning Faints

The Man About Town
*Lord Harrowby has pledged his support of Lord Marsden's Inquiry.*
    *The London Times*

*Offices of* The London Weekly

**T**HE meeting passed as all the others did. Her heart thudded, the butterflies in her stomach fluttered, her eyelashes batted. And above all Annabelle admired. Even his rumored courtship of Lady Lydia, while troubling, was not sufficient to thwart her passion for him.

In fact, for the first time in her life, Annabelle felt . . . competitive. Old Annabelle put everyone else's needs first. New Annabelle fought for her beliefs, and loves, and desires.

Oh, yes, desires.

The meeting proceeded, and she didn't hear a word.

When Knightly wasn't leaning like some devil-may-care rogue with all the time in the world for some Grand Seduction, he stood tall with his wide shoulders thrown back. As someone who usually turned in on herself as if to take shelter from the world, she admired how he always seemed poised to manage anything. And everything.

Knightly was so controlled, too, from the lift of his brow to the tug of a grin. He did not tap his fingers or his foot in idle energy. He didn't run his fingers through his hair rakishly, or fidget in any way. His every movement was restrained and possessed by purpose.

She could only imagine if they made love, what it would be like to have that energy—his blue eyes, his strong hands—harnessed and focused upon herself. In bed. Making love. With Knightly. Honestly, she didn't think she'd survive that.

"Annabelle, are you overheated?" Knightly interrupted the meeting to ask.

She sighed, so mortified there was no point in pretending otherwise. There was no denying the telltale redness of her cheeks.

"Perhaps you should remove your shawl," Owens suggested with a rakish grin and a suggestive nod of his head. Knightly scowled at him.

"I'm not feeling quite myself," Annabelle said, to foreshadow what was to come. But wasn't that the truth! Her own thoughts were making her feel faint. Perhaps a feigned swoon wasn't necessary. She'd just have to keep imagining Knightly. Making Love. In bed. With her.

The clothing would have to go. Each layer stripped off. She vividly recalled how warm and firm his chest was. She could only imagine it uncovered . . . could only imagine his hot, naked skin next to her own. Could only imagine how that faint stubble upon his jaw would feel against her cheek as they kissed and . . .

She did imagine. In great detail. Her face positively flamed.

Other parts of her were rather warm as well, starting in her belly and fanning out. Warm and aching for something . . . she knew not what, exactly. Just that she'd do anything to find satisfaction for this craving.

For one thing, she'd start by fainting into Knightly's arms this very afternoon.

Knightly glanced at her, concerned.

"Owens, open the window," he ordered. Owens did and a rush of cool air stole over her scorching skin. She almost sighed from the pleasure of it.

"Are you quite all right? Should we abandon the mission?" Julianna whispered.

"I'm fine. Just warm," Annabelle replied briskly. It had nothing to do with the temperature in the room, and everything to do with the scorching thoughts in her head. Her. Knightly. Limbs tangled. His lips upon her skin.

"I wonder why . . ." Julianna murmured.

"You wonder no such thing, Julianna," Annabelle hissed. No one could know that she was entertaining the most wanton, lustful fantasies when she ought to be occupying her brain with serious thoughts.

"Oh, Knightly, if I might have a word with you . . ." Julianna requested at the end of the meeting as the other writers were quitting the room. Annabelle lingered by her friend's side.

This was all part of the plan to faint into his arms. She realized now what an extraordinary leap of faith this required. To expect the man who never noticed her to catch her when she fell. This was madness.

What was the worst that could happen? Julianna would catch her. Or she might collapse on the floor, possibly doing herself an injury. Yet she would certainly survive it, and Lord knows she'd already survived embarrassment in front of Knightly.

Like this afternoon, when she thought about him hot and naked, entwined with her . . . His kiss. His touch.

"Oooh," she groaned again. Really, this must stop. Knightly glanced at her, his blue eyes narrowed in concern.

"What is it, Julianna?" he asked. He stood close enough to Annabelle that she thought her plan might just work. His arm brushed against hers as he folded his arms over his chest. She recalled the last time she'd been so close to him—at the theater—and the mortifying brush of her hand upon his . . .

Oh, her skin felt positively aflame.

"It's about Lady Marsden," Julianna said, her voice low. Knightly leaned in. Annabelle groaned again—this time it had nothing to do with her feigned faint or explicit romantic thoughts.

That cursed letter still remained, unanswered, and tucked in a volume of *Belinda* on the highest shelf in her bedroom.

"I told you, no mentions of the Marsdens," Knightly said firmly. Impatiently. He loves her, Annabelle thought wildly, and Lady Lydia loves him. They were star-crossed lovers, with cruel brothers and society conspiring against them! Every reader of romantic novels knew it was a recipe for some Grand Gesture and Bold Romantic Display.

"What if the Man About Town scoops us?" Julianna questioned sharply.

"It won't happen because Hardwicke is quaking in his boots in fear of Marsden and his Inquiry," Knightly said, becoming visibly irritated. That was not part of her plan, but there was no stopping Julianna once she pounced upon a subject.

"Of course that silly man is. But are you?" Julianna challenged.

"Julianna." Knightly and Annabelle said this at the same time, both adopting tones of warning.

Knightly glanced at Annabelle. She wavered on her feet. This was her moment. She knew it like she knew the earth revolved around the sun, like spring follows winter, like the sun rises in the east.

*Be bold*, she told herself. *Let go. Have faith in Knightly and in the advice of Swooning on Seymour Street.*

She fluttered her lashes. In order to bring a feverish blush to her cheeks, she imagined how it would feel to be embraced by Knightly with his strong arms holding her against the muscled planes of his hot, firm chest.

"Are you all right?" he asked, looking closely at her. He pressed his palm on the small of her back. It was amazing how such a small gesture could be felt so intensely and all over.

"No, I don't think I am," Annabelle replied truthfully. She loved him, and he courted another, while she could not restrain the most wicked and wanton thoughts. She was not all right. She was the very definition of wretched, hopelessly in love, desperate to win his heart. "I feel . . ."

*Faint.*

And then she fainted.

Or pretended to.

She let her knees go weak, her eyelashes flutter and close, and then let herself fall.

She even managed to languorously drape a hand across her brow for dramatic effect.

The next thing she knew, she had landed right in Knightly's arms. Right where she had always wanted to be.

She had dreamed of this, and the reality far surpassed it.

The man was all muscle—from his arms to his chest—hard and strong. She inhaled the clean scent of wool suit, the indescribable scent that was just him and that she'd only recently gotten close enough to know. Heaven couldn't possibly be better than this.

When she opened her eyes, his vivid blue eyes were fixed upon her face and Knightly gazed at her intently. The blue had darkened considerably. His lips parted slightly.

When he looked at her like that, she *felt* it. Everywhere. It made her skin feel feverish.

"Annabelle?" he said, and there was a rough quality to his voice. His gaze roamed over her, as if searching for answers. Her lips parted to explain . . . but there was nothing she could say.

Her heart began to pound.

Was this *actually working*? She'd been so accustomed to being overlooked that she hadn't quite considered that this mad scheme of hers might actual succeed.

And yet here she was, in Knightly's arms, as he lifted her up and carried her away, like a princess. He carried her over the threshold to his office, like a bride. He held her like a woman he noticed.

# Chapter 20

## The Dangers of Fainting

TOWN TALK

*Mr. Knightly's courtship of Lady Marsden continues. She has confided to friends that she expects a proposal soon.*

*The Morning Post*

**N**o one actually fainted so prettily, complete with the hand over the forehead. In fact, women did not actually faint as much as the stories would have one believe. Knightly might have allowed that her corset was laced tightly, depriving her of air, for he had noted that her waist was narrow and her breasts were marvelously high and nearly spilling out of her gown.

But he knew a fake faint when he saw one, especially when it swooned delicately into his arms, bringing an end to the world as he had known it.

It was just Annabelle, he tried to convince himself.

Just Annabelle, lovely and luscious in his arms with her soft gold curls escaping from restraint and tumbling down around the soft curve of her cheeks.

Just Annabelle, with her lips slightly parted while he thought of nothing—*nothing*—else but pressing his mouth to hers to discover, to taste, to know, and to claim.

For the first time he truly noticed her blue eyes and dark lashes. He saw the depths of emotion there. Desire. Uncertainty. Hope and fear.

He thought this was how she must appear in the throes of pleasure—tussled hair, desiring eyes, lips slightly parted to share sighs of pleasure. His body responded to the vision as if it were real. As if he had inspired that blush, made her lips part for gasps of pleasure . . .

Knightly wanted to lay her down, have his way with her, and give her that pleasure.

Now that he'd seen Annabelle like this . . .

He knew he wouldn't be able to look at her again without seeing her thusly. That wicked, seductive, wanton, and sensual image was now seared into his brain forevermore.

In the far recesses of his brain shards of logic remained and alerted him to the facts: this was a ruse for her column, for her elaborate seduction. But was this moment just practice? In other words, was this the closest he would ever be to witnessing Annabelle as if in the throes of pleasure?

Or . . .

Was he the infamous object of her affections? Otherwise known, lamentably, as the Nodcock. To that, his heart, his brain, every fiber of his being firmly declared . . .

*No.* No.

"Where are you taking me?" Annabelle asked. He forced a slight smile, even though the world as he knew it was coming to an end. She'd been "the quiet one," and now he wanted to lay her on his office floor and have his wicked way with her.

"I'm taking you to my office," he said. Where we might have some privacy, he thought. *Wrong.* Wrong!

They were going to his office, where she might recover herself and he might have a drink and restore sense and reason in his brain. *Think of Lady Lydia,* he ordered himself. *Think of that damned New Earl and everything you've ever wanted.* Then he promptly ignored the command.

"I'm certain I can walk," she said. Probably because all the other writers were staring as he made his way to his office with Annabelle in his arms. She did seem to have an aversion to being the center of attention.

"Let's not risk it," he said, because he couldn't actually say that he rather liked the feel of her in his arms and in a moment would set her down and probably never hold her thusly again.

*Lady Lydia. Everything he'd ever wanted.*

He set her down in one of the large plush chairs before his desk and proceeded to pour himself a brandy. He took a large sip and tried to convince himself that it was truly Owens she was after, not him.

What the devil did he do now, with Annabelle gazing up at him expectantly?

"How are you feeling?" he asked. That was a safe question.

"Oh . . . I'm fine. Truly. I feel a bit silly," she said sheepishly.

*She had made him see . . .*

Knightly eyed her now. Blond curls pulled back.

Blue eyes full of questions. Her sinfully full mouth making him think of kissing, which made him think of how she'd appeared in his arms just a moment ago. As if in the midst of a damn good ravishing.

Knightly moved behind his desk so she would not see that he was in a state to give her a damn good ravishing.

He'd never thought Dear Annabelle would torture him thusly. Two could play that game, he thought with a slight grin. And speaking of playing the game, he ought to act as if she had actually fainted. Pretending to be obtuse and oblivious to the scheme would afford him time to figure something out.

"We should send for a doctor," he said gravely.

Her eyes widened significantly. Perhaps he'd inherited some of his mother's flair for acting after all.

"Oh no, I feel significantly improved. I'm sure I'll be fine," she said. Which wasn't fair, because he wasn't sure he'd ever erase the image of Annabelle, as if in the throes of passion, out of his head. It was going to drive him mad.

"A real doctor, I promise," he said, and she laughed. It was a girlish laugh, very sweet. She didn't laugh enough—or had he never really paid attention before? What else had he missed over the years? Why did he have to notice now?

"I don't want to cause any more trouble. I've inconvenienced you enough already . . ." Before his eyes, Knightly watched Annabelle in retreat. Her shoulders curved and her voice dropped to nearly a whisper.

"I do hate to be a bother," she said softly. Said the woman who had just faked a swoon into his outstretched arms. It didn't entirely add up.

His gaze locked with hers for one intense second before she looked away. Knightly watched her look around the room, as if looking for some shadows to blend in with.

Had he not noticed her before because she didn't let him?

"You're not a bother, Annabelle." She flashed a shy glance in his direction. She didn't believe him. And why should she? She had just faux fainted directly into his arms and was now keeping him from his work, and life as he had known it.

But he saw daring Annabelle starting to retreat, and he sought to cajole her out of hiding.

"Very well, you are a bother. But I don't mind being given the opportunity to demonstrate my strength and quick reflexes."

And then she treated him to that lovely girlish laugh again. It was shy and nervous and happy all at once. Damn, if it wasn't a powerful feeling to have teased her out of the shadows. But did that mean . . . ? Knightly took another sip of his drink.

"It's important that the other staff be aware of my many talents, including my physical prowess," he continued. "So I do believe thanks are in order."

He raised his glass in cheers to her and took another sip to drown out the words *besides, there are worse things than holding a beautiful woman*. While he didn't want her to feel wretched—and she was clearly the romantic, dramatic sort who would mope for days on end—he couldn't bring himself to say anything that would make things awkward.

And since she was clearly the romantic, dramatic sort who would puzzle over every word for days on end, he did not want to give her Ideas. Not when he had to continue his courtship of Lady Lydia and ensure that Annabelle's column remained the smashing success that it was, so that he didn't lose everything, starting with *The London Weekly*.

At that thought, Knightly took another sip and savored the burn.

"Should I have some of that?" Annabelle asked, and he choked.

"Brandy?" he sputtered.

"In novels, the heroes always force the heroines to drink brandy after they have fainted. Apparently, it is very restorative," she informed him.

"It burns like the devil and will likely make you ill," he lectured. But damn, did he want to laugh. Especially when she pouted so adorably at him. Where had this Annabelle been all these years? And why did she have to appear now?

"I should still like to try," she said.

"I'm not giving you brandy," he told her. It seemed like something done by the vile seducer character in a novel. He would not play that part.

"Very well. What if it was research for my column?" She smiled, pleased with her strategy of selecting the excuse he could not refuse.

"Oh, Dear Annabelle . . ." he said, laughing, and handing over his glass. One small sip remained.

She lifted the glass to her mouth. After one whiff she wrinkled her nose.

"Perhaps I needn't try it," she said. "And pray do not say I told you so."

Knightly grinned, enjoying her company tremendously, even though that was the road to ruin. *Think of Lady Lydia. Think of everything you ever wanted.* But he didn't.

"Come on, Annabelle, let's take you home. No, do not protest," he said to her as much as to himself. "I cannot send you off in a hired hack after you've just fainted. What kind of gentleman would that make me?"

# Chapter 21

## What *Not* to Ask a Woman

### THE MAN ABOUT TOWN

*Lord Marsden was joined by an unlikely guest at White's—Derek Knightly, owner of* The London Weekly. *The two gentlemen were in deep discussion. Was it about Marsden's Inquiry into the reporting methods of the press, or Knightly's courtship of Marsden's sister?*

*The London Times*

ANNABELLE had done it again—she somehow contrived to find herself alone with Knightly and to indulge in the tortured pleasures of his presence. Had she known what to do years ago . . .

She still wouldn't have done a thing, because she wouldn't have been desperate enough to ask for help or to risk taking the advice of Sneaky in Southwark or Careless in Camden Town and especially Swooning in Mayfair.

"Thank you for taking me home," she said. "I am sorry to inconvenience you. Well, a little bit. But this, with you, is far preferable to a hired hack or a long walk. But I sincerely hope this isn't too much trouble for you." She was a bit awed, truth be told, at these situations that she had conjured up. Like she possessed magical powers and was only just discovering it.

"You don't like to ask for things for yourself, do you?" Knightly questioned. "You just fainted, Annabelle. I can't let you walk across town alone. Back in the office, you didn't want me to send for a doctor because you might be a bother."

This was Knightly seeing her. Seeing into her soul, even. Seeing into the dark, quiet parts of her. The part that was forever afraid of being too much of a nuisance and left behind accordingly.

Annabelle was afraid that if she didn't prove useful around the house, Blanche would cast her out, as she had threatened shortly after the marriage. What bride wanted her husband's awkward, orphaned sister lurking around the house? Why pay to send her to finishing school when she could earn her keep—and save household funds—by acting as a servant?

She was afraid that if her column was late or not good enough, she'd demand too much of Knightly's limited time and he'd decide to find a better advice columnist. She labored over each column as if her hopes and dreams depended on each word being perfect.

She was afraid to burden her fellow Writing Girls with these fears in case they found her tedious or hopeless and then cast her aside for more fascinating and fashionable friends.

Having Knightly glimpse these fears was wonderful and terrifying all at once. Before, she could dismiss any slight as simple carelessness or obliviousness. But now that he was learning about her, she had opened herself up to all kinds of hurt and vulnerabilities.

"I hate to cause trouble," Annabelle said softly, finding herself still too tongue-tied around Knightly to say any more.

"How do you get ahead?" he asked, perplexed. The question was blunt; her answer was, too.

"I don't. I get by." She said this with a sigh, of course.

"That's no way to live, Annabelle." Knightly drawled the word in a way that tempted her—forever shy, forever cautious—to throw all caution to the wind and try to be great instead of ducking her head and hoping to get through the day.

"I'm improving," she said, proud, and also relieved to be able to say so truthfully. Yet it was a constant effort to let go of Old Annabelle and adopt New Annabelle. Even now, after having done the most dramatic, daring thing of her life—fainting into his arms—she found herself retreating to more familiar safer, calmer waters.

"You are improving," Knightly said, "thanks to this column of yours." He noticed! Again!

"See, it's taking all of London to instruct me on how to be a bother," she said with a little laugh. Across the carriage, Knightly smiled.

He looked like he wanted to say something, but he didn't. She wondered, desperately, what he was holding back.

"I trust you are succeeding? Is the Nodcock noticing you?" Knightly asked.

How, oh, how to answer! Her heart started to thud because she wanted to declare, *You are the Nod-*

*cock and here we are!* and launch herself into his arms. But she did no such thing, because she was not yet sure how he would take it. Would he kiss her passionately? Or awkwardly untangle their limbs and stop the carriage?

She was still the "Annabelle that just gets by," even though she was slowly, agonizingly becoming bold New Annabelle.

And she also didn't tell him if she was succeeding with "the Nodcock" because that wasn't how she dreamed the moment would be. She had not yet given up her hopes and dreams in which he declared his love for her.

"I am making progress," she allowed. And then she gave voice to the vexing truth. "But not too much . . . you said it's very popular and you'd like it to continue."

"It's the saving grace of *The Weekly* right now. With all eyes focused on the scandal at *The Times*, it's only a matter of time until they examine the journalistic practices at *The Weekly*," he said, plainly stating the facts.

"And then we are doomed," Annabelle said dramatically.

"Not if I have anything to do with it," Knightly said. His voice was calm, but his intentions were fierce. Oh, to be loved the way Knightly loved his newspaper!

Quietly, but steadfast and strong, with a relentless, daily devotion. To know that your beloved would fight to death to protect you. Knightly had taken bullets for the paper.

"You love this newspaper more than anything." Annabelle said the truth aloud.

"It's mine." Plain. Simple. Fact. But there was a world of emotion in that little phrase, *it's mine*.

Knightly might be remote or apparently unfeeling, but if he could say those words, *it's mine*, like that, for a newspaper, then he could love a woman tremendously. She wanted to be that woman more than anything.

"A man. A newspaper. A love story: a novel in three parts," Annabelle said, and Knightly laughed, which gave her the confidence to say more. "What is your story? How did you fall in love with *The Weekly*?"

"It was a second-rate newspaper—yesterday's news, poorly edited—and it was for sale. The editor had married a woman of means and wished to retire. I wanted it, and I had the means to acquire it."

"Starting right at the top," she remarked.

"Actually, I was one of the writers," Knightly said, surprising her. "Before that I worked the printing presses, and before that I delivered them to all the aristocratic households."

Annabelle smiled at the image of a young Knightly standing before a Mayfair mansion with a hot-off-the-presses edition of *The London Weekly* in his hand. Had he known or dreamed then that he would one day live in such a grand home?

"No one knew that paper like I did. The owner offered me the opportunity to buy it," Knightly explained, and she marveled that there was no note of apology in his voice, as there would have been in hers in detailing an accomplishment. That was another reason why she adored him.

That, and the way he made her heart beat a bit faster and heightened her awareness of her every breath, of the rustle of silk against her skin.

When he looked at her, when Knightly noticed her, she felt like she existed.

And she could see the woman she wanted to become.

Starting with not being afraid to ask questions.

"But how did you have money to buy a newspaper? Which isn't to say that writers are not paid enough. But if . . ." Oh, how to ask the question without insulting her wages and the man who paid them? "I do not mean to suggest that you compensate your writers inadequately . . ."

"It was cheap," Knightly said bluntly.

"Not *that* cheap, I'm sure," Annabelle said, daring to contradict him.

He shrugged then, and looked out the window. Drummed his fingers on the seat next to him. Things the calm, cool, utterly self-possessed Mr. Knightly ordinarily Did Not Do.

Had she discovered a vulnerability? Was Knightly *not* perfect? She had thought she'd known him over the years, but apparently there was more to discover. This only made her more enthralled with the man seated across from her in the carriage.

"I had an inheritance, from my father." The way he said it, it sounded like a confession.

In the years, seven months, and a few days since she had loved Knightly, she'd always kept an ear out for information about him. Not even Julianna mentioned much about their employer's family or past. His father had been a peer; Annabelle knew that much. She also knew he was illegitimate. Julianna had told the Writing Girls one day, in the strictest confidence.

"If it was enough to buy a business, wasn't it

enough to just live off of?" she asked now. That's what her brother would do, if he could. Just sit in his library chair with a stack of newspapers and pay no attention to the world around him.

"I could not idly go through life, watching my bank account dwindle and not do something with my time. I have to build and create," he said passionately. "And now I have accomplished something: a successful business. And a bloody fortune, every penny of which I earned my damned self."

"And yet you do not retire," she pointed out.

"It would kill me," he said simply. Knightly paused, fixed his blue eyes on hers, and she knew that what he would say next would be vitally important. "I haven't yet accomplished everything that I intend to."

"What is left?" she asked, her breath hitching as she awaited his response.

He stared at her for a moment, as if debating whether to tell her.

"I want my place in society," he said, and she dearly wished he hadn't. The facts aligned swiftly to reveal a heartbreaking truth. Lady Lydia was high society. Marriage to her—and his bloody fortune—would all but assure his impeachable status in the ton.

"You can't lose your paper now, can you?" she said, referring to the threat of the parliamentary Inquiry. It was the only thing that could ruin *The Weekly*. "Not when you are so close to the ton and everything you ever wanted."

"So close I can taste it," he said, his voice rough.

Annabelle smiled wryly, for they were more alike in this moment than ever before, yet in the most wretched way. Each of them so close to attaining that one thing. Though she had found herself alone with Knightly, and even managed to gain his attention, he had just effectively told her they could have no future together—unless she wanted him to give up his life's dream and burning ambition.

Just for her. Little old Overlooked Annabelle.

She nearly laughed. It was either that or cry.

"Speaking of high society," Knightly began slowly, building up to something. "Lord Marsden has taken a liking to you."

"I suppose he has," Annabelle said carefully, so that she might not betray one of the decoys. She knew, too, what Marsden was to the newspaper at this moment. Possibly its savior; possibly the destroyer.

"He sent you flowers," Knightly stated slowly.

"A gorgeous bouquet of pink roses," Annabelle added, suddenly keen to show that she was *wanted*. Wanted by high society, too.

Perhaps she might even make Knightly jealous.

Also, she wanted him to know she liked pink roses, if he should ever think to send her flowers.

"I have the distinct impression that it is his affection for you and your advice column that has him thinking favorably of *The Weekly*," Knightly said, his meaning becoming plain. Gut-wrenchingly, heartbreakingly plain. "If you encouraged him, Annabelle, it would be a tremendous boon for *The Weekly*. And it would be a great favor to me."

Her heartbeat slowed. The simple act of breathing became impossible.

*Do not ask this of me,* she wanted to plead. But all the words died in her throat.

It was because he loved his newspaper. She knew that. Because he was so close to attaining his life's ambitions, and to lose *The Weekly* was to lose everything. She could make sense of the request, but she could not deny the hurt.

He didn't know her feelings, she rationalized. Otherwise he wouldn't ask this wretched *favor* of her. If he did . . . she couldn't even contemplate such a thing. Not now, in this small, dark, confining carriage with Knightly's blue eyes fixed upon her.

He was waiting for her answer. Waiting for her to say *of course*, because that's what Annabelle did: she solved other people's problems with no regard to the expense to her own heart and soul.

"Annabelle . . ." He seemed pained. Good, she thought. He didn't know from pain.

"I understand, Mr. Knightly." And she did. But that didn't mean she liked it, or would do it, or that it didn't feel like a cold knife blade to her warm beating heart.

The rest of the carriage ride progressed in silence. She was achingly aware of his fleeting glances in her direction. Old Annabelle would have tried to soothe his conscience, even as he'd asked this despicable thing. To hell with Old Annabelle.

"Annabelle . . ." Knightly spoke her name, breaking the silence. He even reached for her hand. She glanced down at that long awaited sight. Her small, delicate hand in his, which was large and warm and strong. But the moment wasn't quite as she had dreamed. She felt deprived, though still wanted her hand lovingly in his.

*If* she were to do this thing he asked . . . it would make him beholden to her. She would no longer be just Dear Old Annabelle, but the savior of *The London Weekly*. How tempting.

"Annabelle . . ." he said again, his voice rough, trailing off as if there were more to say. Vaguely she was aware of her lips parting. *If he kisses me I'll forgive anything . . .*

The carriage rolled to a stop in front of her house.

He wasn't going to kiss her. It didn't feel right. He was probably going to say something wretched and heartbreaking and possibly about Lady Lydia or Lord Marsden or how he loved *The London Weekly* above all else. She knew all of these things.

She also knew that Blanche was likely watching from behind the drawing room drapes.

"I must go," she said, recognizing her moment to employ Mysterious in Chelsea's advice to "leave the Nodcock wanting more."

# Chapter 22

### Newspaper Tycoon Sighted in the Most Unlikely of Places

**DEAR ANNABELLE**

*I'm glad Remorseful in Richmond asked for the best way to apologize to a woman. 'Tis information many men need to know. Flowers wouldn't be remiss; this author is partial to pink roses (in the event the Nodcock is reading this).*

    *The London Weekly*

*The warehouse*

**H**E was not brooding. Knightly preferred to view it as thinking logically and rationally about a frustrating situation. Brooding men paced like caged lions or drank whiskey to intensify the burn.

Instead, he went down to the warehouse and printing presses. Nothing cleared a man's mind like the sweat and strain of manual labor and the roar of machines so loud that thought became almost impossible.

Almost.

The noise of the steam-powered printing presses

generally had a way of drowning out all distractions. Except for Annabelle and that awful thing he'd asked of her.

With a crew of laborers, Knightly lifted and tossed reams of paper that would be fed into the printing press. The warehouse was so hot it felt like an inner circle of hell. The work was tedious. After a while, a long while, his muscles start to holler in protest at him. It was a feeling he craved. Pain. Agony. But damn good all at once.

This soothed more than brandy or boxing.

Usually.

Even over the shout of his muscles and the din of the presses, some damn pesky thoughts persevered. They nipped and nagged at his conscience.

He should not have asked Annabelle to encourage Marsden. Not for him, not for the paper. It was just plain wrong. He resolved to remedy the situation later and then he put the matter aside.

Or tried.

Annabelle. The clang of the machines seemed to rap out her name.

The hiss of the steam engine, sounding like *Miss.* The deep clank of the cast iron upon cast iron: *An . . . na . . . belle.* The rush of paper through the machine sounding like *Swift.*

Knightly bent to lift the next ream of paper and hurled it to the bloke on his right.

He thought of Annabelle.

*I know it was wrong to ask,* Knightly told himself. *It's inappropriate and taking unfair advantage. I will even concede that it might be morally reprehensible.*

Hell, he knew it was wrong the moment he'd said it. And he'd tried to amend it on the spot but the words died in his throat. Her sweet smile had faded. Her sparkling blue eyes dimmed and then she had averted from his gaze. Right before his eyes she seemed to shrink and fade in a desperate attempt to disappear. He'd been the one to extinguish her with his selfish, brutal request.

The fact remained: an apology was in order. He resolved to do it this afternoon.

Thus, at the moment there was no point in thinking about it further.

And yet, he was still bothered, like a stone in his boot or a wasp trapped under his shirt. The damned machines kept it up, churning out issues of *The London Weekly* and sounding out her name.

*An . . . na . . . belle.*

His muscles began to burn from the exertion. He'd been here hours by now. Sweat soaked though his white linen shirt, flattening it to his chest and abdomen. The exhaustion weakened his mental defenses, so the truth was now unavoidable.

It was the way she felt in his arms. Like ravishment waiting to happen. His mouth went dry thinking of her in his arms: warm, luscious, and pure. A man could lose himself in those curves. Spend a lifetime exploring every wondrous inch of her.

It was that innocence. He wanted to taste it. Touch it. Love it. Be redeemed by it.

And he had tainted it with that loathsome request. Sent her off to seduce another man when he wanted to claim that ripe, red mouth of hers for himself. To capture Annabelle's sighs before they escaped her lips.

Knightly wanted to know that purity, that innocence, the sweetness that was Annabelle. He wanted to know every last inch of her pure milky white skin.

Each and every curve, from the swells of her breasts rising above those newly lowered bodices to the less obvious but just as tantalizing dip in her lower back. There was the tilt at the outer corners of her eyes, catlike, with lashes reaching high. Eyes he had seen closed as she swooned. As she might appear in a real swoon of pleasure. As she might appear in a thoroughly satiated sleep.

That damned faint really did a number on him. Making him see her thus.

*Miss. An . . . na . . . belle. Swift.*

He knew it was wrong to ask Annabelle to appeal to Marsden, but that wasn't what made him feel like a damned devil. He didn't get to where he was by worrying about the delicate sensibilities and bloody feelings of others.

He understood now.

The request he'd made was driving him mad because he wanted her for himself.

Wanted her in a wicked, sinful way.

Her innocence and sweetness was like a breath of fresh air, and here he was in the polluted stench of the factories.

Strange, that. Wanting Annabelle all of a sudden with a profoundly unsettling intensity . . . after all these years when she had been around, under his nose, shrinking back and not wanting to be a bother.

Well, she was a damned bother now, though he'd wager she had no idea about it.

On his way out of the warehouse, Knightly passed a group of workers gathered around the new issue of *The Weekly*, steaming hot off the presses, ink smearing under their already dirty fingertips. One worker read aloud to the others as they shifted around, smoking and listening to the news. Seven or eight men, one newspaper.

Knightly slowed, listening, allowing himself to be drawn into their conversation of the news of the day. This might distract him. He might learn something. He listened to the gruff voice of the man reading, and the thoughtful silence of the other men who listened. It occurred to him in an instant: pictures.

If there were more pictures so even the illiterate could understand if no one was around to read the words to them. It would require some advances to the printing press, some experiments.

"That's Knightly. That's the owner," one of them said roughly as he nodded and picked up his pace, now eager to return to the offices. But first: he owed Annabelle an apology.

# Chapter 23

## Writing Girls, Enraged

**DEAR ANNABELLE**

*Perhaps you might do the Nodcock a favor. He'll have
to pay attention to you then.*

   *Helpful from Holburn*

   The London Weekly

*Roxbury House, teatime*

"**H**E asked you to do *what*?" Julianna gasped.
Annabelle shrank back against the settee. One
minute she had been delightfully retelling her fainting adventures and subsequent carriage ride with
Knightly. The next moment an uncomfortable silence had fallen over her fellow Writing Girls when
she mentioned Knightly's request that she encourage
Lord Marsden's attentions for the good of the paper.

"It makes perfect sense if you think about it," Annabelle said defensively. She did understand Knightly's motives, his logic. She had been hurt by it, but he
didn't know how she felt about him, which lessened
the sting. And should she succeed, she might just
get his attention. And everlasting gratitude.

Julianna, even more brash and fiery than usual, scoffed openly. Sophie and Eliza exchanged nervous glances.

"Explain to me how this is anything but a horribly offensive, inconsiderate thing to ask of you," Julianna said sharply. So sharply it hurt, like a knife to the heart. Annabelle was taken aback by this sudden attack. A second ago they were all laughing over her request to taste Knightly's whiskey.

"He loves his newspaper and it's in trouble. He merely asked for help. People help those whom they love," Annabelle explained. Really, it did make sense. Did it not? She didn't like that he had asked this of her, but understood that it came from a place of love or passion. Or something like it.

"Perhaps," Julianna retorted. "But one does not ask them to encourage the affections of another man. That is not love."

"It's not like that. It's not that simple," Annabelle said, because . . . because . . . of course there was a reason why this was all fine. She just couldn't think of it at the moment. Her urge to help him, to demonstrate her usefulness and love, surpassed all else, but she couldn't quite find the words to explain.

"Annabelle, why don't you explain again," Sophie said gently, resting her hand on hers. "Perhaps Julianna is misunderstanding the situation."

Annabelle recognized the diplomacy; it was usually her role. She wasn't usually the one in the thick of drama. With three grave, concerned faces peering at her, she felt like she was on trial. Her crime: idiocy. Her defense: love. Being helpful. Generally trying to prove she wasn't a nitwit.

She wasn't. Right?

"Knightly noted that Marsden seems to have an interest in me, and asked that I encourage it. My column is also a bit of a success, so he asked that I keep up the ruse. It's business and it's Knightly," she said, as if that *explained* everything. The man thought of nothing else.

But did it excuse his behavior?

Doubts began to creep in, like the dampness in a drafty house on a cold wet winter day. Even under Julianna's scorching glare.

"He doesn't know . . . how I feel," Annabelle added, nervously sipping from the teacup she held in her hands, even though she had no idea what Knightly knew. Or didn't.

"How do you know that, Annabelle?" Sophie asked gently. "How did this make you feel?"

"If he knew, he wouldn't ask this of me," she said stubbornly, even though she was well aware that this was based firmly upon the flimsy foundation of her own wishes. Not hard fact.

The doubts continued their march.

Why was she defending him?

What did she know, anyway?. The truth began to dawn: where she had thought herself a noble maiden on a quest for true love, she was probably, in fact, an foolish lovesick girl who was so blinded by the stars in her eyes that she'd hand her murderer the weapon.

Annabelle's head began to throb. A headache.

"Annabelle, he cares about nothing but his paper. Remember when he cast me out—when everyone had turned their back on me?" Julianna persisted, hacking away at Annabelle's illusions, and removing obstacles for the army of doubt to come in, and conquer.

"Because of Knightly's ruthless devotion to *The Weekly*, I almost lost Wycliff," Eliza added. Annabelle glanced sharply at her. Whose side was Eliza on? Julianna's or hers? The shattering of dreams or the preservation of hope?

The throbbing in her head worsened. Her eyes became hot. She would not cry. She would *not* show weakness.

"It just means that he cares. There is nothing wrong with caring," Annabelle said firmly. Yet her hand trembled, and the teacup she held clattered tellingly against the saucer. She had a feeling her friends were right and that she was wrong.

She had feared this moment, in which her friends grew tired of her optimistic infatuation. Of her. Where they no longer thought her sweet, but stupid. She could see it in their pitying gazes and in the worried glances they exchanged amongst themselves.

"Yes, he cares for his newspaper, Annabelle. Not for anyone or anything else," Julianna persisted, driving the point home. Beautiful and bold Julianna. Annabelle felt herself pale and shrink beside her friend, a tower of strength and assurance.

"How did it make you feel when he asked this of you?" Sophie asked gently, again.

"I didn't like it, of course," she said, caving in to pressure because that is what she did. And a little bit of her hadn't liked it. "But he doesn't know how I feel about him, and if he did, I have every confidence he never would have made this request."

She had been confident. Now, thanks to Julianna's

persistent, artful interrogation, she was no longer certain of anything other than her foolishness to persist in loving a man who obviously cared so little for her.

Annabelle leveled a glare in Julianna's direction.

"How can you love a man that would ask that of a woman? No decent man would ask this of a woman, love aside," Julianna said, because she never knew when to stop. If there were a line, Julianna would stomp right across it, turn around and implore you to hurry up and come along.

*What about me?*

Well, maybe it was time she crossed the line. Maybe it was time she defend herself instead of Knightly.

"What is the purpose of this conversation?" Annabelle asked, and her voice had a bold quality to it that sounded strange to her ears. Eliza straightened, Sophie's lips parted, and Julianna fixed her green eyes upon her. "I love Knightly and I have since I first saw him. It's just a part of me and you have known that and now suddenly it's wrong?"

"It was all fine until he asked you to practically prostitute yourself for his bloody newspaper," Julianna replied.

"Julianna!" Sophie and Eliza gasped.

Annabelle took a deep breath. She could do this. She could defend herself.

"What if I want to?" Annabelle challenged. But her hand wavered and tea sloshed over the cup, spilling into the saucer.

"What if you don't, but you have so defined yourself as She Who Loves Knightly that you cannot say no?" Julianna retorted. In the midst of battle, Annabelle recognized that it was a fair question. One she would explore later, on her own.

"Is that what you think of me? That I am nothing more than a foolish girl in love with a heartless man? Perhaps you're right." Annabelle laughed bitterly for the very first time in her six and twenty years. "Look at me—trying to get his attention with ideas from strangers because I have no idea what to do. And now he is starting to notice me and it's suddenly all wrong and—"

"I only want you to be happy, Annabelle, and I'm afraid that—" Julianna said, trying to reach for her hand. Annabelle set the teacup on the tray and stood to go.

"No, you are a know-it-all, Julianna. You may know all the gossip of the ton, but you do not know the contents of my heart nor do you know what is best for me."

And then Annabelle did the unthinkable. She stormed out without even a backward glance.

# Chapter 24

## A Gentleman's Apology

### TOWN TALK

*Lord Marsden has succeeded in rallying his peers to support his Inquiry. If you enjoy reading a newspaper, enjoy it now, for it seems our days are numbered.*

The Morning Post

**A**FTER Knightly knocked on the door to the Swift residence, a meek servant opened it and mutely led him to the drawing room where he might await Annabelle.

The room was sparsely furnished. Everything was useful and plain. No thought seemed to have been spared to comfort, just practicality. He thought of his own home, also simple but designed for ease and comfort, with plush carpets and richly upholstered furniture. Everything was expensive, yet nothing was ostentatious.

This room, however, was thrifty to an extreme.

And then there was Annabelle, standing in the doorway. She wore a shapeless brown dress with a white apron pinned to the front. White flour covered her hands, spotted the brown dress, and there was even a smudge on her cheek.

Her eyes, though . . . instead of sparkling, they were dull. In fact, he suspected she had been crying when he noted her eyes were reddish and puffy, too. He felt like he had been punched in the gut.

"What are you doing here?" she asked flatly. When she did not sound pleased to see him, he realized he had expected her to be, which made him feel like an ass. Like a nodcock.

"Why are you wearing an apron?" he asked. She should not be dressed like a servant.

"Cook and I were baking bread," she answered.

"Don't you have help for that?" She was the sister to a prosperous cloth merchant. They should have a fleet of household help. A woman of Annabelle's position should be occupied with friends and finding a husband, not domestic drudgery.

"I am the help," she answered flatly. This was not the Annabelle he knew; she seemed to be missing her sense of magic and wonder. Something was wrong. Was it the awful request he'd made of her? Probably. He was glad he'd come to apologize.

"Why are you here, Mr. Knightly?" she asked.

"Would you like to sit?" As a gentleman, he could not take a seat until she did.

Mutely, she sat upon the settee. He took a place next to her on the most uncomfortable piece of furniture he'd ever encountered. He reached for her hand and held it in his. Her hand was cold.

"I owe you an apology, Annabelle. It was wrong of me to ask you to encourage Marsden on behalf of the newspaper. Or as a favor to me."

Knightly had expected to find his conscience

soothed upon uttering those words. He had traveled across London, all the way from the Fleet Street office to Bloomsbury to deliver them. He thought she would thank him and say not to worry, for she had understood his request was one of a desperate idiot. A nodcock.

Annabelle narrowed her blue eyes and titled her head questioningly. His breath hitched in his throat.

"Julianna put you up to this, didn't she?" she asked. He could not miss the note of accusation in her tone.

"I beg your pardon?"

"You have come to apologize because Julianna thinks it's wrong of you to ask and *pathetic* of me to agree to it," she said, spitting out the words. At least as much as Annabelle could do. Then she took a deep breath that foretold doom and proceeded to say more to him than she ever had in the years he'd known her. "We all know that the only thing you care about is the newspaper. No one is under any illusions here, Mr. Knightly. Not even me, who has a foolish propensity toward flights of fancy and always seeks the bloody goodness in everyone."

Knightly's jaw dropped. *Annabelle had uttered a swear word.* What next—unicorns pulling hackneys and the King in dresses?

"I knew what you were asking of me. And why. I'm not stupid," she added. Her chin jutted forward. She lifted her head high. Angry Annabelle was impish and magnificent all at the same time. Thinking had suddenly become impossible when all the truths he'd ever known seemed null. This was Annabelle as he had never seen her—and, he suspected, as she'd never even been seen.

"It was wrong of me to ask," he said, because that was all he knew in a world that had just turned upside down.

"It was wrong. You really ought to think beyond yourself and your newspaper for once," she lectured. "I ought to have said so at the moment you asked. I'm very sorry you have come all this way to hear me say that. And listen to me! You are in the wrong and I have just apologized. I am such a . . . a . . . nodcock!"

"Annabelle, what is this all about?" he asked in a calm, measured tone.

She took a deep breath to calm herself. She fixed her pretty blue eyes on him.

"You really do not know," she said, awed. He had no idea what she was talking about. It must have shown in his expression. "Oh . . . oh . . . oh . . . bloody hell!"

She flung herself back on the wretchedly uncomfortable settee and just laughed her pretty blond head off while he marveled that Annabelle, who barely spoke, had just uttered the words "bloody hell."

He did not know what was so funny.

He was about to ask when the laughter ceased and the tears began.

Knightly glanced in the direction of the heavens, seeking guidance. Like many a man, nothing flummoxed him like a woman's tears. With some mixture of horror and terror, he watched as Annabelle wept beside him.

Although she looked tragic and adorable, something had to be done to stop this madness. First, he pressed a clean handkerchief into her palm and she pressed it to her eyes. Her pretty shoulders shook as she cried.

Horrors. Curses.

"Bloody hell," he muttered; then, with a sigh, he pulled her into his arms.

Annabelle burrowed her face into his shoulder. No doubt soaking his jacket and cravat with tears. It didn't matter. He could feel her become calm and still in his embrace.

He also felt her soft curls brushing against his fingertips. He felt her breasts pressing against his chest. He felt powerful for having soothed her. It felt right to hold her so close. Above all he craved more. All he wanted was more Annabelle.

He whispered her name.

They were interrupted before anything untoward could occur. A dowdy, hatchet-faced woman stood in the drawing room entry and cleared her throat. Loudly.

"Would someone like to explain this scene to me?" she asked in a sharp voice. Annabelle recoiled from his embrace and took up the smallest possible amount of space on the far end of the settee.

Knightly replied in kind. He did not take orders anywhere, from anyone. "Perhaps introductions might be in order," he stated after rising to his feet.

The woman lifted one brow at his command, in her house.

Annabelle, on the other hand, interrupted in the softest voice.

"This is my sister-in-law, Mrs. Blanche Swift," she said dully. And then with a pleading glance at him, she added, "This is Mr. Knightly, with whom I work on the Society for the Advancement of Female Literacy."

Society for the Advancement of Female Literacy? *Oh, Annabelle.*

Knightly ached to turn to her and ask a thousand questions. But he recognized a scene when he was in the midst of it. He did his best to play his part.

He schooled his features into what he hoped was a charitable expression; he had not inherited his mother's gift for acting.

"Ah, yes. Your charity work," Mrs. Mean Swift said in a glacial tone to Annabelle. "When I suggested that charity begins at home, this was not at all what I had in mind. Who is supervising the children? Have they been fed? What of the bread?"

Annabelle stood a step or two behind Knightly, as if he might protect her from her hatchet-faced sister-in-law. Frankly, he wanted to.

"Nancy is with them," Annabelle answered, even though Knightly thought she ought to reply that governesses and servants existed for those sorts of tasks, not sisters.

"I see." To emphasize her point, Mrs. Swift glared at Annabelle, who took a step back. She then glared at Knightly, who only squared his shoulders, stood taller, and looked down his nose at her. Intimidating with one's size was a juvenile maneuver, but really, sometimes the situation just called for it.

"Mrs. Swift, I would like to conclude my conversation with Miss Swift," he stated. He paused for emphasis and added, "Privately."

Never mind that he was a guest. In her house.

She stared at him with narrowed eyes.

Knightly confidently met her gaze and held it. Unblinkingly. Really, one did not attain his level of success without the ability to win a staring contest.

"I will insist the drawing room door remains open," she said harshly. "The last thing I need is a moral lapse that results in a poor example for my own children." She turned quickly and quit the room. No one was sorry to see her go.

Had he not been fully in the mode of Haughty Commander of All He Surveyed, his jaw might have dropped open.

Did this woman not know Annabelle? He'd wager his fortune she was the *last* person in the world who might corrupt an innocent youth. She was probably the last woman in the world who set a poor example. She was a paragon.

Or did *he* not know her?

Speaking of the little minx, she'd been hiding behind him during that strange introduction, and he turned to face her now. He smiled. And took a seat on the damned uncomfortable sofa.

"My dear Annabelle, you have some explaining to do."

# Chapter 25

## A First Kiss

*The Duke of Kent dismissed his secretary upon discovering the man was bribed to relay information to writers of* The Morning Chronicle. *The editor and reporter's arrests are imminent.*

The London Weekly

IN the history of bad days, Annabelle was certain this one would rank in the top one hundred. Perhaps even the top ten. It was certainly one of the worst days in her own life, along with the death and funeral of her parents and the day Blanche married her brother.

There was the horrible fight with her fellow Writing Girls earlier that morning. All these years, she'd been afraid they would find her tedious or foolish. Today her fears were confirmed. It was everything she had dreaded, and more.

Even worse, Knightly had asked her to debase herself for him. While she had not agreed, she had not refused. In fact, she had defended him when she ought to have stood up for herself. That he was here in her drawing room, apologizing, only confirmed that Julianna was correct and she had been a fool.

Had she not been so fixated upon Knightly, to the exclusion of all sense, reason, and eligible bachelors, she might have married another by now. She could be a mother of a darling brood with a home of her own. Annabelle thought of Mr. Nathan Smythe and his bakery down the road. She was baking bread anyway; why not in her own kitchen instead of slaving for the ever-unappreciative Blanche?

Worst of all, she had imagined Knightly calling upon her at home a time or two or twenty. But not like this. Not when she wore her worst dress and her eyes were red after sobbing in a hired hack all the way from Mayfair to Bloomsbury.

Not when she ungraciously ignored his apology, bickered, burst into tears, buried her face in his shoulder and sobbed.

He had held her; it was lovely beyond words to have a man's strong arms holding her close and secure, as if protecting her from the world. She had wanted to savor it more but was all too aware that she was soaking his fine white linen shirt. All too aware that a dream of hers was coming true—Knightly, embracing her—but she was too distraught to enjoy a second of it.

Cruel, cruel world!

Then Blanche interrupted and mortified her. Treating her like a servant was one thing, but to do so in front of Knightly? Words could not describe the humiliation of having him see just how worthless and unloved she was by her own family, in her own home.

He could never love her now. She had a prodigious imagination, but even she could not envision how a man so strong and commanding as he could ever fall for a delusional, foolish, and unappreciated girl like her.

"Miss Swift," Knightly said sternly as he sat on the settee. She stood before him, emotionally distraught and utterly exhausted.

"My dear Annabelle," he said, and she wondered if he was mocking her.

She heaved a sigh.

"You have some explaining to do," Knightly commanded. It was as if the Swift drawing room was his office at *The London Weekly*. Well, it wasn't and she didn't have to explain anything. She told him just that.

"This is not your office. I don't have to explain anything to you," she said. For emphasis, she folded her arms over her chest. Was it her imagination, or did his gaze stray to her décolletage?

"Annabelle, you intrigue me more each day," he said, and her lips parted in shock.

"What do you mean?"

"The Society for the Advancement of Female Literacy?" he questioned with a lift of his brow. She sighed again and sat beside him.

"They do not know the truth," she confessed quietly.

"You've kept that secret for three years?" he asked incredulously.

"Three years, seven months, and five days," she clarified out of habit. "They do not read *The Weekly*. I did not care to encourage them. I fear they would not approve of me writing and would forbid me from doing so."

And it was something that belonged to her, and her alone. Writing for *The Weekly* had been her secret, happy life. Advising and helping other people was the one thing she was good at, and it satisfied her deeply to be recognized for her talent. Much as she assisted at home, her family never gave her much credit for it.

"How did you keep such a secret for so long?" Knightly asked, his blue eyes searching hers for more answers.

"Mr. Knightly," she began impatiently. She moved away and began to pace about the sparsely decorated room. "I exist in the shadows, overlooked. I do not bother people. I live to serve. I am a professional solver of other people's problems, often at the expense of my own. And above all, expectations for me are low. Even if you told Blanche now who you are and what I write, it would take a quarter hour, at least, to convince her you told the truth."

"I see," he said after a long silence.

"Do you? Do you really?"

"I'm beginning to," he said. He glanced over at the open door. "And why do you think Julianna motivated my apology?"

"You know, it's awfully audacious of you to call upon me for this interrogation," Annabelle replied, because she didn't want to answer that question and say that Julianna meddled terribly and that she didn't have faith that Knightly would recognize what a wretched position his request placed her in.

"I came only to apologize. This interrogation was inspired by the oceans of domestic drama I have witnessed in your drawing room. Besides, I didn't become so successful by standing aside," he said, to the girl who was an expert at taking one step to the left—or right, you pick!—and generally getting out of the way.

"What's that supposed to mean?" she asked.

"Be bold, Annabelle," Knightly said, his voice all low and urgent and making her want to do just that, in spite of herself. "I like it. And it probably suits you more than you realize."

"I've been trying," she replied, and there was anguish in her voice. Because this boldness didn't come naturally to her. It was a conscious thought, a deliberate action. For every success, she encountered some sort of trouble Old Annabelle never would have succumbed to.

Old Annabelle never fought with her friends. But then again, Knightly never called upon Old Annabelle.

"I know you've been trying. Trying to the tune of four thousand extra copies each week," Knightly replied with a grin. A usual printing was around ten or twelve thousand. This was really good. She allowed herself to enjoy the rush of enjoyment upon the news.

They both cringed at a massive clattering in the kitchen and paused to identify the unmistakable sound of Blanche, grumbling and storming off to the back of the house.

Knightly stood, walked over to the drawing room door and shut it.

Annabelle did not protest.

"You have not answered my question," Knightly persisted as he strolled toward her. "About Julianna. My apology."

"I fought with them," Annabelle said with a shrug. "They think I am a fool. They are probably right. I certainly feel like one. And I don't want to talk about it with you. I cannot."

Knightly took a step closer to her, closing the distance. With his fingertip, he gently tilted her chin so her face was peering up at him.

"So don't talk, Annabelle," he murmured. And then he lowered his mouth to hers.

And then he kissed her.

Knightly. Kissing. Her.

On one of the top five worst days of her life.

She felt the heat first, of his lips upon hers. Of him being near her. It was a particular sort of heat—smoldering and building up to a crackling fire—and now that she basked in it, Annabelle realized she'd been so very cold for so very long.

This heat: a man's warm palm cradling her cheek, the warmth from his body enveloping hers, and the warmth from his mouth upon hers.

At first it was just the gentle touch of his lips against hers. She felt sparks, she felt fireworks. Her first kiss. A once in a lifetime kiss. With the man she loved. This alone was worth waiting for.

Aye, there was a surge of triumph with this kiss, along with the sparks and shivers of pleasure. She had waited for this. She had *fought* for this. She *earned* this. She was going to enjoy every exquisite second of it.

And then it became something else entirely. His lips parting hers. Her, yielding. Knightly urged her to open to him, and because she trusted him implicitly, she followed his lead with utter abandon. She had no idea where this would go, but she knew she would not go there alone.

This kiss was not at all like she had imagined—she hadn't *known* the possibilities—it was so much more magical. She let him in. She dared the same. She tasted him. Let him taste her.

A sigh escaped her lips, and it did not travel far. This sigh was one of contentment. No, she was not at all content. This was a sigh of utter pleasure, experienced for the first time. This was a sigh that only Knightly's kiss could elicit.

He placed his hand upon her waist, just above the curve of her hip. It was a possessive caress. She wanted to be possessed. She clasped the fabric of his jacket. Her whole world was spinning wildly—in a magical way—and she was dizzy with the delight of it. But still, she needed to hold on. Needed to ground this moment in physical, earthly sensations so she'd know it wasn't some flight of her own fancy.

There was the wool of his coat in her palms.

His cheek against hers. A little bit rough. So very male.

The scent of him, so indescribable but intoxicating all the same. She wanted to breathe him in forever.

The sound of his breathing, the rushed whisper of her own sighs. Little sounds, to be sure, ones that spoke of intimacy and passion.

The pounding of her heart.

The taste of him . . .

His mouth, firm, determined, generous, hot, and possessive against her own. She melted against him. Whatever he wanted, she would indulge. And she

wanted, needed, him to know, how much this kiss
meant to her. How she had waited her whole life for
this kiss. She kissed him with years' worth of pent-
up desire. And the amazing, wonderful, exhilarating thing was . . . . he kissed her with a passion to
match.

# Chapter 26

## The Nodcock Begins to Wonder if
## He Is the Nodcock

DEAR ANNABELLE

*While many readers have written with encourage-*
*ment and advice for my quest to attract the love of the*
*Nodcock, many have challenged me to explain why*
*I bother. I confess, this author does wonder if he is*
*deserving of my efforts, or if I should give up. But just*
*when I am ready to admit defeat, some magic occurs*
*to convince me to carry on. Dear readers, please*
*advise! How far does one go for love?*

*The London Weekly*

*Galloway's Coffeehouse*

KNIGHTLY sat with a newspaper and a hot coffee
at Galloway's coffeehouse, as he did every Saturday morning. His love of newspapers extended
beyond his own. He loved, too, the atmosphere in
the coffeehouse—the rich smell of coffee mingling
with the smoke of cigars and cheroots. The rustle of
newsprint. The hum of conversations.

He badly needed the coffee, for he had not slept.

He badly needed a distraction, but this was not to be.

He had kissed Annabelle.

Shy, quiet, Writing Girl number four. Annabelle. Just weeks ago he'd barely spared a thought for her, and now . . .

He had kissed Annabelle.

What madness had impelled him, he knew not. But some force beyond his control had him strolling across her horrible drawing room and tilting her chin to his, lowering his mouth to hers.

It had been a good kiss.

So good he had the damnedest time thinking of anything else since it happened. She tasted sweet, dear Annabelle. She kissed with an artlessness and enthusiasm that undid him.

It was not calculated to please, like that of a mistress, and it was all the more seductive because of it. It was a kiss for the sake of it. Purely for the love of it.

Knightly had discovered all these truths in the moments when her tongue tangled with his, just as he had known then that it was her first kiss. The implications of that kind of kiss made his chest feel tight and deprived of air.

But to hell with the implications, if a certain part of him had its way. The memory of the taste, the touch, kept him awake at night, inspiring wicked dreams. He sought relief. He attained it. And yet still, he craved Annabelle.

In an attempt to restore his world to rights, he would coolly consider the facts:

*Fact: Annabelle was in his employ.* No law prohibited him from ravishing his workforce should he so choose, but it just felt . . . wrong. Like taking advantage. That was not the pleasure he sought—and he had given extensive thought to the pleasures he might have with Annabelle.

*Fact: Annabelle lived with strong contenders for the dubious distinction of London's Worst Relatives.* Her family treated her like a servant. Right before his eyes Annabelle shriveled under the menacing glare of the Mean Mrs. Swift, who put him in mind of a particularly nasty school warden.

Annabelle was no servant. She was a beautiful woman and a talented writer—which all of London seemed to know except her family.

Society for the Advancement of Female Literacy, indeed. Of course they never questioned her—likely never paid her that much mind. As she said, they probably wouldn't even believe her if he commissioned her illustration, placed it on the front page along with a statement confirming her as Dear Annabelle, and had a cartload delivered to their front door.

Knightly was of half a mind to do just that, except . . .

*Fact: Annabelle was delicate.* In the course one afternoon, he watched her act boldly, then retreat. Blossom and then wilt. All right before his eyes. Something was happening with Annabelle. He liked Bold Annabelle, and was glad he told her so, even though Bold Annabelle stalked his thoughts and seduced him with a kiss that was a heady mixture of enthusiasm and innocence. Old Annabelle made his life easy. Bold Annabelle set his life on fire.

Something was happening, something glorious, and he didn't want to wreck it. A picture began to emerge of a woman who possessed hope and optimism and gumption in spades in spite of wretched relatives and a world that never took much notice of her—in real life anyway. On the pages of *The London Weekly*, Dear Annabelle was something else: a delightful minx, a sweetheart of a hellion.

It was bloody impossible to concentrate on facts when Drummond and Gage were having the most infuriating conversation about Dear Annabelle, as they were now. Knightly pretended to read *The Morning Post* while eavesdropping on their idiotic chatter.

"You know, I don't think this nodcock deserves Annabelle," Drummond declared as he set down this week's issue. He paused and sipped his coffee, brow furrowed as if he pondered Annabelle's love life in the same way Newton must have puzzled over calculus.

"Though it pains me to agree with you, Drummond, I reckon you're right. And 'Nodcock' is not a strong enough name for the bloody ungrateful, cork-brained jackanape she's set her cap for," Gage added thoughtfully.

"Obviously, he has bruised her soul and is testing her faith in love," Drummond said, jamming his finger at that particular page of *The London Weekly*. "Positively criminal, that is."

Knightly snorted. Faith in love? Bruised her soul? What sentimental rubbish. But what else would one expect from a playwright? All the same, he shrunk back in his chair and lifted his own newspaper higher.

He had read her column, holding his breath the whole damn time. He had his suspicions. But the cost of confirming those suspicions was too high. He would either give up his lifelong quest to prove he belonged with his peers or break Annabelle's heart.

He was not prepared to do either.

"It sounds like she has attracted his attention but he just took advantage of her, if you know what I mean," Gage said. Knightly's gut knotted.

"It does, doesn't it? You're right. 'Nodcock' is not a strong enough word. You know, I wish I knew who he was only so I could plant a right facer on him," Drummond practically growled.

For years Knightly read the papers and drank coffee with these old friends, and in all that time he'd never heard Drummond react so bloody passionately to a single item in any newspaper. It was worse than when *The London Chronicle* described one of his plays as "entertaining as a severe bout of smallpox" after he'd shelled out six pounds in puff money.

"While you're doing that, I'm going to whisk Dear Annabelle off to Gretna Green and along the way show her the love of a good man," Gage said with a rakish grin that made Knightly want to plant a right facer on *him.*

Knightly concluded it was up to him to bring logic and rationality to this conversation—before his temper flared and he revealed far too much.

"You cannot be serious," he said flatly, lowering the newspaper he'd been pretending to read.

"Oh, I am," Drummond said solemnly, hands clasped upon the rough-hewn table.

"I as well," Gage added with equal gravity. He pounded the table for emphasis.

"You don't even know her," Knightly pointed out.

"Aye, but you do. Fancy introducing us?" Gage asked with suggestive lift of his brow.

"No," Knightly replied firmly. In the name of all that was holy, no.

"Why not? She's obviously a lovely chit who is lonely and looking for love," Gage said.

"And young, pretty, and quiet," Drummond added in a way that could only be described as dreamily, even though it pained Knightly to do so.

"Do you not think she deserves love?" Gage demanded.

"It's her own business," Knightly said, snapping the newspaper shut and setting it on the table.

"Maybe it *was*. But once she started writing about it in the newspaper it became everyone's business," Drummond said. Unfortunately, he had a point.

"Given that it's your newspaper," Gage said, "I'd think you'd be more interested it. Being your business and all."

"Annabelle is . . ." And here Knightly's description faltered. She was shy, except for when she was bold. She was beautiful. Adorable, even when her eyes were red with tears. She was a mystery, ever unfolding before his eyes, which both fascinated and terrified him.

And he had kissed her.

He'd choke before he said any of those things aloud, and he'd choke to death before uttering such sentiments to the likes of Drummond and Gage.

"Annabelle is a very nice person," he finally said. His companions stared at him, slack-jawed. And then they both burst into raucous laughter, slapping each other hard on the back and pounding the table with their fists. Old Man Galloway himself hollered at them to shut their traps.

"It's you, isn't it? You're the Nodcock!" Drummond shouted, and pointed, in the midst of roaring laughter. The rest of the coffeehouse quieted, heads lifted up from newsprint pages to stare at him.

"I'm not the Nodcock," Knightly said hotly, feeling like quite the . . . Nodcock. He cursed that damn faint. Until that moment he could exist in a blissful ignorance, caring only about the Nodcock's affect on sales and not his identity. He could assume it was Lord Marsden or Owens (it could *still* be Owens) and carry on with his plans.

He cursed Drummond and Gage for their laughter and accusations because they brought to the fore an issue he wanted to ignore. He wasn't ready to make that fateful decision. *Belong. Be beholden to no one. Break Annabelle's heart.*

The entire situation was impossible. Their laughter was irritating. Yet Knightly retained a cool demeanor nonetheless, because that's what he did. That's who he was: cool verging on cold. Always in control. The laughter of some louts rolled right off his back, like water off a duck.

But he suddenly thought of Annabelle, and the day Owens declared her too well behaved to be wicked and thus *unworthy* of investigation. They had all laughed.

Shame and remorse kicked him in the gut as Knightly realized, belatedly, how devastating that must have been for her. Was that the day she started to blossom? Had that been the moment she resolved to capture Owens's attentions?

Was their kiss something meaningful, or sweet

Annabelle's determination to be wicked? Was he the Nodcock or just another man she practiced her tricks upon?

So many questions and none of them mattered. He had decided his fate years ago, on an October day in 1808. When he made decisions, he acted and abided by them.

# Chapter 27

## Missing: One Loving Sigh from the Lips
of Dear Annabelle

TOWN TALK

*Mr. Knightly's proposal to Lady Marsden must be imminent. We have it on good authority that he visited a jeweler in Burlington Arcade. However, he left without making a purchase.*

*The Morning Post*

*Offices of* The London Weekly

THE first thing Knightly noticed upon entering the writers' room: Annabelle did *not* sigh. The second thing he finally noticed: she had always sighed when he strolled into the weekly gathering of writers. It was this routine, like clockwork, that he never realized until the watch broke.

For a moment he faltered. She had sighed; he had kissed her; now she did not sigh. The facts explained nothing. Logic and reason failed him. He wracked his brain thinking back over her columns—had there been clues he missed? He tried to tell himself it mattered not.

But his mind wandered to Annabelle.

His gaze strayed to Annabelle.

He craved Annabelle.

Yet his decision had been made and obligations remained. Both Lord *and* Lady Marsden were becoming impatient with him. He drank tea with the lady, drank brandy with the gentleman. He visited the jeweler but found himself unable to find something suitable. Something that declared, *I belong. You can't ignore me.* None of the diamonds, rubies, or sapphires were large enough.

This morning he'd learned that the editor of *The London Chronicle* had been arrested for printing an editorial that questioned the Inquiry . . . . and that relied on facts gleaned from penny-a-liners employed as footmen.

It was clear to Knightly what he must do—would do, because he was a man of action.

Given all that, he should not care in the slightest about a sigh, or lack of one. And yet here he was, standing mutely in front of his staff, pondering the absence of a sigh.

He scowled, mightily.

He would not be undone by the absence of a pretty girl's sigh.

He glared at the room.

That's when he noticed that Annabelle wasn't where she was supposed to be, or where she always was.

They had a routine, he and his staff, and today she had disrupted it, tremendously. He would walk in. Annabelle would sigh. He said, "Ladies first," and then meeting would commence with the Writing Girls rattling off their reports one after another, seated side by side in a neat row.

Today Annabelle sat between Owens and Grenville. Knightly narrowed his eyes—was Owens the Nodcock? How else to explain why Annabelle sat beside him, and touched his hand when he leaned over to whisper something in her ear? Something that made her blush and smile.

"What the devil is going on?" He asked, irritated, and itching to put his fist through the wall. Or into Owens's jaw. No one answered. "Miss Swift, why are you over there?"

Then he remembered how she preferred the sidelines to the center of attention and resolved to not make her uncomfortable before the other writers.

"Never mind," he said gruffly. And then the meeting proceeded mostly as usual. His staff chattered. They debated the Scandal at *The Times*. He stole glances at Annabelle, her lowered bodice. Her lowered gaze.

At the conclusion of the meeting, he clasped Annabelle by the arm as she attempted to slink past him, arm in arm with Owens. He had questions—he didn't know quite what they were—and he suspected she had answers.

It had been his plan to act even more imperiously to remind them both of the Right Order in the world. But when he said her name, "Annabelle," he heard the questions, the sleeplessness, and something like feelings in his voice.

"If you're going to apologize again, I'd rather you wouldn't," she said, stunning him.

"Why would I apologize, Annabelle?" He leaned against the doorway.

"For the kiss," she whispered, and she leaned toward him to keep the words private. He breathed deep, breathing in Annabelle.

He ought to apologize, probably. For taking advantage of a woman in a state of despair, and who was in his employ and thus could not risk rebuffing his advances. But he had tasted her wanting, her desire—along with that intoxicating sweetness. There was no way in hell he'd apologize because he wasn't the slightest bit sorry.

And as anyone could attest, he hadn't become so damned successful by issuing apologies. So he leaned in closer to her and murmured:

"Oh, I'm not sorry for that kiss, Annabelle."

It was the truth. He was bewildered by it, wanted it again, couldn't make sense of it, craved it . . . he had a million thoughts and feelings about that kiss, but regret was not one of them.

"You're not?" she asked. Her expectation didn't surprise him, but it bothered him. She had no idea how beautiful and alluring she was, did she? But then again, why should she if she loved a man from afar, for years, and he never paid attention to her?

"Are you sorry?" he asked.

"You didn't mean to do it, did you?" she questioned. She must have spent hours fretting over what it meant and what his intentions were. When was a kiss not just a kiss? When it was with Annabelle. He meant that in the very best and worst ways. The best answer he could give her was plain honesty.

"I did not drive from Fleet Street to Bloomsbury with the intention, no. But it's not as if I tripped and fell and our mouths collided."

She couldn't help it; she giggled. Progress. He grinned.

The words "Am I the Nodcock" were just there in the back of his throat, waiting to be spoken aloud. But it sounded too ridiculous to actually say aloud. Frankly, he did not want to know.

Because if he knew . . .

If it was he . . .

If she had been pining after him all these years and he was only just noticing her now, when he intended to marry another woman, then fate was a cruel mistress indeed. Knightly could not think of this here, now. Instead he snuck another glance at her bodice to clear his mind. And then his gaze fell on a thick packet of letters in her hands.

"What scheme are you up to this week?" he inquired. What did he have to watch out for? he wondered. Or was it none of his concern? He couldn't rule out Owens—not with those damned winks and whispers they shared throughout the meeting.

"I can't tell you yet," she said, with a nervous laugh. He lifted one brow, questioning. "Because . . . I haven't read them through, all of them. The suggestions are becoming more and more outlandish. Like this one: compose a song and hire a group of singers to serenade him."

"I don't know if that's the way to appeal to men," Knightly said frankly. But it surely would put to rest the matter of who she was after. *Which he did not want to know. Why did he not want to know?*

"I don't know that I'd have time to write my column after composing a song, hiring and training singers, and finding a moment when they might perform for the Nodcock."

"Your advice column must come first," he insisted.

"Then I shan't take this reader's advice to commission a portrait of myself in a suggestive pose and have it delivered to the Nodcock or displayed at the National Gallery. Just imagine those hours of sitting still and not writing. Nor shall I fling myself in front of an oncoming carriage while the Nodcock looks on and presumably rescues me. If he notices me . . ."

It was on the tip of his tongue to say, *Have that put on my schedule, it would make great copy,* but he felt like an ass for presuming it was he, and that she wanted him enough to risk life and limb like that for him. That was the thing; he could not *ask* without sounding like the most pompous, presumptuous nodcock.

"I am appalled at these suggestions," he stated. "And like these readers, the blokes down at the coffeehouse are full of idiotic ideas. They also fancy themselves in love with you."

"Are they suitable gentlemen?" Annabelle inquired, and his jealousy flared. "If so, I may wish to meet them."

"They are not suitable at all," Knightly said flatly. And then he could not resist inquiring further—because one did not attain his level of success without always inquiring further. "More to the point, I thought you were quite taken with the Nodcock, as you call him."

"It's a funny thing, really," Annabelle said in a thoughtful tone. He caught himself holding his breath, hanging off her every word. Because what she was saying wasn't what he expected. He didn't like it either, and he didn't know why, and deliberately avoided a thorough examination of his heart and mind.

"I suppose the question is, is the Nodcock taken with me?" she asked. "And how far is this scheme supposed to go? But don't worry, Mr. Knightly. I'll turn in good copy, as befitting *The London Weekly.*"

Bryson, the secretary, stood off to the left and cleared his throat.

"Yes, what is it?" Knightly asked. He didn't take his eyes off Annabelle.

"Mr. Knightly, you asked that I remind you of your afternoon appointments. Mr. Skelly is here to see you about the new factory acquisitions, Mr. Mitchell requested an interview, and you had promised to visit with Lady Marsden this afternoon."

"Thank you, Bryson. I'll just be a moment," Knightly said. He didn't once take his eyes off Annabelle.

*Fact:* Annabelle did that thing where she tried to make herself invisible. She took a step away from him. She developed a sudden fascination with the hem of her dress. She clasped her arms over her chest, turning in on herself.

It had been the mention of Lady Marsden, no? What else might it be?

*Fact:* He was stricken with the preference to spend the afternoon with Annabelle, rather than call upon Lady Marsden. Rather than issue the proposal that would assure him the success he'd sought all his life. Since the moment the New Earl uttered those crushing words:

*Throw the bastard out. He doesn't belong here.*

*Fact:* Lady Marsden was the golden ticket to all

of his long-held plans. Success. Power. Vindication. Recognition—especially from the New Earl.

*Fact:* Men in their right mind didn't throw the lot of that away, and he'd always prided himself on logical, rational behavior.

"You have a busy afternoon. I shan't keep you any longer," Annabelle said, and she bid him a good afternoon.

*Fact:* He wanted her to keep him longer.

# Chapter 28

### Lady Roxbury's Apology

FASHIONABLE INTELLIGENCE BY A LADY OF DISTINCTION
*The identity of Dear Annabelle's nodcock is the best
kept secret in London, and apparently a secret from
the Nodcock himself. But how much longer must
she—and her readers—wait for him to come to his
senses?*

> The London Weekly

**A**FTER the meeting in which Annabelle cowardly
avoided her friends, Julianna clasped her arm and
tugged her down the stairs and out to her awaiting
carriage. The Roxbury crest was emblazoned on the
side in bright gold. A bullet hole pierced the very
center of it, courtesy of an irate Julianna. Unlike this
version of Julianna, sitting opposite her in the carriage. She appeared to be making a concerted effort
to appear woeful and contrite.

"I owe you an apology," Julianna stated, presumably in reference to their argument the previous week. Annabelle had been in a wretched mood
ever since. It had even dulled the lovely glow from
Knightly's kiss, which was an unforgivable sin.

Old Annabelle didn't have these problems. New Annabelle had considered reverting to her previous ways.

"So much talk of apologies lately," Annabelle mused.

"Who else . . . ? Was it . . . ?" Julianna leaned forward eagerly. Then, remembering herself, she leaned back and folded her hands primly in her lap. "No, that is not the point. I behaved abominably toward you, Annabelle, and it was horrid of me to do so. I am so very sorry. You love Knightly. He just doesn't realize what a treasure your love is, and that angers me."

Annabelle eyed her cautiously. She did seem sorry. Julianna did have the unfortunate habit of shooting her mouth off (and actually shooting—Annabelle took a moment to be grateful it hadn't come to that).

"If you must know, Knightly also apologized. That should answer the question you remarkably restrained yourself from asking. Which means you were right, that it was wrong of him to ask me to encourage Marsden. Upon that we all agree. It's funny, though: I was a fool, and yet everyone is groveling to me."

"I'm sorry that I was right," Julianna said, and Annabelle laughed at the sentence least likely ever to be uttered by her friend.

"Let's not get carried away, Julianna," she cautioned, but a smile tugged at her mouth.

"No, truly. I want you to be happy, and Knightly, too. But only if his happiness is found with you. And yes, I know that's probably the wrong thing to say. But I'm not as goodhearted as you, Annabelle.

And my own experiences with Knightly have been . . . difficult."

"Is that because of him, or because of you?" Annabelle asked.

"Eliza also— What is your point?"

"My point is that it was simple before. I adored, he ignored . . ." Annabelle paused to marvel on the poetry of that. "But now it seems that not only is he beginning to see me, but I am also beginning to see him as he is and not how I have imagined him to be."

"Do you still love him?" Julianna asked.

"Does it even matter?" Annabelle mused, shrugging. "He kissed me, Julianna. And yet now he is calling upon Lady Marsden and probably proposing marriage to her this very moment. I do not know how much more I can bear."

Her love of Knightly, the thrill of her successes, the terror of still losing, was beginning to exact a toll on Annabelle. This past week, after the fight with her friends and Knightly's kiss had lead to hours of musing, pondering, wondering. In the end, she'd barely ate or slept and was none the wiser.

And know Knightly was still going to call upon Lady Marsden after he had kissed her. The Nodcock.

"Did you love the kiss? Was the kiss just delicious?" Julianna asked, eyes aglow.

"Yes," Annabelle replied. The exact details—the taste of him, the heat of his touch—those were hers to savor and hers alone. And yet . . . "However, I fear I may go mad trying to puzzle out what it all means. What do you know about him and Lady Marsden?"

"Would you believe me if I said nothing?" Julianna asked, cringing.

"Not at all," Annabelle retorted. Perhaps she wasn't a fool after all.

"This is part of the reason I behaved so horribly. Everyone believes a proposal is imminent. It was in *The Morning Post* that he was sighted perusing jewelry at Burlington Arcade. He did not purchase anything."

Another matter that had weighed heavily upon Annabelle's conscience was that Letter from Lady Marsden, which had spent days and nights tucked away in a novel, on a very high shelf. It remained unanswered.

But Annabelle knew the contents well: *I am pressured to marry but I love someone far below my station . . .*

She really ought to give her an answer. Or admit that she didn't know what to do. Or do the *right* thing and suggest she hold out for true love.

"Will her brother allow it?" Annabelle asked. Lord Marsden had sent her flowers, and might just forbid the marriage that would destroy her hopes and dreams. She liked him.

"He is encouraging the match! He covets Knightly's fortune and influence, you see. I am so vexed that I can't publish a word of all this drama," Julianna said, scowling and wringing her hands. "And of course, one can't avoid the conclusion that Knightly certainly stands to gain protection for the paper if he makes this match."

She no longer liked Lord Marsden very much. There were not enough pink roses in the world to console her if he forced his sister to marry her own true love . . . lest Knightly risk losing everything he valued most.

But wait . . .

Annabelle frowned, puzzling over these two contradictory pieces of information. Lady Lydia loved one man and was pressured to marry another . . . She had just assumed she loved Knightly because . . . well, of course she did. She found him extremely deserving of that fine emotion.

But Lady Lydia also said she was pressured to marry a man she didn't love. If her brother was pressuring her to marry Knightly . . . it meant that she didn't love Knightly.

Which mattered because . . .

"Who is her lover, then?" Annabelle asked. If her hunch was correct, Knightly was about to shackle himself in a loveless marriage. This struck her as terribly sad.

"What do you mean?" Julianna queried, tilting her slightly.

"She loves someone. But not Knightly. Who?" Annabelle questioned.

"How do you know that?" Julianna asked.

"Never mind how," Annabelle said, waving off the question. "I suppose it doesn't change anything, really. He is still courting her. Lord Marsden is approving of the match. Knightly shall marry her and they'll be so very posh and fashionable and aristocratic and I shall slog out the rest of my days helping Blanche and everyone else."

"Here is what you must know, Annabelle," Julianna said earnestly, leaning forward and clasping Annabelle's hands in hers. " If you love him you must fight for him."

"But what if I want him to fight for me?"

And then she understood why she couldn't derive supreme satisfaction from the kiss or her progress thus far. She had teased and tugged him along. She stalked and hunted, when she wanted him to chase her.

"Why all the talk of fighting when we are speaking of love? You must admit, Annabelle, that you have waited and waited and nothing came of it. And now you've set your cap for him, pursued him, and he has kissed you. Frankly, I do not see why you are wavering."

"I am chasing him and he is chasing Lady Lydia," Annabelle stated plainly.

"And may the best woman win," Julianna urged. "You have a duty to your readers, Annabelle, to see this through, if nothing else. Now tomorrow evening is the charity ball for the Society to Benefit Unfortunate Women. Knightly will be there."

"How do you know that? How do you know *everything*?" Annabelle asked.

"Because I know that he gives a sizable contribution. Secretly he's charitable, that Mr. Knightly. Also, I assisted the hostess, Lady Wroth, with the invitations, so I knew he was invited. And then I may have peeked at Bryson's calendar that he keeps for Knightly, so I confirmed he would be attending."

"Julianna!"

"Can I help it if he left it unattended to investigate the smell of smoke?" Julianna asked with feigned innocence and a delicate shrug. Obviously one could not help it at all.

"There was no smoke, was there?" Annabelle questioned; Julianna's reply was an impish grin, and Annabelle supplied the words: "Of course there wasn't. How do you manage these things, Julianna? If I had half the gumption you did—"

"You are writing about your own trials and tribulations in love for all of London to read. I'd say that's gumption in spades. The whole city is cheering for you to succeed, Annabelle."

Tears stung at Annabelle's eyes. It wouldn't do to disappoint the entire population of London by giving up when she had gotten so far. If Knightly was going to marry Lady Lydia, she vowed that he would at least know how she felt before he did so.

# Chapter 29

## Lady Lydia's Secret, Revealed

THE MAN ABOUT TOWN
*While society on the whole has accepted Lady Lydia*
*after her prolonged absence from London, the rumors*
*still dog her graceful steps.*
   *The London Times*

**K**NIGHTLY thought of Annabelle as he traveled to the Marsden residence. To be more specific, he thought about how he wished to be traveling to the Swift residence. More to the point, he really wanted Annabelle here, in this carriage, with him.

Why the devil did she think he would apologize for that kiss?

What kind of man did she think he was, anyway? Whatever she thought, he was not the kind that apologized for pleasuring them both.

In the far recesses of his mind—the part devoted to decency, which was currently largely overruled by the part devoted to thoughts of lust—it occurred to him that he was planning a seduction of one woman while on his way to court another. It also occurred to him that this wasn't the best example of decent, gentlemanly behavior.

Rather caddish of him, really.

But the facts were thus:

*Fact:* The *London Weekly* was the most important thing to him.

*Fact:* Lady Lydia's hand in marriage would ensure that Marsden didn't crack down on the nefarious reporting tactics of his reporters. Another one had been arrested—this time a reporter from *The Daily Register.*

*Fact:* Lady Lydia's hand in marriage would also assure his prominent place in high society. Like his father before him. The New Earl would not be able to ignore him.

*Fact:* Annabelle's kiss made him want to throw thirty-five years worth of facts aside and ravish her thoroughly, completely, utterly.

*Fact:* He was not going to throw away thirty-five years worth of facts, truths, and plans for a kiss. That was the rash action of madmen. He was the epitome of a sane, logical, practical man.

Or he used to be. Knightly exited the carriage, strolled up to the Marsden's residence, and generally made an effort to ignore the sense of dread in his gut.

"My brother is not at home," Lady Lydia declared when she received him in the drawing room. It was a fair enough slight, for he'd often combined his calls to her with visits with Marsden.

"Actually, I have come to visit with you, Lady Lydia," he replied.

"Of course you have," she said with a sigh.

"Would you care for a walk, Mr. Knightly? I've been sitting here all day, chattering and drinking tea. I fear I shall go mad if I don't get a breath of fresh air. I first must fetch my shawl."

Women and their blasted shawls, he thought. He knew Annabelle had left hers behind as some sort of ploy. But had it been for Owens . . . or another? He did not dare entertain that thought. Not with Lady Lydia present.

"Lord Marsden is with Parliament," she began as they strolled along the streets of Mayfair in the direction of the park. "I suppose you shall wish for an update."

It irked him, that. While their courtship and relationship was never based upon affection, she didn't need to be so obvious about it. Though any romantic streak he possessed was buried deep, Knightly was the product of a love match (if not a marriage), and this cool detachment was uneasy to him. How he planned to endure it for a lifetime of holy matrimony had not been considered in great depth. He thought only of immediate threats, not long-term happiness.

Status, he reminded himself. His peers. He'd be a damned earl if it weren't for a few twists of fate. *Throw the bastard out. He doesn't belong here.*

He did belong, though. Knightly gritted his teeth. He would prove it.

"Would you believe it if my intentions to you went beyond digging for gossip?" he asked Lady Lydia. "I'll ask Marsden myself. Just to confirm if his reports matched those of my reporters."

That was the other thing. Marsden wasn't the only one with information. Owens was on the case, and Grenville, too. The details they unearthed were . . . intriguing. Incriminating. Hints of blackmail and bribery. It seems Marsden had been paying enormous suppression fees . . . until the money started running out.

Those explosive, expensive secrets that consistently eluded him.

Lady Lydia treated Knightly to a long look with those large brown eyes that put him in mind of a startled doe.

"You are not afraid of him. Most people are," she said, and it was clear he had impressed her.

"Most people don't have something that he wants," Knightly replied easily.

"And what might that be?" Lady Lydia inquired. What could the tradesman possibly possess that a peer of the realm could want? He could hear the derision in her voice, and it only made him want to marry her more so he might prove to her, and everyone, that he was not any less than they.

"I have a fortune," Knightly answered. "And influence."

There was a pause, in which undoubtedly they both thought of the rumors that plagued the Marsdens, from her missing season to their evaporating funds, and the ability to stop it.

"Most of the newspapers are terrified of him," she replied, but did not correct his presumption that his wealth was appealing. So much so that his lower status could perhaps be overlooked.

"No one of any sense reads that rubbish," he replied, and Lady Lydia laughed.

"So if you are not here to talk about newspapers and my brother and his mad schemes, then what brings you?" she asked. She paused under a tree and pulled her shawl close around her shoulders. "I know my brother wants me to marry you. But what of my wishes on the matter?" she asked. And there was something desperate in her voice: *What about me?*

"What are they?" he asked.

Lady Lydia paused. Her jaw dropped open. She remembered she was a lady and closed it. Obviously he was the first man to inquire about her wishes.

"My wishes would not be supported by society," she said stiffly.

"Does this have anything to do with your extended stay in the country?" he asked. The reporter in him didn't shy away from questions, even the insensitive ones. Besides, Lady Lydia seemed to respond well to direct and open conversation. He liked that about her.

"Perhaps. You do know, of course, that *The Times* reporter was after me," she told him. He did not know that . . . but he stitched that fact together with what he had learned from Brinsley. Rumors of a pregnancy. An extended stay in the country. A missing season. It was now clear to him what her secret was.

Knightly said none of that. Instead he asked, "Whatever do you mean?"

"Do not play obtuse, Knightly. It doesn't suit you. There were rumors about me, being with child. What better way to confirm them than by disguising oneself as a physician?"

"Other than time?"

"Time will tell, usually. But that is not as lucrative. The rumors were bad enough, but it was the blackmail and suppression fees that have nearly bankrupted us. And still, in spite of that . . . the gossip has been horrendous. I had to go away." She shuddered, and Knightly actually felt a strong stab of guilt for all the gossip peddling he'd done in his day. It had earned him a fortune, which might be the Marsdens' salvation. Funny, that.

"You're intriguing, Lady Marsden," he said. And wasn't that the truth. The web of secrets and gossip was woven thick around him. He imagined Julianna would be beside herself to have this conversation.

"You might as well call me Lydia. Though it will certainly set tongues a-wagging," she replied with a wry smile.

"You never did answer about your wishes on the matter of my courtship," Knightly replied.

"I'm agog that you would mention it again after what I just confessed to you."

"I'll be frank with you, Lady Lydia. There is no pretense that it is a love match. You and your brother would benefit from my fortune, and your brother's political career particularly would benefit from my influence. I want an entrée into the ton. This would be a marriage of convenience, but we could get along."

As far as proposals went, it was certainly a contender for "least romantic" or "the worst." But it was the truth.

It wasn't what she wanted to hear.

Lady Lydia blinked and asked, "What if I want a love match?"

# Chapter 30

### The Hero, at Work

DOMESTIC INTELLIGENCE

*Two newspapers have folded*—The Society Chronicle
*and* Title Tattle—*for lack of staff after too many
writers were arrested for questionable journalistic
practices by Lord Marsden's Inquiry.*

*The London Weekly*

*Offices of* The London Weekly

LADY LYDIA hadn't said yes. But Lady Lydia hadn't
said no either. His fate hung suspended in the hands
of a noblewoman in need of a fortune who wished
for a love match, presumably with some impover-
ished mystery lover.

And then there was Annabelle . . .

His thoughts kept returning to Annabelle.

He kept tasting her on his lips, no matter how
much wine or brandy he drank.

The hour was late, and Knightly was still at his
desk. Candles burned low. A stack of articles begged
for his attention, but he couldn't give it. One sheet of
paper in particular haunted him. Dear Annabelle.

Dear God, Annabelle.

*It was just a newspaper article.* Some femalecentric fluff that appeared on page seventeen, between adverts for medications of dubious efficacy and haberdashery. Or so he told himself, even though he was well aware that Dear Annabelle contained hopes and dreams of a beautiful woman. It was a fleet of devastating words in her girlish script. It was a love story that had nearly all of London riveted.

He picked up the sheet of paper, determined to see only grammar and spelling.

Would she write of their kiss? he wondered. And if she did . . . he leaned back and raked his fingers through his hair.

It all came down to one question, didn't it?

Was he the Nodcock?

Suspicions remained. They lurked in the back of his head, and Knightly did his damnedest to ignore them.

He edited Grenville's twelve-page transcription of parliamentary debates. He corrected the grammar in Owens's news reports on fires, robberies, and other crimes. He edited out the libelous statements from Lady Julianna's "Fashionable Intelligence." He poured a brandy and did the rest.

And it all came back to Annabelle.

Amongst all the articles was a quick portrait of her that he'd requested done, partially inspired by Drummond's and Gage's obsession and curiosity, partly inspired by seeing the men who couldn't read listening to the paper being read aloud. In this sketch she looked pretty. Quiet. Shy. He set it aside, knowing what trouble it would cause her if this were printed and her horrible relatives witnessed such undeniable proof of her Writing Girl status. Knightly placed it in the top drawer of his desk. And when he could avoid it no more, he gave his attention to the newest installment of Dear Annabelle.

> *Dear readers, your suggestions are becoming more outrageous by the day, much to the amusement of my fellow Writing Girls and myself. From moonlit serenades to specially commissioned portraits or even a simple declaration in these pages . . . Yet one writer writes with a suggestion that is utterly simple and unbelievably risky: Do nothing . . .*

Oh no, she did not get to do nothing when he desperately needed a clue, a confirmation. When he wondered what he was to Annabelle. Wondered when he *wanted* to be something to her.

They had kissed, and the whole world seemed askew, like it shifted on its axis and started spinning in the other direction. This new world intrigued him, even though Knightly could see it meant letting go of the old world . . .

*What if I want a love match?* Lady Lydia's question was pointed, the implications devastating. If she married him, it would be reluctantly and he would never again taste Annabelle on his lips. If they did not marry, *The London Weekly* would have to survive on wits and popularity alone in a climate when every printed word risked imprisonment for the writer. These were the tangible things that he could wrap his muddled brain around.

Knightly closed up the offices and set out for home. A walk in the cool night air would clear his head, and somewhere between Fleet Street and Mayfair he would figure out what was to be done about Lydia's love match, his newspaper, and the constant craving for the sweet taste of Annabelle's kiss.

The houses in Mayfair were lit up, with balls and soirees in full swing. Knightly wove his way through streets congested with carriages and drunken revelers until he came to one house in particular.

The one belonging to all the Earls of Harrowby, and where the earl had lived with his other family. Knightly had never graced the halls. He had never been summoned before the desk in his father's study to report on his lessons or receive a punishment. He had never strolled through the portrait gallery to observe the paintings of centuries of relatives whose names and stories were still a mystery to him. He had never slept in the nursery, climbed a tree in the garden, or explored the attics. There was an entire life he had never lived.

As things stood now, he would never dine with his brother in the family home. Nor would they smoke cigars and sip port and make stupid wagers whilst the ladies took tea in the drawing room. They would not reminisce about their father. They wouldn't speak at all.

It was likely they never would, unless he married well.

If he were the Nodcock . . . then he'd have to break Annabelle's heart in order to obtain entry to his father's house.

It was just one kiss. He tried to convince himself of this, and failed. It was so much more than just a meeting of lips one afternoon. If he was the Nodcock, then Annabelle was the price he'd have to pay to live out his life-long dream.

# Chapter 31

## Annabelle Truly Falls in Love

### THE MAN ABOUT TOWN

*It is a small consolation that Lady Harrowby is no
longer alive to witness her husband's illegitimate
child swiftly climbing the rungs of the social ladder.
How mortifying it would have been for the countess
to be confronted by her husband's transgression at
something so civilized as a soiree. One must sympa-
thize with Earl Harrowby, who must encounter this
family shame with an appallingly increasing fre-
quency.*

The London Times

ANNABELLE arrived at the ball with Julianna and
was quickly left to her own devices as her friend
spent more time trolling the private alcoves and
other dimly lit areas where gossip and scandal
lurked. Awkwardly on her own, Annabelle stood
next to a potted palm while she tried to identify
which corner belonged to the wallflowers and spin-
sters, and thus where she would go.

A conversation happening just to her left intrigued her. Temporarily abandoning plans to spend

the ball in a state of hopeful desperation with other imperfect girls, she retreated into the protection afforded by the large plant and eavesdropped.

"They let anyone in these days, do they not?" The man who made this remark was tall, with dark hair brushed back from his face and deep blue eyes. Everything about him screamed overbearing aristocrat, from the perfect cut of his evening clothes to his rigid posture.

"It is a charity ball, Harrowby. Anyone who can afford a significant donation is welcome to attend," the friend said, with a notable emphasis on *afford*.

Annabelle peered out to look at these . . . snobs. But her gaze was drawn to Knightly, standing just behind them. His mouth was pressed in a firm line and the hand holding his drink was a fist. He must have heard. He must have assumed they were speaking about him. Her gaze shifted between the two men and she noticed a similarity in their appearance.

"What is this world coming to?" the man named Harrowby said to his friend, but it was Knightly who replied.

"Welcome to the future, Harrowby, when talent supersedes nitwits with nothing to recommend them other than the name of long dead ancestors," he said easily. But still, Annabelle saw the fierce grip he kept on his drink. She wouldn't have been shocked if he cracked the cut crystal glass with his bare hands.

"A name you'd do anything to have," Harrowby replied with such disdain that Annabelle recoiled behind a palm frond. "I cannot believe you have the audacity to speak to me."

Harrowby glanced uneasily around to see who might be witnessing the exchange. Annabelle shrank back even farther into the refuge afforded by the potted palm.

"Nothing like family, though is there?" Knightly mused in a jovial tone likely designed to be particularly provoking. Annabelle continued to watch his hands, still gripping the glass so hard his knuckles were white. He was anything but relaxed, no matter how he might seem.

"Apparently not," Harrowby said, his voice like ice. "As my father abandoned his *real* family for some doxy and her bastard."

If she understood the conversation correctly— Annabelle never presumed things of that nature— then it seemed that Knightly had a brother. Or if one wanted to be precise, a half brother. Had she heard anything about his family? He didn't seem like a man who had one. It seemed that Knightly had been born all-powerful and fully formed.

"Talk about me all you like, but leave my mother out of it," Knightly said. Or so Annabelle thought he'd said. His voice was low and his expression menacing. But he stood his ground as she shrank back and away from the conflict.

"You are a stain on the Harrowby name," Harrowby uttered viciously. She gasped. But Knightly stood tall, shoulders back, as if he wasn't bothered. Annabelle stood in awe.

"Out, out damn spot," the third man quipped. Both men turned to glare at him. When they realized their identical reactions, both stalked off in opposite directions and pushed their way through the crowd.

It was a miracle to Annabelle that Knightly had

been able to coolly stand there and trade cutting remarks with the half brother who so obviously loathed him. She would have slinked off, or never even approached him, and bent over backward to make sure no one ever felt the same way toward her.

But not Knightly. He was a tower of calm strength, of self-possession. He dared to venture where she never might, and with wit and grace, too.

It was why she loved him.

"Why are you seeking refuge in a potted plant, Miss Swift?"

"Oh! Lord Marsden! Good evening," she replied, a blush staining her cheeks.

"Perhaps you would like to waltz instead?" Marsden offered his hand, and Annabelle accepted.

*On the terrace, in the moonlight*

LATER that evening, Annabelle strolled past Knightly and gave him a flippant glance over her shoulder— or what she hoped seemed a flippant, coy, inviting glance as Flirtatious in Finchley Road had instructed.

Knightly's gaze locked with hers for that brief, potent second. Her skin seemed to tingle with a strange delight, like awakening. Or anticipation. Her heart began to beat faster. Would he follow?

She sauntered outside, where all manner of danger and romance might befall her, if the stories were to be believed. She attempted to lean casually against the cool stone balustrade, as she had seen Knightly do. And then he stood before her and she didn't notice much else.

"Annabelle." Knightly said her name softly. It was

a statement, a greeting, and a question all at once. "I did not realize you would be in attendance this evening."

"I came with Julianna and Roxbury. Yet I seem to have lost them, for it has been some time since I've seen either of them . . ."

"I saw you waltzing with Lord Marsden," Knightly said flatly. Annabelle thought of the advice to cultivate a rival. Or another reader's advice to hold herself at a distance and not throw her heart and soul at his mercy. And another's suggestion to play coy.

"I imagine most of the guests here this evening did as well," New Annabelle remarked.

"It was a stupid suggestion, Annabelle. And I'm sorry I asked you to encourage him to protect the paper," Knightly said urgently, still fixated on his wretched suggestion from days ago. Weeks ago! She had moved past it after his sincere apology. Quite forgotten all about it, really, after he had kissed her. She was forgiving like that.

"Who says I'm encouraging him for you or *The Weekly,* Mr. Knightly? What does it matter, anyway?" she asked. He had apologized, she accepted it, and they had moved on, hadn't they? Or was there another reason?

"I don't know, Annabelle, I don't know," he said, sounding awfully frustrated.

She took a deep breath and straightened her spine, as if it might give her the courage to ask a certain vexing question.

"Is it for the newspaper that you are courting Lady Lydia? So that she will plead your cause with her brother?"

"It's more complicated than that," Knightly replied, which only raised more questions. Did he love her? She wished to express her skepticism, her curiosity, with the lift of one brow arched.

"I really wish I had the ability to raise one eyebrow," she said wistfully, and Knightly laughed. The conversation had been taking a turn for the far-too-serious anyway. "You can do it. Julianna can. All the heroes and heroines in novels can do it."

"It's easy. You just have to look all haughty and superior. Like this." Knightly's demonstration looked remarkably like . . . Knightly did all the time. Lofty, unattainable, wickedly handsome, mysterious.

"Who is Harrowby?" she asked, and Knightly's shock was evident. But how could she not ask, after what she had heard? "I saw you speaking to him. And when I say 'I saw,' I might actually mean that I happened to overhear your conversation with him. I'm sorry."

"I didn't see you," Knightly replied, and Annabelle smiled wryly at that. She gazed at his face, which she knew and loved so well—the slanting cheekbones, firm jaw, dark hair, and piercing blue eyes and dark lashes.

"Haven't I told you that I am Miss Overlooked Swift? There might have been a potted fern standing between myself and the rest of the ballroom," she replied, a touch ruefully. "I understand you and that Lord Harrowby fellow are related in some fashion?"

"You've an awful lot of personal questions this evening, my dear Annabelle." Knightly brushed a wayward curl away from her face. His fingers grazed her cheek, ever so slightly. It was the familiarity of the gesture that made heart beat faster, and it was the possessive *my* in *my dear Annabelle* that thrilled her.

She remembered a time when he addressed a letter to her as "Miss Swift." How far they'd come!

She was his Dear Annabelle, wasn't she? Always had been since he'd named the column she was to write, and named it after her, thus bestowing an identity beyond Spinster Auntie or unfortunate, destitute relation.

Dear Annabelle was a girl of his own creation. She belonged to him and had for three years, seven months, one week, and five days. And now he was finally starting to see.

"It is Julianna's terrible influence, you see," Annabelle explained. "She is encouraging me to have more gumption."

"And how does it feel, Annabelle?" Knightly leaned upon the balustrade. She did so love it when he leaned, for he appeared at ease even though she knew he wasn't. What would it be like to see him truly at ease? To slumber beside him, to wake with him . . .

Really, she had to stop imagining these things when he was right there. Or at least blushing at the thoughts. Because Knightly leaned in close, observed her every blush and grinned wickedly as if he could read her mind.

"It feels exhilarating. Constantly. But don't worry, I shall write all about it," she told him.

"Speaking of your writing, how fares your progress in attracting the attentions of the Nodcock?" Knightly inquired. Wasn't that the question of the hour, the week, the month, the year, the moment?

Annabelle smiled, and her cheeks burned, utterly at a loss about how to answer *that* question. And in her silence, she thought she might have detected caring in the way his breath hitched. As if he were holding it, awaiting her answer. Only she would notice such a thing, thanks to all those novels loaded with such details, and thanks to all those hours in which she was so utterly devoted to loving and knowing him.

But one's breath only hitched like that if they cared. And why should Knightly care about the identity of the Nodcock, unless . . .

Unless he had a wager on the outcome, or something. No, she ought to give him more credit than that.

Unless he suspected that he was the Nodcock? How on earth could she ever tell him now, after that awful nickname? She ought to never write in a fit of pique again.

Annabelle found herself leaning in toward Knightly, drawn to his warmth. She dared to brush an invisible piece of lint from the lapel of his jacket as Affectionate from All Saints Road had told her to, in a letter weeks ago.

"Are you not reading my articles, Mr. Knightly?"

"Of course I am, " he replied, in a tone that affectionately called her silly, and ducking his head a bit closer to hers so he might whisper in her ear. "Perhaps I want to know the secret, Annabelle. Perhaps I want the unpublished version of the truth."

"That's awfully demanding of you, Knightly," she said softly. Oh, he was closer to her now. Their mouths, just inches away, quite possibly close enough to kiss.

"That's how I am, Dear Annabelle," he murmured, and Lord above if she didn't feel the vibrations from his voice all over and deep down inside.

"You told me to keep up the ruse," she reminded him, a bit breathless. He traced one finger along her jaw, down the slender column of her neck. Knightly, touching her. Such a light touch, such a little thing, but she felt it in spades.

"What if I said to hell with it?" he asked. He lifted one brow, and she couldn't help but smile even as her heart was thundering from the thrill of his touch.

"What if I am enjoying it, Mr. Knightly?"

She did not want this moment to end. She wanted to stay here, suspended between knowing and not knowing, where everything was lovely. The final risk she was not yet ready to take.

Knightly traced along her collarbone, dared to trace his fingertip lower, along the edge of her bodice where lace rested against her skin. It was the smallest caress, but so possessive. Her skin felt feverish, and she wondered if he could tell.

"Do you like all that waiting, wanting, anticipation?" he asked. "Do you not want satisfaction?" His voice was low and rough.

"When I am assured of it," she whispered. This moment was magical and lovely. She had an idea of the kind of satisfaction he spoke of, and it was one she mostly dwelled on very late at night.

But there were other kinds of satisfaction, and though she was well aware that beggars shouldn't be choosers, she wanted him to fall in love with her. Not just to discover she was in love with him.

Knightly dropped his touch, and Annabelle missed it intensely, immediately.

"What about Marsden? Was that part of the ruse?" Her heart thumped hard in her chest. Knightly was asking an awful lot of questions that were homing in on the truth. Did he know . . . ?

"Perhaps I enjoy his conversation and take pleasure in his company," Annabelle replied. "And the pink roses he sent me."

But she thought she was allowed to ask questions, too. "Who is Harrowby?"

"Harrowby is my half brother," Knightly said plainly, and then added, "I hope Julianna's influence hasn't rubbed off on you too much because I wouldn't want that talked about."

Annabelle counted to three, summoning up her courage to ask the question she knew would cut to the heart of the matter.

"*You* wouldn't like it, or *he* wouldn't like it?" A quiet rush of mocking laughter escaped him.

"Is there a difference?' he asked skeptically.

"There's a world of difference," she replied. Everything she'd seen and heard—that Knightly had even confided in her—told her that he would declare the news on the front page of *The London Weekly* were it not for Harrowby's refusal to acknowledge the relationship.

If there was one thing she knew even better than the back of her own hand, it was the desperate, driving need to seek approval and acceptance. All these years she had thought Knightly didn't need that. He carried himself like he didn't give a damn.

And now she'd learned that Knightly was not immune to seeking acceptance and recognition, as she was. He was not an impossible, remote god, but a man who was perhaps more similar to her than she'd thought.

He wanted to belong, just as much as she.

This was the moment that she really, truly fell in love with Knightly.

The for better or for worse kind of love. A love based on acceptance of the real person, and not some imagined fantasy.

"I don't want to talk about Harrowby," he said bluntly, and it took Annabelle a moment to place the name and recall their conversation. Once she caught up, she suspected that what Knightly really didn't want to discuss was his humanity, despite all of his efforts to portray himself as above the worldly fray.

"I'm sorry for mentioning it," she said automatically. "No, I'm not. Well, 'I'm sorry' is just a thing to say, you see. I'm trying not to be so apologetic and obsequious all the time. It's just such a habit and—"

"Annabelle?"

"Yes?" She looked up at him, and he pressed his hand against the small of her back and then pressed her close to him. Then Knightly's mouth claimed hers for a kiss. In the moonlight. Oh Lord above, the romance.

Annabelle closed her eyes, blocking out the ballroom behind her and the moonlight above them so that the only thing she was aware of was Knightly's mouth upon hers, hot, searching, and wanting. She was aware, too, of those sparks and shivers at an ever-growing intensity that threatened to overwhelm her, except . . .

She wondered if he was only kissing her because she'd been rambling on a subject he didn't wish to discuss and he wanted to stop her from talking. Or was he overwhelmed by passion? Did the intentions of the kiss matter? Why the devil could she not just enjoy it? How did one turn their brain off?

Knightly pulled back, just a bit. He cradled her head in his hands, his fingers entwined in her mass of curls. Her coiffure would be wrecked. She didn't care. Knightly looked her firmly in the eyes. They were so blue, even in the moonlight.

"Just so we're clear, Annabelle," he said in the calm, self-assured way in which he stated facts and gave orders, "I'm kissing you because I want to, not to make you stop talking, or to avoid the conversation. And you need to stop thinking."

"How did you know that I was—"

"I'm learning you, Annabelle," he said with a knowing smile, and she wondered if there were any words more magical than those: *I'm learning you, Annabelle.* "Now enjoy this because I've been at war with myself over it and I'd like to thoroughly enjoy the spoils."

His lips were firm against hers, his intentions clear. Annabelle could not think this kiss was accident or that he was overtaken by the moonlight.

Could anything possibly matter more than Knightly's arms wound around her, holding her in a haven she had only dreamed of?

He urged her to open to him, deepening the kiss. She responded with a fervor that came from years of longing and loneliness. Knightly wrapped his arms around her, tighter, pressing her close to him. She slid her arms around him, holding onto not just the man but this moment. She had dreamed of this.

This moment, this real moment, was better.

She tasted him, let him taste her. His every touch set her aflame. A slow, ever-growing heat that pooled in her belly and radiated to every inch of her. With her silk-clad body pressed against his, she felt his arousal pressing hard against her, there. Her cheeks flushed, and that blush crept all over her skin, leaving her feeling feverish in a wickedly wonderful way.

"Oh, Derek . . ." She sighed his name. There was so much she wanted him to know—her love for him, this hot, surging desire he was awakening within her, that she wanted to do *everything* with him—but words were impossible. She contented herself with a sigh of his name.

She sighed his name again.

KNIGHTLY tasted that sigh, and understood all the unspoken thoughts and feelings it conveyed. He felt that sigh deeply. He'd never felt so wanted, and because he now did, he could just savor all these little moments adding up to this soul-altering kiss. There was no need to seduce or impress or win; he just needed to kiss like it was the first and last thing in the world.

Or so he tried to reason, but then logic fled, leaving one thought in its wake: no one would ever kiss him with the passion that Annabelle did. No woman would ever sigh his name the same way, and if she did, it wouldn't mean anything. This kiss meant something. What, he knew not. Thinking was impossible. He desperately needed to taste the soft skin where Annabelle's neck curved gracefully into her shoulder, so he pressed his mouth there for a kiss. She murmured her pleasure. He felt like a king.

He ran his fingers through her hair. He caressed the curve in her hip, slid his hands lower still and pressed her close. There was something about Annabelle that required delicacy and there was something about restraining himself that made him feel every little touch, and sigh a thousand times more intensely.

He wanted to feel her, everywhere. Feel her, without this silk dress, without anything at all . . . but enough higher brain functioning remained to tell him they were at a ball. They were in public. He needed to stop this.

But he didn't want to.

# Chapter 32

**Angry Women Storm *The London Weekly* Offices**

THE MAN ABOUT TOWN
*At long last, a clue to the true identity of the Nodcock.*
*The London Times*

*The following day*

**K**NIGHTLY was pretty damn sure that other news-paper proprietors were not plagued by females storming into their offices with all sorts of dramatics, such as he was.

*Drama is for the page.*

Apparently rules do not apply to females, he thought dryly.

Julianna arrived first, a fiery haired, sharp-tongued hurricane in a green dress. This was a habit of hers. Today he was not inclined to deal with such dramatics, which is to say that he was in a bloody good mood. Whistling while he walked down the street kind of mood. It was the effect of Annabelle and her kiss.

Well, one of them. The other effect was a rampant, relentless desire. Nevertheless, his eyes had been opened and he wanted what he saw. He knew, too, that he wanted to know more about Annabelle, and what that knowledge would cost him. The question was, would he pay the price of throwing off Lady Lydia and enraging Lord Marsden?

It was one hell of a question, and he preferred, instead, to whistle and think of kissing Annabelle.

"Really, Knightly. Really," Julianna said, with buckets of sarcasm, anger, and disappointment dripping from each syllable. She threw a newspaper on his desk; it landed with a *thwat*.

Knightly stopped whistling. He looked at the paper.

"*The London Times*, Julianna. Really? No wonder you're upset, if you're reading this second-rate rubbish."

"Read it." Her tone was that of ice, covered with frost.

Intrigued, he picked up the paper.

*At Lady Wroth's Charity Ball to benefit the Society of Unfortunate Women,* The London Weekly's *proprietor Derek Knightly was glimpsed in an extended moonlit interlude with a woman identified as* The London Weekly's *own Dear Annabelle. Readers of that gimmick-laden news rag will know that she is engaged in a public scheme to win the attentions of a man now known by all of London as the Nodcock.*

*The* Man About Town *wouldn't care in the least about the goings on of two Grub Street hacks, were it not for Knightly's well-known courtship of Lady Lydia Marsden. Or has this scandal-plagued female lost yet another suitor, this one with very unsuitable connections (for his suitable ones will not claim him)?*

*Which woman is this by-blow newspaper tycoon after? Will either chit want him now that he is so openly pursuing the affections of two different women? Or is his ton blood showing true, for what aristo is complete without a wife and a mistress?*

"We'll file that under scathing. Or perhaps incendiary," Knightly remarked. He leaned back in his chair, a pose of deceptive ease.

The article was possibly disastrous. Yet he kept his calm because that is what he did and who he was, unlike Julianna, who worked herself up into such a froth over the slightest thing.

"I'd like to file it under inaccurate rubbish, which I presume it is?" she questioned sharply.

"To the contrary," Knightly replied easily. "I ought to congratulation *The Times* for finally getting their reporting correct."

"I am beside myself. Utterly beside myself," Julianna huffed. "This column is—well, it has me speechless with rage, and that is saying something, you must admit."

"No comment," Knightly said. Wisely, in his opinion.

"While I don't really care about Lady Lydia's feelings on the matter—" Julianna started, switching tactics.

"Which is perfectly clear given the columns you've submitted lately in spite of my explicit commands not to write about her."

"Do not distract, Knightly. This is about Annabelle. And you."

And that sparked his temper. He leaned forward, palms flat on his desk, eyes surely blazing.

"So you admit that it is none of your business, then?" he challenged.

"I beg your pardon?" He had flummoxed her, and now resisted the urge to crow in satisfaction. That's what she deserved for meddling in his personal affairs.

"It is between Annabelle and myself. Not you."

"So you admit there is something between you two," she replied, tilting her head inquisitively and thinking herself clever.

"Mind your own business, Julianna," he said, and allowed his irritation to reveal itself in his tone.

"I am employed by you to do precisely the opposite, thank you very much. My task is to mind everybody else's business."

"In that case, I excuse you from doing so in this instance," Knightly replied, pushed aside the unfortunate issue of *The London Times* and picked up the papers beneath. He started to read them in a not-so-subtle clue to Julianna that he was finished with this discussion.

Honestly, if she'd been a man, someone probably would have shot such a vexing, meddlesome creature by now.

Julianna placed her palms on his desk and leaned forward to speak to him in a low, menacing tone.

"Be a gentleman, Knightly. Have a care with her. She's fragile."

And that was not to be borne. Annabelle might have been a delicate flower, treated with the utmost care and handled only with kid gloves. But he was discovering that she was made of much sterner stuff, and treating her as such was a disservice to everyone. Bold Annabelle was something else entirely—

asking the questions no one had ever dared to voice to him, kissing him with a fervor that made him feel more powerful and *wanted* more than anything. Her kiss made him whistle as he walked down the streets.

He pitied those who didn't see that Annabelle.

"We must be talking about different Annabelles, then," Knightly told Julianna. "When I'd rather not discuss Annabelle at all."

"What should I tell her, when she sees that?" Julianna asked, pointing, witchlike, to *The Times*.

"Say whatever you like. Just remember that my personal business is just that—mine."

Julianna left in a huff, of course, and once relieved of her presence, he strolled over to the sideboard and poured himself a generous serving of brandy.

There were a long list of women and their feelings that would need to be soothed, thanks to that damned Man About Town, and a fortifying drink was certainly in order.

Lady Marsden probably wouldn't care, so long as he kept her secrets. He smirked—to no one in particular—because he knew why she had missed her second season, and Julianna did not. He ought to casually mention that to her, as payback for her meddling in his personal affairs.

Annabelle on the other hand . . . As he learned her, he knew that she had a heart that beat in overtime, and a capacity for feeling that verged on excessive. She rambled when she was nervous and possessed an extremely active and vibrant imagination. When he kissed her, he could feel her thinking, puzzling, wondering, and memorizing every second of it.

However, with some reassurance—that being a

firm command to enjoy it—she melted under his touch. Other women responded to him, but with Annabelle it felt like it mattered, and that made it feel . . . just *more*, really. When every touch of the lips counted, when every caress meant something, when every murmur or sigh was a pleasure unto itself . . .

What the devil had happened to him?

Knightly took a long swallow on the brandy and concentrated deeply on the burn. First, on his tongue. Then the back of his throat. Down, down, down to his gut.

When a man thought about some fleeting kiss with a woman the way he had just caught himself doing, it meant that . . . Well, besotted was the word that came to mind. Or worse—*beholden*. And it wasn't a fleeting kiss. It was one of those all-consuming, axis-altering kisses.

Besotted indeed. Bloody hell.

His mother appeared in the doorway just then, strolling in like some fiery-haired demon fairy. If he ever wondered what Julianna would be like in thirty years, he now knew.

Bloody hellfire and damnation. Mehitable, a man of gargantuan proportions who had been hired for the sole purpose of preventing such unscheduled appearances by irate readers, must have been drunk on the job. Or this was mutiny.

"What is the meaning of this?" she inquired, shaking a copy of *The London Times* at him.

Knightly downed the rest of his drink and returned to his desk.

"Mother, I have already had this conversation with Lady Roxbury. It might be a better use of your time to go speak with her, as I can tell you both are far more interested in discussing this than I am. I might also add that I am appalled to discover how many *Weekly* women have exposed themselves as readers of *The London Times.*"

His mother sat in the chair before his desk.

"Utterly appalled," he repeated, and then returned to his work. Or tried to. He looked at the page but didn't manage to read a single word, try as he might.

"You do realize that Dear Annabelle is beloved by all of London," his mother said. "If it turns out that you were the man she was after . . ." Knightly stiffened, held his breath. Why did that thought paralyze him every time? His mother appeared not to notice and carried on.

" . . . Well, I daresay you'll have a mob of angry Londoners at your door." Was it wrong that he thought that spoke well of Annabelle's column and what a great story it would make?

"Mehitable will handle any angry mobs," he replied. After a stern talking-to about the admittance of angry females.

"For all you know, Mehitable may lead the mob," she challenged.

"No he won't. I pay his wages." Knightly stated this as simple fact. He just needed to remind Mehitable of that.

"Nevertheless," his mother persisted, "what are your intentions? Because if you throw over Dear Annabelle, with whom you obviously are infatuated—"

"Obviously?"

"I'm sorry. Are you in the habit of moonlit interludes with desirable young women and then kissing them—but not *liking* them? Especially when it seems you have an understanding regarding marriage with another woman. Have you inherited my talent for acting, after all?"

"Is this really any of your business?" he asked, growing angry now.

"What does that have to do with anything?" his mother asked, so genuinely perplexed by the concept of "minding one's own business" that he was struck speechless. She carried on in his silence: "At any rate, this story reminded me that I need to tell you something about your father. Before you make a mistake."

That got his attention. He set his papers aside.

"Your father loved us," she said plainly.

"I know that—" he began, but she waved him off.

"No, listen to me. He loved us. And he didn't love *them*, and they knew it. How do you think that boy felt growing up, always second in his father's attentions? Can you imagine it, Derek?"

He never had. Not once.

The heir, taking second place to his father's bastard child. He imagined the New Earl wanting to review his lessons, or asking after his father, who was never home. It began to dawn on Knightly what wretchedness the New Earl must have suffered, to be ignored, overlooked, second best. Knightly had always known he was loved.

"And Lady Harrowby was married but never had a husband, not really. But she *chose* that because your father told her about us before they were wed."

"Why did he marry her, anyway?" Knightly asked. If they were in love . . . why did they not make it official? So what if his mother was an actress? Wasn't half the fun of a title doing whatever you damn well pleased?

"Duty. Debts. Lack of courage at the crucial moment," she said, turning to look out the windows overlooking bustling Fleet Street. Did he detect tears? Did he detect more to the story—that her mother had asked his father *not* to marry someone else. Had she asked him to forget about duty and respectability and implored him to choose love instead?

His mother, now composed, turned back to face him. "They live in a world, Derek, where love doesn't matter."

He thought of Lady Lydia's plaintive question: *What if I wish for a love match?* He didn't have an answer for her, but he possessed a deeper understanding of the question now.

"I suppose it goes without saying that I wish you to have love," his mother carried on. "And if you still insist on some marriage for status and wealth, don't do it out of some notion to be like your father. It would be a dishonor to us both."

# Chapter 33

### A Misunderstanding with the Marquis

DOMESTIC INTELLIGENCE

*The total number of newspaper reporters arrested: 38*

*The total number of newspapers that have been shuttered: 4*

*Only* The London Weekly *seems immune. For now.*

The London Times

*White's Gentlemen's Club*
*St. James's Street*

**T**HERE was no point in refusing Marsden's request to join him for a drink at White's. They had business to discuss and it could happen here or there, sooner or later. That Marsden should wish to meet in a place that would display his rank and power was not lost upon Knightly. Clever, too, for White's would remind him of what he stood to gain—or lose.

I ought to belong here, Knightly thought as he strolled up the four short steps to the entrance to this exclusive haven.

The first thing he saw was the New Earl, seated

with a few gentlemen, card game in progress. The look in his eyes conveyed those taunting, menacing words: *Throw the bastard out. He doesn't belong here.*

Only now, Knightly saw beyond the obvious hatred in his glare to see hurt and confusion. When the New Earl leaned to whisper something scathing to his companion—all the while shooting daggers with his eyes—Knightly wondered what his relationship had been like with their father. Did they have the same long conversations? Did they share the same dry sense of humor? Did they go to the theatre together?

His mother had mentioned debts as a factor for the marriage. Had the countess's dowry paid for his own gentlemen's education? Had it provided the inheritance with which he purchased *The London Weekly*?

They were questions he'd never known to even ask. His mother had stormed in and delivered all this devastating information and then made an elegantly cutting exit, as befit one of London's best actresses.

The marquis had claimed a table in a dark corner of the club. He sat there, steely-eyed and seething. If he was supposed to be intimidated, Knightly thought, then the marquis ought to try harder. Or just not bother.

"I thought we had an understanding," Marsden began, without offering a drink. It was to be one of those conversations. "I thought I had been abundantly clear that I would steer the parliamentary Inquiry away from the notoriously unsavory reporting methods at your newspaper if you would marry my sister."

Knowing what he knew now—namely, the reasons Lady Lydia remained impossibly unwed—Knightly knew what a bad bargain it was. Not because she wasn't some pure ideal, but because her heart was otherwise engaged, and that would make for a cold marriage indeed. Certainly it wasn't good enough to violate truth number three: *Be beholden to no one.*

But that was information he had no intention of revealing. Yet.

"No date had been set," Knightly pointed out.

"Which is exactly why I am here," Marsden said. At least he was the sort of man who got quiet when enraged. None of that undignified blustering sported by lesser—though more amusing—men. "No wedding date has been set. Not even a proposal. And I hear that you enjoyed a significant, extended, private interlude with Miss Swift."

"You must be referring to the item that appeared in *The London Times* this morning. Surprising what information such a second-rate paper manages to uncover, isn't it?"

The mark hit home. Marsden visibly reddened. They now both knew that Knightly had learned he'd nearly bankrupted himself paying suppression fees to *The Times* and launched this Inquiry when his funds began to run out.

"I saw you. With Annabelle," Marsden said through gritted teeth.

Ah, now that was interesting. Not that they were spotted, for neither had made any effort at discretion—and why did they need to? Neither were haute ton, with reputations to maintain—but that Marsden gave a damn.

"I believe you are referring to Miss Swift," Knightly corrected.

"Devil take it, Knightly, we had an understanding," Marsden growled.

Knightly only shrugged, and said, "We did not agree upon a date by which I would propose. We did not agree upon a love match or some pretense of romance. We may have had an understanding, but there was no discussion of the terms."

"I assumed your word was that of a gentleman," Marsden said tightly.

"That was your first mistake, Marsden," Knightly said with a laugh—and a glance across the room at the New Earl. "We all know I'm no gentleman."

Marsden went silent. Was Marsden shocked that he had so directly referred to his bastardry when it was something he ought to be ashamed of?

In that silence, Knightly realized, deeply, that he was not a gentleman. He did not belong here, in White's. He missed Galloway's and its raucous company, the rustling sound of newspapers, and the scent of coffee and cigar smoke. He liked the ease one felt there. And the lack of angry glares launched in his direction.

"Pity, that," Marsden said thoughtfully, "because we gentlemen protect our own. And we actively suppress those who are . . . *not*."

The emphasis he placed on that little word, *not*, was remarkable. *Not* suddenly had the connection of rats, dung heaps, mud larks, and rotting corpses.

When Knightly replied, his voice was the drawl of a bored man. Between the glares from the New Earl (which were now, at this point, making it difficult to maintain a shred of that newly discovered empathy) and Marsden's overbearing manner and the restrained silence of this club, Knightly felt his chest tighten, as if a thousand-ton anvil pressed upon his chest, making breathing impossible.

He needed to walk and to get lost in the busy, meandering streets of London until night and silence descended upon the city. He needed the slap of cool air on his face. He needed to think about Lydia and Annabelle and *The London Weekly* and the family he'd never had. And to think about love.

He had no more time or patience for Lord Marsden and his bad bargains.

"Marsden, if you have something to tell me that I don't already know, I'd like to hear it. But the pretentious, heavy hand of the upper orders is not news. If it's not news, then I'm not interested."

"Oh, I have news for you, Knightly," Marsden said with a nefarious grin. "But I think I'll let you read it in the papers tomorrow. *The London Times*, in fact."

# Chapter 34

## Lovesick Female Driven to Desperate Measures

DRAFT:

*Dear Annabelle*
  *What is the proper way to conduct oneself after being discovered in a compromising position?*
  *Composed by Miss Annabelle Swift, unsolicited, on behalf of Mr. Derek Knightly.*

*Offices of* The London Weekly

**K**NIGHTLY must know that he was the Nodcock. No man as successful as he could be so obtuse. Annabelle allowed that all her sighs and blushes and stammers over the years were very missable. But they had kissed, Knightly and she. Twice.

Furthermore, the gossip columns had reported on it, thus mercifully offering concrete proof that such an exquisite event had actually happened and was not some wicked tease from her imagination.

And yet Knightly strolled into the weekly meeting with the same grin and drawling "ladies first" as he had for every other meeting since the dawn of time. He didn't act differently. He didn't give any indication that Something Momentous had occurred.

Annabelle scowled. Why was it all so hard, every step of the way?

A wink would have done wonders. A lift of one brow would have been a simple, unremarkable thing that spoke volumes to her. A knowing smile, perhaps? And really, what was the point of discretion now when *The London Times* printed up the details for all to see? Almost anybody in London now knew that:

1. At the charity ball benefiting the Society of Unfortunate Women, she and Knightly had enjoyed an extended, moonlit interlude, complete with a passionate kiss. Every Londoner was surely imagining the most wanton behavior on both their parts.
2. Knightly was one wicked lothario, dallying with an unmarriageable chit (Annabelle) while his very marriageable intended (Lady Marsden) languished in the ballroom.

Upon seeing her today, Owens had placed his hand on the small of her back and leaned in close to inquire about her extended moonlit interlude. Her response was a breathless "Nice" because she had been too flustered over his affection and concern. She gazed up to his warm brown eyes, searching for a reason why he would be so involved in the trials and tribulations of her little love life.

How to make heads or tales of any of it? A glimmer of anything remotely resembling acknowledgment might have gone a long way. Had Knightly nothing to say to her after that gossip rag? It was ungentlemanly to ignore it. Unsporting not to say something. Unless his silence was the answer she sought.

Sophie was chattering about weddings and the latest fashions; Eliza continued her reporting on the adventures of the Tattooed Duke, the previously unsuspecting subject of her writing, and now her husband.

Knightly warily turned his attentions to Julianna.

"Julianna, what salacious gossip might we find in your column this week?"

"I thought I might comment upon the Man About Town's recent column. Set the record straight, perhaps?" She asked this with a challenging lift of her brow.

"I don't know that there is much more to be said," Knightly replied, leaning against a table. Annabelle wanted to disagree strongly. There was plenty to be said—to her. Knightly added: "I'm certain any member of the aristocracy is engaged in much more scandalous activities that will be of significantly more interest to our readers."

In other words: don't talk about it. In other words: there was nothing to say. In other words: if we ignore it perhaps it will go away.

Julianna scowled. Annabelle did, too, for that matter. And then Knightly fixed his attentions upon her.

"Annabelle, what schemes do you have for us this week?"

It was on the tip of her tongue to say she would offer advice on how gentlemen ought to conduct themselves after passionately kissing women during moonlit interludes at a ball. Alas, Bold Annabelle had not progressed so far as to airing her personal business in public. Though she now entertained wicked and sassy retorts, she was not yet able to voice them.

Instead, she said, "I think it might be time for desperate measures."

"Are your efforts thus far unsuccessful?" Knightly asked with a lift of his brow. Was that a reference to their conversation or just a thing to do? And why did he have to be so impossibly handsome when he leaned?

"Oh, there have been some *small* successes," she replied, making every effort to sound haughty and dismissive. " Nothing grand enough to be *satisfying*."

Beside her, Julianna stifled a chortle, and Annabelle caught Owens's mouth hanging slack-jawed. These things made her rather proud of herself.

"What do you have in mind, Dear Annabelle?" Knightly was grinning, ever so slightly. She saw it in the upward tilt of the corner of his mouth, but mostly she saw it in his eyes.

"You'll see when you read my column," she said, with a little bit of sass, which was all bluster because she had no idea what desperate measures she would try.

"Not sooner?" Knightly asked casually. Oh, he had to know. He must! But she needed more certainty than a lift of his brow or an easily asked question in front of a room full of people.

Annabelle lifted her head higher and replied, "Quite a few of my readers have encouraged me to maintain an aura of mystery. And some even say that if the Nodcock cannot figure it out for himself, he doesn't deserve to know."

AFTER the meeting, the Writing Girls proceeded immediately to Gunther's for some ices. They parked Sophie's open-aired carriage in the shade of a tree, and with raspberry ices in hand proceeded with the important conversation.

"What desperate measures do you have in mind?" Sophie asked.

"Well, there are quite a few options," Annabelle said as she rummaged through her reticule and pulled out a packet of letters. "I have received dozens, but these are some of the more outrageous suggestions. This one says I ought to just print the truth in my column."

"Direct. But not exactly thrilling," Julianna replied.

"Unless you can be there when he reads it," Sophie said. "How fascinating it would be to watch his reaction! I wonder if he knows and would just coolly lift one brow and—"

"Correct a comma and carry on," Julianna added with a smirk.

"If he reads it, that is," Annabelle grumbled.

"You are not still vexed about that?" Eliza asked. "Because I'd wager he's poring over your every word these days." Annabelle hoped that was the case. If he wasn't wondering at this point, then he was more of a nodcock that she had thought.

"Perhaps. At any rate there are significantly more dramatic options than just telling him. For example, this one suggests I make a grand declaration at a ball."

"It's often so hard to hear in a ballroom," Sophie

said thoughtfully. "And if he's in the card room or the necessary when you give your big speech, it would be all for naught."

"With careful preparation, it could work," Julianna said. "It'd be terrifically entertaining."

"If I didn't perish of mortification first," Annabelle replied. She shuddered just thinking about speaking in public, let alone confessing the deep secrets of her heart to a crowd of strangers. "Here's another one: write a sonnet that confesses his identity and my love for him, commission a printing of one thousand flyers with the sonnet and toss them 'like leaves in the wind' from a hot-air balloon."

"That's an awful lot of effort," Eliza remarked. "But I know where you could get a hot-air balloon."

The other Writing Girls peered at her curiously and decided not to pursue that avenue of conversation.

"People have quite the flair for the dramatic," Julianna remarked, twisting a lock of hair around her finger. Eliza shrugged, reached over and selected a few of the pages from Annabelle.

"But a deplorable lack of consideration for logistics and costs," Sophie said. "Especially when they are not paying for it. Not that I blame them for it."

"If I'm to invest in this venture," Annabelle said, "I'd rather just buy more silk dresses and underthings. I certainly wouldn't spend it on printing sonnets or chartering hot-air balloons."

"Especially if you follow this reader's advice," Eliza said, "and run through the streets in broad daylight, wearing nothing but your unmentionables, proclaiming your love at the top of your voice." Sophie reached out for one, too.

"This one literally suggests shouting your love from the rooftops," she said with a laugh.

"I'll be carted off to Bedlam!" Annabelle exclaimed.

"It almost makes this one sound sane," Eliza said, looking up from the page in her hands. "Simply steal into his bedroom at the midnight hour."

"And then what?" Annabelle asked.

"Annabelle, please," Julianna said with a dose of exasperation in her voice. "Surely it's been covered in your novels and our conversations. If it hasn't been, then I am ashamed of our discussions and your reading material."

"Knightly will either ravish you or he will send you home directly," Sophie clarified.

"But when do I tell him? *What* do I tell him?" Annabelle asked, anxious. It was well and truly time for some sort of reckoning. If Knightly wasn't going to figure out that he was the Nodcock and *do something about it*, then she would make it abundantly clear so that he'd have no choice but to explain himself. Yet she wasn't sure how to make such a declaration.

"I can just see it now: 'Oh, good evening, Knightly! I just thought I'd drop by at this outrageously inappropriate hour to let you know that you are the Nodcock.'"

"There would be no room for ambiguity or misunderstanding," Julianna pointed out.

"Oh, he'll know he's the Nodcock the minute she falls off the windowsill onto his carpet," Sophie said. "Why else would she steal into his bedroom at the midnight hour?"

"We'll have to dress you in breeches," Eliza said, apropos of nothing.

"Why?" Annabelle asked, very nervous about the answer.

"For when you climb up a tree to the second-story window." Eliza said this so matter-of-factly that Annabelle was aghast.

"Are you mad?" she said. "Breeches! Climbing to a second-story window! Do you even know if there is a tree to climb?"

For goodness sakes, until recently the most daring thing she had done was lower her bodices or pretend a swoon. This was in another league entirely.

"Grand Gesture, Annabelle," Julianna reminded her. "Think of the great story this will make. Readers will devour it, and if nothing else, there is nothing Knightly loves like a stellar week of sales."

She was, alas, correct. But still . . . Annabelle was not convinced. Obstacles. She needed to present logical and insurmountable obstacles to this corkbrained scheme.

"I'm not sure of his address," she said.

"Number ten, Bruton Street. The red brick house," Julianna answered easily.

"Nor do I have breeches," Annabelle pointed out.

"I do," Sophie said. "They were Brandon's back in the day. Of course you may borrow them."

"You're too kind. But I have no idea how to climb a tree or a wall," she said with some desperation.

"It's easy, I can show you," Eliza said with a mischievous smile.

And that was how Annabelle came to be perched precariously on the windowsill of Knightly's bedroom. In breeches. In the midnight hour.

# Chapter 35

### Annabelle, Out on a Limb

**A**NNABELLE generally believed in focusing upon the positive things in life. Thus, as she dangled precariously in the tree outside of Knightly's house, she thought, At least I'm not in a hot-air balloon. As per Eliza's tree-climbing instructions, she kept hold of one branch at all times and thanked her lucky stars her friend advised her to wear gloves. Her friend did not mention this activity would ruin said gloves. But at least she would get a new pair. A small consolation.

That is, if she survived.

As Annabelle increased her distance from the ground, she had second thoughts. Did love really require grand gestures? Wasn't true love to be found in the little things, like holding one's hand or sitting comfortably around a gentle fire? Inside. On the ground.

When it came time to ease off the rough branch and onto the stone windowsill, Annabelle saw new merit in the suggestion of dashing through the crowded city streets clad in nothing but her unmentionables. Surely that was a much less perilous activity.

She finally reached the window of what she hoped was Knightly's bedchamber. Although, a small part of her hoped she tumbled into an empty room and could slink away and pretend this whole thing never happened.

She held onto a branch and with one hand reached out precariously to open the window. One awful truth was clear:

The window was locked.

"Oh no," she muttered. "Oh no, no, no, no, no."

An unfortunate creaking sound emerged from the branch. The kind of creaking sound before the whole limb threatened to break off and plummet to the ground.

"No," Annabelle told it. "Stay."

She felt it sag under her weight. Awkwardly, she adjusted her position to rely more heavily on the windowsill.

Some bits of gravel and brick broke off, falling ominously to the ground.

Desperately and carefully, she tried to open the window again. It was large, heavy, and very much locked.

She really ought to have run through the streets in her unmentionables instead.

"Okay, Annabelle, you have three options," she

said. Yes, she was now speaking aloud to herself. If she survived this, then she'd go straight to Bedlam and check herself in for the safety of herself and tree branches everywhere.

*Option the first:* attempt to climb down and hopefully pretend nothing ever happened. And never ever complain about a lack of romance or grand gestures again. At the moment both seemed vastly overrated, and it was her noble duty to warn every other young, romantic woman that she ought to relinquish such foolish notions.

*Option the second:* Holler for help. Because when one was in such a mortifying position, drawing the attention of the entire neighborhood was just the thing. Option the second was quickly dismissed.

*Option the third:* knock on the window. And pray that a very blind and mute servant assisted her entry and subsequent exit from the house so no one would be any wiser.

The sound of wood splitting rent through the night air. The branch suffered some fractures. Annabelle's heart missed a few beats.

*Option the fourth:* fall to her death in Knightly's garden. It would make a dreadful mess, and be terribly awkward for him, she presumed. She did so hate to inconvenience people . . . However, she would be dead and presumably no longer plagued by such worries.

Annabelle instead knocked on the window glass. And waited. She knocked again.

Somewhere nearby a cat mewled. A dark cloud passed over the cool, bright moon. A cool breeze rustled the leaves on the tree.

This was his bedroom window, was it not? It had

been a calculated guess based upon Julianna's visit to Lady Pettigrew's home just two doors down.

"Oh blast," Annabelle muttered.

The tree branch cracked and creaked again.

"Curses," she swore. "Gosh darn it to heck."

Annabelle knocked on the window again. And finally, oh finally, Knightly opened the window. She had never been so happy to see him. She had also never wished to see him less.

"Annabelle?" He rubbed his eyes as if he could not believe that she was perilously clinging to his windowsill and a tree branch.

"Hello," she said. *Hello? Oh for Lord's sake.* She was trapped on his windowsill, clinging desperately for her life, in the middle of the night, so *Hello* probably wasn't the worst thing she could have said. She ought to have gone with *Help* instead.

"What the devil are you doing?" he asked. Rightfully so. But truly, not the best time.

"Um, a grand romantic gesture?" she offered. He lifted one brow and didn't say a word. He was going to let her ramble out an explanation, drat the man. Well in that case she would give the only reason he would accept. "This is actually research for my column. For *The Weekly.*"

"I know where you work, Annabelle."

"One of my readers suggested it . . ." Her mouth went dry when she saw that he was not completely attired. He wore breeches. And a shirt that was carelessly thrown on and not one button done up. Not one. His bare chest was exposed. His hard bare chest. It was very flat, except for all the planes and ridges of his muscles. She thought about tracing her fingers along . . . feeling him . . .

And it would be the last thing she ever did. Falling to her death because she let go of her tree branch in order to caress Knightly's bare chest.

"I recognize that this is an unexpected and increasingly awkward situation," Annabelle said. "I considered climbing down and pretending nothing ever happened, but the branch is beginning to break—I'm terribly sorry and you can take it out of my wages."

She paused for breath and to consider the cost of one, lone tree branch. "The fact of the matter is that I'd be much obliged if you'd help me in. It turns out that given the choice, I'd rather die of embarrassment instead of falling and breaking my neck."

"Come inside, Annabelle. But you have some explaining to do."

Knightly held out his hand. She hesitated. The prospect of explaining to him that he was the Nodcock, that she had involved all of *The Weekly*'s readers in a scheme to seduce him, and that she risked her neck to do so, all while he wore naught but fitted breeches and an open shirt was just . . . unfathomable, impossible, and utterly terrifying.

She really ought to have run through the streets in her unmentionables. This was London, no one would have blinked twice.

But the branch cracked further, and a shriek might have escaped her.

She reached for his hand.

ANNABELLE tumbled into his arms, warm and luscious, tempting and maddening.

She was a tangle of long, slender limbs and smooth, alluring curves. Her soft curls brushed against his cheek and he inhaled the scent of her, like roses. He remembered this from the day she had tumbled into his arms during that minor carriage accident. He wanted her then. He wanted her now.

"What are you doing here, Annabelle?" The question had to be asked, even though he wasn't sure he wanted to hear the answer. He reluctantly released his hold on her and took a step back.

She bit her lip. Gazed up at him. Heaved such a sigh, as if so disappointed in the world, her fate, and him. He felt a dull ache in his chest. He didn't want to hurt her or let her down.

"Do you really not know?" she asked, forming each word slowly.

"Know what, Annabelle?" This truth was too important to just be assumed. Too much rested upon it to leave it an understanding. She had to say it aloud.

She mumbled something almost unintelligible.

"I am *a* nodcock or *the* Nodcock?" he clarified. It was a minor but crucial distinction.

"The one and only," Annabelle said softly.

"I am the Nodcock," he repeated, and she nodded her head slowly. *Yes.* He exhaled, all suspicions confirmed and all fears realized. After *years* in which she adored him from afar, while he didn't notice her, it had come to this.

Knightly couldn't think of all the profound implications of this simple, devastating fact—he was the Infamous Nodcock, he was Annabelle's heart's desire and had been for quite some time. He could only concentrate on the facts before him.

Annabelle, standing in a ray of moonlight falling into his bedroom. After midnight. In breeches.

"And you thought the best way to inform me

of this was to climb in my second-story bedroom window in the dead of the night?"

"Well if you had noticed me sooner, I wouldn't have had to resort to such desperate measures," she said, rebuking him.

"You are saying I caused this . . . this . . ." He raked his fingers through his hair and still couldn't think. He was the Nodcock. She had said so. All the sighs, faints, lowered bodices, and affectionate touches had been for him. She had literally and figuratively gone out on a limb to reveal her feelings to him.

And now he was expected to show his.

He felt desire. And a million other things he couldn't make sense of.

"I'll just be on my way, then," she said, stepping across the carpet toward the bedroom door.

"That's all?" he asked. She had come all this way only to leave?

"They said you would either ravish me or send me home. If *this* is ravishment, then it has been vastly overrated," she said. He choked on shock, and mirth.

"Annabelle," he said, because something needed to be said. Volumes needed to be said. But he had nothing to follow it up with. He was at a loss for words. He noticed that the few burning candles in the room added a soft, warm, inviting glow to her skin. But it didn't seem the thing to say.

"My audacity has left you speechless," Annabelle said, punctuated by another one of those sighs. Like the world had met her low expectations.

But that was beside the point at the moment.

"Your audacity?" His jaw dropped open. The fool woman had nearly fallen to her death at his doorstep. From what he gathered, she had escaped her bedchamber in Bloomsbury, crossed London alone in the middle of the night, and then proceeded to climb the tree in his garden and break into his bedroom. What insanity or desperation propelled her, he had no wish to know, though he had a sinking feeling he knew.

All that talk of ignorant nodcocks and desperate measures. He had invited this.

"Audacity, I suppose, is one way to describe it," he said, after taking a deep breath and exhaling slowly. "I was thinking that was a bloody stupid thing to do. Do you have any idea how dangerous that stunt was?"

Knightly caught himself pacing and running his fingers through his hair as if he were actually about to tear his own hair out with frustration.

She could have been hurt. She could have died, twice or thrice over. This forced him to consider a world without Annabelle—his heart stopped for a moment and resumed with the sound of her voice. *A world without Annabelle . . .* It would be bleak and lonely and cold. It was sadly lacking in a young woman's fearless attempts to come out of her shell.

He did not want to know a world without Annabelle.

"It did cross my mind, yes," she replied. "However, it seemed preferable to a hot-air balloon ride or running through the streets in an advanced state of undress."

Knightly stopped pacing to stare at her.

"What does that have to do with anything? No, do not tell me." He shook his head. " I don't want to know."

"Suggestions from readers as to how I might attract the attentions of the Nodcock," she explained in a very small voice.

"I am the Nodcock," Knightly said, needing to repeat the words again. Eventually, the truth would seem real, make sense and take hold.

"Am I not in your bedroom in the middle of the night after risking my life?" Aye, she was. And standing in a puddle of moonlight. Risking her virtue, too.

She had mentioned ravishment, throwing the word out like a lure. She didn't need to. The sight of Annabelle in his bedroom was enough. Annabelle in his bedroom dressed so that all her curves taunted him was further temptation. Annabelle, in so many words saying she wanted him, nearly undid him.

"By some miracle you are here, yes, and not in a mangled heap in my garden," he said, because the thought of a world without Annabelle made him feel as if he couldn't breathe.

"I thought it would make a good story for *The Weekly*," she explained.

"Did you not think of how it could have gone wrong?" he said, voice rising. It was fear of having almost lost her, of still possibly losing her. That decision he had avoided was now here in his bedroom saying words like "ravishment" with her plump lips he wanted to feel everywhere on his body.

Would he choose her, or belonging?

"Of course I considered that! When I was stranded on that branch and your windowsill, I thought about it extensively. But I wouldn't have been there if Julianna and Eliza had not assured me it would be perfectly fine."

"Oh, those two. Those two are trouble. And the

breeches," Knightly said, taking a long, rich look at her legs clad in the fitted kerseymere breeches that clung to her hips and thighs in such a sinful way.

He should not look.

He could barely wrench his gaze away. God, he wanted to strip them off her, to reveal acres of pale skin, bathed in moonlight.

"I'm not sure if your breeches show sense, given your tree climbing escapades or even more madness. What if someone had seen you?" he asked. In the back of his mind he thought that none of this really mattered—she was safe, no one had seen her. But something momentous was going to happen. He and Annabelle were going to make love. There was no avoiding it, really. It had been inevitable, he supposed. He wanted to know her, intimately, more than he'd ever wanted anything.

*Anything.*

And he needed a moment to process that everything was about to change.

"Miss Overlooked Swift, remember? Spinster Aunt from Bloomsbury! So what if I was spotted? What do I have to lose?" There was a note of anguish in her voice, but defiance in her stance. "No one ever *sees* me, Knightly. Least of all you. Which is why I have to do utterly mad and dangerous things to get attention. And now here I am and my intentions are clear. What do you have to say about that?"

He had seen her—or started to, these past few weeks. He'd been driven to distraction by her—but just these past few days. He thought of all the years they met every week when she sighed when he walked into the room, and he had thought nothing of it. Never even noticed.

Of course she had to climb a tree and knock on his bedroom window to get his damned attention. She had risked her life and heart for him.

"I am the Nodcock," he said. Again.

"I'm dreadfully sorry about the name," she said, smiling sheepishly.

"I shan't forgive you for that," he said sharply. Good God, if anyone knew he'd never live it down.

"I wouldn't either," she replied with a shrug. But they both knew her heart was so damn big and loving she would forgive almost anyone anything. Even a bastard like him.

"I suspected as much," Knightly added. "I was thrown off by Owens and Marsden. And I suppose I didn't want to see. But I suspected."

"And yet you let me take it this far?" she asked, horrified. Understandably so.

"Last week you were only fainting in my arms, Annabelle. And now you're risking life and limb to break into my bedchamber in the middle of the night? How was I supposed to know you would go to such lengths?"

If he had seen this coming . . . If he had known that she would resort to this . . . What would he have done? He groaned when his brain supplied the idiotic suggestion of lining the ground with feather mattresses in case she fell.

The truth was, he didn't know what he would have done. The sight of Annabelle in breeches and a thin white linen shirt didn't exactly facilitate rational thought either.

"You let me throw myself at you when you knew!" And then Annabelle folded her arms across her chest and stomped her foot. Bloody adorable.

"Suspected," he clarified. "I suspected but I was not certain. I did not have the facts. And I operate on facts."

"You suggested I give up the ruse," Annabelle pointed out, and it sounded like an accusation. It sounded like he had lured her here. She stepped closer to him. He swallowed, hard. "You asked if I wanted satisfaction," she whispered.

"Be careful what you ask for, Annabelle," he warned.

She took another step in his direction. If she came any closer, he could not be held responsible. A man could only endure so much temptation. As it was, his self-restraint was already straining under the pressure.

He wanted to claim her mouth, sink his fingers in her hair, strip off those breeches. He wanted to feel her skin, hot and bare, underneath his. He wanted to see if one of Annabelle's infamous blushes went beyond her cheeks. He wanted to bury himself inside her. He wanted to know her, possess her, make love to her so thoroughly it would be impossible to move.

"Well, I have given up the ruse," Annabelle said plainly.

There were reasons, good reasons, why all those things he wanted should not happen. He could not think of one now. Not one.

"You want satisfaction, Annabelle?" He looked down at her face tilted up to his. Her eyes were large, searching. Her lips were plump, red, and slightly parted.

"I think so," she replied, revealing that devastating innocence of hers. She was offering that to him,

along with her trust and her faith. That was why
Annabelle scared him, and why he'd been reluctant
to see the truth.

With Annabelle, it would matter.

With Annabelle, there would be no turning back.
There would be no marriage in the aristocracy,
there would be no parity with the New Earl. He still
wanted these things. But in this moment he wanted
Annabelle more.

When Knightly made a decision, it was swift and
sure and he followed through without looking back.
On the spot, in the moment, he chose Annabelle.

His life's ambition, tossed out the window in exchange for the chance to lose himself in her kiss, her
touch, her sighs. That's how much he wanted her.

"Oh, you do want satisfaction, Annabelle, you do,"
he promised. His voice was rough. "I'll show you."

He did not start with a kiss. She had kept him in
suspense, wanting, waiting, and teasing for weeks.
Tonight she would suffer the same . . . though he was
damn sure she was going to revel in every second of
it. He'd make sure of that.

Her hair was pulled into a tight bun, and he began
by removing the hairpins holding those curls back.
A mass of thick blond curls tumbled down around
her shoulders. Annabelle, undone.

His breath hitched. He had known Annabelle
was pretty. But with her hair down she was beautiful. Like a goddess. Like it was impossible that he
should not have noticed her all these years . . .

Well, he was going to discover her now. He was
going to give her years worth of attention, in one
night.

She gazed up at him. It pulled hard at his heart.

No one had ever looked at him like that. She was nervous, and she was putting herself in his care. She had literally gone out on a limb for him when no one else ever had. And she stood before him, waiting . . .

Then Annabelle licked her lip; a nervous gesture that he found unbelievably erotic. She would stay the night and, he thought wickedly, she would like it.

"Annabelle," he said, clasping her cheeks in his palms. There were all these things he should say. All these feelings he didn't have the words for. The woman left him speechless and nearly breathless. "Annabelle."

She tasted like sweetness and trouble. A marvelous combination. She responded hesitantly at first and then he could feel her reservations and nerves calm and fade. He didn't know he could do that with a kiss. Was he drunk on that power? Or just drunk on Annabelle?

They kissed in the moonlight, until he could stand it no longer—a minute, maybe two. He was desperate to know her. How soft was her skin? How did she sound when he pleasured her? How did she taste, everywhere? How did it feel to be inside her?

Knightly needed to know. Knightly sought answers.

One could not make proper love to a woman while she was dressed as a boy. He tugged at the shirt, pulling it from her breeches and above her head. Buttons seemed to have gone flying; he heard them skittering across the floor.

Annabelle folded her arms over her chest.

"Oh no, my dear Annabelle," he murmured. "I need to see you."

Truly, he needed to. Like he needed air. He needed

to know how the real vision of Annabelle compared to the one he had conjured up, late at night when he was alone. He knew this would far surpass anything he'd imagined.

Yet in the far recesses of his mind, Knightly was aware that this was likely her first time. She'd be shy and uncertain and would need an extra gentle touch.

To even things out, he took off his own shirt, dropping it carelessly on the floor.

Her eyes widened as her gaze roamed over his naked chest. Perhaps that didn't put her at ease. Knightly couldn't help it; he grinned. Then he tugged her closer and kissed her some more. Her arms stole around him, tentatively to start.

Slow, he reminded himself, *slow*. He wanted this to be perfect for her. And her hesitant touch set him on fire. Something about being where no man had been before. If he did one thing in his life, it would be to make sure that this moment had been worth waiting for, for her.

When he could take it no longer, he guided Annabelle to the bed; he needed to feel her utterly naked, beneath him. He needed to make love to her. Needed to like he'd been blind, and now had the gift of sight and never wanted to close his eyes again.

WHEN Annabelle had thought about this night, in all honesty, this was the part she had thought about most of all. Never mind that it was her first time and her knowledge was limited to the occasionally illuminating conversations of her fellow Writing Girls. She knew what was supposed to happen. She had wondered what it'd be like.

She hadn't known. Dear Lord, she hadn't known. To feel this close to someone and to feel this wanted was to really know, for a moment, how cold and lonely she had been. Then Knightly proceeded to chase that feeling away every time he uttered her name in a husky voice, looked at her with undisguised craving. That was to say nothing of his kiss, which set her body and soul afire, and his touch, which stoked that fire.

Knightly lead her to his bed and together they tumbled down to the feather mattress. His bare skin was hot against her bare skin. She loved it. Loved the possessive feeling of his weight on hers. His fingers threaded through her own. It was the sweetest thing that he should still hold her hand in a moment like this when they were naked and tangled together. She didn't know quite where she ended and he began.

"I can feel you smiling as we kiss," he murmured, and she laughed softly. Knightly's mouth nibbled oh so gently on her earlobe and it sent shivers down her spine.

"I wanted . . ." she whispered, but then gave up. She meant to tell him how she had wanted him, wanted this . . . But Knightly's palm closed over her breast, gently caressing and holding. He shifted his weight and her protest became a gasp of shock and then of pleasure when his mouth closed around the dusky, sensitive peak.

Knightly did the same on the other side. Annabelle gasped, and Annabelle sighed, and Annabelle took the lesson she had learned from practicing fainting and just *let go*. Those sighs turned into murmurs of pleasure and she writhed beneath him.

It was exquisite what he did to her with his mouth
. . . leaving a trail of hot, scorching kisses from her
breasts down to her belly, across to the indenta-
tion of her waist and lower still. The stubble on his
cheeks was a wicked contrast to the softness of her
own skin.

And then Knightly kissed her *there*. This she had
certainly never imagined . . . didn't even know . . .
He licked the bud of her sex, slowly back and forth
at first. Breathing suddenly became impossible. And
then slow leisurely circles around and around as a
particular heat intensified, and with it a feeling of
increasing pressure.

Annabelle gripped the bedsheets in her palms.
She couldn't breathe. She felt like she was on fire.
Like she might explode. The pleasure was so deep,
so intense, so overwhelming, she simply couldn't
fight it. So she didn't. She let go, cried out from the
joyful release and surrendered.

She had risked her life for this. Risked rejection
and mortification at the hands of the man she loved
more than anything. It had been worth the risk. So
very absolutely worth it.

"Annabelle," Knightly said, his voice rough with
desire. "I want you."

She fixed her gaze upon Knightly. His dark hair
fell rakishly down before his blue, blue eyes. How
she had ached to hear those words from his lips. She
had longed to see him thus: desperate for her.

She grinned wickedly—surely she now deserved
to grin wickedly—and kissed him. It was now his
turn to sigh.

"Annabelle, I need you," he murmured. She felt
his arousal, warm and hard, pressing at the en-

trance between her legs. She arched her back, tilted her hips, intrigued by the sensation of it. Knightly groaned, then claimed her mouth for another kiss. She felt the heat surging again. Felt the sparks. Felt like she wanted more.

"Tell me to stop," he gasped. She wrapped her arms around him, entwined her legs with his. She couldn't get close enough to him. There had to be more. They had to be closer. She wanted more.

"I want to be yours," she whispered. "I want you."

When Annabelle whispered those words, there was no going back. Even if Knightly had wanted to stop, not even the devil and all the angels in heaven could make him. He entered her, slowly, because he didn't want to hurt her and because he did not want to miss a second of this. This one moment, this once.

She was warm and wet and ready for him. He pushed ahead until he was fully inside of her. Until there was no going back. Until he and Annabelle, at long last, were one.

"Oh, God, Annabelle," he rasped, and then he thrust gently. She gasped with pleasure. He thrust again, harder, and she moaned with desire. And then again and again. He lost himself in the rhythm, in the scent of her and the sound of her soft cries of pleasure. Lost himself fully in the taste of her skin and surrendered to the overwhelming need to love her completely, to possess her entirely. He cried out, reaching his climax. She did too. He heard her cries of pleasure and felt her contract around him. He lost himself in this moment in which he noticed Annabelle, all of her.

# **Chapter 36**

### The Morning After

PARLIAMENTARY INTELLIGENCE

*There are rumors that Lord Marsden's Inquiry is*
*about to get worse—much worse.*

The London Weekly

**A**NNABELLE awoke in Knightly's embrace. He held
her close and her head rested on his bare chest. She
heard his heartbeat, strong and steady. She held
him, too, with one of her arms flung over his chest
as if to say *mine*.

She thought she might have been having an extremely vivid dream in which she could experience
the scent of him and the glorious sensation of his
bare skin against her bare skin. But it was real.

This was real.

The world must have altered its course sometime
in the night. Perhaps it started spinning in the other
direction or started to orbit the moon instead of the
sun. The world as Annabelle had known it ceased
to exist.

Good riddance, she thought.

And to this wonderful new world, she practically purred good morning.

She didn't often feel contentment. Usually she woke up slightly disappointed to open her eyes to her attic bedroom and to the chores and drudgery of the day that awaited her. But she summoned her hope and sunny disposition and dared to dream perhaps that day would be different.

The word, *contentment,* now had a new definition, and it was Knightly's arms around her. It was this feeling of nothing between them, not even so much as a chemise or a bedsheet.

Or perhaps, Annabelle thought with a smile as she happily drifted from deep sleep to fully awake, perhaps this was joy. To waken in the arms of the man you loved. What could possibly be better than that?

Hmm . . . She smiled bashfully and blushed. They had made love. She'd had no idea. None at all. He'd teased and seduced New Annabelle to heights Old Annabelle never could have imagined.

Annabelle sighed, and this time it was a sigh of absolute and utter pleasure.

"Good morning," a man's voice greeted her. That never happened in her old world. And it was Knightly's voice, still rough from sleep.

"Good morning," she replied. It was a good morning indeed. She stretched and yawned and nestled closer to him. She loved him, and they had made love. Her heart had always belonged to him, and now the rest of her did, too.

"You are trouble, Annabelle," he said, turning on his side to gaze down at her. He brushed her hair out of her eyes, away from her face. Her hair was surely in a state. But she didn't care, not when he was looking at her like that.

"No one's ever said that to me before," she replied. "I like it. I probably shouldn't but I do."

"Good," he practically growled. But he grinned, too, and claimed her mouth for another kiss. He clasped her breast and she arched her back, pressing herself closer to him, to encourage him to that again, and more.

"You are absolutely trouble," he murmured as he feathered kisses along her neck. "For the first time in history, I will be late to the office."

"At least you don't have to worry about losing your position," Annabelle said, and wrapped her arms around him and pulled him even closer.

"And I have a very good reason for being late," he murmured as he rolled atop her. She parted her legs and felt him straining against her, ready. Oh so ready.

They made love again, trading in the cool glow from the moon for the softness of morning light.

"Annabelle," he whispered, holding her close after they had both cried out in pleasure and lay for a while in each other's arms. "Oh Annabelle."

It was inevitable that reality would intrude. It took the precise form of Knightly's valet, who discreetly entered the bedchamber with a tray of steaming black coffee and a thick stack of newspapers, which he set down on the bedside table before disappearing into what must have been the closet. Not once did he seem to register Annabelle's presence in his master's bed. Naked. Covered only by a bedsheet.

"I would feel better if your valet seemed to find this unusual," Annabelle remarked.

"Part of his job is to maintain an inscrutable expression at all times. At any rate, rest assured that I do not often have women sneaking into my bedroom in the middle of the night."

"I hope you don't mind I did that," Annabelle said bashfully, and Knightly laughed. She loved his laugh. Couldn't believe she was in bed, naked, with Knightly. And they were laughing. Dreams she hadn't known to dream were now coming true.

"Oh, Annabelle," he said, still laughing but pausing long enough to drop a kiss on her nose. "Oh, Annabelle."

"I'll take that as a no, you don't mind," she said with a touch of laughter.

"Good," he said . . . but all trace of laughter was gone from his voice. She peered over his shoulder at the newspaper he picked up and recognized the large masthead of a certain rival paper.

"*The London Times*, Knightly?" she said. She supposed he already knew every word of *The London Weekly*.

"Hell and damnation," he swore.

"What is it?" she asked, peering over his shoulder. She read the headline: THE LONDON WEEKLY UNDER INVESTIGATION. "Oh. That's not good," she said, which may have been the biggest understatement of 1825.

He scanned the lines quickly.

"I have to go," he said, tossing the paper aside, right into Annabelle's lap. He rubbed his eyes and the stubble on his jaw. She saw him glance around the room, bewildered. Worse, she saw that any lovely magical interlude they had shared was over. Knightly might still have been right next to her in his own bed, but in his head he was already at *The Weekly*.

He located his breeches and pulled them on before strolling off toward what she presumed was a dressing room of some sort. When he emerged a few moments later, he was dressed and groomed and looking like the Knightly she had known for years. Perfect, aloof, commanding, and ruthless.

"Stay as long as you'd like, the servants will take care of you," he said, quickly dropping a kiss on her mouth. Her lips were still parted and wanting when he pulled away and headed to the door.

He paused for a second with his hand on the doorknob and glanced at her over his shoulder. His blue eyes focused on her for a moment, as if committing the sight to memory. As if he wouldn't see it again.

"Damn," he said softly.

The door clicked softly shut behind him. Like that, he was gone.

What did *that* mean? She pulled the sheets up higher, as if to comfort herself and ward off the growing cold, which had nothing to do with the temperature of the air, only an unfortunate feeling inside. When Knightly left, it was like the sun stopped shining.

And now he was gone and she was still naked in his bed, alone.

"This is awkward," she muttered to herself. Being a Good Girl her entire life meant that she had never even contemplated what she might do if she found herself naked and alone in a gentleman's bedchamber in broad daylight.

Her first thought was to put some clothes on. Yet the only clothing she had with her was better fit for a lad and in a wrinkled heap on the floor on the far side of the room.

It was one thing for a woman to dress as a boy with the darkness of night to aid her. It was quite another for her to stroll through the streets of Mayfair during midday. Julianna had done it once . . . but Annabelle did not possess Julianna's brisk, determined stride.

Plus, she thought her shirt might have been divested of a few buttons.

Even more perilous than walking through the streets of London at midday in such a state was returning to the Swift household. By now they must have discovered that she was missing, if only because breakfast wasn't set out or fires weren't lit or the children weren't woken at precisely six in the morning.

Annabelle glanced at the clock; it was eleven. Eleven in the morning!

"Oh, dear," she said to herself. The raptures of pleasure and love she'd been basking in were now ebbing, replaced with panic.

She should know what to do. She was Dear Annabelle. She always knew what to do. Matters of practicality were her strong suit. It was in the romance department that she was an utter nitwit. In her head, she positioned her situation as a letter to Dear Annabelle, with half a mind to submit it to Knightly.

*Dear Annabelle?*
  *A "gentleman" left me stranded and naked in his*
*bed. What to do?*
  *Mortified in Mayfair.*

If only Knightly hadn't dashed off, leaving her
like this!

What had she expected? If there was one thing
known about Knightly, one carved-in-stone fact, it
was that *The London Weekly* came first and last. He
spent so much of his time in the office that the Writing Girls had fiercely debated whether she should
climb into his bedroom or drop in to *The Weekly* offices. They only settled on his bedchamber because
Mayfair would be safer than Fleet Street at such an
hour.

She should not take it personally that he had run
out, leaving her naked in his bed with no clothes. It
was just how he was.

Unless he meant to strand her here, awaiting his
return, like some obliging mistress? While there
were worse things than laying about in bed all day,
with Knightly's scent still on the pillows, she knew
she could not wait for him. For one thing, it seemed
undignified. For another, for all she knew it could be
days before he returned.

What to do, oh what to do?

She pulled the silk bell cord. And waited. Pulled
the sheet up higher and waited until a moment later
when an older woman opened the door and behind
her a maid with a tray.

"Mr. Knightly told us to take care of you, so we'll
do just that. I'm Mrs. Featherstone, the housekeeper."

The women acted thoroughly unsurprised to

find a naked woman in his bed. Annabelle scowled. She didn't think he'd been a monk, but why didn't anyone find it at all remarkable?

She considered asking, but decided she did not want the answer. Instead, she requested assistance in sending a note to Sophie.

# Chapter 37

### Quest for Rogue's Heart Leads to Disaster

FASHIONABLE INTELLIGENCE BY A LADY OF DISTINCTION
*Dear Annabelle has launched a craze for feigning
faints and tantalizingly low bodices among the ton's
debutantes. Mothers and determined bachelors are
afraid of what she will do next.*

The London Weekly

**S**OPHIE came to her rescue and arrived shortly
with a dress, stockings, a bonnet, and all the other
items necessary for her to appear in public. It was
lovely that she did not have to explain why such a
favor was required.

"I trust the evening was successful," Sophie inquired after they were comfortably ensconced in
her carriage.

"Oh yes," Annabelle said. At the thought of it,
that warm glow returned. Her cheeks inflamed, as
they were wont to do, when images from the night
before flashed in her mind. But then she recalled
Knightly's abrupt exit. "But this morning . . ." How
to explain this morning?

"I trust you both saw the news. *The London Weekly*

under attack," Sophie said softly. "Did you read the article?"

She had done so while nibbling toast and drinking tea. Mrs. Featherstone had given her one of Knightly's shirts to wear, and she'd been loath to take it off when Sophie arrived with more suitable public attire.

"It's rather bad, isn't it?" Annabelle asked. *The London Times* had reported that Marsden's Inquiry would be expanding to review all newspapers, starting first and foremost with *The London Weekly*. The newspaper's owner and editor would be called to testify. He might be charged with libel. He would almost certainly find himself in prison.

"He might lose the paper, Annabelle." Sophie said this softly, her expression woeful.

"He owns it. How can they take it away?" she asked. More to the point, *The London Weekly* belonged to Knightly in a way that went beyond mere possession. Like it was his heart, or his soul.

"Well, the paper might lose him if the Inquiry determines that we broke the law with our reporting methods. Just think of Owens and Eliza . . ." Sophie said, wincing.

The devil only knew what Owens had done for stories: he'd posed as a Bow Street Runner, a guard at Windsor Castle, a footman at the Duke of Kent's residence. Those were the exploits they knew of.

Eliza had been disguised for weeks as a housemaid in the Duke of Wycliff's household, exposing his most intimate secrets each week (before he married her, that is).

"They couldn't possibly send a duchess to the tower." Annabelle's heart clenched, imagining such an awful fate for people whom she loved so dearly. They hadn't really done anything wrong. No one had been hurt.

"It's unlikely they would go after Eliza. Really, Marsden is just out for Knightly. Rest assured, Brandon is working tirelessly behind the scenes, and even Roxbury and Wycliff have deigned to show their faces at the House of Lords for the first time. But Marsden is furious."

"Why? What has Knightly ever done to him?" Marsden, who had sent her pink roses. Marsden, who had coined the phrase "the Nodcock." Marsden, who had been one of the few gentlemen to ever pay attention to her. She felt betrayed for thinking him kind, a friend. She felt like a traitor to Knightly for her friendliness toward Marsden. She also felt like a fool.

"Marsden is livid because it seems Knightly and his fortune were supposed to marry his sister—whom no one else will have," Sophie said, and with an apologetic smile added, "Then Knightly was seen with you . . ."

"Oh," Annabelle said in small voice, thinking of their kiss in the moonlight at the charity ball. The moment when she really, truly fell in love with Knightly as he was, not Knightly of her dreams. She had thought that hour enchanted, and never considered that such destruction would be left in its wake.

Knightly had been courting Lady Lydia and was her only marital prospect, thanks to all those rumors and the missing second season. Was she now doomed to a life of spinsterhood, because of her? Knightly had been courting her, too, in order to protect his beloved newspaper. Was he doomed to lose the thing he loved most in the world?

It trying to obtain her own happiness, it seemed she ruined the lives of two innocent people.

"Oh no," she whispered as she all too clearly saw how this was her fault. All of it—Marsden's fury, Knightly's fight for *The Weekly*, Lady Lydia's impending spinsterhood. If she hadn't caught his eye and glanced over her shoulder, as per the suggestion of some stranger, when she strolled onto the terrace . . .

If she hadn't fainted into his arms, or left that shawl behind, or lowered the bodice on each dress she owned in a hope to catch his eye, and then his heart . . .

*If she hadn't thrown herself at him week after week . . .*

If Knightly had never noticed her, he would have married Lady Lydia and everything would be fine. There wouldn't be an inquiry or a trial or the threat of prison. He wouldn't be faced with the loss of the thing he loved most of all.

But she had grown selfish and desperate in her loneliness. She had tried tricks and schemes to turn his head. She had forced him to catch her when she fainted. She had climbed a tree and tumbled into his bedroom in the middle of the night.

It had never occurred to Annabelle that she was distracting him from something else or someone else.

She had only wanted his love. Now it seemed that she'd ruined his life in her quest for it.

"What do I do?" she asked. She had to fix this, somehow. Because this disaster was her fault and because she loved him, she had to make this right.

"Wait and see, I suppose . . ." Sophie said with a little shrug.

"No, I must fix this," Annabelle vowed. She would. No matter what it cost her.

# Chapter 38

*The London Weekly Courts Scandal*

FASHIONABLE INTELLIGENCE BY A LADY OF DISTINCTION
*The matrons of the ton are united in their fury against the vice of gossip in the press and have pledged their support to Lord Marsden's efforts to promote a "decent and honorable" newspaper industry. That is, until they must go without their scandal sheets.*

*The London Weekly*

*Galloway's Coffeehouse*

**I**T had been one hell of a day and one hell of a night. Darkness came and went; Knightly noted its arrival and passing from his desk.

He barely slept, barely ate, barely drank.

Barely even thought of Annabelle.

Oh, she was there, in a way—somehow her scent had clung to his skin. When his attention faltered and his gaze drifted to the clock, Knightly thought, *At this hour last night, Annabelle was clinging to my windowsill for dear life. At this time last night Annabelle was climaxing in my arms, from my touch.*

And truth be told, he even thought, At this time yesterday, I was blissfully unaware . . .

He had been blissfully unaware that Dear Annabelle was intent upon seducing him. Didn't know that Annabelle loved him. Hadn't claimed her in the most irrevocable way. He didn't have to do anything about it. But now there was no question that something must be done about Annabelle. But he couldn't think about it. He did not have the time to puzzle it out. Not tonight, of all nights, when he had few precious hours to respond to the direct attack to his beloved newspaper.

Knightly and Owens had taken the unprecedented action of stopping the presses so they might rewrite, reset, and reprint a new edition of *The London Weekly* that included a letter from the editor responding to the attack.

They ended up rewriting nearly the entire issue.

"This isn't working," Owens had muttered, staring down at the draft of a letter from the editor on the table between them. Dusk was settling over the city, and they'd been working ceaselessly since first light.

"You're right," Knightly reluctantly agreed. The front-page story just wasn't hitting the right notes of outrage, defiance, and humor. Instead it came across like a boorish lecture on the importance of a free press.

Knightly rubbed his jaw. He had left Annabelle hours ago . . . Was she still in his bed? What would it be like to come home, knowing Annabelle awaited him?

He refused to consider it. Instead, he strolled across the room and poured a brandy for himself and Owens.

"You know, Owens, we should show them what a government approved paper reads like."

"You mean cut out all the good bits?" Owens retorted.

"Basically. And then we rewrite this first page article to explain. You know, '*The London Weekly* gives its readers exactly what they want. You asked for this piece of rubbish edition of the paper. And the readers who didn't want this know why they should be riled up, and who they should direct their anger at. Enjoy.'"

"I like it," Owens said with a grin. "One hell of a statement. But we won't have time to rewrite and reset the type for the whole issue."

"Black it out. Cross it out. That way there's no change in the pages just black lines showing what they're missing," Knightly said, and then he thought about it more and got excited. "Can you just see it? Most of the paper will be blacked out."

"Genius. There will be hell to pay for this," Owens said. But he was grinning, and Knightly knew he was imagining this utterly defiant edition of the paper with those taunting black lines.

"Publish and be damned," Knightly said, raising his glass in cheers.

It was one hell of a gamble. Give 'em all exactly what they ask for, sit back and watch them howl. Marsden might be on a personal quest against him, but he was going to make this into a public spectacle. Which is why, exhausted as he was after working for twenty-four straight hours, he went not home to his bed, but to the coffeehouse. To Galloway's. His club.

He wanted to watch readers react. Wanted to see what he left a beautiful woman in bed for.

He would go to her. Even though he didn't know quite what to say. The irony that he, a professional master of words, did not know the right ones for this occasion. She loved him. He made love to her.

A proposal of marriage wouldn't be remiss, but . . . what about love matches and half brothers who refused to acknowledge him? What about hopes and plans he'd long possessed, and what about his impending imprisonment? They would arrest him, surely. Especially after the stunt he pulled with this new issue.

Knightly sipped his coffee, flipped through the pages of *The London Weekly*, and more often than not glanced at the other patrons around the room.

He noted with no small amount of satisfaction that most of the blokes in the coffeehouse were reading his newspaper. Some laughed. Some had their brows knit into deep lines as they tried to puzzle out what the damned articles said. Or maybe they were realizing the stranglehold on news that the government was attempting. More than stamp taxes, or window taxes.

Knightly was reminded, then, that this wasn't just a personal battle between Marsden and himself, nor was *The Weekly* just his darling pet. It was the newspaper that was written for the people he grew up with—tradesmen and actors, barristers and shopkeepers. And it was the paper for the people he aspired to associate with. It was, like himself, a mix of high and low. He was not one or the other, no matter what his aspirations might be.

As per their usual routine, Drummond and Gage ambled in and took seats at Knightly's table near the window. They also looked worse for wear, Gage especially, probably after a long night at the theatre and an even longer night at some demimonde soiree. Those routs were much less decorous, Knightly had to say, and thus much more fun than ton parties.

Gage held his head in his hands and groaned. One could practically smell the alcohol emanating from his pores.

Drummond took the paper and wordlessly flipped through quickly until hitting a certain page. Knightly watched, slack-jawed in something akin to horror. All those hours, all the careful deletions, the presses stopped and restarted, a staff on the verge of mutiny, all on a day he could have spent in bed with a beautiful, loving woman . . . and the man went straight to Dear Annabelle.

It was his turn to groan.

"Dear Annabelle," Drummond said with a sigh. "How fares your quest for love?"

Knightly rubbed his stubbled jaw. He leaned back in his chair. This was going to be interesting.

Drummond grinned at Annabelle's words on the page and then laughed at something she'd written. Knightly remembered editing it in an advanced state of frustration. The exact words hadn't stuck with him; just a feeling of confusion, wanting, refusal to engage.

"What's so funny?" he asked.

"She fainted into his arms!" Drummond said with unabashed amusement. "Listen to this," he said, as he read aloud from the paper: " 'Quite a few letters arrived my way, written in a matronly handwriting from Mayfair addresses, encouraging me to feign a swoon in the particular gentleman's arms. I am given to understand that this maneuver plays to a man's chivalrous instincts—to start. But then to hold a comely young maiden in his arms is supposed to arouse his baser inclinations as well.'"

"That's funny," Gage muttered, managing to lift his head from his hands, but only for a moment. Green. The man was positively green.

"This girl . . ." Drummond said, shaking his head and grinning. "I say, I am in love and have never even met the chit."

Knightly fought to keep a scowl off his face.

Annabelle was *his*.

In the only way that mattered.

Memories of that night crashed over him, like waves on a beach.

Annabelle in the moonlight—desperately hanging on outside of his window. He'd heard the phrase "having one's heart in the throat," but hadn't understood it until that moment. He almost lost her, far too soon.

Annabelle in breeches, showing off her long slender legs. Later in the night, she wrapped those legs around him as he buried himself deep inside her. Knightly closed his eyes . . .

Annabelle in nothing. Her skin, oh God, her skin was milky white and pure, and so soft. A soft pink blush, everywhere. Her mouth, her kiss, her tentative touch growing more bold as he showed her dizzying heights of pleasure.

He could still feel her, still taste her. He still craved her.

His lungs felt tight, like he couldn't breathe. It wasn't because of the smoky haze in the coffeehouse either.

He still desired her, still wanted her, and still needed more of her. And yet—how badly? How much? What price was he willing to pay for Annabelle in his bed?

Drummond chuckled and muttered, "Baser inclinations. God, I'd love to show her—"

Before he even knew what he was doing, Knightly had leapt across the table and grabbed a fistful of Drummond's cravat.

Coffee spilled across the table, pouring over the edge. The ceramic mug cracked in pieces as it hit the hardwood floor.

Drummond's face took on a shade of crimson.

"Oi! Some of us are sorely feeling the aftereffects of alcohol," Gage muttered, but no one paid him any mind.

"I strongly suggest you do *not* finish that sentence," Knightly said. There was a lethal tone to his voice he didn't recognize.

"Really?" Drummond asked. Since he managed to imbue the word with some sarcasm, Knightly determined that he still had too much air, so he twisted the bunch of fabric in his fist until Drummond was gasping for breath.

"Really," Knightly drawled. Then he let go, took a seat and waved for another coffee.

"You're the Nodcock, aren't you?" Drummond said.

"Bugger off," Knightly told him. It was the wrong thing to say. It only encouraged him. Even Gage lifted his head.

"How did it feel to have Dear Annabelle faint into your embrace?" Drummond inquired. "Were your baser inclinations aroused?"

Gage snorted, laughed, and then groaned.

"Really?" Knightly replied, lifting one brow for emphasis.

"Really. How have you missed her all these years?" Drummond propped his head on his palm, elbow on the table. Beside him, Gage laid his head on the table in defeat.

"What's wrong with him?" Knightly asked, looking warily at their supremely ill friend.

"Some people think it's a good idea to accept a wager to see if one can drink an entire bottle of brandy in one evening," Drummond explained witheringly.

"I won," Gage grumbled.

"But at what cost?" Knightly mused.

"But let's not discuss Gage's idiocy, as that is expected of him," Drummond said with a dismissive wave of his hand. "I'm more interested in your idiocy, Knightly. How have you missed Annabelle all these years? Is she actually not that pretty?"

"She's pretty," he said tightly. By pretty he meant soul-wrenchingly beautiful, the kind of gorgeous that brought a man to his knees. Actually did, last night.

"Pretty? And you only just noticed this . . ." Drummond pointedly let his voice trail off. " . . . yesterday . . . a week ago . . . a month ago?"

When she started trying to make him notice. When he informally betrothed himself to a perfectly fine woman who possessed no traits that attracted him, other than her high society connections. When it was too late for him.

Aye, he noticed Annabelle not in all the *years* when he could have, but waited until it was absolutely and completely inconvenient to do so. No wonder she called him the Nodcock.

"I take it you've noticed her now, Nodcock," Drummond remarked.

Knightly lunged across the table once more, once again tugging hard on Drummond's cravat, by now a limp and wrinkled scrap of fabric.

"Have mercy on a man," Gage pleaded. "Please. For the love of Annabelle."

"This is serious, is it?" Drummond asked after Knightly released him—but not without a threatening look.

"It's none of your damned business," Knightly said. And still—still!—Drummond blithely carried on, provoking him more with each word he uttered. That was the problem with longstanding friends— they felt utterly free to go too far and to enjoy every step they took over the line.

"*Au contraire, mon frère,*" Drummond declared. "Annabelle's business is all of London's business. If you do not do right by this chit, I will come for you—if you are the Nodcock, that is, and not some desperate pretender—and I will bring the mob. And then I will go and console Annabelle myself. Nakedly."

This time Knightly swung at him; his fist connectedly solidly with Drummond's jaw. Satisfied his point had been made, Knightly quit the coffeehouse.

# Chapter 39

### An Offer She Can Refuse

DEAR ANNABELLE

*Attentions are one thing, affections are quite another.*
*True love cannot be sparked by parlor tricks. A lower*
*bodice will catch a man's gaze, but it will not make*
*him care. A forgotten shawl may afford a moment*
*alone, but it will not lead to love . . . and if it did,*
*would that be fair? This author thinks not and en-*
*courages all—particularly Scandalously in Love—to*
*hold out for true love.*

The London Weekly

**K**NIGHTLY arrived at the Swift household later
that afternoon, after a nightmare-plagued sleep in
which Annabelle fell from that branch and he hadn't
caught her in time.

A maid answered the door. That wicked sister-
of-law of hers made the most snide and horrid comments when he stepped into the drawing room.
This time, children were present. Plump little faces
looked up at him from their books and games with
sullen expressions. They did not seem pleasant.

Her brother reluctantly took his damned issue of

*The London Times* and the rest of the family into another room, only at Knightly's request that he and Annabelle might have some privacy.

The man did not seem the slightest bit curious why his unmarried sister might wish to have a private audience with a gentleman. Really, he ought to have pulled him aside to ask his intentions. That he did not was a black mark in Knightly's book, even though it was to his own benefit.

He needed to take her away from this house, the awful relatives and uncomfortable furniture. He would install her in his town house. They'd make love each night. And during the day she'd easily be able to walk to the Mayfair homes of the other Writing Girls and the shops on Bond Street. She'd want for nothing.

Maybe he'd even marry her. The thought crossed his mind, and for the first time his heart didn't rebel.

Knightly was glad he'd brought flowers. Pink roses. She seemed like a pink roses kind of woman. She had told him that, at any rate. He'd waffled because Marsden had sent them to her. Knightly had no idea that the purchase of flowers for a woman was so fraught with peril.

"Annabelle," he said once they were alone. "Annabelle," he said, with urgency and lust and fear and restraint.

"Good afternoon, Derek," she said softly.

She smiled faintly, with just a slight curve to her lips. Her eyes seemed more gray than blue—he noticed those subtle distinctions now. Something was wrong. He knew it, because he knew her now.

"I'm sorry I didn't come sooner," he said.

"That's all right. You had quite a lot to do with

the paper. I understand," she said softly. Annabelle was always so understanding and generous. In this situation, any other woman would be hollering at him like a banshee. But Annabelle knew what this meant to him and let him have his moment. It was admirable of her—or was it too nobly self-sacrificing?

"I brought you flowers," he said, reduced to stating the bloody obvious. Good God, what did this woman do to him? He mastered tense negotiations, dealt with irate readers, and conducted interviews and interrogations eliciting all manner of incriminating confessions.

"Thank you," she said softly. She took the bouquet and inhaled deeply with her eyes closed, the pink buds casting a pink glow over her skin.

When she opened her eyes, they were still more gray than blue, more haunted than happy.

He exhaled impatiently, annoyed with himself. He should just treat this like a business negotiation in which the goal was to achieve a mutually satisfying outcome.

Yet he was dealing with a woman, with Annabelle . . . A confession of his feelings was in order, which was a problem because he didn't know how to make sense enough to explain them. Hoping she'd favor disorganized honesty rather than artfully arranged sentiments, he plowed ahead.

"Annabelle, about the other night . . ." he said, clasping her hands. "I can't stop thinking about it. About you. Now that I finally see you, I never want to close my eyes. I want to know you."

"Oh, Knightly," she whispered. Those haunted gray eyes were now slicked over with tears. Her eyelashes were dark, damp. Where those tears of joy? A man could hope, but he could not be sure.

Knightly felt as if he were thrust upon the stage on opening night, to perform in a play he had never watched or read. He didn't have a flair for the dramatic, or an ability to improvise.

He stated facts. That was all. He would state them now.

"I want you to live with me, Annabelle. And I want to save you from this awful household. You'll stay with me and spend your days with the Writing Girls and writing your advice column and we'll spend long nights together.

"That does sound lovely," she said, and he heard the *however* that was yet unspoken. And then she sighed—a sigh so laden with feeling that even he felt it deep in his bones. It was a sigh containing heartache, whispering of a cruel, cruel world, and suggestive of utter, unrelenting sadness.

She used to sigh with happiness when he walked into the room. Bewildered, he wondered when that had changed, and why.

"But I cannot." She said the words flatly.

She said no.

Annabelle said no.

For a second Knightly's heart stopped beating. Blood stopped circulating, air ceased to flow. He would have sworn that the earth stopped spinning. Even though he stood on firm ground, the sensation of falling stole over him. In this epic fall, he reached out for Annabelle but she pulled back her hand and turned away.

He stiffened all over, bit down hard. He had felt this before, years before, when he was thrown out of his own father's funeral. *Throw the bastard out. He doesn't belong here.* This feeling was a desperate, driving need to belong. It was abandonment and rejection from the one he needed approval from.

At this moment it was all the more devastating because he'd never expected it—she was Dear Annabelle intent on wooing him, the Nodcock. All of London knew this. All of London had cheered her on. This was her moment, and she refused it.

He had thought she'd throw herself into his arms and kiss him with love and gratitude. He never thought she would say no.

Worse, worse, a thousand times worse, he realized in this moment that he *wanted* her to say yes.

"Cannot or will not?" he asked sharply. His chest was tight. Breathing was impossible.

"I forced your hand, and that wasn't right," she explained in an anguished voice. "And now with this awful business at *The Weekly* . . ."

"Leave the paper out of this, Annabelle," he said roughly. He didn't want any favors or her idea of better judgment. His temper flared, and he didn't try all that hard to restrain the anger. He stepped closer to her, looming above her. There was no anguish in his voice when he said, "You made me notice you. You made me see, and now I can't stop thinking of you."

"I didn't realize the consequences!" she cried, stepping back. "And you *say* forget the paper, but you can't really mean it. I know you, Knightly. I know you better than anyone."

They were both thinking of how he'd rushed out and left her alone in the morning after making love to her. He had not forgotten the paper. It had been at the forefront of his mind even as a beautiful, naked woman who loved him was in his bed. After risking her life and her reputation and her everything to get there.

These facts revealed a brutal and unflattering truth.

"Knightly, you ought to marry Lady Lydia and have your newspaper and forget about me." She said this in such a small, pitiful voice. But he couldn't feel pity, not now.

Not when he only discovered what he'd lost as it was slipping away.

Like he hadn't appreciated sunlight until a month of gray skies and rain, he had the feeling a long, dark winter was only just beginning.

He was angry, and though it was petty and cruel, he needed her to know that.

"I can't stop thinking about you, Annabelle. You wanted my attentions, and now you have them and you're throwing it back in my face."

"I'm so sorry," she said. A few tears streamed down her cheeks. He wanted to kiss those tears away. Wanted to take her in his arms and hold her. They probably both wanted that. But she wouldn't allow it now, would she?

"That makes two of us," he said. With those parting words, he left.

# Chapter 40

### Woman Drowns in Own Tears (Almost)

*If you love something, set it free.*

*Some heartless and unfeeling person*

*Annabelle's attic bedroom*

**A**NNABELLE sat at her little writing desk, tears sliding forlornly down her cheeks. To her left, a bouquet of dead and dried pink roses. To her right, a fresh bouquet all luscious and fragrant. Before her was a sheet of paper and her writing things. She intended a reply to Lady Marsden. And she owed an explanation to London.

But her heart was too broken for her brain to even contemplate words and sentences.

Relinquishing Knightly and releasing him from any obligation to her was the right thing to do. She was certain of it.

But God, oh God, it hurt. Hurt like when they buried her parents, but worse, because Knightly was still living and breathing in the world. Probably hating her, too, which was not the passion she'd been trying to incite in him.

She could still vividly recall what it felt like to be held in his arms. She could still taste his kiss, and her body remembered what it was like to have him inside of her. To be wanted and possessed by him. It was . . . it was a kind of glory that could never be replaced. It was why she had refused Mr. Nathan Smythe from the bakery up the road. She had waited for this and it had been worth it.

Yet she refused him.

She was mad, utterly mad.

No, she was a Good Girl. She was Annabelle who always did the right thing, and who always put others before herself. Old Annabelle or New Annabelle, it was all the same. Her own happiness was the least of her concerns, especially when it came to what was right. Or what was best for Knightly.

She knew the truth: she had teased and tugged his affections from him. Could they ever be happy knowing that she conjured up love like a wicked sorceress? Could they ever be happy knowing that he had sacrificed his life's ambition of conquering the haute ton for marriage to a Spinster Auntie of no consequence?

Annabelle did not believe happiness was possible under such circumstances. She wanted true happiness.

Much as she loved him, she still loved and cherished herself, too. If she cared any less, she would have accepted his paltry offer. She would have sacrificed her body and soul to be his lover. She would be his little mistress who penned the cute advice

column until he tired of her or found a duke's sister
or an earl's daughter to marry.

So parted they must be, however much it might
hurt. Dear God, this hurt.

She'd made him notice her. But she didn't make
him love her.

# Chapter 41

## Breaking News: the Nodcock Finally Falls in Love

*Dear Annabelle,*

*We, the undersigned, think the Nodcock does not deserve you. Nevertheless, we wish that he would come to his senses and love you.*

*Penelope from Piccadilly (and two hundred additional signatures)*

**S**HE made him want her.

She giveth and she taketh away. He wanteth.

He didn't know . . . didn't know . . . until it was gone, all gone.

Last night the wind had blown, knocking a branch against the glass and rattling the windowpanes. The alacrity with which he dashed out of bed and leapt to the window was mortifying when it was all too clear that Annabelle wasn't there, awaiting his rescue. It was just the wind, and he'd suffered from an extreme case of wishful thinking.

He drank, as a man is wont to do when confronted with his innermost emotions, particularly ones pertaining to the heart.

He threw himself into work but found no joy in it, not even when *The Weekly*'s rebellious version outsold all others. Another sales record had been reached. His mantra, *scandal equals sales*, had once again proven to be gold, pure gold. The milestone passed, uncelebrated.

There were rumors he would be arrested. He didn't give a damn.

When it came time for the weekly writers' meeting, Knightly strolled in, taught and tense and determined to show no emotion.

"Ladies first," he said with what he hoped was a good approximation of a grin. He glanced around the room, fighting and losing the battle of where his focus would reside. His gaze landed on Annabelle.

She wore one of the Old Annabelle dresses, a drab frock in a particularly dull shade of grayish brown. The cut and fit of the dress did her no favors. He could say that now because he knew the long, lithe legs hidden under those skirts. He knew the gentle taper of her waist, the flare of her hips, and the perfect swells of her breasts.

It was all hidden away behind a sackcloth disguised as a dress.

The sight of her still took his breath away. He felt a hot, tortured flare of longing.

He saw her shoulders roll forward as she clasped her hands in her lap. Her eyes were downcast. It was the posture of Overlooked Annabelle.

She no longer wanted him to notice her, did she?

Yet she sighed when he walked in; his every nerve was attuned for this one small indication that she still cared. It was vitally important that she still cared.

The meeting progressed. Knightly acted as if nothing had ever occurred between him and Annabelle. His pride was on the line here, his reputation amongst his staff. He was Mr. London Weekly Knightly—cool, reserved, ruthless, and inscrutable. He would be damned, *damned*, if they knew he had been laid low by a woman.

However, he could not ignore her. After the other Writing Girls had mentioned their stories for the week, he turned to Annabelle and fixed her with the Knightly stare. She shrank back a little more. His head lifted higher.

"Dear Annabelle, what's the latest from your column?" He fought to keep any emotion from his voice. His anger, though, started to fade with every glance of her blue eyes.

"I don't think I've written about etiquette enough recently, particularly the proper use of fish knives," she said.

The room fell silent. Nervous glances were exchanged.

"Bugger etiquette and the cutlery. What happened with the Nodcock?" This came from Grenville, of all people. Grumpy old, Parliament-obsessed *Grenville*.

Every head swiveled in the direction of *The London Weekly*'s resident grouch. Julianna's jaw dropped open. Alistair coolly lifted one brow. Sophie and Eliza were grinning, and Owens looked up from his notes, shocked.

"What? I'm the only person here who read Annabelle's Adventures in Love?" Grenville asked gruffly. "Anyone who claims not to have done so is a liar."

"We're all agog that you are interested in something other than . . . Parliament. Something . . . human," Julianna sputtered.

"I'm not dead, am I? I can appreciate Annabelle's low-cut bodices as much as the next bloke." One of the ladies gasped.

"Grenville," Knightly said in a warning tone. She was not to be spoken of thusly, not in his presence.

"I liked New Annabelle and her crazy schemes," Owens said affectionately. He smiled at her, but she didn't see it, as her gaze was studiously fixed upon the tabletop. "She's got that mixture of sweetness and wickedness, if that makes sense. She's funny."

"She wore much better dresses," Alistair added, and he glanced at the grayish brown gown with a wince.

"I'm right here," Annabelle said. But she was Overlookable Annabelle today so her voice lacked any force or volume, and she didn't carry herself in a way that compelled one's attention. It was remarkable to witness. In fact, it was all too clear now how she had escaped his noticed all those years. From the softness of her voice to the quickly averted gazes, Annabelle hadn't made herself known.

"I for one want a conclusion to the story," Grenville said. "Even if it turns out the Nodcock is just that. Or worse."

Knightly bit his tongue. The fellow writers heartily agreed, yet they all carefully avoided looking in his direction.

"The story is over," Annabelle said, this time with a little more force.

All heads swiveled to look at *him*—not her, but him!

At that moment a horrifying truth became clear:

every single one of them had known of Annabelle's infatuation with him, and had for years.

All those weeks when Annabelle had sighed and he'd carried on, utterly oblivious, they had known.

All those weeks when Annabelle tried her "crazy schemes," they had been waiting and watching for him to finally, *finally* notice her.

He truly was the last person in London to know. He deserved this torture of having glimpsed her, and lost her.

"It ought to have a happy ending." This came from Owens, to his surprise. What the devil did a rough and brash young reporter care about happy endings? But even Knightly couldn't miss the affectionate glance that Owens gave Annabelle. It seemed New Annabelle had earned his affections, too.

"Happy endings equals sales?" Julianna offered.

"It's up to Annabelle, is it not?" Knightly challenged.

"Only a nodcock would think that," Grenville stated, punctuated with a *harrumph*. Heads nodded all around.

Knightly glanced at Annabelle looking all wistful and forlorn and heartsick and wearing the most god-awful gown he'd ever laid eyes upon. Old Annabelle was present today: quiet and shy and desperately trying to be overlooked.

Oh, but he knew a different version of Annabelle, who climbed trees at midnight and kissed him like every kiss meant something beautiful and something true, like it was the first time and the last time all at once. That New Annabelle had wrapped her lithe legs around him as he buried himself in her.

She went out on a limb for him, in more ways than one.

New Annabelle had transfixed him, bewitched him.

But she couldn't quite shake Old Annabelle, could she? But was that such a bad thing?

She impressed him with the way she walked steadily and kindly through life, even though more often than not the world didn't spare a second thought for her. He finally saw that Annabelle gave, gave, gave, and asked for nothing in return. She offered thoughtful advice to complete strangers, minded those brats, and slaved away at domestic drudgery.

Annabelle, who could contain oceans of emotion in a little sigh. Who had every reason to be bitter, yet imbued everything with such sweetness and hope.

Annabelle, so often overlooked.

Oh, he saw her now. Did he ever.

Suddenly, he couldn't breathe. The truth hit hard like that.

That was one amazing woman, sitting there, making herself invisible. She was kind, beautiful, generous, daring, and funny. She possessed the courage to ask for help and to share her triumphs and embarrassments with the whole city. She possessed the strength to do the right thing even when it was the hard thing. He could see that now.

At that moment Knightly fell completely in love with Annabelle.

# Chapter 42

### What Would Dear Annabelle Do?

OVERHEARD

*When I find myself in times of trouble, I ask, "What would Annabelle do?"*

*Overheard in a coffeehouse*

*Galloway's Coffeehouse*

**K**NIGHTLY loved her. The thought would not leave, but he didn't exactly wish it away either. The question of his intentions regarding this newly discovered love was another matter entirely.

"You ought to brace yourself for the mob, Knightly," Drummond said grimly. According to Drummond, hurting Annabelle was a crime punishable by a slow and painful death by medieval torture instruments.

Knightly didn't want to hurt her, he wanted to love her.

"When did the whole damn world fall in love with Annabelle?" he wondered aloud. How did he miss this?

"I ought to plant you a facer for even asking that

question," Drummond said. "She's a bloody delightful chit and she writes for your paper. How did you not see this unfolding?"

"You ought to have seen it before anyone else," Gage said. "Do you even edit the paper or just lord over it?" he, smirking.

"Until just recently she wasn't exactly clamoring for my attention and I had my sights set elsewhere," Knightly answered. He knew now that she hadn't let him see her. It was fascinating the way she could blend into the background at will, and even more amazing that she had launched herself into the spotlight.

"Now that's a different matter. More interesting," Drummond mused, sipping his coffee and staring pointedly at Knightly.

"By interesting he means feel free to elaborate," Gage explained.

"Annabelle inconveniences everything I had planned for myself," Knightly confessed. "I was going to marry some aristocratic woman and take my place in society. I had even contracted an informal betrothal. An understanding, at any rate. Everything was just in reach. But I did not plan for Annabelle."

"Change your plans," Gage said with a shrug.

"This is not a matter of what to do on a Tuesday evening, Gage," Knightly retorted. "One does not give up lifelong plans on a whim."

"Are you calling Annabelle a whim?" Drummond challenged, as he deliberately rolled up the sleeves of his shirt and folded his hand into a fist.

"Look, you can drop the Protector and Defender

of Annabelle act," Knightly retorted. That was his job. Or it ought to be.

"I don't think I can. Not while you're still acting like a nodcock," Drummond said with a smirk. Knightly fought the urge to wipe the smug look right off his face in a violent manner.

"I'll never forgive her for that name," he muttered instead.

"I love it," Gage said, grinning. "Nodcock."

"At any rate, Annabelle no longer wants me," Knightly said plainly. Drummond's reply was awfully succinct.

"Bullshit," he said.

"No, really. She told me to marry Lady Marsden to save the paper. After all she did to get my attentions, and she just drops me at the slightest obstacle."

"You're in love with her, aren't you?" Drummond questioned. His expression warned Knightly to answer carefully.

Knightly shrugged and sipped his coffee. It was tantamount to a confession.

"It's about time," Gage said. "Nodcock."

"What am I to do while she has these stupid ideas of noble self-sacrifice?" Knightly asked. If they were such geniuses, let them figure it out. His only idea was to have a reasonable, logical conversation with Annabelle where he would present the facts: they loved each other, they should marry, and it would be pleasing to them both. However, even he knew more romance and more theatrics were needed.

*Drama is for the page.*

Not anymore.

"Funny you should ask that," Drummond began

grandly. "Because lately, when I find myself in a quandary, I merely ask myself, 'What would Annabelle do?' I find it's really the only guiding principle I need."

"Hmm," Knightly said. He took another sip of his coffee.

What would Annabelle do?

More to the point, what *did* Annabelle do when she wanted to attract his affections?

Knightly's lips tugged into a slight smile before breaking into a full grin—because she had left very detailed and explicit directions. She lowered her bodice. Tried sultry glances. Left something behind. Employed a rival. Fainted into his arms. Climbed into his window at midnight.

Annabelle, in her infinite faith in the universe and unshakable optimism, would *try* no matter how risky or scary. She literally would go out on a limb for those she loved.

Suddenly, his course of action was clear. He was going to win Annabelle's affections back. And he was going to employ all the tricks she had.

# Chapter 43

### Fashion Alert from *The London Weekly*

*Offices of* The London Weekly

**A**NNABELLE could not stop staring at Knightly. That was nothing new. What was new, however, was that he was not wearing a cravat, nor was his shirt done up all the way to his neck as it ought to be. In spite of fashion and respectability, he wore his shirt open, exposing a vee of his chest.

It was distracting, to say the least.

She had kissed him there, pressing her lips to his hot skin, tasting him. She remembered as if it was only last night. Funny how the memory brought back all those sensations. She had tried so hard to put those thoughts aside, at morning, at night, during the day, in meetings. Anytime, really.

She had done the right thing in refusing him. She knew this in her heart and her mind. But her body craved him nonetheless.

"Did you see that Knightly did not wear his cravat today?" Julianna asked as they strolled through *The Weekly*'s offices on their way outside.

"Is it a new fashion, Sophie?" Eliza inquired of their fashion-forward friend.

"Not that I'm aware of. And not one that my husband would ever follow, however enticing it may be," Sophie replied. "Not that I am enticed by Knightly."

"Annabelle, surely you must have noticed," Julianna said. All three paused and turned to peer at her. She fought valiantly to keep the blush from betraying her.

Of course she had noticed. She had been riveted. If she were faced with a firing squad that had been instructed to hold its fire only *if* she could relate one item of discussion from that meeting, she would meet her death thinking only of the small amount of Knightly's exposed skin that she had once kissed and caressed during the most glorious night of her entire life.

But Annabelle did not say anything of the kind. It hurt too much to dwell upon it, and she couldn't fathom speaking of it. Plus, they stood near the open doorway to Knightly's office where he sat at his desk, writing. A lock of dark hair fell into his eyes. She folded her hands in her skirts to restrain herself from strolling in and brushing it aside.

He might look up, tug her into his lap, lower his mouth to hers . . .

"Annabelle?" Sophie said curiously. "Are you all right?"

"I'm sure he was merely warm," Annabelle replied. "Or perhaps the cloth had come undone and his valet was not present to attend to him."

Jenkins, his valet, who was paid to be inscrutable. Oh, must she know all these details about him? She had collected them carefully over the years, and months and weeks and days, never knowing how the knowledge would torture her.

KNIGHTLY had overheard them, and he dropped his head into his hands. He resisted the urge to pound his head against the desktop.

"Oh, Annabelle," he muttered. The sweet girl was utterly oblivious to his scheme—thus far. For the first time he had a hint of what Annabelle must have felt every time she sighed or blushed and he didn't notice: utter frustration. Enormous, enraging, frustration. Wanting to howl frustration. She was amazing, that Annabelle.

With a weary sigh of his own, Knightly reached into the top drawer of his desk, where he kept among other things—a loaded pistol, a flask of brandy, pens, important papers, and a list of every trick she had employed in order to gain his attention and affection.

He crossed *Lowered bodice—or the male approximation* off the list.

# Chapter 44

### Gentleman Shows Shocking Disregard for Attire

THE MAN ABOUT TOWN

*It seems that Mr. Knightly's courtship of Lady Marsden*
*has concluded—without a betrothal announcement.*
The London Times

*Offices of* The London Weekly

THE following week, Annabelle dragged her heart-broken and forlorn self to the regular gathering of writers because really, she thought, she did not suffer enough.

Blanche had been especially keen on haranguing her lately, for the parlor wasn't dusted thoroughly, she said, or she couldn't see her reflection in the silver. Fleur had become exceptionally moody, prone to fits and sulks that left the entire household walking on eggshells. Watson and Mason were constantly at odds, which meant a racket the entire household had to endure, compounded by Blanche's fishwife shrieks requesting silence. Brother Thomas continued to read *The London Times*.

Annabelle sought refuge in her attic bedroom,

where she was faced with letters from readers livid at her handling of "the Nodcock situation." She read them all and desperately wished to explain that it was all a misunderstanding. That she had made a noble sacrifice. That they were hurting her feelings, and to what end?

She had been overlooked before but she had never been so cruelly criticized.

*You made a mistake and you will rue the day you threw his proposal into his face*, wrote Harriet from Hampstead Heath.

*You're a cruel, heartless woman. How do I cancel my subscription?* wrote Angry in Amersham.

*My sympathies had been with you and now they are with the Nodcock, you wanton hussy*, wrote some coward who hadn't dared sign a name.

Had she made a mistake? She thought about it and shed copious amounts of hot, salty tears and thought some more (and in all honesty wept more, too). In the end she concluded that she had done the right thing, despite the furious letters. It was love under false pretenses—if at all—and it wasn't acceptable.

She had waited far too long to settle for anything less than true, eternal love.

The Writing Girls had discussed it over a strong pot of black tea and ginger biscuits.

"I think you might be absolutely mad," Julianna had told her. "But that is always what they say of the most courageous."

"I think she is very wise and noble in her actions," Sophie said. "Especially as she was so swept up in the throes of passion."

"You did the right thing, Annabelle," Eliza said, patting her hand consolingly. "He'll come around."

"And if not . . . ?" Annabelle asked. She tried to lift one brow and couldn't manage it. She'd taken to practicing that in front of the mirror and had about as much luck as she did with the sultry gazes. Which is to say, no luck at all. Curses.

They hadn't a reply for that, which was not reassuring in the slightest.

*Would it really be the end of the world if Knightly never truly loved her?*

Yes, she concluded. It was one thing to be a Spinster Auntie to Wretched Relatives, but to do so after knowing, for one night, the most exquisite and glorious passions and the heart-stopping, breathtaking, soul-shattering touch of a devastatingly handsome man? Returning to the dull lonely life of Old Annabelle was unbearable.

Nevertheless, Annabelle endured, because that is what Annabelle did.

Thus she attended meetings even as they were now a particular kind of torture because of the pleasure she had known and forgone.

There was never any thought of giving up her writing, though. Other people's problems distracted her from her own. And it felt good to help other people use the right fork, address a countess properly, find new uses for vinegar, or solve a spat between sisters. With her writing, she made other people happier, and someone ought to be happy, if it wouldn't be her.

The writers had all gathered, waiting. Knightly always made it a point to arrive last. Outside, wind rattled the windowpanes. There was a low rumble of thunder in the distance. The air was positively electric.

Knightly strolled in.

"Ladies first," he said with a grin. She didn't sigh because she was distracted by something particularly wicked in his grin today. She saw a certain light in his eyes. It went without saying she knew all the sparks and dimensions of Knightly's gaze.

Annabelle sat up straighter.

A meeting progressed in which nothing remarkable happened, or so Annabelle assumed. Her attention had been drawn to the exposed vee of Knightly's chest. Once again he was eschewing fashion and modesty and not wearing a cravat. How positively scandalous.

It put her in mind of that night. That one glorious night. She clasped her hands in her lap.

About halfway through the meeting he slowly shrugged out of his jacket. That night he'd allowed his shirt to slide off his shoulders, down his muscled arms and falling to the floor, exposing the broad expanse of his chest. Today he set the jacket on the chair and carried on with the meeting wearing nothing but his shirtsleeves and a waistcoat that highlighted how his chest tapered from his broad shoulders to his waist . . . and lower.

Annabelle's cheeks flamed at her wicked thoughts of Knightly, naked. She bit her lip, hard.

Of course he took his jacket off, she thought; the temperature seemed to have spiked ten degrees. Yet when she glanced around, no one else seemed bothered. Sophie even pulled her shawl tighter around her. She ought to see a doctor about that, for she herself was just about burning up.

Knightly stretched his arms, and she could have sworn she saw the ripple of muscles under the thin white linen of his shirt. Her mouth went dry. She was suddenly parched.

She missed him. Oh, did she ever. She missed his voice and his smile and discovering the real Mr. Knightly. She missed his touch and a whole lot of very unladylike things.

Knightly rolled up the sleeves on his shirt, exposing his forearms. Good Lord, she was now all agog over his arms. Who was the Nodcock now? But those arms had held her—no one else ever held her. Those arms had pulled her close and made her feel loved and cherished, if only for one night. She decided then and there that Knightly would be the only man to know her thus. No matter what happened, there would be no one else.

The heat increased, her skin felt feverish. She was certain her cheeks were pink and that everyone would know she was thinking such wanton thoughts.

Perhaps she did make a mistake. Perhaps she had been too picky and particular about the exact proper circumstances in which love ought to happen. It was a wild thing, wasn't it? Who was she to impose all the rules and strictures on love?

The meeting concluded and Knightly walked out. She felt the loss intensely as she watched his retreating form while still stuck in her chair.

The other writers trickled out and Sophie dawdled gathering her things. The Writing Girls chattered about society gossip and the latest Paris fashions and other things Annabelle was only paying half a mind to.

In the distance thunder rumbled again. It would rain. Perhaps that would cool her heated skin. But even the thought of cool raindrops tumbling on her scorching skin made her breath hitch. She had become far too sensitive lately.

And then Knightly returned.

"I forgot my jacket," he drawled, leaning in the doorway. She fought hard for a gulp of air. God, she loved it when he leaned like that. Her mouth went dry. Words eluded her.

"Oh, goodness, is that the time!" Sophie said. "I have an appointment with the modiste." Annabelle was too tongue-tied to point out that she hadn't even looked at a timepiece.

"Yes, I promised Roxbury . . ." Julianna said, hot on Sophie's heels as they pushed past Knightly.

"Wycliff is expecting me . . ." Eliza said, and she too followed the others out of the room, leaving Annabelle and Knightly alone. Quite alone.

"Hello, Annabelle." His voice was low, and it sent shivers up and down her spine. Goodness, she had better steel herself if he only had to say *Hello, Annabelle* and she nearly went to pieces. She'd do well to remember that he was probably going to marry lady Lydia to save his newspapers.

But she had to reply to his hello; it would be rude not to. Annabelle, both Old and New, was nothing if not polite.

"Hello." Her voice had never sounded so breathless, as if she had dashed through Hyde Park with a vile seducer and nefarious murderer in hot pursuit.

"How are you?" he asked. The question was politeness itself, and yet he managed to imbue each word with a hint of wickedness.

"I'm fine, thank you. And yourself?" she replied politely. Young ladies were polite. Young ladies also did not imagine handsome partially clad men closing the door and ravishing them upon the tabletop. Oh very well, this one did. What had become of her?

"Oh, I'm good. Very good," he said, sounding wicked, very wicked. She longed to fan herself.

"Good," she echoed, as her brain was not up to the task of forming complex thoughts or sentences. It was still focused on him, leaning, against the doorway. She could see the muscles of his chest outlined through the thin fabric of his shirt. That vee of exposed skin taunted her, begged for her to touch. With her mouth.

"Might you need someone to escort you home?" he inquired.

The words were polite, but delivered in such a wicked way. And how torturous would it be to find herself in an enclosed carriage with him for the long ride to Bloomsbury whilst rain lashed at the windows, and the air was so electrified, and when he had mischief in his eyes?

Annabelle could not conceive of a greater torment. Other than his marriage to Lady Lydia. She ought to remember that. She ought not to think of all the privacy his carriage afforded, those plush velvet seats . . .

"I don't think so. Why?" she replied suspiciously.

"Because your fellow Writing Girls just left in quite a hurry," he said. "Which makes me think you may require alternate means of transport."

"I'll just walk," she replied, as if it were really no bother at all. As if Bloomsbury weren't on the far side of London. But really, how was she to restrain herself if she were alone with him and when he was looking especially sinful in a very seductive way, and when she knew how it felt to kiss him as if her soul's salvation depended upon it? Her soul suddenly felt in desperate need of salvation.

The thunder rumbled again. The wind rattled the windowpanes again, darkness drenched the city, and the rain now began in earnest, slapping against the windows.

"Really? You will walk from Fleet Street to Bloomsbury in the driving rain?" Knightly asked skeptically.

"Given the weather, I might hire a hack," she replied. "I am nothing if not sensible."

"Yes, hired hacks are a-plenty when it is raining," he said, which was of course utter nonsense. She thought he really ought to pick her up, sling her over his shoulder, and just be done with it, if he was so intent upon taking her home in his carriage. Her protest would be halfhearted, at best.

Clearly, she was doomed.

"I shall manage," she said, because that's what she did best: she managed to get by. Managed to restrain her passions. Managed to be polite when she wanted to act with outrageous impropriety. She excelled at managing.

"Come with me, Annabelle," he said in a low voice. He was leaning, and he smiled at her. He reached out, clasping her hand in his. The thunder rumbled and the rain picked up and, really, how could she say no?

# Chapter 45

## Love, Restrained. Alas.

THE carriage ride with Knightly progressed exactly as she expected. It was a slow, sensual torture that tested her resolve. The velvet upholstery was soft under her bare fingertips. The rain lashed gently at the carriage windows, which became opaque with steam from the interior warmth of the carriage. The wheels clattered over the cobblestones, and the conveyance swayed in a gentle, rhythmic motion.

*Love under false pretenses was not love at all*, she reminded herself.

Even in the short jaunt from the door of *The Weekly* offices to the door of the carriage, Knightly managed to become drenched in the rain. With his jacket open, his white shirt now clung to his skin, revealing every outline of his sculpted muscles. Annabelle *managed* to steal only a few sly glances, which she prayed he didn't notice in the dim interior of the carriage.

Did other women lust after men like this? It wasn't exactly the conversation of polite or mixed company. Perhaps it would make a good topic for her column . . . if she was feeling wicked.

At this moment she was feeling wicked.

But determined to be good.

She did not want Knightly by hook or by crook.

*Keep telling yourself that, Annabelle,* a cruel voice in her head taunted.

Raindrops clung to his black eyelashes and then dropped off to roll down his impossibly high cheeks. She was struck by the strange desire to lick them . . . before she kissed him and tasted raindrops warmed from his lips.

Oh, for Lord's sake, Annabelle, she thought to herself.

She folded her hands primly on her lap, interweaving her fingers and clasping her palms together so she might not be tempted to touch anything. Be. Good. She would Be Good. She would make polite conversation so that she might be distracted from lusty thoughts of sitting on his lap rather than properly on the opposite seat.

"How goes the scandal with *The Weekly*?" she asked. Politely.

"We covered that in the meeting, Annabelle," he said, smirking, as if the blasted man knew she hadn't been paying the slightest attention all along. How mortifying.

"My apologies. I must have been woolgathering," she replied primly.

"I noticed," he said in a seductive tone that made

her heart skip a beat. "What was on your mind, Annabelle?"

*Licking you. Kissing you. The insane feeling of your hands on my skin. Every sensation from the one night we spent together.*

"Chores. For Blanche," Annabelle lied, shamelessly. Some things were just not said aloud, not even by Bold Annabelle.

"Why do you stay there?" Knightly asked. She wasn't surprised by the question. She could always tell it was on the verge of being voiced by her friends and those who were aware of how her family treated her.

"I have nowhere else to go," she answered with a shrug. It wasn't quite the truth, but she didn't know how to explain the real reason. Because they had almost committed her—a shy, gangly girl of just thirteen—to the workhouse or some other employment where she would have never survived. She worked for her own family instead, *grateful* to have been spared a worse fate.

"That's not true," he said softly. She winced, recalling his offer for her to reside with him—but as his mistress or his pet or his plaything. Not even Old Annabelle would sell herself so short. "I'm sure any one of your friends would and could take you in."

"I would hate to impose on them. Besides, I am needed there, which makes me feel useful. And they are my family. One ought to devote themselves to their family."

"All very good reasons," he said, then he leaned forward, looked deeply into her eyes. "They don't appreciate you, Annabelle."

"I know," she said, even adding a little shrug. Oh,

she knew. But having lost some family, she clung to those she had left. Even if it was Thomas, the most inattentive brother in Christendom, and his harridan of a wife. Annabelle couldn't say those words aloud, and it was bittersweet that she didn't have to with Knightly. He saw. He knew.

"Do you not feel the same way with your half brother?" she asked, turning the tables on him. "As much as he may scorn you, he is still your family. And people tend to stick with their families, for better or for worse."

"He doesn't," Knightly said flatly, and that was the end of that conversation. She refused to feel badly about introducing a sensitive topic, because after all, she had already lost him. She had nothing left to lose.

The silence, however, would not do.

"Well, how is the scandal?" she asked.

"There are rumors I may be arrested," Knightly said, uttering such devastating words as easily as one might say *There are rumors it is going to be cloudy tomorrow.*

"Arrested?" Annabelle gasped.

The carriage rolled to a stop in front of her home. What wretched timing.

She rubbed the steam away from the windows and peeked out. There was a rustle at the drapes in the drawing room window. Blanche was likely watching.

"Oh look, here we are," Knightly remarked lightly, as if he had not just mentioned such an awful fate looming. "Come, I shall walk you to your door."

They dashed madly through the downpour, arm in arm from the carriage to the front door. They stood under the porch, seeking its small refuge as rain tumbled down around them. His eyes were dark in the gray light, but they were locked upon hers.

It was a moment in which every breath, every gaze, was laden with depth and passion and vexing words unsaid. She recognized it from novels. She recognized it because she was living it in this real, heart-pounding moment.

Annabelle tilted her head up to his, and she knew her lips parted, practically begging for his kiss. To be fair, it seemed like he might kiss her. He brushed a wet strand of her hair away from her eyes, his knuckles gently grazing her cheek. His eyes never looked away from hers.

But he didn't kiss her. She'd have sworn that he wanted to. And yet—

"Goodbye, Annabelle," he said in his sultry voice. She stood there in the rain and watched him walk away. There was a swagger in his walk, and that, with the mischief she'd seen in his eyes, made her wonder just what Knightly was up to.

# Chapter 46

## The Arrest

*Dear Annabelle . . .*
*Unfinished letter on the desk of Derek Knightly*

*Knightly's Mayfair town house*

It had been impossible to not touch her. He wouldn't allow himself, much as he wanted to, as part of the seduction. *Leave her wanting more.* Hadn't that been one of the schemes? Knightly knew now that however much he'd been tortured by her tricks, she must have suffered mightily in the execution. Seduction, and the willpower required for it, was no walk in the park.

Such were his thoughts as he wandered from one room to the next. He paused near the fire in the drawing room and leaned against the gray marble mantel. Annabelle, dear Annabelle. He craved her touch and ached to caress her so much that he feared his survival depended upon it. He wasn't sure he wanted to survive if he could not have her.

After that carriage ride in which they both suffered the torment of unrequited love, Knightly had allowed himself to brush one damp curl out of her eyes and indulged in the touch of her cheek, which set him afire. She had reduced him to that mere caress.

His desire for her had not been sated in the slightest by such a benign touch. In fact it only inflamed more, as he was reminded of the softness of her skin. Of how he had once touched her all over, and where no one had ever touched her. Not even Annabelle herself. That he knew of. God, that thought made him hard.

Nevertheless, he continued to stroll from the drawing room across the marble floor of the foyer, into the dining room with its mahogany dining table polished to a high shine. He stared at his brooding reflection in the extremely well-polished silver tureen. An oil painting over the mantel depicted a nude woman at her bath; he thought of Annabelle.

Usually, he felt pride in his home. It was the physical manifestation of his success—and of his bachelorhood. No womanly touches like a half-finished embroidery or fragile little knickknacks made the place seem welcoming.

The house felt downright cold. Yes, it was a rainy night. But fires were blazing in every fireplace in every room. The building seemed cold and empty because Annabelle wasn't here to fill it up with her sighs and laughter and kisses and death-defying escapades and just . . . her.

Annabelle, he wanted Annabelle. Needed her. Craved her.

He understood now why she had to say no to his lust-driven proposal that she move into this museum of a house and become his mistress at his convenience. He had asked her only to share his bed and be around for his comfort. She deserved so much more. She knew that, and he was glad of that.

He knew that now. He needed so much more of her now.

Loss will do that to a man; it'll make him realize what he's missing in a really damned painful way. Since he did not lose, he had embarked on that courtship to win her back.

But hell, it was slow going. He wondered how she had endured for all those years and months and weeks and days. He'd only been at this game of seduction and loving trickery for a fortnight and already his nerves were frayed, his desire overwhelming, his patience worn to a delicate thread. Yet she had steadfastly loved him and patiently waited for *years*.

What a nodcock he'd been. Perhaps he could even forgive her for that unfortunate name. Surely, he deserved worse, and he cursed himself. He definitely deserved this torture of wanting and waiting. Even worse, he knew exactly what he was missing. Intimately.

Knightly pressed his forehead against the cool glass windowpane of his second-story drawing room, overlooking the garden and the tree Annabelle had recklessly climbed.

A pounding at the front door echoed ominously through the house. He idly wondered who bothered to go out on such a god-forsaken night as this. Wilson, the butler, would see to it.

Annabelle? His heartbeat quickened.

No, those were not Annabelle's footsteps he heard

thudding in the marble-floored hall and pounding up the stairs. No, that was the sound of an army; of heavy boots; of men on a mission.

The door burst open, splintering the wood and slamming into the plaster wall. Knightly turned slowly to face the intruders. As if he had all the time in the world. As if he couldn't be bothered to hurry.

"You might have just tried the doorknob. Or knocked," he remarked dryly.

"That doesn't make quite the same impression, now does it?" Lord Marsden drawled. He stood in the doorway, legs apart and arms folded over his chest.

"I'm not intimidated, if that's the effect you sought," Knightly said. He took a small sip of brandy, savoring what would surely be his last taste of the stuff for some time.

"I'm only just beginning," Marsden remarked. And then without even looking, he barked out an order to the officers standing in formation behind him: "Arrest him."

"On what grounds?" Knightly inquired as his hands were shackled with cold metal cuffs behind his back. The glass of brandy had tumbled to the floor, staining the Aubusson carpet.

"Good old libel," Marsden said. "We're taking you to Newgate."

"Splendid. I've heard such great things," Knightly remarked.

"Now you can confirm the rumors," Marsden said, and he sounded happy, too damned happy, to have captured Knightly on such unimaginative charges and to have him carted off to Newgate like some common criminal. Knightly would take the arrest and the imprisonment, but he wouldn't let Marsden get the last word or fully enjoy the moment.

"Wilson," he called to his butler as they led him away, "see to the door and the carpet. Make sure that the invoice for repairs is sent to Lord Marsden, although I'm not sure that he can afford it."

# Chapter 47

### An Exclusive Report from the Confines of Newgate

*Newgate*

THE prison was as dank and disgusting as the stories led one to believe, including those *The London Weekly* had published. Eliza once spent two days in its confines, only to dramatically reenact Mad Jack's outrageous escape. The thought did cross Knightly's mind—he had *plenty* of time for thoughts to cross his mind—but while it would lead to an improvement in his lodgings, it would only delay the inevitable. Plus, given the schemes he had enacted, he might as well plan to stay awhile.

"You have to keep the paper going," he told Owens, who had come to visit as soon as word of the arrest and imprisonment reached him.

"I don't suppose we humbly offer apologies, etcetera, etcetera?" Owens dared to ask in a tone belying that he knew better.

"Have you suffered a head injury?" Knightly retorted.

"I'm just testing your sense of humor," Owens replied. "What's the story here? What's the angle?"

"I'm already in prison. I am already facing trial. We might as well go for broke," Knightly said frankly. "I need to see Lady Marsden. And then I'll need to see Lady Roxbury. We have some scandalous secrets to expose."

"As we at *The Weekly* are wont to do," Owens said cheerfully. "Scandal equals sales."

"And then you'll have to bring me writing things, or I will have to dictate to you. There will be a letter from me, from prison. Won't that be something? And then I'm going to take over Dear Annabelle."

"What?" Owens jerked his head up in shock.

"Is she still writing that rubbish about table manners and whatnot?" Knightly asked. After her absolutely inspired campaign to win his attentions, she was now writing about the proper way to grasp a teapot while pouring a cup of a tea, and a thorough examination of the merits of adding sugar versus milk in one's tea.

"The Nodcock story seems to have met an unfortunate end, and now we're stuck with boring articles on tea parties," Owens said, with one hell of a fiery and bloodthirsty glare aimed at Knightly.

Knightly had no choice but to face the facts: (1) everyone had known of Annabelle's love for him, (2) Annabelle had many champions, (3) he was indeed a nodcock, and (4) those champions were sure as hell going to make sure he remembered that, which would be fine because (5) he was going to win her, and love her.

"To the contrary, Owens. The Nodcock story is about to get interesting," Knightly said with a grin.

# Chapter 48

### The Newspaper Must Go On

ACCIDENTS & OFFENSES

*A rock was thrown through the drawing room window
of Lord Marsden's Berkeley Square residence. A note
was attached that read, "Free Knightly."*

*The London Weekly*

*Offices of* The London Weekly

**T**HE writers of *The London Weekly* were called to
order. From Grenville to the penny-a-liners, they all
crowded into the meeting room to hear what Owens
had to say.

"Knightly has been arrested on charges of libel.
He's in Newgate," he told the group. There were audible gasps and murmured questions and a stunning array of expletives. Annabelle's heart stopped,
which made breathing or thinking or moving or
feeling impossible. Knightly. Arrested.

"Newgate!" Julianna exclaimed above all in obvious shock. Newgate was a horrible, filthy place, and
Annabelle's beloved Knightly was there, locked up
like a common criminal when he was anything but.

"What did you expect, that they'd take 'em to Buckingham Palace?" Grenville retorted. Julianna silenced him with a withering look.

"What are we going to do?" she demanded. "Obviously we must do something."

"I can help him escape," Eliza offered. "I did a series of articles on how to get out of Newgate. Which couldn't happen fast enough. The place is just awful."

"We're definitely going to reprint those stories," Owens said with a grin. "And we're definitely going to keep the paper going. As Knightly said, he's already in prison. We might as well go for broke."

"You saw him?" Annabelle asked. The words were out of her mouth before she thought to censor them for the moment and inquire discreetly later. Everyone quieted and turned to look at her. Everyone knew that her concern went far deeper than anyone else's.

"Aye," Owens said in a low voice.

"How is he?" she asked softly. There was no need to raise her voice, for the room had remained silent. Everyone already knew she loved him. Even Knightly knew it now.

"He's spoiling for a fight," Owens answered, which was to say that Knightly was fine and in good spirits. "Penny-a-liners, you know the drill. Find as much dirt on Marsden as you can, get details from the prison. Lady Roxbury, Knightly asked to see you."

"Me?" Julianna gasped.

"Yes, something about Lady Lydia," Owens said briskly. And then he winced when he realized what he'd said and who had heard it. Annabelle was the recipient of more than a few worried glances.

"What about Lady Lydia?" Annabelle asked, because she was free to ask these things now. But she voiced the question in a small, hollow voice. When she had meant that Knightly ought to marry Lady Lydia it was some vague idea. Some noble sacrifice to save the paper. But now the hour was upon them in which Knightly faced prison or marriage to a highborn woman.

She was going to lose. She had already lost him.

"He asked to see her," Owens said, looking very pained to deliver such news, and she was sorry to have put him in such a position. She wanted to reassure him, *Oh, it's all right. My heart is already broken.*

Instead she said, "Did he ask to see . . . anyone else?" Her desperation to know if he cared for her at all overrode her fear of speaking before a group.

Owens shook his head no. He looked sorry, and she felt ashamed for making him feel that way. But she'd had to know that when Knightly was in jail, he did not ask for her. If there were any questions lingering about how he felt about her, she now had her answer.

She was right to refuse him. This was proof, but she was not consoled in the slightest.

"What does one wear when paying a call to Newgate?" Julianna asked, changing the subject. It wasn't the best most tactful question, Annabelle thought, given the fact that Knightly had not asked for her. But it was the least of her troubles.

"Definitely your worst dress," Sophie answered.

Annabelle's imagination starting spinning awful stories of Knightly's imprisonment. She envisioned rats and mice scurrying about, nibbling on toes of dead prisoners. She imagined the wretched specimens of humanity moaning and groaning (she didn't know why, it just seemed like the thing). All of this, of course, occurring in a relentless darkness, broken only by shafts of gray light from narrow slits placed high in stone walls that were moist from the dampness.

This vivid vision made her shudder with revulsion.

Poor Knightly! Her heart ached for what torments he must have to endure as a Newgate prisoner, keeping company with thieves and murderers.

Poor Knightly indeed, she grumbled silently, asking for Lady Lydia to visit him and not requesting the same of her. Obviously he was going to propose to Lady Lydia. Marsden couldn't very well lock up the betrothed of his dearest sister. Some things were just not done.

Clever, she gave him that, even as her heart positively throbbed in agony.

She had done the right thing, Annabelle reminded herself for the thousandth time. If he was going to marry a woman just to get out of prison, then he was not a man capable of love. And she wanted love, all-consuming, outrageously passionate, fiery, and not-even-death-do-us-part love.

If she wanted anything less, she would have married Mr. Nathan Smythe from the bakery up the road. Though it looked like she might after all.

THE Writing Girls gathered at Sophie's house at the conclusion of the meeting to wait whilst Julianna immediately went to visit Knightly at Newgate.

"Annabelle, are you all right?" Eliza asked. Worry

was etched in her features. She reached out to clasp her hand.

No, Annabelle thought. No, I'm not all right and I'll never be again because I have lost the love of my life. I had a chance and I threw it away and now I must live with this regret until my dying day . . . But she bit back those overdramatic sentiments and said, instead: "I was when I first heard the news. But since he requested Lady Lydia . . . it is clear where his attentions are fixed."

"I wonder what that is about," Sophie said. "It seems strange that he would call for her. Unless it is to plead his case with her brother."

"He must be planning to propose to her, of course," Annabelle said matter-of-factly. She wondered if he had a ring. Or if would be on bended knee when he asked. Probably not in Newgate.

"What an awful proposal. I would refuse," Sophie said with a shudder.

"What if Brandon proposed to you in a prison?" Annabelle asked, rephrasing the question to include her beloved husband.

"Brandon would never find himself in prison. Unless it was to rescue someone," Sophie replied.

"Well Knightly was bound to be arrested," Eliza said frankly, and to murmurs of agreement. "I'm only surprised it has not happened sooner."

Annabelle frowned, annoyed, because she found there was something wild and exciting about a man who might be imprisoned. It meant he was bold, daring, adventurous, as if he could be a hero or a villain in equal measure.

*Do not feel affection for him*, she commanded herself. *He is probably proposing to another woman this very minute.*

But then she thought of how it must feel to be locked up and away. He would feel so frustrated with the lack of liberty, and that must drive him mad. Would he go mad?

No, because he would escape first. He would find a way out. Knightly always found a way to get just what he wanted.

*If only he wanted her . . .*

*No, she was done with that line of thinking—done! Now she was going mad herself, oh blast.*

He was going to marry Lady Lydia. It was the sensible thing to do. Would she be invited to the wedding? Would she have to smile while he recited vows to love and cherish another woman?

"Annabelle, are you all right? You look close to tears," Sophie said, peering closely at her.

Her eyes did feel the hot sting of tears starting, but she would *not* let them fall.

"Or like you're about to cast up your accounts," Eliza added with a cringing expression. Indeed, her stomach was in knots.

"What if he does marry Lady Lydia? What do I do?" Annabelle asked, and she did not even try to disguise the anguish in her voice.

She had spent her whole life waiting for a Grand, True Love. And since she met Knightly three years, eight months, one week, and three days ago, she had been waiting for that Grand True Love to blossom between them.

She could never love another, she was sure of it.

She had always just assumed that he would marry her and love her . . . eventually. For the first time, Annabelle honestly confronted the prospect of a lifetime—a bloody lifetime, for she was only six and twenty—without love, without Knightly. The prospect was bleak indeed.

A lifetime of Blanche's barbs and orders and snide remarks. Forever living in a household where she was merely tolerated because she served so selflessly.

A lifetime in which her brother—her own flesh and blood—ignored her and buried his face in *The London Times*—of all the newspapers in London, for Lord's sake.

A memory of one glorious night in which almost all of her secret wishes and dreams had come true . . . One night in which she was not only wanted, but loved . . .

After which followed a lifetime of remorse.

"You will be fine, Annabelle. You will be loved," Eliza said in a fierce whisper with an affectionate squeeze of her hand.

Annabelle didn't let go, even as Sophie and Eliza chattered on and she made an effort to follow their conversation about dresses and scandals and books they had read and Eliza's upcoming plans to travel to Timbuktu with her adventurous husband.

But Annabelle also watched the clock, awaiting Julianna's return. Watched it so intently that it seemed time would stop if she looked away. Finally, two hours, forty-nine minutes, and twenty-six seconds later, Julianna burst through the doors.

"You would not *believe* what I am now privy to," she exclaimed breathlessly. "Oh my Lord. Be still my throbbing heart. Fetch the smelling salts. Do you remember when I found Drawling Rawlings in that unfathomably scandalous barnyard position with the most unlikely of characters?"

Sophie, her face an expression of awe, replied: "The scene you described as, and I quote, 'The single most scandalous compromising position of your career, second to Roxbury's.' That one?"

"This is better," Julianna said with a broad grin. "Better even than unmasking the Man About Town. This is the biggest story of my career."

Annabelle supposed Knightly's Newgate proposal to Lady Lydia might be classified as that interesting.

"I know what happened during Lady Lydia's missing season! She related it to me directly. And Knightly has given me *orders* to print every last salacious detail!"

# Chapter 49

## A Most Scandalous Edition of *The London Weekly*

**LETTER FROM THE (IMPRISONED) EDITOR**
*London, prepare to be scandalized.*
*The London Weekly*

*The Swift Residence*

**T**HIS particular issue of *The London Weekly* became the most widely read and discussed issue of a newspaper in years. Many would mention it in the same breath as Thomas Paine's *Rights of Man* or the *Declaration of Independence* from the Colonies.

A typical issue of the paper might sell twelve thousand copies, with each one read by a few, then read aloud to many more. The issues in which Eliza revealed the exotic secrets of the man known as the Tattooed Duke in a column set sales records, as did Julianna's very public battle of words and wits with the rival gossip columnist, the Man About Town and her now-husband Lord Roxbury. But neither of those topped this one.

From prison, Knightly authorized the purchase of a new printing press to keep up with the demand.

Even from behind bars, *The London Weekly* plainly belonged to him. His touch, his vision, and his love was apparent in every line of type on this, the most scandalous issue of a newspaper ever printed.

How scandalous was it?

Even the Swift household possessed a copy. It was the second one ever to cross the threshold. (The first was the issue featuring Annabelle's debut column. Only that page remained carefully folded and tucked into a copy of a Jane Austen novel.)

Annabelle wasn't even the one to buy this particular issue. Thomas, a lifelong loyal reader of *The London Times*, brought it home the previous evening, muttering something about everyone at his cloth company offices reading it. It was not until breakfast that Annabelle was able to read it privately, after finding it discarded in the bin.

On the front page was a defiant letter from the editor displaying Knightly's razor sharp wit, slicing and shaping the facts to tell the story he wanted. She could hear it—his voice, strong and commanding and so self-assured—as if he stood behind her and read the words aloud.

She loved him, of course, and admired him because when the world turned against him, he stood proud. Even from the dankest of prisons he possessed wit, intelligence, defiance, and grace. It made her love him all the more.

Annabelle poured a cup of tea and sat at the breakfast table, alone, and began to read *The Weekly*.

LETTER FROM THE (IMPRISONED) EDITOR
*I write this from Newgate, where I am imprisoned on*

*charges of libel. When has it become a crime to print the truth?*

*Taxes keep the prices of newspapers high, in a deliberate attempt to keep information out of the hands of the common man and woman. Yet the coffeehouse culture flourishes, and newspapers are shared, thus ensuring the printed word will be read and discussed.*

*It is foolish to try to put a stop to this. But fools will persist in their madness, will they not?*

*It is a well-known but oft unspoken fact that the government pays newspapers for favorable reports and portrayals. The London Weekly never took a farthing. This publication is beholden to no one but the reading public.*

The London Weekly *has long brought you "accounts of gallantry, pleasure, and entertainment." It has also brought a level of equality and truth to the press. which has resulted in great success—and my imprisonment. I stand by every word in this paper, especially in this particular edition. London, prepare to be scandalized.*

Annabelle caught herself with a wicked, delighted grin. Her heart was racing. Who knew so much adventure and anticipation could be contained in a newspaper? Knightly did. Like thousands of others all over London at that very moment, she turned the page, eager to delve into more.

But unlike the rest of London, Annabelle felt a glow of pride that she *belonged* to this paper and was a part of something so daring and great. She, little old Annabelle Swift, was a beloved member of an exclusive club: the writers of *The London Weekly*. If nothing else . . . she had this triumph in her life.

If nothing else, Knightly was and would always be the man who gave her a rare chance to be more than a Spinster Auntie from Bloomsbury. For that alone, she thanked him and loved him and granted him her undying devotion.

On the second page, she found Julianna's masterpiece. Even though Julianna had breathlessly confessed every last detail, Annabelle still read the printed version. She knew that Owens and Knightly had gone through it to ruthlessly remove anything that would not be supported by fact. The story, so detailed and salacious, occupied the entire second page.

FASHIONABLE INTELLIGENCE BY A LADY OF DISTINCTION

*The mystery of Lady Lydia Marsden's missing season has been solved, and was related to this author by the lady herself. It involves a lover, of course, as all great gossip does. Like the fairy tales, there are unfathomably cruel relatives; lovers, separated; innocence lost. But will there be a happy ending?*

*Lady Lydia took a lover, a man hired to teach her the fine art of dancing. It has often been noted that she moved across ballrooms with an unparalleled grace; that she could waltz better than any debutante, that she possessed such a poised and regal bearing and knew by heart the steps to every dance, even the most obscure country reels. We now know why. Hours spent in practice, in the arms of a man she had come to love.*

*For years their love was expressed only in the hearted gaze of illicit lovers, or hours spent in each*

*other's arms as they danced across the ballroom of
Marsden house. In time, that was not enough . . .*

*Rumors soon surfaced of Lady Lydia's condition
after a particular incident in which she was discovered casting up her accounts in a potted fern during
a breakfast party.*

*A remarkably intrepid reporter from* The London
Times *sought confirmation of the lady's condition by
impersonating a physician (he now languishes in Newgate, awaiting trial). The lady in question was discovered to have been in a delicate condition. Her lengthy
stint in the country—the infamous missing second
season—did nothing to stifle rumors to that effect.*

*As one would imagine, the lady's brother was livid
to discover that his sister was not only with child, but
that the father was a lowborn dance instructor. Even
more vexing, these lovers imagined a happy life together with their child. This was not to be, alas. She
found herself locked in the tower of the country house;
her lover was banished and threatened with deporta-
tion to Australia should he dare to see his beloved.*

*And what of the child? A boy was born and smug-
gled to its father. They live in squalor. 'Tis not merely
a tale of a young woman's missing season, but of love
thwarted. The lesson to be gleaned from this? Love
knows no rules or class or boundaries. And, we hope,
that only fools stand in the path of true love.*

To hear the story related by a breathless Julianna
was one thing; it was quite another to read it in black
and white. It quite explained Lady Lydia's letter to
Dear Annabelle, and she breathed a sigh of relief at
the personal note she had included in her previous
column. She had encouraged Scandalously in Love,

otherwise known as Lady Lydia, to await true love. It had been the right thing to do.

But what could Knightly be about, printing this? Marsden was livid already. What purpose could this serve other than to provoke the man further? Did Knightly *want* to spend the rest of his days in Newgate?

The line of questioning was disturbed when something else caught her eye . . .

On the rightmost column of the page . . .

The headline DEAR ANNABELLE . . .

Usually her column appeared on page sixteen or seventeen, tucked behind all the serious and important news, but today it was prominently featured on page three. This was odd, as she hadn't turned in a particularly interesting article. She had answered Mrs. Crowley from Margate's question about the proper way to hold a teapot, she advised Mr. Chapeau from Blackfriars on which feather to decorate his hat, and settled a dispute between neighbors on who ought to sweep the sidewalk. In other words, it might have been one of her dullest columns to date.

Certainly nothing worthy of page three. Certainly nothing worthy of her portrait. What was her portrait doing in the paper? Owens must have put that in . . .

Intrigued, Annabelle began to read.

### DEAR ANNABELLE: A DECLARATION OF LOVE
#### FROM THE NODCOCK

*Dear Annabelle,*
*You have succeeded in winning my attention.*
*I can think of nothing but you, day or night—and*

*not because there is little else to do in prison, and
not merely because of your low-cut bodices or other
tricks to catch my eye. You are beautiful, Annabelle,
inside and out. You intrigue me, Annabelle. I crave
you, Annabelle. You have succeeded in winning my
affections. Annabelle, I am in love with you.*

*Readers have marveled at the dim-witted and
obtuse idiot you adored. I am a fool to have missed
you for so long, and an even bigger one to have lost
you once I found you. Dear Annabelle, please advise
how I might win your favor, your affections, and your
promise of a lifetime together.*

*Yours always,*
*D. Knightly, the Nodcock*

She couldn't quite believe the marvelous words
just there, in black and white, making her heart beat
hard and her breath catch in her throat. Hot, *happy*
tears stung her eyes because once upon a time, on
one otherwise unremarkable Saturday morning, her
dearest wish came true.

He loved her.

Mr. Derek Knightly, man of her dreams, loved her.

Annabelle knew a Grand Declaration of True
Love when it was printed in black and white. Her
heart continued to pound hard and her breath
hitched in her throat. Knightly loved her! And all of
London knew it!

She had to go to him. Had to find him even if it
meant storming into Newgate. She had to tell him
YES.

# Chapter 50

## Newspaper Tycoon on Trial

TOWN TALK

*The trial of newspaper tycoon Derek Knightly is such a crush, rivaling balls thrown at the palace. Everyone is eager to attend the most sensational trial of 1825. Especially as fears are high that one may not be able to read about it in the newspapers.*

*The Morning Post*

*The Trial*

**K**NIGHTLY sat on a hard wooden chair before a plain wood table awaiting the start of his trial. All around him, people filed into the courtroom finding seats and carrying on tense, hushed conversations. He scanned the courtroom, searching for a lovely woman with milky skin, eyes blue like the sky, golden curls, and a mouth made for sin yet smiled so sweetly.

Increasingly his glances grew frantic—though he disguised the growing fear gnawing at him. Annabelle was not here.

Depending upon the outcome of this trial, he

might be locked away for years. His fortune might suffer. The ton could have no use for him now. So much hinged on the outcome of this farce, in which he would defend himself. Everything depended upon his absolute focus, sharp wit, and keen observation.

Yet he thought only of Annabelle. Where was she?

Had she seen *The London Weekly*? She must have. Owens assured him that every last person in London had read it, or had it read to them, or discussed it at great length. No one was oblivious to its contents.

Had she seen his version of Dear Annabelle? Was there anything more anguish-inducing than a public confession of love with naught but silence in response? He would testify under oath that it was more punishing than Newgate.

Again Knightly deeply, painfully, empathized with what Annabelle must have endured all those years . . . waiting patiently. Always wondering. What she must have endured, each week as she published her exploits and her daring attempts to snare his attentions, when he had been as obtuse as ever. It was, in his mind, the very definition of bravery. To push oneself to great heights, risking such a great fall, with all of London watching.

"Order in the court!" the judge called out. His gray powdered wig shook with the force of his declaration. The gavel knocked hard on the wooden desk and echoed around the room.

Knightly would defend himself. He would do so with the premise that it could not be libel if it was, in fact, the truth. With Owens's help he'd lined up witnesses, including the Lady Lydia Marsden, who might be called to testify against her own brother.

Did he buy her testimony? Perhaps. He preferred to thinking of it as investing in her freedom. In exchange for her story, Knightly settled a small fortune upon her, allowing her to marry and set up a dignified household with her lover and son, despite the wishes of her brother. They thought they might take an extended visit to Italy. They could go first class with the settlement he was providing. He thought it worth every penny, because he knew about love now.

On the other hand, Marsden was going to have a very bad day.

He saw the other *Weekly* writers file into the courtroom and take seats in the gallery. His mother joined them, and she beamed proudly at him from her seat in the gallery. Knightly watched the lot of them obviously peer around the courtroom, murmuring the same question. *Where is Annabelle?*

"We are here for the trial of Mr. Derek Knightly, editor and owner of *The London Weekly* on the charges of libel," the judge intoned. His voice carried across the crowded room and all conversations ceased.

Marsden sat on the opposite side of the courtroom with a smug smirk on his face. Obviously he did not know that his sister—his own flesh and blood—planned to provide the testimony that would devastate his case.

The premise was simple: it was said that *The London Weekly* regularly published false, inflammatory, and libelous statements. Knightly would offer proof of every statement in every issue of the newspaper.

The judge said that would not be necessary.

Marsden's solicitor pointed out that the recent issue provided the most relevant and libelous and false statements.

Knightly said he was glad they brought that up, at which point Lady Lydia Marsden took the stand at his invitation. The courtroom erupted in audible gasps followed by a general uproar.

"Order in this court!" the judge hollered. He pounded the gavel again. *Thwack. Thwack. Thwack.*

Lady Lydia looked to Knightly with trepidation in her eyes. She had already stood up for him, so the damage to her reputation was done. But he lifted his brow, asking the question: Did she wish to go?

Lydia nodded her head. Somewhere, in the midst of their arranged courtship, they had developed a truce, which had led to something like friendship. He had earned her favor when he inquired about her wishes—it was an unfortunate fact of her life that he was only the second man to have ever done so (second to her beloved). When she shared her wish for a love match, he didn't laugh or dismiss her. The question haunted him—until he fell in love himself. And then he knew that nothing was more important than being with the one you loved.

Through her story, Lydia provided him the means to defend his livelihood, and through his fortune she would have the means to live with her soon-to-be husband.

Thus, Lady Lydia took the stand, facing quite a few people who had whispered vicious rumors and snubbed her at every opportunity, so that she might take control of her own story and write the happy ending she so desired.

Knightly stood to address the room.

*Where is Annabelle?*

"Lady Marsden, it is said that *The London Weekly* takes liberties with its facts. Can you confirm that your story, as it appears in this last issue of *The London Weekly*, is the absolute truth?"

"It is the truth as I told it," she said.

The reaction of the courtroom was explosive. Marsden paled. Other men shouted, more than one woman shrieked. The gasps stole around the room like a strong wind.

The judge's face reddened as he called louder and louder for order once, twice, thrice.

"How can it be libel if it is the truth?" Knightly asked the courtroom, which had fallen silent when he began to speak. "By definition, it cannot be. If Lady Lydia's story, which happens to be one of the most scandalous collections of words printed by *The Weekly*, is the truth, what does that say for the rest of the newspaper? We can examine every line. Or we can conclude that occasionally it is not the portrayal that is unflattering, but the actions themselves."

The trial carried on for the rest of the day, reaching ever more sensational heights, in which Marsden alternated between glowering and gloating. Knightly fought the urge to pace, to drink. He scanned the crowds, ever looking for Annabelle. Where was she? Worry set in—not for his fate, but for her. In the end the jury deliberated and the judge pronounced Knightly's fate. Not guilty.

The judge pounded his gavel to restore order before his concluding remarks:

"Good day, Mr. Knightly. You don't belong here."

# Chapter 51

### Dear Annabelle's True Identity Discovered

DEAR ANNABELLE

*This author discourages standing in the path of true love.*

**The London Weekly**

*Earlier . . .*

**ANNABELLE** had grabbed her shawl and was reaching for her bonnet for her journey to Newgate, where she was going to tell Knightly YES. It didn't matter that it was Newgate, the least romantic location in Europe, possibly even the entire Northern Hemisphere.

He loved her. She loved him.

Nothing could stop them now.

An obstacle immediately presented itself: Blanche and her friend Mrs. Underwood, the witch. They entered through the front door, effectively blocking Annabelle's path.

"What horrible disaster is in the news that has you weeping, a fire in an orphanage?" Blanche asked as she absorbed the tears on Annabelle's face and the newspaper she clutched in her hands. Mrs. Underwood hovered just behind Blanche's shoulder with an evil gleam in her eye.

"Nothing," Annabelle said stupidly. Then she cringed. It was tantamount to shouting *I'm not guilty!* or *Look at this!* or *Question me further!*

"Nothing? Nothing has you weeping like a schoolgirl at a rubbish novel? Let me see that!" Blanche said, snatching the newspaper from Annabelle's hands and quickly scanning the lines.

It was the picture that did her in. Owens must have found it and plunked it in to fill space, not knowing the damage it would do. Knightly wouldn't have exposed her thusly.

"You're Dear Annabelle?" Mrs. Underwood said incredulously from her position still behind Blanche's shoulder. She gave Annabelle a once-over and then pulled a face of utter disbelief. "I never would have thought you capable of that."

"What is that?" Blanche asked, frowning.

"Blanche, you are the only one who doesn't read *The London Weekly.* And it looks like you've been living with one of the Weekly Wenches," Mrs. Underwood said, her voice tinged with a cackle.

"I suppose this is the work of that gentleman caller you entertained," Blanche said icily.

"Has the Nodcock been here?" Mrs. Underwood asked, gasping with unabashed excitement. She was obviously going to dine out on this story of months, Annabelle could tell. And she didn't like it. She felt a flush of anger. "Blanche, have you met him? Oh goodness me. 'Entertained' is one way to put it. She had climbed into his bedroom window in the dead of the night!"

Amongst all the things Annabelle felt at the moment, she suffered a particular irritation that she would be so betrayed by a regular reader of the column. She had assumed, in her eternal good faith, that her readers were championing her. Perhaps the rest of them were. Just not Mrs. Underwood. She tried to inch toward the door. To freedom. To true love.

"Allow me to summarize the facts," Blanche said in a voice that allowed no contradiction. "You have been dallying with a man."

"Don't deny it," Mrs. Underwood said, wagging her finger. "All of London knows you did."

Of course they did. Because she thought to pen her most intimate thoughts and actions in the most widely read newspaper in London. Widely read, that is, save for her own household. A fire started to burn in her belly at the unjust treatment of her. So what if she dallied with a man she loved, who loved her back? She was a free, consenting adult in the eyes of the law and everyone else, save for Blanche and her horrid friend.

"You have been writing for this news rag," Blanche gasped with the same degree of horror had, say, Annabelle been caught digging up dead bodies in the cemetery and selling them to science. Not only was the act itself repugnant, but she didn't believe Annabelle possessed the strength.

Maybe I do, Annabelle thought. The fire in her belly grew hotter.

"I suppose all that charity work was a lie," Blanche carried on, her eyes narrowed. Annabelle could see the machinery churning in her brain as she stitched all the pieces together. One could practically see the steam rising from her ears and hear the roar of the engine.

"She's been writing for years," Mrs. Underwood said. "This column started four years ago, I think it was?" she asked, damning her even more. Annabelle decided her next column would be about minding one's own business.

Blanche drew a deep breath and squared her shoulders; the effect made her appear larger and more formidable. Her eyes narrowed and her mouth pinched into a mean line.

Annabelle knew she was meant to be intimated, or feel guilt or shame for her secret. However, instead of cowering as she tended to do, inspired by the brilliant and courageous man who loved her, she drew up to her full height—which was considerably taller than Blanche, she noted. She lifted her head high. She was a writer at the best newspaper in the world and she had the love of a good man. A man who was defiant and proud, and would want her to be defiant and proud, too.

"Three years, eight months, two weeks, and six days," Annabelle said, looking Blanche in the eye. Without blinking. Or blushing. The fire in her belly raged.

"And in that time I have given you room and board out of our own pockets when you have had an income of your own," Blanche said, absolutely aghast.

"Yes, and I did the work of a housemaid and a governess in exchange," Annabelle said. She could feel Knightly cheering her on and the thrill of his pride. Oh, she was so excited to tell him YES and to tell him about this scene in which Dear Annabelle stood up for herself.

He would be so proud of her. But it wouldn't compare to the pride she felt for herself.

Blanche's explosion started with a huff. And then a *harrumph*. And then a wail. She grabbed a fistful of Annabelle's hair, now an option thanks to Owens's coiffure suggestions, and yanked hard. Annabelle flailed, trying to stop Blanche without loosing a significant portion of her hair and scalp.

Mrs. Underwood hovered and cackled.

With a firm grasp on Annabelle's hair, her fingernails digging her scalp, and a wicked twist of her wrist, Blanche pulled Annabelle to the stairs.

Annabelle tripped halfway up and was dragged the rest of the way. She was kicked and shoved and ruthlessly forced up the creaky flight of stairs leading to her attic bedroom.

It was only there that Blanche released her, and she did so with a forceful thrust that sent Annabelle tumbling to the floor, landing with a thud on the hardwood.

"I'd set you out on the doorstep now were it not for Thomas. You just wait here until he comes home," Blanche hissed, eyes blazing with fury. Thomas was on a business trip. It was not certain when he would return.

With that, Blanche slammed the door behind her, and locked it.

# Chapter 52

## True Love Stops at Nothing

MISS HARLOW'S MARRIAGE IN HIGH LIFE
*This author suspects a highly anticipated wedding
will occur—soon. Three years, eight months, two
weeks, and one day after love at first sight.*
The London Weekly

*The tree conveniently growing outside
of Annabelle's attic bedroom
Midnight*

**B**EING a born and bred city boy, Knightly did not
have much practice climbing trees. Logic dictated
that Annabelle didn't have much experience with
it either, and yet she had managed it, therefore he
should be able to as well.

"Here goes," he muttered, grabbing onto the
lowest branch and pulling himself up. He thought
about taking care not to wake Annabelle's awful relatives and then decided he cared more about getting
to Annabelle alive and unbroken than he did about
the quality of their sleep.

If this went according to plan, it would be a loud

night indeed with his and Annabelle's cries of pleasure. He loved her. He needed to tell her, and to show her. Anticipation spurred him on as he grabbed one branch then another and pulled himself up. More than once he uttered a prayer of thanks for Annabelle's column in which she shared tips for midnight tree climbing.

Of course her bedroom had to be in the attic, three stories off the ground. Her fellow Writing Girls gleefully offered this information to him—after he was acquitted on all charges and ordered to find Annabelle and provide a satisfying resolution to her quest to secure the attentions and affections of the Nodcock. The Judge also let it be known he expected to read about a happy ending in the next issue of *The London Weekly*.

That would all have to wait. Some things were more important.

He could have called upon her tomorrow, with an entire hothouse worth of pink roses and sapphires to match her blue eyes. There was time for flowers and roses. But he could not wait any longer to tell her that he loved her or to show her that he would do anything to be with her, including climbing an old tree on a moonless night all the way up to her third-story bedroom.

Knightly finally hauled himself onto her window ledge. Fortunately it was a warm summer night and she kept the window open just a few inches. After all, why would she suspect that anyone would climb three stories into her bedroom? It was the act of a desperate man.

Finally he tumbled into her bedroom. Somewhere, a clock chimed midnight.

ANNABELLE awoke immediately, hearing someone thudding into her bedroom from the window. *The third-story window.* She lay still, her heart pounding and breath held, while considering her options.

She could feign sleep, or death.

She could discreetly reach for the pewter candleholder on her bedside table and wield it as a weapon.

Or she could assume that it would be useless to fight whomever had gone to all the bother of climbing into her third-story bedroom window in the dead of the night. Obviously, the person was determined.

Or insane. She reached for the candleholder and clutched it tightly against her chest. She recalled that the door to the rest of the house was locked. Thus, she would have to fight or climb out the window and shimmy down the tree in her nightgown.

She was about to sigh and curse her luck when a voice spoke in the darkness.

"Annabelle, it's me."

She knew that voice. Her heart pounded hard, but no longer from fear. She sat up in bed, blankets pooling around her waist, her hair a tumbling mess around her shoulders. Of course he climbed into her window on the night she wore some plain, drab, spinsterish nightgown. She thought of all the silky underthings in her armoire and considered asking him to wait whilst she changed.

She sighed and cursed her luck.

"Derek? What are you doing here?" she asked. She set down the candlestick and fumbled to light it. With the candle lit, she blinked, not quite believing the sight of her beloved Knightly in her attic bedroom.

"Well I couldn't very well faint into your arms, now could I?" Knightly replied, grinning. She wondered if this was a dream.

"What are you talking about?" she asked. Men didn't faint and they certainly didn't do so into a woman's arms. It would be impractical. And embarrassing. Injurious. This must be a dream.

"Oh, Annabelle," he said, and she heard warmth and laughter in his voice.

"It's the middle of the night and you have tumbled into my bedroom. I'm not sure if I'm awake or dreaming. Don't 'oh Annabelle' me. What is going on?" she asked, utterly perplexed and not quite her cheerful self until at least a quarter hour after waking. "I thought you were in prison."

"I was. But the courts have found me not guilty," he told her. She released a breath she didn't know she had been holding.

"And so you have come here. At midnight," Annabelle said. He loved her, he had declared so in the newspaper. But it was the middle of the night and she possessed a fantastic imagination, which made her fear she was imagining this entire encounter.

But no, Knightly crossed the room and sat beside her on the bed. He brushed a lock of hair away from her face and brushed his lips across hers. There was no mistaking his touch.

"It so happens that I fell in love with an amazing woman and wanted to capture her attention," he told her. "Being a nodcock, I didn't know what to do other than rely on the experiences of a certain popular advice columnist."

In the dark, Annabelle smiled. A warmth started

in the pool of her belly, radiating through every inch of her. It was the pleasure of being loved, of being wooed. Of being a woman Knightly climbed a tree at midnight for.

"Well that all makes sense now. The lack of cravat—" she said, a laugh bubbling up.

"The male equivalent of a lowered bodice," he replied with a grin, kissing her softly where her neck curved into her shoulder.

"And the day you left your jacket behind?" she asked, tilting her head to encourage him.

"I don't have a shawl," Knightly said, and she laughed loudly and didn't care who heard her.

"And you have climbed into my bedroom. At midnight. You love me," she said. Merely stating the facts. Wonderful, delightful facts.

"I do, Annabelle. I love you," Knightly said, his voice husky. He took her hand in his and squeezed it tight. His mouth found hers for another kiss.

"I love you," Annabelle told him, with happy tears in her eyes and giddiness in her voice. "I love you. I've thought those words so much but I've never said them aloud. I can finally tell you, and it was worth the wait. I love you."

His mouth claimed hers for a kiss, and there wasn't much talking for the rest of the night.

*The following morning*

"ARE you ready, Annabelle?" Knightly asked with a spark in his eye, his mouth in a wicked grin. He carried her in his arms, like a princess, like a bride, like a woman he wanted to hold and cherish for a lifetime.

"Yes, oh yes," she replied, clasping her hands tighter around his shoulders.

He stood before the cursed locked door at the top of the attic stairs. They both eyed the obstacle warily. On the other side lay freedom. And happily-ever-after.

"On the count of three," he said. She nodded.

Knightly never got to three. With a deep breath and a quick, forceful kick on *two*, the door splintered on its hinges. One more deftly executed kick sent the wooden door clattering down the stairs and skidding across the second-floor landing before tumbling straight down the main flight of stairs, into the foyer.

The whole family gathered around the door, looking at it curiously before turning their heads up the stairs to see Knightly descending with Annabelle in his arms.

Watson and Mason watched wide-eyed with awe at this tower of masculine strength. Annabelle saw the delight in Fleur's eyes at the magical sight of a fairy tale come to life in her very own house.

Blanche appeared as always: immensely peevish, appalled, and enraged. Her mouth gaped open, rather like the fish Annabelle used to buy at the market, and no sound emerged. It seemed she had been struck dumb by the site of Annabelle, adored.

Even Thomas had emerged from his chair in the library to see what the noise was about. He carried a newspaper in his hand, and Annabelle's smile broadened because it was *The London Weekly*.

"Thomas!" Blanche shrieked, finally recovering her voice. "Thomas, do something!"

"I think we've done enough," he replied, nodding

to Annabelle before shuffling off to his armchair to resume his reading. The children tugged at their mother's skirt, pulling her out of the path of true love.

Knightly carried Annabelle across the threshold, carrying her from the shadows to the bright light of a beautiful new day and the start of the happily-ever-after she had hoped for, fought for, and won.

### Happily-ever-after

*Two years later*

**I**T began with a letter, and that letter commenced with the shocking words: *Dear Lord Harrowby*.

It had taken hours for those words to emerge from a pen Knightly commanded. He did not write *To the New Earl* or even *Dear New Earl* or avoid a salutation altogether. That he even sat down to compose this letter was a lifetime in the making.

But Annabelle had persuaded him to make this overture.

"You can spend your whole life waiting for someone to notice you or you can do something about it," she urged, idly rubbing her growing belly. She was right, of course. He was surrounded by proof: every morning he woke beside his beloved wife in a home filled with happiness and laughter. All because one day she had dared to ask for what she wanted. It had started with the simple act of pen to paper, with a letter . . .

He was thankful each day for his daring, darling Dear Annabelle.

Soon they would have a baby, and hopefully the

child would be blessed with brothers and sisters. Knightly never wanted them to know the estrangement he had suffered. He wanted them to always feel they belonged, together.

So he wrote the damn letter.

*Dear Lord Harrowby.*

Knightly wrote of never having his father's full time and attention—and how they both must have felt the same. He wrote of feeling competition with an adversary he only wanted to befriend. He wrote of his hopes that blood was stronger than slights or regrets. He thought perhaps their father would have liked his sons to be able to lean on each other.

He signed it simply *D. Knightly.* And he enclosed it with an invitation to a ball celebrating his elevation to the peerage. The title Lord Northbourne had been granted to him by the King in acknowledgment of his service to the burgeoning newspaper industry. "The first of the press barons," the newspapers had proclaimed.

Knightly sent the letter. Then he left his office at 57 Fleet Street and strode determinedly through the city streets at dusk, eager to be where he belonged: home with his beloved wife, Dear Annabelle.